OFF LIMITS

The Books of Hans Habe

PUBLISHED IN THE U.S.A.

Three Over the Frontier

Sixteen Days

A Thousand Shall Fall

Katherine

Aftermath

Walk In Darkness

Our Love Affair With Germany

Black Earth

PUBLISHED IN OTHER COUNTRIES

A World Crumbles

All My Sins (AUTOBIOGRAPHY)

OFF LIMITS

A NOVEL BY

HANS HABE

TRANSLATED FROM THE GERMAN BY EWALD OSERS

NEW YORK

FREDERICK FELL, INC., PUBLISHERS

Manufactured in the United States of America by H. Wolff,
    New York.

Designed by Sidney Solomon

Published simultaneously in Canada by George J. McLeod,
    Ltd., Toronto

Library of Congress Catalog Card No. 56–11971

Published in Germany by Verlag Kurt Desch, Munich
Published in England by George G. Harrap & Co., Ltd.,
    London.

TO THE MEN AND WOMEN

WHO RESISTED MUCH

AND OBEYED LITTLE

THIS BOOK IS DEDICATED

CONTENTS

The Year 1945

FIRST CHAPTER 11
        Dr. Wild Has an American Caller
        A Woman Waits in a Prison
        A Girl Goes on the Street
        Always a Rabbit up his Sleeve
        Colonel Sibelius Is Detained
        The Patriot Thief
        The Mountains Guard their Secret
        Colonel Hunter Learns German
        PW Eber Returns Home

SECOND CHAPTER 40
        Frank and George Meet Again
        Four Women Await Their Fate
        Frank Finds Elisabeth
        Inge and the Negro
        Adam Wild Acts
        George Requisitions a Home
        Sanctuary at Dr. Wild's
        Major O'Hara Saves the Commandeuse
        A License for the "Mücke" Night Club
        SS-Führer Mante Scents the Morning Air

THIRD CHAPTER 94
        That First Winter Was Hell
        The Barbed Wire Remains

Adam Wild Hits Out
A Whores' Rummy Party
Chief of Counterintelligence East is Needed Again
Frank Takes Charge of the O'Hara Case
Hans Eber Speaks the Truth
Mortal Drama in Nuremberg
O'Hara Whips No More
Christmas 1945

The Years 1946·1948

FOURTH CHAPTER 177
Inge Schmidt Is at the End of Her Tether
Mrs. Hunter Is Jealous
The Commandeuse Flees to Berlin
Elisabeth Finds Asylum
Is Obedience a Crime
The Governor Gives a Party
Frank Green Hits Back
A Night without Ghosts
Colonel Sibelius Becomes a Waiter
Spring Comes to Germany
FIFTH CHAPTER 262
Cleaning Out a Monkey Cage
A Murder is Committed in Berlin
The Föhn Turns the Colonel's Head
Adam Stands His Trial
"We Owe That to the Yanks"
The Direction of the Current
Denazification in Full Swing
Second Round to Frank
Tomorrow They Will be Widows
The Close of the Year 1946
SIXTH CHAPTER 348
Black Market Supreme
"I've Always Been a Good Father"
Forgive More and Forget Less

Sibelius Pays a Painful Visit
You Need a Good Stomach
The Colonel Has Three Interviews
Bankhaus Eber Runs Up Its Flag
Black Bird Among the Ruins
The Ghosts Are Stronger
Towards a Splendid Future

The Years That Followed

SEVENTH CHAPTER 437
Colonel Hunter Declines Promotion
Wedemeyer Conjures Again
Sibelius Writes to Adam Wild
In the Air-Raid Shelter All Men Were Equal
Adventure at the Cemetery Gate
Mante Breaks off the Engagement
". . . And All We Want is One Little Thing"
The Unquenched Flame

THE YEAR

1945

FIRST CHAPTER

Dr. Wild Has an American Caller

THE last patient had left. Dr. Wild hung his white coat, no longer quite white, on a hook on the door. The walls of the little surgery were patchy, like a mangy dog.

He walked over to the open window and looked out.

It was May and there was a *Föhn* about. The *Föhn* came in warm waves: July weather with an undercurrent of winter. In such weather the cattle on the Alpine pastures would go wild or lecherous, or both.

The scene painted by the *Föhn* was like that of a child: primitive, with the contours too sharp. Much too sharp were the contours of the ruins outside Dr. Adam Wild's window. It was not as if the sky looked in through the empty windows, but as if the windows had carved out a piece of blue sky.

On the opposite side of the narrow street in the suburbs of Munich there was not a house left. It was like that everywhere: one side of a street was unscathed and the other was razed to the ground. Death had ploughed a straight furrow, like a good farmer.

Dr. Wild turned away. He crossed the stuffy waiting-room which smelled of panel patients and entered the living-room. This was a fairly big room, but it was so crammed full of furniture that it seemed small in effect. Chairs, chests, vases, display cabinets, statues and even pictures were practically touching one another. Frau Wild's antique shop had been bombed out. Now the living-room served also as her antique shop.

Frau Wild was sitting in an antique chair on whose tall, rigid, velvet-covered back a coat of arms was embroidered. In this majestic chair she looked like a tiny old queen. By the side of her son she always looked smaller than she was, for he was a giant: broad, massive and heavy, he resembled the Norman wardrobe by which he now stood.

Frau Wild looked up from the dark antiquarian book she had been reading. It was strange how alike the giant and the slight woman were. Both had pale blue eyes—only hers were much younger, islands in a sea of wrinkles. No doubt she had once been as fair as he, for her hair was not white but yellow.

"It's like midsummer," said Frau Wild.

She went to the window and opened it. Her eyes went down to the street.

"An American," she said.

Dr. Wild looked down into the street over her head. Below, a jeep had drawn up. Next to the driver sat an officer. He wore a khaki shirt and a field cap. In the back of the jeep three or four cardboard boxes were piled up. Mother and son knew what they contained, for these cartons kept appearing again and again in their dreams. The American Army called them rations. For the Germans they were dreams in cardboard.

The officer glanced up at the window. Then he said something to his driver and got out.

"A customer?" Frau Wild asked.

"Maybe," said the doctor.

She went over to the door of the apartment, to be on the safe side, since the electric bell was not working.

The officer's hand froze in mid-air: he had been on the point of knocking when Frau Wild opened the door. He was a man of about thirty, of medium height, slim, with brown hair, fair rather than dark. He had an open face, the kind in which one found one's way as easily as in a modern city: not beautiful, but clean, straight and practical.

"Is Doctor Wild at home?" asked the officer, taking off his field cap. He spoke German like a native.

"Will you come in, please," said Frau Wild.

He regarded the old woman with some surprise. He was used to being met with fear or obsequiousness. But this woman seemed neither afraid nor servile.

She took him into the living-room and left him alone with her son. Evidently he was not one of those customers who traded cardboard boxes for antiques.

"My name is Frank Green," said the officer. He spoke rapidly, as if anxious to get the formalities over. "No doubt this won't mean anything to you, Herr Doktor. It used to be Grün. Franz Grün."

"Won't you sit down?" said Adam Wild. The name Franz Grün did not mean a thing to him either.

The Major looked around. He could not immediately find anywhere to sit down in comfort. To Adam it seemed that he was trying to gain time. At last the visitor sat down on a Tyrolean dower chest.

"I have come," began the officer, "to thank you, Herr Doktor. For looking after my mother to the end."

Now Adam remembered.

"Frau Grün, the widow of the High Court Judge," he said.

The officer nodded.

"I know what you did for my mother." He spoke as if he had prepared his speech beforehand. "I know how difficult it was."

"If I remember rightly, it was before the war. It was not particularly difficult then."

The conversation was beginning to embarrass him. He now remembered the old lady clearly. She had come to him, for the last time, the day before being taken to the concentration camp. "Do help me, doctor," she had said to him. As if there were a medicine against concentration camps. And this now was her son, an American officer, with cardboard boxes piled in his jeep. He said quickly

"Did you find your house again, Herr Green?" He did not know U.S. officers' ranks.

"The spot where it used to stand," replied the Major. "It's bombed out."

Odd, Adam thought to himself, the bombed-out house of an American.

The Major produced a fresh, folded handkerchief and wiped his moist forehead. He wanted to say something, but the doctor forestalled him.

"The *Föhn*," said Adam and attempted a smile.

"Yes, the good old Munich *Föhn*," smiled the officer.

He felt in his breast pocket, fished out a pack of cigarettes and extended it to the doctor. Adam gave him a light and lit a cigarette for himself.

The Major kept the pack in his hand. He was no longer used to pocketing packs of cigarettes. He was also surprised that the doctor had lit his cigarette at once instead of saving it for later. "Saving it for later" was the Germans' request for the whole package, or for what was left of it. This giant with his bushy mustache was not conforming to the rule. The Major regretted that he had come.

"Well," he said eventually, "I just wanted to come and thank you, Herr Doktor. And to give you my address. If I can be of any help to you . . ."

He tore a page from his notebook and wrote on it: "Frank Green, Major, M.I., Headquarters, 45th Division, Ludwigstrasse."

He wanted to give the note to the doctor, but when Adam did not move his hand he put it down on the dower chest.

At the door he stopped once more, as though he had forgotten something.

As soon as he was gone Frau Wild poked her head through the door.

"What did he want?" she asked.

"He wanted to make us a present of a few rations," said Adam.

A Woman Waits in a Prison

"B" Corridor in the Nuremberg prison was like all prison corridors: an endless tunnel with doors along the sides.

Elisabeth von Zutraven was sitting on a bench, waiting. It was four o'clock now and she had been waiting since one. But she was used to waiting, for this was the year 1945 and she was a German.

Elisabeth von Zutraven wore a black shawl over her medium fair hair. Blue eyes or gray would have gone better with her hair, but her eyes were brown like the bark of old trees. Perhaps it was those eyes that made it so difficult to determine her age—twenty-five or thirty, maybe more. They were eyes which not only saw but told of what they had seen.

The MP leaning on the wall opposite her was staring at her, and Elisabeth understood immediately that he did not know what to do with her. He wore a snow-white helmet and looked like an armed cook. That was another thing Elisabeth had got used to—being stared at. His eyes did not worry her, less so than the eyes of her compatriots. It was easier to stand up to foreign eyes; foreign eyes were no concern of hers.

Suddenly the MP smiled. He asked:

"Chewing gum . . . ?"

She tried to smile and shook her head.

And then the MP was no longer leaning against the wall. As if caught in the act he pulled himself up and stood at attention. A door had opened. A young captain appeared in it and said:

"You can come along, Frau Zutraven."

Briskly he walked in front of her. At an iron door stood two other military policemen. The captain showed them the visitor's pass; they saluted and unlocked the door.

The room which they entered reminded Elisabeth of the winter houses at the Zoo. There were three cages, separated from one another by thick walls. They were cages, not cells, divided from the visitor by bars only, and with doors at the back. It was easy to imagine that behind those doors were rocky pits and pools for playful and begging polar bears. But the stench here was not of animals in their winter quarters. It was of human beings.

Outside each empty cage stood a chair. On one of them sat an American soldier, notebook in hand.

Then the door leading from outside into the middle cage was opened. It was a normal-sized door through which a man might enter upright, and that surprised Elisabeth who had unconsciously expected the prisoner to make his entry on all fours, like a bear or a wolf.

There was another chair inside the cage. By that chair Kurt von Zutraven stopped.

She had not seen him since his arrest. She no longer remembered when that was. Berlin had not yet fallen; the Führer had still been alive. And there had still been some people who believed in a miracle.

It must have been a very long time, thought Elisabeth. Because Kurt von Zutraven's blond hair had turned gray. Not white, but as if a can of ashes had been emptied over his head. Even his blue eyes had turned gray. He had a gold tooth in his right upper jaw. It now looked grotesque, like a ring in an ashtray.

"How are you, Elisabeth?" asked the man behind the bars.

"Thank you," said the woman. "How are you?"

She thought it ludicrous the way the soldier was taking down every word.

"When did you come out?" he asked.

"After only eleven days."

"Can you talk to Dr. Leberecht?" he asked after some hesitation. "Maybe he would undertake my defense."

"I will try," she replied.

"Have you got any money?" he asked.

"I don't need any money," she said. "I am still staying at the interrogation villa."

She wanted to say something comforting to him, but could not think of anything.

"Is there anything you need?" she asked at last.

He tried to smile. "I've got everything. The only thing—I should like to have a picture of you. And of Mama." He glanced through the bars at the captain. "It is permitted."

"I'll send them along," said the woman. She wanted to add that she, too, had put up his picture. But it would have sounded maudlin. And it was not true either.

At last she remembered something. "I have brought you some books," she said. "They are being checked."

"Thank you," he said.

Two minutes later the Captain gave a little cough.

They said goodbye.

The captain led her back to his office. He nodded to the MP.

The MP walked beside her in silence, right to the entrance of the Law Court building. As she stepped out into the street he said:

"Chewing gum . . ."

And before she could say anything he had pressed a package of chewing gum into her hand.

A Girl Goes on the Street

The house at No. 56b in St. Martin Strasse in Munich was favorably situated. In the past, the old-age pensioner Alois Schmidt had always considered it fortunate that his two rooms were on the third floor. The Eastern Cemetery was surrounded by high walls, and one had to live high up to be able to look over them into the cemetery.

Whenever it was not too cold Schmidt would lean in the open window, in shirt sleeves, puffing at his pipe—in the days when there still was tobacco—and looking at the cemetery. He would not have exchanged it for the most beautiful park. All there was in a park was shrubs and trees, and perhaps a few flowers. But in a cem￼ y there were wreaths whose brilliance of color was independent ￼ the seasons. Wreaths with purple ribbons and gilt lettering. In ￼ emetery there were funerals, rich funerals and poor, with and w ￼ ut graveside orations, sad ones and business-like ones.

It may have been because of the graves that the old-age pensioner Alois Schmidt became a Block Warden in the Third Reich. The NSDAP, of which he had been a member of long standing, valued a man who was observant. In addition to observing the dead who were entering into the life eternal, he also observed the living who were entering into, or emerging from, the near-by houses.

Now he had returned to the dead, but in unfavorable circumstances. He had been deprived of his pension. And he could not smoke his pipe, for tobacco had become even rarer than money. Fine funerals, too, had become a rarity. No doubt, it was a matter of supply and demand: the more common death had become, the cheaper the funerals.

That day towards the end of June 1945 the clouds were lowering over the cemetery. At last the first thunderstorm of the summer broke. With a sigh Alois Schmidt closed the window.

He had not noticed that Inge was sitting in a wicker chair behind him. She was doing what she always did—nothing.

Inge was sixteen. One might have thought her fourteen: she was so willowy and in need of cod-liver oil. But anyone seeing her eyes would know she was not fourteen. Indeed he would be surprised that she was not more than sixteen.

"Brought anything home?" her father asked.

"Potatoes," she answered.

"That all?"

"Yes."

"No tobacco?"

"No."

Inge crossed her legs, left knee over right. Her knees were almost pathetic: they might have been covered with scabs like the knees of little girls who keep falling down.

Her father sat down on the couch opposite her. It was plum-colored plush with hard cylindrical cushions at each end and with brass lions' heads with rings through their mouths. Except that one of the lions was toothless: he had lost his ring.

"The Donaubauers always have tobacco," said the father. "And yesterday they had beer."

"Old man Donaubauer wasn't a Block Warden," said the girl.

"That's got nothing to do with it," said the father. "It was American beer. He didn't buy that with his pension."

He was staring at his daughter's knees. Inge recrossed her legs, right over left. She said:

"Hilde is running round with an American."

"Nothing of the sort," said the old-age pensioner. "It's forbidden."

"Forbidden or not," said Inge.

Alois Schmidt did not like being contradicted. He said:

"She's going out with Karl Huber. He deals in black-market gas."

The girl shrugged her shoulders. The shoulders went with the knees: they belonged to a fourteen-year-old.

"She's a whore," she said.

It was getting dark in the room. There was a clap of thunder. The girl gave a jerk.

"Just like the bombs," she said.

"Because she goes out with Karl Huber that doesn't make her a whore," her father said stubbornly.

"She had a Negro up with her yesterday," the girl said. "He was drunk."

"He probably brought the beer," said the man.

The girl gazed out the window.

"Do you want me to become a whore, too?" she asked.

"Nobody'll want to pick *you* up," said her father.

The girl got up.

"You can have all the potatoes," she said. "I don't want anything."

She slammed the door behind her.

Always a Rabbit up his Sleeve

By the side of the narrow lane between Tutzing and Garatshausen, not far from the Starnberger See, seven or eight military vehicles were drawn up. There were two jeeps and two command cars; the rest were German civilian sedans, Opels and Mercedeses, confiscated and now bearing military license plates.

One might have thought that some maneuvers were being held nearby, or a general staff conference. But this was June 1945 and there were no maneuvers or staff conferences any longer. Least of all by the Starnberger See at seven o'clock in the evening.

The officers to whom the cars belonged had disappeared. The drivers, standing together in a little group, would not have disclosed their whereabouts.

Occupied Germany was ruled by the Non-Fraternization Law. No American was allowed to talk to a German, man or woman. You started the war—I'm not talking to you. Besides, one could not be sure that the German pestilence was not contagious.

That was why the officers had left their cars on the edge of the wood. The drivers knew where they had gone—to a forbidden German house. But they would not have revealed this information, for there was a tacit conspiracy between officers and men, a conspiracy for the breaking of their own rules. It said: a blind eye for a blind eye.

Walter Wedemeyer's house was situated almost immediately on the lake, surrounded by trees which rejoiced in their fresh greenery like young mothers in their newly born.

It was the kind of farmhouse that no farmer could afford—with antique furniture and inside plumbing. And this was the first party that Walter Wedemeyer had given since the end of the war. He had made his first contacts with the gentlemen of the Military Government some time early in May—first with those in Starnberg and later with some from Munich. Of course, they had wanted his house—an ideal summer house with a sailing boat and a skiff. And there had been all sorts of things they had wanted to know—about his personal relations with the Führer, for instance. Thus, one thing had led to another.

His relations with the Führer had turned out to be lucky for Walter Wedemeyer. To start with, he had been able to prove that he never was a Party member. Very interesting that—a man who had freely walked in and out at the Führer's and had never been a Party member. Moreover, Walter Wedemeyer had dozens of unknown anecdotes to relate about the Führer. For instance that the Führer had had special leopard-skin bathing trunks made for Eva Braun. Real leopard-skin and waterproof. Or that he, Walter Wedemeyer, had once right under the Führer's eyes turned a copy of *Mein Kampf* into a rabbit—although admittedly he had later turned the rabbit back into *Mein Kampf*.

"You've got to show us that trick with *Mein Kampf*, Herr Wedemeyer," the red-haired Major O'Hara was now shouting. "I've promised my friends that you would."

"Just one minute, Major," Wedemeyer smiled.

He spoke English fluently, which was also to his advantage, not merely because it made communication easier but because it was generally assumed that, just as bad men did not sing, nobody who spoke English could be bad.

However, at the moment he could not meet the Major's request as he was busy, with the bustling earnestness of a bachelor, discharging a hostess's duties. Everything that there was had been brought by the guests. The American white bread was cut into miniature squares; half of it was put aside by his housekeeper. Spam from army cans was put into sandwiches. K-Rations yielded cheese, smooth and square like army soap. A major had brought some whisky from Kentucky, bourbon smelling of moth balls, but it quickly went to everyone's head because there had been little to eat. There was also some Moselle wine, out of army supplies, without vintage but eminently drinkable.

"Do you think that there is still much wine hidden in Starnberg?" a fat captain asked the host.

"It'll turn up all right, it'll turn up," Wedemeyer reassured him.

He fluttered from group to group. He really was a wizard: when he raised his glass a common or garden wine would taste like the most precious drop. He had also conjured up some ladies from Munich. They wore light summer dresses with generous necklines and each of them had an American lipstick, even though it might have been used before by an officer's wife.

"These German women!" a major remarked to a captain. "Nothing to eat and they look like a million dollars."

Towards half-past nine the host eventually yielded to his guests' entreaties. They grouped themselves in a circle around him, on chairs and on the floor. He began his conjuring.

He was a man of medium height, with dark hair and bushy eyebrows. He reminded one of the plasticine figures made by children: a ball for the head, a bigger ball for the body, and slightly elongated ones for the legs. His round spectacles over his large dark eyes emphasized the spherical shape.

Never before had the guests seen such conjuring. No tables with double bottoms, no card tricks, no top hat. Everything modern, improvised, individual. One gesture—and all the medal ribbons vanished from the chest of a lieutenant. He was allowed, blushing, to fish them out of the décolletage of a young lady. A captain carefully sealed an empty whisky bottle—and, presto, it was full of wine. "I am a self-supplier," remarked Wedemeyer. "No ration cards for me."

Finally he demonstrated the trick with *Mein Kampf*. He changed the book into a white rabbit. This time he did not change it back.

"We don't need *Mein Kampf* any more," he said. "Rabbits are more useful."

There was universal applause.

Later everybody went down to the boathouse. The night was sultry. The young officers were no longer afraid of contamination.

The red-haired major put his heavy arm on Wedemeyer's shoulder.

"You really must show that one to the General," he said. "In his office." He added with a chuckle: "But you've got to bring your own rabbit."

"I always ahave a rabbit up my sleeve," said Wedemeyer.

Was the Commandeuse at Home?

The face of red-haired Major William S. O'Hara looked like a map. The hundred little red veins were the rivers. The freckles were the villages. The nose was a mountain. It was an absurdly small mountain.

It was the face of a drinker. Back home, in New York, police sergeant Bill O'Hara had drunk like a fish. His superiors could have got him exempted from service, but they had been quite glad to get rid of Bill. True, he was a good policeman, but like so many good policemen he had never, in more senses than one, been far from jail. If a criminal fell into Bill's big red hands he confessed. Sometimes a man would confess even without having committed a crime. That was why they let Bill go when his draft call came. They were not so fussy in the Army. After all, this was war and all enemies were criminals. Nor was there any need for them to have committed the things they confessed to. Within less than three years the police sergeant Bill O'Hara became Major William S. O'Hara.

Oddly enough, the Major's consumption of alcohol had gone down since he came to Germany. A man could get his thrills here even without drinking so much as in New York. The Major had a whole string of nonalcoholic entertainments. One of them he called "feeding the pigeons." He would go to a public park and chuck half a loaf of white bread among the people. Then he watched them fighting over the bread, his pigeons turning into birds of prey. Another form of amusement for the Major was following a man and woman in the streets in the evening, just before curfew hour, sending the man packing and taking the woman home with him. This he called "the curfew game." Finally, the Major would play at interrogating—as it were for professional reasons. After all, he was an MP major, with delicate gilt pistols on his uniform insignia, and he was attached to a counterespionage unit. Most officers in his unit, such as Major Frank Green, for instance, were amateurs. He alone knew the way to deal with prisoners. And he loved interrogating, for he was no amateur.

Now, once again, he was on his way to an interrogation, or rather to an arrest. And it was an arrest that would intoxicate him more than a glass of bourbon.

Next to him in the jeep sat his driver, Harry S. Jones from Houston, Texas. Jones was six foot two tall and his knees touched the steering wheel. He had the reputation of being the best driver in the army and O'Hara was proud of him. In civilian life Jones's occupation, if one could call it an occupation, was that of auto stunt-man. He would test-drive cars. He would steer them through burning hoops, or turn a somersault in them or whip them through running streams. Consequently, Jones was not afraid of the former police sergeant William S. O'Hara. This is not to say that their relationship was in any way simple. For a week the Major might easily treat his driver as his equal and take him along, privately, on all his escapades. They would drink together, do their black-market deals together, and sleep with the same girls. Until the Major suddenly remembered that he was a major. And then, from one minute to the next, he would treat Jones as if he had reverted to the status of Private Jones or even that of a German.

Just now Major O'Hara was in one of his jovial moods. At such moments he confided everything to Jones, even military secrets.

"I'm curious to see that babe," he said. "Some dame!"

Jones asked no questions; he knew that the Major would continue presently.

"She was the commandeuse in a concentration camp," the Major resumed. "That is, she was the wife of the commandant. Quite good-looking, to judge by her photographs. When the prisoners were flogged she had a sofa put out in the yard for her. She'd lie on the sofa and watch the proceedings. When she felt like it she'd get up, pick up her horsewhip and take a crack at the men herself. Her husband said in evidence that she slept with the prisoners. And anyone ordered to sleep with her knew that he'd be horsewhipped afterwards. What d'you think of that, Jones?"

"Some dame," said Jones.

"We caught the husband at the camp, right at the beginning," continued O'Hara. "Had to protect him even; the prisoners wanted to kill him. He tipped us off himself about his wife. She's supposed to be hiding out at the Hotel Nadler. Belongs to her brother-in-law."

They were driving through nocturnal Munich. It was nearly midnight, almost two hours since curfew time. The city slept its early, fitful sleep. There were few lighted windows: everybody was saving electricity and nobody felt like staying up and talking to anybody else. The curfew may have been conceived as a security measure, but in the subconscious mind of the conquerors it was something else besides: the vanquished had to be humiliated by being treated like children. Children ought to be in bed at an early hour, especially naughty children. If you love children you will treat them as adults, and if you hate adults you will treat them as children. It was beautiful to be a child, but it was also a punishment, and the whole thing was paradoxical and confusing. And now the punished children were asleep. But they were sleeping restlessly like adults who want to understand what the punishment is all about. They dared not ask those who punished them, and even less dared they ask each other. They only asked themselves between sleeping and waking. It was not their conscience that kept them awake in the long nights. Their conscience was not yet redeemed and could not make itself heard.

What have you done?—is what their conscience would have asked. But there was no room for that question; it was pushed aside by: Why are you being punished? Now and again the people would wake up in their humble beds without bedding, in their ruined apartments, because the bombs were crashing into their dreams and the sirens were screaming through their visions. They went to sleep again, but they slept no better. Some indeed wished that the bombs might fall again as in the days when the punishment came down from the heavens and not from human hands. Through these dark streets, unlit by any fires, Major O'Hara's car was racing, its headlights full on. The headlights swept over the ceilings of the sleeping apartments.

Major O'Hara knew the way. He had reconnoitered it in daylight and his police instinct now led him through the night. Besides, it was not dark: a full moon shed its light through the empty windows of the ruins. The houses were like human beings in front of an X-ray screen: cold, hopeless, probed to the depth.

They passed underneath a railway bridge, climbed the Giesinger Berg and turned off to the right. The Major was still talking. He would have liked to have shown his driver the photograph in his breast pocket—the picture of a woman with long fair hair, falling untidily to her shoulders, with small narrow eyes and thick sensuous lips. She wore a dress of checked gingham and by her side was a large police dog. O'Hara had a dog like that back home. He could not show the picture to Jones because the moonlight was not bright enough for it, but he could talk about the woman and about the prisoners whom she had first compelled into her bed and then on to the flogging stool. But Jones was only listening with half an ear; he did not understand why the Major had to repeat the story three times, just as drunks repeat everything. And Jones knew that the Major was not drunk.

The Hotel Nadler was at the end of a narrow cul-de-sac. It was in darkness like all the other houses. O'Hara leaped from the jeep. He took his riding crop with him. Strictly speaking, U. S. officers were forbidden to carry riding crops, but an MP major could always claim that he needed one professionally. Apart from his major, Jones did not know anyone who exercised this privilege.

Jones switched off his engine and made as if to follow.

"You stay here, Jones," commanded O'Hara. "I'll call you if I need you."

He began to beat the door with the hard end of his crop.

After a few minutes it was opened. O'Hara flashed his torch into the face of a frightened little man in shirt sleeves. Then he vanished inside.

Harry S. Jones, from Houston, Texas, sat in his jeep outside the hotel in Giesing, waiting. He had not slept the night before and he was tired. He did not understand why the Major was not back after half an hour, nor after a full hour. He glanced up the wall, but no light had come on in the house that called itself a hotel. He wondered whether it was his duty to follow the Major. But he had no fear for O'Hara. And he did not want to poke his nose into things that were none of his business. Just for safety he took his pistol from its armpit holster and laid it on the seat beside him. Then he tried to stretch his long legs.

A near-by church clock struck two. Houses gone, but they have to have clock towers, thought Jones, in whose native country church bells were seldom heard.

At the same moment the door of the hotel opened and Major O'Hara strode up to the car.

"Get going!" he ordered the driver.

Jones started up the engine.

"Wasn't she there?" he asked as he reversed the vehicle.

"No, she ain't there," O'Hara said impatiently.

Jones said nothing. He knew the Major was lying.

Colonel Sibelius Is Detained

This is a letter written by Colonel Achim Freiherr von Sibelius to his friend Dr. Adam Wild on May 26, 1945. The letter was composed in the clear, correct, soldierly manner of the thirty-eight-year-old Colonel, but the style and handwriting betrayed a man of more than average culture. The letter ran:

"My dear Adam,

"A released PW, Feldwebel (perhaps one ought to add: retired) Ernst Stroh, has kindly volunteered to take this letter from Frankfurt to Munich. I am therefore taking this opportunity to assure you that I am still alive and also to say goodbye.

"As a colonel in the General Staff I am, as you are probably aware, subject to 'automatic arrest.' After a certain amount of hesitation and after settling my private affairs I have decided to do my duty and report to the authorities. My address for some time to come will no doubt be the local American internment camp for 'militarists.'

"Looking out of the window of the café where I am writing this—by the way, they don't even have any substitute coffee and there aren't any panes in the windows—I can see on the wall of the ruined building opposite the first proclamation of General Dwight D. Eisenhower. It begins with the sentence: 'We have come as conquerors, not as liberators.' I accept this statement without bitterness, as indeed I do the tragicomical circumstances that I, one of the officers of the 20th of July, should now be subject to 'automatic arrest.' What strikes me as odd is merely the fact that the Americans should be so proud to come as conquerors and not as liberators. I remember very well that when we marched into Yugoslavia by force of arms we took care to display posters everywhere, expressly declaring ourselves to be liberators, not conquerors. That example alone should have taught the nations what to think of the promises of conquering armies—armies which can justify any trickery and deceit by pretending to be anxious to save human lives. The circumstance that there is never so much talk about the value of human life as in wartime is one of those oddities which I shall no doubt have plenty of time to meditate upon during the months to come.

"What precisely the General is aiming at in his proclamation I cannot tell. Perhaps he is afraid that we Germans might derive, from a professed 'liberation,' certain rights which they evidently intend to withold from us. I do not suppose that the General has ever read Rainer Maria Rilke, but only a few days ago I discovered in his Letters to a Young Woman a few lines which I feel I must not keep from you. 'Germany,' says Rilke, 'might have shamed and shaken the whole world in the year 1918, at the moment of collapse, by an act of profound truthfulness and revocation. By an ethical, determined renunciation of her falsely developed prosperity —in short, through that humility which would have been so infinitely in line with her character, which would have been an element of her dignity, and which would have forestalled anything that could be imposed on her in the way of foreign humiliation. Germany omitted to give of her purest, best and most anciently established measure—she did not show that dignity which has devoutest humility as its root, she thought only of salvation in a superficial, quick, mistrustful and rapacious sense. She wanted to achieve, to get up and get on again instead of—as would have been her most intimate nature—suffering in patience, surviving, and being ready for her miracle. She wanted to persevere instead of changing.' Sometimes I fear that, if freedom really were granted to us, we might not know what to do with it, or that we might use it wrongly, and that we are lacking in that 'innermost humility.' From this point of view I could even understand why the victors should act not as liberators but as conquerors. But are they really guided by such considerations?

"Therefore, my dear Adam, I do not wish to complain, even though I could not help being somewhat surprised at the regulations under which I am 'categorized' as a militarist—a new verb which yields nothing in hideousness to the finest neologisms invented by Hitler. A number of the definitions undoubtedly apply to me—such as the one that 'any person who, prior to 1935, was organizing the systematic training of young people for war, or who participated in any such organization,' shall be deemed a militarist. Any German officer, therefore, who—either during the Weimar Republic or the Third Reich—did not happen to be conducting a military band was inevitably training the young people under his charge for the event of war. Indeed, any military training for 'the event of peace' would have been an utter absurdity.

"You must not assume that the Americans, whom I had expected as liberators, will turn me into an admirer of the Unleashed Corporal whom I, together with others, had planned to liquidate. Nor will they convince me that the war which that Corporal so recklessly provoked has been a just war. It is the bitter irony of history that the victors do not wish to speak with 'free' Germans—almost as if they could learn the truth only from those behind prison walls. No doubt I shall be interrogated a few times, and if this is to be the roundabout way by which I shall get into conversation with the conquerors I will gladly accept this. I am afraid merely of the looks, of the outspoken and tacit remarks, of my future fellow-prisoners who will regard my 'automatic arrest' as a confirmation of their Führer's theories. Once more—this seems to be my fate—I shall have to mix with bad company. I am hoping, though, that they will not 'keep' me overlong—as the police jargon has it. You know better than anybody that I have for many years longed to take off my uniform and to serve my people as a 'civilian.' That this has to be done in the present circumstances makes no difference to my endeavors.

"I hope that you are well and that you are receiving the recognition

which you have so richly deserved. Kiss your mother's hand for me: I trust
that she has come through the recent excitements in good health. With
my most cordial regards—

> "Yours as ever,
> "Achim von Sibelius.

"P.S. I should suggest that you destroy this letter; it might cause you
needless unpleasantness."

The Patriot Thief

"Well, this is a surprise. Fancy seeing you, Maurer," said the Colonel. "Make yourself at home."

The former Corporal Josef Maurer sat down uncertainly. He was a
man of medium height, with broad shoulders, arms that were too
long, a wide mouth, a thick nose and an unusually low forehead. But
for his foxy eyes he would have looked like a village idiot. But these
eyes were so clever that one might have suspected the rest of his face
of being a mask, with two slits for his real eyes.

Maurer was not used to sitting down in the presence of his regimental commander. Apart from Colonel Werner Zobel, Maurer re-
spected no one on earth, not even his father and mother. He had
been the Colonel's orderly for twelve years.

"Didn't think you'd be in Munich," said the Colonel. He remained standing.

For a while they measured each other with embarrassment. Neither of them had ever seen the other in civilian clothes. The Colonel
—a man of sixty-one, a slim figure with a short crop of ice-gray hair,
a well-disciplined face but with eyes tired in default of army regulations—wore a perfectly cut, though now somewhat loose suit. His
orderly wore a brand-new brown jacket that pulled across his chest
and back. Like the spoons in certain old-time cafés, this suit might
have borne the legend "Stolen."

Maurer's hand plunged into the large patch pocket of his jacket.

"I have taken the liberty of bringing the Herr Oberst a little birthday present," he said. "I am glad to find the Herr Oberst looking so
well."

This was a good opportunity for Maurer to stand up.

"Fancy you remembering my birthday!" said the Colonel.

"The sixty-first, Herr Oberst," Maurer reported.

"You wouldn't have found me in yesterday," said the Colonel. "But they released me quickly." Clearly he did not want any sympathy.

Maurer's pocket was like a clown's—a pocket cornucopia. First there appeared a box of cigars, followed by six packs of cigarettes—needless to say, American—a red can of pipe tobacco, and finally three eggs. It was a mystery how the eggs had survived whole.

Maurer placed it all carefully on the embroidered velvet shawl which covered the large mahogany grand piano.

"But I cannot possibly accept this," expostulated the Colonel. "That stuff must cost a fortune!"

"I didn't buy it, Herr Oberst," said Maurer. "Everything's stolen."

The Colonel did not know whether to be angry or not. It was quite obvious to him that everything had indeed been stolen or else —which seemed to him even worse—procured on the black market. But for Maurer to think that he, Colonel Werner Zobel, the commander of the glorious 268th Infantry Regiment, would become a receiver of stolen goods on his birthday . . . ! At the same time he did not want to offend Maurer. He went on as if the presents were not there.

"Well, and what are you doing these days, Maurer?" he asked. He sat down in the faded armchair. Unwittingly the natural order of things had been restored: Zobel was sitting, Maurer was standing.

"Stealing, Herr Oberst," said Maurer.

The Colonel thought Maurer was joking—and in bad taste, at that.

The retired Corporal noticed that his regimental commander was frowning.

"Herr Oberst must not mind me talking like this," he said. "I know the Herr Oberst did not even approve of 'finding' things in enemy territory. The Herr Oberst always had a very high view of clean warfare."

"Clean or not," remarked the Colonel. "The war is over, Maurer."

"Beg permission to differ, Herr Oberst," said Maurer, and the Colonel suddenly noticed how his orderly's narrow foxy eyes had turned hard like stone. "The war is not yet over, Herr Oberst; only the enemy territory has come right into our country. Maybe I'm only a stupid soldier, Herr Oberst, but I know this: occupied and de‌feated are not the same thing."

The Colonel regarded his former subordinate with amazement. You think you have known a man for years, and then you discover you know nothing about him. Aloud he said:

"Are you suggesting that you are a thief out of patriotism, Maurer?"

"Not quite, Herr Oberst," Maurer replied. He had overcome his shyness and was leaning slightly against the piano. "I simply take back on a small scale what the others are taking away from us on a big scale. They've plundered the house that used to belong to my brother and me, Herr Oberst. Cleaned it out, like locusts. They've thrown his wife and children out into the street. It's now occupied by some Polish black marketeers. One's got to resist as best one can, Herr Oberst—Herr Oberst used to say so often himself."

"That was during the war, Maurer," the Colonel repeated. It did not sound very convincing.

"Beg permission to differ, Herr Oberst," said Maurer. "As the Herr Oberst knows, I never was a Nazi. As for the Russians, well, we've made their acquaintance. But as for the British, the French and the Americans, I used to think they were people like us. Until I'd made their acquaintance, too. And now, Herr Oberst, there's no more surrender for me . . ."

He was about to develop his theories further when the door opened and Zobel's daughter came in. Martha was the Colonel's only daughter; two of his sons had been killed in action and the third was still in captivity. She was fair, buxom without being plump, and her skin was so clear one would have judged her to her twenty-five, at the most, whereas in fact she was in her mid-thirties.

"Why, Maurer," said the girl, shaking hands with him. "What brings you to Munich?"

"He is here on business," the Colonel said hurriedly. "And he remembered my birthday."

Martha's eyes lit on the piano and caressed the delicacies.

"Well," said Maurer, stiff and shy again, "I had better say goodbye. . . ."

The Colonel stood up and crossed over to the piano. He put his hand on the cigarettes.

The girl immediately guessed his intention.

"Many, many thanks, Herr Maurer," she said hurriedly. "We had not seen an egg for weeks."

The Colonel saw the Corporal to the door. The hall was a long dark passage which smelled of cooking and lodgers. The Colonel was suddenly reminded of Russia. They had often walked through the night like this, shoulder to shoulder, his orderly and himself. But that had been during the war and there had been less danger then.

When he returned to the overcrowded stuffy sitting-room the birth-day presents of ex-Corporal Josef Maurer had disappeared. He looked questioningly at his daughter.

"You know quite well," she said. "Gerd needs it."

At the mention of the name the Colonel seemed to start.

The Mountains Guard their Secret

Snow had fallen during the night in the mountains high above Berchtesgaden. It was as if winter was venturing out of his lair in darkness only. Now the sky was hard and clear and blue. There were so many yellow flowers in the meadows that one might have thought the greenness itself was yellow. If there had been any schools the children would have written essays on the subject "If Winter comes can Spring be far behind?" Spring was indeed not far behind. But the schools were still closed because one could not be sure that the teach-ers had not been Party members.

When Gerd Mante looked out of his cave in the rock he only saw the snow-covered mountains. He saw no sign of spring.

His comrades had descended into the villages around Berchtesga-den and Reichenhall to find something to fill their stomachs with. They had been gone for a long time. Originally there had been thirty of them. Now they were six. And nobody knew whether they would return. One could never be sure. Some were nabbed. Some allowed themselves to be nabbed. Some were swine. Some were just hungry.

Gerd Mante stood in the opening of the ravine and looked out. With a telescope he might have seen the ruins of the Adlerhorst. But it was better that Gerd Mante should not see them. French troops were patrolling the ruins, as if expecting the ghost of the late occu-pier to appear to them.

Gerd smoked a cigarette. Cigarettes had their own fate. They were manufactured in America. Then they crossed the ocean, neatly pack-aged. Then they went to some American soldier. A carton and a half a week. Then the soldier would peddle them on the black market. Or the former Corporal Josef Maurer would steal a few cartons and

make a present of some to his old Colonel on his sixty-first birthday.
The Colonel's daughter would seize them and make her way up into
the mountains. And then one of these cigarettes would be smoked by
SS-Obersturmbannführer Gerd Mante. And a little later there was
nothing left but ash.

At the back of the cave Martha Zobel was pulling her skirt straight.
She did not want to make a noise. She knew Gerd's terrible moods
when their love-making was over. His caresses were like surprising
punctuations in long, grumpy sentences.

"They ought to have been back long ago," Gerd said without turning his head.

"I'll stay with you till they come," the woman said softly.

"I don't need you," said the man. "I'm not afraid."

"I know you're not afraid," the woman echoed.

She came up to him from behind and waited for him to put his
arm round her. She never gave up hope. But the man did not move.

He was about ten years younger than she—twenty-five at the most.
But now he looked older. His head was like a skull with a great many
white teeth.

"Yellow-bellies," he snarled through his teeth.

"Maybe they'll come yet," said the woman. She pressed closer to
him, cautiously but unmistakably. Her big warm breast touched his
open tunic.

After a little while she ventured to speak:

"Gerd . . . you should come with me."

She expected an angry outburst. But he only said:

"Your father put you up to this."

"He hasn't said anything."

He turned to face her. His head became suffused with a purple
flush; it now looked like a painted skull.

"Your father is another cowardly louse," he said. "It's all their fault,
those cowardly lice. Louts in uniform—that's what the Führer put
his trust in!"

She asked humbly: "What could they have done?"

"What could they have done? What could they have done?" he
mimicked her. "They could have held out, the cowards! Or died an
honorable death." He extended his arm in the direction of the villages. The May sun had broken through the glass of the cold blue
sky. At the foot of the mountain the peaceful red-tiled roofs of the

farmhouses were basking in the spring sunshine. "Look at them down there, stuffing their bellies!"

"They're all starving," said the woman.

"They all deserve to starve to death," he said.

She looked up at him. She thought: he has never been so handsome as now in his indignation.

Then she spotted a flicker in his clear gray eyes. She followed his glance. She saw a man in a ragged Wehrmacht uniform pulling himself up by a boulder and making for them. His disheveled hair hung over his face and he was limping.

"Karl," said Gerd. "He's alone."

The man approached slowly, dragging his feet.

Gerd asked: "Where are the others?"

Karl said: "Gone!"

"Caught?"

"No. Deserted."

"The yellow rats," said Gerd.

The woman went softly back into the cave. Her brassiere was still lying on the horse blanket.

Colonel Hunter Learns German

The spacious house in Harthauserstrasse, in Harlaching near Munich, used to belong to a big industrialist by the name of Oskar Mueller. In theory it still belonged to him, and two cabin trunks of his were in fact still standing in the garage. But since May 10 the house had been occupied by Colonel Graham T. Hunter of the U. S. General Staff, Acting Chief of U. S. Intelligence for the Province of Bavaria.

The Colonel was sitting in the garden. He wore an old pair of slacks with his army shirt and he had undone his collar. "Not even at home are officers and men of the U. S. Army permitted to wear items of civilian clothing if there are more than two persons present," it said in army regulations. The Colonel had only a housekeeper, and she came in the morning and left in the evening; for it was forbidden for Germans to sleep under one roof with Americans. This suited the Colonel quite well, especially in view of his predilection for "items of civilian clothing."

His deck chair stood in the shade of an old tree. On a little table at his right elbow were a half-filled glass of whisky and a German dictionary. Piled up on the lawn at his left were three or four bound volumes of the *Simplizissimus*.

The Colonel had found the dusty volumes in the house. They dated from the First World War and were full of jokes about the Kaiser, the army, Germany's allies, and the Fatherland. The Colonel thought the cartoons excellent. He spent a long time on the captions. From time to time he reached for his dictionary. He was brushing up his German with the aid of the *Simplizissimus*.

At last he put down the volume, removed his rimless spectacles, took a short sip from his glass and turned his face towards the sun. He could not stand too much sun: that was why his deck chair was in the shade. He had a pale complexion which matched his features— the face of a scholar rather than a soldier, narrow, finely chiseled, intelligent and urbane.

deep peace had settled on the garden. The peace reminded the Colonel of home—Columbus, Ohio. He only knew Europe in wartime, in two wars. A peaceful Europe might be almost like America, thought the Colonel. But they don't want peace, these Europeans.

A procorious bee was circling round him. He opened his eyes. From the flagstone terrace his housekeeper was approaching.

"There's a woman here," said the housekeeper as soon as she got near enough. "She says she's been sent by the Military Government."

"Sent by the Military Government?"

The housekeeper shrugged her shoulders. "A children's nurse," she said. There was so much disapproval in the words that the Colonel smiled.

"That's right," he said. "Send her out here."

The Colonel replaced his glasses.

A moment later the woman was crossing the lawn from the house. She was tall and slim, and wore a light gray suit. The Colonel did not know much about women's fashions but he knew that this was an elegant suit. Only when she stood before him did he notice that her shoes were well-worn, very shabby, and quite flat-heeled.

He had got up.

"Good afternoon," he said.

"Good afternoon," she replied. "My name is Marianne Artemstein. I have come in connection with the vacancy."

He did not know at once what to do. He could not offer her the deck chair and there was no other chair about.

"Maybe this is a little premature," he said. "But my wife and children are shortly due to arrive from America." He spoke rapidly. "I've got a son of seventeen and a daughter of fifteen. Our youngest is three—a little girl. We need . . ."

"I am a qualified kindergarten instructress," said the woman.

"Shall we go indoors?" said the Colonel.

Side by side they walked to the house.

The woman said: "The fact is, this would be my first job. I have never practiced my profession."

"That doesn't matter," said the Colonel. "Have you any references?"

"I have left them with the Military Government," the woman replied.

The sitting-room opened on to the terrace. It was a large, tastefully furnished room. For the first time the Colonel noticed how derelict it looked with its empty flower vases, the empty bookshelves and the bare walls.

"Won't you sit down?" he asked.

She had raven hair, brown eyes, a nose a little too small and a mouth that was a little too wide. Her hands were well groomed, the first really groomed pair of hands the Colonel had seen in Germany.

The Colonel found her uncanny, without being able to say why. He had met his wife at West Point, during a Saturday Evening dance given by the Military Academy. He had little experience of women and was usually shy and confused in their presence. He did not find it easy to understand German men, but German women were to him a complete mystery. Did German nursemaids look like this beautiful lady whom one did not know how to treat? Back home, in Columbus, they had never had a nurse. When they had gone out a neighbor's daughter had acted as baby sitter. The Colonel did not think that his wife would get along with this nurse. The thought of having her permanently in the house frightened him. He said, discouragingly:

"As I say, the whole thing is premature. I filled in the form, but I didn't think things would move so fast. I could well imagine that you might not wish to wait so long."

"I can wait," she said. "I have nothing to do."

"Do you speak English?" the Colonel asked. "My wife doesn't speak German."

"My English is somewhat rusty," said the woman. "But I manage."

It was not true that her English was rusty. It was excellent English, the kind that is taught in England, but sounding broad and affected to some American ears.

"Well," said the Colonel. "Perhaps you could leave your address."

"It is on my papers, at the Military Gevernment offices," said the woman.

"I shall let you know, Fräulein . . ."

"Artemstein," supplied the woman.

"Fräulein Artemstein," said the Colonel.

She rose. She did not hold out her hand and he made no attempt to shake hands with her. She nodded lightly and said: "Goodbye, Colonel."

He followed her with his eyes. Her movements were confident and graceful. The Colonel was determined not to take her up on her offer.

PW Eber Returns Home

Private Hans Eber had set out at four that morning because he wanted to get to Munich by nightfall.

Three weeks before he had swum across the Elbe. There had been a good deal of shooting on the Elbe then; some people could not bear the thought of not using up what ammunition they had left.

The Americans, to whom he had surrendered, had not let him down. True, there had been little to eat in the PW cage—"No kraut for the krauts" in the words of the camp sergeant whose sense of humor had not seemed greatly different from that of German Feldwebels. There had been little to eat, but instead each man had received two bars of soap a day—one for his body and one for his laundry. Nobody had had enough shirts or enough skin for all that soap. When Private Hans Eber was eventually released he had carried a pack full of soap on his back. The peasants needed soap. Thus the soap had filled his stomach after all.

No trains were running. Even on the autobahns it was easy to make much progress. Many bridges had been blown up and now hung in mid-air with their cables sticking out—rather thin entrails for such splendid bridges. The first English word he had learned was *detour*. The detour in turn had a detour, and that had yet another detour. The word had lost all meaning.

Along those detours rolled the Shermans and Pattons and smashed up whatever the Mark IV's had left intact. The Americans were evidently trying to use up their fuel just as the others, on the Elbe, had tried to use up their ammunition. But now and again the tanks were quite an amusing sight. On top of one of them sat a soldier with a top hat; another twirled a brightly colored parasol; yet another cradled a grandfather clock in his arm. They looked as if they had just been victorious in a rifle range at a fair.

Mixed up with them were convoys of trucks carrying deportees back to their homes: women and children, complete with bedding and booty. The trucks were driven by Negroes from Alabama and Georgia and Mississippi, and people who had been deported to Kassel were riding in them back towards Warsaw. These columns were moving eastward. And in the opposite direction, towards the west, traveled the liberated French prisoners of war, aboard second-class U. S. Army trucks, waving tricolors.

It was a world on wheels: military vehicles and gipsy caravans, tanks and circuses, victory and misery, everything motorized. And in between, like a narrow stream, trickled that other world, the world on foot, the German world. Men and women roaming over the pitted highroads. Some were looking for a crust of bread, others for their children. Some cursed the conquerors, others did business with them. Whenever a convoy stopped the pedestrians stopped also. Now and again a loaf of bread passed down from a truck or a tank. The children begged for chewing gum. Women stood wedged in between the tanks, from which issued blasts of hot air as though they were on fire inside, and between trucks laden with prisoners. Should they give their smiles to the conquerors or to the vanquished? The whole road seemed to be on the move, like Birnam Wood, the asphalt ebbing and flowing like blood teeming through the arteries of the country, from a dead heart to a dead brain.

Like an overfull stomach the PW camps had thrown up their surfeit. And they looked, too, like something vomited up. The dignity of defeat was here only the defeat of dignity: in rags and tatters the beaten army was hobbling back into its beaten country. They had always been on the roads, these men—on the roads of France and Poland, Russia and Belgium. They had advanced together, but they were retreating singly. During their advance the road had borne them; now they were bearing the road. Only yesterday they had run for their lives, running from the enemy. Now they were only limping and the enemy was watching them; they did not know where he was going and they hardly knew where their own sore feet were carrying them.

Among these thousands was ex-Private Hans Eber. And like those thousands he did not know if he still had a home or why he had been walking for the past three weeks.

And then he was outside the wrought-iron gates of the park in which his parental home stood. That the house should still be there in Bogenhausen, the most elegant part of Munich, completely unchanged with mahogany doors, arched windows, marble floors and parquetry—all that Private Hans Eber could have understood. But that his father should come out to meet him, in a correct black suit and stiff white collar, his pince-nez on his nose, almost in fact as if his son were coming home to spend an enjoyable leave from the front—that was rather more than Hans Eber could comprehend in a hurry.

Back in the PW camp, when he had been asked his name, Hans Eber had been glad that his was a common name—not like Goebbels or Goering or Ribbentrop, names which seemed predestined to notoriety. If he had borne one of those predestined names there would have been questions about parentage and kinship. But who was to suspect that this ragged soldier without insignia or rank or honors was the son of that Eberhard Eber who had been called "the Führer's banker"? Here in Munich the name, however common, could hardly offer refuge or cover. No wonder, therefore, that Private Eber should have assumed that with the fall of the despot the purple would have fallen too. He did not know how much more enduring purple is than the men who wear it. It took him several hours to get over his ghostly experience.

His sister Karin, with whom he could have spoken frankly and to whom he could have communicated his discordant emotions, was not at home and Anna, the old housekeeper, who had looked after him since birth, seemed to find nothing incongruous in the normalcy of their life. She apologized for the modest meal she served him on his homecoming and she accepted as a courteous tribute the fact that Hans was overwhelmed by that modest meal.

He was sitting at the long dining table, his tray before him. His father sat down with him.

After a while Dr. Eber observed:

"The university is supposed to open up again shortly." Again just as though nothing had happened.

His tone irritated the son. He said:

"You aren't going to tell me that the bank, too, will shortly be reopened, Papa?"

"The bank's been bombed out—a total loss," said Dr. Eber. He had not understood.

I shall have to be more brutal, thought the son. He said:

"But you have no difficulties?"

"Everybody has difficulties," replied his father. "After all, we lost the war."

So he has noticed that much, thought Hans.

Dr. Eber was polishing his pince-nez. "The war couldn't be won," he said. "We ought to have stopped long ago."

"We ought never to have started," said Hans.

"That is a question only history can decide," said his father. "The living have an obligation to look ahead."

"What do you mean by that?"

"We must face facts."

But he did not face his son. There was no need for it. Darkness had fallen in the meantime.

SECOND CHAPTER

Frank and George Meet Again

𝔍T WAS symbolical that the life of the city, the province, and
the whole nation should be centered on the railway stations
and their neighborhood. Only rarely did trains arrive at these stations, and only rarely did they depart. "Individuals," said the regulations, "may travel only on presentation of an official urgency voucher
or a doctor's certificate." Transport was available only for a public incapable of transportation.

The rails, like hands outstretched between people who could not
reach one another, were one symbol among many. The wheels were
no longer turning for victory; they were turning for the victors.

The few trains which still left the stations were groaning under
their excessive human cargo, but the conquerors were riding in practically empty coaches. A brigadier general might commandeer a
whole train; a colonel could upset the time-table. The German railways were running to American schedule. Just as the country was cut
off from the world, isolated and in quarantine, the German cities, too,
were cut off from each other. Progress had been wiped out: Germany
had slid back into a medieval solitude. Distances were growing again
and vastnesses which had once been conquered were again gaping
wide. Electric trains were running no longer—only snorting and puffing steam engines, weak with old age and stoked with poor quality
coal, as though to demonstrate that technical progress would take its
revenge against those who abused it.

And yet the stations were even more crowded than at the time
when trains were running. It was not only that the homeless, the
black marketeers, swindlers and small-time racketeers were milling
about in the bombed-out buildings which lay open to the scorching
heat of the sun and the chilly light of the moon—instinctively the people felt that it was here that the first signs of life would be seen, if
there was to be any life again. There were people who went to the

station every day to ask irritable railway officials about the departure times of trains which never departed, and which in all probability they did not want to take: they were just putting their fingers on the pulse of the epoch. All Germany stood still, torn out of time and space; and impatience and hope (as if the two were not the same thing) were circling around the stations, those heaps of rubble which nevertheless still symbolized movement, a getting-somewhere.

Germany, in this spring of 1945, was misery and speculation; and misery and speculation met at the focal point of the railway station. In Munich, one time "the capital of the National Socialist movement," there had been twenty-two thousand hotel beds before the war; now there were exactly one hundred. The city had five hundred sixty-three thousand inhabitants: sixty-five thousand homes had been totally destroyed, a further twenty-five thousand were uninhabitable, and thirty thousand houses were badly damaged. These were not statistics that one could pass over lightly: the statistics stood right there in the middle of the city, and anyone who did not have a roof above his head was a stray unit in these statistics. People sought asylum in the railway stations. In the trains they had cursed they slept on wooden seats or amidst the tattered glory of second-class compartments. Outside, on the track, people were pressing round the train doors as night began to fall, in a way they had never pressed in the past, not even one minute before a train was due to leave. In vain did the railway officials try to get some order into this chaos of homeless mothers, infected prostitutes, cunning railway thieves, cripples, prisoners of war, fledgling sparrows and circling carrion vultures—and they only felt helpless and ludicrous. Like everybody else throughout the land, they were adults no longer: they had become children playing trains on mother's living-room chairs.

And shrill amidst this misery flourished speculation. In the bombed-out buildings black marketeers were busy: Germans, deportees, soldiers; exchanging, haggling, offering, cheating. They were not only offering cigarettes, that currency in packages of twenty, one hundred marks a package and sometimes more; bars of chocolate for one hundred marks, a pound of sugar for one hundred and twenty, a pair of children's shoes for two hundred, fat coupons for two hundred and forty per one-pound unit—anything was on sale here: rumors and young girls; travel permits and beds for a night; genuine dollar bills and false witnesses. Now and again a few ragged German police or some white-belted MP's would drift through the vast buildings, but the groups which scattered on their appearance re-formed instantly. Besides, why should the victors prevent the humiliation which they had themselves thought up from running its full and final course, to the self-immolation of the vanquished?

On that pleasant cool June morning Major Frank Green—or Franz Grün, as he used to be—strode through the station building to meet his brother, Captain George Green, who was due to arrive by the military train from Frankfurt at 8:17.

The news that Captain George Green had been attached to his own unit, the counterintelligence section of the 45th Division, had come as an unpleasant surprise to Frank. They had grown up together, in the Munich house of their father, High Court Judge Dr. Karl Grün, but since 1933, when an aunt had brought the eighteen-year-old Franz and the seventeen-year-old Georg to America, it seemed as though their paths had divided forever. Their father's illness had kept their mother in Germany, and when he died a year later—still in office, since several colleagues had courageously stood up for the Jew—Frau Grün had kept postponing her emigration until it had been too late and the gates of the Hitlerite Reich had fallen shut for good. The two sons had been to different universities: Frank had studied history at Columbia University, graduating with honors and being offered a post there immediately as Assistant Professor. George had studied chemistry at Yale but had soon given up his studies when more lucrative opportunities offered. He had also adapted himself more rapidly to the American way of life in that he ran through half a dozen occupations in a short time, moving his home like a nomad, and always with an eye to the main chance. Whenever the brothers had met the sharp differences in their characters had led to almost stormy clashes, but whereas George had not seemed to worry unduly about their evident estrangement and tacit hostility, Frank had gradually preferred to avoid those meetings. When he had last heard of George he had been some sort of contractor in Dallas, Texas, and it had seemed exceedingly unlikely that they would ever meet in uniform, least of all in their native town.

"You're looking fine," said Frank as he shook hands with George on the platform. It had always been his custom to conceal his dislikes behind especial courtesy—not from hypocrisy but because only that excess of courtesy stopped him from showing his true feelings.

"You're not looking so bad yourself, Major," George joked. He grabbed his army duffel-bag which Frank had taken from him. "I can't let a superior officer carry my luggage."

They crossed the big building. Nobody would have thought that the Major and the Captain, walking briskly side by side, were brothers. Although they were about the same height, George was broader and more massive, and thus seemed shorter. His dark hair was cut short in the military manner, his eyes were small and narrow, his forehead surprisingly low and his nose broad and flat. Yet for all that he was more handsome than his brother: although his features were ugly in detail there was about him a virility and vitality which more than offset those flaws. One would notice only the spreading circles in the water but not the stone which had caused them.

They got into Frank's waiting command car.

"Pretty good pasting this place got," said George as the driver was weaving the car through the city. Needless to say, he was speaking in English. "Frankfurt's one big ruin. Well, that's the way they wanted it, the bastards."

"Our house has gone, too," said Frank.

"I'll have a look at it. We must register our compensation claims in good time." He laughed. "By the way, let me assure you that I haven't done anything to get transferred here. I was doing fine in Frankfurt. What's accommodation like here?"

"Not too bad. I believe Colonel Hunter has fixed you up in a bachelor block in Klementiner-Strasse."

"Just my idea of fun—a bachelor block! Sounds like a YMCA hostel. Surely there must be some decent Nazi villas here that one could confiscate? In Frankfurt I had an eight-room villa to myself. Used to belong to an I. G. Farben director. By the way, have you heard the latest joke? The I. G. Farben has been renamed G. I. Farben. It's to become the Headquarters building."

They were driving through the city center. There was a smell of burning about the place. No longer a very penetrating smell—just the smell of a kitchen at night when some food had been burned at lunchtime. Some of the ruins were still looking rather new; they had not yet been fixed up for inspection by visitors. The city had been cleaned up and some order had been re-established, but all of the masonry had not yet been removed: it was scattered about like building blocks on a nursery floor. The naughty children had gone to ped without tidying up. Here and there green vegetation had sprung up among the untidy stones. Now and then a woman would pass, in a white blouse, flowers in hand. Nothing in their stomachs, but flowers in their hands—that, too, is Germany, thought Frank. But he said nothing. He was watching his brother. Only when they turned into the Königsplatz, a square that had always been a little unreal, a ballroom without walls and roof, and which looked even more unreal now without any people in it, did he say:

"That used to be the Brown House."

He said it with some pride, as though he had himself seen to it that there should be no Brown House any more.

"The bastards," said George.

After a while, as if he had delayed the question long enough, he asked:

"Did you find Mama's grave?"

"She has no grave," said Frank.

There was another pause.

"Any people left from the old days?" George began.

"I went to see Dr. Wild. I wanted to take him a few rations, but he would not accept them. Or rather, he gave me no chance of offering them to him. He acted as if my visit embarrassed him. He is a queer fish; I can't make him out."

"Probably turned Nazi, too, in the end," said George. Then he swung round abruptly to face his brother, as if he not only demanded an answer to his question but also wanted to watch the expression of his interlocutor. He asked: "Have you seen Elisabeth?"

Frank evaded the question by asking in turn:

"How could I have seen Elisabeth?"

There was nobody with whom he was less anxious to discuss Elisabeth than George. It had not always been possible to avoid it during those past few years, but even in America he had tried whenever he could to sidestep any conversation about Elisabeth.

They had grown up together—Franz, Georg and Elisabeth—almost as brothers and sister, and yet in a relationship as full of turbulent undercurrents as the sea hiding its whirlpools beneath a smooth surface.

In Nymphenburg the Grün's garden had bordered on the garden of the house occupied by High Court Judge Dr. Joachim Steer, a widower, with his daughter and an old housekeeper. The two judges had been not only colleagues but friends, and this friendship had stood its test even when Dr. Grün's position was becoming more and more precarious with the advent of the Third Reich. Elisabeth was the same age as Georg, a year younger than Franz. The rivalry between the two brothers for her favor had begun when she was three years old and discovered how to play the shy and quiet Franz off against the more robust Georg and vice versa. Later this unconscious, but nonetheless genuine, coquettishness had curiously disappeared— not because the growing girl had decided in favor of either brother, but presumably because with the growing realization of her attraction she had also become increasingly aware of the dangers it entailed. Georg's first passion flared up early, and Franz, too, was now smiling at the sentimental hours he had spent standing by the garden fence: a picture from a neighbor's-daughter romantic novelette which he felt sure he had long outgrown. But the two boys who had told each other about their first adventures, real and invented, in the darkness of their bedroom had invariably fallen silent as soon as Elisabeth's name was mentioned. Suddenly a silent hostility had hung in the nocturnal room. Not only had it harbored the sullen hatred of two rivals, but it had also seemed as though each of them were standing pugnaciously, warning and forbidding, in front of the adolescent fantasies of the other. If it had been possible they would have listened in to each other's dreams. Just as the natural contrasts of their characters had led to these clashes, so that it was impossible to say whether their rivalry had begotten their hostility or was merely an expression of it, so their strange solidarity had similarly crystallized around Elisabeth. They could renounce Elisabeth, but not their common hatred when a third man seemed to step into the girl's life.

They had been barely a year in America when Elisabeth was married to a member of Hitler's intimate circle—Kurt von Zutraven. Their mother had sent them the news without comment, mindful of the censorship. At that time Franz and Georg had still seen each other fairly often, even though they attended different colleges. If they had conscientiously searched their hearts they would have discovered that from that moment onward they began to avoid meeting one another because they flinched from talking about Elisabeth. Each of them knew that the other was following every piece of news about Elisabeth von Zutraven—perplexed or angrily, full of questions or full of condemnation, bent on comprehension or revenge, according to their different characters. And there certainly had been no dearth of news, for the rise of the Führer's aide-de-camp to the post of Reich Commissar, then Cultural Commissar for the Occupied Territories, and finally Governor of France, had been rapid and dazzling. And again everything was as in the old days: if Zutraven's name was in the papers, if Zutraven's picture was published, or perhaps even Elisabeth's, then Franz knew that Georg would see the paper, and Georg would think of Franz, and across thousands of miles the estranged brothers would meet in a common sentiment.

And now George had asked the question: "Have you seen Elisabeth?"

Whether or not the idea of seeing Elisabeth had previously occurred to Frank, he certainly had nipped it in the bud. "Have you seen Elisabeth?" Did this mean that George wanted to see her? The command car had not even reached the billeting office when, like an old familiar friend, a feeling welled up in Frank: he had to warn Elisabeth, defend her, protect her. George must not talk of her; he must not see her.

George did not notice anything.

"I saw in the papers that she's locked up," he said. "I wonder what she's thinking now—the Nazi moll."

Four Women Await Their Fate

If one looked out of the windows of the villa one could just discern in the distance the outlines of the Party Rally Stadium. It looked like the walls of a half-built skyscraper. All that had stood for centuries in this ancient town of Nuremberg now lay in ruins. The half-built folly had remained unscathed.

Elisabeth was standing by the window, gazing out. For the past two days it had been raining incessantly. The rain was like the muslin drapes on an operatic stage. The sentry on his uninterrupted patrol around the house saw the woman's face behind the pane. It was as if the woman were crying; the water streamed down over her face, ceaselessly, disconsolately. But the woman was not crying; only the windowpane was.

Elisabeth had been standing by the window for some considerable time; she did not want to take part in the conversation that had been babbling along in the sitting-room for the last two hours. The wife of the Marshal, the wife of the Reich Minister and the wife of the Foreign Labor Commissar were sitting around the coffee table, talking.

The Marshal's wife was a powerful woman with thick blond hair which now fell loosely on to her shoulders and over her bosom and lap, for she had washed it at noon and was now letting it dry. She was doing this not fortuitously, even with that restricted audience. She had always been very proud of her Lorelei hair, and although she bore little resemblance otherwise to the gentle Lorelei of the legend—indeed she would have towered well above the Rhine cliff and was built more on the lines of a monumental Statue of Liberty—she would sometimes hum a romantic little song as she lovingly and evenly drew her comb through her tresses. Moreover, she was sitting very straight, even a little stiffly, in the faded easy chair; she was enthroned rather than sitting. During the past weeks of arrest and interrogation, far from losing her majestic bearing she had actually emphasized it as far as possible. She sat enthroned even in the cricle of the dethroned, as though afraid that any condescension might be interpreted as weakness. She saw the other women not as fellow-prisoners, at least not in the sense that a common fate levels or even wipes out distinctions of rank. And while her grandiose vanity had been the object of much malicious feminine gossip and unfavorable criticism in "the good days," it now exacted a certain tacit respect from the wives of the other dethroned dignitaries, as all human qualities are apt to do, good ones and bad ones alike, so long as they prove sufficiently enduring and not subject to the quirks of fate.

On her right sat the Reich Minister's wife: small, gray-haired, with unrimmed spectacles, wearing a nondescript, almost cheap, dress, the type of woman one would always describe as "no doubt much older than her husband" whether this was in fact so or not. True, her husband had always displayed an improperly youthful behavior, especially in his choice of uniforms, which he wore on all possible occasions, preferably with white lapels. Their marriage had been childless, a circumstance for which the Frau Minister—no doubt unjustly— blamed her husband as much as for his white-lapelled uniforms. Her criticism of her husband and his escapades, about which there had been much discreet sniggering, did not however take the form of disapproval of his political views and activities. On the contrary, her fanaticism had excelled his, except that she had deliberately directed it into activities which would make his own work appear irresponsible and superficial. She had been the patroness of anything that could be patronized: illegitimate children, air-raid victims and war widows, railway missions and castles belonging to the Teuton Knights. Whereas the Frau Marshal was all out to bewitch the American interrogating officers, not from any lack of dignity but from natural feminine coquettishness, the wife of the Reich Minister remained taciturn and stubborn, endeavoring unconsciously to humiliate the victors just as she had always humiliated her husband.

The wife of the Reich Commissar had settled down on the old settee with its Victorian scroll back and was busy with some knitting. Impassively she let the conversation of the other women drift over her, occupied with herself as she had been for many years past—even though her friends and acquaintances were unable to discover how such an uncomplicated nature could be the subject of such persistent occupation. She was pregnant, some four months gone, but her condition was fairly obvious and she had made no attempt to conceal it. She was a woman of no more than thirty-five, with a robust rustic figure and with almost childlike frank eyes in a broad but pretty face. The Führer had always honored her with his affectionate if slightly condescending favor, probably because among all the wives of the "big shots" she came nearest to his idea of the German woman. Maybe the Führer's favor had also contained a little sympathy: even he must have heard that the Reich Commissar was keeping up an adulterous relationship with a beautiful and worldly aristocrat who had already borne him two illegitimate sons, which brought the total of his children, legitimate and illegitimate, up to six. To the surprise of some and the admiration of other members of high society the Commissar's wife maintained the most cordial relations with her husband's mistress, and indeed—to the utmost disapproval of the Frau Reich Minister—the countess had visited her legitimate rival even here in Nuremberg, at the interrogation villa. Besides, the wife of the Reich Commissar—he was kept under arrest in Nuremberg—was not, strictly speaking, a prisoner any more than Elisabeth von Zutraven. They had been temporarily accommodated at the so-called interrogation villa, whereas the other two ladies were kept at a Nuremberg prison camp and only occasionally brought up to the villa for questioning. It was they, not Elisabeth or the Frau Reich

Commissar, who were guarded by the MP who was on sentry duty in the neglected garden.

When Elisabeth returned to the little group by the coffee table the conversation, as usual, was about the treatment in the camp from which the Frau Marshal and the Frau Minister had been brought to the villa that morning.

"I had to cut my nightgown in half," the Marshal's wife was explaining while continuing to comb her hair. "I couldn't have washed it otherwise. Such a small washtub they've given us. They lack all sense of chivalry."

"Did you expect anything else, Excellency?" asked the Frau Reich Minister. "The Americans are barbarians. That's the most painful thing of all: to have been defeated by barbarians."

The Marshal's wife did not pursue the historical subject. "Of course, there are some human beings among them," she observed. "One MP has smuggled a mirror into my cell." She looked around. The chilly sitting-room, with half its furniture removed, resembled a second-class railway waiting-room. The silver-gray wallpaper was torn in one or two places and the strips were hanging loosely from the wall, as if it had not even been worth while to tear them off properly. But on one wall there was an old mirror in an ornate frame, half-blind with a few wounds like the wallpaper, but a mirror for all that. Pointing to it the Marshal's wife continued: "This place here is paradise by comparison." She was looking steadily at Elisabeth.

The Frau Commissar, however, took the remark to apply to her.

"It's not paradise," she said, glancing up from the baby's undershirt she was knitting, "but they let us have a bottle of milk every day."

Elisabeth was listening inattentively. She had always found it difficult to understand the ladies of the hierarchy; now it seemed more difficult than ever. The Americans would almost certainly not believe her, but she could have taken her oath on it: these women had always talked about underwear and mirrors and milk. Not only now, but in the past, also—when the Germans were in Paris, and when Stalingrad came, and when Dresden stood in flames, and when the gas chambers were busy in Auschwitz. Whenever they met they had exchanged information: about shoes that could be obtained in Holland, or pepper which a courier had brought from France. If ignorance was inno-

»49«

cence, then these women were innocent. But was ignorance innocence? No, the Americans were wrong: these women and the wives of the other high dignitaries were no hyenas. Domestic animals cannot be hyenas. The whole world was talking about them, full of envy or hatred, full of admiration or thirst for revenge—and meanwhile they were talking of Paris fashions and cooking recipes and hairdressers. Their great rise had not made them greater; neither had their great fall. Their menfolk had ruled half the world; their menfolk were now waiting to be tried as war criminals by a tribunal of the world— but they were sitting around a coffee table, having a coffee party without coffee. And myself? questioned Elisabeth. What gives me the right to judge them or even to despise them?

She had no time to follow this thought to its conclusion. Besides, it was a thought of which she had wearied, for its answer lay always hidden in confusion. The Frau Marshal was now addressing her:

"My dear, I hear that you were allowed to visit your husband?"

"Yes," said Elisabeth. "Just for a few minutes."

"Is he all right?" asked the Marshal's wife.

"He is in good health."

"There is, of course, no hope of our getting a visiting permit," said the Minister's wife.

At that moment there was a knock at the door. The women looked up. The MP had not waited for an answer; he had come in.

"Is there a Frau von Zutraven here?" he asked. Clearly, the names of his charges meant nothing to him. He pronounced the name as Vansutreven.

"Yes, me . . ." Elisabeth said in surprise.

"An officer wants to see you," said the MP. "Come along."

Elisabeth got up. For a moment the others followed her with their eyes. Then the conversation babbled on. There was nothing unusual in an officer wanting to see one of them.

Frank Finds Elisabeth

The library of the villa was empty when Elisabeth entered it. Like the other rooms in the house it was only half-furnished: in front of the desk, in the middle of the room, stood a solitary chair. There were no books on the dark shelves. On one of the shelves stood a frying pan which the former owner must have left behind, incongruous in its surroundings. From the center of the ceiling dangled two wires, intended for a lamp which was no longer there. The early evening was creeping into the room.

Elisabeth had only just noticed that the MP held a slip of paper in his hand.

"A Major Franz Grün," he read.

Elisabeth had no time to reply. The Major entered the room at the same moment as the soldier left it.

He approached her with rapid strides. He did not wait for her to shake hands with him but extended his hand to her.

They both searched for an opening remark. At last the man said: "I only learned a few days ago that you were in Nuremberg, Elisabeth. I thought I ought to see you."

"Thank you," said Elisabeth.

"How are you?" asked Frank.

"Quite well, thank you," said the woman. "And how are you?"

"I am all right," said Frank. "I'm stationed in Munich. I had some business in Nuremberg."

They were facing each other, waiting. Frank was acutely aware of the whole pointlessness of his action. Why had he come? Had he been driven by curiosity? Or was it more? Did he want to rejoice in the sight of the defeated? He ought not to have forgotten what experience had long taught him: that there is always an unbridgeable gulf between imagination and reality, that one could never picture anything in advance, neither encounters nor conversations, neither one's own sensations nor those of others. Fantasy was no prophet; its prophecies never came true. He should have known too that the vanquished would be different individually from what they were in the mass; that a bombed town looked different in a bird's-eye view from the bombed streets on the ground; just as a street looked different from the individual house with its entrails protruding, and the house different again from the dead man lying beneath it, with his guts torn out. Hatred was like a large sheet of water; it was colored green and blue and metallic if one looked across its wide expanse; it was calm or turbulent, whipped up or menacing. But if one immersed one's hand to scoop up some of it, it was suddenly colorless and vanished between one's fingers. Or had he come because he wanted to help her? Abruptly he repudiated the idea; his hatred seemed to him an obligation to his mother and all the other dead. There was something wrong, he thought, with the doctrine that love alone was an obligation; for could love not become treason to love? Yet he need not have come here for retribution; retribution was running its course and did not require his help.

Aloud he said: "I don't know why I wanted to see you, Elisabeth. But it would have been cowardly of me not to see you. I don't know what you did during those years—apart from what there was in the papers, over on the other side. But the eighteen years of our childhood cannot be simply expunged. I cannot offer you any help; I doubt that I would even if I could." He was afraid that she might interrupt him and continued more rapidly. "But I suppose that nobody will listen to you today, at least not with . . . let us say, a modicum of understanding. So if you would like to talk to somebody who is prepared to listen to you without prejudice . . ."

He could not go on. It was a terrible sensation to hear himself speak: he thought that he had never before heard his own voice so clearly. At the same time he became aware of the distance which the voice had to traverse from thought to expression, and how it changed and disguised itself on the way. The thought was simple but the words were pompous, and out of a seed of pity had sprung bombastic magnanimity.

They were still facing each other in the dusky room, and the empty chair stood between them.

"It was good of you to come," said Elisabeth. "It has surprised me, perhaps even overwhelmed me. But I have nothing to say to you, Franz. I have been interrogated all day long, and I shall be questioned again. They are treating me correctly: I have nothing to complain of."

She wanted to add: I have admitted more than I need have done, because I despise people who dissemble and distort. More hateful than sullenness are denials; more hateful than stubbornness is groveling. But she said no more because she knew she would be misunderstood. Anybody who was proud now was bound to be regarded as a sinner: they did not suspect what little pride the sinners had left. And if one was not proud then one was an opportunist: too many were queuing up outside the confessionals to make repentance credible. If there was a way out at all, it was that of not seeking a way out.

She said: "I do not think you have come to humiliate me, Franz. But seeing you humiliates me. Please, do not come again."

"As you wish," he said.

She tried to smile because she wanted to tone down what she had said. She gave him her hand.

"You haven't changed a bit," she said with a certain relief as they had moved closer, divided only by the chair. "I should have known you at once. How long is it?"

"Nearly twelve years," he said.

"How is Georg?" she asked.

He said quickly: "He's all right, thank you." He wanted to add: He is here too. But he only said: "He's in the Army, too."

Suddenly he was in a hurry to leave, not because of Georg but because he was afraid she might ask him about his mother. And he would have to answer: You know quite well that she is dead.

He said goodbye and left.

The MP outside the house saluted smartly. Frank returned the salute and got into his car.

Nuremberg was in darkness. Progress was slow because there were deep holes in the streets and some streets were closed altogether. In the middle of the Old City they got mixed up with a convoy. The heavy army trucks were lumbering over the old cobblestones, past the medieval houses of which only the façades were left, as if reality were trying to copy a stage setting from *Die Meistersinger* just as the opera backdrop had once been copied from reality.

On the wet road surface Elisabeth's face danced before Frank's eyes. It was three faces: the face of a girl of sixteen or seventeen, gay and carefree; the mechanical smile on the face of an elegantly gowned woman surrounded by mechanically smiling dignitaries on an official photograph; the tired face of the woman in the empty library of the interrogation villa. The faces were reflected in the puddles, trembling, gyrating and fading, so that Frank could not hold on to any of them.

"Do we spend the night in Nuremberg?" asked his driver.

"No. We're going back to Munich," said Frank.

Inge and the Negro

Nobody will want to pick you up, her father had said.

Perhaps he is right; perhaps nobody will pick me up, thought

Inge, as she sauntered around the Sendlinger-Tor-Platz where, in that spring of 1945, love was being offered for sale as early as mid-afternoon, since the Germans were forbidden to show themselves in the streets after ten o'clock, whether purveying love or not.

Perhaps I really won't get get picked up. Monotonously and dully the thought was hammering on her brain. When she was fifteen she had known a boy who had wanted to take her, and she had resisted him. Now he was dead. And it was odd that what she had considered precious only yesterday she was today ready to cast away. It was even odder that she wanted to give to a stranger what she had denied to the boy whom she had liked so much. But the oddest thing was that it hurt her that nobody wanted to pick her up. It was easy for Hilde and the other girls; they did not think about these things. That was what Inge envied them most: that they did not have to think about it.

It never occurred to Inge Schmidt that nobody picked her up be-cause she did not want to be picked up. Most of the Germans who crossed the square at night were not in the mood for venal love any-way. The girls who were waiting for clients did not want money. They wanted cigarettes or chocolate or coffee or at least a few ration coupons. The eternal question of whether a rumbling stomach or a rumbling hunger for love was the stronger had long been solved in postwar Germany. Nobody who had any ration coupons would part with them for the sake of love; lust began with a sufficiency of calories. The Americans, on the other hand, who possessed the currency of love—cigarettes and cans of food—waited to be accosted. Mostly they were hanging about in groups, propped against the wall of a bombed-out movie theater, waiting. They were strange soldiers: they were evidently unable to stand upright. They would generally lean against a wall, standing on one leg like storks, with the other leg bent at the knee and the sole of the foot lying flat against the wall. Others would crouch, always in the same position, their haunches on their heels; for hours on end they would sit there like frogs. These storks and frogs would smoke cigars or chew gum, rarely talking to each other, and when some girl addressed them they would usually just utter a few obscenities. After all, obscenities could hardly be regarded as a violation of the Non-Fraternization Law. For the most part the men leaning against the bombed-out theater wall were Negroes, and many of them were generous: they would toss a cigarette to the pass-ing girls, follow them with their eyes and laugh among each other, but they would not go with them. It was too dangerous to go with them.

Inge Schmidt had passed these groups a dozen times, but she nearly broke into a run as she passed them, dropping her eyes at the same time. The men's glances did not follow her: she looked too slight and too childlike and asked for nothing, not even a cigarette. Yet something drove her out to the Sendlinger-Tor-Platz night after night. It was not just because her father had said that nobody would pick her up. She was hungry. It was rumored that every standard consumer would shortly obtain one thousand three hundred and fifty calories. Inge did not understand about calories. She only knew that there were no one thousand three hundred and fifty calories available at the moment, and that she was hungry. Her father was hungry too, and whenever there was anything to eat he would eat it, for he did not consider Inge a standard consumer. She had been hungry before, during the war, but looking back to that time now her hunger then seemed like repletion. Now she was constantly and painfully conscious of her hunger. Her hunger reminded her of a dead mouse. It was as if she had a dead mouse in the mouth. And her stomach was like a painful pit. She could not tell where the hunger hurt her, because the pain traveled from her stomach to her chest, and from her chest to her neck. It was as if the void were aching. Her brain, too, was empty and aching. Only when she was asleep did the pain relent, but then came the dreams—the dreams which were driving Inge into the street. For in her dreams the soldiers were crouching around a cooking pot, and from the pot rose the smell of goulash and dumplings. Or the soldiers by the theater wall produced sausages from their pockets and handed them to her. There was one soldier in her dreams who conjured up hundreds of sausages from his pocket, yards and yards of sausages, the way they used to hang in the windows of cooked-meat shops in the old days; he was chasing her around the Sendlinger-Tor-Platz with his string of sausages, until they formed a huge circle right around the square, like the trolley lines that used to be there once.

It never occurred to Inge that she might have chosen an "honest" occupation—for one thing, she could not think of an honest occupation and for another, all honest occupations were paid for in money, those ridiculous scraps of Reichsmarks for which one could not buy anything. Other people were selling their possessions: the pensioner

Alois Schmidt had already parted with a grandfather clock, an ala-baster bust, a suit, two pairs of shoes and a canary complete with cage. But Inge Schmidt had nothing to sell except her body, and that was thin and flat and sixteen-years-old.

Every evening for a whole week she had been wandering around the Sendlinger-Tor-Platz. She possessed only one pretty summer dress, of blue artificial silk with large yellow flowers. Every afternoon she put it on. Hilde, the girl from next door, lent her her lipstick. She often spent half an hour in front of the gilt-framed living-room mir-ror, making up. Strictly speaking, the lipstick was for her lips only, but she also drew a red circle on each cheek and then spread the color over her whole face, until she looked like a feverish child. Her father watched her making up in silence, but she knew that he rum-maged through her handbag when she came home at night, and that he knew then that again nobody had picked her up.

Incidentally, it was this handbag that she began to blame for the total failure of her enterprise, so that eventually she developed an almost physical hatred for it. It was a small, shiny, red patent-leather handbag, quite dainty in a way, but unmistakably a child's handbag. And in fact Inge had received it as a birthday present many years before. The women in the Sendlinger-Tor-Platz all carried enormous handbags, black, spacious and heavy—signs of their trade, as it were. Inge felt sure that some soldier would have accosted her long before if it had not been for her brilliantly-red child's handbag.

It was getting on towards eight o'clock on a heavy July evening. In the blue summer sky stood a crescent moon, modestly and shame-facedly reporting for night duty, yet also a little impatiently, since it would not be dark for some time yet and day was only reluctantly getting ready to depart.

Inge was just considering whether she had better make for home when a female voice rang out beside her:

"High time you beat it, child!"

Inge turned in alarm. One of the women she had often noticed had followed her and was now marching by her side. She was a tall blonde of about forty, with far too numerous curls, her bulging figure squeezed into a tight suit, which was moreover too short and revealed to the knees a pair of unattractive legs of considerable girth. Like most of her colleagues, the tall blonde stalked about the pavement on excessively high heels, and since the heels were made of wood they clip-clopped like a horse's hoofs. From her right arm dangled a large black handbag.

"Take it easy, child," the woman continued, aware of Inge's alarmed start. "I'm saying this for your own good. The others are beginning to get annoyed and one of these days they may well lose their patience." She was talking not exactly cordially but by no means threateningly, and her speech was careful rather than vulgar. "It's not as if you were robbing anybody of their livelihood; after all, you haven't hooked a man so far. Nor are you likely to, the clumsy way you're setting about it. But if by any chance some man decided to go with you, just because you looked like a decent girl, or if someone were to give you a present—well, then it might easily happen that the girls would give you a terrible hiding. You see, business is bad, downright disastrous, and they don't want any competition, even if that competition looks as emaciated as yourself."

"I don't know what you're talking about," said Inge. She could not think of anything else to say.

"Oh yes, you do," the woman said patiently. "I don't care if you want to become a whore—after all, you're not my daughter. And before the occupation it was quite a decent profession." She glanced at the men who were standing propped against the wall of the bombed movie theater like storks or crouching on the ground like frogs. "If you get entangled with one of those you'll get an entirely wrong idea of the profession, and that would be a pity." She slipped half a piece of chewing gum into her own mouth. "No respect for our profession—not those gentry. They'll tell you full of pride that they've got no prostitution back home, and then they go all maudlin and tell you about their wives and the 'decent girls' back home, and they're scared stiff of you as if you were a leper. And then they'll demand things of you of which you've had no inkling, child, enough to make you vomit, especially if all the while they keep telling you how decent their women are and how they would lose their girl if she knew of this . . ."

They had twice circled the square. At the Sendlinger Tor stood a group of colleagues watching them: they put their heads together, whispered and giggled.

Inge wanted to say something impertinent, but she said only: "I've got to go home now. I live a long way off."

"Now you go home like a good girl, and don't come again," said the blonde. "Besides, I'm willing to bet you haven't been to the police yet. They won't give you a ticket at your age. And if the others get you into trouble with the police you won't get off so lightly." At the corner of Lindwurmstrasse she stopped. She took a step backwards as if to scrutinize Inge more carefully. Suddenly she began to laugh. She laughed noisily, in a deep, masculine bass, and her voice echoed back from the ruin at the street corner. "Do you know what I'm thinking, child?" she asked.

"I don't care what you're thinking," said Inge.

The woman was not offended. "I'm thinking that you might still be a virgin," she said.

She paid no attention to the girl who was standing there trembling all over. The prostitutes across the square need not beat Inge up any longer: the way she was standing there, grown even slighter in her pretty summer dress, with the child's handbag in her hand, she looked sufficiently beaten. The woman opened her handbag and said:

"Here—you must be hungry."

She gave her half a bar of chocolate. Inge had no time to think whether to accept the present or not. There was a screech of brakes at that moment and a jeep had pulled up by the curb.

The man at the wheel signaled with his hand. He was a giant of a Negro, much blacker than most colored soldiers, so that the white of his eyes and his teeth seemed even whiter. The tall blonde left Inge standing and moved towards the vehicle. She swayed her hips and smiled. The chocolate had been swiftly slipped back into her bag.

The Negro pushed her aside, not roughly but unambiguously. He pointed his long thin fingers towards the ruin. The tall blonde turned in surprise. The Negro said nothing, but uttered an impatient sound like a man who had no time for being misunderstood.

"He means you," the tall blonde said to Inge.

Not until the blonde took her by the hand did she understand.

The Negro smiled. He gave the tall blonde two cigarettes and thought she was thanking him, whereas in fact she was cursing. Then he pulled Inge on to the seat by his side. Almost without a will of her own she yielded. She only pressed her child's handbag against her, as if it provided a last refuge.

Next morning the pensioner Alois Schmidt found two packs of Chesterfields in the red handbag.

When a German entered the U. S. headquarters building in Ludwig-strasse he had to fill out a regular questionnaire. True, the young lady who presented the questionnaire was German herself, but for that very reason she made sure that the American regulations were obeyed with German thoroughness. Dr. Adam Wild spent two hours filling out the form and going through a string of further formalities that were to clear the road for him to the office of Major Frank Green.

At last a waiting-room sergeant had sent his name in to the Major.

The Major rose at once and met him in the door. He offered Adam a chair and resumed his seat behind an American steel office desk.

"I am glad you have come, Herr Doktor," he said. "What can I do for you?"

Adam made himself as comfortable as possible on the little army folding stool.

"You are quite right, Herr Major," he began. "I have indeed come as a suppliant. One of my friends has been detained in Frankfurt for a number of weeks, under what is called 'automatic arrest.' He is a colonel in the General Staff, Baron Achim von Sibelius."

"A former colonel," corrected Frank.

"Very well, a former colonel," continued Adam, not in the least disconcerted. "I remembered that you'd left me your address, Herr Major. I thought perhaps you might be able to do something for my friend."

He regarded Frank openly with his big blue eyes, as if he thought his request in no way improper.

"And who is this Baron Sibelius?" asked Frank.

"He was one of the officers of the 20th of July," said Adam.

"And what happened to him after the 20th of July?" asked Frank.

"He was lucky," replied Adam who had been ready for this question. "His superior sympathized with the conspirators, although he did not himself belong to them. He covered up for Achim, so that he was able to sneak off to the Eastern front."

The Major did not reply at once. At last he said:

"Herr Doktor, I am not doubting your word. But it does seem strange that the whole Wehrmacht should have consisted of conspirators and that these conspirators should nevertheless have held out to the end. Can you explain this?"

"No," said Adam. "I cannot explain it. At least not so that you'd believe it." Quite simply, without any irritation, he added: "I have not come, Herr Major, to convince you of the innocence of the German people. I wanted to bring to your notice the case of my friend, the former Colonel Sibelius."

"Do you know our attitude to the 20th of July?"

"No . . . not exactly . . . ," said Adam.

"We take the view," said Frank, "that the 20th of July, 1944, was a damned late date for an awakening. With the exception of the Lunatic nobody had any doubt left by the 20th of July that the war was lost for Germany. The men who wanted to liquidate him hated him not because he had started the war, but because he had lost it. Even though much bloodshed might have been avoided, we still take the view that the failure of the attempt was a blessing in disguise. If it had succeeded the question of responsibility would have become quite insoluble."

"And now, Herr Major?" asked Adam. "Now you believe that the question of responsibility can be answered?"

"Certainly," said Frank. "Now everything is perfectly clear."

I won't argue with him, thought Adam. To him everything is perfectly clear. To all of them everything is perfectly clear. To the Lunatic, too, it had been perfectly clear that the whole world was only waiting to be redeemed by the German spirit. To his followers it had been perfectly clear that he was the new Messiah. To the German people it had been perfectly clear that things would turn out all right in the end. And later it had been perfectly clear to most of them that there was no point in resisting. Then again it had been perfectly clear that the whole nightmare would be over as soon as the Americans liberated the country. To the Americans, in turn, it had been perfectly clear that we were all Nazis and did not deserve liberating. It is also perfectly clear to them that there had been no resistance to the regime and that thousands of Germans had been swept into the concentration camps by pure chance. It is perfectly clear to us that we knew nothing of concentration camps, and it is equally clear to them that we all personally turned on the gas chambers. It is perfectly clear to us that we lost the war only because we set human hands against steel; and it is perfectly clear to them that they won the war because they represented divine justice. How can there be any understanding when the whole world is full of people to whom everything is perfectly clear . . . ?

He said: "If I had come on my own business I should try to convince you, Herr Major. I could then get a few things off my chest and we should probably part as enemies. In the business of my friend Sibelius I cannot afford this. You came to see me some time ago and asked if you could do anything for me. I am not asking anything impossible: just have a look into the Sibelius file and help him out of jail if you think he deserves it."

Frank regarded the doctor with ill-disguised astonishment. He had not heard that kind of language since had had crossed the Rhine. He had met kowtowing and obsequious Germans, people who would recount their deeds and sufferings under the late regime; others, those who stood to gain or lose nothing, had been presumptuous and sullen; still others had been curiously indifferent. But this slum doctor, who had looked after his mother, was carefully avoiding all conversation about himself, although he seemed to have a clear conscience, and now that he was asking a favor it was for someone else. However, Frank was determined not to let himself be impressed. The doctor had spent the past twelve years in Germany, and he did not seem to have been to prison or to a concentration camp. How often, wondered Frank, had this blue-eyed giant raised his arm during those past twelve years and shouted "Heil Hitler"? How often had he stood passively by the curb as the trucks rolled past with Jews packed into them like cattle being taken to the slaughterhouse? How many of his colleagues had he watched moving anxiously along the streets, marked with the yellow Star of David? Possibly he had a conscience. But a conscience was like singing: anybody could sing inwardly, but only the voice issuing from the throat made the singer. Evidently Dr. Wild's voice had not rung out. Such were Frank's reflections, and they were accompanied by growing anger. He felt deceived. He had been impressed by the doctor's recent cool reaction to his presents. But in fact he had merely regarded cigarettes and rations as insufficient—he at once demanded liberty for a militarist.

Aloud he said: "The other day, Herr Doktor, you avoided talking about my mother. You must know more about her."

Adam had a bitter taste in his mouth. He's trying to compel me to pay for Achim's freedom by my heroic deeds, he thought. And he's trying to compel me to advertise them.

"I have looked her up in my card index," he said. "She first came to see me in 1933, shortly after Hitler's rise to power. I treated your father, the Judge, to begin with, and after he died I saw your mother several times."

"How did my parents come to you?"

"Judge Steer had been a friend of mine, or rather a friend of my parents. He was a neighbor of yours."

Frank struggled to hide his excitement.

"Then you must know Elisabeth too?"

"I've known her since her earliest youth," said Adam.

There was a moment's silence in the room. The windows were wide open and the afternoon sun was flooding in. Now and again a truck rumbled along Ludwigstrasse.

"We have been told that you were a real friend to my mother," said Frank.

Adam got up. In his ill-fitting suit, which had become too tight for him, he looked like an overgrown schoolboy.

"Look here, Herr Major," he said. "You won't get any heroics out of me. I don't know why you're trying to. Perhaps you are determined to make the acquaintance of just one decent German, just as some Germans in the past had picked out 'their' Jew. Perhaps you are really prepared to do something for me—but only on condition that I am entirely 'different' from all other Germans. I have to disappoint you. I thought nothing of becoming your mother's medical adviser. She was an old lady, she had angina pectoris, and she paid her fees like everybody else. It is true that I continued to treat her after I had been forbidden to do so—but again I thought nothing of it, except that I don't like people forbidding me to do things. The day before she was taken to the concentration camp she came to me and asked me to help her. I gave her kind words, and nothing else. I did not hide her; I did not smuggle her across the frontier. I only went to Judge Steer and interceded for her, just as I have now come to you to intercede for Achim Sibelius. I don't know if Judge Steer did anything, or if he could have done anything. That's the whole story, Herr Major, and there's no point in bringing it up again. If you can help Sibelius then you'll be doing so not for my sake, but because it is idiotic to lock him up—completely and utterly idiotic."

Frank had also risen during Adam's speech. He now escorted him to the door.

"I will look into his file," he said.

For a full hour that afternoon he sat pensively behind his desk.

George Requisitions a Home

In the *Münchner Zeitung,* a daily run by the Military Government, the banker Eberhard Eber had read the following announcement:

"In view of the acute housing shortage an appeal was recently made to all active National Socialists to content themselves with fewer rooms and to share their houses, so that accommodation should become available before the advent of winter for those people who have hitherto been compelled to live under the most primitive conditions. This appeal has had no effect. The very people who not so long ago boasted of their 'national community' and presumed to instruct others in readiness for sacrifice are now failing when unselfish and collective action is needed to weather this difficult period. An Order has therefore been issued to the effect that the homes of all persons incriminated through their position in the Party, State and economic life, or through their special relationship to National Socialism, are to be vacated. Details will be found on public posters."

Munich was not a ghost town like Cologne or Essen, but this perhaps had been its misfortune. Into the desolate city poured people from cities even more desolate. More than three hundred refugee camps had to be created from nothing in Bavaria. They provided the barest shelter for one hundred thousand people; but the number of refugee children alone was one hundred and forty-two thousand. More than six hundred thousand refugees were vainly trying to find shelter. The word "reconstruction" had still a bad odor. Without batting an eyelid the *Münchner Zeitung* reported that Bavaria "would like twenty thousand peasants from the Banat, now in Württemberg" and was "offering in exchange twenty thousand Sudeten German textile workers." Nobody could buy anything, except perhaps on a barter basis—and thus human beings, too, had become the object of barter. Sudeten German textile workers sold cheap for clearance in exchange of Banat peasants.

There were some roofs and walls left in Munich, but these roofs and walls put human solidarity to a test it could not possibly stand. The moralizing communiqué had spoken of "persons incriminated through their position in the Party, State and economic life"—but in their grim defense of their small square of "living space" the upright differed in no way from the incriminated for whom "living space" had once held a much vaster meaning. Sound walls and intact ceilings were defended with false vows and false vouchers. It would have taken an army, bigger even than the conquering armies, to provide roofs and walls for the people who wanted to sleep. Only from chaos did a natural order of priorities arise: food before love, and sleep before food. In the air-raid shelter by the station people slept in shifts: after four hours a nursing mother would yield her place to an aimless wanderer, and he would yield to some homecoming soldier without a home, and he to another nursing mother. In the houses around the devastated university block the occupants had been driven from their apartments by "slave workers": bedding, lamps and even furniture were thrown after them from the windows. Indeed, the ejected might consider themselves lucky, for this gesture at least amounted to a recognition of past ownership. If a house or a villa suited the requirements of an Allied officer there was practically no valid appeal against requisition. The Allied authorities, though officially opposed to arbitrary action, were unable to control it in practice. After all, once a whole nation had been found guilty, how could anybody hope to prove that one particular owner of an apartment was innocent . . . ?

Since early morning, when he had read the paper over breakfast, as was his custom, the banker Eberhard Eber had had a premonition. True, his son Hans and his daughter Karin were back home again, his brother Oskar had come to stay and a married couple, relations of Anna, the housekeeper, had moreover moved into the house—but that the spacious, almost pompous villa in Bogenhausen could indefinitely escape official seizure seemed too hopeful a thought even for the banker's legendary optimism.

He was not therefore unduly surprised when a Captain George

Green of the Military Government was announced. A circumspect man even in difficult situations, the banker first sent his excuses—or rather, he sent Hans and Karin in to fight the vanguard action, chiefly because they both spoke English fluently whereas he himself had enjoyed a Gallic and classical education and only had an inadequate command of the English language.

The Captain sat down without waiting to be asked and scrutinized the two young people with undisguised curiosity. Hans, who had cast off his uniform without regrets, wore gray flannel trousers and an exceedingly well-cut brown jacket and suggested much more an Oxford or Cambridge undergraduate than the tattered infantry private he had been a few days before. The nineteen-year-old Karin, with her light-brown hair cascading loosely on to her shoulders, with her pert little nose, her full well-shaped lips and her close-fitting cashmere sweater, might easily have been one of those teen-agers who populate America's cheerful colleges.

"So this is the house," the Captain said. He came straight to the point. "How many rooms have you got?"

"Twelve," said Hans.

"And how many people are living here?"

"Papa, Hans, Uncle Oskar, myself . . . eight in all," said Karin.

"And the house hasn't been requisitioned so far?" the Captain asked.

"I don't think so," said Hans.

The Captain gave a little cough. "Your father *is* Eberhard Eber?" he asked. Some doubt seemed to have struck him.

Hans and Karin confirmed.

"This must have escaped the Military Government's notice," the Captain said. He looked around. "I shall move in tomorrow. I presume the house can be vacated by five P.M."

He got up, but something seemed to hold him back. He remained leaning against the mantelpiece. There was a white Capo di Monte porcelain figure on it. He picked it up and began to turn it in his hands.

"Do you need the whole house?" asked Karin. It sounded disarmingly naïve.

"That's beside the point," said the Captain. "We are not permitted to live in the same house as Germans. Does that surprise you, Fräulein Eber?"

"Frankly—yes," said Karin. "How do you expect to get to know us if you won't even talk to us?"

"We have no particular desire to get to know the Germans," said the Captain. "For that matter, the world has come to know them well enough."

Karin did not reply. But Hans said:

"That's just the way the Nazis used to talk in the occupied countries, Captain. We thought the Americans would bring us democracy."

With a gesture that was much too brusque for so fragile an object the Captain put the porcelain figure down on the marble mantelpiece.

"That would suit the Nazis fine," he said. "First they wreck democracy and then they want to profit from it. Democracy, Herr Eber, is for the democrats. You are not suggesting that democracy ought to protect the house of Herr Eberhard Eber?"

Karin bit her lips. She wanted to remain silent; but this was the first American she had met face to face. She was nineteen and believed that people got closer to each other if they talked to each other. Besides, she felt that she stood to lose nothing: the moment the man had picked up the porcelain figure he had taken possession of the house. She said:

"It depends on the purpose that the house is requisitioned for. To requisition even Eberhard Eber's house would not, I think, be very democratic if you merely wanted it for yourself."

She blushed at her own boldness. The Captain looked at her: the insolence of this German girl was beginning to get his goat. At the same time he observed that she was pretty, exceptionally pretty. Wouldn't hurt at all if she stayed in the house, he thought.

"I want to see your father," he said curtly.

Karin and Hans exchanged glances. Since their earliest childhood they had never needed words to understand each other; looks had always been enough. When Eberhard Eber had been divorced from their mother Hans had been twelve and Karin nine. It was then that, embittered and determined on opposition, they had formed their mutual defense alliance. Hans had taught her a secret language, the kind used by "Red Indians," at least in the imagination of the authors of westerns. They still remembered many words of their exciting private language, but they had long since had no need of them. People, events and words produced in them such similar, sometimes quite alarmingly twin-like reactions that each of them knew the other's thoughts better than their own. Now, too, the same thoughts had come to both of them: that their opposition, their resistance to arbitrariness, had driven them to the defense of the house they did not love and of their father whom they did not respect. Only the day before they had had a stormy scene with him, within the bounds of his traditionally impenetrable discipline, and they had pressed him to report the house to the Accommodation Office. And now, they thought, the usual thing would happen: the man by the fireplace would confirm to their father, and symbolically also to them, that he had been right in basing his philosophy on contempt for the human race.

Karin rose to call her father, unwilling to bear any longer the flag she did not believe in, when the door opened and Dr. Eber entered the drawing-room with a smile and measured tread.

"I apologize," he said in his broken but carefully construed English. "I did not want to keep you waiting so long, Captain. May I inquire to what circumstance I owe the pleasure of your visit?"

Hans and Karin noticed that the officer was eyeing their father curiously—with a good deal of curiosity but also with that certain respect that is usually paid even to the notorious when they step out from the columns of newspapers into actual life. He even accepted Dr. Eber's invitation to sit down, much to the surprise of the young people who acutely sensed their own eclipse in the presence of their father's stronger personality.

Meanwhile the Captain had recovered from his first impression.

"I have come to requisition the house," he said. "It must be vacated by tomorrow afternoon."

"That surprises me," Dr. Eber replied, entirely collected. "Unless, of course, you are acting on behalf of General MacCallum."

"What's General MacCallum got to do with it?" George Green asked irritably. But it was obvious that the mention of a general's name had much the same effect on an American captain as it would on a German Hauptmann.

"I am negotiating with the Herr General," Dr. Eber replied politely, "about equipping an officers' casino. If that is what you have come about . . ."

"This has nothing to do with any casino," said Captain Green. "Besides, can you prove that story?"

"Perhaps I may refer you to the Herr General," said Dr. Eber.

The Captain rose abruptly to his feet. But he was prevented from doing or saying whatever he had intended to by the events which unrolled during the next few minutes with the speed of a film sequence in which a skilful director had replaced an excess of dialogue by lightning-like action.

The piercing wail of a siren, evidently a military jeep, suspended the action in the Ebers' drawing-room. When the startled actors peered through the open window out into the sunlit park, they saw indeed a military police vehicle, painted all white, swinging round past the gracefully curved balustrade and coming to a stop with the screech of brakes that belongs to the sound-track repertoire of such dramatic moments. A military police officer, accompanied by two MP's leaped from the jeep—he really leaped, he did not just alight—and rushed at the house, as though afraid that any slower form of locomotion might waste several yards of valuable celluloid. Anna the housekeeper, who was about to receive the unexpected visitors, was literally swept aside and the three men burst into the drawing-room. The MP officer, momentarily startled at finding an American captain in the place, produced his credentials—again at top speed—and presented at the same time a warrant of arrest adorned with many rubber stamps. The banker, who had been struggling hard and not quite unsuccessfully to keep his composure, was accompanied by the two MP's to his bedroom where he was allowed to pack a few indispensable articles; a few minutes later he was handed over to the MP lieutenant in the drawing-room, all packed and ready to depart. Karin and Hans had meanwhile gathered from the conversation of the two officers that "an inexplicable oversight" was being hurriedly rectified: General MacCallum had personally ordered the arrest of "Hitler's banker."

Dr. Eber said a hurried goodbye to his children, without losing any of his dignity. Almost as though setting out on a business trip that had suddenly become necessary, he walked out of the room, flanked by the soldiers.

Captain Green was also at the door. He turned once more and said:

"Well, this simplifies matters. Till five P.M. tomorrow, then . . ."

Sanctuary at Dr. Wild's

The foregoing events in Dr. Eberhard Eber's house took place on a Wednesday afternoon. Every Wednesday evening a group of young people were in the habit of meeting at the lodgings of Stefan Lester, a young law student.

Hans's first call after his return from captivity had been to the Adelheidstrasse in Schwabing, where Stefan occupied a room that was undamaged in the sense that it never had a window that might have been shattered by the blast of the crashing bombs. Now that his parental home had been requisitioned and his father taken away Hans once more hurried off to see Stefan. He found him in conversation with a man of about twenty-five, one Horst Kallegher, whom he had met once or twice before being called up by the army.

Not even in the days of the *Volkssturm*, not even when the agonized Führer of the Reich reviewed ever fresh drafts of baby-faced youngsters amidst the ruins of Berlin, prior to sending them to their death, had Stefan Lester been enrolled in the forces. Stefan was a hunchback; he had been born a cripple. If a crippled figure is usually seen by people as an incomprehensible mockery of creation, then this was doubly so in the case of Stefan Lester. He had a hump without being crookbacked: the hump which deformed his narrow back contrasted with an otherwise normal, though frail, body and with a face whose noble symmetry suggested the statue of a young Greek god. In this paradoxical body, which looked as if the devil had wanted to spoil a piece of divine creation one moment before birth, but had no longer been able to do so entirely, lived a soul which Satan had clearly been too late to mar. Even modern psychologists would have tried in vain, in the case of the cripple Stefan Lester, to discover those complexes and overcompensations which they are so ready to derive from physical malformation. Indeed, if there was any connection at all between his physical defect and his personality, then it was only in the early maturity which had marked him almost since childhood.

It was in line with Stefan Lester's nature that he should bridge the first few awkward moments of Hans's encounter with Horst Kallegher by means of a little cheerful and tactful conversation. When Hans had last met young Kellegher he had been a broad-shouldered young student with brown curly hair, merry eyes and boyishly gawky movements—the type that went over big with the girls who, in those glum and perilous days, regarded "being fun" as the strongest of male attractions. This "amusing" young man now seemed to have aged by some twenty years: his face was sunken and lined, and his right leg had been shot from under him, so that he could move only with the aid of a strangely constructed and somewhat primitive crutch. The injury must have dated from the last year of the war, as Hans, a former infantryman, was quick to diagnose: before the final act of the tragedy the wounded had been patched up rather more carefully. Like the ruins of the towns, the human ruins, too, bore a clear date to the expert: the further the war progressed the more painstaking grew the work of destruction and the less painstaking became the tidying up of the wreckage, both structural and human.

Face to face with this young human wreck Hans was ashamed to confide his worries to his friend, but within a a few minutes Stefan extracted from him an account of the afternoon's happenings.

"I can get a mattress from Frau Huber," Stefan said. "And you can sleep on the divan."

"We'll do it the other way round," said Hans. "But your hospitality is gratefully accepted."

"Incidentally, I think we can also find a hide-out for Karin," Stefan continued. "Dr. Wild will be here in a few minutes, and I am sure he'll fix up Karin without any bother. He's got sleeping accommodation for one in his surgery."

"What makes you so sure that your Dr. Wild will give her shelter?" asked Hans. He had heard a lot about Dr. Wild before going into the army, but had never met him.

Stefan smiled. "Dr. Wild's divan!" he said. "If that divan could speak! Jews have slept on it and officers of the 20th of July, escaped political prisoners and members of the resistance movement, and sometimes just people who had been bombed out." He sat down on the only chair, which stood by a rickety table. "If anybody needed him Dr. Wild was always there, but don't ask me what sort of person he really is or what he has done, because I don't know myself. Take the 20th of July. I am convinced that he had no idea of the plans of the conspirators, but once the thing had misfired he harbored those officers who had made for Munich. Or the revolt at the university. We just told him what we intended to do and he hid our leaflets in his apartment till we needed them. Or the conspiracy of the Interpreter Company. Several groups had been meeting in his mother's antique shop and later impersonated patients at his surgery."

Horst Kallegher had been silent so far. Now he said:

"A regular saint. Or a hypocrite. God, how I am sick of them, those people who are always right and always do right!"

"Why should you be sick of them?" Stefan asked calmly.

"Because they only bring more chaos into the world," said the one-legged man. "You know that I never joined your so-called resistance movement. You confided in me, Stefan, and you've had no cause to regret it. I held my tongue—but that was all. Your talk and your doings always made me sick. What made you so sure that you were right? Weren't there enough people being shot up at the fighting fronts? Did you have to produce more martyrs on the home front? True, you stuck out your own necks—so what? I had a colonel once, a real swine if ever there was one, and he too had to frisk about in the front line all the time to 'set a good example' or some such heroic nonsense. So what? Since when has personal courage been an excuse? Because he was so convinced of his sacred duty I had to have my leg shot off. And if you think that my leg will grow again merely because he had himself shot dead in the process then you're mightily mistaken. They make me sick, all those people who 'set an example,' and I don't care which cause inspires them. Every time somebody is convinced of some 'sacred cause' a few thousand poor fools who allow themselves to be persuaded are shot dead."

Stefan was about to reply when there was a knock at the door and the man whom Horst had referred to as a regular saint or a hypocrite entered.

He greeted Stefan and the two strangers. Stefan introduced Horst as a medical student. Presently Adam began to rummage in his pocket.

"I have brought you some tobacco, Stefan," he said. "Unfortunately there's no cigarette paper. But if you didn't smoke like a chimney you'd have some left. Incidentally, my mother has instructed me to bring the wrapping paper back."

Stefan thanked him and carefully emptied the tobacco into an old cigar box.

"A chimney indeed!" he said. "I haven't smoked anything for a couple of days."

"And very good for your health, too," said Adam. "If we go on like this we'll be a surprisingly healthy nation one day. By the way, you may roll me a cigarette."

He sat down on the sofa between the other two men. His extended legs very nearly touched the opposite wall.

"My friend Hans will have to go soon," Stefan explained. "He is in an awkward spot." And he began to broach the subject of accommodation for Karin.

"But of course," Adam interrupted him even before he had finished. "The divan is free." With a smile he added: "As you see, Stefan, things are looking up."

Hans watched him keenly.

"I am grateful to you, Herr Doktor," he said, almost moved. "But may I ask a question?"

Adam raised his eyebrows.

"Don't you think it rather odd that you should give sanctuary to the daughter of Eberhard Eber?" Hans asked.

Adam inhaled deeply from the cigarette which Stefan had rolled for him.

"Herr Eber," he said. "Do I look like a man who believes in hereditary guilt?" And when Hans was silent, covered with confusion, he launched on an explanation which was not immediately clear to those present. "It happens every day that a doctor wants to kill a bacillus, but the bacillus won't play and instead infects the doctor. We all get infected by the things we fight against." He rose and began to pace up and down, a pursuit for which the room proved much too small. "Only yesterday," he said, "I read the following story in the paper of the Military Government. The daughter of a former German Governor-General of Poland, a girl of nineteen, married a young actor. Whereupon the proprietress of a well-known provincial theater company gave the young man the sack: she was having no dealings with the son-in-law of a war criminal. No doubt the good lady feels that she has acted like a thoroughbred democrat. She doesn't even suspect that she has applied the Nazi principle of hereditary guilt and family liability. The bacillus had got into her bloodstream."

"In other words," said Hans, "you don't believe that the end justifies the means?"

"The very phrase seems to me a monstrous absurdity," said Adam. "The end is always confused, vague and arbitrary. Do you know if your ends are right, valuable or enduring? Do I know? Does anybody know? What a presumption, Herr Eber, to regard any end as good enough to justify crooked means! And what guarantee have you that the end will ever be reached, that you won't get stuck in the crooked means? All you can see is the means. From the means you may draw your conclusions as to the end—but not the other way round. A surgeon who tries to tell me that he operates better with unsterilized instruments is a fool or a knave."

Horst, leaning on his crutch, had been watching the doctor. Now he said:

"If one may judge the end from the means, Herr Doktor, then the ends of the occupation are just as dirty as those of the late regime. They, too, are operating with unsterilized instruments."

Adam stopped in front of Horst. It was obvious that he had no intention of sparing the invalid, but it seemed to Hans that this lack of special consideration was more tactful in the circumstances than any respectful sympathy could have been.

"And what, Herr Kallegher," said Adam, "makes you think that I admire the methods of the occupation?"

"As far as I know," said Horst, "you helped to get us an occupation."

Adam sat down. Stefan wanted to intervene, but Adam forestalled him. "Let him be, Stefan," he said. "I am not touchy." And turning to Horst he added: "Herr Kallegher, it is too early to blame me for contributing—very much on the fringes, by the way—to the fall of the regime. That day may come, but it is not yet. If you think that I wanted this occupation you overestimate my foresight. I worked against the regime because I was convinced that it was a thoroughly and utterly rotten regime."

"In other words," interrupted Horst, "you too presumed to know what was good and what was 'rotten.'"

Stefan answered for Dr. Wild. "We did not examine the aims of the regime," he said. "There was no need to. Its method betrayed it: that's why the fight was justified."

Adam lounged back. He said: "I'm not trying to dodge your charge, Herr Kallegher. If you will permit me another medical parallel: I do not believe that we can cure people altogether. The mere attempt would be presumptuous. We can only cure specific diseases, and we must hope that the next disease will be a little less serious than the last. When it strikes we've got to attack again. And so forth. And if this doesn't appeal to you as a sufficiently positive program you had better become a theologian, not a doctor."

"Whether I become a theologian or a doctor," said Horst, "makes no difference anyway. The decisions are made without me. That's the point you have missed, Herr Doktor. Nobody asked me if I wanted Hitler or if I wanted the war, and nobody has asked me if I want this occupation." A little more calmly and softly he added: "I have nothing against your theories, Herr Doktor, except that they are theories. You cure this and you cure that; and in fact you don't cure anything. Sickness comes and goes independently of you."

"Ah, the theory of the humble man," said Stefan. "We've discussed it a hundred times with Dr. Wild . . . that cursed theory of the humble man!"

Hans got up. He would have liked to have listened to the end of the argument, possible even to have contributed to it, but he could not leave Karin alone all evening. There were a thousand things he had to do by five o'clock the next afternoon. He thanked Adam for his hospitable offer, made a note of his address, shook hands with the young people and left.

The time was half-past eight but it was still daylight. Soon it will be the longest day of the year, thought Hans. The thought seemed to pain him. Summer was the season of childhood. He could not remember the springs, autumns and winters of his childhood, at least not clearly, but all his childhood summers were still alive in him, with their scenery and their smells, their voices and their moods. The summer house on the Tegernsee, evenings on the lake in his skiff, the spume and spray of the North Sea, the trilling fireflies, the smell of the box tree by the fence, sultry afternoons and sudden thunderstorms, the crunch of the gravel in the spa park, the dawn chorus of the birds under his window, his first kiss—all these were part and parcel of his early summer memories, and all these suddenly engulfed the former infantryman Hans Eber as he made his way homewards past the ruins of the Pinakothek. He also remembered summers in Munich: the heat weighing heavily on the city, men in shirt sleeves carrying beer across the street, boys and girls leaning against their bicycles, the whispers of lovers from the Englischer Garten. The curfew and the dead houses and foreign police patrols and the frightened silence—these might possibly fit into the picture of a chilly, wintry town, but the summer rebelled against them. And because everything was quiet now and dead, the street looked as if mortally wounded and dying, after a crushed rebellion.

Hans walked fast: the ruined streets allowed of many short cuts. He reflected on what he had heard, but only a vague impression was left in him. In a thousand stuffy rooms of the city, he was thinking, such and similar conversations were now being held—conversations and soliloquies. People were talking cleverly or stupidly, aggressively or apologetically, with asperity and with hope—and they were all talking merely because they could not face up to themselves. Why were so few of them asking how all this had come about? Why, Hans asked himself, are we all feeling sorry for ourselves: because we did not oppose the lunacy, or because we opposed it in vain, or because Hitler drove us into the war, or because we lost the war, or because we are outcasts now and occupied? Why are we so thorough, we Germans, and still fail to get at the root of things? The occupation is the result of the lost war, and the lost war is the outcome of the Third Reich, and the Third Reich is the outcome . . . but this is where we get stuck, and most of us do not even get that far. We observe the circumstances and analyze them, and yet we remain on the surface because we are careful not to probe into the causes. Even what Dr. Wild had said seemed to him rather defeatist, and perhaps the one-legged Horst Kallegher was right: perhaps all cures were in vain and it was mere quackery to attempt them.

He had scarcely thought of his father all evening, but now the picture of Eberhard Eber rose before him, walking erect and with stiff dignity out of the door of his drawing-room. Hans felt he could almost envy his father. Eberhard Eber conducted no discussions or soliloquies He did not meditate over good and evil, truth and falsehood. He was Eberhard Eber, a man who had jettisoned character like an irksome encumbrance and, together with character, all questions and doubts.

It was getting dark, but as Hans walked through the gate at the end of the drive he immediately spotted the car by the front door. It was a smart blue Mercedes, but on its dark-blue hood a large white star had been painted, marking it as a requisitioned vehicle.

"That officer's here again," Anna whispered as she let him in.

And indeed, there was Captain George Green sitting in the drawing-room, opposite Karin. A half-empty bottle of wine stood on the table before him. He did not rise when Hans entered, but he returned his greetings with friendly condescension. He offered Hans a cigarette.

"I've been thinking," he said. "Under certain conditions you can remain in the house. . . ."

Major O'Hara Saves the Commandeuse

Everybody in the occupied land had his or her secrets. And just because they were all being dragged behind the X-ray screen for their hearts to be inspected and their brains and their bones and their very marrows, they were now trying to hide away both from others and from themselves.

For hours on end they would sit over the grotesque questionnaires, painfully searching for answers which escaped and eluded them the more they tried to pin them down. Were you a Party member or a probationer for membership, or did you belong to any affiliated organization? By the hundred these probing questions were staring at them, in black on white, and the blank space was to receive their secret which spelled punishment or disgrace or hunger or the whole lot together. The "space for answer" was too big or too small, according to one's point of view. It was too big because it made the little word "Yes"—the admission of past Party membership or probationership or membership in some organization or other—float more solitarily and hence more brilliantly and more finally in the large white space. Yet it was also too small, for it ought to have been big enough for a whole biography, indeed for world history . . . why one had marched with them or not marched with them, or been a fellow-traveler, or traveled with them halfway, or right at the tail end, or in front with the vanguard. Why, why? Because one had been an opportunist, or an idealist; because one had hoped to get a brother out of a concentration camp or get a business rival inside; or because one had not dared to turn the enrolment official away from the door; because one had tried to hold on to one's job; because one had hoped to impress a woman; because one had felt patriotic; or because one had been hypnotized or enthusiastic or cowardly or fanatical or misguided or embittered or just a dreamer . . . There ought to have been room for all that in those blank spaces, but circumstances demanded that one should surrender one's secret with a bare "Yes" or

"No." Life was like a bad novel, in which everything happened and nothing had a motive.

Everybody had some secret or other. One person merely concealed the fact that he had a few dollars hidden in his mattress, while another kept quiet about his presence at the shooting of innocent people in Lidice or Oradour. One person concealed the fact that twelve years before he had been a Party member for three months, and another that he knew where some money was buried. There were also some whose secrets moved about a strange maze: men and women who had suffered under the Third Reich and who had waited for retribution, but who now kept their knowledge of this person or that to themselves. They had been ashamed of Germany's victories and did not wish to profit from her defeat. And there were others still who hoped for the safety of their own secret, or even for impunity, if they betrayed the secret of a friend. People denounced one another; they shielded themselves and each other; and that secrecy game became more and more absurd as in the occupied country everybody knew everybody's else's secret, whereas the inquisitive strangers knew nothing except what their paper questionnaires and some dubious tipsters told them.

Everybody had his secrets, even the conquerors. They had made laws for themselves which they could not keep or which they would not keep. It was forbidden to speak to the defeated, to do business with them and to sleep with them, or even to feel sorry for them and to show understanding. "Don't gum up the victory," said the leading article of the *Stars and Stripes*, the Army paper. Chewing gum distributed among German children, it maintained, would cheat the victors of the fruits of victory. Against such diabolical madness even the common sense and feelings of the conquerors rebelled. They resorted to secrecy. They spoke to Germans, they did business with them, and they slept with the women. Occasionally they even felt sorry for them and had some understanding for them and some chewing gum. And since among the conquerors, just as among the vanquished, everybody knew everybody else's secret, the ties of discipline were slackened: superiors and subordinates became accomplices and fellow-conspirators, and presently they became fellow-conspirators with the occupied country.

But the secret which Major Bill O'Hara, the former police sergeant, had been carrying about with him for some days was of a totally different nature from the secrets which custom and circumstances had long hallowed on both sides.

Pfc. Harry S. Jones of Texas—Private First Class, as his full military description had it—the Major's driver, knew perfectly well that the Major had lied when he denied having found the concentration camp commandeuse Irene Gruss at the Hotel Nadler.

Her brother-in-law Herr Nadler, the proprietor of the hotel, had been frightened to death that night and had not for a moment denied that Irene Gruss was in his house. Breathing heavily, he had conducted the Major up the stairs, with many assurances that he had had no idea his sister-in-law was wanted by the authorities.

What precisely occurred in the attic, whose door Herr Nadler obsequiously opened to the Major, was revealed only several years later, under the most unusual circumstances. When Herr Nadler, immediately after the Major's sudden departure, climbed up to the attic again, together with his wife, Irene's sister, Irene was wearing only a lilac-colored kimono which barely covered her naked body, and was vociferously demanding that her brother-in-law leave the room as she wanted "to show something" to her sister. Frau Nadler, of course, later revealed to her husband that the Major's riding crop had wrought "terrible havoc"; but at the same time that naïve lady, never greatly attached to her sister, related an astonishing version of what had taken place. Without in the least understanding the occurrence, Frau Nadler reported that Irene had accepted her thrashing not only without protest but evidently also without regrets and that she had boasted she knew exactly how that American had to be "handled." And indeed, on the following morning Herr Nadler discovered two packs of American cigarettes on the bedside table of the maltreated woman. To the hotelkeeper's growing amazement Irene, though physically in a pitiful condition, wore that morning an arrogance which clashed noticeably with her humble modesty during the preceding weeks. Wrapped in her kimono and hiding neither her nakedness nor her weals, she sat in the Nadlers' sitting-room, smoking one cigarette after another, demanding real bean coffee, and bragging that she would soon be able to repay her in-laws' hospitality with interest. In the afternoon she packed her belongings in a little fiber suitcase which she had brought with her, and shortly after nightfall, just as Irene had foretold it, a Horch limousine, evidently once the property of some Nazi official, drove up in front of the hotel in the cul-de-sac and the red-haired major stowed the woman away in the interior of the luxurious vehicle.

All this had happened nearly a fortnight before. For two weeks now Irene Gruss had been in hiding at the villa which Major William S. O'Hara had requisitioned in a secluded back street of Pasing near Munich. Since then not a day had passed, and not even an hour, when the Major had not considered handing his mistress over to the authorities. His superior officer, Colonel Graham T. Hunter, was convinced for more than one reason that the commandeuse was hiding out somewhere in Bavaria, and he was accusing the Major—never a favorite of his—of gross incompetence. On one occasion Colonel Hunter had even remarked that he would put Major Green in charge of further investigations—a threat which had deeply wounded the policeman's pride and had almost made him betray his secret. Besides, the popular American slogan "Crime Does Not Pay" had been drilled a thousand times into O'Hara's brain and he was genuinely convinced that his crime would not pay in the end. Yet the urge which drove O'Hara was stronger than ambitoin and morality; it was stronger even than fear.

It had all begun during his—at that time—theoretical investigations into the case of Irene Gruss. The more O'Hara had learned about her, the more he had put himself in her place: but instead of identifying himself with the victims of the commandeuse, he had identified himself with her. On the way to the hotel in the suburbs he had been gripped by an excitement which, while not unfamiliar and indeed habitual whenever he was able to inflict or witness pain, had never before possessed him with such intensity. When at last he had faced the woman whose photograph with the legend "Wanted" he had, almost like a lover, carried in his breast pocket, his excitement had reached a climax that completely overpowered his senses. The thought that he was inflicting on the woman no more than she had inflicted on others a hundred times—a fleeting thought at the most— gave his urge a thin veneer of righteous indignation, while in fact his brutality and the pleasure he derived from it were mounting at the same rate as when his victim had herself once practiced that same brutality and tasted the same pleasure. In Irene Gruss there was still an echo of the experience which O'Hara was seeking, and before her he became like a beast that had always lived among other animals and was now for the first time scenting a partner of its own species.

But for all that, O'Hara might have taken her to prison after that night, instead of to his secluded villa, if she had not symbolized for him the fulfilment of his lifelong unconscious ambition. Through a paradoxical concatenation of circumstances Bill O'Hara had always represented the law, although in fact there was nothing he hated more than the law. True, the law had made him the executive organ of justice, but at the same time it had subjected him to that justice. The accused, the prisoner in the dock, the offender or the criminal had never been Bill O'Hara's private property: the law had only lent them to him, and presently snatched them away for good. This time O'Hara wanted to be master of the law: this prisoner did not belong to the State, the army, the police, or any other impersonal institution. This prisoner belonged to him, personally and exclusively; to him, the former police sergeant William S. O'Hara of New York.

Now it was too late. The former commandeuse had lived at the Pasing villa for a fortnight, and the Army would accept no explanation of this private arrest.

Irene Gruss realized that. She realized even more. Bill O'Hara needed her just as she had once needed her victims. Except that the mad machinery of the Third Reich had constantly supplied her with new victims, whereas she was Major O'Hara's only prisoner, only victim and only mistress.

On his return in the evening the same spectacle would be repeated again and again, though with many minor variations thought up by his diseased fantasy. Almost invariably he would start with an "interrogation." She knew that he not only expected but indeed demanded stubborn denials on her part; for the more stubborn her denials and the more brazen her provocation, the more severe would be the punishment which he could mete out to her under his own private law. When she had been denying long enough he would order her to undress in a hurry, except when his excitement was speeding towards its climax too quickly and he would just order her to bend with hastily bared abdomen over the "whipping stool" in the living-room. Standing behind her he would count aloud the strokes pelting down on her from his riding crop or leather belt, until her flesh was lined with deep purple weals and she began to cry for mercy. At other times he would "sentence" her to lick his boots. Sitting in a chair while she knelt in front of him, licking or pretending to lick one boot, he would push his other boot into her breast or stomach, brutally yet at the same time careful not to injure her. When she had been sufficiently tortured in one way or another the next act would begin: she had to "confess" and, whimpering, ask for harder punishment. On all fours she would then crawl into the kitchen where a plaited dog whip lay ready and bring the whip to him between her teeth like a dog, so that he could chastise her once more. But what he loved best was the re-enactment of scenes from the concentration camp. Wearing only a bathrobe over his bare red-haired body he would lie on the divan, while she was one of the prisoners brought before him—or rather, before her, since he was impersonating her former role. Now and again she had to "deny" or "misbehave," or provoke him in some other way that would allow him to leap to his feet and subject her to the flogging which the commandeuse had used to inflict on her victims.

Yet not for a moment did Irene Gruss feel that she was paying too high a price for her relative freedom and her life. She did not fear the night, partly because she would have immunized herself from early in the evening by the consumption of ample quantities of alcohol, and partly because the curious pleasure which her sufferings gave the Major confused his senses more rapidly than her own diseased desires had found satisfaction in the past. When he "sentenced" her to twenty-five strokes she knew perfectly well that the whip would come down only five or six times: he would then drop his instrument of torture almost helplessly and take the woman into his arms with an over-heated and quickly-spent passion. Besides, Irene Gruss knew the beast in her partner like her own reflection in the mirror: she knew the exact limits of his brutality and hence faced her nights without terror.

Altogether, she had settled down very comfortably in the secluded but well-equipped house of her tormentor. All day long she would drift about the place in her lilac kimono; she would spend the afternoons lying on a sofa, reading some sentimental romantic novel she had found on the bookshelves; she would eat Hershey chocolate by the carton; she would prepare enormous meals from the sumptuous U-Rations which she ordered from the Major as if he were her housekeeper; she would smoke her favorite Lucky Strikes and empty whole bottles of French perfume, bought for her by the Major at the PX, into her bathwater. Sometimes, pouring precious oil on to her maltreated body in the privacy of her bathroom, she would burst into noisy laughter. With every day that passed Bill needed her more than she needed him. She held the key to Major William S. O'Hara's secret. And her realization of the danger entailed by that secret gradually got blurred.

A License for the "Mücke" Night Club

Every time that Colonel Hunter had his program for the day submitted to him at eight o'clock sharp in the morning he reflected how far his sphere of activities had spread beyond his proper functions as Deputy Chief of Intelligence, or G-2 as the Army called it. In addition to counterespionage work, of which he had been in charge for some time, he was now also responsible for controlling the press and all other organs of public life—and since G-5, the Military Government Department, was hopelessly understaffed the experienced professional soldier was expected to make a great many additional decisions which had hardly any connection with his own field of activity. Should a theater be licensed; was a certain conductor politically reliable; should a brewer be allowed to brew again and a surgeon to operate—all these questions converged on the office of Colonel Graham T. Hunter, for there was always the problem of preventing the re-emergence of "incriminated elements" and the need for a most careful examination of their political past.

Moreover, Colonel Hunter was the Deputy for a Chief who did not exist. The post of Chief of G-2, which would have to be held by a brigadier general, was vacant. This now permanent vacancy immediately above him—a circumstance behind which Hunter's mild optimism suspected a deliberate intention—spurred him on to even more energetic work.

Hunter, a man of fifty-three, had had a rapid career. Or more correctly: his career had been rapid until the moment in 1930 when, barely thirty-eight, he had been made a "chicken colonel," as that rank was jocularly called in the American Army because of the plucked eagle insignia on the shoulder. A man who wore the little silver bird at the age of thirty-eight, and moreover in peacetime, could be practically certain of the general's star. Yet for the past fifteen years Colonel Hunter had waited in vain for his elevation out of the mass of senior officers and his enthronement on the coveted pedestal of the highest rank. For many years he used to scan the biannual lists of colonels whose promotion was recommended to Congress, his shortsighted eyes looking for his own name with tense and hopeful expectation, and for many days after their publication he used to walk about disappointed, almost dazed, but soon taking fresh heart, until the next list again dashed his hopes.

Yet Hunter was not an ambitious man—at least not in the sense that ambition sacrifices character and principles to advancement. Looking back over the past fifteen years he had to admit to himself, sometimes with bitter self-recrimination, that he had never interested himself sufficiently in the game of uniformed bureaucracy, even though he knew perfectly well that the army might march with flags and bands but did not essentially differ in structure from a vast post office. Also, as he admitted to himself with advancing years, he was not what is usually meant by the "general" type. Perhaps the Army was right in not promoting him, just as it was as a rule averse to turning a first-rate sergeant into a second-rate lieutenant. The numerous generals under whom Colonel Hunter had served in the course of many years, and who seemed to be getting younger at the rate that he was getting older, invariably wrote excellent, even enthusiastic, reports about the Colonel; but always there was in them the clear suggestion that a man of such outstanding ability should at all costs be kept in the post he was holding.

For the past few years the Colonel had given up reading the lists of recommended promotions; he had become resigned, as was his nature. He would have contented himself long before with the part of an esteemed, indeed an indispensable, second fiddle if Mrs. Hunter, his wife, had not kept him under a ceaseless pressure which he could not escape by wisdom or humor, anger or jokes. Betty, once tender and merry, but now quickly fading and embittered, had taken out a kind of endowment policy by marrying the promising West Point cadet and son of a general. Now she regarded the Army as a defaulting insurance company which had robbed her of her savings. She reproached the Colonel not so much with his failure as with his unrebelling acceptance of it; but since rebellion was not part of his mental make-up he did not rebel against her either, so that his life proceeded in twofold resignation. Even so, the Colonel would have liked to please Betty and the children by snatching that eagerly-coveted general's star from the hierarchical skies, and his new functions seemed to him to provide his last chance of doing so.

Even though he was afraid of another disappointment—or rather, that he might once more find himself in the grip of painful ambitions from which he had escaped into a less painful resignation—Colonel Hunter could not this time disregard the indications all of which clearly pointed to promotion. T/O, "Table of Organization," was the name of that fiendish table worked out in Washington and prescribing a definite rank for each post. Thus, the Chief of Counterintelligence for Bavaria had to be a brigadier general, regardless of qualifications, and Hunter could not therefore occupy that post at the moment; if he were to be appointed to it, on the other hand, he would have to be made a general. Lieutenant General Theodore F. MacCallum, the Military Governor of Bavaria, could have easily appointed a chief over Hunter's head, especially as young brigadier generals were then springing up like mushrooms, but from his attitude, and also from casual remarks, Hunter felt justified in concluding, without indulging in wild hopes, that the general's chair was this time really being "kept warm" for him.

On that sultry summer morning in 1945 the Colonel was therefore studying his extensive timetable for the day with a certain sense of gratification, yet also with the unspoken conviction that a man cannot fairly be expected to shoulder all burdens himself without eventually receiving the recognition due to him.

"That Herr Wedemeyer is waiting again in Major O'Hara's office," his German secretary announced. She was a middle-aged spinster with a narrow pair of glasses and a nose that seemed frozen even during the hot season: a Fräulein Bauer who had been unconditionally devoted to the Colonel from the start. "But first you must tell me, Herr Oberst, if you wish to see the Countess Artemstein." She always called him "Herr Oberst," never "Colonel" as Hunter had repeatedly asked her to do: one could not say "Herr Colonel" and plain "Colonel" struck her as too familiar.

"Countess Artemstein?" asked the Colonel.

"Yes—the children's nurse who called on you at your home."

"She is a countess?"

"Yes," Fräulein Bauer said pointedly. "A countess and the daughter of a general. He was killed in Russia. I thought instantly that she was quite unsuitable."

"And why should she be quite unsuitable?" the Colonel asked irritably.

"A general's daughter!" Fräulein Bauer was horrified.

"Surely she's not responsible for her father?" said the Colonel.

Fräulein Bauer shrugged her angular shoulders. She did not wish to contradict her boss, but was nevertheless emboldened to remark:

"Countesses don't make good children's nurses. At least that's my opinion, Herr Oberst," she added.

"If she's efficient and reliable," he replied, "it should make no difference whether she's an aristocrat or not. We Americans," he went on to lecture her, "have no prejudices—neither one way nor the other."

"Quite so," said Fräulein Bauer. "I only thought . . ."

The Colonel acknowledged her retreat with a nod and remembered at the same moment that he had decided not to employ Fräulein von Artemstein. There would be no end of complications. Prejudices or no—it would be impossible to relegate her to the kitchen. That meant she would have to sit between him and Betty at table every night. He would have to make conversation with her, under the eyes of his wife; and she, for her part, would no doubt listen to his conversation with Betty. Later she might even live in. Suddenly before the Colonel there arose an absurd picture which he instantly confined to the deepest dungeon of his puritan soul: Marianne Artemstein emerging from the bathroom, in a dressing gown, a towel elaborately knotted over her raven hair.

He said sharply: "Who examined her questionnaire?"

"Major Green," said Fräulein Bauer.

"Ask Major Green to see me afterwards," the Colonel commanded. "And now send in that Herr Wedemeyer."

"Is Major O'Hara to come in with him?"

"It doesn't matter," said Hunter.

Bill O'Hara gave a smart salute as he entered his chief's spacious room, in spite of the fact that the Colonel had more than once deprecated such formalities at the office. As Wedemeyer, round and rubicund, toddled in after him it was as if a child playing soldiers were pulling a cuddly teddy bear on wheels along behind him.

Wedemeyer bowed, not too deeply but respectfully, and sat down in silence as the Colonel pointed to a chair in front of his desk.

"It's about the night-club license for Herr Wedemeyer," said the Major.

The Colonel carefully took off his unframed glasses and put on his reading glasses. He flicked through the file on his desk.

"So you want to open a night club," said Hunter. "And you believe that this will meet an urgent demand?" It did not sound very encouraging for Herr Wedemeyer.

"Colonel," said Wedemeyer in his smooth English. "In my application I have outlined the advantages of such a place. The difficulties which you gentlemen are encountering seem to me to be chiefly, if I may put it that way, of a geographical nature." He smiled, pleased with his elegant formulation. With the Colonel staring at him uncomprehendingly, Wedemeyer continued: "The black marketeers, the politically unteachable, the profiteers of our misery—in short, all those people who will not understand that a new era has begun are hiding in our ruins. The night is dark, Colonel. If in that dark night you switch on a light it's bound to attract all the moths and midges. I have even considered calling the place 'Die Mücke'—the midge." He looked around him, radiant and a little self-satisfied, as he was wont to do whenever he produced a rabbit to a surprised audience.

"In other words," said Hunter, "you want us to create a place where the 'midges' can meet."

"Well," interposed O'Hara. "It really might make things easier."

The Colonel switched back to his ordinary glasses and cast a sidelong glance at his subordinate. Wedemeyer noticed at once that O'Hara was not perhaps the best champion of his cause.

He said: "I have mentioned the geographical problem, Colonel. There are a dozen illegal night clubs in existence in Munich. The kind of place I have in mind would ruin them all."

"But maybe your 'midges' prefer illegal dives?" Hunter suggested quickly. "A place that's been licensed by us might not suit them so well."

"One need not advertise the licensing aspect too much," replied Wedemeyer. "And if you so desire, perhaps one or two of your German agents . . . as waiters perhaps . . ." For the first time he floundered; he felt that he had gone too far. Major O'Hara had instantly kindled to the idea of specially setting up a night club in order to keep a closer watch on suspicious elements—a kind of "concentration night club." But this colonel, who looked like a professor of mathematics, evidently had no imagination. Or perhaps he had enough imagination to recognize Wedemeyer's bait at once and to see through the scheme. In either case it would be wiser to keep quiet for a while and to approach the man more cautiously.

To Wedemeyer's surprise, however, the Colonel did not pursue the point. He asked:

"And what do you intend to offer the people, Herr Wedemeyer?"

"Light and warmth, Colonel. Light and warmth above all, and a little illusion. After casting around for a more innocent occupation—because I am really a lawyer—I did a spot of conjuring in the Third Reich, the sort of thing the French call 'l'illusion.' Je suis illusioniste, mon colonel," Wedemeyer said with a slight bow towards the desk. He was gaining ground again. "Intoxication and a full stomach, Colonel, these today are illusions. And I may claim to be a bit of an expert where illusions are concerned." After this digression he turned again to the Major. "If the Army could provide me with a generator . . . Winter is approaching, the long nights . . ."

"Yes, I know," Hunter interrupted him, as if to say that he required no instruction on the nights growing longer in winter. He performed another change of spectacles and in silence turned the pages of the Wedemeyer file.

Neither the conjurer nor the Major stirred. Wedemeyer's hands were in his lap, his short pudgy fingers intertwined.

"You say here that you have special qualifications for this business," the Colonel took up the thread again. "How do you make that out?"

"I have a very wide circle of acquaintances," said Wedemeyer. "Certain connections which I made during the Nazi period—though I never was a Party member myself—are fortunately being misinterpreted by those people. They trust me. I could count on a considerable clientele."

Hunter looked up. He scrutinized the man with undisguised interest. Wedemeyer wore a well-cut suit—not too short like most German suits, not too loose for a figure that had grown thinner. The Colonel had learned to pick the wearers of such suits out of the crowd: if they were shrewder they would not wear them, he thought. They were mostly the suits of the newly-arrived of the Third Reich, or of profiteers, or at any rate of people who had managed to escape the general misery and profit by it. Questionnaires and party cards were important in the Colonel's eyes; but just as important to him was the soft cloth of which Wedemeyer's suit had been carefully made. But then this man did not even deny having "made certain connections." An illusionist . . . Mentally the Colonel repeated the word to himself and the thought suddenly struck him that he was not up to his task. This man with the round dark eyes under the bushy eyebrows had been outspoken where others were not: but, he thought, they were all illusionists, conjurers and enchanters. How could one trust them or sit in judgment over them or guide them? What was one to do with all that circus crowd of sword-swallowers, magicians, trapeze artists and tightrope walkers who merely pretended to speak the same tongue as he but who conversed with one another in an exotic secret language.

He said: "I can't give you a final decision, Herr Wedemeyer." To postpone a decision always seemed the best way out. A little while before he had postponed his decision about the Countess Artemstein; now let the illusionist wait for a change. "A night club ranks as a place of entertainment," he said. "We take the view that the Germans should reflect more and amuse themselves less. It's true that the theaters are to be reopened shortly, but then theaters are cultural institutions."

Wedemeyer smiled. "If I know my Germans," he said, "they will amuse themselves at the theater while in the night club they will either debate or do business."

The Colonel cleared his throat. "Well then," he said. "I'll see the General about it. I shall let you know the decision through Major O'Hara."

O'Hara saluted again and Wedemeyer bowed, again not too low. The Colonel dismissed the German with a nod but kept O'Hara back.

"One moment, Major," he said. "What news about the commandeuse Gruss?"

The Major blushed, not only to the roots of his hair like other people, but almost as if the color of his hair had flooded his freckled face.

"Still no news, I'm afraid," said the Major.

"I want to see some results within the next forty-eight hours," said the Colonel, and his voice held a new note. "I'm sick of this unfinished business."

But that was a sentence which Major O'Hara did not understand.

SS-Führer Mante Scents the Morning Air

There were still some people who talked of Werewolves and centers of resistance, but by August 1945 even the last stragglers had crept out of their lairs. In any case, they had hidden there not with were-wolf-like intentions, nor in the hope of getting away in the end, but simply because they wanted to postpone the moment of the last reckoning. Senselessly they delayed what had become inescapable.

When the very last of his faithful followers had forsaken him, SS-Obersturmbannführer Gerd Mante had eventually agreed to Martha Zobel bringing him a few civilian garments from her father's wardrobe and, dodging the police checks since he had no papers, had made his way to Munich along the wrecked autobahn.

Colonel Zobel had had a refugee family billeted on him, so that the three-roomed apartment was now reduced to a bedroom and a living-room. The Colonel slept in the bedroom, though under protest, while Martha had hitherto contented herself with the narrow and uncomfortable divan in the so-called sitting-room.

It was the special confinement that precipitated the first conflict between the Colonel and his daughter. In the bedroom, which was furnished in heavy German baroque style, were two beds: and when Colonel Zobel finally waived his opposition and agreed to accept the SS officer into his home it seemed to him a matter of course that he and Martha would move together while his daughter's fiancé would have his makeshift bed in the sitting-room. But Martha would not hear of such an arrangement. Gerd, she said, had too long lived in a mountain cave and before that his couch had been the frozen soil of Russia: he had more than earned his right to a featherbed. When the Colonel declared that he had no intention of sharing his bedroom with his hated "son-in-law," Martha observed that she had never expected him to do anything of the sort. She and Gerd would "of course" occupy the bedroom. This produced from the Colonel an outburst of choleric fury: his pent-up anger, possibly with a touch of jealousy, erupted in an explosion such as occurred only on the rarest of occasions. The veins at the Colonel's throat swelled alarmingly and his words began to get blurred. The expression "brothel" occurred at least half a dozen times, together with references to the late Frau Oberst Zobel, née von Schimmelhausen, dead for the past twenty-five years, who had been "fortunate enough" to die of influenza after the first war since she would not have survived this kind of thing that was now spreading like a plague.

The more cholerically the Colonel behaved the more certain Martha became that he would surrender in the end. Even his threat that he would give the young man "a piece of his mind" she interpreted as a rearguard action designed to maintain his parental prestige.

She was the more surprised when the Colonel received the SS-Obersturmbannführer almost without greeting and insisted on having a talk with him that same afternoon. Gerd Mante had arrived shortly after lunch, at a time when Martha had made sure the billeted refugee family would be out, looking for work. He had greeted the Colonel courteously but distantly and had asked Martha to show him his place —just as if this were her home entirely and the Colonel merely another lodger. He had spent half an hour in the bathroom, which opened off the dark narrow hall, and with ill-controlled displeasure the Colonel had watched his daughter busily carrying piles of towels and even a bathrobe to the bathroom—treasures which had been cherished these past few years like the family porcelain and which were irreplaceable at the moment as there was not even a soap ration. The Colonel himself had been using some soap which appeared to consist of little pebbles. Only when Gerd had shaved and carefully brushed his hair—the Colonel even believed he could detect the almost forgotten aroma of hair lotion—did he find himself ready to listen to his future father-in-law.

"Herr Mante," began the Colonel, struggling for self-control. "I'm not used to dissembling; I have always been one to speak my mind. I have received you into my home—" he slightly stressed the word "my" —"because Martha implored me to do so and because, in your difficult position, you are in need of help. Besides, I have no reason to doubt your serious intentions with regard to my daughter—even though I am rather surprised that you did not make use of the opportunities which existed for the contraction of marriage during the last few months before the collapse."

He stopped short. His own speech, even the sound of his voice, suddenly struck him as grotesque. He watched the young man with the straw-colored hair sticking to his head and forehead, who was lounging in a chair opposite him and who wore his—the Colonel's —suit, shirt and shoes with such calm matter-of-factness that for a moment Zohbel felt he was seeing himself in some strange distorting mirror. And to this crooked image of himself he was now lecturing on "serious intention" and the state of matrimony as if he were still Colonel Werner Zobel, holder of the Knight's Cross, commander of his regiment and within his limited kingdom master over life and death, and as if the other man were still SS-Obsersturmbannführer Gerd Mante, a product of the peeriod washed up to the surface, but also the representative of the new State which one had to serve without understanding it. But in reality even the new concepts had become outdated, swallowed up by the chaos and ground into dust: how empty and ludicrous his words rang in this room where respectability had once reigned and where he would now spend sleepless nights while his daughter lay in her lover's arms next door . . . Would this corruption never end? One had painfully got used to one kind of chaos, one had come to accept it as a hard and ineluctable law, but already that void was being swallowed up by an even bigger void in which apparently there was no law at all. As he looked at the mask-like inscrutable face of the younger man, Colonel Zobel realized with a shock that he was standing at a lost post, far more hopeless in fact than the other man who was at home in chaos and had nothing to lose but a void.

The Colonel rose and went over to the open window. He dropped the moralizing tone and took refuge in military precision.

"Herr Mante," he said. "I am prepared, for the moment, to give you shelter, but not to harbor you. I could not do so even if I wanted to. The refugee family that lives here would gossip about your presence and someone would very soon report you to the authorities. Besides, we can't manage on our rations as it is and I can't allow Martha to let you have hers."

"That's been seen to, Papa," interposed Martha who had sat down on a revolving stool in front of the dark-red grand piano.

The Colonel looked at her in surprise, but was afraid to lose the thread of his argument. He continued:

"I suggest that you take a few days to recover from your hardships of the past few months and then give yourself up to the Americans."

Martha jumped up.

"You can't be serious, Papa!" she said.

"I don't see any other way," said the Colonel.

Martha went over to Mante and put her arm protectingly round his shoulders.

"It's unbelievable!" she said.

"Please, Martha, don't upset yourself," said Mante. He freed himself from her caresses, crossed his legs and calmly lit a cigarette. When he spoke he addressed himself to her, as if to emphasize that the Colonel was not worthy of a reply. "There's no need for your father to worry about our future: if I give myself up I'll get twenty years at the least. They may even put me up against a wall. That, in itself, wouldn't worry me, because if a man's still alive today it serves him right. Only, unlike your father, I am not convinced that we are definitely and finally defeated. Not by a long shot."

"You don't call that defeated?" The Colonel was speechless.

He stretched out his arm towards the scene outside the window. There was the city, under the heat haze of the dying August day. The bombed circular twin towers of the Church of Our Lady looked like two empty bird-cages. And what was it that still supported that wall in Kaufingerstrasse, which seemed to be leaning over under the evening breeze? The city looked as if it had been cut out of cardboard—a cheap toy, crumpled, temporarily propped up, makeshift. The whole picture was enveloped in dust: the dust of crumbling walls, the dust of crushed masonry, and the dust whirled up by the American vehicles racing through the town in all directions. Across the empty space beyond the Marienplatz two children were wading through the dusty desert. They wore motorcycle capes which were much too big for them and which flapped against their legs; evidently they were not wearing anything underneath. A man, too, waded through the dust, stooping from time to time as if picking flowers, but he was only picking up butts. Right in the center of the square stood a solitary tree; a strange tree with strange branches, each branch an American signpost, pointing the way to a hundred authorities which administered the victory of the ones and the defeat of the others.

Gerd Mante did not even raise his head. He said:

"Terror raids ensure no victory in the long run." He was at last addressing the Colonel. "Before long there'll be an awakening. Soon the Americans will march against Russia. Then they're going to need us. Even if our people limp they still march better than the Americans with all their jeeps and tanks. Then there'll be an end to all this tomfoolery. No one's going to ask then who was or wasn't in the SS or if some SS man has perhaps knocked off a few Bolshevik swine." He got up. "That's what I want to live to see, Herr Oberst. And at liberty, because I've no desire to waste time. When the signal comes we shall have to be ready. One day, Herr Oberst,"—his tone was almost menacing—"you may well be thankful that you've given Obersturmbann-führer Mante a bed and even a piece of soap."

Mante never learned what Zobel had intended to reply, for there was a knock at the door, determined and twice repeated. The three people in the room looked at one another and the hostility which had hung in the air evaporated before common fear. A moment later, however, the door opened and the Colonel looked shamefacedly out of the window while his daughter and her lover cordially welcomed the visitor.

"Somebody must have left the outer door open," said the former Corporal Josef Maurer. He clicked his heels as he bowed to the Colonel and shook hands with Martha and Mante.

His appearance had come as a surprise to the Colonel, but what surprised him even more was that his former orderly was evidently expected. Now he understood Martha's remark that she was not worried about rations for the illegal lodger. He realized that Martha had got in touch with Maurer, and evidently with some success. He was now dragging in a huge carton from the hall—the carton itself a precious possession—and from it emerged American food cans; a package of two hundred cigarettes, a whole stick of shaving cream, the yearly ration of a German citizen; a chunk of cheese, half a sausage, and finally a bottle of schnapps. Like a commercial traveler invitingly displaying his collection, Josef Maurer was arraying these treasures on the Colonel's divan, while Martha, like an overwhelmed purchaser, accompanied his movements with shrieks of delight.

"I am to give the Herr Obersturmbannführer the best regards of Captain Green," said Maurer when he had finished his labors. "At twelve o'clock tomorrow the Captain will call."

Flabbergasted, the Colonel watched the group: his daughter, rummaging with flushed cheeks among the delicacies, as he had not seen her since her childhood Christmases; the complacently smiling Gerd Mante whose hand was resting jovially on the orderly's shoulder; his own orderly, finally, who was paying scarcely any attention to him and whom he hardly recognized. And the backdrop to this panopticon scene was the divan—a divan bright with cans of food.

The Colonel turned away towards the window. The August sky was crimson with the setting sun. Through the dusty desert an old woman was pulling an empty cart.

That First Winter Was Hell

During the summer everybody had avoided talking about it and in the early days of autumn the subject was mentioned only in whispers, just as in the middle ages people had anxiously and superstitiously avoided talking about cholera and plague—yet everybody knew that winter would inevitably fall upon Germany.

Winter was no longer a season; it was the plague. And just as the plague used to strike at a town without warning, insidiously, overnight, so winter had come after a short and deceptively mild autumn. In November the first frosts burst into the towns from the countryside. All deception and delusion were over: the struggle for one's bare existence had begun. Three hundredweight of coal was the ration each German was supposed to get for the whole winter: no matter how long the pestilence would rage, no matter how furiously it struck, this was all the medicine there was, and that was the end of it. Now and again the coal trucks rumbled through the streets. Picking up coal and stealing coal had become a life-saving activity. "Coal chaperons" was the popular name for the men whom the Allies employed to guard the black diamonds. But now and again a lump of coal dropped off a truck. Soon everybody was running after the vehicles: men and old women and children, citizens and beggars; some shyly to begin with, but presently with all dignity gone; at first stooping casually as if picking up something they had dropped, but presently shouldering each other away, tripping each other up, risking blows and enmity for the sake of a black lump of warmth.

German life revolved around window and stove. The misery, as happens invariably, produced its new aristocracy—the privileged class of glaziers. Any person possessing a piece of glass and capable of fitting it between the outer cold and the cold within could name his own terms. In the unpaid advertisement columns of the first papers appeared the notice: "Would offer riding boots in exchange for window glass." Some optimistic advertiser evidently hoped that there might be a glazier somewhere with cold feet. Some naïve character, perhaps a poet himself, offered Goethe's collected works, in excellent condition, for a few windowpanes. Military expressions were shunned, but the field stove was achieving ironical triumphs over central heating, steam heating and oil heating, just as the lumber-room with its despised articles from the past was triumphing over technical progress. The essential had become a matter of life and death; thus the superfluous had become doubly superfluous. One advertiser offered a marble fireplace in exchange for a handcart, another an evening gown, as good as new, for firewood.

People talked about the cold so as not to speak of their hunger, and they talked about hunger so they should not think of the cold. It was rumored that the Americans would supply five hundred thousand tons of foodstuffs. Five hundred thousand tons was like talking in terms of light-years. More comprehensible was the communiqué of the Military Government defining a new concept. "The unit of energy, one Calorie, is defined as the quantity of heat necessary to warm one kilogram of water by one degree centigrade. By consuming 100 grams of butter we supply 745 calories to our body. Sugar provides 400 calories, chocolate 518, bread 225." It was not meant mockingly, and indeed the communiqué may well have been a slight tribute to the Germans' thirst for knowledge and love of statistics. But the words themselves were full of mockery: quantity of heat, unit of energy, butter and chocolate. Calories warming water, and sugar providing calories, and food supplying warmth, and warmth giving pleasure—it was as if the starving were to be reminded of the cold, and the freezing of their empty stomachs. Just as people tracked the coal trucks to collect the black crumbs, so they searched for food among the refuse. And even if they found nothing to eat among the garbage behind Allied buildings, villas and offices, they might find some paper or a can, and from paper and cans food could be conjured up. But at many refuse dumps there was a notice: "Chlorinated refuse—unfit for human consumption"; for everybody was hygiene-conscious and care was taken that no human should consume the rubbish.

Never before this impending winter of 1945 had it been so obvious that misery and comedy held no contradictions. Not fortuitously had clowns and comedians of all ages arrayed themselves in rags: they perceived the comic element of misery. On October 6 the *Süd-deutsche Zeitung* carried the following announcement: "All persons entitled to rations within the orbit of the Food Office for Munich City, who are in possession of Munich purchase coupon No. 6, will receive one pound of apples." Surely only an ungrateful public could miss the irresistible joke of the news: one pound of apples for those "in possession" of purchase coupon No. 6, provided of course that they could also boast of being "persons entitled to ration." And was there not sidesplitting humor in the report, published by the same paper in its local news column, that a woman of twenty-eight who had hitherto received but scant attention from the male sex had been flooded with 2,437 proposals because her advertisement had offered to those contemplating marriage a heated room and her entire rations for the whole winter? However bad times are, there is always some good news: on November 30 a dancing school was at last opened in the city on the Isar, coyly inviting the public to "dance themselves warm"—naturally only till curfew time, but this difficulty was overcome by the announcement that the warmth-generating proceedings would start daily at eight o'clock in the morning. It was as easy to view events through rose-colored as through smoked glasses, for there were many promising signs in the air even at the beginning of winter. On October 25, for instance, it had been stated that there would be no beer in Bavaria, since some thirty per cent of barley would have to be admixed to bread flour; yet five weeks later, on a historic November 30, the ban on brewing was officially lifted and surely only inveterate grumblers could object that this new beer had been purged of that enemy of the people, alcohol.

There were circuses, too, in the early winter of 1945. Not only in the sense that the "Zirkus Krone" began to rebuild its tents on November 2—16 elephants, 110 horses, 8 lions, 6 camels and 12 bears—and not only in the sense that Shakespeare's *Macbeth* and Franz Molnár's *Play in the Castle* were staged by the Munich Kammerspiele; and not, finally, only in the sense that the political parties had been permitted again in the Provinces, no doubt as a well-meaning attempt to get the freezing public heated in that way. Much more than that: in the city of Nuremberg a veritable Circus Maximus was ceremonially opened: on November 20 the Nuremberg Trials were due to begin.

On that November 20 Frank, who had been sent to Nuremberg

by Colonel Hunter, met there Elisabeth von Zutraven, whose husband was to be one of the principal actors in "the greatest show on earth."

When the Reich Marshal was first taken prisoner—or rather, when he strutted into captivity with such naïve lordliness as if this had been a pleasant old-fashioned war and he himself a kind of modern Napoleon III—Frank had been in charge of the first interrogations. Now he was to clear up a few remaining details by questioning the Marshal's wife. For although the prosecution had accumulated mountains of material against the "war criminals," hundreds of questions still remained unresolved at the opening of that "greatest show on earth." It was as if rehearsals had to go on in the circus caravans while the public was already crowding into the big top.

In the detention camp on the outskirts of the city, where only the wives of high dignitaries were accommodated, Frank learned after the conclusion of his business that the wife of Governor Kurt von Zutraven was also held there. Since his visit to the "interrogation villa" Frank had done nothing to see Elisabeth again. The news of her renewed arrest had not been published in the still scanty papers, but even when he discovered her name on the blackboard Frank was determined to respect her wish and not approach her again.

But, his interrogation over, as soon as he stepped out of the wooden barracks—an unbearably hot barracks it was, heated on American principles—he ran into Elisabeth outside the door. Carrying a large clothesbasket with both her hands she was on her way between two barracks. Naturally the Major could not relieve the woman of her burden she was laboriously supporting on her abdomen, but neither could he watch passively as she carried the basket past him. In this difficult situation Elisabeth collected herself more quickly than he: she put the basket down on the frozen ground and greeted Frank with a slight smile. Perhaps this casual greeting would have been the end of the encounter if a huge MP had not emerged from behind the barracks and, anxious to prove his zeal to the officer, had tried to prod her into renewed activity with a rough "Come on, now!" The Major thereupon put the soldier in his place by telling him that he himself had ordered the woman to put the basket down. The MP saluted and withdrew with a faint shrug of the shoulders.

"What are you doing here?" asked Frank, trying to cover up the incident. "I thought you had been . . ."

"No," said Elisabeth. "I was brought back here again a few weeks ago."

"Any reason?"

"No. Except that the trial has started today; perhaps I behind barbed wire."

Frank hesitated for a moment. Then he said:

"Come in here. I want to talk to you."

With a sudden decision he got hold of one of the plaited handles of the basket while Elisabeth seized the other, so that the American major and the wife of the war criminal now carried the full basket between them and put it down right in front of a completely bewildered sergeant in the anteroom of the barracks.

"Is the room still free?" asked Frank, ignoring the sergeant's surprise. And he stepped into the little office where he had questioned the Marshal's wife a few minutes earlier.

"Sit down," he said to Elisabeth, offering her the chair in front of the desk. He remained standing.

"That was nice of you," Elisabeth said.

It was the first familiar sound Frank had heard from her lips. It was the speech of his childhood companion, thanking him cordially and yet distantly for one of the many little services which had always been more important to him than to her. He did not reply, but he no longer regretted having asked her, on some uncontrollable impulse, to follow him into the barracks.

"I know you didn't want to see me again, Elisabeth," he said, "but in the meantime I have learned a few things about you, and you would do me a favor by clearing up one or two points for me."

"May I take my coat off?" she asked.

Only now did he notice that she was wearing a heavy gray army greatcoat. Round her neck was a coarse but warm woolen scarf. He helped her out of her coat. She was wearing drill slacks which contrasted with a well-cut suit jacket. Under the jacket she wore a thick sweater. Her motley and utterly unfeminine collection of garments did not seem to worry her. He put the greatcoat, which smelled of soldiers and wet, down on the desk and said:

"I've made inquiries about you, Elisabeth—out of a personal interest which I hope you will not resent."

"Why should I?" she said.

"And this is where my mystification begins," he went on. "I am

»98«

told that you 'behaved very well,' as the phrase goes nowadays. You are said to have made nothing but friends in Paris and even to have prevented the deportation of Jews." The word "even" had a slightly ironical ring which Frank had not intended. He continued quickly: "They say you had a rather sharp exchange with Hitler."

"Supposing all this was true," she said, "why should it surprise you?"

"Because you aren't defending yourself, dammit all!" he replied. He turned away. "I asked to be shown the records of your first interrogations. There's not a word in them about all this. What on earth are you trying to do—become a martyr?"

He faced her again.

"You wouldn't understand," she said calmly. "You would not understand if I explained it to you a thousand times."

Frank noticed that she was talking quite differently from that time in the gloomy library of the Nuremberg villa a few months before. She looked different too. In the brown eyes with the green-edged pupils there was no flickering restlessness any longer, not even sadness or resignation. These eyes, undoubtedly, had once been sick, but they were now the eyes of a person who has known great sickness and who knows that one neither dies of it nor does one ever fully recover.

"And why wouldn't I understand?" he asked.

"Mainly because you can't imagine all those years in Germany. When I was young, Franz, in our day"—she smiled—"I used to have a secret game. I suppose everybody must have played it at some time or other. I tried to imagine that I was somebody else—our cook, or a man in the streetcar, or a film star, or you. Not only for one moment, but for always and since all time. And do you know, Franz, what I realized even then, when I was barely seventeen or eighteen? That it is enough to drive one to distraction, that fruitless attempt at being somebody else even for a moment. That it is easier to picture some fabulous beast or an inhabitant of Mars than another human being. And now you come along, the lot of you, from America and want to be able to imagine everything. Absolutely everything. Indeed you've gone further than that. You've already imagined everything."

She stopped. The sudden silence was heavy with mistrust.

"Go on," he said. "Never mind me: go on. I shall be offended if you don't."

"You can't imagine a thing while it is happening," she said. "And now you want to imagine it long after it happened. You are unrolling the film backwards, but we have lived through it from beginning to end. Do you understand? You ask: How can anyone go out into a street where a murderer is lurking? You have first seen the murder, then the murderer, then us, and last of all the street. But to us everything happened from one day to another, from yesterday to today. You think in terms of years, and proceed from today to yesterday. Why then should I speak out, Franz?"

He sat down on the table before her and said:

"Perhaps you are right, Elisabeth; perhaps we don't understand you. But do you understand yourselves? Perhaps we really can't get into your skins, not even for a moment. But what about yourselves? Can you get into your own selves, you Germans? You can't even do that. Already you ponder about us, about God and the world . . . But why do you walk past your own reflection in the mirror?" It sounded hard but not harsh, because he seemed to be putting the questions to himself. Suddenly he too broke off, just as she had done a moment earlier. Then he said: "Why should you speak out? Simply because you've got to get out of this camp. If you are innocent, or even comparatively innocent, this is no place for you. And that's a fact all your philosophizing won't change."

She smiled. It was the old smile, and he lowered his eyes to avoid it. She said:

"You haven't changed, Franz. It almost frightens me, how little you've changed."

He looked at her questioningly.

"You have always had an almost panicky fear of injustice," she said. "You see: I don't understand you either. I have seen so much injustice that I can no longer imagine why anybody should be shocked by it."

"I don't remember clearly what I was like then," he said, a little confused. "But I don't see why I should get accustomed to injustice." He got up and started pacing up and down the little room. "I shall demand that your case be re-examined. Understand: I shall not interfere in any way with the investigation. I believe that you Germans have sinned horribly and must do penance for it. But there's got to be some sense and measure in everything." He stopped in front of her. "You must promise me that you will shake off this apathy. Defend yourself! We'll see if it's any use or not."

He picked up the greatcoat which smelled of steamy dampness and helped her pull it on over her sweater and jacket. She had to wedge herself into the coat, which was much too tight for her, and thus he stood behind her for quite a while, close to her, holding his breath so it should not touch her neck. Nevertheless, it seemed to him that she was prolonging unduly the simple act of getting into a coat, and it seemed to her that he was transforming this simple process into a solemn ritual.

In the anteroom of the barracks they each picked up a handle of the clothesbasket, now as a matter of course and as if acting in secret accord, and carried it out into the raw November afternoon.

Presently Frank left, and she was once more carrying the basket towards the barracks where she was to deliver it. He did not turn his head till he was outside the barbed wire. As he watched her go it seemed to him as if the barbs went right through her body.

The Barbed Wire Remains

Everything had changed since that day when "on May 7, 1945, at 1:45 P.M. Central European Time, the German land, sea and air forces unconditionally surrendered to the Allied forces in the west and, simultaneously, to the Soviet High Command."

Everything had changed in Germany—only the barbed wire remained. It had its own tough life. The masters of yesterday had valued nothing, and the conquerors of today valued nothing. The only thing that was unassailable was the barbed wire. Gold was first surrendered in exchange for iron, then iron for bits of tin, then the tin for bread. But nobody exchanged the barbed wire for anything. Gasoline and food stores were destroyed, bridges and roads blown skyhigh, the earth itself seemed to shake. Only the barbed wire survived. The gates of concentration camps were thrown open; barracks were burned down; PW camps were liquidated and prisons leveled to the ground. Only the barbed wire remained. Gates could be opened and shut: the liberated passed through them on their way out and presently another lot passed through inward-bound. It was all very simple and convenient because that most vital thing had been saved from the deluge—the barbed wire. And that was just as well: for if it had been uprooted and spread out it would have made a carpet of crowns of thorns the length and breadth of Germany.

That barbed wire! Yesterday it had held Jews in its grip and slave laborers, foreign prisoners of war and German resistance fighters. Today it held Nazis and persons politically incriminated, fellow-travelers and refugees, and the soldiers of the defeated. New guests were staying at the Grand Hotel Misery, but, as was only proper with a conservative hotel, nothing betrayed the change from the outside. All there was to be seen from the outside was the barbed wire.

On a certain November evening in the year 1945 two men were standing by the barbed wire: one of them inside the cage, the other outside in the field.

The moon had completed her short course and the night was dark. The first snow had melted and frozen again. Puddles covered the ground like scattered mirrors. They cracked if you stepped on them. The two men did not move.

Their encounter was not accidental: encounters by the wire never were. A discharged prisoner from "No. 4 Detention Camp for Militarists" near Frankfurt-on-Main had smuggled a letter from Colonel (retired) Achim von Sibelius out of the camp with him and had passed it on, without further difficulties, to Dr. Adam Wild in Munich.

In this letter Colonel von Sibelius explained that he was getting sick and tired of spending his time behind barbed wire—not so much because of the physical discomfort as for the fact that he had a number of plans which he could not pursue behind the wire. Besides, he had more and more come to doubt the victors' sense of justice, or, for that matter, their good sense generally—and this brought him to the purpose of this note. Letters, documents and newspaper clippings (he explained) which conclusively proved his implication in the 20th of July—at least, as far as anything was considered conclusive nowadays —were in safekeeping in Munich with his sister, a Countess Deidesheim. Before his A.A.—automatic arrest—he had not been able to get hold of them; besides which he had assumed, to be perfectly frank, that the Americans themselves would be anxious to collect all such evidence. Anyway, after nearly six months in the stockade, and after a couple of dozen unsuccessful attempts to get the Americans to start the legal proceedings against him, there was now nothing left to him but laying claim to the services of his friend Adam. Would he please, if this could be accomplished without undue risk, collect his papers from the Countess Deidesheim and bring them along to a certain spot along the wire enclosure one Sunday evening between eight and nine. There was no legal way of getting the papers inside the camp; on the other hand, an American corporal, a splendid young chap, was ready to turn a blind eye. And since it was he who patrolled the eastern side of the compound on Sunday evenings it would probably be quite safe for Dr. Wild to pass the bundle of papers through the wire then. Just to be on the safe side he—Achim—would take a stroll along the barbed-wire fence on the next four Sundays, since he realized that Adam might not be able to make one definite Sunday.

Adam Wild, who had a good deal of experience in such matters and who was also annoyed at the failure of his intervention with Major Green, managed to be on the spot on the very first Sunday. He got a sympathetic colleague to sign a medical certificate to the effect that he urgently required treatment by some Frankfurt specialist and, having thus cunningly obtained a travel permit, he covered the distance between Munich and Frankfurt in less than forty-eight hours.

No doubt everything would have gone according to plan if Adam could only have denied himself the luxury of a nice chat in these inappropriate surroundings. But he could not bring himself to do that. When he had tossed the well-tied bundle over the wire fence—as well as two pairs of warm pants, a woolen scarf and a pair of ludicrously dainty ear-muffs, the last a thoughtful present from Frau Wild—he engaged his friend on the other side of the wire in lively conversation, just as if they were both facing each other in a pair of club chairs in front of a blazing library fire.

Needless to say, Achim too was anxious to make contact with the outside world, and moreover with his best friend. He related how he had been questioned on the very first day after his arrest: he had been treated correctly, almost courteously, and altogether he had nothing to complain of so far as his treatment was concerned. But after this first interrogation two months had passed, with the Americans showing no further inclination to talk to him—a circumstance which might also have been due to the fact that the camp command had been changed three times during that period. Evidently the Americans saw no reason for settling down any more permanently in this foreign land than they were wont to do back home. The third commandant had soon launched a paper campaign against the camp, so that Achim was at present engaged in filling out his thirty-second questionnaire. It was amusing enough to keep a tally of them, except that there was nothing on that new form that he had not already stated thirty-one times. But, demanded Adam, had he had no further live interrogations? Oh yes, three of them during the past three months: the first by an entirely well-meaning lieutenant who had, however, wanted to know what this talk of that "summer day," the 20th of July, was all about; the second by a hard-bitten lieutenant colonel who had assured him that only "downright swine" ever rose above the rank of captain in the Hitlerite army; and finally by a captain who had been both well-meaning and well-informed, but had explained to him with regret that in the case of a colonel in the General Staff the Americans were under an obligation to ask the British, the French, the Russians, and in Arnim's special case also the Yugoslavs and the Belgians, if they did not by any chance have a claim on the Colonel. But at least the captain had intimated to him that any documentary evidence in his favor would be desirable and useful, and had advised him to get hold of it—how, was his own business.

Throughout their conversation, which had been going on for about forty minutes, the friends had at regular intervals heard the steps of the patrolling sentry, but without ever catching sight of him in the thick fog which even hid each of them from the other. Only the cracking of the thin sheet of ice told them that they were not alone. But now they pricked up their ears: the sound of the breaking ice had become louder and the footsteps seemed to be coming nearer instead of withdrawing. Adam, on the point of addressing a question to Achim, suddenly fell silent and Achim instinctively shrank back from the wire fence.

The deceptive security into which the two men had lulled themselves suddenly split like a thin cloth. The challenge "Halt!"—uttered in English—rang out from quite close and at the same moment the bright beam of an oversize torch alighted on Adam.

"Raise your hands!" commanded the soldier whose outlines now emerged from the mist. Adam, blinded by the light, could not see him clearly, whereas the other held his torch well in front of him in his outstretched left hand. But Adam did not need to know that the soldier's right hand held a weapon; he hardly expected a sentry to be unarmed. Although ignorant of the English language Adam did not find it difficult to guess the meaning of the order and, without further futile argument, he raised his arms.

The soldier was alone. The beam of his torch performed a quick circle round Adam, but the soldier would not risk losing the stranger by the wire even for a moment. Adam had therefore every reason to assume that Achim had either flung himself down in good time or had crept away from the fence.

Adam did not understand the soldier's question, but he gathered from the gestures that he was to turn about. A moment later he felt the muzzle of a rifle pressing into his back, and then began a march around the camp, a march that seemed never-ending to the arrested man, but which finally terminated at a lighted side entrance. There, Dr. Adam Wild was taken over by several soldiers and led to an over-heated hut where half a dozen MP's interrupted their card game to receive him. A telephonic report was immediately made to authority, with all signs of extreme excitement, and presently a lieutenant appeared with two MP's to conduct him to the interior of the camp.

When he had been carefully searched and relieved of his watch, keys, a little money, his identification papers and his shoelaces—he did not wear a tie—Adam was left alone. The soldiers withdrew and bolted the door.

Adam Wild Hits Out

The part of the camp where Adam Wild had been kept for the past seventeen days was carefully separated from the rest, and there could have been no question of getting in touch with Sibelius even if Adam had thought such a step advisable. The detention camp was earmarked for "militarists" and only the one odd compound serve as a place of arrest for the somewhat motley crowd which consisted of anything but former Wehrmacht dignitaries.

On his first evening the Lieutenant had taken down Adam's particulars and questioned him briefly as to the reasons for his suspicious presence near the fence. Adam had made some flimsy excuses and eventually refused all further information. Since then he had waited in vain for another interrogation. The seventeenth day had dawned, and still nobody was showing the slightest interest in this particular prisoner.

During the first fortnight—Adam had carefully counted the days—everything had gone well.

He shared his room with five other prisoners. The adjacent rooms of the long and narrow barracks held many more prisoners, some twenty or thirty, but these rooms were so crowded that, in spite of the notorious elasticity of prison accommodation, it had been simply impossible to squeeze any more people in. A small room, evidently a former junk-room, had therefore been made available for the "new boys"—and one of these was Dr. Adam Wild.

The company was mixed in more senses than one. The only bunk, a two-tier affair, was occupied by a writer named Hannes Glück and a merchant named Alfred Rabenkopf. A secondary schoolteacher, Paul Müller, and a boy of fifteen, Jürgen Stuckenschimidt, shared the cold floor with Adam. Strictly speaking, Jürgen was the "oldest" inhabitant of the room, but Glück and Rabenkopf had dislodged him from the bunk originally put there for him. The remaining occupant of the former junk-room was a Dr. Heinrich Zille, to Adam's surprise a medical colleague.

Just as the inmates of a nursing home delight in exchanging their medical history, so the occupants of Room 8, Barracks C, spent a great deal of time discussing the offenses they were charged with.

It had not taken Adam long to form an opinion about the writer Glück. As soon as Adam appeared among his new companions the arrested author had clicked his heels and introduced himself as "Glück, Aryan"—a habit which this writer of stirring National Socialist verse had adopted during the Third Reich to prevent any misunderstanding arising from his not absolutely Aryan-sounding name. Glück (Aryan) was the victim of infernal bad luck: on the very day before the Americans entered his little Hessian town his local paper had published a "Stand-fast" poem by him. The paper, fresh off the press, had fallen into American hands. A variety of camps, however, had wrought no change in Glück's views: he still spent his time composing mournful odes on the Führer's demise.

Alfred Rabenkopf, a businessman, was not suspected of any political activity: as he himself was only too ready to admit, his offense had been the circulation of dollar bills, which he had sold for valuables to people who could bear the privations of the postwar months no longer and were getting ready to emigrate. Although Rabenkopf had some complaints to make about the standard of accommodation, he assured Adam that the acquaintances he had made with numerous Americans on the camp staff would prove invaluable for his business activities which he intended to resume upon his discharge.

Rather more complicated was the case of Paul Müller, the secondary schoolteacher, who—like many a sane man interned for some time in a lunatic asylum—was beginning to doubt his own sanity. Müller had fled to the American Zone from Leipzig, after the victorious Russians had raped and murdered his wife and daughter. At the zonal boundary he had been promptly arrested and had since been moved from one camp to another, as the victors could not understand why a German could not live just as well in the territory of another victorious power. Paul Müller was continually expecting deportation to the East.

The least communicative of the "patients" was Dr. Heinrich Zille, and this may have been due to a certain shyness he felt in the presence of a professional colleague. However, after a few days Adam managed to extract the doctor's curious history. Dr. Zille, a man of thirty-four, during the war a major in the Wehrmacht Medical Corps, repeatedly wounded and having almost by a miracle avoided capture in the Stalingrad bulge, had recently been caught performing an abortion on a girl of fourteen. The operation had been entirely successful, as Dr. Zille made a point of emphasizing to Adam, and no aspersion had been cast on his medical skill. The point was that this doctor, who came from Breslau, had established himself in Frankfurt as an abortionist because he believed that it was high time to stop mankind from propagating itself. It was true, he admitted, that he had occasionally accepted payment for his services, from persons well able to pay, but he was not motivated by material considerations. Nor did he mind the occupation in the least, although his patients were almost exclusively violated girls and abandoned "Occupation mothers" —"but this, my dear colleague, is quite beside the point: I was at the front for nearly six years and have come to the conclusion that it is better to strangle embryonic life than to help bring human beings into this rotten world." Even though such remarks were not entirely devoid of logic, it was clear to Adam that his floor-fellow, with his repeated serious demands for a "world-wide abortionist movement," should indeed be kept safely behind bars, though not perhaps in a detention camp.

The worst muddle, however, was the case of the fifteen-year-old

Jürgen Stuckenschmidt. It was not surprising, therefore, that it was this acquaintance that finally led to the complications which prolonged Adam's stay in the camp.

Jürgen was a blue-eyed boy with a straw-colored thatch; he was not ugly, but his head was much too big and swollen, not by any means from excessive nourishment but through constant starvation: his large head sat precariously on an emaciated throat and a frail childish body. Jürgen had lost his parents and sister in one of the last air raids on his native Würzburg; through a quirk of fate he escaped entirely unscathed from the completely gutted building. A "hero-snatcher," as the recruiting officials were called in the late stages of the war, had put the thin but tall young lad into uniform; moreover—since Jürgen Stuckenschmidt's bad luck moved in curious ways—into the uniform of a freshly killed lieutenant of the Waffen-SS. To make matters worse, the dead lieutenant appeared to have been something of a hero, for the empty uniform into which Jürgen was hastily put bore all sorts of ribbons and decorations. The irony of fate reached its culmination when an elderly German Home Guard man, scared stiff of the "Panzerfaust" entrusted to him, thrust this antitank bazooka into the hands of the fifteen-year-old. Dressed in the uniform of the dead hero and carrying his dangerous weapon the young boy was captured by the Americans on their entry into Würzburg. He had since been interrogated at five different camps: because he possessed no papers the Americans suspected him of being a particularly cunning war criminal. Thus Jürgen Stuckenschmidt, schoolboy and son of a cobbler, drifted about the camp uncomprehending and puzzled, with his fair hair and blue eyes reminiscent of those Russian peasant lads who, in the role of perplexed country bumpkins, move through the pages of the Russian classics. Like all children—and Jürgen was still a child—he was attracted by strength, which he sensed instinctively, and he therefore not only confided in Adam but followed his every step, even—if groundlessly—expecting his freedom at the hands of his fellow-captive.

For a fortnight, then, everything had gone well—provided the adverb is understood relatively. After a night spent in a vain attempt to snatch some sleep—the two thin army blankets were just enough to prevent a man from freezing to death but not from freezing—a snappy Prussian "*Raus!*" would ring out at five in the morning. The guards, otherwise ignorant of the German language, had soon acquired this useful word of command. After everybody had been standing in the square for two hours, in total darkness, in the snow and cold, while an American soldier would read out the names in a way that made it impossible to recognize them, a hot liquid was distributed, called breakfast coffee, but otherwise indistinguishable from that called soup at lunchtime. The morning roll call was not the last of the day: once more, sometimes even twice more, the prisoners were driven out into the square between the barracks, where the unimaginative conquerors repeated their name-reading game until some captives collapsed from exhaustion or had to be taken to the infirmary with symptoms of frostbite. Adam Wild, placing himself during these endless roll calls behind Jürgen Stuckenschmidt, ever ready to catch the reeling boy in case he hit the frozen ground, found it difficult to remind himself that, in contrast to Nazi concentration camps, an inmate here was at least not in immediate danger of his life and that detention would probably lead to liberty, and certainly not to the gas chamber.

Adam's reluctance to overdramatize his experience and his readiness to attribute the conquerors' lack of humane sentiment to the crimes that used to be committed in the name of the vanquished found a welcome support, during that first fortnight, in the person of Sergeant White. This compound sergeant, in civilian life an electrical engineer in a small town in Nebraska, "stuck his neck out," as he himself put it, in his efforts to mitigate for his charges the hardships of prison life. Sergeant White used the tremendous power wielded by an NCO—especially if he represents the victors in a camp for the defeated—for good; not because he felt any special sympathy for the Germans but because he believed that the business of an army was to win wars and not to play prison guard.

On the evening of the thirteenth day Sergeant White said an almost tearful goodbye to his charges, handing over to them his own rations, cigarettes and a few more blankets. With Professor Müller, who knew some English, acting as an interpreter he assured the inmates of Room 8, Barracks C, that he should be happy to welcome them all to his place in Nebraska some day. Finally he added a little warning: Corporal Crane, his successor, had never smelled a whiff of powder and occupation soldiers fresh from home must, paradoxically, be handled with care.

Corporal Crane, who had thus been awaited with misgivings, in fact soon revealed himself as a beast furnished with superhuman full powers. On his very first appearance in the former junk-room he dropped a remark about a "new reign"; an hour later he returned to collect all "surplus" blankets and, after an inch-by-inch search, also all accumulated "treasures." On the next day he had a new idea: on the grounds that the room was too small to hold a "double-decker" the bunk was removed, so that the poet Glück and the businessman Rabenkopf now had to bed down on the floor as well. Crane was a man of medium height, about twenty-five years old, with a crew cut and a face which betrayed no sort of mental life, and thus not brutality either, but which was reminiscent of those newspaper pictures which reveal only to the expert physiognomist the buried instincts of a criminal type. Corporal Crane—nobody ever found out where he came from and whether he was a regular army man—soon began to pick on Jürgen Stuckenschmidt as his victim in a long series of small but perfectly obvious displays of chicanery.

But it was not until the third day of his reign—the seventeenth of Adam's detention—that Crane's hostility to the fifteen-year-old boy erupted openly.

The small separate compound had no mess of its own; the food was was doled out in the barracks. Three times a day two or three captives were detailed to bring from the cookhouse a large pot containing the coffee-soup or soup-coffee. Under Corporal Crane's watchful eyes the food was then ladled out into old Wehrmacht mess kits and the empty cooking pot carried back to the cookhouse. In Adam's barracks the distribution always started in Room 8, because that room opened directly on to the yard.

That afternoon the steaming pot had been brought over by Jürgen, Dr. Zille and Glück. The frail boy, inadequately supported by the raving doctor and the lazy poet, was carrying most of the weight. As he squeezed through the door with it he tripped over one of the "beds" on the floor and in his fright let go of the handle, so that some of the steaming soup ran over the floor and on to a couple of army blankets.

Jürgen's roommates looked at one another. Only then did they dare to raise their eyes in the direction of the door where the Corporal had stopped with clenched fists. Panic hung in the air, and it was doubly strong because it seemed as if the boy had only acted out what an inescapable fate had cruelly decreed for him.

With a curse Corporal Crane approached Jürgen. His movements seemed elements in a well-produced and much-rehearsed play. As the boy quickly tried to straighten himself up Crane caught him by his slender shoulders and flung him against the wall like a ball. For an instant it looked as if it was going to end there. But then Jürgen made a fatal mistake. He said something in his mother tongue, instinctively, a kind of apology; but Crane assumed, or wished to assume, that his prisoner had the effrontery to contradict him or even to resist him.

The large battered ladle, which had been in the cooking pot, was lying on the ground where Jürgen had dropped it. Crane now lifted it up. The men, pressed motionless against the wall, thought the Corporal was going to strike Jürgen with it. Perhaps that had been Crane's original intention—but the cowering men, the trembling boy by the wall, and his mounting intoxication with power made him conceive a diabolical idea.

The lid had slid off the steaming pot. Crane dipped the ladle into the hot liquid. And before the prisoners understood what was happening he had flung some of the boiling contents of the pot into the boy's face.

Jürgen was pressed flat against the wall. The steaming liquid was trickling down his face, singeing his eyes and scalding his lips.

Instinctively he raised his hands to shield his face. Infuriated even further by this defensive gesture Corporal Crane once more dipped the ladle into the steaming broth: with a semicircular movement of his right arm he splashed the hot liquid into the face of the boy screaming with pain.

The prisoners did not stir. Rabenkopf stood pale and trembling; Professor Müller had shrunk into himself; Glück's hands were ludicrously pressed against his sides, as if he were standing at attention. But Zille, still in the door, burst out laughing: a hysterical laughter that resounded through the hut.

But for that laughter Adam might never have freed himself from that rigidity into which he had frozen together with the others. But now he went into action, almost like a soldier leaping a ditch and flinging a hand grenade.

With a jump he stood in front of the Corporal. Crane, himself a man of not inconsiderable strength, almost disappeared in Adam's gigantic hands. The attack came so suddenly that Crane could not, as no doubt he would have done, reach for his pistol. Adam wrested the ladle from him, pinning the Corporal's arms behind his back with his other hand. Uttering curses and threats Crane began to struggle. With his free left hand Adam caught him by the neck. And his petrified fellow-prisoners saw him getting ready to force the man's close-cropped head into the still steaming pot.

At that moment, however, Adam came to his senses. He let go of Crane's head and bodily lifted the man who was furiously kicking his feet. Like a wriggling child he carried him to the door; he kicked it open and flung the Corporal, like a bulky sack, out into the yard.

Still no one moved. Jürgen stood by the wall, whimpering. Completely blinded, he was trying to wipe the liquid off his scalded face with the cuff of his uniform tunic. His large childish head rocked more loosely than ever on his thin neck.

Adam stopped, facing the door. He could not think clearly, but he expected to see Crane appear in the door with his pistol drawn.

But nothing happened. A moment later the prisoners heard the Corporal's receding footsteps.

Adam wiped the cold sweat off his forehead. He turned and said to Jürgen:

"Lie down. I want to have a look at you."

The sober sentence at last broke the tension. Dr. Zille was laughing no longer Professor Müller knelt down by Adam's side to give what help he could. The black-marketeer Rabenkopf began to rummage among his possessions as though he kept a first-aid box hidden there. Only the poet Glück remained erect against the wall and said:

"Heil Hitler!"

Adam turned his head. He said:

"Shut up! Run over to the infirmary. I can't do anything without bandages."

He was trying to clean up Jürgen's eyes when the door burst open. Four MP's, with rifles on their shoulders, stood in the door.

Adam rose to his feet.

"See he gets taken to the infirmary," he said to Dr. Zille.

Then he followed the soldiers.

They took him across the icy yard, past barracks and staring prisoners, to the commandant's quarters.

The office they entered was so hot that for an instant Adam was afraid of fainting. He looked about for a chair, but eventually rallied all his strength to pull himself together. He knew that it was not just a manner of speaking if one referred to a man's shaking knees; only his knees had never shaken before. Now they were rattling together, almost like chattering teeth. Adam realized the absurdity of the fact that he feared nothing so much at the moment as that his knees might be seen shaking.

Almost half an hour passed. At the two desks sat two disinterested soldiers reading the Sunday comics. The hands of the lazily ticking clock formed an exclamation mark. It was six.

At last the door of the commandant's office opened. Corporal Crane came out. He did not look up. But as he passed Adam he said something between his teeth, in English. The MP's smiled.

Adam entered the commandant's office. To his surprise the four MP's withdrew at once. He was alone with Lieutenant Colonel Lee E. Perry.

The lieutenant colonel, whose name in gilt letters stood on a little wooden board facing the visitor in the middle of the desk, scrutinized Adam carefully for some time.

He looked like a Trappist monk who had not spoken for years and who had only taken the most indispensable nourishment. Adam began to wonder if the man would ever start speaking.

"Do you speak English?" the lieutenant colonel finally broke the silence.

"No," said Adam.

"I understand German," said the lieutenant colonel. He spoke slowly, in measured periods, like someone who had mastered the rudiments of the language in painful study, but who did not like to waste words even in his native tongue.

Adam was silent.

"Well," said the lieutenant colonel. "What have you to say for yourself?"

Adam began to relate the events of the past few hours. He was as succinct as possible, speaking slowly and calmly, anxious to make himself understood. The man behind the desk listened to him without interrupting.

"I am sorry," Adam concluded his account, "but I could not act otherwise."

Still there was no movement in the thin ascetic face.

"There's no need for you to feel sorry," the lieutenant colonel said at last. "I should have done the same thing."

The two men looked at each other. Adam had to rally all his strength spent during the last few hours not to be overcome by emotion. Only now did he realize that he had been sick with fear, naked fear, as naked as his fury a little while before. He made an effort to suppress his emotion, to stop it from showing in his eyes. One was too easily moved when one had been badly afraid.

"But you are out of luck," said the lieutenant colonel. "You were on the discharge list. The prisoner Sibelius has told us why you came here. For that, seventeen days was enough. Now I have to keep you in. Physical assault against a uniformed member of the Occupying Power in a serious offense. I am sorry." He dropped his eyes. "I shall have Corporal Crane put before a court-martial. You have merely confirmed his account. Have you anything else to say?"

"Yes," said Adam. "I should like to thank you."

"Nothing to thank me for," said Lieutenant Colonel Perry. "We try not to make concentration camps. You may find that surprising, Herr Dr. Wild. But it is easier to make concentration camps than not to make concentration camps. You understand?"

"Yes," said Adam.

"Very well," said Perry. "Go back to your barracks. Corporal Crane won't be on duty for the time being."

He touched the bell on his desk. To the sergeant who appeared in the door he said:

"The prisoner can return to his barracks by himself."

A moment later Adam was outside in the yard between the low wooden barracks. The light from their windows fell on the ice-covered ground. The last roll call was over: the camp was deserted and desolate.

He had nearly reached Barracks C when three figures loomed out from the dark.

Adam knew at once what was going to happen. He squared his shoulders, tensed his muscles and got ready. But he had no time to resist. Two men whose faces he could not see seized him and with a practiced twist dislocated his arms so that they formed a knot on his back.

Corporal Crane was facing him. Without saying a word he struck Adam in the face with his clenched fist. Once, twice, three times. Adam felt no pain, only warmth engulfing his face. His blood poured from his nose into his mouth.

Adam never found out what was to have followed. The sound of marching was heard in the darkness and the two men let go of him. Crane's hand, raised to strike again, dropped. The three made off on the double.

Adam opened the door of his room. Jürgen was no longer there. "For God's sake, what have they done to you, Herr Doktor," said Müller the teacher.

Adam wiped the blood from his face. For an instant he thought of returning to the Colonel to report the incident. But he immediately rejected the idea. He could still hear the officer's foreign accent: It is easier to make concentration camps than not to make concentration camps. You understand? Yes, thought Adam; I understand.

A Whores' Rummy Party

Inge was sitting in the room of the tall blonde, playing rummy.

After that summer evening, when she had gone off with the Negro, Inge had not ventured near the Sendlinger-Tor-Platz for weeks. Perhaps she would have never gone back if she had not run into the tall blonde one day, on the corso outside the "Mücke."

The Negro had been from Annistan, Alabama. Once Inge sat up next to him in the jeep he had let her guide him. He did not understand that she had no address. They drove right across Munich first one way and then another, along the Isar, till they came to the Hellabrunn deer park. The grass was deep and the bushes along the edge of the park were thick. Moreover, darkness had fallen. And then the Negro from Alabama understood even less.

His name was Lincoln Washington Haymes. His parents had given him the two presidential names as a compensation for the color of his skin. Now, in occupied Germany, Lincoln Washington Haymes felt worthy of his Christian names for the first time. He was happy in Germany, and because he was happy he was kind to Inge. Then he was moved to Berlin. And Inge began to ply up and down the corso in front of the "Mücke."

That was where she had one day met the tall blonde who had likewise given up the Sendlinger-Tor-Platz for, as it were, higher spheres. Inge's heart missed a beat as Ilse approached her with the firm tread of a grenadier. But Ilse Joachim—that was the blonde's name—was a realist. She was no longer young herself and she knew that it was wiser to support budding talent if one could not crush it. She took Inge under her wing.

Four months had passed since then. Inge still lived with her father, the pensioner Alois Schmidt. She still slept in the sitting-room, on the divan with the two lions' heads. But whereas the divan had once been her only possession, she now owned the entire furnishings, including the pensioner himself.

She had been six when her mother had run off with a hairdresser's assistant, in the winter of 1935. It had been a very severe winter. And although the seasons changed in due rotation, the climate had since persisted severe for Inge Schmidt. The pensioner—forty-five years old when Inge was born and fifty-two when his young wife failed to return from the hairdresser's one day—had poured out all his hate of the unfaithful woman on the child, especially as she was getting more and more like her mother no matter how much her father tried to stamp out any resemblance to the sinner. The border line along which Alois Schmidt moved was about as narrow as all border lines between good and evil. He might have enveloped the child in the love he had felt for the wayward woman, the only love he had ever been capable of. But he had buried the child under the hatred which had replaced his love.

Just as the father had taken his revenge on the girl, so the girl now took her revenge on her father. He had sent her out on to the street: now she brought the street home to him. Ilse Joachim had offered Inge her room in a half-wrecked building behind the Sendlinger Tor for temporary use, but a bitter impulse, an almost perverted pleasure, drove the girl home to her own apartment by the cemetery. On her second or third meeting she had brought the startled Lincoln Washington Haymes to the paternal home. He had been followed by a black marketeer from the "Mücke," then by another Negro from Harlem, then by a white major who had three daughters back home in Chicago, all of them older than Inge. She kept her father as he had kept her throughout her childhood years: she did not let him go hungry, thirsty or without cigarettes. But the tune in the home of the domestic tyrant Alois Schmidt was now called by Inge. She took literally what he had taught her: that he who provided the bread could give the orders. And it made no difference where the bread came from.

But her afternoons, and sometimes all day, Inge would spend with the tall blonde. Ilse lived on the third floor of a house which, strangely enough, only had a third floor. It was the kind of architecture created by incendiary bombs which, though they had ripped through that floor also, had only burned out the lower two floors. But as the staircase had been destroyed at the same time there was now a kind of emergency stairs, not unlike a chicken-ladder, leading up to the third floor. As a result, the women—all of them girls of easy virtue—lived there like hens in a chicken coop and only fluttered down the ladder to the yard in the evening.

The room of the tall blonde was a spacious and comfortably equipped chicken house. There was a deep green couch; a small round table by the window had a slightly yellowed but clean lace-work centerpiece; on the walls hung several massively-framed oil paintings representing implausibly lugubrious landscapes. A cheerful note was provided by three or four photographs of American soldiers with dedications such as "Thanks to Ilse, from John"—gentle mockery of the law which forbade the Americans all contact with the sinful nation. On the dark-brown wardrobe five to ten rosy-cheeked apples were invariably lined up, which underlined the domestic atmosphere and also served as stakes in the unending games of rummy played by the two friends. In the way that hazelnuts are distributed among children for stakes in party games, the domesticated Ilse would always hand several apples to her companion at the beginning of their session—without, however, seriously jeopardizing these presents from a rural relative since she invariably won and presently returned her reconquered apples to their neat row on the wardobe.

On that frosty afternoon towards the end of November Ilse Joachim had once more won back the six apples which she had generously put at Inge's disposal. Now she was opening the wardrobe to cast an eye over clothes. Inge meanwhile stood by the little iron stove in which a fire was merrily crackling—the firewood having been supplied by a rural client who paid in kind. The sickly smell of the rotting apples was mingling in the room with the pungent odor of the burning wood.

"The trouble is that everything's three times too big for you, child," sighed Ilse. "Although you're looking well, very well indeed, considering your miserable hangdog appearance when I first spoke to you. Walking the streets is doing you good."

"Having something in my belly is doing me good," said Inge.

"Your improvement isn't due to food alone, child. It's the recognition."

"Your recognition makes me sick," said Inge.

The tall blonde laughed. "Who's talking about my recognition? I'm talking about men."

"I'm sick of men," said Inge.

"Now you're talking rubbish," said Ilse. "When I was still a mannequin . . ."

"I know your stories by heart," said Inge.

Ilse did not mind. "I'm not weeping tears over the past," she said. "Not me. I used to feel God knows how important waddling down the gangplank . . ." She turned about and, swaying her hips, walked down an imaginary gangplank.

"Any gangplank would collapse under you," Inge said.

Ilse paid no attention to this either. "The men goggled at me," she said, stopping in front of the wardrobe. "But did one of them pay? No fear! Now I know what I'm worth. Never mind about losing your virtue, child, but don't lose your independence." Her glance took in the photographic trophies on the wall and came to rest on the iron stove which was glowing dull-red. "Now who else can earn a carton of 200 cigarettes in a day nowadays? Not every day, perhaps, but then it might be two cartons on a Saturday. Who else can get a chap to lug a sack of firewood up two flights of stairs? The other day they found a carton of Chesterfields in the apartment of a minister— there was hell to pay! It makes me laugh. A minister! Now who's got more self-respect: the minister or me? And it's the same with you, child. He who has something, has self-respect; he who hasn't got anything, hasn't any self-respect. Think of your father . . ."

"You were going to lend me a coat," Inge said.

From the wardrobe she took an overcoat which was dyed navy-blue, but which nevertheless immediately betrayed the fact that it had been made from two GI blankets, those warm dark-khaki blankets used by the American army. In a few places the dye had not penetrated the material and the masculine khaki was showing through the feminine blue. But such trifles did not shake Ilse Joachim's professional pride.

"Just think: some chap may have been court-martialed for pinching these two blankets," she said, lovingly fingering the material. "That's recognition, I tell you—real recognition. . . ."

She helped Inge on with the coat. Although the girl was really no longer so thin and helpless as she had been in the spring, she could still have wrapped the coat round her twice. Lost in the sea of material she looked small and miserable again.

"Perhaps you needn't button it up," Ilse remarked thoughtfully. "It certainly is a warm coat."

"All right," said Inge. With a gesture towards the divan where her own coat was lying she added: "I'd freeze to death in that childish thing."

It was wise of her to wrap herself in the former army blankets. It was bitterly cold outside. The moon had risen and it was bright in the streets because there were fewer houses now in the way of the moonlight. The cold was more noticeable because it was more visible. Only a few vehicles had left their tracks on the glassy ice of the roadway: the sheet of ice was unbroken like the reflecting surface of some rural landscape. The streets were frozen streams, the wide avenues were frozen rivers and the squares were frozen lakes. The November sky seemed even colder above the dead city; the humble rivals of the stars—street lamps and lighted shop windows—were so pale and dim that one looked up instinctively to the stars which stood twinkling and remote behind the moon.

The two women were walking along quickly, the younger one almost at a trot with her shorter steps, the older one with her customary strut unimpaired by her hurry. They had nearly reached their beat and had turned behind the ruin of the brewery into a back street down which, invisible from the road, the "Mücke" was situated. The night club was screened from the street by the solitary wall of a bombed-out building; the "Mücke" itself was a low wooden hut that had been placed amidst the debris, just like the temporary huts put up by the building workers on a construction site.

Suddenly a jeep pulled up alongside the women.

"Hey!" called the officer at the wheel. "Is there a night club hereabouts, called the 'Mücke'?" He spoke without a foreign accent; in fact there was just a tinge of Munich in his speech.

"Perhaps," replied Ilse.

The officer dipped into his breast pocket, pulled out a pack of cigarettes and passed two of them to the women.

"Down there, through that gate," said Ilse.

"Might as well leave the car here," the officer said.

He climbed out and opened the hood. He thrust his hand into the engine, unscrewed a round brown box and pulled out a short rubber tube. He pushed them into his pocket and let the hood fall shut again.

"Just to prevent anyone from stealing it," he said to the women who had watched him in silence.

He was about to follow them when a shout of "Captain Green! Captain Green!" rang through the empty street and made him stop. From the little square at the end of the street a man was running up to them.

"Beg to apologize most humbly, Herr Hauptmann," the man said breathlessly as he reached the waiting group.

"Quite all right, Maurer," said the American. "I was a bit early."

Only then did the former Corporal Josef Maurer notice that the Captain was not alone. Without being disrespectful he made a questioning gesture.

"It's all right," said the Captain with a smile. "The ladies are also on their way to the 'Mücke.'"

Chief of Counterintelligence East is Needed Again

George Green had been mistaken in thinking the "ladies" were on their way to the "Mücke." It was true that they had both been inside two or three times, but the night club for which Walter Wedemeyer had at last got a license after protracted negotiations was restricted to a clientele to which Ilse and Inge could not boast to belong.

The "night club," which closed its doors at half-past nine in the evening, consisted of two rooms, one a little bigger than the other. Both had been exceedingly tastefully furnished with the most modest materials. Walter Wedemeyer had known how to make a virtue of necessity: the walls were covered in rough sacking which lent the place a rustic character. And since in a night club things do not have to make sense, a few life-belts suspended from the walls, three or four cleverly placed carriage-lanterns, a few ultramodern paintings and, lastly, a gigantic midge cunningly fashioned in rope were sufficient to give the place the intimacy which Wedemeyer's guests sought. There had at first been a small jazz band, but Wedemeyer had soon dismissed it because the players' delight at being allowed again to play music had led them to express their enthusiasm in a more-than-American noisiness. Wedemeyer, who did not like musical servility, had instead hired a pianist who rendered German and English songs with a tinkling sentimentality.

For reasons connected with the conditions of Wedemeyer's license, but which were known only to him and American Intelligence, the Occupying Power turned a blind eye, and often a pair of blind eyes, to the fact that a great deal of cheerful fraternization was going on at the "Mücke." The place was patronized chiefly by black marketeers, prostitutes and members of the occupation forces, and was exclusive in the sense that only the cream of these three categories was to be found there. The military came chiefly for the sake of the barmaids whom Wedemeyer had chosen with exceptional care and astonishing expertness; the black marketeers came principally in the hope of doing their business with the conquerors mellowed by wine. Besides, the "Mücke" served quite amazing meals—scrambled eggs, made partly of American egg powder and partly of fresh eggs; boiled beef, from cans, and sometimes even real pork; white bread and butter— and all, needless to say, without coupons. A considerable part of the food was supplied by the military visitors, in payment to the girls; the girls then sold the foodstuffs to Wedemeyer, and he in turn sold them to the black marketeers. Sometimes the economic cycle worked in a different way: the black marketeers might acquire cigarettes from the troops, or Wedemeyer might give the girls cans of food in exchange for cigarettes. Since in the few restaurants that were left in the city all food was served exclusively for coupons, and moreover for a whole collection of coupons, Wedemeyer would explain to any inquisitive American that his guests had "brought along" the food they were eating. In actual fact the "Mücke" owed its phenomenal success to the fact that a guest need neither "bring" anything nor possess any food coupons.

As soon as Captain George Green, followed by Josef Maurer, entered the crowded restaurant he was cordially welcomed by the proprietor and conducted to the smaller room. There was a good reason for the deliberate attention which Herr Wedemeyer was showing his new guest. At the time when Wedemeyer submitted his project to Colonel Hunter and when the plan began to pass through the long official machinery, the pretext that the "Mücke" might serve American Counterintelligence as a hunting ground had come to him like an inspiration. In fact, Wedemeyer had no such adventurous and far-reaching plans: he simply knew a good thing when he saw one, and this had been his chance of opening a place where human flesh could be converted into pork by way of tobacco. Nevertheless, he had been disquieted by the fact that his licensers, at least as far as he knew, had not yet made use of his place; it was in Wedemeyer's nature to want to give good service to his customers. When therefore one of his favorite guests, Herr Josef Maurer, informed him that "an influential Intelligence officer" would visit the night club that day Wedemeyer assumed that he was on the way to discharging his obligations.

Captain Green and Maurer sat down at a corner table in the small room, and with a "hey presto" gesture Wedemeyer—wreathed in smiles and looking more like a diplomat than a restaurateur in his pinstriped trousers and black jacket—had conjured up a water jug full of bubbling champagne. The circumstance that the champagne was not served in its original bottle had nothing to do with its quality—it was indeed excellent champagne—but was simply due to the fact that at the "Mücke" even the drinks appeared camouflaged and that the tables were mostly empty either because food and drink had hurriedly been cleared away or because the guests had altogether preferred it to be placed discreetly on stools and benches.

"Well, here we are," said Maurer, not very brightly, as soon as Wedemeyer had withdrawn.

"Any of the people here?" asked Green.

"Not seen any yet, Herr Hauptmann," Maurer said apologetically. "Turn up without doubt any minute."

Green offered Maurer a cigarette.

"If I may make so bold," said Maurer and picked up the champagne glass at the same time. "Your very good health, Herr Hauptmann."

Green took a sip without replying to the toast. He said:

"I hope Herr Mante is going to keep his promise. Otherwise I might find it difficult to guarantee his freedom any longer."

"Beg to assure the Herr Hauptmann that everything is under control," Maurer said eagerly. "Herr Hauptmann must please understand the difficulties. Anybody who was anybody in the Gestapo is either in jail or in hiding. The people are suspicious. They think it's a trap. They won't understand that they are needed again."

" 'Needed' is putting it too strong," Captain Green interposed.

Maurer shifted impatiently on his chair. From their table they could watch the rest of the restaurant through the open door. The pianist was a haggard man in a shabby Wehrmacht jacket. His profile was like a triangle: from his forehead a steep straight line went down to the tip of his nose, and an equally steep line went from there to his receding chin. One of Wedemeyer's girls was leaning against the piano. She had red hair which fell loosely down to her shoulders. In her décolleté evening gown, which had seen better days, she looked like a girl desperately trying to impersonate a cocaine addict. She was trying to attract the attention of two men at a near-by table. Maurer knew them: they dealt in butter. One of them had supplied him with a consignment of seventy-five kilograms of butter: fifty kilograms had been rancid. Their relations had been somewhat strained since then.

Maurer's features suddenly came to life.

"That's one of them," he said to the Captain.

Green glanced towards the entrance. A man in a black leather coat had entered the night club. He was a broad-shouldered man with a flat face pitted with pock-marks, but strangely enough the scars were not repulsive; in fact, they emphasized the masculine character of the brutal features. The man stopped at the door and pulled off his thick leather gloves. He did not pocket them but stood holding them in his fist.

"I'd better speak to him alone first," Maurer said.

George Green nodded agreement.

Maurer and the stranger sat down at the last free table, close to the pianist. George Green could watch them from where he sat.

Clouds of smoke hung in the air like fat white balloons. In the middle of the restaurant a few tables had been pushed aside and three or four couples were making rhythmical movements. The soldiers danced with their revolvers strapped on. Now and again a girl would rub her behind because the holster of some dancing soldier had dug into her hip. Rifles were leaning against several tables. The soldiers to whom the rifles belonged were sitting behind the tables, their opened fingers on their girls' breasts, almost as though trying to gauge their circumference. One or two, drunk with the cheap wine, had plunged their hands into the girls' blouse fronts. They had forgotten about their weapons. From time to time some dancer would trip over a propped-up rifle and it would clatter noisily to the ground. The pianist had switched from jazz to a sentimental German song—"A Rhenish girl and some Rhenish wine." The girl by the piano crooned:

"This must be paradise divine . . ." Every time a rifle crashed to the floor the girl gave a little start.

Maurer and the man in the leather coat rose. The stranger knocked his head against one of the dangling life-belts. They came over to George Green.

Maurer dispensed with the formality of introduction. They sat down. Green offered them cigarettes; the stranger declined.

"Herr Maurer has told you what this is all about?" George Green began.

"Yes," said the man. "I am to get you in touch with the General." Green nodded.

The pock-marked man said: "What guarantee have I that this isn't a trap?"

"But I keep telling you," interposed Maurer. "Mante vouches for him . . ." He was all eagerness.

George Green pretended not to hear that Mante had to vouch for him.

"Suppose that I can talk to the General," the stranger said, still suspicious, "what am I to tell him?"

"We want to organize a new secret service," said Green.

"With us or against us?"

"We are looking for people with experience of the East. The General is reputed to be an expert."

The man in the leather coat smiled. "There isn't a greater expert." Then his smile vanished again from his hard features. "There is a case pending against the General."

"We might quash it," said Green.

"That won't be enough for the General," said the stranger.

Green raised his eyebrows questioningly.

"The General stands by his old colleagues," said the man. From his coat pocket he produced a German cigarette—it seemed to Green like a deliberate gesture—and lit it. He looked straight into Green's face. "Many of his people are Nazis. Some belong to the Gestapo." He pronounced "Nazis" and "Gestapo" in the way the Americans did. He seemed to be trying to make a contemptuous pronunciation sound contemptible itself.

"We shall discuss with the General the selection of his people," said Green.

»124«

"If the General is to set up anything he'll need money," said the stranger.

"That's no news," said Green.

"Green dollars?"

"Sure."

"Very well," said the man. "I'll try to speak to the General." His eyes lighted on Maurer. "Who's paying him?" he asked.

Maurer smiled. When he smiled his wide mouth turned into a moronic grin. The contrast between his village idiot's face and his cunning eyes became particularly striking.

"I work out of idealism," he said.

"We're paying him," said Green.

The stranger started to get up.

"If possible I should like to talk to the General this week," said Green.

For the first time there was an almost merry twinkle in the stranger's eyes. He asked:

"Is the balloon going up so soon?"

George Green knew what the man was talking about. But he asked:

"What do you mean?"

"Against the Russians," said the man.

"What the General may know is of interest to us today rather than tomorrow," said George Green. "That ought to be enough for you. We could meet at Herr Mante's place."

The stranger got up.

"I can't make any promises for him," he said. "I'll do what I can."

George Green did not rise. His glance swept over the man, upwards from foot to head.

"Do you need an advance?" he asked.

"No," said the stranger.

He nodded briefly, turned quickly and marched out through the restaurant.

A few minutes later Maurer and the Captain also left. In the door they collided with a huge American sergeant. Maurer noticed casually that the sergeant's arm was round the waist of the small pale girl they had seen earlier in the street. In her much too big army-blanket coat she looked like a rag doll in the hands of a grown-up.

Frank Takes Charge of the O'Hara Case

"And now you know the whole story, Frank," said Colonel Hunter to the Major across his desk. "That woman's in Munich." He made a scornful gesture towards the papers in front of him. "That's quite obvious. But there's nothing in these reports. It's like groping through raw cotton. You got any idea what's the matter with O'Hara?" It was typical of Colonel Hunter's relationship with the two men that he referred to the one major as O'Hara while he called the other by his first name.

"My relations with Major O'Hara are entirely confined to business," said Frank.

"I know," said the Colonel. He shrugged his shoulders. "Anyway, you've got to look into this business, Frank. You've got the photographs and the descriptions. Take my car. Comb the whole town. In particular those places specially marked in the papers. This business is beginning to get me down."

Frank rose. During the four years that he had served under the Colonel he had only seldom seen Hunter betray any sort of emotion. His reserve had not weakened under the fire of the Normandy landings or at the triumphal moment of entry into Paris; neither in the relaxed atmosphere of the officers' mess nor during nerve-racking interrogations or prisoners. There were many who interpreted the Colonel's austere reticence and severe self-control as coldness, either innate or acquired; others simply believed that it sprang from conceit. But Frank had always felt that behind the grave, almost schoolmaster-like features lay a sadness through to which one might penetrate neither with nor without permission, simply because there was no keyhole into which a key or even a skeleton key could be inserted. He felt a certain affection for Hunter, the affection of a man who had lost his father early, and even Hunter's anger was to him a welcome confirmation that the inner life of his superior officer, though perhaps pathless and craggy, was certainly not arid and void.

Nevertheless he considered it his duty to point out to the Colonel that the Irene Gruss case had been entrusted to Major O'Hara and that he, Major Green, would prefer not to be charged with the search for the commandeuse until O'Hara had been fully informed of his irregular mission.

"You will kindly let me decide when to inform O'Hara," said the Colonel. In a more conciliatory tone he added: "I may have my reasons. . . ."

"All right, Colonel," said Frank. "I shall report to you as soon as I can."

"Good luck," said Hunter and dismissed the Major.

It was snowing heavily when Frank got into the olive-green Chevrolet which had waited for him in the yard of the headquarters building in Ludwigstrasse. Although the cold was far less severe than during the first few days of November, the temperature was still below freezing, so that the snow did not melt but remained lying on streets and roofs. The heaps of rubble were white and looked like snow pyramids; the piles of paving stones looked like huge blocks of ice. Even so, the scenery seemed less eerie than it did before: it was the details in the destruction that were most shocking, and hence the covering blanket of snow had a softening effect.

It was into this new scenery, which held some of the beauty of rural winter landscapes, that Major Green drove off that November afternoon, unaware of the curious adventures which his estranged native city had in store for him.

The German Museum which, in obedience to the Colonel's somewhat surprising instructions, he chose for his first stop provided his first adventure. UNRRA, that organization set up by the young but already fossilized United Nations to provide relief for the victims of the Axis powers and to help the repatriation of displaced persons, maintained in this scarcely damaged building a university for "forcibly displaced foreign students" of eighteen nationalities. Believing correctly that the Roman adage *plenus venter non studet libenter*, if indeed it had ever been true, was certainly inapplicable nowadays and that nobody could study on an empty stomach, the charitable UNRRA made issues of foodstuffs and cigarettes to those in its care. But instead of the academic activities which he had expected, Frank found himself amidst the bustle of a stock market, of a noisy and busy mart where goods and valuables were being bartered, bought and sold. The serious students—for there were some of that category—were being jostled and pushed aside by men and women whose thirst was not for knowledge. The unloading of gift parcels, which the Major witnessed, had nothing about it of the touching humanity of similar manifestations of neighborly love; rather, the scene was reminiscent of an impatient market hall where the supplies had arrived with a delay and were now being snatched from the hands of the vendors. A little man, not unlike a frog in coloring and gestures, was hopping from recipient to recipient, haranguing those fortunates party in German and partly in Rumanian, all in a frantic hurry; he haggled hurriedly and paid hurriedly, and thus piled carton after carton of American cigarettes into the outstretched arms of a second man who followed him from stall to stall. Another man, who was talking Hungarian to two women, evidently his assistants, seemed to specialize in cheese: he was making inquiries about the arrival of cans of cheese, and Frank, who had followed him inconspicuously, heard to his amazement that he was negotiating for a whole truckload of cheese. An UNRRA official, a gray-haired woman, American in appearance, in a blue uniform and rimless glasses, the typical missionary who hastens from mission station to mission station, partly to bring humanity to others and partly to escape from her own loneliness, was standing helplessly amidst the turmoil, still with a benign and charitable smile, unable to understand that the needy had become speculators, that alms had become an object of barter, and that her own mission had become a farce. She wanted to chase the dealers away like naughty boys and protect the innocent—but she just remained a small motionless point in a crazily spinning whirligig. But what impressed Frank most was the fact that this tower of Babel was being built with an uncanny precision; that among the confusion of tongues the tower did not by any means remain unbuilt; that Hungarians and Poles, Czechs and Rumanians, with an occasional sprinkling of Germans, were swiftly and methodically piling up packing cases, cigarettes and food cans; and that, though ignorant of each other's language, they yet managed to understand one another perfectly in the language of barter, deception and profit.

Not for nothing had Colonel Hunter picked on the German Museum as one of the places for Frank to look into. It was known to American Counterintelligence that certain elements, living in hiding and therefore not entitled to any rations, were in the habit of doing their "shopping" at these black-market centers. Here anybody could obtain sufficient supplies for weeks, without bothering about the meager official rations. It was rumored that quite close to the American PX, in the once elegant Brienner Strasse, a certain Herbert Fischhopp was running a special organization solely for the purpose of supplying the "submarines"—people living in hiding—with fuel. This Fischhopp, against whom nothing could be proved although there was no doubt as to the nature of his business, gained added interest and significance from the fact that he had been doing much the same thing under the Third Reich: he was presumably interested more in his fuel deals than in the "submarines." It was with the intention of getting at this character, whose acquaintance he thought might prove profitable, that Frank went to the PX and hung around there as long as he dared without attracting special attention.

The spectacle before him was no less strange than that at the German Museum, though entirely different. Normally, when he collected his PX rations once a week, Frank was in a hurry to leave the premises and get back to his jeep. But now he lingered among the people milling outside the entrance; he was fortunate in being able to listen to the talk without anybody suspecting him of eavesdropping. Although a few patrolling MP's kept trying to disperse the crowd of gapers, beggars and dealers outside this American treasure-house, it re-formed almost immediately. Major Frank Green was experiencing an ambivalent feeling which he quickly tried to suppress, accusing himself of unpermitted sympathy with the defeated. It seemed to him that the humiliation displayed by the vanquished rebounded on to the conquerors, just as in the relationship between beggar and donor, between the recipient and the giver of alms, the humiliation of the one frequently turns into a confession of guilt by the other. The children who, clad in thin coats, and some with no coats at all, were running after the soldiers, who were muffled up to their ears, in order to beg a piece of chocolate, a little candy or a slice of chewing gum—these children humiliated the victorious servicemen much more than they did the vanquished nation to which they were condemned to belong. Every time some Negro soldiers left the well-heated and well-lit building, that wonder-house of a thousand undreamed-of luxuries and delicacies, they looked about them expectantly; a moment later they were surrounded by women and girls reaching up for a can of food, a package of Kleenex, a single cigarette, or even an empty carton and a little wrapping paper. Laughing and begging they addressed their imploring requests to the Joes and Jims, while pushing each other aside and squabbling among themselves. The white women's calculations were correct: the Negroes were far more generous than the white soldiers. A smile, a word of thanks, a pressed hand meant so much more to them. But here, too, what a fatal relationship between the women begging for a scrap of paper and the Negroes begging for a tiny smile. Who was the conqueror here and who the vanquished? Frank was unable to decide. Just then a man had detached himself from the crowd—Frank only saw his back: a dark, tousled, unkempt head—and was dragging a woman away by her hair. He was nearly hauling her along the snow-covered street, shouting "Yankee whore" all the time. A few stood as if turned to stone; others laughed; the MP's did not know what was going on and whether they should arrest the man or be grateful to him for helping to break up the crowd. A moment later everything was the same again: the brightly-lit entrance, the uniformed Father Christmases stepping out of it, the helpless MP's, the dark street, the waiting women, the begging children, and the silent men with downcast eyes.

After several unsuccessful attempts to find out Fischopp's address, or possibly even to make his acquaintance, Frank decided on a last, and indeed an obvious, step: he would drive out to Stadelheim where, as far as he knew, Irene Gruss's husband, the concentration camp commandant, was under detention.

It was dark by the time Frank had himself announced to the prison governor, an elderly man of courteous though by no means obsequious manners, who much regretted to have to inform the Major that the camp commandant had been transferred to an American military prison some time ago. Certain interrogation records, however, were still at hand—as a matter of fact, some other American major had already inspected them. Perhaps the Herr Major would not mind waiting a few minutes while he had them found.

Thus it happened that Frank learned some more facts of German life that day—not from personal experience, but emerging none the less strikingly from the account of the prison governor who seemed more than anxious to seize this opportunity of unburdening himself to a senior American officer. American red tape, the governor remarked candidly, seemed to be no less entangled than the German version: his complaints went through so many hands that by the time they had reached their final destination the remedies had become useless.

"Conditions are desperate," said the governor, settling back in his armchair. The office was unheated and he was wearing his winter coat; about halfway through their conversation he pulled off his thick mittens. "Conditions, Herr Major, are quite desperate. Persons brought in for detention pending questioning, and who are therefore allowed to keep their own clothes, arrive with bundles of dollar bills and other hard currencies sewn into the lining of their suits. In the old days—before Hitler, I mean—a prison used to be an institution for punishment or rehabilitation, according to how you looked at it. But now it has become—under my own eyes, as it were—a clearinghouse for business transactions. I have replaced guards, punished them, locked them up—with hardly any effect, Herr Major. The prisoners send the guards outside to run errands for them, to collect money or goods, and to clinch deals—and before I know it the prisoners and the guards are all of them keen partners. One can't blame the men, Herr Major; not really. By running an errand a guard will earn food for himself and his family for a week; if he resists the temptation then he will merely make himself the only true convict among a host of convicts. The daily exercise in the prison yard and even divine service are occasions for a veritable stock exchange. A prisoner detained here for questioning told me to my face the other day that not until here, under my custody, had he managed to make the right contacts for his future. During divine service last Sunday we caught two men—you'll hardly believe me, Herr Major—who exchanged their suits. Wedged in among their fellows, they stripped to the skin during the sermon. One of them, due to be discharged shortly, in this fashion 'bought' a good suit from the other prisoner whose company we shall be enjoying for a little longer. I spent four years in a concentration camp, Herr Major," he concluded resignedly, "and I am not saying this to boast. Your fellow-countrymen have found me and restored me to the post from which the Nazis had sacked me. I am grateful to them. But it is not enough, Herr Major, for conditions to change; they also ought to improve."

Frank tried to say a few polite words, but he knew that this was a bad day for polite conversation. He was relieved, though also a trifle ashamed at his relief, when a prison official turned up with the wanted file.

From this dossier Major Frank Green discovered—and he was almost unable to conceal his boundless surprise from the German—that Commandant Gruss in his evidence had named a certain Hotel Nadler in Munich as the most likely hiding place of his wife Irene.

But nowhere in Major Bill O'Hara's reports, which Frank had studied by Hunter's orders, had this hotel been mentioned; nowhere had there been any indication that inquiries had been made there.

A few minutes later the olive-green military sedan was speeding over the snow-covered road. Inside the well-heated vehicle was Major Frank Green, trying in vain to get some order into the chaos of his recent experiences and emotions.

It was just on midnight, about the same time that Bill O'Hara had first rapped on the door, and again the chimes rang out from near-by church towers, when Frank shook the Hotel Nadler out of its sleep. A few moments later he was in possession of all the details of the red-haired major's two visits. But just as it had not been a good day for polite conversation, this did not promise to be a good night for sense and comprehension.

Hans Eber Speaks the Truth

Nothing probably was more typical of that period, which will go down into history as the era of Germany's occupation, than the confusion of human relationships.

During the twelve years of the "Thousand-Year Reich" the world had seen Germany as one vast complex, believing that in the ever-increasing German Reich the life of every individual was linked with that of the community. Just as human imagination is too poor to grasp greatness, it is also too weak to comprehend the smallness of the small: it cannot understand the individual's isolation amidst world-shattering happenings. The detonations which shake the world are no more than faint vibrations by the time they reach the middle-class homes and proletarian hovels; if the nations do not revolt more frequently it is only because they do not know what to revolt against. The optimistically conceived phrase that "life goes on" is in fact a measure of the damnation of the world: life goes on because human conscience is lifeless. Birth and death, pregnancy and sickness, poverty and toil, a roof, warmth, copulation—even in the most glorious hours of mankind these remain the symbols of a life that goes on, of hope springing anew, and of rebellion withering.

For twelve years Germany had looked from the outside like a huge puppet theater, with marionettes all suspended from the fingers of the great wire-pullers. But what distinguishes a puppet theater from the great theater of the world is the fact that every puppet dangles from numerous strings which all meet in the hands of the showman, but that there is not a single string by which one puppet is linked to another. In the world theater, on the other hand, countless strings connect man to man, and only few of them end up in the flies. Only in wartime did human beings become puppets in accordance with the invariable design and law of the war lords of all ages. A few interconnecting strings continued to lead from one person to another, but each of them hung on the wire of the great producer. The period of occupation, finally, completed the confusion: birth and death, and all intervening happenings, were inextricably linked to the life of the community, and the strings which the clumsy showmen held between their fingers got hopelessly tangled with the string slinking one living puppet to another.

If ever there had been a straightforward relationship then it was that between the student Hans Eber and his sister Karin. The more bewildering to him then was the confusion which now beset it.

From the moment of their first encounter there had been a smoldering hostility between Hans and Captain Green. It would not have been so bad if Captain Green had merely symbolized the conquerors —the hardships, mistakes and injustices of the occupation. Whether it had been his rebellion against his father, or an early glimpse into the machinery of the Third Reich, or simply an innate tendency to clear thinking and independent judgment—the infantryman Hans Eber, and before him the student and indeed the boy, had passionately hated the whole rotten system to which Dr. Eberhard Eber had sold himself. Captain Green, the German Jew who had returned to his country in a foreign uniform and who was acting as if he did not know any German; who had arbitrarily requisitioned one of the finest houses in the city for his own private use; who turned up almost every day with some "liberated" objects, such as paintings or gramophone records, jewelry or "souvenirs"; who invited shady characters, black marketeers and secret agents to the house and entertained them noisily—this man had shattered Hans Eber's expectations and hopes of a true liberation. Hans Eber was allied to the Americans and the Jews both by his revolt against the old system and by the prohibited but highly prized literature of his youth. But the revolt had spent itself, and the letters, however vivid, were now confronted with a reality that was personified in Captain George Green.

But the real source of the confusion was Karin. That it was for her sake that the Captain tolerated the continued presence of the other residents had been obvious to Hans from the start; what he could not understand was the nature of the attraction which the stranger was visibly exercising on Karin. With every day that passed the nineteen-year-old girl seemed to fall more and more under Green's hypnotic spell, and with every day she withdrew more and more from her brother in whose eyes she saw nothing but disapproval and, at best, incomprehension. Hans had repeatedly urged her to leave the house with him, calmly at first and then with growing impatience, but Karin, at one time prouder than he, would not hear of such a gesture. He would have moved in with Stefan Lester long ago if it had not been for an obligation he felt of protecting his sister. Although at times he felt somewhat old-fashioned and ridiculous in the role of the censoriously wrathful brother, and although he had no illusions about the effectiveness of that role, yet he persisted in acting it through to the end. Even now Hans was feeling certain that nothing irrevocable had yet passed between Karin and the Captain; but at the same time he felt clearly that things were moving towards the inevitable.

What role am I playing? It was from this question that Hans's confusion sprang. He told himself that his sister's virginity or future love had never been a problem for him, and he began to wonder if his objection was not perhaps to the Jew and the American. He wanted to free his sister from the circle of corruption, but he was not certain what constituted corruption nor whether, in attempting to liberate her, he was not getting entrapped in it himself. He stayed at the house, playing a part that was distasteful to himself, but since he stayed he ate the bread of the seducer. And by eating the seducer's bread he was losing the authority he had hoped to exercise in the part of the elder brother. He hated George Green the man, but he tried not to hate the Jew or the American. In the end, however, he was unable to distinguish between the principle and the special case. He had always despised his father's house, but he was now catching himself endowing it with an aureole in his memory. Even at the time when, an unwilling soldier of the Führer, he had dangled from the puppet wire of collective fate, he had not felt himself so utterly bound hand and foot as now when the fettering strings were tying him to other hands.

When the news of Dr. Adam Wild's arrest reached him, it seemed to Hans that he would get himself entangled more hopelessly still. It was Stefan Lester who had found out the fact and the circumstances of Dr. Wild's detention. In the spring Adam had told his young friend about his first meeting with Major Frank Green, but he had not mentioned to him his subsequent disappointing intervention on Sibelius' behalf. It seemed therefore perfectly natural to Stefan to appeal for help to the American officer who had seemed so favorably disposed towards Adam. He suggested to Hans that he should get George Green to fix up an interview for him with his brother Frank. At first Hans protested: he could not stomach the idea of asking a favor of his "landlord." Besides, he had gathered from stray remarks of the Captain that relations between the brothers were by no means cordial, and Frank had not once called on his brother at the Ebers' house. In the end Hans yielded to Stefan's insistence and, having got the Captain to make an appointment for him, set out on his errand feeling exceedingly unhappy.

For reasons connected with his ever-extending range of activities Frank had asked the young Eber not to his office but to his private apartment for seven o'clock in the evening.

The apartment was Han's first surprise. Frank lived in a former barracks block on the Tegernseer Landstrasse, where the former married quarters of German NCO families now served as accommodation for a number of single American officers. Hans, who had expected a requisitioned villa, entered an apartment which, though scrupulously clean and overheated in the American fashion, was in every other respect an ordinary lower-middle-class home of two rooms, whose furnishings—a particularly unfortunate blend of tastelessness and unfriendliness—the officer had evidently left unchanged. Only the shelves, on which no doubt a playful china cat, a rococo figurine, or at best an incomplete set of a popular encyclopedia had once reposed in splendid isolation, were crammed full with books, English and German, among which Hans spotted at once a number of his favorite authors.

Frank offered his visitor a chair and Hans explained his business. The Major listened to him attentively.

"The chain continues," he said with a faint smile when Hans had finished. "Dr. Wild intervened with me for Herr Sibelius, and now you are intervening for Dr. Wild. You all overrate the powers of an

American major. I have gone through the Sibelius file and have come to the conclusion that there are no grounds for keeping him under arrest. I have therefore recommended his release. Evidently my recommendation has merely swelled the file."

"Are you going to rest content with that, Herr Major?" asked Hans.

"To be perfectly frank—yes," said Frank, calmly facing the man opposite him.

"And Dr. Wild?" Hans asked in some confusion.

"Dr. Wild has undoubtedly made a mistake," said Frank. "But it so happens I shall be near Frankfurt the day after tomorrow. I think I can manage to get him out."

Now that's the end of my mission, thought Hans. But he could not resist the temptation to say:

"I don't quite understand, Herr Major."

"What is it you don't understand, Herr Eber?"

"You say that Colonel von Sibelius is innocent but nothing can be done for him; you say Dr. Wild has made a mistake but you'll get him out."

"Dr. Wild," said Frank, "is an individual case. The fact that he tried to help a friend doesn't mark him. He doesn't come under any of the categories, such as active Nazis, fellow-travelers, beneficiaries of the system, or militarists. Categories are like walls; it's useless to kick against them." He stopped and dropped his eyes. "I know what you are thinking now, Herr Eber. You're thinking: just as in the Third Reich! I would ask you to remember that we aren't setting up any gas chambers or any concentration camps. It may take a few more months, but in the end Herr von Sibelius will be released safe and sound. And for another thing, you mustn't forget that Germany has lost the war."

"I could not forget it even if I wanted to," said Hans. "Even if our ruins didn't remind us of it every day the Occupying Power is doing its best not to let us forget it."

He thought: I must have gone out of my mind to speak like this. Yet at the same time he had a strange feeling—strange because it was not rationally founded—that he could speak openly to this man. He tried in vain to spot any resemblance between the two brothers. But this narrow face with the severe straight nose, the pale but deep eyes and the by no means embittered mouth contained not a single feature that was reminiscent of the brutal face which Hans had grown used to seeing every day and every evening. This was not a soft face, not even a friendly and obliging one; but it was so frank and unambiguous that one had to respect its owner even if one did not love him.

Now too the face remained calm and transparent. The Major was saying:

"The occupation, Herr Eber, is a thankless business. We aren't here for our amusement—even though far too many occupation officers and men behave as if they were. Put yourself in our position. If we proceeded with kindness and clemency, fastidiously anxious to avoid all hardship and injustice at any price—do you believe, Herr Eber, that your fellow-countrymen would understand it? I think not. They would probably forget from one day to the next that Hitler and his vassals precipitated the world into the greatest disaster of our epoch. On the other hand, if we proceed firmly and ruthlessly, at times unjustly as is inevitable—won't you then accuse us of using the methods which we had set out to fight? I happen to be a teacher of history, Herr Eber; soldiering is very much a sideline with me. History has taught me that the tearful phrase that the defeated are always wrong is no more than a phrase. It is the victors who are always wrong. Go and read the great war novels in world literature, from Tolstoi to the present day: they are one and all heroic epics of the vanquished, almost to the paradoxical point of suggesting that only the defeated had fought bravely. This is not saying that history is unjust. But what is one to do with victory? This question, Herr Eber, naturally only worries the victors. The defeated don't have to do anything: things are done with them. Success, however, is not a good counsel, any more in the life of nations than in that of the individual."

"I understand that," said Hans. This was his first talk with an American, not counting George Green or the sergeants in the PW camp. He leaned forward and spoke with all the intensity he could muster. "I have not studied history, Herr Major, but law. Maybe that's why I see things differently. And that's why I'd like to speak practically, not theoretically—that is, if I am not keeping you . . . ?"

"On the contrary," said Frank. He offered Hans a cigarette.

"Perhaps Captain Green has told you who my father is," said Hans.

Frank nodded. It was a slight, indifferent nod which appealed to Hans; it seemed to say: I know who your father is; it is neither in your favor nor does it count against you, and it is certainly of no interest to me.

"Herr Major," said Hans, "I have not come to plead for my father. Not merely because you probably couldn't do anything about him, but also because I regard what is happening to him now as a just turn of fate. Perhaps you do not care for this cool detachment on the part of a son; but without it we Germans could not survive today. But I have come deliberately to plead for Dr. Wild and perhaps for Colonel von Sibelius. These men had been waiting for the liberation. I can understand all injustices towards the defeated, Herr Major; and, who knows, I might have been more ruthless in your position and, at the moment of victory, probably even more unjust. But Dr. Wild and Colonel von Sibelius are not defeated: in my eyes they are victors. In fact, they ought to be your allies. But you are turning them into losers and hence into allies of my father. Perhaps I am too young to understand," he added, "but I very much doubt if I should understand this if I lived to be a hundred."

"You are confirming what I said a little while ago," retorted Frank. "You are forcing the victor into the defensive." Across his thin lips flitted that almost shy smile which was so encouraging to Hans. "I have lately spoken with two Germans—with Dr. Wild and with the wife of a war criminal. Both of them, just as you are doing now, forced me into the defensive. It sounds paradoxical, but it is quite understandable." He leaned back, rested his head against the top of his chair and fixed his eyes on the ceiling as if speaking to himself. "We talk about victors and vanquished, but we might just as well speak of the knowing and the ignorant. The vanquished are always those with knowledge; the victors are the ignorant. You say your father is rightfully under arrest, but Colonel von Sibelius is wrongfully detained. I presume that you say so because you know it to be true. But what do I know? I know nothing. I don't even know if you know what you are talking about—I merely presume so. There is that woman I mentioned: I should like to help her. But do you suppose she is telling me the truth—or even the subjective truth? And what about your friend Dr. Wild?" He straightened up and faced Hans. "Do you know why I am going to Frankfurt to get him out? Because for three months I have dug into that man's life, or his 'antecedents' as the idiotic jargon has it. And do you know what I found? I discovered— mind you, I say: discovered—that this man is a hero next to whom many of our and your bemedaled heroes would look puny and pitiful. But I had to discover all this because he deliberately misled me—out of his offended German sentiment, or because he didn't want to howl with the opportunist wolves, or for some other reason so complicated that only a German brain could think it up. Of course he is a victor, Herr Eber! But how the devil am I to know it if he himself keeps it dark? The modest heroes and the importunate informers, the proud men who keep silent and the sycophants who talk too much—they are a plague, all of them, Herr Eber, and nothing would please me better than to chuck this whole business and get back to my history books where I can read about the foolishness of others instead of committing foolish acts myself."

He got up and began to pace up and down, not like a man crossing a room but like one who is anxious to get his destination. He was clearly pursuing his own train of thoughts without expecting a reply from his visitor.

Hans also rose. With a resolution so sudden that he became aware of it only when he heard his own voice he said:

"Herr Major . . . if you like I will come and tell you the truth from time to time, so far as I know it. May I start right now?"

Frank nodded, but continued his march through the room.

In a controlled voice, that was yet trembling with excitement, Hans said:

"Herr Major . . . for many days I refused to call on you. I was convinced that you'd be just like your brother."

Frank stopped before Hans.

"What do you know about my brother?" he said.

Hans Eber began his recital. He spoke of the day the unknown captain had appeared at the villa in Bogenhausen, the day on which Dr. Eberhard Eber was arrested. He related how, on his return in the evening from Stefan Lester's lodgings, he had found the Captain in conversation with his sister. He suppressed nothing: neither the arbitrary requisition nor the illegal permission for the family to stay on at the house. He spoke of Captain Green's growing stock of merchandise and his mysterious callers; of his own anxiety for Karin and his suspicion that his sister was gradually falling under the incomprehensible spell. They had sat down again, facing each other, the German who was ashamed of his father and the American who was ashamed of his brother. Hans Eber spoke breathlessly, without pause, as if afraid that if he once stopped for an instant he would never be able to continue. Presently he broke off in the middle of a sentence and he felt as if he could not utter another word. He looked at the man opposite, the man in the uniform of the conquerors, with three rows of colored ribbons on his chest, the stranger to whom he had fled in his hour of need and who could yet be nothing to him but an enemy.

The Major stood up again, with an abrupt gesture which Hans could not interpret. In a hoarse, almost inaudible voice he said:

"If everything you have told me is true, Herr Eber, then I can promise you that Captain George Green is going to be taught a lesson he won't forget for the rest of his life."

Hans could not make a reply because the large wooden clock, a structure of massive hideousness reposing on the top of the bookshelves, insistently struck ten. The two men exchanged glances. The clock brought them back to the realities of everyday German life, out of which their conversation had arisen but from which it had also drifted away. It was ten o'clock, curfew hour.

Frank laughed. "Now it'll be my fault if you go to jail," he said. "Perhaps you could bed down on the couch here." Then something seemed to occur to him, evidently in connection with their recent talk. He turned away deliberately so the other should not guess his thoughts so easily. "On second thought," he said, "you had better go home." He snatched up a bunch of keys which lay next to the clock. "Come along," he said. "My jeep is still outside. I'll run you home."

Is Obedience a Crime

Snow was lying deep in Colonel Graham T. Hunter's garden. The silver birches outside the windows looked like emaciated snowmen, their meager arms stretched out helplessly. It had turned cold suddenly, and the leaden snow clouds hung over the landscape as if they had been frozen at the moment when they were about to discharge their burden.

It was Sunday and the Colonel had invited Major Frank Green to lunch. They were now sitting at a little table by the window, in a recess of the sitting room. The Colonel was smoking a cigar and gazing out into the snow-covered garden.

"Where are you going to spend Christmas, Frank?" asked the Colonel.

"I don't know yet," said Frank. "I'm supposed to go to Frankfurt and Nuremberg for a few weeks, as you know."

The perfect host, Hunter had not mentioned any official business throughout the meal. Now he said:

"Don't know if I can spare you that long, Frank. . . ."

Frank knew what the Colonel was driving at, but he had no intention of making things easy for his superior. As if he had not heard the Colonel's last remark he said:

"May I mention a bit of business, Colonel?"

"Of course."

"Through personal circumstances," Frank began, "my attention has been drawn to a certain Baron Achim Sibelius, a former colonel in the Wehrmacht, who is now being held at the Frankfurt detention camp for militarists. He's been inside since the end of May. I have gone through his file, insofar as the Frankfurt people put it at my disposal. That man is innocent."

"What do you call innocent?"

"He took an active part in the 20th of July."

"You know what we think of that."

"I'm not convinced that we're necessarily right."

"And in what are we wrong?"

"Tying up guilt with a date seems to me fatal," said Frank. "Take the question of Party membership, Colonel. We punish people because they belonged to the Nazi Party at an early date. The later they joined the more lenient are we with them. In other words, it is more pardonable for a man to have joined the Party at a time when its criminal character had already become clear!"

The Colonel got up and returned with a bottle of brandy which had been standing on the piano. He poured out two glasses. He said:

"But for the early members there would have been no *Machtergriefung*." He used the German word for the seizure of power, like a technical term.

"That is a practical criterion, not a moral one," said Frank. "This may be a personal fad of mine, but the inadequacy of all judgments on other people strikes me with particular force when it is coupled with concepts of time. Even as a young man I always thought it ludicrous that parents' concern for the moral welfare of their daughters should only start at eight P.M. I don't know if I make myself clear

—but clocks and calendars appear to me poor frontier posts between right and wrong. What is pardonable and what is unpardonable? The question can no longer be waved aside when it arises in its most extreme form, namely: Until what date is evil pardonable, and from what date onward is it unpardonable? Besides, there is a further inconsistency here: if a civilian had left the Party no matter at how late a date we should count it very highly in his favor. But the men of the 20th of July did more. They stuck out their necks for their conviction."

"Let us say: for Germany," interposed the Colonel.

"Is that necessarily a contradiction?" asked Frank.

"In this case, certainly," replied the Colonel. "The 20th of July was an opportunistic affair—if you want to talk of moral criteria. Why, do you suppose, it was the officers who rebelled and not the civilians? Because the officers knew more. After our successful landing in Normandy they realized that the war was lost for them. The civilians may have gone on believing what they were told, and expecting all kinds of miracles—but the military men wouldn't swallow such fairy-tales. And that, don't you see, is the reason why we must exterminate German militarism, maybe even more thoroughly than Nazism. German militarism is like a pistol that's lying about a house openly. Anybody, from the cook to the little children, can pick it up. And so, for that matter, can any burglar who's got into the house. Even if Germany were ever to become a democracy—which I personally doubt—the democratic masters of the house would no doubt go on leaving the pistol lying about freely. The only question is: who's going to use it?"

"I should like to pose a heretical question," said Frank. "Are these not the characteristics of any militarism?"

Hunter ground the end of his cigar into the large marble ashtray. Frank watched the Colonel's long sinewy hand, a typical American hand that is found equally among intellectuals and cowboys, bank presidents and factory workers. On the little finger of his left hand Hunter wore the deep-red fraternity ring of a West Pointer.

"You know what Mark Twain said about the Jews," said Hunter. " 'The Jews are people, too, only more so.' I've never worried about the Jews, but his words are certainly true of the Germans. There is a story that Kaiser Wilhelm II used to boast that all his colds were tremendous colds. With the Germans everything has to be of gigantic dimensions. It may be true of certain materials that their substance remains unchanged by their quantity, but man is not one of those materials. German militarism differs from any other militarism by the dimensions which it assumes and which, ultimately, remain uncontrollable."

"Supposing that is so," said Frank, "there still remains, in the individual case, the question of a man's duty. Colonel von Sibelius was a soldier. He did his duty until, one day, he could no longer reconcile it with his conscience. I might point out that I am not myself convinced of the correctness of each one of our measures in Germany. But I perform my duty. In other words, I am obeying blindly—the very thing we are accusing the German soldiers of."

In the Colonel's well-controlled face, which sometimes looked as if it were made of ancient yellowing parchment, there were countless lines. They were like the tracks in a switchyard. They did not move. Only when Hunter was annoyed was there a movement among the rails, just as if some invisible switchman had thrown a switch. Frank knew at once that he had gone too far. His relations with Hunter had never been those of a young officer and an elderly army colonel. Just because he had a lot of respect for Hunter he had counted on his understanding. But now he had probably crossed the invisible border line. He was not surprised therefore when the Colonel said:

"What's bitten you, Frank? You know that I never held that narrow-minded view. But there are times when I think that the occupation would really function better if not a single occupation officer knew any German. You know the meaning of 'going native'? Assimilation to the locals—that great danger of diplomats, colonial administrators, officials abroad and explorers. You're talking now as if you'd met too many natives lately." He waved aside the protest Frank was about to make. "The point at issue is not obedience, but the cause a man serves. A lot of people nowadays—and I hear similar comment even from the States—are acting as if we were accusing the German soldiers of obedience. In fact we are accusing them of being Germans. Like all other Germans they have served the regime and have failed to resist it. Their obedience is no more objectionable than anybody else's—but that ought to be quite enough. Or do you suggest that military obedience should be an excuse, but not civilian obedience?"

Hunter got up and Frank likewise took the opportunity to rise.

Hunter is right, he thought; one should not understand a word of German. It is bad for the occupation. In fact one should not understand anything; it is bad for one's self. A thought rose up within him, bitter and unjust; he tried to chase it away but he did not succeed. Did the Germans put Hunter's mother in a concentration camp or mine? Did he have to escape or did I? Has his house been wrecked or mine? But perhaps this was the point: a house that had stood in Germany and had been bombed together with other German houses. One had grown up in that house; one used to speak German. One ought to hate, a thousand times more than the good-natured colonel from Columbus, Ohio. But one's obligation to hate, and even one's avenging instinct, were being weakened by understanding. Inability to understand was the most important ingredient of hate. Did they say hatred obscured understanding? No; it was understanding that obscured hatred. But did one really understand? Providence be thanked: one did not, or not fully. But even the attempt held a temptation. Hunter was right: one had to put the temptation behind one.

Thus thought Major Frank Green, formerly Franz Grün of Munich, as he paced up and down the room in the house at Harlaching while the dusk of the winter afternoon was slowly descending. But it was not in his character to lay down arms without a struggle; besides, there was still in him some echo of his conversation with Hans Eber the day before. He suddenly halted and said:

"Colonel, you have honored me with your confidence for four years . . ."

Hunter, connecting this remark with their argument and already regretting his sharp tone, interrupted him:

"And nothing's changed in that, Frank. You'll see that in a minute when I tell you the reason for asking you here today." His brandy glass in his hand, he sat down again by the window. "I have studied your report on O'Hara most carefully. Have you any explanation?"

"None whatever."

"And you've questioned that man Nadler again?"

"Twice more. Unless he or I have gone completely crazy O'Hara took the commandeuse away with him."

"But what's he done with her?" asked Hunter. "She can't just vanish from the face of the earth."

Frank shrugged his shoulders. "What does O'Hara say?"

"He doesn't say anything. Chiefly because I haven't asked him.

Only yesterday he put in another report about his unsuccessful investigations. Do you think the man is mentally deranged?"

"I know him too little to say, Colonel."

Hunter put down his glass.

"Frank," he said, "I have a nasty feeling. A very nasty feeling." He almost sounded as if he were looking for help when he continued: "I can't afford a scandal in my unit just now. You know that I don't accuse a man until I am quite certain of my facts. But I can't grope in the dark any longer. You've got to find out what this O'Hara business is all about. I know what you're going to say: that you can't spy on a fellow-officer. But I can't entrust the matter to the CIC. That would bring on just that scandal which I am anxious to avoid. Can you see a sensible way out?"

Frank had known for some time that the Colonel would put this question to him. He had come to his house determined not to find "a sensible way out" and to avoid at all costs being drawn into the O'Hara affair. But the subject of Colonel von Sibelius seemed to him by no means concluded, and the subject of George Green, which he had on the tip of his tongue, had not even been mooted yet. He said:

"Maybe I can. Suppose, Colonel, you announce at a staff conference that you're relieving Major O'Hara of the investigations and are putting me in charge. This will force O'Hara's hand—without my having to spy on him. If he is innocent he will let the matter rest there. If he has something to hide he will try to prevent me from pursuing the investigations. He will either try to spike my guns or he will get round me in a friendly way. In either case the next move will be with him."

"Excellent," said Hunter. "Quite excellent. Drive over to Nuremberg tomorrow, but be back here on Tuesday. We aren't having a staff conference till Wednesday anyway. It would be imprudent to call one for earlier."

"I'll be back on Tuesday night."

The Colonel heaved a sigh of relief.

Frank went over to the window.

"By the way," said Hunter, "I am sorry for what I said a little while ago. If you think that this colonel . . . what's his name?"

"Sibelius."

"If you think that he is such an exceptional person have him transferred to No. 2 Detention Camp in Bavaria. If the Hesse Military Government lets him go you may release him for all I care."

"Thank you, Colonel," said Frank. "I'll ask them at Bad Homburg."

So Hunter had after all taken him by surprise with his sudden concession. While the Colonel was talking about German militarists Frank began to wonder about those sinister characters whom his brother George was receiving at Eberhard Eber's house and about whom Hans had told him. Frank knew that George had come to Munich on a special assignment, but it was not customary in G-2 to ask questions about the assignments of others. Even so it was clear to him that the men whom George was meeting had served the late regime in secret, important and doubtful functions. If George's orders came from Colonel Hunter, as he assumed they must, then there was an inconsistency here which Frank was anxious to clear up, the sooner the better. At the same time he knew that he had achieved what he had set out to achieve that day, and that he might jeopardize Colonel von Sibelius' liberty and the rectification of a patent injustice if he now overreached himself. He decided to speak to George direct and to find out more from his brother before resuming the offensive.

"Another glass of brandy?" the Colonel asked.

"No, thank you, Colonel," said Frank. "I've got to be on my way."

Hunter accompanied him through the cold hall. For a moment they stood in the open door. The garden was white. More snow was falling, softly and slowly, as if the heavens wanted to spread a thick white blanket over the cold earth.

"Perhaps we'll have a white Christmas," said the Colonel.

"Will Mrs. Hunter be here for Christmas?" asked Frank, just to say something.

"Hardly likely," said the Colonel. "It would be improper for my family to come first. Even though everything's prepared. Do you know, Frank, I've even engaged a nursemaid for my little daughter. . . ."

Mortal Drama in Nuremberg

This was the tenth day of the great trial in Nuremberg, with Kurt von Zutraven as one of the accused, but only the smallest trickle of news filtered into the detention camp where Elisabeth von Zutraven was held. The camp was situated only a few miles from the square-block building of the Nuremberg Court House where on November 20, 1945 began the proceedings which were to last for nearly a whole year and which were to decide the fate of twenty men accused of having deliberately hurled Germany and the world into war and misery.

It was a grandiose spectacle, but with what a miserable cast! As Kurt von Zutraven, the son of an Imperial German ambassador and a Brandenburg countess, himself a Doctor of Letters, a scholar proficient in five modern and two ancient languages, and a traveler on three continents, looked about the dock, his perplexity and fear, and even his instinct of self-preservaton, gave way to a sense of shame which he was uable to fight down. It was not shame for the deeds he had committed as the Cultural Commissar of the Third Reich or as Governor of a defeated France; for the charges leveled at him by the Four-Power tribunal were so exaggerated that in the unfortunate proportion of fact and accusation he was aware only of the injustice done to him and not of that done by him. It was not therefore shame in the sense of repentance that now filled Kurt von Zutraven, but shame of his alliance with the men with whom he was doomed to share the dock.

If the country which he loved with every fiber of his heart had been ruled merely by criminals, as the indictment tried to make out in four languages, Kurt von Zutraven would have been able to bear it. But the piteousness of their puny stature was now brought home to him with alarming suddenness. Immediately before him, on the front bench, sat the former Foreign Minister of the German Reich, a sickly, weak man, trembling and pale, and devoid even of that dignity which death lends to nearly all men bearing his mark. This man, who was so flat from head to foot that he seemed to have only two dimensions, had represented Germany in the world: he had dispatched and recalled ambassadors, drafted and presented ultimata, and all the time he had shrunk with every grand gesture and every grandiloquent word. Not even a cheat—just a pathetic carnival figure who seemed as bogus as a prisoner in the dock as he had been in the role of master. And further down, next to the defoliated Reich Marshal, sat that strange and possibly crazy bird with the bushy eyebrows, the restlessly flickering eyes and the scrawny neck in a wide collar, an undernourished vulture, perched on his seat in the dock as on a dry branch. The man who had once deputized for the Führer and then betrayed him, a person of ill-defined views and powers, at one time seemingly master over life and death, but in fact looking rather like a neurasthenic concierge. And then, on the extreme left, the baldhead, incessantly chewing gum as if this imported habit might save his forfeited life, the obscene Jew-baiter of Nuremberg, his minute eyes even now darting over to the well-groomed stenotypists, the typical surreptitious Sunday visitor of small-town brothels, a drinker without refinement and with weak kidneys, a glutton without discrimination and with a belching stomach. It was no consolation for Kurt von Zutraven that on the long benches there were also others, more akin to him. That the professorial gentleman with the pince-nez and the high starched collar, who was all the time trying to edge away from his gum-chewing neighbor, was a man of vast knowledge and profound erudition; that the gentleman in the well-cut double-breasted suit with the impeccable handkerchief, who looked like a distinguished aged race horse, was even now in the dock showing the same dignity with which he had represented the strange Reich abroad; or that the ancient admiral in his dark naval uniform, though bereft of his decorations, still maintained the ramrod stiffness of his now scuttled office—all this made Kurt von Zutraven's confusion worse confounded, since the defendants of his own class did not even leave him the illusion that he alone had taken the ghostly spectacle for reality.

Kurt von Zutraven did not believe that he was himself a criminal, that he had committed crimes against human beings and humanity, as the indictment asserted; but the thought that he had been fooled by these masks around him occupied him ceaselessly during the days when the reading of the indictment rambled on and on. He had known them all at the peak of blind power and triumphal glory; he had seen them in their gigantic and yet petit-bourgeois homes; at their conferences, which had been endless rivalries of petty vanity; in their offices, where nothing had been great except their desks. What he had or had not known about shameful offenses against humanity or the cynical preparation of mass murder had not yet become the subject of the dialogue which Kurt von Zutraven was conducting with his hardened conscience. But one thing he could no longer understand: that he had not seen what those twelve years amounted to.

That a macabre carnival party, disguised as kings and hangmen, generals and jailers, diplomats and revolutionaries, had gained control of offices and public functions, the army and the police, the railways and the schools, and that they had stayed there for a full twelve years, continuing the carnival revelries in deadly earnest, through winter and spring, summer and autumn. Kurt von Zutraven was reminded of a story by Edgar Allan Poe, in which the author describes his visit to a lunatic asylum, a lonely building which he reaches after a ride of several days. There he is received by the director of the institution, entertained by the doctors and nurses and orderlies—until at supper a curious suspicion springs up in him as the director and staff, in a fit of macabre jollity, begin to mimic and caricature the lunatics. Suddenly, during supper, a tremendous noise is heard from the depths of the cellars and a moment later some men and women burst into the room, seizing the bogus doctors and nurses—the deranged inmates who had for a few hours acted the parts of sane people. But what even a writer's imagination had dared to present as the nightmare of a few hours only now seemed to have been the German reality for twelve long years. Moreover, it had come to an end, here at Nuremberg, not as in Poe's story through the sane people liberating themselves, but only after foreign armies had released the sane Germany from the depths of its cellars.

Such thoughts, confusing rather than clarifying his view, occupied the defendant Kurt von Zutraven, who never suspected that they proved convincingly that he had lost all contact with the people he loved.

The confusion into which the Nuremberg trial hurled the German people was of a different kind. Thus, the man who was busy outside the square pile of the Court House clearing the dirty slushy November snow with unpracticed movements, not perhaps reluctantly but grumpily and amateurishly, had less than a year before been a teacher of mathematics at a high school. But Law No. 8 "prohibits the employment of former Party members in commercial enterprises and responsible posts and sanctions their employment as manual laborers only"—thus ran the text of the notice which had thrust the snow shovel into the hands of the Herr Studienrat. The Herr Studienrat was a great believer in discipline, which he had not only always demanded but also practiced—an inclination that might account for his early sympathies for the Nazi party. This snow-shovelling mathe‹

matician therefore, engrossed though he was in his physical labors, still tried to put two and two together, a silent occupation which he was not debarred from but which, on the other hand, led to no result. Two and two, as the Herr Studienrat discovered to his alarm, no longer made four. If the men now sitting inside the overheated Court House (while his own ears were going numb with cold) had indeed despicably deceived the German people, as the indictment claimed they had, then surely something must be wrong with this much-advertised collective guilt. To maintain that the seduced was at the same time the seducer seemed poor logic. Ten thousand pages the Nuremberg protocol would run to, it was said: to print it in full—this was the kind of arithmetic the Herr Studienrat amused himself with—a daily paper would have to devote a full page to the trial for three years, five months and two days. Ten thousand pages to prove that the arch-criminals were in fact criminals—whereas the criminal responsibility of the entire German people was taken for granted without any further protocol!

That two and two no longer made four was now obvious to the Herr Studienrat. But no higher mathematics was needed to spot the error in the calculation. In vain did the new German papers, freshly created by the Allies—in particular the official American *Neue Zeitung*—publish pages and pages of reports on the proceedings in the Court House: the people walked apathetically past the building where judgment was being passed on their destroyers, except those who previously had sat in judgment over themselves. The idea that the nation should look back, questioning and repenting, was the concept of a conqueror, conceived with a full stomach and in a warm room: in reality, the people only worried about how to fill their stomachs and their stoves. There was no pity for the death candidates in the small Nuremberg courtroom, for they had never themselves pitied the suffering people. But likewise there was no anger, no shame and no indignation, especially as the rulers of yesterday were now in the grip of a well-functioning foreign precision machine. The desire to see the truth did not arise until much later, when the defendants of Nuremberg had long been dead or buried alive. But this was the first winter of the occupation and such questions as: would one go to bed hungry again, would there be milk for a new-born baby, would there be a hospital bed for a mother, would one find a job or would one have to queue up, overshadowed the historical spectacle. Besides, the ponderous procedure, thought up by the victors to demonstrate their strict objectivity and to give the legally ignorant Germans a taste of Anglo-Saxon law, utterly missed its effect. The spectators grasped instinctively that the verdicts were a foregone conclusion, and the long road to the gallows seemed no whiter to them for being so long.

The indifference of the public outside, this defeat of historiography at the hands of hunger, presently also invaded the gray building in Nuremberg, even though the Allies had been confident that the circuses would be a substitute for the bread for which the people outside were queueing up in vain.

Over the dark-paneled courtroom hung the weariness of winter afternoons. The simple wooden benches which had been built for the defendants, surrounded by a hoarding of plain boards, clashed with the fine old room and gave the impression that fugitives had knocked up some temporary stabling in a church. The men inside the oblong stable took no part in the macabre ceremonies that went on outside the wooden partitions. The chief attraction was lacking, the one attraction that would have swept aside all lethargy: the actor playing the lead had made his excuses and had been left behind in Berlin, charred in the Chancellery shelter. His absence gave rise to the 1945 version of the legend of the stab in the back. He alone, asseverated his one-time vassals, had wielded the dagger; he alone had known everything; he alone was guilty. The others, the living, sat staring and being stared at, some only captured and others already embalmed; no more related to their own names than the animals in the zoo are to the Latin appellations on the bars of their cages; stripped of the greatness of legend and thrown back into the petty existence from which they had sprung. It was true that the press tickets were all sold out and that all the big papers and news agencies throughout the world had sent their correspondents to Nuremberg; but the intimate little press gallery by the side of the dock was occupied only by the conscientious reporters of the new German papers, while the uniformed correspondents of the foreign press were looking around for other sensations. Translators, women secretaries and press officers were busy stirring up artificial excitement and the monotonously humming mimeograph machines spewed hundreds of bulletins into the press room. But in the pigeonholes with the names of the correspondents the unread paper accumulated until it overflowed, dropped on to the floor and was swept up. The foreign journalists, in British, American, French, Russian, Czech and even Brazilian uniform, mostly stayed only for a few days: to have seen the peep-show characters in the flesh satisfied their curiosity. The fact that they had actually existed, and were still there, was more interesting than what was happening with them. Oddly enough, the uniforms of the correspondents did not make the spectacle any more lively, but on the contrary more lethargic. The circumstance that only about one reporter in ten wore civilian clothes stripped those in uniform of their impartial dignity and made them into fellow-prosecutors, just as on the other hand one could not overlook the fact that the German defense counsel in their black gowns were fellow-defendants. These counsel for the defense, whose solemn black attire concealed the shabbiness of their suits, had themselves been put on starvation rations and, as Germans, had themselves been arraigned—even if only in a collective sense. They were discharging their functions with the resignation of physicians administering a heart stimulant to a dying man, knowing all the while that the injection cannot help him any more. The lunatic idea of collective guilt had turned the stars of the Nuremberg show into extras; judges, prosecutors, MP's and journalists seemed like conspirators, and the courtesy with which the other judges treated their Soviet colleagues deceived no one about the underlying clashes. It was hardly surprising in the circumstances that the trail dragged on lamely and hopelessly.

The only thing which occasionally relieved the paradoxical monotony of this historic event was the rumors which fluttered out of the courtroom. The Reich Marshal, it was said, had fired some shots at a witness—a Field Marshal who had turned up like a ghost from the grave out of Russian captivity and who presently vanished again. The British, French and American judges, others maintained, were at daggers drawn with the Russian judges; the Soviet prosecutor had been recalled and war with Russia was imminent. Fear and wishful thinking, mingled with conjecture and fact, centered on Nuremberg.

These and similar rumors, discussed more eagerly in a Germany starved of newspapers and passed on more swiftly than the less colorful news, also penetrated to Elisabeth von Zutraven through the barbed wore of the "Detention Camp for the Wives of War Criminals."

Since Frank had left her that afternoon she had been pursuing her struggle for freedom, not with eager haste but with growing determination. It was not so much Frank's words which had given her new strength as the realization that had gradually come to her.

She could not tell Frank the truth—him less than anybody else. Whatever she might have said would have remained incomprehensible without the central truth, the one truth around which all other truth revolved—the fact that the only reason why she did not hate the man who was now facing his judges at Nuremberg was that she despised him too deeply. Perhaps she had loved him once, for a very brief time, and after that she had hated him for many years. And as hate had supplanted love, so contempt had supplanted hate.

She had been barely seventeen when she met Kurt von Zutraven. Even the circumstances of her acquaintance with him and her early love were incredible—or were bound to seem so to Frank. How was he to understand that she had been fascinated and inspired and convinced by that gigantic cheat they had called their Führer; that together with other boys and girls she had gone to all the rallies which he addressed in the "capital of the Movement"; that she had carried torches and sung songs in those days when it all began. There had been no deep-rooted reasons for this confusion and delusion: it was difficult to understand why the daughter of the benign, wise and moderate High Court Judge Steer should have fallen a victim to the psychosis which then swept the country. But she had been seventeen at the time, and all around her had been misery and despair, or at best a philistine spirit and false contentment. Everything which the man from Braunau had planned he had wrapped in a cloak of idealism, and Elisabeth Steer had believed him. Let other women assert that they had acted merely as the docile pets of their husbands, unthinkingly and obediently—it did not apply to her, and she had no intention of pretending that it did. On the contrary, it was not so much Kurt von Zutraven, by ten years her senior, that she had fallen in love with, as the symbol that he stood for. She had met him at a rally which she had attended in defiance of her father's prohibition and, again in defiance of her father, she had married him a year later. If things had been different, if she had not seen Kurt von Zutraven as a symbol, her marriage might have turned out happier. But as it was, she had begun to see him clearly at the moment her eyes had been opened to the great folly. Naturally, this had not happened suddenly, from one day to another. The "Machtergreifung" had washed Kurt

»153«

von Zutraven up to the crest and Elisabeth had been lifted up with him. Then she had not known everything, not nearly everything. But with every day that passed she had learned more, and every day she had demanded more insistently that her husband should cut adrift. That had been act two of her marriage: the time when she had seemed clear-eyed and he had seemed blind, and when she had begun to hate him for his blindness. But even then she had believed that he would make his decision once he realized what was happening also in his name. And finally the curtain had risen over the third act—on a summer day, when she discovered that Kurt von Zutraven had known everything all along, from the very start, and that realization could not cure him. That was when her hate had turned to contempt.

But why had she done nothing, or seemingly nothing, in the days of her hate or those of her contempt? This was another thing nobody could understand—certainly not Frank Green. Dramatic decisions were not in line with her character. But quite apart from that, by the time she had finished with Kurt von Zutraven she had already been so deeply involved in secret opposition to the regime and so many human lives had depended on her, that open opposition on her part, in the sense that courage was generally understood, would have seemed like cowardly desertion. Her opposition may have been insignificant, possibly infinitesimal—which was why she declined to mention it now. But just as the giant Gulliver had been held down to the ground by thousands of tiny threads tied about him by pigmies, so she had been held down by the threads she had herself spun around her. To rise she would have had to burst those bonds. It was irrelevant now to ask if she could have done it; the truth was that she had not wanted to break them.

And now Kurt von Zutraven was sitting in the dock at Nuremberg, only a few miles away, and his guilt, which had wrecked their marriage, held them together. She had been with him in "the good days," as the other women in the camp called the past few years. Who was to know that she preferred even the hardships of the camp to those "good days"? If she left him now she would be leaving a man in his adversity. This was how it stood, and neither her indifference to malicious tongues nor her indifference to the fate of her long-estranged husband could alter it.

These and similar thoughts occupied Elisabeth for the hundredth time, in ever new shapes, while she sat on her wooden bunk in the dormitory she shared with two other women. To escape from the unceasing train of her thoughts she put down her knitting and went over to the small window in the thin wall. A soldier was trudging up to the hut through the snow.

The soldier knocked and without waiting for a reply opened the door.

"Frau von Zutraven," he said, "get your things packed!"

Elisabeth looked at him in astonishment. The other women, too, looked up in surprise.

"Look sharp about it," said the soldier. "Orders have just come through. You're released."

Still incredulous, Elisabeth asked:

"Back to the interrogation villa . . . ?"

"No," the soldier said impatiently. "Take everything. You're free."

O'Hara Whips No More

Officers were not allowed to drive their own cars, but there were more important things on Major O'Hara's mind that December afternoon in 1945 than such trivial regulations. A few minutes after he had hastily left Colonel Hunter's staff conference—though skilfully dissembling his haste—the Major was behind the wheel of his requisitioned Horch limousine. Even as he drove into the garage of his villa in Pasing it seemed as if the car would not pull up until it had reached the gates of hell; but then O'Hara slammed on his brakes and the car came to a halt, its bumper touching the garage wall.

Using, as always, his own key the Major unlocked the back door into the kitchen and burst into the sitting-room.

Irene Gruss had not been expecting him. The Major did not often get home before seven o'clock, and sometimes it was late in the night. He had never been home at five o'clock before. Shortly before his arrival the commandeuse had decided to kill time by enjoying the amenities of a well-scented bath. She had emptied half a jar of bath salts—obtained cheaply by the Major in the PX—into the warm water and had now been lying in her spacious bath for nearly half an hour.

The Major glanced into the sitting-room, which contained a partially decorated Christmas tree, and without knocking thrust open the door to the bathroom.

The sight of the naked woman lounging comfortably in the violet-tinted bath water provoked a state of wrathful frenzy in O'Hara.

"What d'you think you're doing?" he yelled at her, unconscious of the ridiculousness of his question.

"I'm taking a bath," said the woman, letting herself glide deeper into the water.

"Get out at once," roared O'Hara.

Still she did not move. She could not know that the game was over and that O'Hara was in earnest. During the past few weeks there had been very little real matter of conflict between the Major and the commandeuse, and she realized, or at least she felt instinctively, that her existence depended on her ability to furnish fresh nourishment to his inclinations. Her stories of the concentration camp, even though she gave them ever new and more garish colors, had begun to pall. His imagination was inexhaustible in the invention of new tortures: sometimes she would have to play "ashtray" and he would stub out his burning cigarettes on her arms; another time he would force her to wash his soiled underwear stripped stark naked in the wintry garden. However, Irene Gruss had discovered that perverseness was just as subject to weariness as any conventional partnership in bed. She had therefore begun, like a naughty child, to commit deliberate offenses, ranging from the breaking of a porcelain dish to refusal to obey O'Hara's orders. Thus she enabled him to act as the punisher and to find satisfaction in the chastisement of the intentional offender.

The Major was standing bent over the bathtub and repeated his command: "Get out at once!" But she only wriggled in the water, stretched her legs, covered her ample breast with one arm and with the other hand splashed some water out of the bath—just enough to wet his well-pressed uniform. Even when O'Hara stooped down, caught her by the hair and began to drag her out of the water, like a woman drowning, she still did not suspect that her lover was for once not just responding to her cunningly exciting provocation, but that his excitement sprang from circumstances outside her control.

He let go of her only when, dripping and groping with both hands for her bathrobe, she stood in front of him.

"What's the matter, Bill?" she asked. The treatment she had just suffered seemed to run off her back like her bath water.

"You've got to get out of here," panted O'Hara. "You must be gone in half an hour."

She went pale. O'Hara had never seen her go pale before. Her complexion was yellowish; at times she might flush pink, but O'Hara had not believed that she could turn white. The intoxicating perfume of the too liberally applied bath salts and the hot steam which pervaded the room went to his head. For an instant the desire to see her tremble was stronger than his own fear.

"They'll be here in half an hour," he said. "They'll come and get you. They know everything."

He knew that none of these statements tallied with the truth or that, at best, they were considerably in anticipation of actual fact. Barely an hour had passed since Colonel Hunter had relieved him of the investigations into the case of Irene Gruss and handed the business over to Major Frank Green. It had all been done in a most business-like way, without reprimand of suspicion, as an ordinary routine matter. Hunter had even muttered something about O'Hara having too much on his plate—a polite phrase customary on such occasions. There was no evidence, and very little indication, that they "knew everything," let alone that they would "come and get" Irene Gruss. It was even less probable that they would start off on the right track and "be here in half an hour," or that they would force their way into Major William S. O'Hara's private residence. But panic needed an outlet and O'Hara had found his more quickly than he could have hoped. The panic which had at first gripped him had not only vanished but was turning into cold-blooded pleasure as he transferred his fears to the woman. Now that, for the first time since their first meeting, there was genuine alarm in her usually expressionless eyes, O'Hara experienced the same rapture that had driven him to his fateful decision in the suburban hotel. This was different from the games which his diseased fantasy and her inventive cunning had thought up, and the Major had to rally all his strength to resist the temptation of castigating the trembling woman before him and, as would inevitably happen in the end, weakly succumbing to her in her chastisement.

O'Hara did not suspect what was passing in Irene Gruss's mind. She suddenly realized that something had occurred to turn her lover from hunter into hunted. And even though the fear that was written on his flushed and heated face sprang from an outside source, even though the agonies he was suffering had not, as she would have preferred, been inflicted on him by her—the sight of the pitiful creature aroused in her a sensation of delight which she hailed like a long-lost friend. Her realization of her own awkward position had not yet crystallized into recognizable shape; it was still submerged in a glowing sense of satisfaction over her return to her proper role.

She had hurriedly left the bathroom and was beginning to dress in the adjoining bedroom.

"Where shall I go?" she inquired of the Major who had stopped at the door of the bedroom.

"Away!" said the Major. "Into the street, where you belong."

She was in the process of putting on her girdle. The comic element inherent in most dramatic moments was underlined when, halfway through the grotesque movement of squeezing herself into the belt, she stopped and looked into his face.

"I'd make you sorry for that," she said. She did not sound at all frightened now.

"Are you trying to threaten me?" he said.

She had forced her bulk into the girdle.

"Yes," she said firmly.

He laid his hand on the pistol holster which he had not yet taken off. It was a calm gesture and therefore doubly menacing.

"I could shoot you down," he said. "No one would hear the shot. It'd be the simplest way out."

She had put on her dress. It was the dress in which she had come to his house: gray, with a small white collar, a severe modest dress, slightly reminiscent of the uniforms of Prussian girls' boarding schools. Instead of retreating before his gesture she advanced a step.

"They'll find you out," she said. "They'll hang you."

"So what? So long as you're dead," he said. But he took his hand off his holster.

She walked calmly past him, through the bathroom and the hall, into the sitting-room.

He followed her heavily, shut the door behind him and went over to the window. It was night outside. He drew the curtains. The floor lamp by the bulky radio spread a warm, biscuit-colored light. The army Christmas tree stood on the radio. She had half-decorated it with red, silver and golden balls, with glittering tinsel and with blue, yellow and green electric fir cones. But the wire leading from the fir cones was not yet plugged in and the room was lit only by the floor lamp.

"Get ready," said the Major. He spoke softly now, through his teeth. "You've got to be outside in ten minutes."

"Not till I know where I'm going," said the woman.

"You're going now," he repeated. "And you're taking all your stuff. If you say another word I'll strangle you with my own hands."

"I can prove that I know you," she said, "and a great deal more."

"Nobody's going to believe you," he said.

"I can prove everything," she repeated.

Slowly he moved towards her. She was standing still, motionless, just as she had always waited for the gradual or sudden start of the frenzied prelude of his passion—lying in wait, without realizing it. She did not know it herself, but she was lurking. What she wanted to discover was whether his motions of brutality were still a gratifying necessity to him, whether he was still enslaved by making her his slave, or whether he was already using brutality towards a clear and unemotional end. If he had pounced on her with his bare hands, if he had threatend her life by squeezing her throat—perhaps she would have run out of the house and out of his life. But O'Hara stopped for an instant, and in stopping he committed his last mistake. With an unsure hand he opened a sideboard, a ludicrously philistine cupboard in the sitting-room of the requisitioned house. Inside, almost as neatly arranged as an orderly housewife's cups and saucers, were the instruments of torture which he had accumulated in the course of the past months: cat-o'nine-tails and coiled ropes and a slender steel whip and leather thongs, large and small, wide and narrow. It was a wooden-handled whip with thin leather strips at one end, a ridiculous instrument of the Inquisition, almost looking like a feather duster, that the Major now snatched from the sideboard. He approached her with big strides. But she was no longer afraid. Because she was made of the same stuff as he, she had been able to suffer what she would really have liked to inflict. First, he had got right inside her part and then she had got into his: her great deception had been her pretense of being a victim when she had long become a partner. But this kinship also enabled Irene Gruss to predict with deadly certainty what was bound to happen now. With his hate and her torment, with his brutality and her humiliation, the passion which alone bound the tormentor to the tormented, would spend itself. But this time there would be no time for its renewal, a time which passion born of delight in pain needed just as much passion springing from love. The sobering-up would come, and once sobered up the pervert would no longer differ from a sane person. It was not the man who was now approaching her with bloodshot eyes, his white fist clutching the whip, that the woman feared; it was not his frenzy but his cooling down. But he had lacked the strength to turn away from his cruel routine, even at a time when his own life might have been at stake; faced with her alarm, he had succumbed to the rhythm she knew so well; and even now his lust was blinding him to his predicament—that was why Irene Gruss was able to consider her position and choose a way which offered a last chance of salvation.

As if from a burst cesspool, the filth was pouring from O'Hara's lips. The former commandeuse understood less than a tenth of the curses which he spat out in his native language, but she understood his meaning. Suddenly she was the temptress, the cause of his troubles and his disaster; and he was the victim, resisting belatedly, but perhaps not too late. Irene Gruss understood it all, and at that moment occurred the turn which O'Hara could not have foreseen.

What she did, she did not do only out of calculation. O'Hara, the defeated; O'Hara trembling, fear-ridden and helpless; O'Hara, the flagellator, ludicrously unable to free himself from his victim; O'Hara with the whip, but himself chased by a weapon a thousand times more dangerous—this O'Hara filled Irene Gruss with an unsuspected bliss. And because her decision to do the unexpected was now reinforced by the intoxication that O'Hara's humiliation engendered in her, she acted in accordance with her most primal instincts.

The strokes were falling on her thick and fast. In the past he had flogged only her trunk, forcing her into unresisting humility as she had been wont to do with the concentration camp inmates; but he was now thrashing her blindly, across her face, her neck and her breast.

She was standing next to the radio. With a lightning-like movement, dodging one of his blows, she snatched up the Christmas tree on top of the set. Holding it by its trunk she hit out at O'Hara, again and again. The thin branches snapped. Pine needles flew through th air and dug into the face of the man. The colored balls, made of thinnest glass, burst and tore open his cheeks. The brightly colored electric pine cones exploded on the ground. The tinsel got mixed up with his red hair, and the blood which trickled down his short nose washed along a jetsam of green pine needles, iridescent glass and silvery threads.

O'Hara could easily have overcome her. But he did not try to. He stopped in front of her. The whip fell from his hand. She understood the sign at once and snatched it up. And presently there was re-enacted, with an eerie similarity, the scene that she had always had to tell him about—the scene from the concentration camp. But this time he did not take over her part: this time she played it herself. He retreated under her blows, step by step, back to the long table which stood against the wall.

"Across the table!" she commanded.

He obeyed.

And she struck.

Then she flung the whip to the floor. She was standing in the middle of the room and he was coming for her, no longer threatening but only full of desire.

She evaded him.

"Later," she said, brooking no opposition. "You're taking me away now."

He stammered: "Hurry up! Quick!"

And while she packed her little suitcase he picked up from the floor the fragments of the Christmas tree that was not destined to see Christmas.

Christmas 1945

A few days before Christmas the following paragraph appeared in the *Süddeutsche Zeitung*:

"This is no Christmas story but an official announcement: Food offices in the American Zone have been instructed to issue one kilogram of white flour and 400 grams of sugar to each consumer."

It was indeed no fairy story. The "consumer"—as the former "Volksgenosse" was now more soberly called, though not without a touch of reproach—could now indeed "consume" a slice of white bread and perhaps even a piece of sweet cake for Christmas. Altogether, the first German peacetime Christmas was by no means wholly joyless. There were, of course, no traditional Christmas markets—but anybody able to cycle just beyond the outskirts of a town could obtain a modest fir tree from a peasant or, simpler still, he could steal one on the way.

If any proof had been needed that the time of Advent wrought a magical change in human beings, allowing the exceptional in them to ring out loud and silencing their everyday nature, at least for a few days, then such proof was furnished by the Advent of 1945. "Offering electric iron, 220 volts, good as new, in exchange for well-kept baby doll with clothes. Klipstein, Friedenheimer Strasse 18"—thus advertised a mother who wanted at all costs to put a baby doll, complete with clothes, under her meager Christmas tree. "Offering Russian boots in exchange for rocking horse" was the advertisement of a selfless father, while a generous young lover offered to exchange "two made-to-measure suits, size 48, against engagement ring." During the first winter months the utilitarian had been trumps—"Willing to exchange evening gown for bicycle inner tube," "Chandelier offered for pair of boots," "Cooker hot-plate wanted in exchange for elegant desk set"—but now the time had come for light-hearted luxuries, and warm leather gloves were cheerfully bartered away for glittering Christmas decorations. Admittedly, there was not much to buy in the bombed-out shops and empty department stores. But at least there was a notice announcing: "Novelty! Tobacco shredder! The most magnificent present for gentlemen!"—and rumor had it that coat hangers, curtain rods, wicker baskets, a reprint of the *Struwelpeter* and even dachshunds on wheels were available in the open market.

To this must be added the fact that the festival, which throughout human memory, had always been celebrated most noisily by the Pharisees, the same who had sent out their police to search for the newborn babe and murder him, had in the defeated country once again become the festival of the poor, as indeed it had always been intended to be. In the public squares of the German towns stood huge, electrically illuminated Christmas trees as they had always done; but whereas in the past these trees of the poor and homeless had themselves remained lonely and deserted—for no one had been quite so poor and homeless on Christmas Eve as to have to warm himself by such collective illumination, there were now men and women and children standing under the tree, presenting and exchanging gifts, herded together by need but still imbued with the festive spirit. Just because there was nothing in the scantily decorated shopwindows, except now and again a few artistically turned wax candles, some drooping felt slippers, or an occasional second-hand book, Christmas had again become a cheerful anxiety. A present was the bravely won result of a long and troublesome search, and amidst the jubilation the only worthy price of jubilation was sacrifice. In other countries, in countries that were more fortunate in the ordinary sense of the word, the birth of the Redeemer was traditionally celebrated as if in ignorance of the subsequent fate of the newborn babe; behind the German Christmas of 1945 was Gethsemane, the road to Calvary and the Crucifixion.

The last few days before Christmas had been mild, but snow had fallen in most parts of Germany—a piece of good fortune in all the misfortune. Homes were not quite so cold as they had been previously, and outside the stuff of heaven covered a savaged earth. Unwittingly or deliberately, most people had put their little Christmas trees more carefully than usual into their windows, as a modest greeting to those who possessed none themselves. And since many trees stood in the windows of half-wrecked houses a passer-by might get the impression that the sparkling trees were suspended in mid-air, between heaven and earth, luminous signposts in the darkness. From cellar windows too—for many people still lived in cellars—came the glow of Christmas trees. Frequently these windows came halfway above gound level, so that only the tops of the trees were visible and the streets appeared edged with glittering stars, stars fallen to earth, a string of pearls bordering the streets.

Christmas Eve 1945, the Year One of the occupation of Germany, brought a Christmas surprise to the student Hans Eber. In the afternoon, as he and Karin were decorating their tree, an excessively tall Christmas tree contributed by Captain George Green out of army supplies—a circumstance which rather spoiled for Hans an activity he had loved since childhood—there was a ring at the door and presently Dr. Eberhard Eber walked into the sitting-room. He greeted his children in the same matter-of-course fashion in which he had left them; he made no mention of how and why he had been released, nor did he treat them to an account of his captivity. Yet he seemed to wear that optimistic air which characterized him in all situations. He soon withdrew to confer at some length with his brother Oskar, and from casual remarks made by his uncle Hans gathered that the two brothers proposed to reopen the banking firm in the New Year. For the time being it would be known as "Bankhaus Oskar Eber"; for not without good reason had Eberhard Eber years before forbidden his elder brother, who had always been slavishly devoted to him, to join the Nazi Party. Thus the good banking name of Eber could now again bear fruit. Hans's astonishment over his father's release from arrest, not only unbroken but evidently with a good bargain to boot, grew even further upon Captain Green's return late in the evening. Not only was the Captain not surprised at Dr. Eberhard Eber's appearance on the scene, but he acted almost as if he had expected to see him. True, he did not give up his bedroom to his lawful host, but on the other hand he saw no reason to forbid him the house. When finally, at midnight, the Captain—usurper, guest and host all in one—produced from his room several bottles of excellent champagne, which had traveled there from the Ebers' cellar a few months previously, and began to uncork them *en famille*, as it were, Hans Eber could stand it no longer and escaped from the paternal home into the street which was busier than usual since the occupation authorities had suspended the curfew for one Holy Night.

Christmas Eve brought an unusual celebration also for Inge Schmidt, whose fate was to be linked so strangely in the New Year with that of Hans Eber. Lincoln Washington Haymes, the Negro soldier who had picked Inge up on the Sendlinger-Tor-Platz one sultry summer evening, had unexpectedly turned up in Munich on Christmas leave from Berlin—a black Santa Claus whose sack of presents contained a veritable mountain of luxuries. Lincoln Washington Haymes's business deals with the Russians in Berlin had proved exceptionally lucrative. "Ivan," as the Russians were universally called, had fallen victim to the fascination of a revolutionary new invention—the wrist-watch. And although "Ivan" was rather particular in certain respects—the watches had to be round, as it was obviously impossible for the hands to go round square dials, and moreover for aesthetic reasons the dials had to be black—Haymes had been able to meet those demands. From back home, in Alabama, he had entire cratefuls of Ingersoll watches sent to him, the type popularly known as Mickey Mouse and sold at every drugstore for ninety-eight cents.

They were not perhaps very durable, but they were indubitably round and had a black dial. The "Ivans," quick on the uptake, had soon learned that the quality of a watch was determined by the number of its jewels, and so Private Haymes, like many of his fellows, invariably ordered a bottle of red nail polish to be sent over with each consignment. With this quick-drying polish any desired number of rubies could instantly be conjured up in the watch's movement. No wonder therefore that Lincoln Washington Haymes, uniformed representative of Mickey Mouse, returned to Munich with rich treasure. It was typical of his loyalty that he immediately looked up Inge to share his wealth with her. And because the Negro from Alabama, like most of his race, was a family man at heart, he insisted on celebrating Christmas at Inge's home—a request that was gladly acceded to. In addition to Ilse Joachim, the tall blonde, two other girls from the Sendlinger-Tor-Platz had been invited: Olga, no longer quite young and active in the neighborhood chiefly as a maternal adviser, and the young and graceful Helga who brought along her boy-friend, a certain Paseto who, kept by her, had led a comfortable and immoral life till the end of the war, but who had recently begun to earn an honest living by the sale of black-market cigarettes. These were joined by Duke F. Smith, from Harlem, a colleague of the host, who for his part contributed sugar, flour, coffee beans, cigarettes, a multitude of useless and beautiful presents such as perfume, lipstick and powder, and even a pair of liberated opera glasses. The pensioner Alois Schmidt, who had been permitted to help Inge, Ilse, Olga and Helga decorate the Christmas tree, became so maudlin under the effect of the unaccustomed quantities of American whisky that before long, with tears in his eyes, he joined in the singing of "Jingle bells, jingle bells, jingle all the way . . . ," in English, while at the same time successfully teaching his two American guests to sing "O Tannenbaum, O Tannenbaum."

Christmas Eve was also an opportunity for Walter Wedemeyer, conjurer and proprietor of the "Mücke," to rest after his wearying work of the past few months. He was, at heart, a tired and lonely man who had spent his life in the exhausting endeavor of being cleverer than the rest of the world and who feared his hours of contemplation just as trapeze artists and tightrope walkers fear their leisure hours because of being reminded alarmingly of the dangers of their daily occupation. And because, carefully hidden within him, he had a conscience—a possession as dangerous for a man of Wedemeyer's type as a disturbance of the sense of balance is for a circus artist—the last few weeks had caused him a good deal of worry. Although he was a discreet host, genuinely anxious to eavesdrop on his guests' conversations only in so far as they concerned him, at least indirectly, he had heard rather more than pleased him. He had put his night club at the disposal of the Americans in order to get them to license it; if they used it as a convenient and inconspicuous hunting ground for shady characters with political or business connections, that was part of the bargain and suited him all right. But Walter Wedemeyer had certainly not bargained for the kind of shady characters that had been walking in and out of the "Mücke" since the first visit of Captain George Green, and it was particularly awkward that he knew those people better than he or they cared to admit. Moreover, the fact that there could be no question of a hunt and that, quite on the contrary, the hunters seemed to be eating out of their quarries' hands, shocked Wedemeyer's natural sense of propriety. He had always in the past managed to keep within those bounds where man lived in a state of friendly argument with his conscience without having to clash with it violently and irreparably. The fact, therefore, that the "Mücke," now increasingly the boxing ring of his conscience, had closed its doors for the next two days was a welcome break for him, and he had arranged matters in such a way as to be spared all business problems during the holidays. As he was also a filial son he had managed, with ineffable difficulties and at even greater sacrifice, to have his aged mother smuggled out of the Soviet sector of Berlin through the rather tricky corridor into Munich; at the Starnberg house, which had still escaped requisition, mother and son were celebrating their joyful reunion on Christmas Eve, a reunion sweetened by all manner of worldly gifts.

Christmas Eve also saw the candles burning on a tree in the apartment of Colonel (retired) Werner Zobel. True, the festival was quite different from how the Colonel had pictured the first postwar Christmas in his dreams. Shortly before Christmas 1944 the Colonel's regiment had been pulled out of the costly fighting that marked the German retreat through the Polish plains and hastily—though with many delays due to the precarious situation of the Reich—switched over to the West to take part in that Christmas offensive which, much against the Field Marshal's will, was to become known as the "Rundstedt offensive." True enough, this reckless and senseless attempt to stay the wheel of history had got stuck in the snow of the Ardennes on Christmas Day—but the troops had nevertheless advanced a few hundred miles during the preceding days and this advance, fatal though it was to prove in the end, had rekindled in the regimental commander certain hopes to which he had clung obstinately. It seemed fantastic now, but a year ago he had still, superstitiously and against his better judgment, believed in final victory and imparted this confidence to his men. It might have been thought that the disastrous year that was now drawing to its close would have given Colonel Zobel time to get used to the idea that Christmas 1945 would not be a festival of victory, and not even one of heroic steadfastness, but finally and irretrievably a Christmas of defeat; and he would indeed have reconciled himself to this fact, had not the fate of his vanquished nation become so confusingly interwoven with his own life. There he sat, in his accustomed easy chair by the window, while his daughter Martha, his future son-in-law Gerd Mante and his former orderly Josef Maurer were grouped round a table piled high with presents. The confusion which overcame the old man at this sight was made worse by the fact that, even during the past twelve years of confusion, he had always followed what had seemed to him the orderly road. For him and Martha not to celebrate the festival this year, not to have a Christmas tree or a table with presents, would have seemed quite in order. For Martha to spend this evening in thoughts of especial devotion and grief for the young SS leader whom the Allies must surely have arrested and sentenced, would have been understandable to Zobel and hence bearable. But the carefree and tipsy cheerfulness which was displayed before his eyes was to him utterly and completely incomprehensible. What punishment was deserved when deserved punishment was not imposed? How deep was the cleft which divided victors and vanquished and how wide, at the same time, was the avenue that led across the gulf? Did the morass have to spread so fast that not an inch of his native soil remained unaffected? And he himself, Colonel Werner Zobel, had he merely simply become a figure of ridicule, a pedantic caricature and a peep-show character from the past by his refusal to understand and to join in? These questions troubled the former regimental commander at the very moment when his former orderly started up the gramophone he had brought along with a record of "Holy Night."

A certain disorder, though of an entirely different nature, also came into the life of another colonel that Christmas Eve—a victorious colonel, Colonel Graham T. Hunter. In the afternoon the Colonel had attended a Christmas celebration in the barracks of the occupation troops in Munich and he was glad that this indifferent event had dragged on into the early hours of the evening. He feared the lonely evening that lay ahead at his large and unfriendly house at Harlaching. He had dismissed his driver and set out to walk home, hoping that the long walk through the city and the suburbs would take his mind off things and tire him out. But instead the strange city aroused a certain emotion in the Colonel. Dim lights were still burning in the windows of the shops, and the empty shelves conveyed the illusion of having been stripped bare by eager purchasers; one quite forgot that they had been empty before. Several shopkeepers were busy lowering their steel blinds and locking them conscientiously—an absurd and pathetic gesture as these blinds only protected articles which did not exist. The Colonel had not expected to find so many children about; though still early, it was quite dark in the streets. Dressed up as Nativity players, the children were going from house to house: on their heads they wore paper crowns and in their hands they carried a cardboard stable of Bethlehem with a lighted candle inside. Carefully they climbed over the debris, anxiously protecting the flickering flame in the crib. As the streets were dark the candlelight illuminated the young players, and as they advanced through the night of ruins there was about their crowns a gleam of real gold, and their shadows, and that of the crib, grew to gigantic size against the background of the white heaps of rubble. In the suburbs which the Colonel had to cross there was in some places still a smell of fire and bombs; the cold pungent odor mingled with the warm and cozy smell of the Christmas trees. The Colonel thought of his children, his home, his country, and also of the woman whom he had not loved for many years but to whom he was growing more attached with every day of separation. He thought that on this evening the defeated must be especially envious of the victors—the victors eating turkey and drinking coffee and punch, and exchanging wonderful presents in their well-heated homes. He did not understand their envy, for he knew that destiny had a way of restoring the balance: the defeat had brought the defeated closer together and torn the victors asunder. It was not true that one dominated a foreign country; it was the foreign country that dominated the conqueror and thus every individual was paying a heavy price for his country's victory. Such were the Colonel's thoughts and feelings as he unlatched his garden gate and stamped up the snow-covered path to his house. The housekeeper, who had worked for him since May and who, like all his subordinates, was devoted to him, welcomed him with a "Merry Christmas" and handed him a little parcel tidily done up in creased tissue paper. The Colonel, who had not expected a present, undid the package under the jealous eyes of his housekeeper and discovered a book, evidently second-hand but in good condition, containing a history of the city of Munich and illustrated with some excellent copper engravings. On a little card, which had been slipped into the book, was written in a good and, so to speak, smiling hand the English inscription: "I thought this book might amuse you during the holidays. A Merry Christmas from Marianne von Artemstein." Hastily the Colonel carried the book and the note into the sitting-room; he was hoping that his housekeeper had not noticed his blush.

Christmas Eve was a lonely time also for another American—Major William S. O'Hara. He, too, had spent the afternoon attending various official celebrations and casting about desperately for some company for the evening. But nobody had seemed to want to invite him. Even his faithful driver, Pfc. Harry S. Jones, had made some excuse when the Major asked him to his home for the evening. Nothing had happened since the previous day, when he got Irene Gruss out of his house—at least nothing of what he had expected. After a furious drive he had taken the woman to the apartment of a German, the former Gestapo chief Dieter Griff, the very man whom George Green had contacted in the "Mücke" through the mediation of the ex-soldier Josef Maurer. O'Hara had been in touch with Griff long before George Green approached him, and had kept him on tap as a valuable source of information. Griff, mistrusting Captain Green, had gone to O'Hara for information about him—and thus it came about that the Major was fully informed about the contacts between U.S. Intelligence, to which he himself belonged, and the former Gestapo chief. He had on more than one occasion done Griff a good turn and felt entitled to hope that the man would give Irene

Gruss at least temporary shelter. At the same time O'Hara realized that his outfit's contacts with Griff ran counter to the publicly proclaimed policy of the United States and the Occupation Army and belonged to that category of operations which Intelligence was instructed by higher quarters to perform but for which it might well have to carry the ball itself. The knowledge of this secret was a valuable weapon in O'Hara's hand, and he was determined to make full use of it if he found himself in an awkward situation. That he would so find himself now seemed inevitable to him on that first lonely evening. He had started drinking early; he was trying to drown his fear in quantities of bourbon unusual even for him; he gulped his whisky in big mouthfuls, finally even without water, but the alcohol which had so often got the better of him in the past was now getting the better of him in quite a different way. Intoxication, which had often come when he would have liked to stay sober, now refused itself to him like a capricious beauty; the more O'Hara drank the more sharply were the contours of the living-room outlined to him, and the vision of what was going to happen was before him as clearly as if it were a picture from the past. This clairvoyancy, in the original meaning of the word, had nothing speculative about it; O'Hara was not contemplating what might happen but he knew what was bound to happen and he realized that it was futile to resist. He was no longer ranting against the woman whom he had blamed for his misfortune; he was not even ranting against himself. He was merely trying to hide, and on his restless wanderings from room to room, from one place to another, it came to him clearly that there was no hiding place. At last he felt driven out into the street, but the lights of the Christmas trees in the windows, the peals of the church bells and the chanting of the worshippers drove him back into the deserted house.

Christmas Eve saw a deep and blissful peace settling on the apartment in the Schwabinger suburb where Dr. Adam Wild lived with his mother.

Adam had returned from Frankfurt the previous day. He had embraced his mother—he had to lift up the tiny woman in order to kiss her, and she almost disappeared in his arms—and asked her if she had worried about him much. Not at all, Frau Wild had replied with an almost naughty twinkle; she had realized that he must have got himself into trouble again with the authorities, but then she was used to that, and trouble was trouble even if the authorities changed. Of course, until his letter arrived from the detention camp she had indeed had a few uneasy hours, but she might have known that the devil would look after his own and that Adam would probably come back, a little the worse for wear but all in one piece. Ever since childhood he had had more luck than sense and had got out of the most unlikely scrapes. Besides, she had been busy in his absence—not only reassuring his impatient patients but also, as he would see in a moment, organizing a nice little Christmas sale of antiques. Quite a number of Americans had turned up and had amply supplied themselves, and hence also her, for the holidays. No further explanations were needed: considerable gaps had appeared in the overcrowded living-room, and at the same time the whole apartment, including his surgery, was pervaded by a warm Christmasy smell of all kinds of delicious cakes. Needless to say, she had not got through her Christmas preparations yet, and the conversation which continued thenceforward for the next few hours—since he wanted to tell her everything and she to hear everything—had to be conducted in the kitchen, where Frau Wild darted to and fro like a weasel while Adam leaned against a cabinet which almost entirely disappeared under his arm.

"One particularly curious thing," Adam was saying, "is the way one goes on, time and again, misjudging people—especially if one underrates them. I had completely written off that Franz Grün, a very silly and humiliating thing to do considering the way he suddenly turned up like a rescuing angel and snatched me from the camp contrary to all rules and regulations."

"I'm glad you realize that," said Frau Wild. She cast a maternally proud and at the same time reproachful glance at the giant by the kitchen cabinet. "You might have broken every bone in that fellow's body!"

Adam dropped his eyes. He was not shamed by his mother's reproach; secretly he still regretted not having broken every bone in Corporal Crane's body. But he had kept from his mother what had happened in the darkness of the camp after he had left the lieutenant colonel's office. The blows no longer stung his cheeks, and he thought sometimes that a man who had never been humiliated could never have dignity. But he was afraid of his mother's belated sympathy and preferred to let her believe that he himself had emerged unscathed.

He said quickly: "You're quite right; it was no trifle. Without Lieutenant Colonel Perry's help even Grün wouldn't have got me out: quite a few blind eyes had to be turned. Of course, Grün couldn't quash the proceedings even if he tried. It's not impossible that I may get locked up again; in fact, I should think it probable. After all, an occupation soldier is an occupation soldier. I am not even sure that Grün didn't make improper use of his boss's name to get me out; Perry dropped a sort of hint when he made out my temporary discharge slip. Later, when we were in his jeep, Grün gave me a dressing down as if I were a little boy—but I had the distinct impression that he was doing so because he was afraid I might thank him too profusely. I judged that this was no suitable moment to talk about Achim —but just imagine: he didn't say a word till we got to Munich and then, all of a sudden, he just remarked incidentally that my friend Sibelius had been transferred to Bavaria and, if it was at all possible, he'd get him out at Christmas. A very strange fellow, that Grün—or Green, as he now calls himself—and I'd give a lot to know what makes him act that way. . . ."

Frau Wild, who liked to pretend that she was not listening but who followed each word attentively, suddenly looked up from the baking pan she had pulled out of the oven and interrupted her son.

"He probably is a good man," she said. When Adam did not reply she went on, busying herself once more about her baking: "I can see you're thinking that the old woman is again simplifying things which aren't nearly so simple. That's the trouble with you youngsters: you keep looking for motives. . . . You must have a motive for everything. You find so many motives for evil that it ceases to be evil; and you keep searching for motives behind every good deed till it has lost its value. You smile in your superior way when people talk about good and evil, as if they were talking of corsets or buttoned boots or some other old-fashioned rubbish, whereas in fact there are good people and bad people"—she resolutely smacked her empty baking pan down on the stove—"yes indeed: good people and bad people. And you'd all be a good deal wiser if you only stopped trying to analyze evil into its good and bad components."

Adam laughed. "You're quite wrong, mother, but your wrongheadedness is exceedingly endearing." He picked up the struggling woman and kissed her on her flushed wrinkled cheeks.

Thus, with lively argument and cheerful preparations going on, Christmas Eve descended. Frau Wild and her son were on the point of lighting the candles on the small tree when the doorbell, which was working again though somewhat erratically, rang.

"Good evening, Frau Wild," said Frank Green. "I thought perhaps I'd better bring you a Christmas present."

Out of the dusk of the corridor emerged the figure of the former Colonel Achim von Sibelius.

"Do come in, please," said Frau Wild cordially. Adam had also come out into the hall. "You can't just run away like this."

Adam shook hands with Frank and took Achim's arm. The baron was of slight and delicate build and might have been more easily taken for Frau Wild's son than Adam. His snow-white hair, which he wore brushed close to his skull and meticulously parted, contrasted pleasantly with the youthful features of the man who was still on the right side of forty. His small gray mustache looked as if its wearer was trying to make himself look older. He wore his civilian suit—the only civilian suit of a man who had worn uniforms all his life—as self-consciously as a young recruit would his first uniform. The thoroughly military impression conveyed by the very erect short man vanished only when he began to speak: partly because he expressed himself in unusually lengthy, well-construed phrases which were often adorned with literary flourishes, almost as if he were reading a script, and partly because he accompanied his words with eloquent gestures from an exceptionally long, white and well-kept hand which seemed to be rooted in an almost boneless wrist.

"I should love to stay a little longer," Frank said to Frau Wild who was forcing a piece of still warm cake on him, "but I've got to go to my unit's Christmas party, and afterwards to my lonely colonel. But I would like—" his voice was a little uncertain—"I would like to have a word with Dr. Wild first . . . that is, if it isn't inconvenient."

He quickly said goodbye to Frau Wild and Achim, embarrassedly waving away their thanks, and followed Adam into the surgery whose much-tried divan was no doubt going to serve as a comfortable temporary bed for the ex-Colonel.

"Do sit down, Herr Major," Adam invited.

"Thank you. As I said I've got to be off again in a minute," said

Frank and remained standing. "This won't take long. It is—" there was again hesitation in his voice—"it's about Elisabeth von Zutraven, that is Elisabeth Steer, with whom you are acquainted. . . ." He was speaking rapidly, carefully avoiding Adam's eyes. "As far as I know she was released from the Nuremberg detention camp a few days ago and, unless I am greatly mistaken, she must now be on her way to Munich. I don't think she's got a place to go to and it seems very probable therefore that she will call on you. I want to ask her a few questions, only partly of an official nature and partly personal . . ." He did not know how to finish the sentence. He broke off and continued: "An official summons would seem out of place in the circumstances, and I should be most grateful to you if you would let me know when she arrives. I could then call on her here, or choose some other neutral meeting place; at any rate . . ." He again failed to finish.

"But of course," said Adam. "I only hope she really will come and see me. It's by no means certain—we've lost touch a little . . ."

"I understand," said Frank. "Just in case . . ."

"Of course," repeated Adam.

He saw Frank to the door. When he had closed it behind his visitor he stood still for a moment in the dark hall. From the living-room he could hear the excited voices of his mother and his friend. From the near-by church came the peals of Christmas bells. A broad smile spread over Adam Wild's broad face. And what does it matter, mother, he thought, if a good man has some other motive as well as pure goodness. . . .

THE YEARS

1946-1948

FOURTH CHAPTER

Inge Schmidt Is at the End of Her Tether

ALL DAY long it had been *Föhn* weather. The snow had suddenly started to melt and the streets were like dirty canals. The snow shovelers were standing in the water to their ankles, watching the snow floating away under their hands. The warm wind crept over people's necks and under their shirts. It was a promise of spring, like the whispering of a woman who is flirtatious, depraved and desirable, and yet unattainable.

During the day the sky had been deceptively blue; now rain was beginning to fall. The fine warm rain was washing the gray snow away. It was difficult to say whether the evening mist was rising from the ground or descending from the sky.

Inge had been walking through the rain and mist for an hour. The water was oozing through her thin soles. She did not stop until she had reached the bridge over the Isar.

In the glow of the pale lamps on the bridge she saw the river and the craggy fragments of ice that were being swept downstream. She did not know whence the memory rose, but she had to think of her early school days. On winter mornings she used to stand at the trolley stop, waiting for the streetcar to emerge from the darkness. Like the eye of a one-eyed giant the headlight of the trolley car had come to her through the yellow fog. An almost irresistible urge to throw herself in the path of the monster used to grip her; sometimes she had to clench her fists and forcibly dig her heels into the ground to resist the temptation. Now the dark waters were drawing her with the same mysterious power and she knew that it was this temptation that had brought her here.

She did not know if she wanted to die, but she knew for certain that she did not want to live.

It had been like this for weeks. At night, when she switched off the light and slowly went to sleep on the living-room divan, which she had hurriedly got ready and which often still bore the smell of a man, she had only one wish: not to wake up in the morning. But every morning she was awakened by the same noise: her father padding through the room in his felt slippers, and carefully groping his way past her towards the bathroom. She did not open her eyes, but she knew that he would cast a glance at the apparently sleeping girl and then at the handbag, a black roomy handbag, a PX present from Lincoln Washington Haymes. Nowadays he dared not go anywhere near the handbag; he shuffled on, she heard the toilet flush, and then he went back to his bedroom and waited patiently for her to wake up.

That was how the day started. At breakfast her father would face her in silence. She hated his humility as she used to hate his bullying. She felt no shame at being a whore; she was ashamed that everyone seemed to be a whore. Her father was a whore; she spent all her day with whores; and her night visitors were whores too. Whenever she walked past the PX, there were women outside, waiting for an oblig-ing American. Whores. In the "Mücke" the waiters would keep the Germans waiting but would dart about like weasels as soon as an American bawled at them. Whores. When ration cards were issued at the food office the officials would snap at the men and women who had queued up there for hours, but they would jump up obsequiously as soon as a conqueror entered the room. Whores. Sometimes she lis-tened to her father's conversations with the neighbors when they as-sured each other and themselves that they had never been Nazis. Whores. The Americans who came to visit her would dodge along the walls when they left. Whores. And on the walls of the houses a new inscription was more and more frequently being chalked up: "Yankee whore." Who then was a Yankee whore, Inge wondered, when every-body was a whore?

The revulsion which had been choking her for some weeks was physical only in the sense that it passed on to her body. She was no longer afraid of men: they were too miserable to fear. The married men had a bad conscience; the single men hated themselves for pay-ing; the soldiers were afraid of infection. Once one saw through them they all became meek. But they were no less repulsive for being meek.

Her disgust sprang from causes other than physical: it was a con-stant sense of having to free one's self and escape from one's self be-cause wherever one stopped there was a stench. She had never belonged to anyone she had loved; she was not unfaithful either to a lover or to a memory. She shivered in the arms of her visitors, but her sensation was too slight to make her suffer. It was something else: a sickening disgust of the turgid mess in which people seemed to float like dead flies. Nobody seemed to mind the stuff being full of dead flies. And who could tell if one had not oneself become a dead insect in the putrid malodorous mess?

There was no despair in Inge as she looked down into the black noisy river. It would be cold down there, but it would be just as cold in the house by the cemetery. Except that the cold down there would be clean, icily clean. And it would not last long. The other cold, the living one, would be succeeded by a new cold wave the following morning. Eternity was brief and life was long.

Nevertheless she turned away from the parapet. She was standing with her back to the river, trying to think without looking into the water, just as in her childhood she had always turned away from the approaching monster.

"What do you think you're doing here?"

The voice came from quite close to her. She had not heard anybody coming along.

"You can see for yourself what I'm doing, can't you?" said Inge. Hans Eber scrutinized her in the glow of the street lamp.

"I suppose you want to jump into the river," he said.

"I can't do the backstroke," said Inge.

"You've been staring into the water for half an hour," said Hans.

"Anything to do with you?" asked Inge.

"No," said Hans. "If you've set your heart on it . . ."

She looked at him. He was of medium height and had dark-brown hair with a big friendly wave above a high forehead. He wore no hat. She could not see his eyes, but they were certain to be light-colored. He was wearing a trench coat of the kind that was only rarely seen nowadays—a well-cut, almost new trench coat.

"Like to come along with me?" said Inge. That ought to scare him off, she thought.

"I see," said the man.

"What do you mean: you see?" said the girl and shrugged her shoulders.

"Nothing," said Hans. "I apologize. I evidently made a mistake."

Inge laughed. It was an almost girlish giggle.

"What are you laughing at?" asked Hans.

"Isn't a whore allowed to take her own life?" said Inge.

"So you did want to jump in?"

"Maybe," she said and turned to face the water again. Now that she had somebody to talk to she was no longer afraid of the monster.

Hans did not know what to say. Awkwardly he stammered: "But you're still so young . . ."

"You from the Watch Committee?" she said.

"I meant, to die," he said.

"You know you're talking nonsense," she said. "What's that got to do with one's age?" She did not wait for an answer but continued: "You can run along. I'm not going to do away with myself now. Thanks for interrupting me."

"Come along," he said. "There's a restaurant on the other side. You ought to have a hot drink."

"I'm telling you, you needn't worry. There won't be a paragraph in the paper."

He took her arm. He said:

"If I'd said 'Yes' a moment ago you would have come along!"

She turned her head to look at him.

"But that would have cost you at least a pack of cigarettes," she said.

"I've got no cigarettes," he said. But he did not let go of her arm. She let him have his way and pretended not to notice it.

They crossed the bridge, towards the city center. Near the vegetable market was an eating place that was still open. They sat down in a corner and Hans ordered soup. He dropped his eyes when she looked at him.

"You look like a child," he said.

"You aren't exactly in a wheel chair yourself yet," she said.

"But then I don't want to leap into the river," he said.

She was slowly peeling off her coat of army blankets.

"Why not?" she asked.

"Funny question," he said. "Does one have to be tired of life?"

She began to gulp down the hot soup.

"Good luck to you if you aren't," she said.

He was watching her out of the corner of his eyes.

"Was that true—what you told me before?" he asked.

"Oh no—I was only bragging!" she said sarcastically.

"And since when . . . ?" he asked.

"You're asking a lot of questions for a plateful of soup. Got a cigarette?"

"Only a German one," he said, digging the twentieth part of his monthly ration out of his pocket.

"I bet you haven't got any matches either," she said.

"You're wrong there." He gave her a light.

"Now then," she said, "you can calmly go home now. You have a clear conscience. You've saved my life."

He asked: "What's your name?"

"Inge. And yours?"

"Hans."

The hot water which went by the name of soup had driven the color into her cheeks. She was looking like a feverish child. When she looked at him he turned his gaze away; he did not want her to think he was staring at her.

"All right," she said. "Go ahead with your questions! All gentlemen of good family start asking questions after a while. Questions are included in the price. Only most of them ask their questions afterwards. But you can have your questions free of charge."

"You'd probably not had anything to eat," said Hans.

"That was one reason," she said.

"And now . . . ?"

"Now I've had something to eat."

"Well then, before—why did you want to . . . ?"

"To start with, I didn't want to," she said. "I was merely considering it. And secondly, one gets sick of the thing even if one's stomach is full. Especially then." He was about to say something but she anticipated him. "I know that question, too." Imitating the intonation of some stranger, she said: "And why don't you look for a decent job, child? That's what they all ask afterwards, the ones that make you sick. Why, why? Because there's no point in it. Or do you know of a decent job? Do you happen to hold down a decent job? Didn't you sell something in exchange for that coat, something that wasn't yours? At least, I sell only what belongs to me." She buttoned up her coat. "It's getting late," she said. "I live a long way off. It'll soon be curfew time."

She got up. Hans paid the bill.

"I'll see you home," he said.

He expected some opposition, but she said:

"If it gets too late you can come up with me."

He took her arm.

"I'll get home all right," he said.

First Round to George

The Eber family had retired. George and Frank had the drawing-room to themselves.

"What can I offer you?" asked George.

"Nothing, thank you," said Frank. "I want to talk to you."

"That sounds very serious," smiled George. He sat down by the fireplace, facing his brother.

"I haven't come here for the fun of it," said Frank. "I would like to ask you some questions."

"Go ahead . . . , if I can answer them."

"I'll start with an easy one," said Frank. "You have requisitioned this house. Have you got an authorization from the billeting office?"

"You can't be serious," said George.

"Indeed I am."

George crossed his legs. "I'm not, of course, answerable to you," he said, "but needless to say I have no authorization. They had the gall to expect me to live in one of those holes in the Tegernsee barracks. That may have been good enough for German NCO's—but now they're accommodating American officers there. They must be crazy, the boys in your billeting office."

"And therefore you've arbitrarily acquired this house?"

"Naturally. You must be living on the moon, Frank?"

"What do you mean by that?"

"I mean that your question is childish. Thousands of officers have 'arbitrarily,' as you so prettily put it, requisitioned houses and apartments. You're acting as if we were in an allied country. What did we win the war for?"

"Evidently so that you can live in an elegant villa," said Frank.

"That was one of the reasons," said George. "For your information, by the way—unlike many of our colleagues I proceeded with great circumspection. Most of them chuck the people out haphazardly. I have chosen the house of this arch-Nazi."

"But you are permitting this arch-Nazi and his family to stay on," said Frank. "As you are aware, this would be an infringement of the Non-Fraternization Law even if you had not arbitrarily confiscated the house."

"For one thing, if I turned them out I should have to find them alternative accommodation," said George. "Secondly, they are looking after me and I'm saving myself the expense of servants. Thirdly, I intend to go to bed with the daughter of the house. Is that clear now?"

"Abundantly clear," said Frank. "I hope that what I'm going to say to you now will be just as clear. You will vacate this house within twenty-four hours. I shall see to it, without getting you into trouble, that it is requisitioned in the proper way. If you have not left this place by tomorrow evening I shall make a report to Colonel Hunter and call for your immediate transfer. Is that clear?"

Calmly, just as he had done on his first visit, George picked up the little white porcelain figure from the mantelpiece and turned it about in his fingers. He said:

"Major Green, you're evidently suffering from megalomania. The gold leaf on your shoulder and the few ribbons on your chest must have gone to your head. You're talking like a general—except that a general wouldn't talk such nonsense."

Frank made no move to rise.

"Does that mean," he asked, "that you are not prepared to accept my proposal?"

"Just that," said George. "But your proposal, as you are pleased to call your threat, interests me nevertheless. I should like to know why the Jew and American Frank Green should be defending the Germans?"

"You're trying to reverse roles now, George," said Frank. "You won't get far that way."

George stood up and leaned against the fireplace.

"I'm not reversing anything," he said. "Nine months ago, when Germany surrendered unconditionally, it was intended to turn the whole country into a vast area of ploughland. But with every day that passes we are getting softer." He sounded almost sincere and anxious to convince as he continued: "Can't you see what's going on, Frank? Our occupation officers are all idiots. All the people who're any good are getting out of the Army and getting themselves repatriated as fast as they can. They're quite right: the war's been won, so why should they sit around here for five hundred dollars a month, re-educating the Germans? That leaves the scum. You know Colonel McLellan, don't you? He's crazy about model electric railways. Any German who brings him a new engine is a gentleman. In Frankfurt I had a general who'd already had twelve hideous oil paintings made of his wife, on the basis of photographs. Portraits of his wife, in all sizes, are littered about his castle, and the painters, most of them Hitlerite court painters, are receiving double rations." His face hardened. "Our American fellow-countrymen," he said, "are silly children —you know that as well as I do. They are tremendously good-natured, or tremendously malicious—but in either case they're tremendously stupid."

Frank rose abruptly.

"And now you're going to burst into the National Anthem," George said calmly, "but that doesn't change matters. Our fellow-countrymen are letting the Germans twist them round their fingers. It isn't all corruption. The fact is simply that a German street girl is cleverer than an American colonel. Besides, our fellow-countrymen see the world from a toilet perspective. They hated France because the toilets were stopped up, and they love Germany because the water comes flushing down when they pull the chain. And what's more, Frank, the Germans know it. . . . You have always seen people as you wanted to see them. But it is time you grew up. We are living here among Americans who have no brains, and among Germans who have no spines. You can choose yourself which you prefer. But surely you don't believe that the Germans are going to change, just to please us? They'll pick up a few jazz tunes from us, they'll drink Coca-Cola, they'll blow their noses into Kleenex, they'll copy the construction of the jeep, and the German women may possibly discover that it is a good idea to treat one's husband as a servant. That, at most, will be the result of re-education. We failed to crush the worm when it squirmed, and now we shall have to pay for it."

Frank sat down again. He said:

"It would take more than a few hours to reply to you, George. It often seems to me that the cynics have grabbed all the cleverness for themselves. There is a peculiar brilliance in negation: it shines through the night. But it shines only at night. But I haven't come to discuss with you the problem of Germany, America and the occupation . . ."

"No," interrupted his brother. "You've come to chase me out of a house."

"That among other things, but not only for that purpose," said Frank. "And what's more, I'm going to do it. I should have liked it better if you had not dressed up your irregularities, to use a polite term, in an ideological cloak. But since you suddenly insist on having a political conscience I should be the last person to deny it to you. For the moment, therefore, I will assume that you've told me the truth, George—the whole truth." He sought his brother's eyes and did not continue until he had found them. "How then do you explain that you are in touch with black marketeers and Gestapo agents?"

"Have you been spying on me?" asked George. His square skull was flushed.

"Maybe," said Frank. "It makes no difference how I got to know about it. The fact is, I know."

George replaced the white porcelain figure on the mantelpiece. He controlled himself quickly and said:

"Now you're only amusing me."

"I demand an answer," said Frank.

"You're boring me," said George, "and you're beginning to try my patience. First you come here and make me sick with your big-mouthed talk about army regulations and their observance or infringement. Now you're questioning me severely about my contacts with black marketeers and Gestapo agents. I could simply tell you to go to the devil, because you know as well as I do that I'm not authorized to discuss my job. But I'll answer your question: I am meeting black marketeers and Gestapo agents because I have been ordered to do so. Regrettably the Army has omitted to obtain Major Green's kind permission first—but it is busy building up an espionage organization with, if you must know, the help of a former German general and half the Gestapo. The fact that this has not been rubbed under your nose speaks, for once, for the discretion of our fellow-countrymen. And now that I have answered your questions be a good boy and run along home, and sob your grief over the wicked world into your army pillow."

Frank did not move. He was as white as a sheet and was doubtful if he had the strength to rise.

"Is this true, George?" he asked eventually.

"Why don't you ask Hunter of whom you have such a high opinion? Only don't tell him I told you."

"And you're lending yourself to all that, George?"

George shrugged his shoulders. He sounded condescending, almost pitying when he said:

"I told you you were living on the moon, Frank."

At last Frank rose.

"George," he said: "I want to ask you one thing."

"Yes?"

"Do you never think of Mama?"

"What do you . . . ?"

"These are the people who murdered Mama, George!"

"Why these?" said George. "Why not Herr Eber whose house you're defending? Why not the young girl about whose honor you seem so concerned?" He took a step forward and stood quite close to Frank. "And why not Elisabeth von Zutraven whose release you have engineered?" The name hung in the air for an instant, like the blade of a guillotine. Presently George continued: "You're not fooling me any longer, Frank. All your life you've tried to throw dust into my eyes. I was always the black sheep and you were the white lamb. But that's all over, Frank. Don't you dare ever mention Mama's name, d'you understand? I hate the Germans who have killed her. But I hate them all. And I take my revenge where I can. I ransack them and I humiliate them, and I sleep with their women, and if necessary I even join forces with them to squeeze them dry like a lemon and throw them away afterwards. America, and the Army, and your whole stale justice mean nothing to me, Frank. I have come here to avenge Mama, and if you're trying to stand in my way, why I'll . . ." He did not finish. He turned away from his brother and made for the door. "You'd better go now," he said, "before I forget myself."

And Frank went. He picked up his greatcoat and cap in the dark hall, and a moment later he was outside in the cold January night.

As fast as his legs would carry him he walked through the snow-covered avenue down to the Isar. He was feeling ridiculous: the correct Major Green, always concerned about law and justice, who had set out to expel his brother from an improperly requisitioned house, and who had been chased out of that requisitioned house like a whipped dog. He knew too that he would not have made such an ignominious exit if he had been absolutely certain of being in the right. That was the worst of it—not being absolutely sure of one's position. He knew George, but perhaps this very fact was dangerous, for knowledge meant also prejudice. Since childhood he had never attributed to George any motives other than selfishness and greed and egotism. Had George taken him by surprise and was he still motivated by what had always motivated his actions, or had he just seen a new George, or perhaps one who had never quite been as Frank had seen him?

But it was not just George. He, Frank, had believed in the war, almost as if it had been a holy war; he had believed in the country which had first offered asylum to the young man and then lent him arms to fight the holy war. Frank knew quite well that the holiest of wars still was a dirty business and he did not deceive himself by denying that he, too, had been soiled by the craft of soldiering. But what George had said was obviously not a lie, nor an invention on his part: while an American soldier was still not allowed to sleep under the same roof as a German, man or woman, fine threads were already being spun not only to the Germans, and not only to the Nazis among them, but to the guiltiest of the guilty, to the informers and murderers. How was he, the grotesque Major Frank Green, to keep his sanity if he remembered how he had had to cajole and trick Colonel Hunter into releasing Colonel Sibelius, when the same Colonel Hunter had instructed his brother to enrol yesterday's spies and agents into the service of the victors? Frank had arrived in the occupied country convinced of the collective guilt of the Germans; yet from day to day he had been revising his preconceived judgment with a growing sense of happiness. And now, suddenly, everything seemed to point again to Germany's collective guilt, redeemed only by the collective guilt of mankind as a whole. The fact that he had spotted the weak points in George's argument offered little comfort —for instance the point that while revenge was human, or at any rate understandable, this did not mean that it was justified or that it would stand up under scrutiny. Or the point that any alliance with the enemy was questionable, even if it was destined to serve a subsequent retribution. And lastly the point that collective guilt, if indeed it existed, could not be punished individually, and certainly not to the personal advantage of the punisher.

He walked quickly through the deserted streets and reached the city center before midnight. When he picked up a car at the transport pool in the Ludwigstrasse, to have himself driven home, he knew no more than he had known when he left his brother's house all in a turmoil. But as he sat next to the driver in the open jeep, with the icy January wind whistling past his ears, it seemed to him as if the wind were carrying to him the rhythm of a long-forgotten poem by Walt Whitman. That the lines should now be rising up from the deepest depths of his subconscious mind was a mystery to him and a miracle. "To the States or any one of them, or any city of the States, Resist much, obey little . . ."—thus ran the first lines, and that was all he could remember. But the words, and even the letters, were to Major Frank Green like steel pitons driven by daring climbers into the sheer rock-face, to enable other climbers to get a secure hold when benighted in the mountains. He did not know to whom he ought to resist much, or whom to obey little; the confusion in him and about him was still too great. But one thing he knew: that he would resist and not yield to the confusion.

Mrs. Hunter Is Jealous

The weather was warm, almost springlike, as Colonel Graham T. Hunter drove to the station to meet his wife and children.

Betty will get the wrong idea about the Bavarian climate, the Colonel thought.

He wanted to feel nothing but expectant joy, but he was unable to dismiss the worries which had been weighing on him more and more during the past few days.

"Operation Family," launched a few weeks before, had, as far as he could judge, been a failure—possibly the most disastrous mistake in occupation policy. Complaints and unfavorable reports prepared by psychological warfare officers had been piling up on Colonel Hunter's desk.

Whether it was in the nature of things, or whether the American women now pouring into Germany were to blame for it—the occupation music, hitherto sad and majestic, grim and discordant, now took on a frivolous note. The uniforms of the victors, always clean and freshly pressed, and of first-rate material, had nevertheless been uniforms, and the contrast between them and the ragged uniforms of the repatriated or the gray, shabby clothes of the civilian population had at least been bearable. But between the clothes of the occupation women, conspicuous and with an air of elegance even if they came off the peg of some American department store, between their cuban-heeled and high-heeled shoes, their smart handbags, their colorful scarves and their fur coats on the one hand, and the flat-heeled, worn shoes of the German women, their threadbare colorless overcoats and their gray felt hats—that contrast was violent and provocative. The American women were groomed in a way that required much time and extensive cosmetics aids, and even if they wore their lipstick and rouge with moderation they still looked like fashionable mannequins disporting themselves among the destitute and homeless.

Together with the American women their cars had arrived, sleek Chevrolets and Fords and Buicks in all kinds of glittering colors—back home the natural appurtenances of middle-class comfort, but here fantastic symbols of undreamed-of luxury. The jeeps and command cars and light trucks of the Army had aroused the admiration of the vanquished, as part of that American mechanization in which the Germans saw one of the reasons for their defeat; the vehicles of the American women, however, became provocative splashes of color in the grayness of the German scene.

The Army, moreover, belonging as it did to a country where male achievements are pre-eminently put at the service of the women, had provided facilities for the wives of the victors such as the victors had never claimed for themselves. In several towns "Commissaries" had been set up, shopping centers for American families. These had been located in public business premises, so that the starving populace could look through the wide, glittering shopwindows into a wonder-world of plenty. Bottles of sterilized Danish milk were piled up in tall pyramids; there were dewy-fresh lettuces from the south, tender pink hams and even brilliant oranges—a fruit which many German children had never seen before and which they thought was a strange kind of rubber ball. In Berlin some thoughtless commanding officer had set up one of these Commissaries in a suburban Underground station, right in the middle of the platform, so that the public hurrying about their fruitless occupations could press their noses against the brightly-lit plate-glass windows while waiting for their few and irregular underground trains. There was probably no deliberate provocation, only thoughtlessness, in the way the victors' wives emerged from these Commissaries into the wrecked streets, carrying enormous brown paper bags which alone would have aroused envy and anger even if they did not nearly burst under the colorful load of unlimited luxury.

The requisitioning of houses, too, was now proceeding at a faster rate. Entire squares, blocks and residential quarters had to be vacated overnight to make room for family reinforcements. The Germans had always been a patriarchal people, and in their homes the defeated men had yet remained victors. Nothing, therefore, could hurt the pride of a German more than the order to pack up his belongings and clear out of his home, with his wife and child, just because the accommodation was required for foreign women and children.

Needless to say, the feminine element—to wit, the American women—did nothing to mitigate the hardships of "Operation Family." Men, aware that success and victories are achieved step by step, through struggle and compromise, are more ready to realize the frangibility of their achievements; their pride in their triumph is nearly always tempered by a realization of its dubiety and impermanence. The victors never took their victory quite literally; but the women, taking more pride in their menfolk's victory than the men themselves, frequently displayed tactless arrogance. The soldiers, even though hatred and contempt for the enemy had been inculcated into them, yet preserved a certain respect for the vanquished—especially since most of the occupation officers and GI's early in 1946 had been fighting troops not so long before and had wrested their victory from the opponent with much effort and many sacrifices. But the women had never known the opponent; they only knew the defeated.

Even in the British and French Zones the latent tensions were exacerbated by "Operation Family," although these foreign women, who had themselves passed through the hard test of war, clashed less conspicuously with their new surroundings. In the American Zone, at all events, the operation redounded to the detriment of the conquerors. Just because the psychological national costume of the women of different countries differs more strikingly than that of the men, everything foreign now gained a new poignancy. And because anything strange is apt to seem ridiculous there developed a crisis of respect. The American women had a new part to play as the representatives of victory in a strange land; but they were familiar only with the part of ruling their own husbands. The victorious soldier pushing a baby carriage with his wife idly strolling by his side;

the master of the house bringing his wife her early morning cup of coffee in bed; the soldier pushing a chair under every female's bottom; the officer eclipsed by a mountain of parcels while his wife drives his car—these strange and ludicrous customs could not exact any respect from the Germans, and while they hated the feminine invasion army more than the masculine one they acknowledged with malicious pleasure that there existed human beings who could humiliate the conquerors into the role of vanquished, right under their eyes.

All this was very much in Colonel Hunter's mind as his car pulled up outside the wrecked Munich station and as he made his way to the platform where the military special from Frankfurt was due to arrive in a few minutes.

Hunter spotted his family at once in a window of the almost empty train. Betty was holding little Beverley in her arms. Behind the woman, with a tiny flower-decked hat on her richly curled gray hair, was the pretty dark head of fifteen-year-old Ruth and the fair cheerful boyish face of seventeen-year-old Bob.

The Colonel's driver had rounded up an army of porters to deal with the luggage and Hunter was able to devote himself fully to his family, principally to Beverley who was not yet four.

It was she who held all his affection. The sentimental phrase that you could tell from a child's looks if it was a child of love proved entirely false in the instance of the golden-haired blue-eyed little girl who had been born twelve years after her sister and certainly more than twelve years since love had sneaked out of Colonel Graham T. Hunter's marriage, like one of those wedding guests whom one remembered vaguely only from the wedding-day photographs. Beverley had been born during the war and Hunter had spent no more than a total of a few months in her presence, yet he loved this angelically beautiful child, who might have been his grandchild, with a tenderness he had never shown for his two elder children. To Beverley, of course, her father was a stranger, a courteous gentleman in a smart uniform with countless gaily-colored ribbons on his chest and with a curious bird on his shoulders. The more was the Colonel delighted when the child instantly took to him and settled herself on his knees with cheerful familiarity.

Betty Hunter possessed that extraordinary faculty of most American women of not finding anything unusual. While Ruth and Bob were plying their father with innumerable questions, Mrs. Hunter's frameless spectacles turned only casually towards the windows of the car which was making its way through the ruined city towards the Isar at the moderate regulation speed. She reported about their crossing aboard the "General Brooks," a not uncomfortable troop transport, about their bumpy flight to Frankfurt and their uneventful train journey thence. She conveyed the regards of friends, relatives and colleagues of her husband's, and already appeared to view the occupied city as one of those "military posts" into which to move and from which to move was the natural fate of a soldier's wife.

"I hope you'll like the house," said Hunter. "As I told you in my letter, it's spacious, and the garden should be very pleasant in the summer. I've left it to you to find a maid; I've only engaged a children's nurse. And I'm sure you'll like old Paula who's been looking after me."

"A maid?" said Mrs. Hunter. "Is that necessary?"

"We are entitled to a staff of three," said the Colonel. "They're paid by the Army." He was glad that Betty had asked no further questions about the children's nurse.

The car had crossed the Isar and climbed the Giesinger Berg, and was now swinging into Grünwalder Allee.

"Not much damage here," said Betty.

"No, we're lucky," said Hunter. "Very lucky in fact, because this whole district—it's called Harlaching—is shortly to be requisitioned by the Army. Most officers will have to move out here."

Harthauser Strasse, into which the car had now turned, seemed to illustrate the Colonel's words. American trucks were standing in front of several houses, unloading furniture, refrigerators, lamps and sacks of coal or firewood. Now and again there was a small handcart on to which the ejected owners were stowing their possessions.

The Colonel would have preferred the drive to have taken longer. For several days now he had regretted employing Marianne von Artemstein, but he had been reluctant to cancel the arrangement. His anxiety over the forthcoming meeting between his wife and the young countess grew more acute as the vehicle approached its destination.

The gate was open, the car swung into the drive and came to a halt by the front door. Beverley, tired out by the long journey, had fallen asleep in her father's arms. By the time he got out carefully with his youngest child, Ruth and Bob had jumped from the car.

In the hall Paula, the housekeeper, and Marianne were awaiting the new arrivals.

"That's our Paula," said the Colonel.

Betty gave her a nod, reserved but not unfriendly. Paula greeted her new mistress courteously but not without some suspicion.

"And this is Fräulein von Artemstein," Hunter made the introductions. "My wife . . ."

For a moment the two women measured each other in silence. Marianne was a good head taller than Mrs. Hunter. She was wearing the simple suit in which she had first presented herself to the Colonel, a summery attire no longer appropriate to the cold season. With her deep-black hair brushed straight back, her absence of make-up, and her clear white skin she nevertheless looked like a hostess politely welcoming a guest in the hall, whereas the short woman with the overflowing curls under her cheap flowered hat, with her aging face all-too-carefully made up, wearing a clumsy and mediocre fur coat, was standing before her almost as if applying for a position. The Colonel's discomfort increased to acute embarrassment. He stood there, the sleeping Beverley in his arms, awkward and apart. He wanted to break the silence but no words occurred to him.

"How do you do," said Betty eventually. "Do you speak English?"

"Yes I do, Madam," said Marianne.

"That's fine," said Betty without shaking hands with her.

Now Marianne woke from her immobility. She stepped up to the Colonel and gently took the sleeping child from him.

In the course of the afternoon, which he had taken off to celebrate the event, Hunter came to regret Fräulein von Artemstein's engagement more and more. Without showing any signs of fatigue Betty, experienced in the organization of new homes, had taken possession of the house which the Colonel had occupied by himself for more than six months. It seemed to Hunter that she made no distinction between the cook and the nurse: she was giving both of them her precise and explicit instructions. Before Hunter could raise the subject she had instructed Marianne to take her meals with Beverley in her room, while the family would have their meals somewhat later in the dining room. Although there was nothing unusual in a mistress making her own dispositions in her private domain the Colonel had the feeling that the children's nurse was watching him with pitying sympathy. Betty, Hunter's junior by several years, made him realize his own age in the presence of the younger woman; he thought that during his past encounters with Marianne he must have acted as her coeval, for why else should her glance be traveling with impertinent astonishment between him and his wife? But what surprised Hunter most was that his growing resentment was directed not against the beautiful intruder but against the woman with whom he had spent a whole lifetime and whom he had long been looking forward to seeing again. He thus spent most of the afternoon with Bob and Ruth, strolling with them through the house and garden, giving them a hand with their unpacking, and mustering just about enough interest to listen to their tales.

During dinner Hunter kept asking himself whether he was imagining things: if his conscience was anticipating his conscious mind or if Betty was really acting queerly. She seemed to show no joy, however restrained, over the end of their prolonged separation; several times she relapsed into a broody silence, and finally pulled the children up more sharply than was her usual even-tempered way.

Left alone with her after dinner, when Hunter attempted a more cordial note over their habitual evening glass of whisky, he realized at last that he was not a victim of his imagination.

Marianne had knocked once more and inquired if there was anything else; Mrs. Hunter had coldly told her that she would not require her any more. As soon as the door had closed behind the young woman she turned on her husband.

"How long has she been in the house?" Betty asked.

The Colonel looked at her in amazement. "Since this morning," he said.

"And how long have you known her?"

"She came to present herself for the first time last summer," Hunter replied with growing astonishment.

Betty, who had put on a housecoat, lit a cigarette before the Colonel could give her a light. She smoked seldom and drew at her cigarette in the manner of the inexperienced smoker.

"I don't want her," she said.

"What have you got against her, Betty?" asked the Colonel, not allowing his irritation to show.

"I just don't like her," said the woman.

"Isn't that a rash judgment?"

"No. I want her to leave tomorrow."

"Well," said Hunter, "it won't be easy to find a replacement for her."

"There must be plenty of German girls who'd be glad of something to eat."

"Sure. But even the position of children's nurse in the home of the Chief of Intelligence is a confidential post. The file of Fräulein von Artemstein was under examination for several months."

"I can look after Beverley quite well by myself," said Betty. "After all, it's nothing new to me."

"As you please," said the Colonel. "If you really think . . ."

He was thoroughly disgusted at his own weakness. Nevertheless he raised his glass and said:

"To our new home, Betty!"

Mrs. Hunter took a little sip at her glass.

"You must ring up Daisy MacCallum first thing tomorrow," said Hunter. "She only arrived a week ago." He was talking about the General's wife. "Ted has been particularly pleasant to me of late."

"Ted's always very pleasant if it costs him nothing. Is he getting his fourth star soon?"

"I suppose so," said the Colonel.

They were facing each other in front of the fireplace. And as their conversation moved from one indifferent subject to another it seemed to Hunter as if a glass partition had been erected across the room. He had not expected any passionate scenes of reunion: they had both quietly reconciled themselves to the fact that their marriage had become a meeting place of common interests, a playground of their children, and a resting place through habit—but the very frankness of this realization was also typical of their understanding affection. But Hunter did not experience that affection now: instead of a cheerful, if not exuberant, reunion there appeared to be cold reserve, and perhaps even hostility.

Suddenly there was a lull in the conversation. Betty had left Hunter's last question unanswered. Instead she said:

"You've nothing to tell me, Graham?"

"I don't know what you mean."

"I'm surprised at your bad taste, Graham. At your bad taste, if nothing else."

"I really must ask you, Betty, to explain yourself."

"You need not have established your mistress in our home. Or is that the local custom?"

The Colonel leapt up.

"Betty!" he said. He could not utter anything else.

The woman lit another cigarette. Her lips were trembling.

"It wouldn't surprise me, Graham. There are sensational stories circulating back home, about conditions out here. Having a mistress seems to be good form; after all, everybody knows that a German woman will sell herself for a pack of cigarettes. The officers' corps seems to be behaving like a state convention of the American Legion. Your letters were very revealing. I ought to have been prepared for it."

"Now that's enough," interrupted Hunter. "You're making accusations without any justification at all."

Betty felt in the pocket of her housecoat. She gave a short bitter laugh.

"It's almost a joke that I should find this during my first hour here. I wasn't being inquisitive. It was in a book on your bedside table." She passed him the envelope. It contained, as he instantly realized, Marianne von Artemstein's Christmas greetings.

He did not extend his arm; the letter remained in his wife's hand.

"And what's that supposed to prove?" said Hunter. "I think I might be entitled to a little more trust. Fräulein von Artemstein sent me a book for Christmas. That's all."

"Does a nursemaid in this country send a Christmas present to her prospective employer?"

"Nursemaid, nursemaid," said Hunter with mounting annoyance. "Nonsense! She is a Countess Artemstein and the daughter of a general. It was very kind of her to remember me at Christmas."

Betty got up.

"A countess and the daughter of a German general!" she said. "Just the thing for the Chief of U.S. Intelligence. Please, Graham, spare me further argument. It's all too obvious and too painful. I make no claims on your love, but I do not wish to be insulted in my own home. I don't want to see the countess at breakfast. Good night, Graham!"

For a moment Hunter did not know if he should detain her. Detain her for what? To convince her of the groundlessness of her suspicions?

To explain to her that matters here were not so simple, either in this or in many another case—that a nursemaid was not a nursemaid and a countess not a countess, and that standards, concepts and conclusions were inapplicable? Or to tell her that he did not intend to commit an injustice just because she was not yet acquainted with these standards and was drawing wrong conclusions?

But he let her go. He sat down in his chair by the window. Suddenly it seemed to him as though the house were standing alone in the night, as though there were not another house for miles and miles, not a human soul, not even a dog. He had thought that the strange surroundings would yield to the familiar faces. He had been mistaken. The familiar faces had turned strange.

The Commandeuse Flees to Berlin

Slowly and deliberately, with the ineluctable certainty of fate, the net was closing around Major William S. O'Hara.

He knew it, but he could not break free.

Dieter Griff, the former Gestapo boss, had taken the Major's protégée to his apartment that night before Christmas. He had done so neither out of sympathy nor out of conviction, but because this course of action had offered certain advantages too tempting to Griff for outright refusal. Griff occupied a couple of rooms in a Munich suburb, in Untersbergstrasse—rooms which he had occupied in better days—and since he was out for most of the day the commandeuse lived there, perhaps not quite as comfortably as in the Pasing villa, but in considerably greater comfort than she would have done in an American military prison.

O'Hara visited her only rarely, and then with the utmost precautions. On these occasions Griff would discreetly disappear and leave his apartment to the couple. These visits, risky in spite of all precautions, had become an indispensable necessity to O'Hara. On his earlier visits he still tried to recapture the role he had played since his first encounter with the ex-commandeuse. But Irene Gruss immediately realized that his attempts were not meant seriously, and that he was now in the grips of a passion which had all the charm of novelty. She treated him like a prisoner.

That February evening in 1946 the Major had crept into the house as early as seven o'clock. Griff had left a few minutes previously; Irene and O'Hara were alone as usual. He had drunk heavily during the day, a habit he had lately been getting into, partly to dull his senses and partly to give himself courage for his risky visits. He had brought a bottle of bourbon with him and was now sitting opposite Irene Gruss in the living-room. It was a strange room and provided an exceedingly odd and uncongenial background for the commandeuse's rendezvous with her lover. Throughout the war the bachelor Griff had practiced his profession in foreign countries, from where he had returned with countless trophies: not perhaps the scalps of the men who had been dispatched into the hereafter on the basis of his denunciations, but souvenirs of a more harmless character such as fake oriental carpets, Turkish daggers, embroidered Serbian shawls, a bronze Eiffel tower complete with thermometer, and a hideous copy of a Rembrandt from Holland. It was in this museum that O'Hara and Irene Gruss were now facing one another: she on the divan covered with an African rug, and he in a wing armchair which Griff had purloined from a French house furnished in the empire style.

"Griff wants to talk to you," said the woman. "You're to wait for him."

"What's he want?"

"You must get that scrap metal collected from Lindau at long last."

"And how does he think I can swing that? I can't send another truck out to Lindau just yet."

"Griff doesn't care how you do it. You've managed to do it twice and you can do it again."

"I won't be blackmailed by Griff!"

"You're just a coward," she said calmly. "He can easily find someone else to do it."

O'Hara drained half a tumbler of whisky.

"You're defending Griff," he said, glassy-eyed. "You sleep with him!"

The woman knew at once what O'Hara was after. He had come to wrestle with her. He had nothing to lose in the contest: if he stayed on top he had a chance of humiliating her, and if he succumbed he would taste those pleasures which he had discovered rather late but which he now sought the more eagerly.

"You sleep with Griff," O'Hara repeated. "You're not trying to tell me that you spend your nights without sleeping with him."

"What business is it of yours if I sleep with him?" said the woman.

"After all, you haven't even got the guts to get me out of here. This hole is getting me down."

"I'll get you out all right," O'Hara said weakly.

She rose. She was wearing her prim gray dress with the white collar. She put her hands on her hips and said:

"You'll never get me out. You're too yellow. You can't even get hold of a truck. At first I hated you, Bill; then I despised you. And now I don't even despise you. One doesn't despise a piece of dirt. I don't even feel like punishing you."

She knew that this was his cue.

"But I want to be punished," said O'Hara. "I didn't get the truck. I haven't got you out of here." He advertised his failings as if they were virtues.

She turned away from him.

"Go away," she said. "I'm not in the mood."

He got up, reeling.

"I don't want to go," he said. "I want to be punished."

She was still not looking at him.

"Say: 'I'm a yellow pig!'" she commanded, suddenly turning to him.

He said: "I'm a yellow pig."

"Say: 'I'm a yellow American pig!'"

"I'm a yellow American pig."

"Say: 'I request to be thrashed!'"

"I request to be thrashed."

"On your knees!"

He sank down on to his knees.

Slowly, savoring every minute, she sat down in the empire arm-chair which he had occupied. She stretched out her leg towards the kneeling man.

"Shoe!" she said.

He took her shoe off: a heavy clumsy shoe, suitable for winter wear, which he had bought for her at the PX.

"Fetch and carry!" she said.

Still on his knees, he took the shoe between his teeth. On all fours he approached her. Then, as she took the shoe from him, he turned round. He was following a well-established rite, almost as if he were going through some ancient pagan ceremony of which he knew every detail. On his hands and knees he really looked like a big red-haired dog. She began to beat him with the shoe. She had got hold of it by the toe and was hitting out at him wildly. She was following no ritual—only a rhythm which grew faster from second to second, from blow to blow.

"Say you want more!" she hissed through her teeth.

"More, more," he whined.

With the shoe in one hand she stood up and, in addition to hitting him, began to kick him as well.

She was now in a frenzy. The border line between the detached, deliberate humiliation which she had intended, so as to bind him to her and appease him, and her own lust—first eclipsed by her fear and now waxed stronger than her fear—was obscured. Mistress and slave, flagellator and flagellated became one in the perverted ecstasy which allotted the parts in such a way as to ensure its passionate renewal.

Half-raising himself under the blows the man was loosening the belt of his uniform trousers when the scraping of the key in the lock sobered them up suddenly and icily. The woman dropped the shoe and slipped her foot into it. The man straightened up, with a purple flush on his face, and hastily buckled on his belt.

Griff entered the room without knocking. As always, he was wearing his black leather coat. He had no hat and his hair was wet. His pockmarked face was even paler than usual. Without a word he sat down on a low stool by the octagonal Egyptian coffee table. He did not take his coat off.

O'Hara, expecting an attack and anxious to ward it off in advance, said:

"I haven't been able to get the scrap metal collected yet, but I'll . . ."

.He did not get any further. Griff interrupted him:

"We'll discuss that later." He pointed to the commandeuse. "You've got to get her away from here. The lid's off. They're on our track."

O'Hara turned white. The contrast was strikingly abrupt: the blood vanished from his red face and pallor, like a leper's, spread over his flat features.

"You've been watched for weeks, O'Hara," said Griff. "You must have been completely blind not to have noticed it!"

"How do you know . . . ?" stammered the Major.

"My contact man with the Americans heard of it by mere chance. A captain told him that his brother was in charge of the investigation."

"Green . . ." said O'Hara.

"Correct," said Griff.

"What shall we do?" asked O'Hara. He cut an even more pitiful figure now than when he had whined for punishment.

"That depends," said Griff. Again he pointed to Irene Gruss. "I could hand her over to the MP's." He talked of her as if she were not present. "First of all, how much money have you got, O'Hara? I mean in dollars."

"On me . . . two hundred dollars. But . . ."

"It'll cost five hundred," said Griff.

"I can find that," said O'Hara.

"Very well. I'll get her to a friend of mine. He'll take her to Berlin tomorrow. He gets a hundred dollars for that. You will bring me the six hundred tomorrow morning."

"I thought you said five," O'Hara said weakly.

Griff got up.

"Five for myself. Get ready now, Frau Gruss."

But the man Griff, the former Gestapo official who believed himself to be acting with a lively sense of business and with confident prudence in making available to the hard-pressed American major and his mistress his now somewhat congested but still passable channels of former connections, had considerably underrated Major Frank Green, the man in charge of the O'Hara investigation. At the very hour when Dieter Griff, omitting not a single precaution, was taking the ex-commandeuse to her fourth Munich hideout, whence she would be spirited the following day into the former capital of the German Reich, the city now ruled by four powers, where hyenas prowled round the houses and carrion vultures screeched from the ruins—at that very hour Major Frank Green was aboard a converted bomber, flying to Berlin.

With merely the school learning that Frank Green had acquired in America's Army Intelligence Schools and that he had repeatedly applied in wartime practice he would probably have never got on Irene Gruss's track. Espionage work, by whichever country, was—as Frank knew only too well—one long story of frivolous deceit and skilful propaganda, of reckless incompetence and hushed-up fiascos.

Frank Green's special mission was moreover made more difficult by the fastidious consideration he had to exercise with regard to a fellow-officer who had not yet been convicted of an offense and who enjoyed a good reputation. There was also Colonel Hunter's explicit instruction that a scandal was to be avoided, if at all possible, and the need of first rounding up the wanted woman criminal and only then apprehending O'Hara. All these considerations put a brake on the Intelligence major's pursuit. At last chance came to his aid; it made Frank think that one could not really blame the writers of cheap spy-film scenarios—men who were as ignorant of the facts as they were endowed with a lively imagination—for making such generous use of coincidence. Success in espionage work was indeed, more often than the layman would believe, the exclusive result of highly suspect coincidence.

One such coincidence was the fact that one day in the "Mücke" Frank had made the acquaintance of ex-Corporal Josef Maurer. Since his disturbing encounter with his brother George, Frank had been determined to pursue his own function the more conscientiously the more he was convinced that invisible forces inside his own camp were diverting it into criminal channels. His visits to the "Mücke," where he had become a regular patron, had led him on to the trail of Dieter Griff, for whom a warrant of arrest was still out while in fact he had long been enjoying the protection of American Intelligence. Just as Frank was about to strike and arrest Griff he was informed by Josef Maurer—an agent for everybody and against everybody—that the former Gestapo chief maintained excellent relations with the Americans and that Frank would be wise to make inquiries about this privileged German with his brother or with Major O'Hara. Although Frank's surmise was wrong—he assumed that O'Hara's connection with Griff and the commandeuse had some political background not yet clear to him—he nevertheless concluded correctly that the Gestapo man was bound to be informed about Irene Gruss's whereabouts. The temptation of green U. S. dollar bills, which Frank supplied from his own pocket, proved too strong for Josef Maurer who, moreover, realized that any self-respecting agent must work for at least two sides. Thus, acting on Frank's behalf, he probed into the Irene Gruss case while at the same time sending Griff a well-rewarded warning. Arranging the facts a little in accordance with his own plans Maurer then informed Major Green that the commandeuse was already being harbored by a Gestapo agent in Berlin, a man named Jäckel, who was at present earning his living as a waiter in the "Mademoiselle" night club. If—calculated Maurer —Major Green were to bag the commandeuse in Berlin there would certainly be some commendation and reward for him, while on the other hand all danger would have been averted from Griff with whom the ex-Corporal was associated in other and far more important enterprises. Thus he put Frank on the right track, even though prematurely.

At a time when Irene Gruss was still only on her way to Berlin, Frank Green, equipped with a photograph of Jäckel, walked into the "Mademoiselle." Even before entering the night club, which was on the first floor of a half-wrecked building, Frank had seen a strange spectacle. Outside the house, which was not far from the Potsdamer Platz, a queue had formed—German men and women, and soldiers of the four victorious powers. The women and the few German men, used to queuing up for bread and milk and a piece of meat, stood in line patiently, queuing up for a small helping of entertainment. The troops had priority; they pushed the waiting women and civilians aside, so that some who had been right at the head of the queue would now have to wait for some time before the gates of "Mademoiselle's" paradise opened to them. Now and again a soldier would pick a girl out of the line of the dance-starved, and she would follow him without asking any questions.

At the cloakroom Frank witnessed an unusual scene. A British soldier insisted on handing in his carbine. He was waving the weapon in front of the aged attendant's nose, but she, though badly frightened and retreating a step or two, resolutely refused to accept it.

The dance floor was reached through an oblong, gilt-decorated outer room in which the tables stood so close to one another that Frank picked his way through with the utmost difficulty. The gilt splendor had crumbled off the walls of the old night club in many places, and at some spots even the white distemper had gone, but a resourceful management, unable to procure new paint, had covered the flaking patches with odd bits of red plush which now conveyed the impression of blood-soaked washing hanging out on a line. In the dance hall the cracks caused by bomb bursts were too big to be covered up with plush, and the walls here looked like stained sheets. From a minute hole just above the bar, which for some reason or other it had been impossible to plug, a fine trickle of sand drizzled into the restaurant. On the bar stood an ice bucket and into that bucket the dust was drizzling with the slow regularity of an hourglass. Whenever it was full of loose crumbly dirt the barman would take it over to a window and, without glancing down, tip it out into the street.

Through the fine curtain of dust Frank instantly recognized the former Gestapo man behind the bar. He was a tall square man with short hair and strikingly prominent ears; he looked like a shrunken robot. He was wearing a white jacket. He was dispensing red wine, but at the same time keeping an eye on the slowly filling ice bucket. Frank decided to wait for closing time—which, in Berlin, was nine o'clock, not ten—and to follow him then.

At last he found a seat, immediately by the band. It was playing noisily, the saxophone dominating, at a monotonously loud noise-level. It was playing tunes that had been fashionable a long time ago, the wreckage of songs from before the Third Reich with its ban on jazz. And since the clothes of the German men, the dinner jackets of the band and the evening dresses of the women looked as if they had been dug out of crates filled with old garments, Frank was suddenly reminded of the era of the silent film. The scene before him might have been a sequence from any silent film.

But on the dance floor, gyrating and milling, was a world unknown to the days of the silent film: the uniformed world of the conquerors. An American airman, fair and well-built, was pressing his cheek against that of a German girl whose all-too-rosy complexion, plaited hair and fat calves made her look like a malicious caricature of a German girl. A British sergeant insisted on grabbing a hurriedly passing waitress, whose gold-embroidered red uniform suggested a circus attendant, and whirling her around the unwaxed floor. A French officer demonstrated some new steps to a beautiful blonde twice his height, pushing the other dancers off the floor. The majority of the dancers were Russians. Majors with golden epaulets, privates in stained tunics, officers in full dress and sergeants in high boots, all of them covered with medals, were pressing German girls to their breasts as though everything had been forgotten: Stalingrad and the Ukraine, the siege of Berlin and the horrors of the summer. The Russian Army, which had fallen on Berlin ransacking, looting, brutalizing, seemed tamed: German whores and American jazz had conjured up sentimental smiles on the dull faces of the victors from the east.

At Frank's table there was a Russian soldier between two German women. The one, fair and plump, had put her hand on his right thigh; the other, dark and thin, had put hers on his left thigh. They were indifferent hands, suggesting anything but erotic passion. On his stained gray blouse the soldier wore five or six orders, including the Stalingrad Medal. He was dull with drunkenness; he was muttering disjointed Russian sentences and his left hand was plunged into the décolletage of the dark-haired girl with the brown eyes with shadows round them. She was taking no notice, almost as if her breast were a dead object, as dead as his short unclean fingers. Across the victor the two women were chatting about ration cards and housing problems.

"Frau Krahl and her three children are out in the street," said the dark one.

The Russian had found her nipple and was trying to take it between two fingers. She took no notice.

"He'll be under the table in a minute," said the blonde, smiling at the Russian as if murmuring some pleasantry. "Perhaps she could move in with the Schulze's," she continued.

"She mustn't leave the Russian Sector," said the dark girl, who reminded Frank of the undernourished plants in the sunless windowboxes of working-class tenements.

Frank lit a cigarette and passed the pack to the girls across the table. The blonde, showing the shyness often found in prostitutes when they are out of their element, began to smoke her cigarette avidly; the other let the cigarette slip into her handbag. The Russian was too drunk to notice the American's interference.

"Do you come here often?" asked Frank, just to start the conversation.

"Whenever I can," said the blonde.

"Always with Russians?"

"No; just as it happens," she replied factually. At the same instant she realized that this American major spoke German suspiciously well. She attempted a smile. "You speak German very well," she said.

Frank turned to the dark-haired one.

"And you?" he asked. "Do you come here often?"

"This is my first visit."

The blonde explained: "She was in a concentration camp. Half-Jewish. They killed her father."

Almost as though he had understood, the Russian withdrew his hand from the girl's décolletage. But he merely wanted to pick up the wine glass in front of him. He drained it. Then he fumbled again for the girl's breast, could not find the top of her dress, and with an angry snarl let his hand fall on her knee.

The blonde wanted to continue the conversation with Frank. She said:

"A pity there aren't more Americans here." Forgetful of the Russian-American alliance she continued: "The Russians are swine. They raped me fourteen times in one night. That was in the summer. They laid Rose on her back three times within an hour of her coming out of the camp."

"Shut up!" said the dark girl.

"Why?" asked the other. "Just because we go out with them nowadays? At least they've got to pay now." And turning to Frank: "Or should one be too proud? You wouldn't be all that proud if you'd been had fourteen times. . . ."

Frank did not know what to say. How could he know what it meant to be raped fourteen times in a night? He looked away and was silent.

"Wine," yelled the Russian. The passing circus waitress took no notice of him. Neither did the two girls. He was sprawling on his back between them, his arms dangling limply, like one of those string puppets that wave their arms and legs while one pulls the strings and which collapse limply the moment one lets go.

All this while Frank had been keeping his eyes on the bar. Now he got up and strolled over. He had to force his way past American, British, Russian and French rifles leaning against the tables. They were almost like the piled rifles on maneuvers or at roadblocks.

It was unbearably stuffy. The windows to the right of the bar, shuttered with wooden boards, were hermetically closed.

Frank pushed one window open. The sharp air of the winter afternoon flowed into the room, the incomparable, keen and bracing air of the city of Berlin. Only now did Frank realize that it was daylight outside. While men and women in the electrically-lit rooms had surrendered themselves to the illusion of night, a bright winter sun in a cloudless blue sky was sending his warming rays down on the tormented city. All round there was nothing but ruins. Of a tall department store across the road only one wall was left, and in the wide, oblong and empty windows the dirty black rubble lay several feet deep. The fragile letters spelling out the name of the store had, as so often happened, survived destruction; giddily they hung from the fourth to the third floor. There was almost something human about them—the two ends of the "M" dangled from the wall like the kicking feet of a man suspended high up from a window. In an open area—and most of Berlin's areas were open—next door to the department store, women with scarves over their heads were clearing away the rubble in buckets—a tragicomical endeavor, ludicrously puny compared with the scale of destruction. On top of the heaps of debris the children were building mountains, tunnels and castles; but their endeavors, too, were inadequate, for the sand of wrecked houses was not suitable for the building of sand castles.

The conqueror in American uniform was overcome by the misery. The ruined city with its walls without houses and its houses without roofs; the women below who seemed part of a Russian village that had marched into Berlin; the women in the night club whose shrill laughter rang in his ears; the provincial quietude of the wintry Reich capital and the hysterical noise of the jazz music behind him; the victorious soldiers drunk with victory and drinking victory away, using brute force against the innocent and fraternizing with the guilty; the hangover without awakening and the sobering-up amidst renewed drinking; and he himself, vacillating between revulsion and pity, satisfied revenge and unsatisfied justice—was there a way out, and if so where was it? The story of prostitutes being raped had been grotesque—but the girl from the concentration camp had been a specter. It was grotesque that he should feel so much more kinship with a German tart than with his ally in uniform—but the toiling women in the empty square reminded him of his mother. It was grotesque that the band should be playing while the sand was running into the ice bucket— but perhaps this dance of death was really a sign of new life, and perhaps the confusion existed only inside him, Major Frank Green, or Franz Grün of Munich.

He shut the window and turned back to the bar. He remembered his mission. An American major had smuggled a Nazi commandeuse to Berlin and entrusted her to the care of a Gestapo agent who was just now dispensing red wine behind the bar of the "Mademoiselle" night club. That was what would be called "a résumé of the facts." Perhaps it was just as well that there were facts, no matter how deep they were. Maybe the chance of doing right in a small way relieved one of the need to practice justice on a big scale.

Frank glanced at his watch. Almost automatically his hand went to his pistol, making sure it was still in its holster. He did not expect resistance. And anyway, what did they signify, these physical dangers, beside the dangers which this peace had brought about . . . ?

Elisabeth Finds Asylum

Dr. Adam Wild had been right in assuming that Elisabeth von Zutraven would not seek him out even if, as Major Frank Green had supposed, her way were to lead her to Munich. Not till February 24, 1946 did Adam meet the wife of the man on trial for war crimes at Nuremberg, and even then it was a coincidence—if there are such things as coincidences—that brought them together.

Adam had been summoned, not for the first time either, before the American Military Court which was going to hear his case on a charge of "insurrection, acts of violence against a member of the occupying forces, and infliction of grave bodily harm." So far the indictment had not yet been framed and, although Adam had already been questioned four times about the same incident, he was evidently going to be interrogated for a fifth time.

As it happened, only a propitious fate saved Adam Wild on that cold and crisp winter morning from getting into fresh trouble; his already considerable string of misdeeds might very easily have been increased by a new, aggravating offense.

That morning Adam had visited several patients who all lived in the Schwabing district. The epidemics expected with certainty for the winter of 1945–46 had almost miraculously failed to materialize; but the past few days had witnessed a rapid rise in the incidence of sickness and there was still an alarming shortage of doctors and medicines. The Munich Health Authority was advertising in all papers for "politically nonincriminated doctors," but Adam had not come forward—partly because the idea of having to undergo a test of political reliability, on top of all the medical examinations he had had to pass, was distasteful to him, and partly because he was reluctant to take over, as no doubt he would have been obliged to, the practice of a politically incriminated colleague. In addition to which he was being kept busy enough by his own patients.

Finally, it had to be admitted, he was not an enthusiastic physician. He would not even have readily agreed that he was a good doctor. To be a great doctor, a man possessed with his profession, he lacked the necessary conviction of the infallibility, or at least the adequacy, of medical knowledge. With that sobriety which is the enemy of professional genius he realized that the easing of physical suffering did not mean much, and certainly not everything, while on the other hand he had too much respect for the mysteries of the soul to try to approach them in a quackish way. During the war, most of which he had spent in a Bavarian military hospital, Adam had come to the conclusion that people did not know what was wrong with them; that pain was not always seated where they experienced it most clearly; that they did not suffer where they believed or pretended to suffer. And since even self-diagnosis, on which all medicine rests, failed so dismally Adam would not presume to claim that he could make any confident or helpful diagnosis for his part. If he was always pushing his nose into matters which were "none of his business" then it was chiefly because he believed that his patients were only partly sick in themselves and for the other part ailing of the world, and that medical specialization really began with the separation of a patient's individual pains from those of the community. If he had nevertheless devoted himself to his work with growing zeal during the past few months, indeed with much self-sacrifice, then it was mainly because of the challenge represented by the unnatural difficulties besetting the pursuit of his profession. It was no longer sufficient to put some Latin names down on a prescription form; one had to find out where the necessary preparation could be obtained. One would prescribe not whatever one considered indicated, but the next best thing that was in fact available. If it was a case of modern medicines such as sulpha drugs or penicillin, the general practitioner had to turn suppliant, briber or black marketeer and try to cadge these preparations by guile, low cunning or dulcet words from the magnificently equipped American hospitals.

Adam had arranged his rounds that morning so that his last patient lived not far from the Military Court. He was making his way there through Theresienstrasse, a street chiefly inhabited by lower-middle-class families, and it was there that he witnessed the scene which very nearly caused him to intervene and rush into new difficulties.

Outside a three-story house, next door to the Technical College, a crowd had collected to watch the depressing spectacle of the eviction of all the occupants of the building. Why this house, of all places, should have been chosen for requisitioning, a house the shabby walls of which still seemed to exhale the goulash cooked between them for the past decade and which was as surely inhabited by retired small officials as an emaciated body is by tuberculosis, was one of the unfathomable mysteries of the occupation. From the conversation of the gapers around him Adam gathered that the occupants had been given notice of eviction the previous evening and had been instructed to be ready to leave shortly before noon that day, to move out of their apartments into a roofless existence. The removal, designed to provide accommodation for DP's from Poland and Czechoslovakia, had been made considerably easier by the regulations of the Occupying Power: those evicted were not allowed to take with them anything except their personal clothes, a few kitchen utensils, and their stocks of food, if any. A dozen GI's were supervising the move which proceeded without opposition and with that matter-of-course discipline which comes natural to the Germans in any situation. Three or four farm carts were pulled up on the right side of the street immediately outside the house, and one of the occupants had even managed to round up a horse cab with an undernourished nag between the shafts —a curious and somehow symbolical black vehicle that had served in more peaceful times as a conveyance for funeral guests. Luckily, the DP's due to move into the building once the funeral cortege had left had not yet arrived on the scene; the authority of the State was represented by the American soldiers and there was, one would have thought, no source of friction that might supply the spark for a sudden rebellion.

There was no source of friction—at least not until the toys belonging to the children of one of the families were brought out. Until then the crowd—some twenty people on the opposite pavement—had watched the spectacle in silence. There was no revolt in this mob of shivering men and women, and there was not so much sympathy in them as fear and the disturbing knowledge that the same thing might easily happen to them the next day, suddenly and without warning. In this respect the crowd resembled those bunches of curious spectators which invariably collect outside a house where a death has occurred: partly glad that they do not belong to the mourners, and partly awed by the suddenness and the finality of demise. In the days of the Gestapo people had feared the ring of the doorbell, with anxiety even if their conscience was clear. It had been hoped that the "liberation" would free the law-abiding citizen of his "doorbell psychosis," but the ring on the door continued to be the symbol of fear: even though one's thoughts did not nowadays run to concentration camps and violent death, the ring at the door was still too often the overture to arrest, eviction, confiscation and homelessness. The ominous bell had tolled in the Theresienstrasse, and the crowd stood gaping, frozen with fear of a similar fate.

Then came the toys. A sturdy man of about forty, with a big mustache, every inch a family man, was dragging them out of the house towards the black cab which he had evidently secured through particularly useful connections. They were not very numerous toys: a toy kitchen, two dolls, a clockwork motorcar without key, and a rocking horse—all of them rather the worse for wear, with that nursery patina that inevitably marks one's favorite toys. He was followed by his little son, a boy of about four, a fair and rather pale child in clothes that were much too "grown-up" for him, just as one would expect a child to be dressed who was born in this goulash-pervaded lower-middle-class tenement and who would, in the normal run of things, end his life there.

His father had stowed the other toys inside the cab and was on the point of loading the rocking horse when an American soldier, one of those in charge of the removal, walked up to him and conveyed to him by word and gesture that he could not take the rocking horse with him because it represented part of the inventory of the apartment and had to be handed over intact to the next tenants. From the man's hesitation and the gestures of the soldier the crowd realized what was going on, but it only awoke from its torpor when a regular tug of war ensued between the owner of the rocking horse and the uniformed soldier for the miserable brightly painted object. To the one it was a matter of sentiment or perhaps of parental authority before his child, while to the other it may have been a matter of principle—in any event, the toy became the symbol of resentment hitherto suppressed by discipline. The father had got hold of the wooden horse's head and the soldier was gripping the wooden tail; like dogs fighting over a bone they pulled one way and another, the civilian determined not to let go and the soldier equally determined to take it away from the insubordinate German. The little boy was hanging on to his father's coat; he had understood the situation and set up a heart-rending howl. Tears of fury and fear, and possibly also of affection for his old toy, were streaming down his face—a circumstance which spurred the father to renewed efforts but made it more difficult for the confused, and probably ashamed, soldier to give in now.

It was at that moment that Adam Wild, whose indignation had reached boiling point, came very close to intervening—a very risky undertaking since two other soldiers had arrived to take a hand in the business and decide the fight by brute force. Adam had in fact detached himself from the muttering but still inactive crowd and taken a step forward when a strong arm brushed him aside. There were not many arms that could brush the giant aside like that and Adam turned in surprise. But then he was surprised no longer: a Negro soldier, evidently taking an idle stroll, had joined the crowd unnoticed by Adam—a man of about Adam's height but slimmer and with that stringy and muscular physique which betrays the champion boxer even under a suit and overcoat. As the Negro crossed the road Adam—now more knowledgeable in such matters—noticed the boxer was no ordinary private, but wore the silver bar of a full lieutenant on the shoulders of his dark-brown officer's greatcoat. With long strides, unhurried but resolute, the chocolate-colored lieutenant made for the contestants, caught the rocking horse at its middle and with a single movement snatched it from the two men who staggered backward like drunks.

Neither the protagonists nor the spectators knew at once what had happened. The civilian believed that the Negro had decided the issue against him; the soldier thought that support had come for him from an unexpected quarter; and the people on the far side of the street were completely bewildered. Only the little boy, seeing his toy disappear between the huge black hands, began to sob even more loudly; a moment before he had almost calmed down, but now he was crying with renewed vigor.

The Negro did not say a word. He put the rocking horse down on the stone pavement, picked up the kicking and struggling child and, with a simple and tender gesture, sat him down on the wildly rocking toy. The American soldier, supported by two of his colleagues, tried to argue. From Adam's side of the street one could not hear the colored officer's words—but it was clear that he was not having any argument and calmly and confidently relied on the weight of the silver bars on his shoulders. In the end the soldiers withdrew with a shrug.

The Negro bent down to the child on the rocking horse. The tears on his cheeks were soon dry. He laughed. The Negro, crouching with bent knees, gave the horse another push and sent it rocking. Now they were both laughing, the boy and the Negro. Then the officer straightened up, picked up the child under one arm and the rocking horse under the other, and loaded them both on to the waiting black cab.

It was at that moment, just as he was about to hurry on since he was by then late, that Adam became aware of a woman by his side who had watched the scene with bated breath and now heaved a great sigh of relief.

"Elisabeth!" said Adam. "What are you doing here?"

"I'm just out for a walk," said the woman, shaking hands with the doctor.

"What I meant was: how long have you been in Munich?"

"Since Christmas."

"And you didn't come to see me?" He took her arm. "Unfortunately, I've got to go to the Military Court just now. But you come along and keep me company. They aren't going to keep me long."

Brooking no opposition he piloted her along. Outside the Court building he stopped.

"I've got to have an urgent chat with you, Elisabeth," he said. "You must not escape me now. There's a café across the road—or a place that ironically calls itself a café. You sit down in there and wait until the gentlemen in their great mercy let me out again."

He was gone before she could argue. An hour later he returned triumphantly.

"Managed to slip through the red tape this time," he said. "My evidence was taken down, and then they let me out again."

"Tell me, what have you been up to?" asked Elisabeth.

"Nothing very special," said Adam. "Something rather like that business back there with the Negro lieutenant."

"And didn't it warm your heart?" said Elisabeth. "I wouldn't have missed that for anything." Suddenly she stopped short. "Don't misunderstand me, Doctor . . ."

He looked at her questioningly. "Why should I misunderstand you?"

She dropped her eyes and nervously fidgeted with the sugar caster on the table before her.

"I understand that the people must clear out of their homes," she said.

"Oh?" said Adam. "And why should you find that understandable?"

"Think of the thousands of people that we threw out into the street," she said. "Only we sent them straight to prison or to the concentration camp."

"And that's a reason for requisitioning rocking horses?" said Adam. "Surely this nonsense has got to stop some time."

"Yes—but we've only been saying this since our defeat," said Elisabeth.

"Quite a few of us said so long before that," retorted Adam. "Besides, the injustice of it worries me only to a lesser degree. But unfortunately it has the effect of an acquittal. Of course you're quite right: the Allies can't do anything that would even be half as horrible as the things that were committed by this country. But what do you think the people who witnessed the incident in the Theresienstrasse, before the Negro intervened, were saying to themselves? The others are no better either—that's what they are thinking; at least those of them who are conscious of any sense of guilt at all. The injustices of the victors obscure the guilt of the defeated—that is what I'm complaining of, my dear Elisabeth, just as I am wholeheartedly convinced that we shall be going to the devil unless we spontaneously admit our past crimes. A moment ago you asked me what I'd been up to that got me into trouble with the Military Court. Well, whatever it was, I have since harvested all kinds of applause from the wrong quarters—I feel like climbing up the walls in the face of that applause and all that misunderstood solidarity. I have as little sympathy for the crooks who have ruined us as ever I had —and I blame the conquerors not for their more or less understandable misdeeds but for their colossal stupidity in failing to realize they are playing into the criminals' hands by depriving a child of his rocking horse."

He stopped abruptly. He blushed—a thing he did only seldom—and the realization of blushing made his face even redder.

She said: "Please go on, Doctor Wild. It does me good to listen to you. I haven't had anyone to talk to me like this for months."

He looked at her in surprise.

"To turn one's eyes away from a cripple is not considerate but inconsiderate," she said. "People turn away 'considerately' when they hear my name. But that's not the worst. Nor, for that matter, are the humiliations. The worst is that people do not dare name the criminals when I am about. That is the misundertood solidarity you spoke of just now." She looked straight into his eyes and said: "Do you take me for a National Socialist, Doctor Wild?"

"I don't know," he said.

"Thank you for your honesty."

"That's no reply."

"There is no reply," she said. "But if you will listen I shall tell you a story."

"Of course," he said.

"It was in the summer of 1943," she began. "Zutraven was then Governor of France. I was in need of a rest. A lot of things had happened to throw me into confusion, and I wanted to get out of the country which my husband ruled with the help of French traitors. I went to some friends in Holland. There was no complete escape: after all, half Europe was ours. The Governor there, an Austrian, gave a reception in my honor—I couldn't get out of it although I thoroughly disliked that devil who always looked to me like a student who can't get through his exams. There, the wife of one of the officials on the Governor's staff told me that one could buy gold cheap at the Hague—a real bargain she said. Unthinkingly, just for the sake of conversation, I remarked that this was interesting—and the following afternoon that woman came to collect me in the Governor's car. Soon after we'd started driving I had an uneasy feeling: we were going through suburbs and working-class districts—not the kind of street where you'd expect a jeweler's shop. At last we pulled up in front of a red brick school building. The place was guarded by SS men. We climbed the stairs, past stuffed animals and glass cases full of butterflies, the woman leading and I following. I understood less and less. Then we entered a classroom. It was an ordinary classroom, with maps and botanical charts on the walls, with desks, and with a dais and a blackboard. On the desks, beside inkwells and inkpots, neatly arrayed . . ."—she broke off, pulled herself together, and continued—"neatly arrayed were gold teeth. Hundreds of gold teeth, Doctor Wild; perhaps thousands." Her voice failed her. Again she recovered control: "The order of it was diabolical, Doctor Wild. Some groups of teeth had been put together to form entire sets;

and there they lay in little semicircles, leering at me, the teeth of the dead Jews who had been gassed in the concentration camps. Price tabs had been tied to the sets of teeth, neat little tabs, and the prices were indeed amazingly low. The official's wife stood by my side, chatting with an SS officer about the prices, and quite unmindful of what was going on inside me. I ran from the room and tore down the stairs to the car—the woman barely managed to catch up with me—and in the car I broke down and cried, and the woman still did not understand what the matter was."

She interrupted herself as if she had been telling a story without a point, and as if she had only just realized that it had no point.

"And what did you do then?" asked Adam. He sounded severe and not at all encouraging.

"I flew back to Paris the same day. Zutraven was not at home. I drove to his office, demanded to see him at once, and faced him. 'Did you know that?' I asked him. 'Does the Führer know that?' He laughed. 'You're living on the moon,' he said. 'You can't make an omelet without breaking eggs.' Those were his words. Eggs he called them, the millions of murdered people."

"And then?" said Adam. "What did you do then?"

"You know what I did then, Doctor Wild."

"I only know the rumor about your famous scene with Hitler."

"That was not decisive. But then, what was decisive? I did not leave Zutraven; I did not flee the country. I did what I considered right—and I don't know if it was right." She seized Adam's hand. "Please believe me, Doctor Wild—and I think you do believe me— that I did what I could. I prevented half a dozen trainloads of Jews from being deported from France. I sheltered French Resistance fighters. In the end our entire household was made up of men and women of the Resistance. I know how insignificant it all was compared with the scale of the monstrosities of which the men in Nuremberg—including Zutraven—now disclaim all knowledge . . ."

"Elisabeth," said Adam, "I do not propose to investigate whether you did right or not. It is not for me to do so. But will you answer me one question?"

"Yes."

"Are you really saying that until the summer of 1943 you did not know what was happening in the name of all of us?"

"I did not want to know, Doctor Wild."

»216«

She looked at him as if awaiting judgment.

"We did not want to know," he said after a little hesitation. "And what's worse, we still don't want to know." He did not let go of her hand and continued suddenly: "I have one more question, Elisabeth, and I have a reason for it; it is important that you should answer it."

"Go ahead."

"Early in the war I went to see your father. It was about an old lady, a Jewess. Your father had been a colleague of her husband's. She was your neighbor: Frau Grün. I asked your father to intervene with you on her behalf. Zutraven was Reich Commissar at the time. Did your father's intervention ever reach you? Did you do anything about it?"

Frau Grün. The dead woman's name hung in the air of the empty unheated café, like a ghost at a spiritualist séance, visible and yet invisible, invisible to some and almost tangible to others.

Elisabeth released Adam's hand.

"Why are you asking?" she said.

"It doesn't matter," he said. "Will you give me an answer?"

She still did not reply.

"You know what happened?" she asked in the end.

"Yes," he said. "She died in the concentration camp, of angina pectoris."

She said: "My father came to see me. I went to Zutraven. He told me Theresienstadt was a transit camp where Jews were being assembled prior to their emigration. He promised me that Frau Grün would receive preferential treatment."

"She did," said Adam. "She was not killed. She was allowed to die a natural death."

"That is all I did," said Elisabeth.

Tears were running down her cheeks. She did not seem to be crying, for her body was motionless and even her face was motionless. Only the tears were streaming down her cheeks. She made no attempt to quell them or to dry them. It was not even certain that she knew she was crying.

"Franz Grün is looking for you," said Adam. "That is why I too was looking for you."

"I know," said Elisabeth.

"Well . . . ?"

"I don't want to see him."

Adam put some money on the table.

"Let's go," he said. "Come along with me. I should like my mother to have a talk with you!" He took her arm, almost roughly.

As they stepped out into the street he asked:

"Where do you live?"

She attempted a smile, but it somehow slipped off her face.

"Just as it chances . . ."

"You can stay with us," said Adam. "A divan has just become vacant." When she tried to argue, he added: "We'll see about it. But first of all you've got to talk to my mother."

"About Franz Grün?" she asked, on the defensive.

"Perhaps," said Adam.

"It's no good," said Elisabeth. "It can't be undone. What happened to his mother will always stand between us."

"I know," said Adam. But he also knew that she had given herself away.

The Governor Gives a Party

Colonel Hunter, who knew little of women and their unpredictable reactions, found it difficult to understand that Betty yielded almost without opposition when, on the morning after her arrival, he informed her that he was not prepared to meet her demands.

"I am sorry, Betty," he had said over breakfast, "but I do not intend to make a fool of you or of myself. Moreover, I do not wish to perpetrate a palpable injustice. I shall not dismiss Fräulein von Artemstein."

What the Colonel did not suspect was that Betty Hunter was glad to hear him say so. She had regretted her rash words of the night before. Throughout the many years of their marriage Hunter had given her no cause for mistrust, and she felt ashamed for having allowed herself to give such a violent expression of lack of confidence on the first doubtful occasion.

Sober considerations had now gained the upper hand. If the children's nurse was her husband's mistress then he could continue their adulterous association just as easily, or more easily, outside the four walls of his home. He would, thought Betty, have given in to her request if he had had something to conceal.

On the other hand there was that strange Christmas letter. No doubt everything that was being said in America about the German women who were out to capture American men, and about the ease with which the Americans became their quarries in the occupied land, was entirely true. Nevertheless, once her first anger had evaporated, there awoke in Betty her latent feminine instincts. These instincts told her that nothing had occurred, or that nothing had occurred yet, between her husband and the countess and that her arrival had nipped the danger in the bud—at least for the moment. There could be no doubt that the intentions of the German woman who had wormed her way into Betty's home were of an immoral character. But there was in Betty Hunter something of the spirit of the wives of the American pioneers who knew how to protect their menfolk against all sorts of dangers. The idea that her husband might be the seducer, however timid, never occurred to her; he could be nothing but the seduced, and it would be her duty to shield him against seduction. To accept defeat was not in accordance with the traditions which Mrs. Hunter represented. During that first sleepless night in the strange house Betty had come to the conclusion that she had not spent a hard and frequently joyless life by Graham's side only to let the first pretty face turn her to flight. She was a soldier's wife, accustomed to careful judgment of strategic possibilities, tactical ratios of strength, and the potential of both sides' arsenals. The other woman was young and beautiful, at home in this country, and probably determined to go all the way. But she, Mrs. Hunter, represented victorious America, home, family, the past, and probably also the future. It was therefore wiser to keep an eye on the enemy—for that, without any doubt, Marianne von Artemstein was—than to force a premature decision. She had been prepared to effect a tactical retreat when the Colonel relieved her of the necessity.

Hunter knew nothing of these calculated and at the same time typically feminine considerations, but he followed the subsequent developments in his home with growing astonishment.

Betty displayed a strange behavior, one that was quite new to the Colonel. She would appear at breakfast with her hair carefully done and her face made up—a thing she had not done for many years. Several times during the day she would ring him up, for no particular reason and just to make some friendly inquiries. For the first time in years she was more concerned with his personal comfort and welfare than with that of the children, on whom all her attention had been focused in the past. What struck him more forcibly than anything was that she never asked any reproachful questions about his position or his unpromising chances of promotion. If within the privacy of their matrimonial bedroom her caresses were confined to the measure that had long been the measure of their married life, she nevertheless displayed in public—within the limited public sphere of her home— a degree of affection which he had missed for years, or, more correctly, which he had gradually forgotten to miss.

Marianne von Artemstein for her part took up the gauntlet with an equally instinctive feminine gesture of opposition. Whether she had ever been out to conquer the Colonel, her troops were certainly re-deployed now and were facing those of Mrs. Hunter. As far as this was possible without discourtesy or disrespect she entirely ignored her employer and devoted herself wholly to her mistress. She gave patient and skilful German lessons not only to the children but also to Betty; she showed Mrs. Hunter round the city and its surroundings; and she opened up for the American woman, who was eager to make pur-chases, a number of unusual sources by bringing into the house dealers offering leather shorts, stein tankards, Munich dolls, Nymphenburg porcelain, loden raincapes and all sorts of Bavarian delights. Much to the Colonel's discomfiture and disappointment—for he shut his eyes and ears to such barter trade—the countess knew how to use packs of cigarettes, PX coffee and scrip dollars in a mildly illegal manner, never for her own benefit, but in a way that made the various collections which Mrs. Hunter had embarked upon with a newly discovered enthusiasm grow to considerable scope in a short space of time.

The Colonel, who had long tired of his mode of existence and had unrebellingly resigned himself to it, now found himself to his grow-ing amazement in the center of subterranean female intrigue, and he would not have been a man if he had not tasted of the muddy, turbu-lent and disturbing, but at the same time refreshing and rejuvenating waters of being the object of such wooing.

His changed personal circumstances were brought home to Hunter with particular force that evening. Dressed in his best uniform, wear-ing all his decorations, he was sitting in the drawing-room, casually flicking over the pages of the *Stars and Stripes*, while Mrs. Hunter was upstairs getting ready for an evening out. Lieutenant General Theo-dore E. MacCallum, Military Governor of Bavaria and Hunter's im-mediate superior, had invited them to a dinner party at Schloss Seehöhe, his private residence, and Betty was now getting into her evening gown. In this, as Hunter was well aware, she was having Marianne to advise her in every detail of corsage, jewelry and make-up, and when she finally stepped into the drawing-room—rather late, which was unusual for her—the Colonel was speechless at the elegant and, as it seemed to him, transformed and rejuvenated woman. Had it not been that Marianne, her lady's wrap over her arm, had entered on Betty's heels, Hunter would undoubtedly have voiced his delight in a compliment—but in the presence of the children's nurse he could not bring himself to do so. With some irritation he realized that he was in fact acting like a man anxious to spare his mistress's feelings.

Only when they were seated in the car, which carried them through the winter evening towards the Starnberger See on whose shore stood King Ludwig's historic castle which now served the Military Governor for his residence, did the Colonel make up for his omission. With shy affection he took his wife's hand and told her how very pretty she looked in her dress.

All the windows of the castle were brightly lit and dozens of army vehicles were drawn up in the big courtyard whose stone-carved glory still reflected the days of the mentally unhinged and romantic Wittelsbach king. It was by no means strange that this castle, with its crenellations and turrets, its wide flight of stairs and its many winding staircases, its vast halls and dungeons, the petrified dream of an extravagant and art-loving king, should have become the Court of an American general; for the castle, curious though it seemed to the late king's countrymen and indeed to most Europeans, was entirely in line with the ideas which MacCallum and Americans generally had of romantic Europe.

Several dozen guests had turned up for the General's "buffet supper"—an occasion that was remarkable not only for its scale but also because this was the first time that the General had invited Americans and Germans together. The General and his wife received their guests at the door of the vast, much too heavily gilded, much too brightly lit and altogether much too regal drawing-room: the General in full uniform with eleven rows of brightly colored ribbons on his immense chest; his wife—out of an intended gesture of courtesy but somewhat grotesque in the effect—in a black silk dirndl, a stylized version of the local national costume. Mrs. MacCallum kissed Betty on both cheeks

»221«

and paid her a genuine compliment, which sounded false only because of its formulation. The two ladies, as far as was possible with their different ages and very different origins, were in fact good friends. Daisy MacCallum, a stately blonde, now in her late thirties and her husband's junior by fifteen years, was the daughter of a plantation owner from the South, one of those "southern gentlemen" whose families had saved a considerable fortune from the Civil War and had come without a scratch through the horrors of the emancipation of the slaves.

The General shook Hunter's hand. They had passed out of West Point at almost the same time and the General always felt a little guilty that Hunter, only two years younger than himself, was still only a colonel while there were three pretty silver stars on his own shoulders.

"Glad you could make it, Graham," said the General. "But your day's work never seems to come to an end. Berlin's been trying to get you over the army wire twice already. Let them know you can take the call now. The Lieutenant here is going to show you to my study. Have a good time," he added, as he was turning to another couple to welcome them; "I'll be seeing you."

The Colonel followed the Lieutenant to MacCallum's study while Betty attached herself to some other Army wives.

Daisy MacCallum, as all the ladies ungrudgingly agreed, was a first-rate hostess. And indeed this party, which reflected so clearly the contrasts of the occupied country, needed the guiding hand of an exceptional hostess.

Apart from the American officers and their newly arrived wives, those present included chiefly the members of the recently established Bavarian Government, and some members of the Bavarian, Prussian and Silesian nobility who enjoyed the special favor of the General and Mrs. MacCallum. The American officers in their smart, but to German eyes rather civilian-looking, uniforms; the Bavarian Ministers in their ill-fitting dress suits; the officers' wives in white or pastel-colored tulle dresses which, though evidently new, had a small-town air about them; the women aristocrats in black silk, tasteful but old-fashioned; a great deal of genuine jewelry about the necks and wrists of the defeated women; very little jewelry, and that mostly paste, in the décolletages of the victorious women; Mrs. McCallum, finally, in her rustic attire—

this was the picture that some contemporary artist might have immortalized under the caption of "Occupation, 1946."

It was up to the hostess to smooth with a skilful hand the unspoken tension that vibrated beneath the music in the royal reception room.

In a way the American officers and their ladies felt superior to the German guests, and yet they moved uneasily and racked by a sense of inferiority among the counts and the princes, the Serene and the Most Serene Highnesses. At the same time, the German guests were not at their ease either. A Prussian princess, for instance, had come primarily in order to make the acquaintance of a certain lieutenant colonel who was in charge of granting Germans exit permits. An Austrian count had accepted his neighbor's invitation in the hope that this new social contact might save his house on the Starnberger See from being requisitioned. Many wearers of coronets were simply hungry and thirsty. Among the guests there was even a member of the Bavarian royal family, a descendant of the king who had lost his life in the Starnberger See; with a little luck the prince might have been the host in this gilt-laden house, and he was clearly making a deliberate effort to conceal his embarrassment at the paradoxical situation behind a large dose of charm.

Both sides were trying hard to act as naturally and unconstrainedly as possible, but on both sides these endeavors failed in the face of the continuous struggle for dignity. The republican conquerors were just as unwilling to admit that titles and names made a very great impression on them as the Germans were to admit that they had come to the party chiefly for opportunist reasons. This desperate clinging to one's own dignity resulted in mutual malicious, though never voiced, criticism. The German noble guests derived much quiet satisfaction from the ignorance which the Americans displayed on historical matters—a subject that was almost unavoidable in the setting—while the Americans noticed with much malicious pleasure the barely-controlled appetite of the aristocratic guests. Political discussions about the late war were, of course, avoided since the German guests, no matter how innocent they might be personally, were still under the accusation of collective guilt and the Americans were too conscious of being hosts to remind their guests of their nation's disgrace. If the talk, as was occasionally inevitable, happened to drift to the Third Reich and the war then recourse was made to certain well-tested conversational clichés—the remarks, for instance, that Hitler had ruined his own nation as much as the world, or that it had been lunacy to blow up those splendid bridges on the autobahn at the very last minute, or what a happy thought it was that this fine cathedral or that should have escaped destruction. Harmless subjects on the whole, and matters on which one could agree without difficulty.

Perhaps the only person who was perfectly at ease was Walter Wedemeyer, proprietor of the "Mücke," owner of a summer house on the Starnberger See, himself neither an American, nor a member of the Government, nor an aristocrat. He owed his invitation to the circumstance that a senior officer had one day introduced him to the General to whom he had shown some of his conjuring tricks. The General had immediately fallen for Wedemeyer hook, line and sinker. His interest went considerably beyond mere admiration for the king of amateur conjurers: he was seized by a passionate wish to take up conjuring himself and he jumped at this opportunity of learning the magician's trade. Although most conjurers invariably guard their tricks and ideas as strict professional secrets, this particular defeated magician had been quick to realize that to share at least part of his illusionist sleight of hand with the victorious general might be sound business. Since then Wedemeyer had appeared at King Ludwig's castle twice a week, complete with a little black suitcase, to give private conjuring lessons to the Governor.

That night then, it was Wedemeyer who was to provide the highlight of the party by giving a conjuring display—including his most exquisite turns which were still unfamiliar to his keen disciple. In the meantime he had made himself useful by providing four excellent musicians who were now playing dance music in the big reception hall. The music and the dancing relaxed the tension: the officers' wives, mostly from provincial cities in the American South, were delighted to be dancing with the bearers of unbelievably ancient names, and the noblewomen were not all averse to swaying in the arms of the uniformed, brawny young savages from Texas, Nebraska and Georgia.

At the buffet, where the culinary miracles of the Army were piled up in generous mounds, Hunter and MacCallum again ran into each other.

"Did you get your call from Berlin?" asked the General.

"Not yet," said the Colonel. "Something wrong with the line. I've left word with the operator that I'm available here."

The General, whisky glass in hand, nodded. "If I may snatch you away from the ladies," he said, "I'd like a few words with you."

Hunter followed the General to his study, which adjoined the large drawing-room and whose white-painted gilt-stuccoed double door stood half open.

The General pointed to a chair by the large ebony-lacquered writing desk.

"Telephone at your elbow," he said.

Hunter sat down. It struck him that the field telephone, a handy instrument in a leather case, contrasted oddly with the antique furnishings.

"There's never time for anything at the office," the General continued. "I' e been wanting to talk to you for days about this so-called Denazification Law. I presume that you understand the new instructions—because I can't make head or tail of the thing."

He paced with long strides up and down the room. He was a man of about fifty-five. His chest, which looked almost like an oak chest, was adorned with countless decorations, which the general had won in hotly contested tank battles. He had gradually come to look like a tank himself. It had been due chiefly to military reasons that he was made Governor of occupied Bavaria: his tanks had thrust into Germany from the south, and nobody had seen any reason why he should not be entrusted with the political administration of the country he had conquered.

To know that MacCallum was in Germany was, moreover, a source of reassurance to many Americans, especially back home in America, for the General was a national hero and the subject of many military legends, legends which drew ever fresh nourishment from his colorful personality. Rough and noisy, but also jovial and a good colleague, MacCallum made extensive use of the privilege of American generals to wear any uniform they pleased. His subordinates had long been amusing themselves by guessing the costume that Ted would display the following day. That evening he was in regulation pinks with dark green blouse, but over it he wore a Sam Browne belt—a smart and impractical outfit from the first world war, as worn by that immortal hero, Pershing.

"What's the point of this law?" began the General. "We ought to put a thousand of the bastards up against a wall and let the rest starve to death. Just picture what would have happened if that lot had won the war! I should have been strung up on a street lamp long ago and you would be serving a life sentence. But what are we doing? In Nuremberg we go on trying them till judgment day, and now I'm supposed to set up 'Denazification Tribunals' manned by Germans who are then to 'administer justice' to other Germans. If you ask me, the gentlemen in Washington have rocks in their heads, if they've got anything in their heads at all. Remember the fuss there was when I made the Germans from Dachau march through the concentration camp a few times? But by God, we ought to make a few thousand Americans march through that camp every day so they get rid of their goddam humanitarianism."

Hunter had been listening attentively. Looking out past the marching and countermarching general into the drawing-room he could see the buffet with the greedy guests crowding around it. For a moment he was tempted to ask the General if this was the way he intended to let the Germans starve to death. But instead he only said:

"I don't know, Ted. Maybe they think they know what they're doing in Washington. I'm glad of the chance to talk to you. I'm supposed to dig up that General Stappenhorst now, the man who was in charge of their Eastern Counterintelligence. He has even been assured of immunity. Do you believe the Russians are going to stab us in the back?"

"It's quite possible," said MacCallum, continuing his tank-like advance through the study. "God knows I wouldn't have minded. I was just nicely in my stride when those idiots pulled me up—I could have gone right on to Moscow. For all I care the thing can start again to-morrow—after all, those Bolsheviks are no better than the Nazis. But I don't need help from that army of cripples! All the Germans want is to get the Russians to rebuild their houses for them and to steal their carpets back again. Of course, Germany today would be an ideal deployment area since there's nothing left to smash up—but I wish they wouldn't expect me to go to war with that wreck of a Wehrmacht on my side."

"But I shall have to set up those so-called Denazification Tribunals, if we like it or not," Hunter said soberly.

"That's one of the things I wanted to talk to you about," said MacCallum. "Set up anything you like, but spare me the details. Above all, I don't want any softies on those goddam tribunals who'd whitewash every German again in no time. I don't care if you pick on a lawyer or a streetcleaner, but I want to see men who're not afraid to act tough."

"I get you," said Hunter. In the other room the band was playing again. White organza and well-pressed uniforms and ancient dinner jackets flitted past the open door. Hunter asked: "About this General Stappenhorst . . . ?"

"I don't want to know anything about him," said MacCallum. "If I had my way I should have pulled that bastard in long ago and strung him up on the nearest tree. I've simply passed on to you the instructions which those armchair soldiers in Washington sent me; it's they who have picked on him. Do what you like; I don't want to have anything to do with the dirty business." He came to a halt. "By the way, Graham, I've recommended you for promotion. Naturally, I can't tell what the Pentagon people will do about my recommendation: maybe they'll think you've smelled too much powder and have a blackened face, and they'd rather send me one of their own lily-skinned experts. But in my opinion you ought to have had your star long ago, and my name's not MacCallum if you don't get it this time."

"Thanks, Ted," he said.

"Nothing to thank me for, Graham," said the General. "For one thing you deserve it, and for another I'm acting in my own interest." He laughed. "I'd rather have a brigadier do all this nonsense for me. I'd like it even better if they made you Governor at once; then maybe I could go home and turn the heat on those bastards back there. At home, at least, there's still some work to be done; over here I shall soon have nothing to do but throw dances for the krauts." He turned towards the door. "Well, I've taken up enough of your time. By the way, don't miss the magician—he's a great guy. You'll fall flat on your ass when you see his tricks!"

With a wave of his hand he left the room.

Hunter was unable to follow him at once. A warm wave was flooding over him. General Graham T. Hunter! The long-buried dreams rose up again. They had been buried alive, and out of fear to see them dead, ultimately and finally dead, he had kept away from their tomb. Now they were beating against their coffin lid, anything but dead. Ought he hurry out into the big room where the couples were now swaying in waltz time, to seek out Betty and tell her what the General had said to him? Or had he better keep the great news to himself so as not to shake her out of her resignation which he had lately acknowledged with something almost like gratitude? He was not sure that he would be able to resist the joyful temptation, but at the same time the old fear came on him again, the familiar fear of disappointment.

He was still wavering when the field telephone began to ring. He pulled the folding receiver from its leather case and answered.

"Is that Colonel Hunter speaking personally?" the army operator queried at the other end.

"Speaking personally," said Hunter.

"I've got Berlin on the line now."

Almost immediately, as he had expected, he heard the voice of Major Frank Green.

"Sorry to trouble you so late, Colonel," said Frank. "The fact is I've found Garbo." Garbo was their code name for the commandeuse. "She arrived here with some delay, but she is where we expected her to be. Only I wouldn't like to act without your instructions."

"What is it you want to know, Frank?"

"The connection between her and Gable has broken off." The second film star's name was their arranged code for O'Hara. "It's doubtful if we shall ever be able to prove anything against Gable if I pick up Garbo now."

"What d'you suggest?"

"I spoke to our office in Munich an hour ago. A few days ago Gable applied for an assignment in Berlin. We ought to pick up the two together."

"What guarantee have you that Garbo won't meanwhile slip through the net?"

"As instructed, I'm cooperating with Captain S. She's being watched day and night."

Hunter hesitated for an instant.

"Very well, then," he said at last. "After all, we can send Gable up whenever it suits us. Fly back here tomorrow morning and report to me. In addition to S. himself put his two men on the job as well."

"That's been done already, Colonel."

"Thanks, Frank. Look me up as soon as you get back."

"Yes sir. Good night."

"Good night, Frank."

He replaced the receiver but remained sitting at the desk. There was an uneasy feeling in him, as though his body temperature had suddenly dropped below freezing point. The O'Hara case! What effect would the O'Hara case and its inevitable scandal have on his promotion? One of Colonel Hunter's officers in league with a concentration camp commandeuse!

»228«

He turned to the door. Even before he reached it he had determined not to say anything to Betty about his conversation with Mac-Callum. By the door he stopped. In the big room the music had fallen silent. The guests were grouping themselves around the raised dais. On the dais a short dark man, who looked like a large plasticine figure, made his bow. The General gave the signal for applause.

Frank Green Hits Back

Martha Zobel had made some real coffee: the steaming pot stood on the table in the living-room. She herself, at the behest of her betrothed, had withdrawn to the bedroom. Around the neatly laid coffee table sat General (retired) Ferdinand Stappenhorst; the former Gestapo chief Dieter Griff; the former Lieutenant Colonel Wilhelm Gebauer; Helmuth Hueber, the former Gestapo chief of Budapest; and Obersturmbannführer Gerd Mante.

Colonel Zobel, as usual, was in his wing armchair by the window. In recent weeks this plush-covered armchair had increasingly become his refuge: an odd island amidst the turbulent seas roaring around him. All day long he would sit there with his back to the room, and behind his back—in the most literal sense of the word—unrolled the disquieting spectacle which he, his opposition worn down, had allowed to be enacted there.

Gerd Mante had not cleared out of the flat where he had found asylum several months previously. He had not reported to the Allied authorities. On the contrary, he had seized unlimited control of his future father-in-law's apartment. He occupied the Colonel's bed with Martha, and he had transformed the crowded living-room into an office humming with activity. Former Wehrmacht officers, Gestapo agents, SS men, and functionaries of the SD, the Security Service, walked in and out of Colonel Zobel's living-room, just as if it was right back in the war and the young Obersturmbannführer had set up his command post in Munich. Sometimes the strangers would arrive early in the morning, with heavy steps and bulging brief cases; in a rasping voice they would make their reports to Gerd Mante, reports of which the Colonel could not make sense, and a moment later they would hurry away again like company runners. In one corner of the room they would already be earnestly negotiating while in the other the Colonel, still in dressing gown and bedroom slippers, was hastily tidying up the sofa from which he had only just risen. Frequently Gerd Mante's friends would stay till late at night: they would sit at the table, bending over documents or arguing noisily and without constraint in an atmosphere that was thick with smoke. And the Colonel would sit by the window, his back turned on the room, staring out into the darkness—just as if he were no more than a portrait of the late Colonel Werner Zobel hanging deaf and dumb and forgotten on the wall of his former living-room.

His future son-in-law and his friends ignored him with respectful indifference or with impertinent tact. When a new visitor appeared—an almost daily occurrence—he would be introduced to the Colonel, but usually in such a way that the Colonel's name was uttered clearly while that of the visitor was mumbled indistinctly. Gerd Mante made no attempt to hide anything from him or to involve him in anything, and Martha, who had at first tried to kindle his enthusiasm, now treated him increasingly as an eccentric old fossil whom one might leave undisturbed so long as he in his turn did not disturb anybody.

Whenever he could the Colonel left the house, either to take long walks through the wintry city or to collect his meager rations from the empty and overrun shops. He would queue up for hours, chatting to the other people on the queue, and oddly enough these excursions became his only relaxation. Among the housewives, old-age pensioners and civil servants he felt again that he was a living particle of a suffering but real community of human beings, instead of being the spectator of a world of bustling ghosts. With what was left of the tenacity that once characterized the regimental commander he now clung to formalities: he insisted on eating nothing except his own rations, on smoking nothing beyond his own twenty cigarettes a month, and he refused to touch the real bean coffee whose aroma tickled his nostrils day and night.

On the evening in question the Colonel again kept himself aloof from the conference which was being held in his sitting-room. If the gentlemen around the coffee table occasionally dropped their voices and, in mutual accord, cast a furtive glance at the motionless figure in the wing armchair, their caution was quite unnecessary. The Colonel had long acquired the knack of not listening; indeed he would occasionally give a start when someone addressed him, so deeply engrossed was he in the subjects on which his thoughts had lately become fixed:

memories of genuine peacetime days and of the war, and visions of battles fought. Like specters on horseback they seemed to be galloping over the ruins on which he gazed from his window.

But the General, who as usual conducted the discussion, was not speaking softly out of consideration for Colonel Zobel, nor out of mistrust. To speak almost in a whisper was his habit, as though to intimate to his listeners that they could catch his words only if they kept absolute and complete silence.

He was a man of no more than forty, and one would not have thought him older in spite of an entirely bald head without even the usual shadow of lost hair around the top. He had a long narrow face which was almost as hairless as his skull. He had hardly any eyebrows, almost no lips and almost no ears. If the General had slipped a wig over his telltale bald head it would have been almost impossible to apprehend him even with the most exact and detailed warrant of arrest.

"Gentlemen," the General was saying, "our moment has come. Captain Green will probably turn up in the course of the evening. We are to move into our offices next week and start work in earnest. I have worked out a number of conditions under which we agree to set up a German Counterintelligence Service. The present state of affairs, needless to say, must come to an end. We have already rendered invaluable service to the Americans, and we must now make them realize the one-sidedness of our relationship."

There was a murmur of approval around the table. The General picked up a sheet of paper that had been lying on the table in front of him and began to read out his conditions:

"One: German Intelligence shall be under German control and shall employ Germans exclusively. Two: All decisions on matters of personnel shall be made by me alone. Three: All members of my organization shall receive immediate amnesty. Four: The organization shall receive a dollar appropriation, the sum to be determined later, and I alone shall decide how it is to be spent. Five: The work of the organization shall be directed against the East exclusively; it shall not be involved in any activity that might result in the defamation of Germans or members of nations associated with Germany in an auxiliary capacity, in respect of any acts or functions under the Third Reich." The General paused. "Do I make myself clear, gentlemen?"

The gentlemen nodded. Only Gerd Mante asked:

"Do you believe, Herr General, that the Americans will accept these conditions?"

"Of course," said the General. Over his naked features flitted a smile. "This is a case of, as it were, unconditional surrender. The Americans have no choice. They are facing a new enemy of whom they know next to nothing. The treasonable Roosevelt Government deliberately omitted to build up an Eastern Intelligence Service. Even if they worked hard at it for the next ten years, the Americans could still not set up a secret service that would be a patch on the German Intelligence I can create within six months. With your help, gentlemen, we can trace a considerable number of our old people and employ them in our service."

For a moment there was silence. Then Mante said:

"If you will permit me one other question, Herr General. Do you believe in a genuine change of heart on the part of the Americans? What guarantee have we that the Americans will not just exploit us and then chuck us out?"

"War with the Soviet Union is inevitable, Herr Obersturmbannführer," replied the General. "That is a thing that I know even better than the Americans. Naturally, an intelligence service without an army is as much of an absurdity as an army without an intelligence service. I should never organize my service for the Americans, or put it at their disposal, if I did not know that the Stappenhorst Bureau will, within a very short period, be part of the new German Wehrmacht. My guarantee is not the Americans, but the inescapable demands of our epoch. My guarantee is the Wehrmacht."

Among the men around the coffee table Gerd Mante was the only one who had not formerly belonged to the closer circle of General Stappenhorst's collaborators. He was the only one who occasionally ventured to interject a skeptical remark.

"I am not doubting your foresight, Herr General," he said. "I would merely point out that the so-called demilitarization is at present being pushed forward with renewed vigor."

The General slightly inclined his head, correctly and politely, as if to say that he was always open to intelligent comment.

"You must see matters in their wider perspective, gentlemen," he said. "America is a democracy ruled by the mob. That mob is at present urging the destruction of the German military machine. At the same time, the American mothers are clamoring for their boys to be sent home. Thus, by smashing the German Wehrmacht the Americans are disrupting their own military strength. The Americans, who won the war only because of their material superiority, can at a pinch afford the luxury of being the stupidest nation on earth—as in fact they are. We, gentlemen, must look ahead." He dropped his voice even further, though it hardly seemed possible, as a signal that he now required particular attention. "I have a theory of my own, gentlemen—I might call it the 'theory of roots.' A peasant may not be able to prevent the boots of brutal trespassers from stamping across his fields. All he can do is make sure that they do not tear up the roots of his crops. So long as the roots are intact there is a future. I have not the slightest intention—I don't wish to leave any doubt on this point—of doing the Americans a favor. What matters to me is the preservation of those roots from which, at some future date, the new Wehrmacht shall spring, and hence a new, strong and powerful Reich. Do I make myself clear, gentlemen?"

The gentlemen nodded and murmured.

"I pay unreserved homage to your concept, Herr General," said Mante. "Yet in the very spirit of that concept it seems to me important that we should keep our ranks free from all traitors, in particular the officers of the 20th of July and the saboteurs within the Wehrmacht."

The General frowned. There were three wavy furrows on his forehead.

"Herr Obersturmbannführer," he said, now every inch the commanding general, "if we are to work together then you must understand me aright." He did not say: we must understand one another; it was clear that Mante had to understand him. "We can have but one aim, and that aim is Germany. As far as the future Wehrmacht is concerned, we want to try to find friends and not to cold-shoulder any German soldier. The Occupying Power is doing its best to drive the men, who until the collapse stood aloof from us, into our ranks. We must learn to forgive. We want to offer a haven even to those who have found their way to us belatedly, and only under the effect of defeat, defamation and humiliation."

He rose abruptly and turned round. He had sat with his back to the window and to the Colonel's chair. With his back to Mante and his staff he was now addressing the Colonel:

"Herr Oberst Zobel," he said. "I don't know if you have followed our conversation."

The Colonel turned round and looked at the General standing before him. His only thought was whether he ought to stand up. But he was too tired to stand up.

"No," he said, "I don't think I have, Herr General . . ."

"Herr Oberst, I am appealing to you," said the General.

The Colonel got up and stood leaning against his red plush armchair. He did not want anybody to appeal to him. He had just been dreaming of that first winter in Russia. There had been black spots on the boundless expanse of snow. From afar one might have taken them for ravens in the white fields. But they were dead soldiers.

"Men like you, Herr Oberst . . ." said the General.

He was not allowed to continue. In the hall a woman's voice screamed. It was Martha's voice. The men around the table sprang up. The General turned towards the door. The Colonel seemed to have been turned to stone.

An American major, his pistol drawn, entered the room. Behind him appeared a lieutenant, followed by three or four American soldiers with their rifles at the ready.

"Hands up!" ordered the Major.

Automatically the men raised their arms. Martha, who had entered the room behind the soldiers, did likewise. She was leaning against the wall, white as a sheet.

The Colonel thought: there is something wrong here. Such scenes only occur in books; they never happen in real life. At the same time he felt a certain relief.

The Major stepped up to the General.

"Lieutenant General Ferdinand Stappenhorst?" he asked. He spoke German.

"I am he," said the General, not without dignity.

The soldiers were frisking the pockets and bodies of those assembled. Except for Lieutenant Colonel Gebauer nobody had any identity papers.

"My papers are in my bedroom," said Colonel Zobel.

"I don't need your papers," said the Major. "You can sit down." And to Martha: "You too."

"No arms," reported one of the soldiers.

The Major turned to the Lieutenant: "Take these men along." Turning to the lieutenant colonel he said: "You may go home, but leave your address." He was now standing in front of Zobel, replacing his pistol. "I would like a word with you alone, Herr Oberst Zobel."

The General had at last recovered from his surprise.

"What is all this?" he asked. "Is this a trap? Have you a warrant, Herr Major?"

"If you insist," said the American. From his breast procket he produced two pieces of paper. One of them he showed to Stappenhorst. He added: "The other is for Obersturmbannführer Mante."

"These warrants were made out in May 1945," said the General.

"They are valid," said the Major.

"The warrant against me has been withdrawn," asserted the General. "You can ask Captain Green in Intelligence, in the Ludwig-strasse."

"My brother has told me nothing of a withdrawal of the warrant," declared Frank. "Any such withdrawal would be in your file. Besides, you're being taken to the Ludwigstrasse."

"You'll pay for this," said Mante.

In silence the two Gestapo men put on their overcoats.

"I am so sorry," said the General, bowing slightly to Colonel Zobel.

The Colonel sat motionless in his chair, his hands gripping the arm rests.

Lieutenant Colonel Gebauer withdrew.

Martha was sobbing. She tried to follow Mante, but one of the soldiers barred her way.

"I'll be with you in an hour," Frank said to the Lieutenant.

When the door had closed behind the group Frank turned to Martha:

"I should like to speak to the Herr Oberst privately."

Still crying she went into the other room.

Frank went over to the window.

"If you'll allow me . . . ," he said. "Too much cigarette smoke." It sounded sarcastic. "Her Oberst Zobel," he went on hurriedly, "I don't have to tell you that I could have arrested you too. You have given shelter in your apartment to a group of conspirators, and moreover the war criminal Mante, for whom a warrant is out, even lives in your apartment. What have you got to say to this?"

"Herr Mante is my daughter's fiancé," said the Colonel.

"Do you know what Herr Mante is accused of?"

"He was an SS officer."

"Is that all you know?"

"Yes."

"Herr Mante took an active part in the atrocities of Oradour. He ordered innocent women and children to be shot. In Russia, two hundred prisoners of war were murdered on his orders." Frank shut the window. "The most shocking thing, Herr Oberst, is that you may really not have known it. Nobody has known anything in this country." He did not sound sarcastic now. He turned again to the Colonel. "What would you do, Herr Oberst, if I proved to you that what I have just told you about Herr Mante is the truth?"

"I should break off all connection with him."

"Is that all?"

The Colonel hesitated. "What else could I do?" he asked.

Frank sat down.

"What do you know about the men who were meeting here in your apartment?"

"Nothing much," said the Colonel. He rather liked the young major who spoke German with such a pleasant southern accent and who was obviously making no secret of his German origin. He said: "May I ask a question, Herr Major?"

"Please do."

"Did these men walk into a trap?"

"I don't know what you mean by that."

"I mean: were they beaten out of their hiding places under false pretenses so that they could all be imprisoned together?"

"Would you mind being more explicit, Herr Oberst?"

"Very well," said Zobel. "You were referring to a conspiracy a moment ago. I assure you, Herr Major, that I know nothing of a conspiracy. I am not saying this to exonerate myself. I had the impression that the gentlemen were employed by your . . . by the Americans."

"Is that what the gentlemen said?" asked Frank.

His question sounded so genuine that it made the Colonel sit up. For the first time that evening he did not feel weary. He began to understand why the major was treating him with consideration. He said:

"But of course. Did you really not know, Herr Major?"

"No," said Frank.

"I don't understand at all," said the Colonel, rising. "You mentioned that Captain Green is your brother."

Frank nodded.

"Captain Green has been walking in and out of this house for
weeks past," said the Colonel. "The money, the cigarettes, the curfew
exemption vouchers . . ." He broke off abruptly.

"Go on," said Frank.

The Colonel settled himself once more in his armchair. He looked
out of the window and was silent.

"You are trying to be correct, Herr Oberst," said Frank.

"It is hardly for me . . . ," said Zobel.

"That's where you are mistaken, Herr Oberst," said Frank. "It is your
duty to speak up. Whose side are you on? Those murderers? Or perhaps
the American secret service? For God's sake, Herr Oberst, surely a man
must know where he belongs."

The Colonel did not meet his eyes. He said:

"Who can tell today where he belongs?"

"There are more such people than you think," said Frank.

The Colonel was facing him again.

"Herr Major," he said. "You are a conqueror, while I belong to the
vanquished nation. You are wearing a uniform, while mine has been
trampled underfoot. But I am an old man, and you are still young. I
believe that you are honest. I will be honest with you, too. The
things that have been going in my home for I don't know how long
have made me sick with revulsion and made me blush with shame. If
these men had walked into a trap I should have drawn a little hope.
Perhaps the use of such a ruse would not have been quite the thing,
but we've got used to such methods. The worst of it is, Herr Major,
that it was evidently not a trap. I have an awful feeling that there has
been a mistake. I hope you won't mind my saying that I think you are
in a worse position than I." With every sentence he seemed to shed
more and more of his constraint; he spoke like a man who was at last
able to give vent to his pent-up feelings. "That pack of gangsters will
be free again tomorrow, Herr Major. I shall be facing a Denazification
Tribunal next week—and Herr Mante is employed by the Americans!
What you have done this evening, no matter how lawful, was an individual action. We know from the Third Reich what to think of individual actions. Can't you see, Herr Major, how hopeless everything

is? What are you going to say, and what am I going to say, when Herr Mante takes possession of my apartment again in the morning?" His long thin fingers made a resigned gesture. "You will probably go home, Herr Major Green. For you, all this will have been a nightmare the memory of which will gradually fade. But what about us? We've got to stay here, Herr Major."

"Please continue, Herr Oberst."

"What's the use of it?" asked Zobel. He got up again and began to pace about the room. "Just before you arrived General Stappenhorst was about to make me an offer. I don't know what it was going to be. But if Herr Mante is a free man again tomorrow or the day after I may well accept his offer. In fact I shall have no choice." He laughed briefly and bitterly. "As you so rightly say, Herr Major—a man must belong somewhere."

Frank got up.

"Let's put it to the test," he said. "I am extremely grateful to you, Herr Oberst." He did not say what he was grateful for.

The two men, the old colonel in mufti and the young major in uniform, stood face to face for a moment. Each waited for the other to extend his hand. At last Frank made the first move.

"Good night, Herr Oberst!"

"Good night, Herr Major!"

No sooner had the door closed behind Frank than Martha burst into the room. Her eyes were red with crying, but she seemed to have regained control of herself.

"What did he say? What did he want?" Anxiously she plied her father with questions.

The Colonel evaded her questions. The room was still full of tobacco smoke. He went to the window and opened it. Without turning to look at his daughter he said in a hard voice:

"Get my bed ready. I'm sleeping in my own bed tonight."

A Night without Ghosts

It was the last Saturday in February. Winter was still lying on the ground, but spring was in the sky.

Inge and Hans had left Garmisch-Partenkirchen at lunchtime. Hans was moving on skis: on his shoulders he carried Inge's skis, or rather

Karin's pair which he had borrowed, for Inge did not know how to ski. He was going to give her her first lesson that afternoon.

That night, when he had met her on the Isar bridge and seen her home afterwards, Hans Eber had been determined not to meet her again. He had always poured scorn on the philistines, but he had equally mocked those moralizing tales from the turn of the century in which people were forever saving the souls of prostitutes. His question when they should meet again had been no more than a polite gesture, rather out of place in the circumstances. Sunday afternoon, she had replied, she would be at home. If he liked he could come about four o'clock.

He had had no intention of keeping the appointment. But on Sunday at four o'clock he was climbing the creaking wooden stairs of the house by the Eastern Cemetery. She had sent her father out; they were alone. She had evidently expected him, for the table was laid for afternoon coffee. At first they talked merely to cover their embarrassment. She spoke about the nights of the bombing raids and he of the nights at the front. Both of them were matter-of-fact and free from self-pity—just two young people reminiscing, as in other days they might have been recollecting summer nights. Then she spoke of her mother who had run away from her father, and he mentioned his father who had left his mother for another woman. She did not know the name of Eber; indeed, he asked himself if she knew anything beyond the cemetery, the bombing nights and the whores at the Sendlinger-Tor-Platz. She listened to him, surprised not so much at what he said as at the fact that anybody was telling her anything at all.

When her father returned Hans left. Since then they would meet in small chilly cafés. They were so false with each other that they never in a single word referred to their first meeting and their first conversation, and yet so frank with one another that, hand in hand as it were, they skirted around that lie. One day, suddenly, they were calling each other by their first names, but he never thought of touching her and she feared the moment when she would have to shake hands with him on parting. Time and again they resolved not to see each other again, and time and again they broke their resolution. The greater the gaps were between their meetings, the more definite grew their fear that one day the thing would happen which they must not let happen; for the supreme hour of the first encounter between man and woman cannot be expunged from memory or banished from thought.

Hans did not know what made him suggest the weekend excursion to the mountains. "How about a skiing trip on Saturday?" he had asked her. The casual question was typical of the tender deceit which marked their relationship: he did not want to know that Saturday was the peak day in a prostitute's trade, and when with childlike delight she agreed to his plan she forgot for a moment to withdraw her hand from him.

About noon on Saturday they met at the station and took the train for Garmisch-Partenkirchen. Perhaps the only thing in Germany, during those winter days of February 1946, that was reminiscent of life before the war and before the occupation was the Saturday trains. The Allies set out on their gay weekends in their jeeps and special troop trains—but even though the only winter sport special that left Munich was composed of ancient rolling stock that seemed to burst under its load of fresh-air fiends; even though the clothes of the sports enthusiasts suggested a carnival procession; even though all eyes in the compartment were enviously and curiously turned on a man eating a piece of genuine salami, there was throughout a mood of gay abandon as though this train, bound for no practical destination, was evidence that life would come out triumphant in the end.

The days were noticeably getting longer. The snow was what skiers call "ideal"—crisp, powdery, not too deep and free from ice. It was resilient snow: the brilliant sun in the blue sky, far from melting it, seemed to be making it firmer. Like a cheerful group of white-capped pastry cooks around a vast cream-topped cake the Alpine peaks towered around the snow-covered valleys.

Hans put the skis down.

"Now you've got to try," he said.

"Must I really?"

"Well, I didn't lug the things up just for the fun of it."

Karin's skiing trousers and sweater were much too wide for Inge. Yet in her colorful garb—black trousers, yellow sweater, red scarf and pale-blue cap (her own)—she did not look in the least helpless or pitiful. On the contrary, she seemed amused at her own disguise, like a little girl who had dressed up in her elder sister's clothes.

Hans knelt down and fixed the skis to her boots.

"Now take the sticks," he said.

Swaying, she stood on the narrow boards.

"First of all, you've got to learn to walk," said Hans.

He took her hand and led her to a slope.

She proved a docile pupil, skilful and fearless, responsive to every hint and grateful for all help.

"Now try it by yourself," he said after a little while.

"But I shall fall down at once," she said.

"Don't worry—it won't be the last time."

She pushed herself off with the sticks and slid down the slope. Almost at once her skis refused obedience, described an "X"—and there she sat wriggling in the snow.

"Up you get!" he called out to her. "Try to get up by yourself."

He was only a few yards behind her, ready to help her up on to her feet in case she could not manage. But as his glance took in the girl and the sun and the snow a cold shiver ran down his spine and suddenly he did not know how and why he had come here. Reality seemed to him an apple cut in half—one half sound and fresh as the dew, and the other rotten and discolored and diseased. The girl in the snow, her cheeks flushed with fresh air and excitement, laughing at her own discomfiture with a pealing laughter of helplessness and enjoyment—she was real enough, like one half of the apple. But equally real was the other half—the prostitute who walked the streets in the evenings, soliciting Negroes, who took them home with her to the house by the cemetery, and who had one night stood on the bridge over the Isar. But I am not a philistine, he kept saying to himself; to hell with all philistines! But there was no comfort in this self-mockery. Besides, he had never been outraged by the truth: he was simply confused faced with both truths at once.

She had almost got up by her own efforts when he slid down to her to help her. He lifted her up with particular gentleness, brushed the snow off her and passed her his handkerchief. He acted with the tenderness of a bad conscience.

She did not notice anything. After a little more instruction she said:

"But this isn't much fun for you. Let me wait for you somewhere and you go and enjoy yourself on your skis."

"There's tomorrow," he said. "Plenty of time for that tomorrow."

They descended, half skiing and half walking, into Garmisch.

The charming little Bavarian town, with its angular streets, its wood-paneled houses, its figures of the Virgin set in niches, its steep gables and the gaily painted walls, resembled an American Army camp. The German visitors were lost among the hundreds of troops who had taken possession of this winter sports paradise. The doors of hotels and restaurants bore notices "Off Limits," "Prohibited to Germans," "Only for Allied Personnel." Munich, of course, was also full of such notices—on the doors of restaurants and public authorities, at the entrances to apartment houses and bars and on garden fences—but in the big city they did not seem so insulting as in this Bavarian village which showed hardly any traces of the all-explaining war, and which was as German in its architecture, its position in the landscape and its rural character as a girl from Hamburg, a poem by Mörike, a Rhine wine or a Wagner opera. The interdictory notices did not only make it difficult for the visitors to find food and lodgings—that, after all, was no different in the big cities—but they also gave them a sense of guilt. What?—they seemed to say—You Germans want to enjoy yourselves? Have you forgotten Hitler and the war, and your crimes, and your misery?

Hans and Inge eventually found a small restaurant near the station, where they sat down to a supper served for food coupons. They shared a table with six or seven other young people in the kind of exuberantly gay mood that comes after a day in the open air. Their cheeks were flushed, their ears were burning, and their carefree conversation was about the weather, the sporting achievements of the day just ending and the promising prospects for the next. Hans and Inge, too, were soon drawn into the noisy and cheerful argument; only rarely did Hans cast a surreptitious glance at the happily babbling girl at his side, and in her happiness—in which he must have had a good share—vanished his fear of the two realities. For him there was only one truth left.

Over supper they had been told that on a dead siding by the station there were several discarded railway coaches which some enterprising speculator had bought or hired, and where he now offered tired winter sport enthusiasts accommodation for the night—not perhaps in great comfort but nevertheless safe from wind and weather. Hans decided there and then to leave the restaurant early and have a look at this novel kind of hotel. As soon as he rose to pay he realized the true reason for his hurry: he had received the information with relief not because he had been afraid of having to spend the night in the open, but because he assumed that in this hotel-on-wheels he would be able to avoid being alone with Inge.

Even so there was an anxious silence between them as they emerged from the smoke-filled restaurant, heated with the exhalations of human bodies and steamy with the dampness of drying boots and skiing suits, out into the icy winter night. The moon was nearly full; the starry sky stretched brilliant and wide open; the white roads were bloomed with a ghostly blue, and the snow had frozen into rigid shapes. They walked side by side, towards the station: the young man with long strides, pretending confidence, the girl almost at a trot, slipping and stumbling in the skiing boots that were too big for her. They had avoided talking about accommodation for the night, and even now that the situation they had been afraid of seemed averted they still could not discuss it.

They had almost reached the station when the incident occurred that Hans had subconsciously feared for many weeks and that Inge had, for just as long, been waiting for in terror.

They were passing a small inn, one of the many with a notice "Forbidden to Germans," just as a group of Negroes left it. A bright yellow neon striplight shone above the entrance. There were five Negroes—three privates and two corporals, all of them giants with their caps askew, and two of them obviously under the influence of some warming alcohol. Perhaps it was simply that Hans wanted to give a wide berth to the noisy, singing soldiers, or perhaps it was an instinctive gesture—but with his free hand he caught hold of Inge's hand and drew her closer to him.

The sudden intimate gesture of the civilian out with his girl—a gesture invariably annoying to the womanless soldier in a foreign land—attracted the Negroes' attention, or at least that of one of them. They stopped. The tallest of the soldiers, a well-built broad-shouldered man of almost white skin-color, and entirely sober, reached out for Inge. It was not a vicious grab by any means, and not even provocative, and providing no cause for intervention by her protector. He simply spun the girl round so she faced the neon light and he could look at her more closely.

"Well, I'll be goddamned," said the Negro, "if this isn't Inge."

Inge did not understand what he said; she only understood her name.

Hans had understood. He let go of her hand.

The soldier was explaining something to his comrades, but he was speaking too fast and with the singsong intonation of the American South: Hans was unable to follow. The drunken soldiers, for their part, seemed to show very little interest in their friend's account; they were anxious to find another bar and, taking the sober man between them, moved off. The tall Negro waved his hand at Inge, called out after her something like "See you in Munich," and then the whole group reeled on, across the ice-glazed roadway, to a soldiers' bar on the other side.

For an instant Hans and Inge stood frozen into immobility. They did not look at one another. At last Hans moved on. He was walking slowly and she was following, always one step behind him. The confidence had gone from his stride and the gaiety from hers.

When they got there the station was in darkness.

"Hadn't we better take a train back home?"

"There isn't a train," said Hans.

They found the hotel-on-wheels. It was situated, or rather pulled up, a little way out of the station. They had to follow the line for a short distance, and then they had to cross a track. The hotel, 1946 style, consisted of three discarded third-class coaches. On the track by the coaches stood a corpulent man with his even more corpulent wife, selling "room tickets" in the way of a carnival barker making his pitch for the attraction inside the tent. Not many words were exchanged. The man thrust the tickets into Hans's palm and the woman climbed aboard the train with Inge and Hans, ushered them past several compartments and finally unlocked one of them. The stationary train was in darkness. Only through the grimy windowpanes, insofar as the windows were not just boarded up, did the pale, wan moonlight filter into the coach.

A moment later they were alone.

Inge sat down in a corner seat by the door. Hans took two blankets from his rucksack. One he spread on the wooden seat where Inge sat, and the other he kept for himself. He put the half-filled rucksack on Inge's seat, by the window, as a pillow.

They were still silent.

He lay down. He was lying on his back, his eyes open. The moonlight fell on his face. He could not see the girl: she was sitting in the far corner, in the shadow.

A couple passed along the corridor, laughing.

Hans closed his eyes. He lay like that for a while, as though asleep.

Then he heard the girl lying down. He could almost feel her breath now, for her head was quite close to his: only the narrow gap between the seat divided them.

Seen from the compartment door, he occupied the right-hand seat. His right hand hung down from the seat and he had the impression that her left arm was hanging down likewise. He kept quite still, so their hands should not touch.

Suddenly he heard her voice. She asked:

"Are you asleep?"

"No."

But still he did not open his eyes.

After a while she said:

"I had nothing to do with him. He was a friend of Haymes."

"I don't know who Haymes is."

"It doesn't matter," she said.

"It doesn't matter," he said.

Although his eyes were still shut he knew that the moon had set or at any rate moved away from the triangle of the half-boarded window. It was dark. He opened his eyes.

He felt even more clearly now that her hand was quite close to his. Their two hands seemed like lips slowly being drawn towards each other. The two hands seemed to be breathing, their breath bringing them closer together.

"It's got to be over and done with," he said.

"What?" she asked.

"Everything," he said.

She understood. The compartment was as cold as ice, but she felt feverishly hot. She supposed it must be the effect of the sharp mountain air that had buffeted her all day. But she knew at the same time that this was not so. Just as her hand, almost touching the filthy floor of the carriage, was feverishly drawn towards his hand, so her whole body was feverishly crying out for the man on the seat opposite. Desperately she tried to conjure up the pictures of the men she had known in the past few months. The men in the streets, the men on the divan with the lions' heads. She wanted to see them. If she could see them, she thought, the fever would leave her. But their faces would not come to her. The night was without ghosts.

He, too, was trying to see the men in the room overlooking the cemetery. And the girl in their arms. Soldiers and civilians, Negroes and others. The man they had met in the street and the man called Haymes. The girl on the bridge and in the restaurant by the vegetable market. But he, too, saw nothing.

Neither of them knew which had made the first move—the movement of a hand towards its mate by the fraction of a thought. But suddenly their fingers touched and frantically intertwined.

From outside came the sound of footsteps crunching in the snow. Then the voice of the man selling tickets for the dead train.

"It's all over now," said Hans.

"I know," said Inge.

He stood up without letting go of her hand. He sat down on the wooden seat beside her.

"No," she said. "Let's go to sleep." She sounded almost imploring.

"We can't go to sleep," he said. "We don't want to go to sleep. Otherwise it'll never be over and done with."

She straightened up. He did not know why she straightened up: whether to embrace him, or to be ready for his embrace, or to escape from him.

He did not await her decision. He took her in his arms.

The wooden seat was narrow; Inge pressed herself against the curved back of the bench.

He said: "I love you."

And then the stationary train seemed to take wings and to carry them off at fantastic speed towards unseen distances. He knew that they were leaving the menacing ghosts behind, maybe at the station whence they had set out on their breathless journey. But she only knew that everything was different . . .

Colonel Sibelius Becomes a Waiter

Strange and utterly confusing were the experiences gained by ex-Colonel Achim Freiherr von Sibelius towards the end of February and the beginning of March 1946. The activities of the erstwhile General Staff officer and former conspirator were eminently suited to the gaining of experiences: he was looking for a job.

With Adam's help Sibelius had found a furnished room in Schwabing, not far from his friend's home, and there he now lived as a lodger, while vigorously trying to build himself a "civilian existence."

His first way had been to a camera factory, or more correctly to the ruins of the factory, a medium-sized enterprise which had just resumed production with Allied help and for Allied purposes. Sibelius knew no more about cameras than any other keen amateur photographer, but an acquaintance whom he had run into on the street one day had told him that the management was looking for a liaison officer with the Americans, and since the Colonel's knowledge of English was rather more than average he decided to try his luck. Of the old factory only the front wall was left, but the temporary hut that had been erected in the yard was humming with activity. After a considerable wait the applicant was taken to an office pleasantly redolent with fresh paint and calcimine, where he was received by the manager, a young man in a sports suit and horn-rimmed glasses, who was continually smoking American cigarettes when he did not happen to be chewing gum. The manager, whose contact with the Americans must have been at least of one month's standing—for he repeatedly began his sentences with a thoughtful "Well" and made extensive use of the expression "O.K."—showed himself from his jovial side, at least until the moment when Sibelius confessed to having been a colonel in the General Staff. Few previous occupations, the manager thereupon remarked, were less apt to inspire confidence among the Americans and he was not shaken in this opinion even when Sibelius, somewhat hesitantly, observed that he had been discharged as "nonincriminated" after extensive investigation. Busy though the young man was, he condescended to add the explanation that, while he had every sympathy for the awkward position of his visitor, it was surely now the turn of "the others," those who had suffered under the Third Reich and had not held any prominent posts. Sibelius felt tempted to inquire about the manager's own actions or sufferings under Hitler, but he saw little point in prolonging the one-sided conversation and thus took his leave, accompanied by the manager's good wishes.

The next time he was more careful. Equipped with a letter of recommendation from his brother-in-law in Munich, he went to the newspaper publishing firm of Bacher, which had also only been functioning for a few weeks and which was looking for intelligent, though not necessarily experienced, employees. He was received by the personnel manager, a certain Herr Güntter, a square-built man with a half-shaven head and a clipped Northern German accent. When that gentleman wanted to know further details about the Baron's past, Sibelius hastened to explain that, though he had been a professional soldier and a colonel in the General Staff, he had belonged to the circle of Count Stauffenberg and played a certain part in the events of the 20th of July. Even before he had concluded his brief biography he realized his mistake. Herr Güntter turned out to be a former officer on the active list, lieutenant colonel in an armored division and holder of the Knight's Cross with Oak Leaves. He himself, Herr Güntter explained, had never dreamed that one day he would have to "act the part" of personnel manager in a newspaper firm. While emphasizing his unpolitical character, his objectivity and his democratic leanings, he also pointed out that, in some respects, a business firm did not differ substantially from the army: loyalty was expected even from an employee of a newspaper business and one could hardly expect a man who had betrayed his government to show loyalty to his civilian employer.

After a few more attempts, which came to nothing for rather more factual reasons, Sibelius further enlarged his store of experience by a visit to the Veltheim porcelain works which supplied the Allied officers' messes in all three Zones. There his dealings were with a very pleasant man, a Herr von Güstloff, with whom he got on instantly and who assured him of his personal favor even when Sibelius had cautiously unfolded his life-story. Unfortunately, Herr von Güstloff explained apologetically, he was unable to act in this matter according to his own judgment. The Veltheim factory was at present run by a Board of Trustees since Herr Veltheim senior had been "an old Party member"; it was general knowledge, however, that he would return to his factory before very long, and he would scarcely wish to have a prominent figure of the 20th of July among his senior staff members.

That he did not find a post in the Thalia Art Printing Works was due to the scruples which the Colonel was unable to shed entirely, even in his hard-pressed situation. In this instance it was he who had been approached and a prospect of a relatively comfortable and rewarding post had been dangled before him. The proprietor of the plant, a very impressive gentleman named Herr Böller, had called on Sibelius in his little room and had proposed that they should conclude a bogus agreement. He himself, Herr Böller explained, was rather badly incriminated as his firm had worked exclusively on NSDAP orders for twelve years—"I am not a politician, Herr Oberst, but a man's got to live"—and the printing works would therefore be confiscated by the Occupying Power unless Herr Böller hurriedly managed to find a suitable trustee. Needless to say, the Colonel's visitor added, a gentlemen's agreement would have to be arrived at between them: after all, in a year or two conditions would be more normal again. When Sibelius remarked that he was scarcely qualified for the role of a dummy, Herr Böller departed with the half-angry and half-regretful assurance that it would not prove very difficult to find a "more realistically-minded" substitute for Sibelius.

"It's curious," Sibelius observed to his friend Adam Wild a few days later, "how surely a man sinks step by step when he is on the lookout for a job. All the time he is, as it were, haggling with himself. He reduces his own demands, material as well as moral. Anything he declined yesterday he would be glad to accept today, and anything that may seem an imposition today might look most tempting by tomorrow. At first one does not want to conceal anything, then one conceals a lot, and finally one is not quite sure that one will not resort to lies. And yet, the experience is not entirely unprofitable. Today, for instance, I am going to call on a Herr Wedemeyer, the owner of a night club called the 'Mücke,' where they need a reliable headwaiter. A little while ago I should have regarded myself in a waiter's tails as a somewhat odd picture, but now I am hoping to get the job. And you may believe me if I tell you that I could fill it without any loss of so-called dignity—first, because it is by no means an undignified occupation, and secondly, because I am glad I have resisted the temptation of more profitable but in fact far less dignified positions."

Adam Wild encouraged his friend in his resolution, and thus the former Colonel in the General Staff Baron von Sibelius arrived at the "Mücke" just before midday on a fine March morning in the year 1946, to present himself to Herr Wedemeyer.

The night club in the ruins showed itself from its least attractive side that morning. Only a circus could have looked more depressing at that hour—and indeed the "Mücke" was in many ways reminiscent of a circus in daylight. The windows, usually covered with a variety of cheap but colorful rags, stood open and the rays of the weak March sun penetrated soberly into the bare rooms. The dust on the dance floor, the piano, the tables, and the chairs which had been stacked on top of the tables, was almost as thick as the sand in a circus ring.

The life-belts suspended from the ceiling, the half-emptied bottles behind the bar, and the large midge fashioned of rope looked like the lifeless articles in a stage property store.

Even Walter Wedemeyer, who received the applicant at a table that had only just been hurriedly scoured, looked dusty and as if left over from the night before. His smooth round face, turned to the window to catch what sun there was, was now full of wrinkles, almost as though the lines which appear with a smile and normally disappear again were frozen on to his features. His professional courtesy and joviality displayed throughout the night had left deep traces, and the conjurer's face was like that of a clown rehearsing without make-up.

"I have been through your papers, Herr von Sibelius," said Wedemeyer, "and I am willing to take you on. As for the terms, we shall have no difficulty in coming to an agreement. I like to live and let live. You would receive a dollar a day, in Reichsmarks of course, but worked out according to the black-market rate each day. In addition, you will have a free supper, and of course your tips which are mostly in cigarette currency and thus of not inconsiderable value. I think that's very fair, and no one can reasonably ask for more these days."

Sibelius inclined his head to indicate that he appreciated the offer.

"The question is only," Wedemeyer continued, "whether you've any scruples about performing your job in the way I have in mind."

"There are plenty of ex-officers," said Sibelius, "who are glad to accept far humbler positions."

Wedemeyer was playing with his exceptionally fleshy ear lobes.

"You are aware, Herr von Sibelius," he said, "that the 'Mücke' is a licensed establishment. That means that the Americans can withdraw my license whenever they feel like it."

"Surely that applies to most enterprises?" said Sibelius.

"Quite so. But matters are rather more involved in this instance. I will be quite frank with you. The 'Mücke' was supposed to give the Americans an opportunity of keeping a close eye on certain groups of people—Gestapo men, black marketeers, people who like fishing in troubled waters. But now the Americans are working with the selfsame Gestapo officials, black marketeers and shady characters. You may say that that's their business. But again matters are not quite so simple. For they are also working against those people. Altogether, everybody seems to be working with everybody else and against everybody else. I could tell you some things that you wouldn't credit. There are two brothers, for instance, both of them officers in the occupation army, who keep giving me diametrically opposed orders."

He paused, as if waiting for a curious question. Sibelius did him the favor and asked:

"What has that to do with my functions, Herr Wedemeyer?"

"I must know what's going on in my place," replied Wedemeyer. "Four eyes see more than two; four ears hear more than two."

"So I am to snoop on your guests," said Sibelius. But there was no indignation in his voice.

"If you want to put it that way," said Wedemeyer.

Sibelius considered. At last he said:

"It's an unusual proposition, although it shouldn't surprise me really. After all, you didn't pick on me because I am such an experienced headwaiter. You mentioned scruples. My scruples, Herr Wedemeyer, are relative; that is to say, they are in accordance with our time. I should like to ask you a question, though."

"Please do."

"I have no moral objections to watching the kind of people you have described, or to snoop on them, which is, after all, the same thing. But I should like to know for what purpose I am to snoop on them."

Wedemeyer blinked at the sun.

"That I don't know, Herr von Sibelius," he said, and it sounded convincing. "Knowledge is power—that's a platitude and like all platitudes it contains a grain of truth." He looked about himself. "I want to know what's going on here. This place, and the goings-on here, have begun to frighten me. I am acquainted with your past, Herr von Sibelius, and that past differs very considerably from mine. You used to swim against the current; I have always swum with the current. Now, for the first time in my life, I no longer know which way the current is flowing." Over his round face flitted a smile, a little resigned and self-mocking. "I don't want to find myself in the position of swimming against the current. It would run counter to my character and I should probably get drowned. Does that satisfy you?"

At least he speaks out what others are only thinking, thought Sibelius. He smiled, too.

"It's good enough, Herr Wedemeyer."

Wedemeyer got up. Sibelius noticed that he heaved a sigh of relief, like a man who had got an unpleasant conversation over with. He also noticed that Wedemeyer was about to shake hands with him, but then changed his mind and saved himself that intimate gesture of sealing a bargain.

"Very well, Herr von Sibelius," he said. "You can start tonight." For a moment his eyes measured the slight man with the well-kept mustache, the carefully brushed gray hair, and the straight soldierly bearing. "Very well," he repeated. "Come along this afternoon about three o'clock and we'll fit you out with a tailcoat. We'll invent some story about you for the benefit of the rest of the staff. We'll keep the name Sibelius, because of your identity papers. But we'd better leave out the 'von.' "

"I shall try to bear it with fortitude," smiled Sibelius.

Wedemeyer saw his new headwaiter out into the street. The March sun stood at its zenith. The hut housing the "Mücke," built right among the ruins with its now paled neon light above the entrance, looked like a barracks in a refugee camp. In the front door opposite, a doorway that seemed like something out of a box of building bricks as it led from nowhere to nowhere, lounged two adolescents, smoking cigarettes with such concentration as if smoking were a full-time occupation. Between the two sides of the street hung a curtain of dust.

"I shall put you in charge of the back room," said Wedemeyer. "We have a particularly interesting booking for tonight. General Stappenhorst, the former Chief of Eastern Counterintelligence, was arrested in sensational circumstances a few days ago. The newshounds got wind of it somehow—probably you've seen the report in the *Süddeutsche Zeitung*. What the papers do not know, or what they are not allowed to report, is that the General was released again yesterday. He is going to be our guest tonight. . . ."

Spring Comes to Germany

A few minutes after getting word from Adam Wild that Elisabeth von Zutraven was at his house, Major Frank Green was summoned to the office of Colonel Graham T. Hunter.

Even the attitude of the angular Fräulein Bauer, the Colonel's secretary, boded no good. The sharp-nosed Fräulein was one of those secretaries who reflect their bosses' mood in a vastly magnified and cruder form. She was like a typing icicle as, almost without looking up from her machine, she said:

"The Colonel is expecting you, Major."

Hunter was behind his desk when Frank entered the office, but he had clearly not been working there but mentally preparing himself for his interview with his subordinate.

"Sit down, Frank," said the Colonel. "I want to talk to you." And, almost before Frank had sat down, he added: "Tell me, Frank, have you completely gone out of your mind?"

"I presume that you are referring to the Stappenhorst affair, Colonel," said Frank. "I hear he has been released again this morning."

"That's just what I am referring to," said Hunter.

"Through a German agent," Frank began his explanation, "I learned the whereabouts of the wanted general. I also learned that he had collected around him a group of ex-officers and Gestapo men. I inspected his file. There was nothing in it of a warrant being withdrawn. I considered it necessary to strike before he slipped through our fingers."

"You didn't realize he was working for us?"

"No, sir."

The Colonel began to polish his glasses with exaggerated care. "Frank," he said, "you've got me into a mighty awkward situation. The General is bound to think that in my department the right hand doesn't know what the left is doing. Well, maybe we can explain that away by the nature of our work." There was no severity in his voice—barely reproach. "As always, you have acted with complete correctness. You have moreover hunted down the SS officer Gerd Mante for whose extradition we have a request from the French and the Russians." He sounded almost as if he had called Frank to his office to commend him. Then he continued: "At the same time you have displayed a complete lack of judgment. If nothing worse. Tell me, Frank—did you deliberately fail to inform me of your action beforehand?"

"Yes, Colonel."

"What's the idea?"

Frank looked into his superior's eyes. He said:

"I was afraid you would stop me."

Frank noticed the slight tremble in the Colonel's hand as he put on his glasses.

"So you knew that you were acting without authority?" said Hunter.

"I have told you, sir, that I knew nothing of a withdrawal of the warrant for his arrest. At the same time I knew unofficially that certain officers of our branch were negotiating with people like Stappenhorst. I have used my official ignorance to do what seemed to me right."

"Are you trying to disarm me with your frankness?" asked the Colonel.

"No, Colonel," said Frank. "Officers whose length of service and decorations rate eighty points or more are entitled to apply for their transfer. I sent in my application to you this morning."

"What the devil do you mean by that?"

"Colonel," said Frank. "You know that I was prepared to stay with you so long as you needed my services. Until this morning I never thought of leaving. General Stappenhorst's release proves to me that there's nothing left for me to do in Germany. I have lived in the illusion that the war was a crusade. I should like to keep my illusion."

The Colonel rose. Frank, too, got up.

"Sit down again," Hunter said curtly. He began to pace up and down the room. "You know quite well why we are releasing Stappenhorst. We need him. It's not our fault that our allies of yesterday are revealing themselves more clearly as dangerous enemies every day. You can't choose your enemies, Frank. Yesterday we were menaced by the Nazis; tomorrow we may be menaced by the Communists. I am assuming that you are an American first and foremost."

"Perhaps we can't choose our enemies, Colonel," said Frank. "But we can undoubtedly choose our allies. First we fought the Nazis together with the Communists. Are we now going to fight the Communists with the Nazis?"

"We don't want to fight at all," said Hunter. "But we may well be forced to. That is very regrettable, a mere ten months after the end of one war—but it is also very true."

"That may be correct in the grand concept of world politics, Colonel," Frank retorted. He was looking for words. "I have studied history, not applied politics. Maybe politics allow us to get entangled in contradictions which to me are incomprehensible. We have locked up about two hundred and fifty thousand Germans—but we are releasing, of all people, Stappenhorst. We have sent out almost a million questionnaires—but Lieutenant General Stappenhorst is exempted from answering all questions. We are already regarding the Russians as our enemies—but in Nuremberg they are still sitting in judgment over our enemies of yesterday. We are acting the part of protector to five million slave workers—but we know quite well that fewer than five hundred thousand have really been abducted against their will. We declare publicly that Poles, Czechs and Hungarians are morally superior to the Germans by virtue of their nationality—but since last week we have been organizing alarm squads in the Bavarian countryside because the farms are being pillaged by vagrant 'slave workers.' We talk about justice—and we evict innocent people while criminals are lording it in luxury villas. We have still not repealed the Non-Fraternization Law—but in the 'Mücke' hundreds of GI's are consorting with German whores every month. We want to bring to the Germans the blessings of our democracy—but we are teaching them boogie-woogie." He stopped short, but immediately continued with heightened emphasis. "No nation, Colonel, has ever gone to war more unselfishly. Back home they are still regarding us as armed missionaries. We have the best intentions. I know it, and you know it. But how, in God's name, are the vanquished to believe it?"

The Colonel was standing at the window. He said:

"We make mistakes, Frank. Naturally. We are a young nation and we aren't practiced in the business of occupation."

"Maybe," said Frank. "And again: maybe not. Maybe there is no nation that is capable of educating another nation."

"And what do you suggest?" asked the Colonel. "Are we to leave this ill-starred country to its own devices? Must we not at least make an attempt at giving the Germans our better way of life, which they have been unable to achieve for themselves?"

"I don't know," said Frank. "I am not suggesting anything. Only I don't want to be a 'humble man.' You know best how many German prisoners I interrogated in the course of the war, and how often I asked them the question: How is it that you did not resist; how could you allow such things to happen in your name? And you know how I used to come to you when I got that stereotyped reply from them, the reply that turned my stomach: 'But I am only a humble man.' That's what they all said—a hundred times, hundreds of Germans. That was why they appeared to me so hopeless, so utterly forsaken by God." He stood up. "And now, Colonel, you expect me to become a 'humble man.' I hate 'humble men.' I will try to understand, naturally—but I want to be able to make my protest if I still don't understand in the end. I do not want to submit to anything I don't understand. There

»255«

is not the slightest chance of my understanding the Stappenhorst affair. Not the slightest." More quietly he added: "Perhaps you think I am being impertinent, Colonel. But I don't think I am. I am convinced that I was entitled to speak out. That is my American creed." Almost imploringly he added: "Let me go home, Colonel."

Hunter did not turn to face him. He was still by the window, gazing out. Between the two men hung a silence that seemed to Frank to last eternally. From outside came the monotonous hammering of the workmen repairing the road. At last Hunter said:

"Frank, you must not let me down. The confusion is great. It is perhaps greater than you suspect. It creates new concepts, and the clearer these concepts become the greater is the confusion. Not long ago I accused you, more or less openly, of being pro-German because you pleaded for some officer involved in the 20th of July. I know that you are now accusing me of complicity in a pro-German conspiracy because I have released the General. Yet in fact neither accusation is true. Unsuspecting, we keep stumbling into the snares of clearly defined concepts. It is like thinking one has found a road in a thick fog, but in fact it is a ditch. The occupation is ten months old, Frank. Give us both a chance to find our way out of the fog." He turned round. Suddenly, as frequently happened with him, he looked much older than he was. The uniform no longer seemed to go with that narrow gray head. "Frank," he said softly, "the Stappenhorst business is as distasteful to me as it is to you. I did not shut an eye all night. Over there—" he pointed to the desk—"lies the draft of my own application for transfer back home." He continued earnestly, almost imploringly: "But what will happen, Frank, if we go home? I don't mean only to you or to me. But to ever thinking person. Are you sure that the men who will replace us will do the right thing? Are you sure that my place won't be taken by somebody who would rather hush up the O'Hara business—to quote just one example of many?" He pointed to the window. "There they go, the defeated Germans, looking up at our windows, some with hatred and some with confidence, and all of them with envy—and without the least idea how difficult it is to conquer."

Instinctively Frank took a step towards him. Now he too was standing by the window. It was not the first time that he felt a warm affection for the man with whom he had had nothing in common initially but who, even in his hesitant uncertainty and in his vacillating doubts, seemed to him like a father.

"I know," he said cordially. "And the most difficult thing of all, I sometimes think, is the legacy of the vanquished. I don't know if you see what I mean. I would not hesitate for one moment, Colonel. But then I ask myself whether, maybe in this very room, a German colonel and a German major were not perhaps facing each other not so long ago, persuading one another to hold out although they knew that everything was lost and wrong and pointless. Whether they did not perhaps say to each other: we must stay, because those who will take over from us will be no better. And so they stayed. And now we are indicting them for staying and thereby permitting the machine to run on. Where is this going to lead, Colonel?"

"We shall see where it leads," said Hunter. "It certainly won't lead anywhere if we desert now. Can I count on you, Frank?"

Frank dropped his eyes. Already he had made up his mind to stay, but he still wanted an answer for himself to the question whether he was staying out of weakness, whether he had never seriously intended to rebel, or whether he was genuinely convinced. It was strange for Frank, who usually so methodically analyzed the motives of his actions, to find himself in the position that he did not know whether he was spurred on by a courageous resolution or whether he had just lamely given in to a weak impulse.

The Colonel took his silence for concurrence. He returned to his desk. Deliberately he changed his tone of voice and his subject. He said:

"This O'Hara business. I let him drive over to Berlin this morning. He took a jeep. Can you take the plane tomorrow morning?"

"Yes," said Frank. "At eleven, I think. I can be in Berlin in the afternoon."

He took leave of him quickly and departed. Fräulein Bauer, who had expected a violent argument and had perhaps even hoped to see a humbled major leave her boss's office, looked after him in surprise. She understood those Americans less and less every day.

Frank went to his office, rang up the Adjutant General to tell him he needed travel orders for Berlin for the following day, at the Colonel's request, and set out for Schwabing.

Frau Wild opened the door to him. Adam was out, she told him, but Elisabeth was expecting him. Then she left him alone with her in the room crowded with antiques.

"I've been looking for you everywhere," said Frank. "I very nearly had you run to earth by the MP's. Why didn't you show up?"

She smiled. "I find it so difficult to say thank you."

He blushed. "That's not what I meant. I had nothing to do with your release."

"I know that you had," she said.

He was in a hurry to change the subject.

"How about going for a walk?" he said. "It's almost like summer outside."

"But can we . . . ?" she asked.

"The Non-Fraternization Law doesn't apply to Intelligence. That is, if it still applies to anybody."

He waited in the drawing-room while she went into the next room to put on her coat. He looked out at the ruins which appeared even more unreal under the afternoon sun. Without knowing why, he was reminded of a visit he had paid as a child to some place of pilgrimage. It had been in the summer. The cripples, who had come from far and wide, had been sitting in the sun. The torsos of the buildings were just like those sun-bathing cripples.

Elisabeth returned, wearing an attractive light-gray raincoat and a white scarf on her dark-blonde hair. The delicacy of her regular features was enhanced further by the frame of white material. Frank was reminded of the portraits by Guido Reni who loved to paint his Italian noblewomen with just such shawls over their hair. How different she looks from the last time in the camp, he thought to himself. And how little she has aged.

Side by side they walked down the Barer Strasse, towards the wrecked Pinakothek gallery.

"There was a definite reason why I wanted to see you," said Frank. "One definite reason, and a lot of indefinite ones," he added hurriedly. "You'll have to appear before a Denazification Tribunal next week."

"I know," she said.

"I'm not giving away any secrets," he said, "when I tell you that the preliminary inquiries are very much in your favor. I can't tell you any particulars, but investigations in Paris have given you an exceptionally good record. Your chances of acquittal are very good, provided . . ."

"Provided I wash my hands of Zutraven," she finished for him.

"That isn't necessary. Provided you don't make a point of standing by him."

For a moment she walked beside him in silence. Then she said: "Franz, do you think he'll be sentenced to death?"

"I don't know. I hardly think so."

"One ought not to hang anybody, Franz."

She said it simply, without grandiloquence. He could not answer at once. He thought: if these passers-by knew what the American major and the German woman are talking about! One ought not to hang anybody, Franz.

"Maybe so," he said. "But we don't want to talk about that now."

"If they hanged him I would have to stand by him," she said harshly.

"You'll come up before the Tribunal long before sentence is passed in Nuremberg. The verdict isn't expected till the end of September." Only now did he realize what she had just said. "And if the sentence on him is lenient?" he asked.

She avoided his eyes.

"I have nothing in common with Zutraven," she said. "Nothing."

They had reached the ruins of the Pinakothek. All of a sudden he realized what had made him choose that direction. Both of them, in their early youth, had shown a more than usual love of painting. She had frequently said she would like to become a painter. In the summer there had often been an easel in the garden next door. He would cautiously creep up and watch her at work, for she would never show him a picture she had painted. Many a time they had been to the Pinakothek together. George had never taken part in those expeditions—and perhaps that was one of the reasons why Frank remembered them so affectionately. But he was determined not to remind her of those days; it seemed cheap to him to take out a loan on the past.

Just then she said: "Don't you remember?"

"Yes," he said.

They crossed the street and, almost as if they were carefree tourists at an ancient Roman site, climbed over the jumble of stones, the fragments of an old iron gate, rusted girders and smashed plasterwork.

"Spring is in the air," she said.

Looking about, he too noticed the first green shoots on the shrubs which had sprung up amidst the stones. The bushes had thin branches—thin like the arms of undernourished children—but some of them already bore leaves, impertinently and delightfully triumphant amidst the waste of destruction. From the clay soil sprang the first yellow flowers. They seemed to creep up from underneath the stones, more timidly even than the other shy harbingers of spring.

She had stepped up on a large square block and halted for a moment before venturing the short jump. He gave her his hand.

When she had jumped down he was going to release her hand but she held on to his. She looked at him and said:

"Franz, why are you doing all this for me?"

He said: "I love you."

They stopped, facing each other, at a lost for words. But he looked more embarrassed than she. She may have expected those words, hopefully or fearfully, though perhaps not that day or in that place—at any rate, they did not come to her as such a surprise as they did to him as he uttered them. Had he admitted to himself what he had now admitted to her, his words would have been forced along many devious detours before reaching his lips. And now he had uttered them, possibly only because he could not lie to her. In answering her question he ought to have embellished or modified his motives. But the truth was infinitely simple and infinitely bewildering.

A smile passed over her face. "I knew it, Franz," she said. "Maybe that is why I asked." And before he could say anything she added: "It's good to hear, Franz. It doesn't have to make sense."

She released her hand and made to move on.

"Will you forget it?" he asked.

"Why?"

"Zutraven," he said. "This is no contest."

"It's not Zutraven," she said. "It's the twelve years. They remain."

"They don't have to remain," he said.

"Yes they do," she said. "Perhaps I can explain it to you one day. But not today."

"Are you afraid of people?" he asked.

"Among other things. The wife of the war criminal and the American major. No comment needed."

"But the comment is just what matters."

"Only if one has a lot of courage," she said. "I have none. I've proved it."

"That's not true," he said.

"It is true," she said. "Some other time, Franz. But it's good to know, all the same."

They were once more out in the street. Looking about themselves they discovered to their surprise that they were not alone. On the debris sat a few workmen, eating a meager meal. Others were clambering about the ruins. American soldiers passed by, scrutinizing the major and the German woman. They did not salute.

Dusk was falling as, instinctively delaying their return, they turned into Adam Wild's street. Abruptly she stopped. He followed her glance and saw two white-painted MP jeeps pulled up outside Adam Wild's house.

"Don't come with me," she said. There was panic in her voice. "They've come for me."

"Nonsense," he said.

He remained at her side as she walked up to the house. Four or five MP's were leaning against the vehicles. They let the Major and the woman pass.

In silence, full of forebodings, they climbed the stairs.

They were about to ring the bell when the door of Adam's apartment was opened. An MP lieutenant emerged. For a moment he stared at the two in surprise. Then his hand went up to his cap. He turned to the Major.

"Frau von Zutraven?" he asked.

"Yes," said Elisabeth, anticipating Frank.

"Come along," said the Lieutenant curtly. "You're under arrest."

"Have you a warrant, Lieutenant?" Frank asked in English.

Still perplexed, the Lieutenant produced the form.

"May I get my things together?" asked Elisabeth.

The Lieutenant looked at the Major and nodded. A few minutes later Elisabeth reappeared, carrying a small suitcase. Quickly she hurried past Frank, down the stairs.

Cleaning Out a Monkey Cage

𝔚EEKS PASSED before Elizabeth von Zutraven found out why she had been taken to the detention camp near Augsburg, and even then the information was scanty and inconclusive.

Compared with the barracks to which she was now allocated, the accommodation in the women's camp outside Nuremberg had been utter luxury. There had been wooden bunks and camp beds there; but here the women slept on the floor, on straw mattresses which were weak with old age and had lost most of their straw stuffing. In Nuremberg the inmates had all been wives of war criminals—a society which Elisabeth had disliked even in the days of the Third Reich but which nevertheless compared favorably with the company in the Augsburg camp. True, during her very first hour Elisabeth had once again met the wives of the Nuremberg defendants—indeed the Marshal's wife had her "bed" next to hers, and the straw mattress of a Gauleiter's wife was along the opposite wall—but generally speaking the society was not very exclusive. On Elisabeth's right was a certain Frau Kein, a former concentration camp wardress, a huge person of masculine features and masculine physique, who was reputed to have been personally responsible for the martyr's death of hundreds of Jewesses. A couple of days after Elisabeth's arrival two young women were assigned to her hut who, as so-called "antisocial elements," had seen the inside of many a concentration camp even during the Nazi era: they were, in fact, Lesbians who, somewhat paradoxically, were being pushed from camp to camp and who had come to derive considerable pleasure from their joint detention. There were still others in the long narrow barracks: a woman radio operator who looked like a mannequin and did not know how she had got inside; a "Flash-girl"—as the women auxiliaries were called in the Luftwaffe—neglected and covered with dirt, who sat by herself all day staring dully in front of her; yet another ex-wardress of a women's concentration camp, many months pregnant; the film actress Lia Rehn, once a much-envied favorite among the many much-envied favorites of the former Propaganda Minister; and finally a Frau Begel, the wife of a top-ranking officer who was himself interned in the adjacent detention camp for men, only a few yards away from her barracks.

It was the nights that Elisabeth feared most in this company.

One night, almost at the beginning, the beam of a torch swept over the straw mattresses. A soldier, one of the camp guards, stood in the door.

"Frau Begel, come along with me," he said.

The women sat up on their mattresses.

Frau Begel was a tall dark woman who seemed to consist only of bones. Her emaciated face was dominated by strong cheekbones and her excessively large hands were bony too. Elisabeth had learned Frau Begel's story on her first day in the camp; she was therefore doubly alarmed when her fellow-prisoner was led from the barracks in the middle of the night. The wife of the SS general had killed her two children. This had happened in a wood, in the mountains near Berchtesgaden, in 1945. The Begel family had fled there before the advancing French, and there the SS general had decided to kill himself and his family. At the last moment he had found it impossible to point his pistol at his nine-year-old son and his three-year-old daughter; the woman had thereupon taken the weapon from his hand and shot her children through the head. A few moments later, as she had been about to execute herself and her husband, the victorious Allies had come swarming through the forest and the SS general had chosen captivity in preference to death. Ever since the woman's life had been filled with nothing but hate: she hated the conquerors fanatically, but even more fanatically she hated the man who had omitted to die. She had not, under the Third Reich, been one of those whom Elisabeth called "domestic pets"; she had known of her husband's actions and approved them. Mass murder, homicide, and even infanticide she accepted as "the harsh law of our time," but she despised the man whose heroism had fallen short of suicide.

When the soldier had left with Frau Begel the other women got up from their mattresses. Frau Begel was wearing nothing except a nightdress patched together from sacking: the guard had not allowed her to dress first. Through a small window in the door the women saw their fellow-prisoner cross the yard, keeping step with the soldier. From the watchtowers the beams of the searchlights swept over the yard and the barracks—coldly, slowly and regularly. An hour later her figure appeared again, was swallowed up in the darkness, and re-emerged in the beam of the searchlight; but now, to the surprise of the women in the barracks, she was wearing a thick pullover on top of her nightdress—a grotesque apparition as the wide nightdress flapped against her bony knees. In her hand she carried something indefinite and glistening.

She entered the darkened barracks, felt her way across to her straw mattress and settled down. Nobody spoke. Only when the beam of the searchlight swept again through the barracks did the others see that Frau Begel was sitting upright on her mattress. She said:

"The swine is dead."

Silence. She continued without waiting for questions:

"At last he's hanged himself. Over there. I'd have loved to have seen him. Did it with a wire. Cut clean through his throat. His pullover's still full of blood."

The beam of the searchlight had left the barracks plunged in darkness. The mistress of the Propaganda Minister began to scream hysterically. The Lesbians tried to calm her. The pregnant concentration camp wardress was sick. The Marshal's wife said in a commanding voice: "Be quiet!" But for the rest of the night the woman kept repeating: "The swine is dead!" She went to the morning roll call in her nightdress, wearing the dead man's pullover. It really was covered with bloodstains.

This was not the only night which left its mark on Elisabeth's mind, and many years later her memories still turned into nightmares.

The concentration camp wardress's confinement came about in the middle of March. She was a blonde woman of about thirty-five, with tiny eyes and a wide mouth, not unlike an overfattened and diseased duck. She possessed no dress and could not obtain one; she wore the coarse gray slacks issued to her at the time of her arrest. But with every day the male trousers were getting tighter and tighter for the pregnant woman, and the cord she had tied round her waist grew longer and longer. But as her belly swelled the gap widened between the two halves of the trouser front, until her bare body, covered only by a dirty shirt, projected more and more prominently from her clothes.

It was at night, about eleven o'clock, when her pains began. It was a month premature, and there was no hope of getting medical help. Anybody venturing outside the barracks at night, except in the company of a guard, was fired at from the manned watchtowers. Only the Marshal's wife decided finally to open the door and to call out for help. Her shouts rang through the night, dramatically but not quite convincingly, like someone requesting help but not needing it for himself.

There was no reply. Elisabeth and the Gauleiter's wife stripped off the woman's trousers. She was squirming. There were plenty of midwives, but their work, performed laboriously and inexpertly, was further complicated by the tricks of the searchlight, whose beam, like a malignant imp, would flit from the barracks just when it was most needed. It was a miracle, therefore, when Frau Begel, still wearing her dead husband's pullover, lifted a live child from its mother's womb. The Marshal's wife was still standing in the open door, and the noise of her shouting mingled with the first cry of the newly-born. The Gauleiter's wife bent down over the blood-covered body of the mother and bit through the umbilical cord, for it was forbidden to own sharp objects and no other suitable instrument was at hand.

Just then the probing finger of light swept through the barracks again and the women beheld a pitch-black Negro baby with thick black hair, a small bundle of thin dark skin over small, sharp bones, strange, miserable and unwanted, in the almost refusingly extended arm of the white mother.

The concentration camp wardress and her baby, kept alive by some diabolical miracle, were taken away in the morning, but a few days later two other women moved into the barracks with their screaming infants. One of them was a Frenchwoman; twenty-four according to her own statement, but of an age that was difficult to determine since her head was shaven clean: the inhabitants of her native village in Lorraine had deprived the "German whore" of her crowning glory. During the past few months, which she had spent moving from one camp to another, her dark hair had grown just a little—but this, oddly enough, made her skull look even barer because the short stubble gave her the appearance of a man convict. The other girl was from Berlin, in a tattered uniform, pretty in an arrogant and provocative way. Both women had given birth to infants a few months previously—two little girls. The Frenchwoman's baby was said to be by a

German, whereas that of the German girl was by a Russian who had raped her. The first time they had stepped into the barracks Elisabeth had not realized that they had babies with them, for they only carried two large brown cardboard boxes bearing the letters CARE; this American gift carton served the little mites as a cot and a carriage. On their wanderings from camp to camp, the young mothers related, they had met countless other young mothers who were lugging their children about with them in CARE cartons—the children of their dead husbands, the children of occupation soldiers, the children of conquerors and vanquished, the fruits of a great love, of a single night, of brute force, or of a bargain for a crust of bread.

Elisabeth found little sleep at night and the day in the camp was tiring. It was the sadistic invention of the roll call, that senseless and humiliating reading-out of names, thought up by the military of all countries and practiced by the camp commandants of all countries, that formed the hub of the lives of the women in the Augsburg camp. Twice or three times the women were ordered to fall in: in the morning they were frequently roused from their straw mattresses so early that they had no time to dress and had to stand there in their nightdresses, in endless ranks, in strict military order. Nor was it the purpose of the exercise to establish if everybody was present: nobody could have got past the electrically charged wire that surrounded the compound. Besides, it was not the complicated German surnames that were called out but, both for simplicity's sake and to make the humiliation doubly painful, the women's Christian names, so that a dozen women would shout "Present!" in a farcical melee of voices in response to such names as Elisabeth, Maria, Grete, Inge or Bertha.

There were humiliations in plenty—natural and general ones such as the roll calls in nightgowns, but also more brutal ones and more cunningly devised ones. When the women were busy washing the dirty underwear of the camp guards—and that was their principal occupation—their work was not only accompanied by insulting remarks on the part of the soldiers, but a modern instrument of torture came into its own: the camera whose sneering eye time and again captured the "high-up women" at lowly occupations. But many of the guards invented their own personal jokes. Private Brown one day brought a portrait of Hitler into Elisabeth's barracks, laid it flat on the floor, and made the women lie down on their bellies and lick off the paint until the color had left the features of their erstwhile Führer. Corporal Flanagan's great and often repeated joke was to distribute tiny little swastika flags to the prisoners and make them clean out the latrines with them.

Even though Elisabeth waded through the morass with dry feet, as though she had no part in what she was doing or what was done to her, she could not remain untouched by the humiliation. Her sense of shame, however, sprang from sources unsuspected by the camp rulers. It was the company, above all, that humiliated her: being forced to share the fate of concentration camp wardresses and prostitutes, and being unable to proclaim to the women who kept coming to her with their lamentations and confidences: "I have nothing in common with you, absolutely nothing." She was offended less by the sadism of the guards than by the utter lack of feminine dignity displayed by her fellow-prisoners—the mistress of the Propaganda Minister, for instance, who boasted that she would earn her liberty by sleeping with a certain lieutenant on the camp staff; the dirt-encrusted "Flashgirl" who at night on her straw mattress noisily and unrestrainedly enjoyed the favors of one of the guards; the Lesbians whom Elisabeth had to chase more than once from her mattress when they approached her amorously, while the children were crying, the Gauleiter's wife was praying loudly and tearfully and the Marshal's wife was snoring.

With the Marshal's wife—who regarded Elisabeth as her only equal, though with a certain reserve—Elisabeth had many a conversation, and these conversations were nearly always worse than the most cunning tortures.

The wife of Kurt von Zutraven's fellow-defendant in Nuremberg was a mixture of dignity and lack of dignity which Elisabeth found it difficult to understand. She still possessed an elegant black coat of the French couturière Mme. Lanvin, whom she had once greatly patronized, and she disported herself exclusively in that garment. At the same time she had an incredible appetite which she was quite unable to control. In the evening she would frequently be seen, her Lanvin coat over her flowing nightdress, creeping along the fence by the adjacent men's camp in order to pick up a piece of bread or sausage which the male prisoners, evidently more plentifully supplied with food, had chucked over. As Elisabeth turned away from the woman greedily consuming this illegal food in a quiet corner she clearly perceived her own conflict: on the one hand she regarded this fall as just, and on the other she wished the victors would not have such an opportunity to gloat over the misery of the fallen.

"I am not hungry," said Elisabeth to the Marshal's wife one March morning when, for the first time, she offered her a piece of cheese she had found by the wire the night before.

The morning roll call was over and they used their free hour to stroll up and down the camp.

"I know what you are thinking, my dear," said the Marshal's wife, hiding the rest of the American cheese ration in her coat pocket. "But I have a duty to get out of here alive. My husband needs me, and one day our nation will need me."

Elisabeth stopped. "Are you serious?" she asked.

"Why shouldn't I be serious?"

"Don't you know what awaits our husbands?"

"They won't dare! I am told they will be banished to some island in the Mediterranean. And when we return from that island it won't be just for a hundred days!"

They walked on.

"I don't understand you," said Elisabeth. "Don't you see that, whichever way the verdict goes, all is over and finished? Not only because we are defeated, but because our people have had their eyes opened. What happened in the past could happen only because the majority of our nation did not know about it."

"So you too have become a victim of Allied atrocity propaganda, Frau von Zutraven," the Marshal's wife said bitterly.

"Atrocity propaganda?" Elisabeth replied calmly. "Do you really mean to say that you are still, to this day, ignorant of the things that have passed?"

"Undoubtedly we made mistakes," said the Marshal's wife. "And some of them were grave mistakes. No doubt about it. We would manage things better next time. But we built up a world-wide empire, Frau von Zutraven."

"We built up an empire of criminals," said Elisabeth.

"I decline to discuss the matter with you any further," said the Marshal's wife. But she could not resist the temptation of convincing Elisabeth. After all, if she could not talk to the wife of the former Governor whom was she to talk to? "Isn't this camp sufficient proof to you, Frau von Zutraven, that the conquerors are worse than we ever were?"

"No," said Elisabeth firmly. She too felt the need to utter her innermost thoughts. "Even if I do have to wash Captain Smith's dirty underwear I never forget that the steam boilers in this camp do not emit lethal gases. Moreover, the millions who were gassed at Auschwitz and Belsen and Mauthausen were innocent, whereas you and I are not innocent. I am sorry to see the conquerors behaving like rascals, but I am sorry only because they humiliate people like yourself instead of putting them to shame." More quietly she continued: "I am not feeling sorry for myself. I am sorry for the victors because they are missing a chance of demonstrating to you and me, through a little more kindness, how bad we were ourselves."

The Marshal's wife stopped. She drew herself up to her full height and said:

"I am sorry for your husband, Frau von Zutraven. And I shall not forget your words when the day of reckoning comes."

"The day of reckoning has come already," said Elisabeth.

She wanted to say more, because she felt genuinely sorry for the woman before her, though not in the way the Marshal's wife expected sympathy. Elisabeth felt sorry for her and envious—and for the same reason. She was blind, the wife of the Nuremberg defendant, blind to the injustices and crimes and atrocities of yesterday, and she was going to have a terrible awakening. At the same time she was just as blindly in love with the man who had made her his wife in the Third Reich—and because she loved him her life had a firm and secure pivot.

Elisabeth had no opportunity to say anything, for just then the women were summoned to a new surprise roll call.

"One hundred prisoners are required for work outside the camp," announced Sergeant Haigh, a tall fair lad from Texas who was popular with all camp inmates because, as far as his duties permitted him, he invariably tried to help, and on one occasion had dressed down a brutal corporal in front of the entire camp. "If there aren't enough volunteers," he added, "we shall have to appoint some."

Far more than a hundred women volunteered, including Elisabeth, for the prospect of getting out of the camp for a few hours appealed to most of them. Besides, the work outside the barbed wire could scarcely be any harder than their daily duties inside.

Two armed soldiers were at the head of the column, two at the rear, and two out on the flank. The procession moved off. It was a strange procession, even for those days when strange processions were nothing out of the ordinary. Many of the women wore their coarse working slacks, while some wore discarded items of American uniforms and others the dresses in which they had been arrested last spring or summer. Brooms, shovels and buckets had been thrust upon them, and now they were trudging through the main street of the city of Augsburg: old women and young, ugly and pretty, nearly all of them hanging their heads.

Elisabeth held her head high, not out of pride or defiance, but simply because even in her present situation she could not entirely suppress her interest in human beings. The pedestrians stood at the edge of the pavement as the column of women passed. There was neither sympathy in their faces nor antipathy; neither solidarity nor hate; only a dull curiosity and occasionally an ill-concealed gloating over the discomfiture of others which they, for once, did not have to share. The most shameless gapers were the women, the same who had cheered yesterday's rulers most loudly. Elisabeth reflected how incapable of loyalty her own sex was and that, while men fallen from greatness at least seemed tragic figures, women fallen from greatness usually did no more than tickle the mob's curiosity.

Elisabeth's neighbor in the marching column, a native of Augsburg, soon guessed their destination. They were making for the zoo. On their arrival there they had another roll call, whereupon they were allotted to different cages with instructions to clean them out. The orders were given in a matter-of-fact manner, as if the scheme was not the fruit of a diseased military brain but the most natural thing in the world.

The Gauleiter's wife, a corpulent German housewife from the Rhineland, and Elisabeth were detailed to a monkey cage—a circular structure not unlike a large bird-cage, situated at a little distance from the other cages, right in the middle of the grounds. To Elisabeth's relief she found herself alone in the cage with her fellow-prisoner when the door was barred behind her: the monkeys had been taken to their winter quarters.

It was just after two o'clock and the March afternoon was brilliant and clear. A friendly pale-blue sky, like a large parasol over an open-air breakfast table, floated above the garden and the shrubs all round were clad in fresh verdure.

The monkey dung, which covered the stone floor, the wooden slats, the suspended rings and the ropes dangling from the roof of the cage, had been largely dried by the sun and stank no longer. A smell of monkeys still clung to the cage, but it reminded Elisabeth of her childhood visits to the zoo and was not necessarily offensive. Now and again a bird alighted on the trees or shrubs outside, and the idea occurred to Elisabeth that these free birds, straying by chance into the zoo, were perhaps mocking the caged animals, just as free humans might goggle or laugh at the inmates of the cages. Just then—almost as though reality wanted to pursue Elisabeth's fancy—the first afternoon visitors drifted into the zoo and stopped in astonishment in front of the monkey cage. Instead of the customary lithe mimics of the human race performing their amusing and malicious tricks behind the bars, there were two human beings working there.

The crowd outside the cage grew fast. At last a little round lover of animals ventured a question. He called out to the women:

"What are you doing in there?"

"We're cleaning up," replied Elisabeth without looking up. She felt that a coy silence would do too much honor to the questioner.

"Why do you have to do it?" asked the little round man, this time not unsympathetically.

"We are Nazis," replied Elisabeth. "We are being punished."

She said it in a business-like manner, to discourage any nascent sympathy. Smiling, she got down on to her knees to scrub the stone flags.

There was a thick circle of people around the cage now. A disabled ex-serviceman in a tattered uniform; two women with their children; the little round man who obviously had nothing to do; an old man holding a little boy's hand; four university students, two men and two girls, with brief cases under their arms.

"Are they monkeys, too?" the little boy asked his grandfather.

"No, silly!" the old man replied with a blush. "They're Nazis."

A titter ran through the crowd, an unhealthy embarrassed giggle.

"Don't answer them," the Gauleiter's wife hissed into Elisabeth's ear.

They were both stooping down, piling the monkey dung into heaps

»271«

with their small shovels. The Gauleiter's wife, who had been converted to religion while in the camp, was muttering prayers under her breath as she did in the barracks at night.

"Are you hungry?" one of the men by the bars eventually asked. He was a middle-aged man with a pince-nez and a scholarly appearance. His voice was friendly.

The two women did not reply, but the onlookers interpreted their silence as an admission that they were in fact hungry. There may have been Nazis among them or anti-Nazis, indifferent people or philanthropists—but sympathy for the punished prisoners in the monkey cage overcame everything else. Suddenly food was being thrust at the two women from all sides: bread, a piece of sausage, and even a piece of chocolate. Gapers turned into givers, and even the monkeys would have envied the prisoners, so generous were the gifts pushed through the bars. Carefully—for their hands were dirty, and also they were afraid that their guards might suddenly appear, the two women pushed their hands through the cage, and in the face of this demonstration of sympathy it never occurred to them that only now had they become animals in the zoo, monkeys being fed in their cage.

Elisabeth collected herself more quickly than the wife of the Gauleiter. Four long-forgotten lines from a poem by Rainer Maria Rilke rose up in her mind:

"His glance, so tired from traversing his cage's repeated railings, can hold nothing more.
He feels as though there were a thousand cages and no more world thereafter than before."

She had learned the poem at school—it was called "The Panther." Her glance, too, had tired from traversing the railings. At the same time there came to her the realization that there was no escape from these bars: wherever she went the bars would go with her, and behind them there was no world but only a gaping crowd.

Ever since the collapse, but especially during the past few weeks, since the MP's had taken her away from Franz's side, she had fought a winning battle against self-pity, and now it seemed as if she were to succumb to it after all. There was nothing left for her but to look out through the cage. In the eyes of the men and women and children who stared at her through the bars was pity—that well-meant affront which she hated almost as much as the vicious, cruel or indifferent looks of her guards. She almost heaved a sigh of relief when a woman, evidently a working-class woman who had just joined the curious throng, called into the cage in a hysterically shrieking voice:

"Come on, swing from that ring, you Nazi bitch!"

With her right hand Elisabeth had just cleaned the monkeys' trapeze ring; in her left hand she held a precious piece of sausage which a little girl had shyly pushed through the bars for her. She dropped the sausage.

The little girl burst out howling. The disabled soldier said to the working-class woman:

"You ought to be ashamed of yourself!"

"Big-shots' wives, that's what they are," said the working-class woman.

"And you're a heap of monkey shit yourself," the little round man turned on her.

Some of them laughed; others swore.

Although she had turned her back Elisabeth could hear the tumult which developed outside. She did not want to see or hear—but the cage was round and the curious crowd followed her about on the other side of the bars.

At last the MP's came. They had been busy with other prisoners, but the commotion around the monkey cage brought them up in a hurry and they quickly dispersed the crowd.

Half an hour later the cage was unlocked. Again the prisoners marched through the town. The evening sky was red like the face of a feverish child. Only when they had entered the camp again through the gate in the fence did the night scatter the crimson clouds.

Sergeant Haigh was standing outside the barracks, checking the prisoners in. As Elisabeth was about to pass in front of him he stopped her:

"Frau Zutraven, an officer wants to speak to you. A Captain Green."

Elisabeth's heart was in her mouth. She glanced down at her hands which were full of monkey dung. She felt herself reeking like a monkey cage.

"Major Green," she said instinctively.

"No," he said. "A Captain George Green."

A *Murder is Committed in Berlin*

Shortly after his arrival in Berlin Frank Green experienced his first surprise—and the string of surprises was not to break throughout his stay there.

He immediately got in touch with Captain Symington, the Intelligence officer in charge of the Berlin branch of Hunter's outfit, who had been entrusted with watching the commandeuse pending Frank's arrival. Major O'Hara, reported Symington, had arrived in Berlin with his driver Pfc. Jones, but had not yet resumed contact with Irene Gruss who was still hiding out at the apartment of the former Gestapo man Jäckel. That in itself was not surprising; no doubt O'Hara intended to wait for nightfall before going to the apartment in the Alexanderplatz neighborhood. What was surprising was that O'Hara, who had reported his arrival to Captain Symington in accordance with official procedure, had dropped a hint to him over lunch that he was going to land an "undreamed-of-coup" in the former Reich capital and that he was going to surprise the "Berlin boys" with "a sensational arrest."

Frank could not have guessed O'Hara's intentions.

Although his mistress's escape to Berlin had come off, O'Hara had no illusions about the danger in which he still was. He did not underrate the efficiency of his own service, nor—any longer—that of Major Green. The arrest of the Gestapo man Dieter Griff had been a forceful reminder of how close to the wind he had been sailing, and even though Griff was released a few days later O'Hara could rid himself of his fear of inevitable discovery only by drowning it in a sea of alcohol. Colonel Hunter and Frank, who had assumed that O'Hara applied for the Berlin assignment—connected with the final establishment of the circumstances surrounding Hitler's last hours in the Reich Chancellery—in order to meet Irene Gruss and provide for her some secure sanctuary, presumably in the Soviet Zone, had failed to make allowance for O'Hara's character and mental state.

The former police sergeant had in fact decided on a far more desperate step. To continue his association with Irene Gruss was impossible: she was bound to be arrested sooner or later. To arrest her himself seemed therefore the only way out. Although O'Hara had for the past few weeks been permanently under the influence of whisky, his speculation was not entirely wrong. If the commandeuse were to tell her interrogators about her life with the Major—a probability but by no means a certainty—the Army would then have to decide between the word of a Nazi criminal and an American field officer of good reputation. This was where O'Hara enjoyed a clear advantage; it would be turned into an overwhelmingly strong position if he brought the commandeuse in himself.

What was even more important, O'Hara's plans were in line with his personal inclinations. His delight in inflicting pain and suffering, and his inability to find satisfaction in anything but torture, whether playful or in earnest, had long ceased to seem abnormal to him, let alone a perversion. Like many an invalid he regarded his malady as a decided advantage. O'Hara's personal likes and general philosophy lived cosily together: brutality was to him not only a source of pleasure but also the quintessence of his convictions. Lust turned into brutality, and brutality gave rise to new lust—so that there was no clash any longer between his days and nights. But all this had changed abruptly when O'Hara discovered that his pleasurable experience, though always centered on pain, humiliation and chastisement, reached an even more delicious culmination if he himself became the object rather than the subject of the physical and psychological tortures. This was the beginning of O'Hara's crisis and fall. To inflict pain, humiliation, punishment or castigation fitted perfectly into the former policeman's supposedly masculine philosophy; his perversion began to trouble him only when it ceased to fit into the picture he had made for himself of himself. Thus it happened that, since that Christmas Eve, when chance ascribed to him a new part in his relationship with the commandeuse, he had been struggling to regain his original role. If his dreams still returned time and again to the tortures inflicted by him on a suffering Irene Gruss, then these dreams had become a form of wishful thinking now that he had been thrashed himself. In his night-long fantasies he would see Irene Gruss being interrogated, beaten up, tortured, and finally hanged. He wanted to send her to the gallows not only for the sake of self-preservation, but also because he felt sure that the sight of her execution would revive that old pleasure which, by comparison with his new perversion, appeared to him as a return to normalcy.

Unsuspecting that he was being watched at every step by no fewer than four officers, including Frank Green, and a number of enlisted men—ironically enough by the secret service methods so familiar to O'Hara—the Major had gone to the "Mademoiselle" night club, where the new barman had slipped him the key to Jäckel's apartment. On March 21, 1946, at seven o'clock in the evening, O'Hara therefore unlocked the door to the apartment which was to become the scene of a rapid sequence of events quite unlike those planned and foreseen by him.

The Berlin apartment where Irene Gruss lived differed most unfavorably from the patrician villa in which O'Hara had once installed her; nor, for that matter, could it compare with Griff's two-room apartment in Munich. It consisted of two rooms in a cellar below a totally wrecked house. Looking at it from the street one would not have thought it possible that any form of human habitation could be concealed underneath that heap of debris. One had to move along a swaying wall and climb over piles of rubble to get behind the gutted house: here the approach had been cleared to a staircase leading below the ground. Even as O'Hara unlocked the wooden door at the end of the staircase he still thought he must have made a mistake, for there was complete darkness around him; only after his eyes got used to the dark did he discover a faint line of light showing below another door at the far end of a long corridor. The place smelled of fire and scullery and urine. With his hands touching both walls of the narrow passage the Major groped his way forward to the door of the apartment.

He knocked.

"Come in!" replied Irene Gruss.

She was sitting by a table in the center of the room which was lit only by a smoking oil lamp. Two candles stood on the table, but they had burnt down. Irene Gruss was wearing her lilac kimono which looked even more grotesque as underneath she had on a pair of men's gray trousers and a thick pullover. She did not get up. Without showing surprise she said:

"So it's you."

"Didn't you expect me?" he asked.

"Sure," she said indifferently.

He looked about. The room must have been a coal cellar at one time. The walls were black and there was still a little coal dust in one corner. The more astonishing were the furnishings—well-made, if haphazardly matched, furniture, a comfortable broad brass bed, even a few pictures on the wall, suspended from nails driven between the bare bricks. In one corner was a battery of empty wine bottles, in another an unlit field stove with a flue ending in a hole in the wall. On a coat hanger hung a man's fur-lined coat.

O'Hara sat down at the table, facing her.

She asked: "What do you want here?"

"A fine reception," he said, clumsily attempting a joke.

"Otto says it's silly to come here," she said. "You may be watched."

"Who's Otto?"

"Jäckel, of course," she said.

"You're coming with me," he said.

For the first time there was some movement in her face. He watched her sharply from the corners of his small deep-set eyes. Her face looked old and sunk. Her skin, always the ugliest part of her, was utterly neglected; it was as though cheese had deliquesced on her features.

"What do you mean?" she asked.

"I've found better quarters for you," he said. "In Munich. I can't keep you here for ever—with your Otto."

He acted as if he were really concerned about finding better accommodation for her. He also feigned jealousy, for in a similar situation he would have been jealous in the past, and he was anxious to pick up the thread where it had broken.

She got up, crossed over to the stove and took up a bottle that stood on it.

"Schnapps?" she asked.

He nodded.

She took a dirty tumbler and half-filled it. As she put it down on the table in front of him she said:

"I don't believe a word of it."

"What do you mean?"

"You're glad you're rid of me. I'm staying here."

"Out of the question," he said. "These Berlin guys are pretty hot. They're sure to find you."

"I'm staying here," she said.

He got up, glass in hand.

"Don't be difficult," he urged her with ill-concealed impatience. "I don't want them to nab you. I've got my jeep outside."

"Leave me alone," she said, not by any means coyly but with a threatening undertone. "Otto is looking after me. I'm not such a fool as you think I am."

"That's gratitude!" he said.

"You're trying to trap me," she said. "Otto knows all about it."

The schnapps began to have its effect on him. All day long, and the preceding day, he had drunk bourbon; now the bourbon and the cheap schnapps did not agree inside him. So far he had not given any thought to Jäckel. But now that she had twice referred to "Otto" it suddenly seemed important to find out more about him.

"You sleep with him!" he said. This time his fury sounded genuine enough; his jealousy was no longer an act.

"Naturally," she said.

"Do you beat him?" he asked.

She laughed.

"What business is it of yours?"

"Do you beat him?" he repeated.

"No," she said. "He beats me."

"I don't believe you."

"Want to see my bruises? My behind is like raw meat."

With a gesture whose obscenity surprised even O'Hara she undid the belt of her dressing gown and began to undo the belt of her trousers as well.

O'Hara's face flushed crimson.

"But you like beating," he said. "You don't like being beaten."

"I like being beaten by him," she said. "He doesn't give up right away."

O'Hara could feel his fists clenching. He did not clench them; they seemed to clench of their own accord. For a moment he was tempted to drop the whole plan which he had so subtly woven during the days of separation from her. It seemed a hopeless proposition now, even if he succeeded in luring her out of the cellar. They would arrest him. The familiar excitement seized him, so much so that he tried to convince himself that there was no point in exchanging the present calm, no matter how uncertain its duration, for a rather risky stroke. She need not hang. It would be enough if he recaptured his old position. It would be enough if he thrashed her within an inch of her life.

But presently his reason prevailed—or at any rate what Major O'Hara thought was reason. He said:

"You're trying to make me jealous. We've got no time. Get ready."

And he repeated his well-rehearsed text: "We can cross the zonal frontier during the night. My own people are on duty tonight."

She retreated towards the stove, her eyes never leaving him for an instant.

"The answer is still 'No,'" she repeated.

"I'm ordering you," he said, making for her.

"You're lying," she said. "You don't want to save me."

"Get a move on!" he commanded.

"You're trying to trick me," she said. "I know you American swine."

He halted.

"Did Otto say that, too?"

"Perhaps."

He did not know if she was speaking the truth, but he realized that she had seen through him. He felt as foolish as only a man does who has regarded someone else as a fool and suddenly realizes that the fool is cleverer than himself. It was no longer enough for her to be thrashed within an inch of her life. She had to hang.

At the same time he realized that it was no use to set traps for her into which she would never fall.

"You're coming with me, you Nazi bitch," he said.

She too was playing a dangerous game. She had her back to the stove. On the floor by the side of it lay a heavy, bent poker. Swiftly she bent down and lifted it up. She asked:

"Want a hiding, you American swine?"

His hand went to his revolver.

"You're coming with me," he said. "You're under arrest."

She laughed out loud. He did not know what made her laugh, but he felt ridiculous, and there was nothing he feared more than ridicule. "You're under arrest" was indeed a ridiculous sentence, not only because of the past intimacy between them but also because the hackneyed police formula lost its effect between him and her. For the first time in O'Hara's experience the terror-inspiring police formula had fallen to the ground like an empty crock and shattered into a thousand fragments. The hollow laughter echoing from the damp cellar walls hit not only O'Hara the man and the major, but also O'Hara the police sergeant.

With a single movement he had whipped out his revolver from its holster. He was advancing on the woman.

"You're going to hang," he said.

Her laughter ceased abruptly. The light of the oil lamp did not reach into the corner of the room. They were standing in semidarkness.

The woman took the poker in both hands.

The Major's finger was on the trigger. He was not yet sure whether her eyes betrayed fear, rebellion or murder. All he thought was: She shall not hang. I'll do for her myself.

When he wanted to fire it was too late. He had got too close to her. She had straightened up. With all her strength she brought the poker down on his head. The pointed bent end of the poker caught him above the forehead. The revolver fell from his hand. He staggered back. Between his red hair the wound was a gaping gash from which a red stream poured over his face. Blindly she kept on hitting him, again and again. Even when Major William S. O'Hara was only a red lump on the black cellar floor her arm was still raised for another blow.

She was standing thus over the dead man when Frank Green and half a dozen military police burst into the cellar.

The Föhn Turns the Colonel's Head

Pressure of work, as had been the case so frequently during the past few weeks, again caused Colonel Hunter to work at his home till late at night. About nine o'clock, after his family had withdrawn, he had received Major Green to hear his report about the happenings in Berlin. Although neither officer referred to that aspect, they were intensely grateful to fate—especially after the revealing interrogation of the commandeuse—for having taken the matter out of the hands of the occupation authorities. The press had been given no information about the incidents in the cellar by the Lützowplatz. The arrest of Irene Gruss and the former Gestapo official Otto Jäckel was announced in a laconic communiqué, while another reported the death "in pursuance of his military duties" of Major William S. O'Hara from New York.

Frank had left the Colonel about half-past ten. Hunter was sitting at a little table in the drawing room, drafting his report to the General.

Behind him the door opened, and quickly closed again.

"Who's there?" asked the Colonel, turning round.

Marianne von Artemstein's head appeared round the door.

"I am sorry, Colonel," she said, evidently confused. "I wanted to get a book for myself."

"Can't you sleep?"

"No. There's a strong *Föhn*."

"Go right ahead," said the Colonel. "I'm still working."

She was fully dressed; she wore a close-fitting navy-blue jumper and a tweed skirt.

He heard her rummaging among the books on the shelves—rather protractedly, he thought. He turned round.

"I've been wanting to have a word with you for some time, Fräulein von Artemstein," he said. "If you could spare me a moment . . ."

"Of course."

He offered her a seat and she sat down on the couch by the fireplace while he settled in the armchair facing her.

"It's about my wife's purchases," he began. "Her purchases on the black market . . ."

She smiled. "One can hardly call it a black market."

"The concept is elastic," said Hunter. "Foodstuffs from the PX and the Commissary are used for barter deals with Germans. I call that black market."

"There are so many little things that give Mrs. Hunter pleasure," said Marianne.

The Colonel made rather heavy weather of lighting a cigarette. He said:

"Are you really interested in giving my wife pleasure, Fräulein von Artemstein?"

Marianne dropped her eyes. "No," she said. "I'm interested in keeping my job." After a little hesitation she added: "Mrs. Hunter was not at first favorably disposed to me."

"What makes you think so?" asked Hunter.

"A woman knows these things," said Marianne.

"My wife has spoken of you in the most flattering terms," the Colonel said, a little confused. "I only wish it had nothing to do with those 'business deals.' "

"They aren't the main reason," said Marianne.

The Colonel looked at her inquiringly. She continued:

"She knows that I am no danger to her."

Hunter looked away. The woman's forthrightness baffled him. She had uttered the last sentence as if he was bound to know what she was thinking. So she might have been a danger: that was the thought that underlay her words. Ought he to be annoyed? Ought he to put her in her place? But before he could make up his mind she continued:

"Don't misunderstand me, Colonel. The American women regard all of us German women as seducers. It's not Mrs. Hunter's fault."

"What makes you say that?" Hunter asked, just to say something.

"The American women are right," said Marianne. "You don't know what's going on in the houses around here."

"I don't wish to know it," Hunter said sharply.

"I didn't mean it literally," replied Marianne, completely ignoring the Colonel's reproof. "Not exactly these houses here. The German women are starved. Principally for bread, naturally—but not only for bread. The men have gone. Killed or crippled or captured. And those that are left are themselves starving. Do you ever see German men laughing, or even smiling? Very seldom. We are starved for a little gaiety. And for a little tenderness. Hungry men aren't tender."

The Colonel flicked his burning cigarette into the fire.

"And the American men succumb to every temptation," he said. It was not clear whether it was a statement or a question.

"Why not?" she asked. She looked into his eyes without a trace of embarrassment. "It's the charm of the exotic."

"What do you mean: exotic?"

She smiled, almost unnoticeably, only with her eyes. She said:

"Tenderness for instance."

Hunter rose. He wanted to close the discussion. But he said irritably:

"You mean that American men need German women in order to know what tenderness is?"

"That would be a generalization," she said. "All I meant was that we are in fact a danger. We are not so exotic as Japanese women or Arabian women. We are white like the Americans; we wear similar clothes and have similar manners. But for us a man is still our lord and master. Perhaps even our god. Our world revolves round him. We are happy if we can make him happy. So to the Americans we are exotic."

Hunter went to his desk, pulled out a drawer and pretended to be looking for cigarettes. He could not understand why he had not closed this conversation long ago. The confusion that had seized him was the stronger because—as he well realized—it ran counter to his precise and methodical nature. He felt like a healthy man suffering from a sudden heart attack—the first one, unfamiliar and alarming.

He thought: If she really wants to tempt me, how clumsily she is setting about it! She talks so coolly of these difficult and secret things, so entirely without illusion, as though she were still discussing the black market. Do these women really offer themselves on their own black market? Do they believe they would be taken in the same fashion that coffee is bartered for a porcelain figurine? But he also thought: What strange personal undercurrents this sober conversation has suddenly taken on! How cleverly she stirs up the depths without, seemingly, going below the surface! In what an impertinent, superior manner this German woman speaks of our women, and how cunningly she contrives to talk of Betty and me and herself without mentioning our names! Yet at the same time he thought: How right she is! I might have just as well spoken about the black market at breakfast—moreover, without endowing the matter with an importance it does not merit. I did not really want to talk of Betty's improper purchases; I simply wanted to seize the opportunity to be alone with the woman. He thought: She speaks contemptuously of the American men "all around here," the Americans who have taken German mistresses, and she even invites my censure on them. But at the same time he thought: And why should I be the only one who, either for the sake of a principle or out of ludicrous thin-bloodedness, misses his last opportunity?

When he had found his pack of cigarettes and turned round to face her again she had got up. She said:

"Please forgive me, Colonel. I don't know what made me start such a personal conversation." She smiled, not only with her eyes but also with her wide mouth. "It is getting late. Good night!"

He glanced at the clock on the mantelpiece.

"I've still got a lot of work to do," he said, although he really wanted to remark frostily that he had not taken the conversation personally.

Instead of going she said:

"You work too much."

"It can't be helped. We've got too few people."

"I don't believe you've seen the country yet," she said. "You even work Sundays."

"I've made a few official trips."

"This is the time when the countryside begins to look lovely," she said. "You ought to take a house for the summer by one of the lakes."

"One requisitioned house is enough," he said.

"Yes," she said; "but you're the only one who thinks so."

"It ought to go without saying," he said, embarrassed.

She was smiling no longer. "A lot of things ought to go without saying," she said.

Why isn't she going? thought Hunter. Suddenly he saw before him the whole house in whose drawing-room this nocturnal conversation was taking place. It was before him like one of those modern stage settings showing a house sliced in two. Upstairs, in one of the high twin beds of their joint bedroom, Betty was sleeping. Her hair, carefully curled, was covered with a silk scarf and her face was smothered in cream. In the next room Ruth and Beverley were sleeping. In the small attic Bob was probably still reading a whodunit. At the end of the first-floor corridor Marianne's room was still empty. Sometimes, when he passed the room, the door would be only half-shut and a strange perfume would waft out into the passage. It was not scent, nor even soap or eau de cologne: it was less sweet and less definite, like a woman's warm hair in summer. And then the Colonel saw himself and the woman facing one another in the drawing-room, discussing personal and impersonal matters, hostile rather than friendly, and united only in an inexplicable attempt to prolong the cold and pointless conversation. The other rooms were in darkness, just as on the stage only the room is lit up in which the action is taking place. He saw the room from outside, as though he were in the audience. But he was not in the audience: the room had four closed walls and outside a dry spring gale was tearing at the trees.

He caught himself standing there clumsily, still clutching the pack of cigarettes without having taken one from it. He made a step towards her and extended the package.

"Cigarette?" he asked, although he had never seen her smoking before.

She took a cigarette. He, too, took another one and put the pack down on the table by the fire. Before he could reach out for the matchbox she had struck a match. He took it from her as she was about to give him a light. Their hands touched. Quickly he withdrew his hand; he first lit her cigarette and then his own.

"You are afraid of me," she said.

"No," he said.

"That's all right then," she said. "Then I'll not have to go."

Hunter did not know whether it sounded trite or helpless, or both.

"You don't have to go," he said.

"I wasn't really looking for a book," she said. "But I really couldn't sleep."

Once more he tried to impose his own limits on the conversation. "The gale's getting worse," he said.

"I won't disturb you any longer," she said. "And I'll not make such clumsy excuses again."

Hunter looked at her and once again an unfamiliar and disturbing sensation crept over him. There was a great weariness in him, so great that it seemed to engulf his whole life and his whole personality. But his body burst the bounds of that weariness, and like the action in the only illuminated room in the exposed house so the movements of his body now became doubly spotlighted by the fact that all around was darkness.

She wanted to flick the ash off her cigarette or to crush the half-smoked cigarette in the ashtray, and to get to the ashtray she had to pass him. Her shoulder brushed against his shoulder. She turned abruptly and her face was only a hairbreadth away from his face.

The cigarette dropped from her hand, on to the table.

When their lips touched there was in their kiss the whole breathlessness, ruthlessness and abandon of a suppressed, forbidden and belated confession.

Hunter did not know how long the kiss lasted. All he knew was that from out of his blackout there suddenly reappeared before him the sliced house—but this time it was like just before the final curtain, when the lights go on in all the rooms. He saw the whole house: the bedroom with Betty, and the nursery with Ruth and Beverley, and Bob's room, and Marianne's empty room.

He released himself from the woman's embrace, and he released her from his.

A moment later she had left the room. The Colonel collapsed into his armchair. He buried his face in his hands.

Adam Stands His Trial

The occupation was a year old in Bavaria. On April 27, 1945, the "Bavarian Freedom Movement" had seized control of the provincial capital, Munich, and on April 30, 1945, some forty thousand defeated Wehrmacht troops laid down their arms. On the same day the Allied armor rolled over the Isar bridges.

That had been a year ago.

For a whole year Germany had been occupied to it furthest corner. For a whole year there had been no bombs. The nights had become quiet again, and blackout and conflagrations had given way to peacetime, though still rather dim, street lights.

The cities in the occupied country were not much changed since the days, a year before, when the last fires were burning and the last walls crumbling. Some order had invaded the chaos: the masonry had been piled into neat heaps here and there, and in one or two places the debris had even been removed so that sporadic open spaces arose where stones, girders, glass and timber had formed a jungle of destruction in the very heart of the city. The buildings were still shamelessly exposed: stairs that led nowhere; grotesquely preserved, elegantly papered walls between wrecked rooms; a ridiculous column of toilets suspended in mid-air one above the other; doors leading from half-preserved rooms into the void; and paradoxically unscathed kitchens without apartments to them. But at least the mocking perquisites of daily life had been removed from the ruins: no longer did a bed hang out of half a bedroom; no longer did a frying pan hang on the only surviving kitchen wall; no longer did a family portrait scowl, somewhat askew, from the wall of a gutted drawing-room; and no longer did bathtubs dangling from the plumbing threaten the lives of pedestrians clambering over the debris. But there was little sign so far of new life springing from the wreckage. The buildings which had been lucky enough to be subjected only to artillery fire, and not also to the bombardment that fell from the skies, still showed their gaping wounds and their flaking walls were pock-marked like a leper's skin. "Bavaria," stated an official communiqué, "is short of 17,000,000 square meters of window glass; her monthly production totals 400,000 square meters, but only 80,000 square meters out of that total is available to Bavaria." But there was no need for such incomprehensible statistics: the language of the boarded-up openings and of the unglazed window frames was comprehensible enough—a permanent exhibition of frames without pictures.

On that anniversary the wounded land seemed torn asunder for all time. For centuries it had been stated at the beginning of each war that the frontier posts would be torn up—but instead, new frontier posts had been planted right across Germany—Russian and American, French and British. True, in January 1946 "limited traffic" had been resumed between the occupation zones, but communications were as cumbersome as in the middle ages and four different sets of victors were endeavoring to impress their own character upon the defeated country. In the Russian Zone the population was rapidly turned into miserable muzhiks, chewing gum and Coca-Cola became the glories of the U. S. Zone; in the French Zone women, mothers, aunts, mothers-in-law and entire numerous *familles* were pushing the Germans out of their homes; and in the British Zone the spirit of the colonial overlords of India, Burma and South Africa had made its entry aboard the British lorries. Once again Man proved to be an exceedingly poor export article, deteriorating more and more with every mile that divided him from his home, and the acquaintanceship between different nations, of which idealists and dreamers had entertained such high expectations, was like opening a crate of oysters which had traveled too far and had gone high and malodorous.

A year was not a long period of time and there was no justification for impatience, among victors or defeated; but to those directly affected it seemed nevertheless as though the conditions which had been accepted, during the first few weeks or months, as the immediate and temporary effects of the war were destined to become solidified and permanent. A rebellious stomach was not like a watchdog who gets used in time to the same visitor: instead of getting used to hunger it growled and barked ever more angrily. The emptier the stomachs, the more fully stocked was the black market. In the elegant residential quarter of Bogenhausen a regular bazaar sprang up in the Möhlstrasse—a piece of Istanbul or Lvov on the Isar. It was quite true that this motley international crowd of profiteers of starvation could not have pursued its trade if the German peasants had delivered the food they grew or if many a reputable tradesman had opened his secret stores more readily—but the fact was that human solidarity failed miserably in the face of hardship and that most people were only too thankful to be allowed to pay out eighty marks for a pound of meat or two thousand marks for an indispensable bicycle.

Moral principles were jettisoned like so much needless ballast. During the first year of occupation the Munich police records—by no means the worst in Germany—listed six hundred assaults with robbery in the streets of the city; one man walked into a police station stark naked, for his assailants had not even allowed him to keep his shirt. The crack of revolver shots rang through nocturnal farmsteads as gangs of criminals roamed the countryside; after the opening performance of a municipal theater all electric bulbs were found to have gone from the lavatories; along the Belgian frontier juveniles formed the legendary "Rabatz" gangs; gangs of children, living among the ruins and building up secret stores of stolen goods underneath the debris, called themselves "Bubbles." On the anniversary of the occupation the Munich police were searching for 3 murderers with robbery, 3,823 burglars and 2,674 bicycle thieves.

The political cleansing had barely begun by that first anniversary, but comedy and tragedy were already so close to each other as their symbolic masks above the gates of ancient Greek theaters. The race was on for the "Persil voucher," as the certificate of a clean past was wittily called. "Principal culprits" were trying to be only "incriminated"; these in turn tried to pass themselves off as "moderately incriminated"; these in turn as "fellow-travelers," and these finally as "nonincriminated." The definitions turned many a dangerous somersault: thus, for instance, a "militarist" was defined in Article Eight of the Denazification and Demilitarization Law as "any person who had devised military teachings or programs," while Article Seven of the same law described as an "active Nazi" any person who had successfully "evaded military service or employment at the front" through his National Socialist connections. For many years to come the legend that the small criminals had been hanged while the big ones had been allowed to escape continued to be believed. That, at least would have shown some system, however absurd; in actual fact the muddle was far more complete: small and big criminals escaped while innocent people, small ones and big, were caught up into the crushing machinery. In the course of world history Justice had frequently been an opportunist prostitute without, oddly enough, ever losing her respectability. But in the spring of 1946 she had lost the last vestige of respect and had become a babbling idiot.

One year after the occupation of Germany the words war criminal were still written without quotation marks. The past hung heavily over every German, guilty and innocent alike. The past had at last become known. Some were already mocking the victors, but many were taking the defeat seriously and hence also the victors. People were hanging their heads, even more so than in the beginning—either because they felt humility or because it was expedient to pretend humility; because they were ashamed of what had happened, or because they were ashamed of the hypocrites; because they did not wish to look into the eyes of other knowing ones, or because they did not want to stand out among the crowd of the unknowing.

On that anniversary of the occupation of Munich, on April 30, 1946, at three P.M., the occupation major Frank Green and the German doctor Adam Wild entered the building of the Military Government, where the case against the doctor was to be tried. He was charged with violent assault on a member of the Occupying Power, at the Frankfurt detention camp, and with inflicting serious bodily injury on him. Adam Wild had availed himself of his right to be defended in the American military court by an American officer, and had chosen Major Frank Green for his counsel.

The hearing took place in a small hall and was public: about a dozen people had in fact turned up, no doubt because they had nothing better to do. Behind the bench stood a huge Stars and Stripes and on the walls hung pictures of George Washington, Franklin D. Roosevelt and Harry S. Truman. The Court was composed of a lieutenant colonel, a lieutenant and a sergeant; a major was in charge of the prosecution. Major Frank Green, experienced in such matters, regarded the very fact that a so-called "small military tribunal" was presided over by a lieutenant colonel as a bad sign—even the lowest-ranking officer could have performed that duty—and he implored Adam Wild to confine himself to a factual defense and avoid all general declarations.

Dr. Wild pleaded guilty within the meaning of the indictment. He did not deny having struck Corporal Francis D. Crane and perhaps even having knocked him about. At the same time he had fully described the incident in Barracks C of the Frankfurt detention camp in his earlier oral and written statements, and insisted that his action had prevented an attempted murder, or at least something very near an attempted murder.

The prosecutor, Major Martin B. Boise, set out—as both Frank and Adam instantly realized—to belittle the importance of those circumstances. The Major was a professional soldier, a man of about forty-five, who had risen from the ranks, of short but massive build, intelligent and quick-witted, and gifted with such a pithy, colloquial manner of speech that Frank was beginning to worry lest this fact alone should impress the Court. Although the circumstances surrounding the Frankfurt incident were favorable to the defendant, Frank knew quite well that it was within the power of the military court to impose a sentence of five years' imprisonment on Adam Wild. The choice of prosecutor was not calculated to dispel his anxieties.

There was only one circumstance that favored the defense from the very outset. Lieutenant Colonel Lee E. Perry, the officer commanding the Frankfurt camp, had had the Corporal put before a court-martial, for the very same incident, and the man had been deprived of his two stripes and sentenced to four weeks' detention. This information, with which Frank surprised the Court right at the beginning and which the prosecution could not deny, appeared to make some impression on the three judges.

For two hours the proceedings were devoid of all sensation. The indictment and the written depositions were read out and translated by the interpreter; prosecutor and defending counsel examined the defendant in what was now only a routine manner; and Frank was just beginning to accuse himself of unwarranted pessimism, when Major Boise rose and asked the Court's permission to submit some circumstantial evidence not perhaps related to the case itself but of importance with regard to the defendant.

"The man you have before you," he said, "as with your permission I shall prove presently, is a dangerous Nazi—a circumstance not without importance in the assessment of the case you are trying. The defense has tried to depict the incident in the camp as though the defendant had acted out of justified indignation. That's no more than I expected in view of the sentence passed on the ill-treated Private Crane. Now if Dr. Wild really were the kind of person we have been told he is, we might perhaps expect justified indignation on his part. If, however, he is a notorious Nazi then his violence against a representative of the Occupying Power appears in a wholly different light. I trust that this consideration is sufficient justification for my request to the Court to be allowed to put to the defendant a number of questions relating to his character and his past."

The lieutenant colonel, a much-decorated officer of an armored unit, no more than thirty years old, with wind-bitten, open and uncomplicated features, nodded agreement.

"Is it correct, Dr. Wild," the Major, satisfied, turned to the defendant, "that from April 20, 1945, until May 6, 1945, you had two members of the Waffen-SS in your apartment and supplied them with civilian clothing?"

The interpreter translated. Frank looked questioningly at Adam. "That is correct," replied Adam.

"Is it correct, Dr. Wild," the Major continued, "that during the war you maintained friendly relations with Professor Wilhelm Voberg, one of the leading members of the Nazi Medical Association and at present under suspicion of crimes against humanity?"

"That is correct," said Adam.

Should he object to the questions? Frank asked himself. He looked at Adam and that clear serene face suddenly seemed to withdraw into a misty distance.

He had now been in Germany over a year. He had arrived full of prejudices, arguments and hatred. But the chaos was in the element of hatred: whenever the shadows lifted and the whirlpools stopped eddying there would be human faces rising up from the receding chaos, and with every clearly outlined human face some of his hatred would vanish. One of the faces that had taken shape in the dark swirling waters, perhaps the clearest and best of all, had been the face of the German Adam Wild. But now it was once more the face of a drowning man, appearing for a last time above the water before being swallowed up forever by the waves. What if the clarity of that face had only been a delusion, a mirage in the chaos? Then only hate, born of chaos, would remain in the spinning vortex.

No, Frank decided; he would not interrupt Boise. He wanted to know whether the man he had got out of the camp, the man whom he had volunteered to defend, had lied to him—if only by means of the great German conspiracy of silence.

He heard the prosecutor's next question:

"Is it correct, Dr. Wild, that you got into conflict with the occupation authorities once before: when in the house next to yours you tried to obstruct an officially authorized eviction?"

"Yes," replied Adam.

"Is it correct that you tried to smuggle documents into Detention Camp for Militarists No. 4, for the benefit of a former Colonel Achim von Sibelius, then under detention there?"

"Yes; that was how I got into the camp," said Adam. "I was arrested in the act."

"Is it correct," the Major concluded triumphantly, "that, following her release, you hid one of the leading women of the Third Reich, the wife of the war criminal Kurt von Zutraven, at your home until she was rearrested by the Military Government?"

"I did not hide her, but I gave her hospitality," said Adam.

"Do you admit having been a convinced National Socialist?" asked the prosecutor.

"Objection!" Frank interposed before Adam could answer. He turned to the judges. "None of the questions put by the prosecutor so far is relevant to the case being tried here. The last question cannot be said in any way to supply fresh evidence."

"Objection sustained," said the lieutenant colonel. "Have you any more questions, Major Boise?"

"No more questions," said the prosecutor.

"Major Green, have you any questions for the defendant?" asked the presiding judge.

Frank turned to Adam: "Can you explain to the Court your action in the matter of the two Waffen-SS soldiers?" He tried to hit a note suitable to his role of defending counsel, but his question sounded almost more aggressive than the prosecutor's. He did not look at Adam.

Adam's light eyes were calm, almost serene. He said:

"I would like to deal with that in my general defense."

"I wish you would answer my question," said Frank irritably.

"The Court notes that the defendant wishes to make a concerted defense," the lieutenant colonel cut in.

A few minutes later Major Boise rose to make his final speech. Skilfully he built his indictment upon two points: one, that in the person of Private Francis Crane the authority of the Occupying Power had been attacked and that only by making an example of Dr. Wild could the German population be discouraged from similar misdeeds; and two, that the defendant was one of those incorrigible

Nazis who, though they had never entered the Party, were venting their resentment in attacks on the Occupying Power and thus represented a permanent danger unless a resolute stop was put to their activities.

"Does the defendant wish to make a personal statement or will he leave the final plea to his counsel?" asked the presiding judge.

"I would like to speak myself," said Adam before Frank could object. He got up and said: "May it please the Court! First of all I should like to apologize to my counsel, Major Green, for electing to speak for myself. This is not due to any lack of confidence in Major Green, who has indeed gone out of his way to give me every possible help. But certain facts which Major Boise has brought up, and which are not known or only partly known to my counsel, can only be elucidated by myself. That is why I prefer to conduct my own defense now. I had hoped that this Court would concern itself, not with my person, but only with the incidents in Detention Camp No. 4. But now that these things have been brought up I shall have to speak about myself, though I shall try to keep that as short as possible.

"The two Waffen-SS soldiers whom I sheltered at my home from April 20 until May 6, 1945, were—as the prosecutor omitted to state—deserters from the Wehrmacht. They were brothers, the sons of an old friend of mine, Professor Lohn of Munich University. Their ages were eighteen and nineteen. They belonged to the 'death or glory' unit of Colonel Waldmüller and were to have been driven to the slaughter in those very last pointless engagements. After unspeakable difficulties the brothers Lohn, scarcely more than children, made their way to Munich, where I sheltered them unhesitatingly until the arrival of our supposed liberators. No doubt, gentlemen, you will ask why the two boys did not surrender to the Americans upon their entry on April 30 and why, on the contrary, I supplied them with civilian clothes until on May 6—and that is another point the prosecutor failed to make—the two surrendered to the authorities of their own free will."

He was speaking softly, almost monotonously. He paused for a moment and then continued:

"I have only one justification for my action, gentlemen: that I was no more convinced of the wisdom of the Occupying Power than I was of the morality of the late regime. Only a few weeks ago a colonel in the U. S. Army surprised me with the observation that the Waffen-SS and the SS were the same thing—both consisted of concentration camp guards. Every German knows that the Waffen-SS was a recently created Wehrmacht unit which a man joined no more voluntarily than he did an infantry or artillery unit. No Waffen-SS soldier ever had anything to do with concentration camps. I am guilty, gentlemen, of having suspected that, together with your supplies of ammunition and food cans, you also brought a good portion of ignorance with you into this country. Thousands of Waffen-SS troops—as guilty or as innocent as any other German soldier—were, out of sheer ignorance, subjected for many months to the kind of treatment that might have been justified in the case of the SS, and then probably not all of it. I saved my two young friends from this unwarranted treatment, to the best of my ability. I first snatched them from the hands of a sadistic Nazi colonel, and then from those of an uninformed American. If, like so many of my fellow-countrymen, I have any regrets at all, then it is that our resistance to brutality and stupidity was confined to so pitifully few isolated cases."

Adam made a pause to give the stenographer an opportunity of getting everything down verbatim, for the subsequent translation.

"The second charge," he continued, "is more complicated. Professor Wilhelm Voberg, my former teacher, was one of the most dangerous creatures nurtured by the Third Reich. The prosecutor has referred to my friendly relations with Professor Voberg. I have answered his question in the affirmative, although in fact such relations never existed. But for three years I worked at the professor's military hospital. This hospital was exclusively for wounded members of the Wehrmacht. Voberg's criminal activities, of which he now stands accused, were performed in the course of his private research work. I was entirely ignorant of Voberg's experiments on concentration camp inmates; but I knew his political views. I did not oppose those views. On the other hand—and I am now compelled to mention this—I used the professor's trust in me to allow a dozen officers, who were directly or indirectly implicated in the attempt of the 20th of July, to find sanctuary in the hospital on the Chiemsee. At the PW hospital, which was attached to our military hospital, I sheltered the American Lieutenant McNamara and the French Lieutenant

Miramont who provided the liaison with the 'Bavarian Freedom Movement' and thus prevented further pointless bloodshed in this country."

He continued hurriedly, as though unwilling to lend his statements the character of sensational revelations.

"If the prosecutor had not brought up the Voberg business I might have saved myself the enumeration of my actions. I should have preferred to do that—not out of misplaced modesty or out of immunity to the present wave of opportunism, but for reasons which I should like to outline briefly. The resistance which we Germans offered to the criminal regime seems to you, gentlemen, extremely slight. I wish I could prove you wrong. But the resistance was not quite so slight as it was individual—and that perhaps makes it appear in a wrong light. Collective resistance, as the world expected it of us, a resistance on the barricades, would have looked more impressive— but that is about all. Our individual resistance, in turn, might have been heroic—as was expected of us—but instead it was practical. In the course of those three years I could have killed Professor Voberg a hundred times: instead of now standing my trial alive I should then have a bronze bust in the Square of the Victims of Nazism. I chose individual, unheroic, practical resistance. We Germans cannot expect you to understand the paradox of this situation. To you, resistance and compromise must seem irreconcilable and I am not deluding myself into believing that I could make you see how little they in fact exclude one another."

He was speaking urgently, struggling for comprehension.

"How can I make you understand it, that German resistance? I know a man who hid a Jewish doctor in his cellar for four years—and so as to be able to do it he gave sumptuous parties for the Nazi bosses in his villa above the cellar. I know another man who became a Peasant Leader in order to sabotage drastic Nazi measures in his village. Finally, only officers who had distinguished themselves in the service of the Third Reich and thus had access to Adolf Hitler could hope to organize the 20th of July with at least some prospect of success. How, gentlemen, are you to understand these things? Are you not bound to assume that the resisters—and they were, of course, a minority—backed all the horses in the race? That they ran with the hare and hunted with the hounds? How are you, who come from outside and find the gory specter exorcised—how are you now to distinguish between compromise for the sake of resistance and compromise for the sake of private gain?"

He noticed the officers whispering impatiently with each other and returned to the matter in hand.

"I did oppose the eviction of a family from the house next to mine. I did so for the same reason that I helped Colonel von Sibelius get hold of the papers which eventually assured him of his freedom. And I extended hospitality to Frau Elisabeth von Zutraven. All three of them—the writer Ernst Helm, my evicted neighbor, who languished in Hitler's prisons for four years; Colonel von Sibelius, an officer involved in the 20th of July; and Frau von Zutraven who, as the wife of the Governor of France, saved dozens of people from deportation, concentration camp and certain death—all three of them were victims of the injustice of the victors. Who am I, the prosecutor will ask, to decide what is right and what is wrong? But why then do you expect our conscience to have spoken up yesterday if we are to condemn that same conscience to muteness today? If you have discovered another yardstick of justice, in your fortunate America, than that of the human conscience, then I wish you would bring it to us. Myself, I know no other."

He took a deep breath and launched into the peroration of his plea.

"May it please the Court. If, by the violent action of which I stand accused, I have undermined the authority and repute of the Occupying Power, then I am truly sorry. I am not, however, indulging in empty oratory when I say that you would undermine the authority and repute of the Occupying Power far more by convicting me and acquitting the uniformed beast in your own ranks. I freely admit, gentlemen, that the German disaster was brought upon Germany by herself. I admit that there were thousands on our side just like that Corporal Crane. I admit that in your camps people are not gassed, executed, or even tortured on higher orders. I admit that there might have been one disaster a thousand times worse than the German defeat—a German victory. But I refuse, and shall continue to refuse, to put one injustice on one side of the scales and another on the other side, or to believe that injustice can be weighed up only by injustice. Conditions change, and I am not denying that sometimes they improve. But they do not change or improve without resistance.

Smug contentment with change is the very enemy of change. To my defending counsel, Major Frank Green, whom I may perhaps call my friend, I owe my knowledge of a few lines written by your great poet Walt Whitman: 'To the States or any one of them, or any city of the States,/*Resist much, obey little,*/Once unquestioning obedience, once fully enslaved,/Once fully enslaved, no nation, state, city of this earth/ever afterward resumes its liberty.' That is how Walt Whitman's verses run. We Germans once gave unquestioning obedience, and once we were fully enslaved. The danger that we may never resume our liberty is great. Some of us are resolved to stand up to it."

He sat down.

At a gesture from the presiding judge the interpreter stood up and translated what Adam had said. The spectators, breathless, tried to read the judges' faces. They remained inscrutable. Major Boise smiled superciliously. Frank tried to catch Adam's eyes: in his own eyes was joyful gratitude and a request for forgiveness.

Walking up and down the corridor, Adam and Frank awaited the verdict.

"Please forgive me for choosing to speak myself," said Adam.

"I am more than glad that you did so," said Frank.

After only half an hour's consultation the judges filed back into the courtroom.

"In the name of the United States," began the lieutenant colonel. "The defendant is found guilty of having undermined the authority and repute of the U. S. armed forces in Germany by attacking a member of the Occupying Power. In view of extenuating circumstances he is hereby sentenced to eight weeks' imprisonment. The sentence is deemed to have been served by the defendant's arrest at Detention Camp No. 4."

Two women among the audience began to clap. The lieutenant colonel gave them a reproving glance. He added:

"Motivation of the verdict will be forwarded in writing."

Quickly he picked up the files in front of him and walked out of the room, followed by his fellow-judges.

The white-helmeted MP who had stood at the door stepped aside. As Adam and Frank descended the stairs Frank said:

"You have now seen the best of America, Doctor Wild."

Adam smiled. "Individual resistance . . ." he said. But in his features, too, relief was plainly visible.

On the following day the Munich papers published a brief announcement:

"Dr. Adam Wild, a Munich physician, was sentenced to eight weeks' imprisonment, allowance being made for extenuating circumstances, for an assult with violence on a member of the Occupying Power."

Not a word was said about the extenuating circumstances or about Adam's speech in court. The occupation of Germany was a year old.

"We Owe That to the Yanks"

The summer day lay heavily over the city. The windows of the tall blonde's room behind the Sendlinger-Tor-Platz were open. But not a breath of air came through them. Tired flies stuck on dusty pieces of furniture. Ilse Joachim was lying on her sofa, clad only in a dressing gown. She was airing her ample bosom and her massive thighs.

"Don't stare at me like that," she said to Inge who was sitting at the table in a light printed cotton dress. "Have you never seen a naked woman before?"

"I've got to talk to you, Ilse," said the girl.

"Sounds ominous," said the tall blonde. She sat up and pulled her dressing gown together.

"I'm not carrying on," said Inge.

"Carrying on with whom?"

"No one. With streetwalking."

"Are you crazy?"

"I haven't been out for weeks."

"And you're looking quite starved again, too."

"I can't do it," said Inge.

"Because of Hans?"

Inge nodded.

"Does he want to marry you?"

"I don't know."

"What does he want? Can he keep you?"

"I don't know what he wants," said Inge. "I only know what I don't want."

"In short, the great love."

"You wouldn't understand."

Ilse lit a cigarette. "Rubbish," she said. "I understand it better than you. Before, everything was all right. Now you feel you're deceiving him."

"Maybe," said Inge.

Ilse lay down flat on her back and blew a smoke ring. "I had a great love once," she said.

"I know—Karl," said Inge.

"But he at least took my money," Ilse continued undismayed. "That makes things simpler. It lulls the conscience."

"I'm not interested in your Karl," said Inge.

"He was a decent lad," said the tall blonde. "Didn't interfere with my profession. But you're a hopeless case anyway. You've never really enjoyed streetwalking."

"Do you?"

"What is enjoyment . . . ? Does anybody enjoy his occupation? I've known many men, but only one of them ever enjoyed his work. A painter in Schwabing. And he starved to death. Does a postman enjoy delivering letters? Well then. But on the other hand he isn't sorry for himself. That's what I mean, child. I'm not sorry for myself because I sell my lily-white body. Amateurs make me sick." She sat up again. "I can't think what made me take you up. And what do you propose to live on, child?"

"I'll work."

"Congratulations. You're just the one they've all been waiting for!"

"Others manage to live," said Inge.

"And your father?" asked Ilse.

Inge stood up. She walked over to the window, pushed the potted geraniums to one side and sat down on the sill. She was now behind Ilse; she did not want to face the tall blonde. She said:

"He has beaten me."

"The swine!" said Ilse. "Because you've not brought any money home?"

Inge did not reply.

"We owe that to the Yanks," said Ilse. "Fathers as pimps. Compared with your father my Karl was a gentleman."

"Do you have to talk about Karl all the time?"

"I hope you told him where he got off?" said Ilse.

"Since I stopped bringing money home he's had the whip hand again. I dare not go home."

"Have you told your Hans?"

"I'm going to, today," said Inge. She looked down into the street.

"Can he take you to his place?"

"I'm sure he can't."

"Then what's all this in aid of?" Ilse asked irritably. She turned to face Inge. She regretted her harsh words. "You can stay here. Only you'll have to scram when I have a visitor."

"Thanks," said Inge. And after a little pause: "How do you suppose he'll take it?"

"Hans?"

"Yes."

"I know men," said Ilse. "He'll probably let you down. They're all hypocrites. Best of all they like a whore who doesn't say she is a whore. Always running away from responsibility."

A whistled signal came from the street. Inge turned.

"Coming," she called down.

She waved. Laughing and waving, she was transformed: a young girl being called for by her young man.

"Good luck," said the tall blonde. "You can always sleep here."

Hans was waiting for her on the far side of the street. He wanted to kiss her but she only shook hands with him.

They walked down the Sendlinger Strasse, towards the Marienplatz.

"What's wrong?" asked Hans.

She looked straight ahead. She said hurriedly:

"I can't go home. I didn't tell you because you wouldn't have believed me: but since that time I haven't walked the streets. I just couldn't."

He took her arm. He laughed, and his laughter was so merry that involuntarily she looked at him. He said:

"Of course I've known it. Was this 'confession' so difficult?"

"No," she said, trying to smile. "But my father . . ."

"Your father is sending you out, is he?" he said.

She nodded.

"I'm going to talk to him," he said. "Come along, we'll go to your place now."

"You can't talk to him," she said.

"I'd like to take you to my home," he said. He was laughing no longer. "I've thought about it a lot. But our house is requisitioned. We're there only on sufferance."

"I know it can't be done," she said.

They got on a crowded streetcar. They stood among sweating, smelly people. The trolley jolted along, as if it were running not on rails but over irregular cobbles.

He had taken no notice of her objection; they were approaching the Eastern Cemetery.

Presently they were outside Inge's house.

"Come along," said Hans. "Let's get it over."

The pensioner Alois Schmidt had already spotted them, for he was leaning out of his window in his shirt sleeves. He turned round as they entered the room. Inge knew at once that he had been drinking: his eyes were bloodshot as always when he took too much. He did not return Hans's greetings but said:

"So you're the one . . ."

"Yes," said Hans. "I'm the one."

"And who invited you here?" asked Schmidt. He seemed to know at once what Hans had come for.

"We'll skip that," said Hans. "I would take Inge with me if I could. For the moment I can't. Until then she will stay here, and you will leave her alone."

"I will, will I?" said Schmidt. "Because you say so?"

"No," said Hans. "Not because I say so. But because you can go to prison for procuring."

Schmidt advanced on him threateningly. "Who's a procurer here? You or me?"

"Don't do anything foolish, Herr Schmidt," said Hans. He was still trying to control himself. "You're an old man; you'd come out second best if we came to blows. That's not what I have come for."

Schmidt stopped. He had drunk a lot, but not so much as not to realize their unevenly matched strength. He said:

"If you want the whore, you can have her. But she's got to get out of here."

Inge was leaning against the sideboard, trembling.

Hans did not know what to reply. That she had become a whore because her father had driven her out on to the streets? But would that not be tantamount to admitting that she was a whore? And was there any point in observing that his moral indignation had begun only when she was no longer willing to ply her trade? He moved over to Inge and said:

"Very well, Herr Schmidt. Tomorrow I shall take her away from here. You will never see her again. But until then I wouldn't lay hands on her if I were you!"

Alois Schmidt, now on the defensive, suddenly seemed to realize that he was losing the goose that laid the golden eggs. He pulled himself up and spoke almost with the authority of an injured father.

"I'm the one to decide what happens to my daughter. She's still a minor. I don't know who you are. I don't even want to know it. But if you think that my daughter is going to walk the streets for you . . ."

"Have you ever heard of the banker Eberhard Eber?" said Hans.

He did not know why he had uttered that name. Since early childhood he had been ashamed of the name of Eber, and never before had the name of Eberhard Eber been so discredited as at present. Yet now, in this stuffy lower-middle-class apartment by the Eastern Cemetery, championing a girl who was a prostitute, he had thrown the name into the balance. Was his father's name his only asset, after all? He asked the question too late: but he hoped that the pensioner Alois Schmidt would shrug his shoulders at the name, or sneer at it.

Instead, the pensioner's features reflected startled respect. He said: "Of course. But what have you . . . ?"

"Eberhard Eber is my father," said Hans. "Is that good enough for you?"

"If it were true . . ." Schmidt said in confusion.

"I shall call for Inge tomorrow."

"If you are the son of Eberhard Eber . . ." began Schmidt.

"I shouldn't try any blackmail," Hans interrupted him. "You'd be sorry for it. You've far too much to answer for as it is, Herr Schmidt." He turned to Inge. "I'll be here in the morning. Don't worry."

Hurriedly he touched the girl's hand. Only then did it occur to him that he had never revealed his true identity to her. But she would not know who Eberhard Eber was anyway.

Quickly, almost instinctively, he went to Stefan Lester, the friend to whom one could appeal in every situation.

Stefan was lying on the sofa in his little room, reading a book. The windowless room was like an oven, but it did not seem to worry him. He received Hans with the cheerful cordiality which, in spite of his physical disabilities, was his invariable mood.

»302«

"You look as if you've come straight from the grave," said Stefan. "What's up?"

Hans sat down in the only chair. He mopped the sweat off his forehead.

"Shall I roll you a cigarette?" asked Stefan.

"No, thank you. You've got to help me, Stefan. I'm in an impossible situation. Will you be patient with me? If I start at the beginning it's going to be a long story. It was in winter . . ."

He began with the day when he had picked Inge Schmidt up on the Isar bridge.

Stefan listened patiently.

"Is that all?" he asked at last.

"Isn't that enough?" said Hans, but he felt relieved already.

"It's enough," said Stefan, "but it's no tragedy." He glanced at the clock. "I'll go and see Dr. Wild presently. I ran into him a couple of days ago." He laughed. "His famous divan is vacant at the moment. It's no problem at all: we'll get Inge installed there tomorrow."

"What would I do without you," said Hans.

"Nonsense," said Stefan. "There's only one point I don't quite understand. Don't be angry with me—but why the devil haven't you told me all this before? Be honest: Were you really ashamed?"

Hans nodded.

"It wasn't meant to be an awkward question," said Stefan. "But you ought to know how silly it is."

"You mean I am a philistine."

"That's not the worst of it. But you don't seem to know whether you can get over it."

"Is that so surprising?"

Stefan did not make a straight reply. "You think her fate touching and horrifying," he said. "But it is neither horrifying nor touching. It is merely typical. You'll never get over your inhibitions if you think hers is a very singular fate."

Hans dropped his eyes. "Not every girl . . . ," he began.

Stefan interrupted him. "That's not the point. We are all responsible for Inge. That is the point. Hunger alone did not turn Alois Schmidt into a swine—hunger does not work that fast. But twelve years of denunciation have made him a swine. And do you think she would have gone on to the streets if she had not spent a childhood in the morass? We're all of us pretty well depraved, and it is high time we realized it."

"And what use would that realization be?"

"A great deal of use. You and I, to start with, would cease considering ourselves superior to Inge Schmidt. We all prostitute ourselves in one way or another. Only she put a clean end to it. That's what we've got to do. Put an end to it. We've got to drag ourselves out of the mire by our own hair—like Baron Münchhausen out of the water. Altogether the baron ought to be our idol—I much prefer him to our other national heroes. Unless we do this individually, each for himself, the German community won't do it for us, and neither will re-education."

Hans stood up and began to pace about the room.

"You're right, Stefan," he said. "Perhaps I ought to make a start at home."

"What do you mean?"

"I mean that I am myself like Alois Schmidt," said Hans. "Throughout that scene with Inge's father I had to think that I was not much better than him. I've sold Karin."

"You did nothing of the sort."

"I watched what was happening between her and Captain Green. I lied to myself and thought up a hundred excuses. Then I wearied of it and simply accepted the accomplished fact. Just as we used to do in the Third Reich. We are so busy we never find time for rebellion."

"We'll discuss that some other day," said Stefan. "Now we'll go. I'm sure to find Dr. Wild in at this hour."

It was evening when they walked out into the street. It was still sultry and the asphalt seemed to melt under their feet. The city smelt like stale beer.

"Till tomorrow morning then," said Stefan as they parted. "And try not to do anything foolish."

Hans walked quickly through the gathering dusk. A great serenity pervaded him. He did not feel the heavy heat; it was as if the sky had released its burden and he were walking through a refreshing summer shower.

He noticed with relief that the Captain's blue sports car was not at the door. The fact that his father and Uncle Oskar had withdrawn seemed to him a further propitious omen. Miss Karin was on the

terrace, the housekeeper informed him. As he stepped out he saw
Karin in a light summer dress by the wicker table on which stood the
record-player. It was playing American dance music. The darkness was
beginning to engulf the trees in the garden.

He sat down in a wicker chair and said:

"Turn that thing off. I want to talk to you."

"Does the music worry you?"

"Yes."

"I can't turn it down any softer." She reduced the volume but
kept the instrument playing.

"Karin," he said, "what's got into you?"

"I don't know what you mean."

"We used to be friends," he said. "Before I went off to the war."

"And . . . ?"

"Please, Karin, don't be difficult," he said. "You know quite well
that everything has changed since Captain Green requisitioned the
place."

"You've behaved abominably ever since," she said. "He extended
his hand, and you've rejected it. I don't understand you any longer."

"He extended his hand only for you. And you know it. We are all
here on sufferance only because . . ."

"Because . . . ?"

"Must I say it? Do you deny it?"

"No," she said. "Why should I deny it?"

He could feel her getting up in the dark. He was afraid she would
leave him, but she merely put on another record. "I'm dreaming of a
white Christmas," crooned a woman's voice.

"And why, Karin?" he said. "For God's sake, tell me why."

"And why not?" she said. "Are you going to act like Papa?"

"I don't know how Papa is acting."

"I'll tell you." She sat down. She spoke so softly now that at times
her voice was submerged in the tune of the music. "Nothing had
happened between me and George until father returned from detention. George had behaved like a gentleman. But Papa could
not understand that. On the very first day he made a scene. Do you
remember finding me in tears one day? I didn't say anything to
you—there didn't seem any point in it. He just raved. Against the
Americans, and against the refugees, and against the Jews. Probably

he meant well. But I had heard his speeches a hundred times during the past few years. I was sick of them. That night I went to bed with George."

Hans did not reply. His throat felt constricted. The soft music came to his ears like the roar of a vast orchestra.

At last he said: "You're not in love with him . . . ?"

"I don't know," she said. "I haven't thought about it. Love is a luxury. Thinking is a luxury, too."

"But it started before then," he persisted. "While Papa was still under arrest. That's why he allowed us to stay on."

"Naturally," she said. "It started with cigarettes and chocolate, and lipstick, and American records. And the house. I used to hate it—but I didn't want to leave the place. A Yankee whore, if you like." She was still speaking softly, without indignation and without bitterness. "So what? You didn't experience those last years, Hans. I don't mean the privations, for Papa did not deprive himself of much. I mean the deadly boredom." She gave a short laugh. "Those are the very words. 'Boredom' and 'deadly.' The only young men I ever saw were in the military hospital. Papa, as you know, insisted on my hospital visiting. You only saw them die. You don't know the stench of those who had limbs amputated. No, don't interrupt me. You've asked your questions; now you'll have to listen. They were deadly, those young heroes at the hospital. The only ones who were deadlier still were the ones on home leave. I can still see them sitting in the drawing-room, with the same gestures time and again. With their hands they described the deadly flight of their bombers. Or how their fighters were chasing the Yanks. When they laughed there was fear in their voice. When Papa came in they clicked their heels and babbled about ultimate victory. Then they sat in the air-raid shelter, longing to get back to the front."

"That'll do," said Hans. "I know the whole story. It just comes to this: that there is no greater sex appeal than victory."

"Perhaps," said Karin.

This was not the Karin he knew. Her answer should have been challenging, but instead it was merely resigned.

"It has nothing to do with Papa, then," he said sharply, anxious to draw her out of her resignation. At the same time he thought: So Eberhard Eber and I are allies again.

"But I think it has," said Karin. Again she got up to put on another record.

"Oh, do stop this filthy noise," said Hans.

She changed the record and continued:

"It has something to do with Papa. To be totally defeated and yet to be impertinent. That's typical of us Germans."

Hans rose abruptly.

"It's you who're typical of us Germans," he said savagely. "It is typical of us that we can't resist a single temptation." Inge's picture rose up before him. He felt as though he must see her at once and ask her forgiveness. "The fellow who chalks 'Yankee whore' on a wall means the poor little wenches who are hungry and who sell themselves for a pack of cigarettes. He is a fool. Papa's politics, your so-called wartime experiences, your joyless youth and your yearning for fun—all these are just rotten excuses. Only the thing about the house and the cigarettes and the lipstick and the chocolate is true. And those dance records." Doubly blind in the darkness he made for the little table with the record-player. "You are a Yankee whore!" he said and kicked the table savagely.

It fell over. The instrument hit the ground with a crash. Sliding and falling, it still played "The last time I saw Paris"; it was sentimental and the needle screeched. The rest of the records were shattered on the stone flags. Now the machine was silent.

He stood amidst the wreckage. The heat of the July day seemed suddenly to have vanished. There was cold sweat on his forehead.

From the silence came the sobbing of the girl.

"What are you crying about?" he said roughly.

"Nothing," she said softly. "You don't understand . . ."

"What don't I understand?" He fought against his compassion.

She stood up. He could feel her standing before him, quite close to him. She was no longer crying. And it was Karin's voice, the familiar voice of their childhood, that said:

"Hans, you've got to help me. I'm pregnant. . . ."

The Direction of the Current

Colonel Achim von Sibelius was not in the habit of shirking difficult or obscure situations. Therefore when he received a letter from a Colonel Werner Zobel, formerly commanding officer of an infantry regiment—with whom he was not acquainted—asking him to visit him at his apartment, "in connection with your work at the 'Mücke' night club," Sibelius at once decided to meet the request.

Thus, on August 3, 1946, at three P.M., the precise time of his invitation, Baron Sibelius climbed the stairs to the Colonel's apartment. The door was opened by Martha Zobel who, however, presently left him alone with her father.

Colonel Zobel complied with the ancient rules of politeness: he avoided coming straight to his subject. Briefly and almost negligently he outlined his own career, but he showed himself surprisingly well-informed about his visitor's past. Colonel von Sibelius accepted the conventional gambit and soon the two gentlemen were discovering several mutual acquaintances among senior Wehrmacht officers, living and dead. Only when sufficient names, regimental numbers and battlefields had been quoted and Martha had put some fragrant real coffee on the table, did Colonel Zobel come to the purpose of his invitation.

"Herr Oberst," he said, "I am exceedingly grateful to you for coming here and I trust you will not regard what I have to say to you as an impertinent interference in your private affairs. You see that I am informed about your work in the 'Mücke,' and I consider it my duty to point out to a brother officer the dangers of that work."

Sibelius said nothing; he merely looked questioningly at his host.

"Perhaps you believe, Herr Oberst," Zobel continued, "that you have remained unrecognized in the disguise of a head waiter."

The baron did not know whether to be angry or not. He decided not to be angry and said with a smile:

"Why do you call it a disguise, Herr Oberst? I am a head waiter."

The Colonel knit his bushy white eyebrows. "Surely only in appearance, Baron. A number of patrons of the 'Mücke' believe that you have been employed to listen to the conversation of the visitors, to report on certain meetings—in short, to spy on the visitors. Please let me finish, Herr Oberst. I am deliberately using expressions which, in different circumstances, might be offensive. My firm belief that I am doing you a service by my frankness entitles me to dispense with unnecessary ceremony."

"May I be permitted to know," said Sibelius, "on whom I am spying and in whose pay I am supposed to be?"

"It seems to me, Herr Oberst," said Zobel, "that you are unaware of the gravity of your position. The special interest which you have been showing in Lieutenant General Stappenhorst and his friends has caused some attention and displeasure both in our officers' circles and in certain American quarters. It is an interest which I might describe as unhealthy."

Sibelius sat up straight in his armchair.

"Herr Oberst," he said. "A moment ago you showed yourself reasonably well-informed about my past. A somewhat more thorough knowledge on your part and on that of your employers—for I have no doubt that you are acting on instructions—would tell you that even under the Third Reich, when people were inclined to regard them as extremely dangerous, I was not very amenable to threats. Even assuming that your suspicions and accusations are justified—which I don't concede for a moment—I would point out to you that the Thousand-Year Reich of our glorious Führer is finished for good, and that if the Herr General Stappenhorst is dissatisfied with my service the most he can do is complain to the proprietor of the 'Mücke.' It would be more than absurd if I allowed myself to be intimidated by any kind of obscure allusions."

To the baron's surprise Zobel did not react violently. He calmly poured himself another cup of coffee and said:

"Herr Oberst, you appear to misunderstand the situation entirely —and that brings me to the second reason, the real reason, for my invitation which you have been kind enough to accept. I am about to build up an ex-servicemen's association, under some neutral name to start with, and I have asked you here to persuade you to join us."

Sibelius sank back into his armchair.

"You bewilder me completely, Herr Oberst," he said. "First you accuse me of spying, very nearly to the extent of using threats, and a moment later you invite me to collaborate with you in your ex-servicemen's association. Before commenting on your offer, may I ask you for some explanations?"

"By all means," said Zobel, offering Sibelius a Chesterfield. In a very genial tone he continued: "Baron Sibelius, I am old enough to be your father. Even though we hold the same rank in the Wehrmacht"—he said "hold" not "held"—"I might perhaps claim the privilege of age, if not seniority. I've seen a thing or two in my lifetime, and I know the meaning of ambition. You may believe me, therefore, that I am trying to help you when I say that you are misreading the signals of our time. This blindness, if you will forgive that expression, reduces the two subjects which I wish to discuss with you to a common denominator. The future, Baron Sibelius, belongs to the Wehrmacht. If you are today compelled by circumstances to serve certain dubious characters—and I quite understand how it is—believe me, you are ill-advised to antagonize such men as General Stappenhorst. You would be equally ill-advised if, out of prejudice against your old comrades, you refused your cooperation to the kind of ex-servicemen's association that I intend to organize."

"I must confess, Herr Oberst," said Sibelius, "that there is no end to my wonderment. As I was glad to note at the very beginning of our conversation, you are not deceiving yourself as to my outlook as an officer of the 20th of July. May I ask why you wish to enroll in your secret organization a man who, to your way of thinking, is surely a notorious traitor?"

"First of all," retorted Zobel, "let us be clear about the fact that there can be no question of a secret organization—or at least only in a very superficial meaning. The rallying of former Wehrmacht officers and other ranks is desired and promoted by the Americans, even though it seems to run counter to Washington's official policy at the moment. For another thing, Herr Oberst, I do not regard you by any means as a traitor: if I did you would not be sitting at my table. Adolf Hitler—and there's no need to waste any words on that point —was the ruin of the German people; he, if you like to put it that way, was the traitor. There can surely be no doubt that, but for that lunatic amateur, we should have won the war; least of all, it appears to me, is there any doubt about it among the military experts of the Allies. This is not the most suitable moment to discuss the different opinions about our oath of allegiance to that Herr Führer." With warm emphasis in his voice he continued: "We, who have got together during the past few months, take the view—though I admit that there are different shades of opinion—that the last thing that can be allowed to divide us is the person of the cowardly suicide of Berlin. Anyone who wishes to restore the honor of the German soldier and to collaborate, to the best of his knowledge and ability, in the building up of the new Wehrmacht is welcome to us. And we expect that men like yourself, Herr Oberst, will lead into our ranks all those who are still sulking on the sidelines."

Sibelius crushed the cigarette, which he had smoked nearly to its glowing point, in the ashtray. He said:

"May I ask a few questions, Herr Oberst?"

"Of course."

"All around me I see nothing but radical demilitarization. So-called militarists—and I was one of them—are being locked up. Generals are sweeping the streets; senior army and navy officers are charged with war crimes. The soldier's honor which you have just mentioned —if indeed there is such a specific kind of honor—is being trampled underfoot. How can this be reconciled with the toleration or even the promotion of an ex-servicemen's association—let alone a new army?"

"Your logic, Baron, is too logical," smiled Zobel. "You forget that the Americans are ranged alongside their former allies—the French and the Russians, and partly also the British—all of whom are interested in the permanent suppression of our nation. For another thing, American democracy—like every democracy—is divided into what I might call the shortsighted and the farsighted. The shortsighted are still organizing war crime trials, while the farsighted are already busy organizing a new European army with which they hope to meet the danger from the East. The war crime trials and all the things that go with them are, of course, a great mistake and it won't be easy in the future to convince our nation of the integrity of America's intentions. It is up to us, who are better informed than the rest, to hold back our understandable sensitiveness for the sake of Germany's future."

The baron tried to conceal his emotions. He merely said:

"Then the Americans are now our friends, Herr Oberst?"

"They are the enemies of our real enemies," said Zobel. "Even in our defeat we exacted respect from them. The crumbling British Empire and the totally rotten France are no use to them. We depend on their superior mechanization, and they depend on our brains and on our army. A marriage of convenience, like this one, is usually more enduring than an association based on love."

"One last question, Herr Oberst. How do you and your friends stand on the Nazis?"

"Would you care to define your term more precisely?" said Zobel.

"It does not require any more precise definition after twelve years of Nazi rule," said Sibelius.

"I have mentioned already that we dissociate ourselves from Hitler and everything that ill-fated name stands for. We likewise repudiate the things that have happened in the concentration camps. The wheel of history cannot be turned back, but a broken thread may well be knotted again. W do not wish to have anything to do with the methods of the Third Reich—the indispensable aims of the Greater German Reich can be attained through decent means." He leaned forward and spoke with all the intensity he could muster. "Herr Oberst Sibelius, you see before you a man who is ready to admit that only a few months ago he thought quite differently . . . perhaps essentially the way you are seeing things today. Like the rest of us, I too was stunned by the great disaster. In the deep depression in which we found ourselves a man was apt to view things in a wrong light. I felt like someone standing on a bridge, unable to decide which way the current flowed. Certain experiences, which it would be premature to discuss now, have opened my eyes. I realized, not gradually but all of a sudden, that the current is flowing our way. I wish I could open your eyes too, Herr Oberst Sibelius."

The little baron got up and crossed the room once or twice under Zobel's attentive scrutiny. At last he stopped by the dark-red piano, the same that some eighteen months before had been piled high with the presents brought by Corporal Josef Maurer for his former CO's sixty-first birthday.

"Herr Oberst," he said, "I am grateful to you for your invitation, and even more for the frankness you have shown me. I cannot make you any promises, either in connection with my humble position in the 'Mücke' or as regards your ex-servicemen's association. There is only one thing I should like to say now—because, strange though it may seem to you, it touched me most deeply of all. The conspiracy which failed so tragically on July 20, 1944, was not a conspiracy against Adolf Hitler, or at least not against Hitler alone. Yours, Herr Oberst, is the American version: it makes the men of the 20th of July appear as a ridiculous society of anarchists, believing that a regime can be liquidated by the liquidation of one individual. The 20th of July—and that's a point the Allies are unwilling to accept—was the conscious expression of the unconscious feelings of the majority of our people. For that expression the Staffenbergs and the Witzlebens died a hero's death. That is all I can say at the moment—

but you may rest assured that, until I take the liberty of commenting on your remarks, our conversation will remain strictly private."

Colonel Zobel rose also.

"I would ask you not to hesitate too long, Baron," he said. "Events are moving more swiftly than is generally assumed."

For the rest of the day Achim von Sibelius could not get his conversation with the Colonel out of his head. When he arrived at the 'Mücke' in the evening, to put on his tails, Colonel Zobel's words still rang in his ears. As he stood in the little dressing room behind the bar, tying his white tie with military precision, his eyes went to the minute mirror on the wall and for the first time since his engagement at the 'Mücke' there came to him a feeling of absurdity and humiliation. He had tried not to show it—but a cold shiver had run down his spine at Colonel Zobel's mention of the bridge and his discovery of the direction in which the current flowed. He had used almost the exact expression Herr Wedemeyer had used when hiring the former General Staff Colonel Achim von Sibelius as his head waiter. There they all stood on the bridge, watching the current and making their decisions, arranging their lives and modeling their opinions in accordance with the direction of the current. And what was worse: the current was evidently flowing in the same direction as ever. To what purpose had he risked his life in those dangerous days? Merely so that, dressed in a waiter's greasy tailcoat, he could now minister to Lieutenant General Stappenhorst, the man who had stuck to his Führer to the end and who once again seemed to have the power of threatening the life and livelihood of Baron Achim von Sibelius? What was he still waiting for? The Zobels were back again in their comfortable apartments, drinking real coffee and smoking American cigarettes, coming to terms with the new masters and building up a new Wehrmacht just as after the first war they had built up their secret Reichswehr. They did not even get into conflict with their consciences: on the contrary, they were again convinced of serving Germany. They had thrown their memories overboard and magnanimously pinned all the responsibility on a single individual and on certain vague methods. Even on coming out of the camp for militarists, after a good many disappointments, he had still hoped to be able to serve the new Germany which, outside the barbed wire, seemed to be awakening from its stunned stupor—but the months had passed by and it had become obvious that no one needed him, with the possible exception of Colonel Zobel, who knew which way the current was flowing.

Sibelius put on his coat and cast a last glance at the mirror. Outside, business at the "Mücke" had begun. During the next hour the place would begin to swarm with black marketeers and spies, occupation troops and prostitutes. The spies would be watching him, the black marketeers would give him a few cigarettes, the occupation soldiers would bawl him out, and perhaps only the prostitutes would recognize him under his masquerade.

He turned and entered the restaurant. Herr Wedemeyer was standing behind the bar, talking to the pianist. Sibelius waited for the pianist with the triangular face to sit down at his instrument. Then he said:

"If you can spare me a moment, Herr Wedemeyer . . . I believe I have found an answer to your questions."

Denazification in Full Swing

It was probably a coincidence that the Denazification Tribunal hearings in the cases of Walter Wedemeyer, Eberhard Eber and Elisabeth von Zutraven were all held within a week of each other, but the denazification machine was indeed running at full speed.

The President of the Tribunal which tried Walter Wedemeyer, proprietor of a night club and erstwhile conjurer, was a former senior civil servant by the name of Paul Eckschmidt who had been relieved of his office in the Third Reich for an improper remark about nepotism and who had subsequently spent a year at a military prison for "undermining the morale of the armed forces." Wedemeyer realized from the start that it would be pointless to try to influence a man of that type in the more primitive, but by no means unusual manner. Instead he used one of his visits to General MacCallum—whom he was still instructing in the art of conjuring and who was indeed making remarkable progress, being quite capable now of producing, unaided, rabbits from his top hat—for dropping a remark about his imminent trial, in the hope that the Governor would tactfully see to it that the Tribunal was favorably disposed towards him.

When Wedemeyer entered the room where the hearing was to take place he tried in vain to read the face of the President, a man of about forty-five, of dyspeptic appearance. Herr Eckschmidt was fully aware of the dignity of his judicial office and was not giving anything away.

The verbal duel between prosecutor and defendant soon developed into a scene of some humor, although Wedemeyer realized early in the proceedings that the prosecutor, a professional lawyer and in many respects superior to the judges, was determined to label him as a "beneficiary of the regime" or even an "active supporter." That meant that Wedemeyer's license as a night-club proprietor was at stake, and the conjurer was therefore determined to fight for his skin.

"Gentlemen," said Wedemeyer, "the prosecutor has proved to you that I was exempted from military and front-line service because the Führer's Chancellery intervened on my behalf. But what this proof really means is that I preferred conjuring to shooting. Let him who objects to that cast the first stone. I happen to belong to the company of regular malingerers; besides, as I am glad to admit, I had no ambition for rank and honors in Hitler's army."

"Herr Wedemeyer's verbal slight of hand," the prosecutor retorted promptly, "cannot change the proven facts. Herr Wedemeyer was invited to the Berghof at least eleven times; he even entertained the King of Bulgaria and the Regent of Hungary. The whole system of entertainments for the forces was based on the idea that it was easier to send men to their death if they were entertained occasionally. Compared with some entertainer who does his clowning at the front—how much more guilty is a man whose endeavor it was to entertain Adolf Hitler himself!"

"The prosecutor credits me with motives that were far from my mind," replied Wedemeyer. "Only my modesty prevents me from pointing out that, though I am an amateur, I enjoy the reputation, rightly or otherwise, of being one of the best conjurers in Germany. The illustrious gentlemen simply used to order the best magicians to their presence, just as they stole the best pictures from public galleries and the best wines from people's cellars. Believe me, gentlemen: Adolf Hitler did not like me, just as he did not like our best actors. I was tolerated merely because I had an international reputation. No doubt, our applause-hungry Herr Führer regarded us all secretly as rivals and would have preferred to see us strung up. As for me, I enjoyed his particular disfavor because I could do all the things he could not: I conjured up money and foodstuffs, and on one occasion

I even ventured to produce a toy airplane from Fat Boy Hermann's nose. That, gentlemen, was a piece of subtle irony—and I now take the liberty of submitting to you a written deposition by Friedrich Stoss, the Duty ADC at the time, showing that this prank very nearly go me into a concentration camp."

"Herr Wedemeyer acts as if he had become the Füehrer's conjurer out of sheer love of his art," interposed the prosecutor, "but he remains silent about the fact that, at a time when the German people were starving, he was plentifully supplied with the most exquisite foodstuffs and that his villa on the Starnberger See was exempt from billeting obligations."

"And the prosecutor is keeping silent about the fact," retorted Wedemeyer, "that the French prisoners of war who had been put to work at Starnberg were enjoying my hospitality almost continuously. I have submitted to the Tribunal three affidavits to this effect. I am no hero, gentlemen, and if I were merely accused of having swum with the current I should be perfectly willing to admit it . . ."

"I request that this remark be put on the record," interjected the prosecutor.

"By all means," said Wedemeyer, taking the conduct of the case more and more out of the President's hands and turning it into a debate between himself and the prosecutor. "By all means. A man who swims with the current is no more than an opportunist; and an opportunist is defined in the dictionary—" here he produced a slip of paper from his pocket and quoted from it—"as 'a man aiming only at what is immediately attainable, seeing which way the wind blows, pursuing a policy of expediency devoid of ideals and principle.' If seeing which way the wind blows is devoid of ideals and principle, then so is sitting down on a hot stove with a bare bottom. The truth is that an opportunist is a modest man who only aims at what is immediately attainable: if it rains, for instance, he will open his umbrella. But, gentlemen, I do not propose to develop any philosophical theories here, but to make a perfectly frank confession. Whenever I was able to obtain for myself some insignificant and trifling advantages from the fact that I was Hitler's hoodwinker then I was not surly enough to decline them. Fundamentally, I did no more than the highly respectable Abbé Sieyès—who did not have to defend himself before a Denazification Tribunal—who, asked about his behavior during the French Revolution, replied 'J'ai survécu.' I too have survived. . . ."

As he sat down Wedemeyer was far from convinced of the effect of his opportunist frankness, but a few minutes later he drew some justified encouragement from an episode barely noticed by most of the people in the courtroom. The prosecutor was about to deal with the accused's present activities, in particular the fact that he still owned his villa in Starnberg and was evidently not exactly sharing the privations of the sorely-tried German people, when the President, silent and icy up to that moment, intervened with the remark that Herr Wedemeyer's life since the surrender was not under discussion. Whether Wedemeyer's optimistic conclusion that the General had dropped a gentle hint to the Tribunal was correct, or whether the judges simply had a greater sense of humor than might have been supposed—at any rate, the conjurer and night-club proprietor was classified as a "fellow-traveler" and fined five thousand marks, to be paid into the Restitution Fund. Being a cautious man he did not immediately hand over to the Tribunal three cartons of two hundred cigarettes each—the equivalent of that sum—but sent in the money on the following morning without revealing how he had come by it.

Far less entertaining but much more dramatic was the hearing of the case against Dr. Eberhard Eber. This took nearly a week and involved the hearing of more than thirty witnesses and the reading of over forty written depositions.

The drama of the trial, which was extensively reported in the German press and to which even some foreign papers had sent their reporters, was of a peculiar kind: it concerned all the participants with the exception of the accused.

The Tribunal, consisting of a President and four assessors, was presided over by a man named Jeremias Helferich, formerly the owner of a Lower Bavarian printing plant, who had served a two years' prison sentence under the Third Reich and then spent another two years at Dachau concentration camp. The political past of his future judge was bound to discourage Dr. Eberhard Eber, the more so as the Helferich Tribunal had a reputation for implacable severity. During the preceding few weeks it had passed a three years' sentence on a theatrical manager accused of promoting Nazi literature, a two years' sentence on an innkeeper charged with making warmongering speeches, and a sentence of as much as five years' labor camp detention on an "Aryanizer" found guilty of expropriating several small businesses. But since Eberhard Eber observed the well-tried banking principle of collecting detailed information about a partner in a business deal he discovered that Jeremias Helferich need not necessarily be regarded as a victim of the late regime. The Occupying Power, firmly convinced that anybody who had remained at liberty between 1933 and 1945 must have come to terms with the regime, was equally convinced that any person who had spent some of that period behind bars or barbed wire was invariably a man of honor. In this way Jeremias Helferich had succeeded in persuading the Americans that he had been a resistance fighter. In actual fact his provincial printing plant had been manufacturing pornographic paperbacks and pictures which had enjoyed a brisk demand, especially among the sex-starved Wehrmacht. His crime of "undermining the morale of the German armed forces," which had gained him the favor of the Allies and earned him his present office, had not, therefore, been of an ideological character.

Having established these facts and provided himself with sufficient evidence to support them, Dr. Eber dispatched his brother Oskar to the President of the Tribunal a few days before the hearing was due —not by any means with a view to blackmail, but to convince that gentleman with a few friendly words that it might be wiser to temper justice with mercy on both sides.

At the same time the journalists were not entirely wrong in allowing themselves to be impressed by the dignified and calm attitude displayed by Dr. Eber in the dock. After all, there was no telling how far Jeremias Helferich would be able to influence his four fellow-judges; nor could he check the veritable flood of evidence submitted by the prosecution. At least two of the nine sections of Article 5 of the Denazification Law, Sections 4 and 6, indubitably applied to Dr. Eber: he had "been active in a leading position in the NSDAP, or one of its formations or affiliated bodies, or any other National Socialist organization" and he had, even more certainly, "lent exceptional political, economic, propagandist or other support to the National Socialist tyranny."

However much the personality of the banker differed from that of the conjurer, their defense had one characteristic in common: Wedemeyer had tried to slip from the category of "partly incriminated" into the more desirable one of "fellow-traveler," while Dr. Eber was making an all-out effort to escape from the class of "principal culprits" and only too anxious to accept with due repentance a classification of "incriminated." The banking firm was to be re-opened in a few weeks under the management of his "nonincriminated" brother Oskar: Dr. Eber did not therefore expect to escape being debarred from professional employment; all he was trying to do was escape the labor camp.

Besides, the banker was a man of foresight. The busy correspondence he had lately been conducting with old business friends in America, in England and even in France; his instructive conversations with the reserved but well-informed Captain Green; the visits paid him by certain former high officers whose material difficulties he had luckily been able to alleviate a little—all this convinced Dr. Eber that his paramount object must be to gain time. Very soon—so all his contacts led him to believe, openly or unwittingly—patriotic colors would again be shown. That was one of the reasons why Dr. Eber did not overact his repentance and penitence in court: of course he regretted having served the criminal regime, but he had been motivated primarily by his love of the fatherland. The fact that Adolf Hitler and his vassals had profited from his advice and financial transactions, especially with regard to currency matters—Dr. Eber explained —had been a more or less inevitable concomitant of his endeavors to benefit the German people. He caused distinct hilarity among the public and some ill-suppressed chuckles on the bench when he described the Führer as an egregious ass whose decline began at the moment when he dispensed with the sound advice of his bankers. The accused moreover dropped a hint or two to the effect that the present material, if not the moral, ruin of the German nation might be remedied if the victors and their German contacts were only perspicacious enough to turn to an expert of his own ability and experience.

The verdict, pronounced on September 13, 1946—the same day that Elisabeth von Zutraven's case came up before the Denazification Tribunal in Augsburg—surprised no one less than "the Füehrer's banker." He was classified as "incriminated," not as a "principal culprit," and allowance was made for a number of extenuating circumstances. A number of penalities were imposed on him, but most of these his realistic instinct had foreseen. His entire property was declared forfeit;

but even while the National Socialist regime was still going strong Dr. Eber had transferred considerable portions of his fortune to Switzerland and to Argentina, or else assigned them to his innocent brother. He was declared "permanently unfit to hold public office, including that of notary or attorney"—but then Dr. Eber's ambitions had never run towards public office, let alone that of notary or attorney. He was deprived of the right of voting and of joining a political party—but, again, his enthusiasm for the political parties which were just rising from the dust was not so great that this ban would have broken his heart. Dr. Eber was further deprived of the right of "being active as a teacher, preacher, journalist, author or radio commentator" —but he had never intended to take up a new occupation. The punishment that pained him most was the ten years' ban on "practicing a profession, or independently directing an enterprise or commercial undertaking of any kind, being a partner in any such enterprise, or exercising control of supervision therein." But here again he had realized from the start that he would be unable to be in the limelight for some time to come. Finally, on the grounds of Article 16, Section 10 (Penalties against "Incriminated" Persons), Dr. Eber was also deprived of "the right to keep a motor vehicle." That, he had to admit, was the only punishment he had not foreseen, but he was determined to bear that too with fortitude.

The case against Elisabeth von Zutraven opened in circumstances very different from those of the hearings *in re* Wedemeyer and Eber.

The defendant, taken to court straight from her detention camp, knew nothing about the three judges who were to decide her fate. The Tribunal was presided over by a trade-union leader, the ex-miner Leopold Roller, a man of about fifty-five, broad-shouldered, heavy-boned, and with a huge white mane. Under the Third Reich he had not been imprisoned, but he had suffered political persecution and been compelled to earn a meager livelihood as an odd-job gardener. The prosecution was represented by an elementary school teacher named Heinz Golling, a Communist according to general rumor, a slight man with a hawk's nose supporting a pair of glasses which he was in the habit of taking off impatiently at the slightest emotion of any kind. He was a prosecutor of exceptional shrewdness; on the preceding day he had got a former colleague six years' labor camp detention for a trivial offense—authorship of a little book of silly National Socialist songs.

The courtroom, an exceptionally large one for a Tribunal hearing, was packed to the last seat as two policemen escorted Elisabeth von Zutraven to the dock. She wore the same gray skirt with a white blouse she had worn on her walk with Frank through the ruins of the Pinakothek. Her darkish fair hair was, as usual, carefully parted in the middle and brushed straight back. She had lost a little weight, but her skin was white and evidently well-kept, and generally her calm, graceful movements suggested to the hostile spectators provocative self-assurance rather than penitence or lethargy.

There was no doubt that most of the one hundred and fifty or so spectators were indeed hostile: they had come to witness the humiliation and probable conviction of the once powerful "wife of a high-up." As she looked about the courtroom, her gaze steady, Elisabeth felt as if she were still in the monkey cage of the Augsburg zoo: her appearance was greeted with surprised and sneering mutterings, and the curiously staring eyes might have been fastened on a strange animal rather than a woman fighting for her existence. From where she stood Elisabeth could not see that in the last row of the gloomy, dark-varnished seats Major Frank Green had sat down; deliberately, so as not to influence or intimidate her, Frank had chosen a place right at the back of the public seats which were filled predominantly with German civilians.

When the indictment had been read out the President started his examination of the defendant.

"Frau von Zutraven," he asked, "what have you to say to the assertion of the prosecution that you were a member of the NSDAP as early as 1932, that is before its rise to power?"

Elisabeth spoke softly as she replied:

"I was scarcely more than a child then. The aims of the NSDAP were not clear to me."

"When did these aims become clear to you?"

"They did not do so suddenly. I did not see them in their full clarity until after the outbreak of the war."

"Did you do anything then to obstruct the criminal aims of the NSDAP?"

"Yes, so far as was in my power."

"Your power, as the wife of the Cultural Commissar and the Governor of France was very considerable."

"No; it was extremely limited."

There was derisive muttering in the courtroom.

"Can you give us some examples of your allegedly anti-Nazi attitude?"

"I learned of what was happening in the concentration camps by a mere chance in Holland, in 1943. A few days subsequently my husband and I were Adolf Hitler's guests at the Berghof. I asked Hitler if he was aware of those happenings."

"You are suggesting that until then you assumed that he was unaware of them?"

"Yes. Hitler had a raving fit. He declared in the presence of twelve men and Eva Braun that people like myself were the gravediggers of the German Reich. He spoke of cowardly sentimentality which was worse than open sabotage. He bid my husband to take 'that hysterical female' home and teach her a lesson she would remember. After that we were never received again."

"What else did you do?"

"Shortly after that scene I learned from one of our servants that a group of Jews was being assembled at the Renault works in Paris for deportation. I drove over to the Renault works, but the transport had already left. Another transport was scheduled for the following week."

She was talking so softly now that the President had to request her to speak up so the Tribunal could hear her.

"I forged the signature of my husband and prevented the departure of that transport."

Indignant noises were heard among the audience.

"What happened to the Jews?" asked the President.

"They were taken to a French camp."

"Did they thereby escape extermination?"

"I do not know."

The commotion in the courtroom grew. Someone laughed out loud.

"Proceed," said the President.

"In Paris I employed several members of the French Resistance in my household, so that they should escape the Gestapo."

"Can you name any of them?"

"I only remember one René d'Alambert. But that was probably a cover name."

The President looked at his assessors. All three were smiling.

»322«

"Did you do the obvious thing? Did you try to induce your husband to stand up against the regime or to resign his office?"

"I should prefer not to answer that question."

"On what grounds?"

"As Kurt von Zutraven's wife I declined to give evidence against him in Nuremberg. Anything I might say now could be used against him there."

"And that you don't want?"

"No, I don't."

"Is it true that you repeatedly entertained leading figures of the Vichy regime at your house in Paris?"

"In my position it was inevitable."

"Is it true that, as late as 1945, you invited such members of the Embassy staff as were not yet NSDAP members to join the Party?"

"I allowed an official circular which had arrived from Berlin to circulate among the wives of the German employees."

"Did you have any contact with the German general commanding Paris?"

"Yes. I called on him in the spring of 1944 and entreated him not to defend Paris."

"Did you know at that time that the war was lost for Germany?"

"Yes."

"Since when had you known it?"

"Since our visit to Hitler in 1943. We left the Berghof about midnight. There was a complete black-out. Through the night came the sound of heavy explosions. There was no air raid on at the time. As our car descended the Bergstrasse I asked my husband what the noise was. He did not know. In the dark the explosions seemed louder and louder, and more and more eerie."

"Come to the point, please," said the President.

"Suddenly our car was stopped. The SS officer who flashed his torch into the car recognized my husband. In reply to my husband's question he said that some trial blastings were being carried out. In the event of an Allied invasion the defense of the Führer's home had to be safeguarded. Then I knew that Hitler was sitting on dynamite. I realized that the war was lost."

The President leaned forward. Quickly, as if trying to take her by surprise, he said:

"And yet you held out for another eighteen months and more?"

"I had no choice."

"The prosecution maintains that the French Resistance fighter Jean Lacoste offered to take you to England in June 1944. You refused."

"He made me the offer because he knew how I felt," said Elisabeth. "But I was Kurt von Zutraven's wife. This was also the reason I gave Capitaine Lacoste for my refusal. As far as I know he got through to London unscathed."

"Capitaine Lacoste's written affidavit confirms this point," said the President. "But he also quotes you for the remark that you could not let down the German troops at the front. Did you say that?"

"I don't remember, but I might have said it."

The hearing of the witnesses began in the afternoon. Witnesses for the prosecution and witnesses for the defense trooped into court, and when the hearing was adjourned in the evening until the next morning Elisabeth's fate still hung in the balance.

It was on the following morning that the event occurred which the papers described as the "sensation" of the Augsburg Tribunal proceedings. A new witness had come forward, a certain Abraham Singer, and—announced the President—wished to give evidence. Did defendant know the witness, he asked. No, said Elisabeth; as far as she was aware she had never heard the name.

Frank, once again in the back row of the public seats, was unable to say whether the murmur that greeted the witness was friendly or hostile. He was a man of such full years that his age could scarcely be guessed at: he might be seventy-five but he might equally well be ninety. Tall and gaunt, with an aquiline nose dominating his bony, sunken face, with small but by no means weary eyes and with a long white beard, the old man in the slightly worn but meticulously clean black caftan presented a picture of majestic dignity. When Herr Roller invited him to sit down he declared in a firm though low voice that he would prefer to make his statement standing up. Throughout the ensuing half-hour he stood upright, supported on his stick, a primitive knobby staff.

"I have come," he began, vainly trying to speak an accent-free German but relapsing time and again into the guttural speech of the Eastern Jew, "to give some evidence that may interest the Court. I was living in Lodz when the Germans broke into it. I fled to the West, hid out, and got to Paris to my son. When the Germans got to

Paris, they arrested me. My son and I were taken to a camp at the Renault works. I was intended for extermination. One day my son, who worked in the office, came to see me and took me with him to the office. There we heard, in the next room, how Frau von Zutraven, the wife of the German Governor, spoke to the camp commandant. She said to him she was ashamed to be a German. She gave him a paper which said he must not deport the interned Jews to Germany. Then the camp commandant said something which my son and I could not understand. Then Frau von Zutraven said that she would pray that the blood of the Jews should not be upon Germany."

The President had been watching the old man attentively. Now he interrupted him:

"Witness, you say you heard the conversation from the next room. But can you identify the defendant? Do you understand me?"

A smile went over the old man's features.

"I shall never forget her," he said. "As she came from the camp commandant's office she walked past us. And she looked like the angel of the Lord sent from above. I wanted to kiss her hand, but my son held me back, because I would have betrayed that we had been listening at the door." He made a short pause. Then he turned to the defendant. "I came to Augsburg from Paris when I heard that the trial was taking place here. I said to myself that God has bidden me to kiss her hand."

It seemed as though no one in the room dared to breathe. The only sound was the old man's stick tapping on the parquet floor. His journey seemed to take an eternity. At last he stood before her. Without waiting for her to extend it, just like a doctor taking up a patient's hand to feel the pulse, he took her hand. He did not bend down, or only very slightly: with a gesture of old-world courtesy he raised the woman's hand to his lips. Then he turned away from her to face the judges—a little abruptly, as though trying to avoid seeing her tears.

"My son is dead," he said, "and also his wife and his two daughters. They were exterminated. That happened much later. I do not know why I have remained alive. But perhaps I have remained alive so that I could come to tell you that you are trying the wrong woman. I have seen your country ruined. I belong myself to a stricken people. I cannot feel sympathy with the murderers of my children, but I can understand a stricken people. I have walked through your streets and

I have seen your people, and your land looks like a ghetto and your people look like people from a ghetto. If you understand the curse that has fallen upon you, then you will learn. But I am an old man and I have learned that vengeance belongs to the Almighty. But if a man can bear witness to a good deed, then he should go and bear witness."

He left Elisabeth and slowly returned to the center of the courtroom. Still nobody moved. The Jewish accent, the caftan, like a living illustration of those mocked and doomed figures depicted a thousand times in the journals of the Thousand-Year Reich; the old wailing voice, almost like a parody of the heartless parodies of the past—all that paled, and there was left nothing except that vision, risen as though from the dead, a specter and yet more alive than the reality of that Augsburg courtroom in September, 1946.

After the midday recess the Tribunal heard the final pleas for the prosecution and the defense. The prosecutor dealt in detail with the evidence of the aged Abraham Singer: the defendant, he suggested, had wanted to reinsure herself by her action at the Renault works—after all, most Nazis were known to have had "their" Jew. On all other points of the defense the Tribunal had been left entirely dependent on the uncorroborated evidence of the defendant.

"Have you anything else to say?" the President asked Elisabeth.

"As the wife of a high dignitary of the Third Reich," said Elisabeth, "I feel partly responsible for what happened between 1933 and 1945. Within the meaning of the indictment I am not guilty."

At four in the afternoon the Tribunal withdrew to consider their verdict. An hour and fifteen minutes later the President, Leopold Roller, declared Elisabeth von Zutraven not guilty on any of the counts of the indictment, and thus classified as "nonincriminated." He ordered her immediate release. A few men in the audience began to clap. A woman shouted: "The high-ups are allowed to get away!" Roller ordered the court to be cleared.

Frank fought his way through the crowd of departing spectators. At the bar he stopped and called out:

"Elisabeth!"

She turned. He stretched out his hand and she came to him.

"There's a café just opposite," he said softly. "Get your things: I'll wait for you there. I'll drive you to Munich."

She said: "Thank you." Instinctively she looked behind her for the

policeman who had sat next to her throughout the hearing. But there
was no policeman left in court. Elisabeth von Zutraven was free.

Second Round to Frank

Startled, Frank stopped in the door of the all but empty café. At one
of the little round marble-topped tables sat George Green.

"I didn't know you were in Augsburg," said Frank, coming up to
the table.

"Sit down," said George with a smile. "I thought I'd find you in
Augsburg."

Frank sat down. "Were you at the trial?" he asked.

"No. I've only just arrived. My congratulations!"

"What do you mean by that?"

George was still smiling. "Elisabeth told me what you have done
for her."

Frank turned color. "When did you see her?"

"I visited her twice at her camp. Any objections?"

Frank did not reply.

"Besides," continued George, "I didn't come here to disturb your
reunion. I don't suffer from puberty fixations."

"As always, you're in bad taste."

"Perhaps," said George.

Frank pricked up his ears. It was not like George to concede a
weakness or to allow his brother to rebuke him.

"I've driven over, Frank," said George, "because I need your
help."

"My help?"

"I know it must come as a surprise," said George. "Perhaps I'd
better tell you right away what's happened. To start with, I've fa-
thered a child on the Eber girl." Without waiting for Frank's reaction he continued: "Well, she didn't tell me in time. It's too late for
an abortion now. That wouldn't matter so much; after all, the
Americans are begetting a few thousand illegitimate children every
month. It won't hurt the Germans to have their blood freshened up
a bit. It isn't even as if I'd got myself in trouble with the law. As
you know, we can't be sued in German courts. . . ."

Frank felt revulsion. "What then do you expect me . . . ?"

"Old man Eber has good connections with the General. And he's denazified now. Luckily he hasn't gone through official channels so far, but has asked for an appointment with Hunter instead. You are very friendly with Hunter. Can't you get him to chuck the old man out?"

"What are your intentions about the girl?" asked Frank. He could not face George.

"What do you suppose my intentions are? I'll give her some money, of course, and she can have her baby somewhere in the country. I don't care what she does then."

"And what does she think?"

"She imagines that one day, when the laws are repealed, I'll marry her."

"And you . . . ?"

"I'm not crazy!"

"And the other thing?" asked Frank.

"There was a raid on a place in the Möhlstrasse yesterday and a certain Jakob Steiner was arrested. A black marketeer on a considerable scale. None of your little foodstuff racketeers. Foreign currency business; dollar transactions. For certain reasons I am anxious to know what the man said under interrogation, but I don't want to ask any questions myself. I know you are well acquainted with Lieutenant Colonel Wallace of the Provost's Office. If you could make some tactful enquiries . . ."

"I presume you've done business with the man?" said Frank.

His revulsion had gone: Frank could feel it being swallowed up in the stronger feeling of satisfaction—a gratification that, however, gave no pleasure. At the same time he was trying to resolve, within those few minutes of silence, the conflict which that satisfaction had brought with it. The satisfaction, once experienced, seemed insatiable: it was seeking ever-new satisfaction, and Frank was asking himself ruthlessly whether such satisfaction would spring more readily from any help he might give his brother, or from its refusal. Would it be more humiliating for George if he now magnanimously came to his aid, or should he seize this opportunity to lecture him on all the things that had been on his mind for weeks, months and years?

George made the decision for him. He said:

"I know how you feel about me, Frank. But you're acting in your own interest."

»328«

"What should your affairs be to me?"

"We bear the same name," replied George. "Besides, you're not such a pure little innocent yourself. Not that I mind. Quite the contrary." He was smiling again. "It's good to know that you too are made of flesh and blood. At times I have doubted it."

"I never claimed to be a pure little innocent. But, if you wouldn't mind being more explicit . . . ?"

"Surely, Frank, that's unnecessary. Only the other day you sermonized me about ourselves and the Germans, and all the time you were after Elisabeth yourself. Not that I have anything against it. I've always known that you haven't grown out of your puberty complexes. Very likely you've never been in love with any woman except Elisabeth. The true love for the neighbor's little daughter—it fits your character perfectly. But there's more to it, of course, and it doesn't take a psychologist to understand it. None of us is free from sentiments of revenge against this nation of murderers—not even you, and perhaps you least of all. You believe that Hitler robbed you of your beloved—and now you're taking her back. You've got my blessings. They'll string up Zutraven in Nuremberg. After a few years you'll marry his widow. You'll be telling yourself that a higher justice had been at work. Slow fade-out. And so they lived happily ever after. . . ." He turned away from Frank, but he did not stop. Quickly, as through his words sprang from an ambush, he added: "But for the moment the Non-Fraternisation Law is still in force. It would look damned awkward if it came out—the wife of the war criminal and the Intelligence major. You're as deep in the soup as I am, Frank—only you don't know it. It probably is the fault of the occupation. It drags us all in."

Frank lit a cigarette. As he brought up the match he saw that his hand was trembling. For an instant he had no other thought than to control his trembling hand. Then he said:

"I am grateful to you, George, for having once again shown your true colors. I was almost tempted to help you."

George interrupted him: "You can't take the truth."

"You don't know the truth, George. While you were talking I was listening to my own thoughts. What you said would have struck home if it had been true. But it slid off me just as your hidden threats. Puberty complexes. You bandy words about without understanding them. Only immature men see a woman as an object of conquest or rape, barter or humiliation. You've never matured, George, and that's why you don't understand Elisabeth and me."

He had only just got started but he did not mind George's interruption.

"The other day you spoke of Mama," said George. "What would have hurt Mama more—you and your 'mature' love for Frau von Zutraven or I with my 'immature' adventures?"

Frank seemed to bear even his mother's mention with equanimity.

"George," he said, "our conversation at the Ebers' house is deeply engraved on my memory. I didn't know how to answer you then; I don't mind admitting that you impressed me. I didn't see a lot of things clearly then, and only our conversation made me realize them fully. Only the day before yesterday I had to think of you again, on my drive here from Munich. I was held up on some diversion, in a little village. There was a great deal of excitement because of some marauding GI's. As you know, they don't need any shooting license in the occupied country and so they roam through woods and fields, shooting anything that moves. They don't care what they are doing and why they're doing it, and they are causing a terrible shambles. A fine company of avenging gods, I said to myself. And then I thought of you. What you are doing has no more to do with retributive justice than the marauding vandalism of our soldiers. Between what the Germans did and what our marauders are now doing there is no connection. They had concentration camps, and they started the war, and no doubt a lot of innocent people have to suffer with the guilty ones. One accepts that. But because there were beasts among them, and perhaps even a disproportionately large number of beasts, this does not mean that they are all fair game now. Marauders aren't judges; pillage and devastation are no punishment—neither in intent, nor by their scale, nor yet in their effect. Whatever Eber is guilty of, it does not entitle you to get his daughter with child and then cast her aside."

George was about to interrupt him again, but this time he did not let him.

"Let me finish," he said. "You maintained that you went in for your deals with former Gestapo people and the new profiteers because there was no sense anyway in distinguishing between them and the rest of the Germans. Or words to that effect. I've thought about that too and I've come to some conclusions since. You can't muddle me any longer, George. Because I came to know people like Dr. Wild more closely I have come to realize that the struggle against the Stappenhorsts can't be waged too vigorously. This is no more than the outcome of your own logic, even if you don't see it. If they were all collectively guilty then, for all I care, use the Stappenhorsts and throw the others, those you don't need, to the wolves. But because there are people like Adam Wild I shall not rest, so far as is in my power, until the Stappenhorsts have all been devoured by the wolves. Anything else would be treason to us and the Adam Wilds." He paused and added more calmly: "It would also be treason if I were to help you, George. I derive no satisfaction from the fact that you are as you are, or that you act as you act. I shall not do anything against you—maybe because I am too much of a coward and don't want to be drawn into yet another conflict of conscience. It'll suit me if you get out without a scratch. But it'll also suit me if you get yourself court-martialed. There are too many people about who are ashamed of others, their brothers for instance—in the literal and the metaphorical meaning of the word. I have enough mistakes of my own to bear with: I have no intention of feeling ashamed of you as well."

"You realize what you are doing?" said George. His lips were almost as pale as his face.

"Entirely," said Frank.

"You also realize that war has now definitely been declared between us?"

"Maybe that was inevitable, George."

"Your situation is not so good as you think, Frank. You think you're standing on a pedestal, a bronze statue of integrity. Maybe. I keep my feet planted on the ground, not on a pedestal. You may crash from your pedestal of proud security—I can't. You're wearing a freshly pressed tailcoat, while I'm wearing dirty overalls. You can work out for yourself who'll come out on top with those handicaps."

Just as he was brusquely getting up the door of the café opened.

Elisabeth stopped in the doorway. In her embarrassment she put down her small suitcase and stood motionless. Frank, too, had risen. She looked at the two men, standing rooted to the spot, staring at

»331«

her. She appeared to guess what had occurred. But at the same time, as the three looked at one another, they saw before them the same picture. There, in a flash-back, were George and Frank by the garden fence; and on the other side, in the garden of High Court Judge Steer, a girl was running across the lawn. They were all about seventeen. The empty Augsburg café was as unreal as the years that had passed: the flying swastika flags, the palace in Paris, the defendant at Nuremberg, the American college, the landing in Normandy, the Denazification Tribunal and the American uniforms of the two men.

Elisabeth was the first to free herself from the spell. She picked up her suitcase. Attempting a smile she approached the two brothers.

Tomorrow They Will be Widows

Sentence in the chief war crime trial in Nuremberg was pronounced by Lord Chief Justice Lawrence on behalf of the Four Power Tribunal on October 1, 1946, at 3.55 P.M. Those sentenced to death were to be executed on October 16; the remaining defendants were to start their prison terms on the same day. On October 14 they were permitted to say goodbye to their families.

Kurt von Zutraven had been sentenced to lifelong imprisonment. The sentence had been accurately foreseen by the world press and was accepted by the German public without surprise or emotion.

At 10 o'clock in the morning on that 14th of October, a rainy and prematurely chilly autumn day, the wives of the war criminals, after waiting in a large room since an early hour, were taken by MP's to a long corridor which was entirely cut off from the rest of the Nuremberg prison building.

Their husbands were waiting for them. They were standing on the left side of the corridor, at accurately measured intervals of ten feet, along the gray wall. Most of the men were so gray they looked like bas-reliefs chiseled into the wall.

The wives, some of them with their children, took up position along the opposite wall. The passage was about six feet wide and sentries were posted at both ends of it to make sure no one transgressed the invisible barrier.

Ghostlike, just as their regime had been, was also their last farewell. There was no Robespierre among them; no Danton, no Saint-Just and no Desmoulins. Not one of the men about to die believed that the idea he had once represented would live on after him. Whether they felt guilty, partially guilty or not guilty, it was a common crime that they were feeling guilty, partially guilty or not guilty of. What they called justice was, at best, hope of personal rehabilitation. The idea, in so far as there had been such an idea, had died before them—unlike the men of the French Revolution who had died before their idea. The fact that there were no such scenes as in the Paris jails of 1789 to 1799, no dramatic outbursts, no curses on a hostile fate, no fist-clenching protests against defeat and no triumphant prophecy of ultimate victory to come had little to do with dignity, self-control or Nordic toughness. It was simply that these men on the threshold of death had themselves always been the end of their Revolution and now possessed nothing to which they might cling with their curses, protests or triumphant vows.

Other women, in the course of history, had shared with their defeated husbands an idea, or an illusion, or both. But the giddy rise which these women had experienced at the side of their menfolk had been little more than a leap from a lower-middle-class apartment into a well-to-do upper-middle-class town house. Between them and their husbands, in that dimly lit corridor of the Nuremberg prison, lay not, as the world supposed, the fragments of a Reich or of an imperial concept, but the shattered crockery of a comfortable household.

Kurt von Zutraven had been placed right at the end of the corridor, and Elisabeth had to pass nearly all the condemned men before taking up her position opposite him. She wanted to feel pity for these men who would be dead or buried alive tomorrow, or at least admiration for their bearing—but she was unable to feel either. With the exception of the Butcher of Nuremberg who, left alone with no woman opposite him, leaning against the wall with shaking knees, was pleading for his life although there was nobody present who could have granted him his forfeited life—with the exception of that whining monster the condemned men were all successfully struggling for composure and dignity. And yet it seemed to Elisabeth—though she accused herself of injustice at the same moment—that there was a marked difference between dignity and greatness and that, even in death, dignity was not identical with greatness. The upright, courageous behavior of these men seemed to her to have something of the stiff and rigid correctness of the duelling students whose code forbids them to flinch under the blows of their opponent's saber.

Like the faces in some nightmarish carnival procession, like masks moving through the dream vision of a sleeper—large staring eyes, bulls' heads with horns, clowns, bony skulls, enormous noses, powdered wigs, orientals with coolie hats, judges and hangmen—the heads of the doomed men slid past Elisabeth von Zutraven. The man who looked like a vulture, once the Führer's deputy, waved to her without recognizing her; the Foreign Minister was a white mask in which only the eyebrows seemed to have been drawn in deeper color; the Colonel General and the Field Marshal seemed like a pair of wizened old twins; the Youth Leader was as pale and wan as a tubercular child; and the aged Governor, next to the young man, was staring in front of him, remote and uncomprehending. On one side of Kurt von Zutraven stood the Reich Marshal, and as Elisabeth passed him he gave her a quick smile, hurriedly clapping his fleshy and yet emaciated hand over his mouth, for he had lost his teeth in prison and did not want to give her a toothless leer. On the other side of Kurt von Zutraven, the last in the row, was the Reich Commissar for Foreign Labor, a stocky man with close-cropped dark hair, the face of a boxer and an inappropriately cheerful check jacket. He cast a contemptuous glance at Elisabeth and she noted with surprise that this man, who was to die in two days' time, had evidently still not forgotten a violent scene she had had with him several years ago, perhaps even eternities ago.

"I'm glad you've been acquitted," were Kurt von Zutraven's words of welcome to his wife. He tried to smile but it did not come off. Like a pair of spectacles that have dropped out of their case he quickly pocketed the smile again.

"I have prayed for you, Kurt," said the woman. "While there's life there's hope."

"I know," said the man. "But it will be years, perhaps decades. You are young. I want you to apply for a divorce, Elisabeth."

Across the invisible barrier, the woman looked at him in some bewilderment. Did he know anything? Did he suspect anything? Her conscience seemed to be a living thing within her, pressing dully and heavily on her heart. Her conscience had nothing yet to accuse her of; but, as with the heart, once you felt it you knew there was something wrong with it. Maybe it was weighing so heavily and expectantly on her soul just because it still had to remain silent.

"No," she said. "I'll not do that, Kurt."

The man attempted a light note:

"Let's have no pointless sentiment, Elisabeth. It won't be desertion on your part. Peace has come: there's no such thing as desertion any more."

"Let's change the subject," said the woman, and the trite sentence seemed doubly trite to her.

"We'll not see one another for a long time," the man persisted. "We've long drifted apart, Elisabeth. Don't you remember the last six months in Paris? We scarcely spoke to each other."

He seemed impelled by a delight in tormenting himself. There, in the corridor of the Nuremberg prison, between men sentenced to death and men sentenced to lifelong imprisonment, standing up against a stone wall, more than two steps away from his wife and thus forced to speak so loud that his neighbors were bound to hear him—some incomprehensible urge seemed to impel him to utter the words which he had never spoken while at liberty.

"I don't want your sacrifice," he said. "I was selfish enough to accept it while I was able to offer you something in return. I shall keep an affectionate memory of you, Elisabeth. But to wait for a once-yearly visit . . . It'll be better for me, too, not to wait."

A peal of laughter rang out. The Reich Marshal was laughing. Chuckling, he was saying to his wife who stood next to Elisabeth:

"All my life I've tried to lose weight. Now, when it is too late, I've succeeded."

And with the gesture characteristic of men priding themselves on a successful slimming cure he picked at his gray tunic which had grown too wide for him.

His wife turned to her teen-age daughter by her side and said:

"Always be proud of your father!"

It sounded not heroic but rather pedantic; moreover, there was a macabre comic element in it, as if the wife of the man sentenced to the gallows were enjoining her daughter to be proud of her father's successful slimming cure.

"Please make sure that Mama's grave is kept up," said Kurt von Zutraven. "Was Dr. Kresse at the funeral?"

"Yes. All the family went," said Elisabeth.

"You can send someone round to pick up the books," said Kurt von Zutraven. "When I am allowed books again will you send me the Hölderlin volume?"

"I hope you'll stay friends," came the voice of the slave-labor Commissar on Elisabeth's right.

He was talking to the two women at the end of the corridor, next to Elisabeth and closer to her than the official ten feet since there was not enough room for the two women and five children. The sixth child, about a year old, was sleeping in the arms of one of the women—the same who, pregnant at the time, had stayed with Elisabeth at the interrogation villa. The three children of this fair, solidly-built peasant beauty were crowding round her, while two other children, dark and graceful like Florentine pages, were hiding behind the elegant pale woman in the black dress. It was to her that the condemned man had addressed the last sentence. The buxom blonde was the Commissar's wife; the dark countess was his mistress of many years and the mother of his two illegitimate children. Whether it was from a spirit of mockery or out of humaneness that the Allied authorities had permitted both women to make their farewells at the same time—at any rate, the secret acknowledged by the vanished hierarchy but discreetly guarded had suddenly become a melee of fair and dark childish curls, boys and girls, half-comprehending and a half-excited, surrounding a stiffly erect wife and a sobbing paramour.

"Time's up," called the sergeant at the far end of the passage. His voice re-echoed twice from the narrow walls.

Elisabeth turned once more. The men were still motionless, but already they seemed to step out of the gray bas-relief. Like the burghers in Rodin's time-defying group they stood next to each other, turned into stone. The nerve-racking effort to dissemble their fear of death and their desperation had driven all other emotions from their features. Presently, as the call of the white-helmeted soldier was repeated, one of them began to smile; another prayed aloud; yet another spoke rapidly, anxious to make the most of this last minute; one of them laughed out loud; and only one of them cried.

Facing them, the line of women and children had begun to move. The infant next to Elisabeth woke up and began to howl in his mother's arms. A little girl of perhaps two or three laughed. A big boy protectingly put his arm round his younger sister. But the most macabre picture, for Elisabeth, was a nine-year-old girl who dropped a polite curtsy to her father. Only now did Elisabeth notice that most of the women were wearing black—a premature and tactless mourning. The chain of women along the wall was like a string of black beads. One could clearly tell now whose husband had been sentenced to death and whose to lifelong imprisonment: hate and envy leaped across like a spark from the hopeless to the futilely hoping. Troops swarmed into the corridor, trampling along the invisible barrier, and at a word of command the condemned did a right turn and began to file out like a company on the march. One woman raised her hand to wave; another called out a name in a shrill voice; an old woman collapsed—it was just like an army train pulling out of a station, leaving behind tomorrow's widows.

"Do as I ask you," said Kurt von Zutraven.

"I'll visit you as soon as I am allowed to," said Elisabeth.

Then the ash-gray head, the last but one, vanished through the steel door.

Elisabeth was afraid of the other women, who had read about her trial and had been measuring her with eyes full of suspicion or hatred or envy. As fast as she could, she hurried down the corridor, through the waiting-room, along more passages, and down endless stairs towards the exit. For a last time she had to produce her visitor's pass. Then she stood outside.

She was glad it was raining: the monotonously gray sky contrasted but little with the monotonous gray of the prison building from which she had emerged. A prison wagon with barred doors and windows was standing outside the gate. Elisabeth knew that many of the women in mourning would presently be taken back to their own camps and prisons. With a desperate effort, gritting her teeth and clenching her fists, she tried to think of Kurt von Zutraven from whom she had parted forever; of the men round whose necks a noose would be slipped in two days' time; of the women and of the children. She did not want to think of crime and punishment; she wanted to share their suffering. But she could not do it. Only now, she felt, was it all over—the confusion and errors, the specter of the twelve years and the specter of the time that followed. Mightier than any other sensation was her certainty that, no matter what was to befall, she was free at last.

She stood still for a moment, bareheaded, with the rain lashing her face and wetting her hair. The rain felt good. Then she began to walk, faster and faster, till she ran. Aimlessly she ran out into the October morning.

The Close of the Year 1946

Towards the close of the year 1946, Elisabeth von Zutraven was living with Frau Müller, the caretaker of the house next door to Adam Wild's. Frau Wild's skilful persuasion had eventually succeeded in getting Frau Müller, whose husband had died a few months previously from pneumonia or malnutrition, or both—to take Elisabeth in as a lodger. She occupied a divan in the living-room of the Müller's two-room ground-floor apartment; but most of the day she spent at Dr. Wild's who employed her as a receptionist and where she was now learning her new trade with much ability and even more application.

She had not filed divorce proceedings against Kurt von Zutraven. She had more than one reason for putting off the decision, but the most cogent of them was a sense of shame for her own emotions. The man with whom she had spent more than a decade was behind bars at Spandau, guarded by the troops of four victorious powers, with no hope of ever seeing liberty again. He had spoken the truth among the gray walls of the Nuremberg prison: their marriage had long ceased to be a marriage and had only been held together by the conventions of a crumbling Reich. Even if their last years together had not been a fight they would have had nothing to say to each other; indeed the fight had been the last link in the chain that had once bound them together. Nevertheless, Elisabeth was torturing herself with the thought that she had denied that living corpse in the corridor the compassion to which he had been entitled on leave-taking. At night in the caretaker's apartment in Schwabing she tried to conjure up the pale face of the prisoner; she spurred on her lame fantasy to fly out to the jail; instead of oblivion in sleep she courted the nightmare. But her fantasy failed her and the nightmare would not come: all that was left was the pain of being unable to suffer. In this fashion Elisabeth was punishing herself for her return to life and for her future, dimly surmised, happiness.

She saw Frank seldom. He was away a good deal, in Frankfurt and in Berlin. When he was in Munich he would make shy, sometimes touchingly awkward, attempts to see her at Adam's, but she avoided being alone with him the more anxiously as she was becoming increasingly aware of her love. Even if it had been possible to get over the things that stood between them—things which a Tribunal finding could not alter—her emotions were like a babe lost in the jungle of reality. The judgment of the world, which she had no right to disregard on his behalf; his career as an officer and his future in America; his Jewish friends who would never cease hating her; the rather too obvious expediency of changing sides—these were the entrapping creepers, the impassable undergrowth and the lurking beasts of the jungle; these were the visible and concrete aspects of the matter, and no amount of knowing that things were quite different really could alter them.

Towards the close of the year 1946, Frank, too, had reached that trough of depression commonly known as resignation. His promotion to lieutenant colonel, celebrated at a special party given by Hunter in his honor, left him cold. He was more and more obsessed with the idea of returning to America and resuming his academic career. His range of functions had grown, and thus also his chance of doing the right thing in small matters—but always only in small and very small matters. There was open talk now of a "cold war" between the former allies, and in Berlin, where he spent two weeks every month, he too had been infected by the restlessness of the Four-Power city. He had concerned himself little with applied politics—not so much because of a lack of interest, but because the struggle against National Socialism had dominated his entire youth and because to him the concept of enemy meant the enemy recently defeated. The Marxist philosophy and Russian Bolshevism were alien to him and distasteful; but his own slow and judicious rhythm and the galloping rhythm of a new hostility did not blend in him into a harmonizing pace but resulted in loathsome cacophony. His anxieties—and that, too, precipitated the American Frank Green into a bewildering conflict—were more and more concerned with his old native land. And one thing he saw clearly: whatever the cold war might mean to America, for Germany it was bound to spell disaster.

His nature was, above all, methodical: he was ready to modify his preconceived ideas about the number of guilty men and the extent of their punishment, but he could not understand why the process of rehabilitation should start before that of punishment had been completed. A man who, in the course of carefully rectifying one mistake, would discover a hundred new sources of error, he was unable to reconcile himself with the mistakes of the occupation. He would find a livelihood or a post for this or that old resistance fighter or silent opponent of the regime—but in the meantime a hundred others would turn away from democracy, disappointed. Irene Gruss, the mass murderer, had been sentenced to death, but the punishment had been commuted to lifelong imprisonment because she appeared in court with a swollen abdomen: one of the prison guards had got her pregnant. Denazification had become a farce. Conceived originally as a healthy and promising cleansing of Germany from National Socialism, and practiced subsequently with much severity and little discrimination, it had now become a means for National Socialists to remove the taint of their past. Lieutenant General Stappenhorst resided in a palace near Munich, guarded by American troops: the road from the prison cell to a desk in the office of the secret Intelligence Chief seemed short and smooth for many a discharged prisoner. To hunger and eviction was added a new feature—dismantling. Hundreds of working-class families became unemployed at Salzgitter, on the Rhine and in the Ruhr—but Rhine and Ruhr industrialists were already negotiating with Britain and America about new and better war machines. Major William O'Hara's post had been filled by a Captain Oliver Y. Yates, one of those young liberal students from Harvard, who to Frank represented the best America—but the ships which brought new occupation officers over from home carried not only good will and earnest, informed minds, but also much ruthless rapaciousness and blatant ignorance.

That it was his love for Elisabeth that was keeping him in Germany Frank would not admit to himself. He knew, of course, that the Non-Fraternization Law would be rescinded at the beginning of 1947, but from there it would still be an incalculably long way to permission to marry a German woman, let alone to take her home with him to America. Besides, more than once when talking to Elisabeth he had suddenly felt that they were speaking different languages. When she said "we" and "to us" she was not thinking of the same "we" that Frank had in mind. Time and again he was tempted to justify to the German woman some Allied measures which, back among his colleagues, he would denounce more vigorously than she; some inexplicable compulsion seemed to make him pronounce collective accusations of which he would be ashamed the moment he was alone. Like a serpent raising its head from among the flowers on the forest floor, the poison of generalization would hiss into their private conversations.

Towards the close of the year 1946, Colonel Graham T. Hunter was still waiting in vain for his promotion to brigadier general, although his superior had done all he could to expedite it. Hunter was still doing a brigadier's job, but there were times when he suspected that Washington must be aware that he was implementing the orders transmitted to him with hesitation and a marked lack of enthusiasm. His difficulties in performing his job to his own satisfaction were growing almost hourly. His counterespionage work, originally directed against National Socialist conspiracies, was now increasingly aimed against the Communists; yet to watch and apprehend persons suspect of Communist sympathies or activities he required the help of the very National Socialists still on some blacklist or other. Never-ending confusion arose further from the clash between the political past and the professional qualifications of Germans, especially as the directives from Washington kept contradicting each other. One moment, in the interests of speedier rehabilitation of the occupied country, professional qualifications alone were to be decisive, and the next moment licenses were to be granted exclusively on the grounds of political ethics. Politics, into which the old soldier thus found himself precipitated, were governed by entirely different rules from military matters which were his métier. Warfare was an interplay of strategy and tactics; the staff and the rear would submit to the needs of the front, or at least base their decisions on information obtained from the front lines. But in politics the front line, with all its experience and needs, appeared of little consequence; only the strategic concepts and considerations of the remote rear seemed to matter.

That night, after the Governor's ball, Hunter had not been able to keep the General's words to himself: after a little hesitation he had told Betty of his impending promotion. She had received the news, for which she had waited so long, with skepticism; and the more her skepticism seemed justified, the more did she gain the upper hand again over Hunter. If he spoke to her of his work, if—as was inevitable—he brought some of his work home on Saturday to deal with over the weekend, he would find no support from Betty. Explicit or implicit, there would hang between them the question of why he should go on wasting his time, health and ambition without reward.

But while the Colonel was coming to look increasingly foolish to himself, Betty for her part did not escape looking foolish to him as well. The Harlaching house was beginning to be more and more like a museum of bad taste. To start with, Betty had taken delight in Bavarian mugs, and beer mugs of all sizes were accumulating on a table specially put up for that purpose in the drawing-room. Next, she had discovered a passion for landscape painting and allowed third-rate painters and unscrupulous dealers to talk her into buying their canvases. In the end, she had become interested exclusively in "antiques," by which term she understood articles from the turn of the century. Marianne von Artemstein continued to encourage Mrs. Hunter's grotesque hobbies, but she managed at the same time to allow the Colonel to understand what she thought of them.

Her presence was intolerable and yet indispensable to Hunter. Again and again she succeeded in being left alone with him, if only for a few minutes, and what had happened during that spring night was repeated five or six times, always in circumstances which seemed to surprise the Colonel although he had played a deliberate part in bringing them about. In the summer he had after all, just as she had suggested, taken a villa on the Tegernsee and life by the lakeside brought opportunity and temptation. When they went for a swim Hunter could not help seeing the woman undressed, and her slender but shapely figure, the brilliant and youthful whiteness of her skin which seemed to radiate electricity even at a distance, and her casual yet modest nudity threw him into turbulent excitement. Nevertheless, nothing occurred beyond surreptitious kisses and hasty embraces, and this very circumstance led Hunter into a hopeless impasse. His excitement, never satisfied, became a permanent condition; the burden on his conscience was no lighter for the fact that, in the strict sense of the word, he was not deceiving his wife, while on the other hand, by avoiding the road of supposed vice, he accused himself of cowardice. He felt like an immature college boy and, for the same reason, like an old man; yet he lacked the strength to put an end to the state of suspense, either through the consummation or through the severance of this dangerous liaison.

Towards the close of the year 1946, Hans Eber was able to record a gain which was to affect his entire future life: a firm friendship had developed between him and Dr. Adam Wild. Dr. Wild had taken Inge Schmidt into his home, and Hans was in and out of the house. Inge was now working as a counter-hand in the PX, a position arranged for her by Frank at Adam's request and which turned out more favorably than all those concerned had dared to expect. The PX girls did not enjoy a good reputation any more than most German women in daily contact with the conquerors—but in Inge's case the bad reputation soon proved an unjustified prejudice. The fact that now and again a humiliating but unrefusable present was forced on Inge; that now and again she had to endure the importunate or coarse attentions of a soldier; that from morning till nightfall, she was exposed to the temptation of treasures which she must not touch, treasures such as did not exist outside those premises—all these would have been dangers to a girl less experienced, but Inge met the humiliations and allurements with a dignity that sprang from conquered indignity. Slowly she lost the fear, which had at first beset her, of encountering any of the soldiers who had been her guests on the divan with the lions' heads, but she did not meet any of them with the exception of Lincoln Washington Haymes who acknowledged her social rise not only good-naturedly but with genuine pleasure and innate tact. Hans met her almost every evening in the Brienner Strasse, and their relationship had become so free from disguise and inhibitions that she caught herself, surprised, telling him without any false shame about her accidental and unconstrained meeting with the Negro soldier.

But while his relationship with Inge was happy and carefree and his endless discussions with Adam fruitful—and occasion for the latter seemed to arise almost every evening—Hans Eber's life at his own home had been increasingly difficult. It had been his task to break the news of Karin's pregnancy to Dr. Eberhard Eber. He understood the pain and indignation of the old man who seemed to forget his own affairs over his outraged paternal pride, but he did not approve of Dr. Eberhard Eber's attitude to Karin, an attitude devoid of the least understanding. Hans was also disappointed over the all-too-careful consideration which eventually led Dr. Eber to control his anger; the banker avoided a direct confrontation with Captain Green and chose, wisely as he thought but nevertheless somewhat oddly in this most private of private matters, the official approach. Colonel Hunter, after receiving Dr. Eber, promised to start an investigation and to question his subordinate—but autumn had turned to winter, Karin was seven months pregnant, and Captain Green, evidently untroubled, was still living with the Eber family. It was a strange company that inhabited the elegant house: Dr. Eberhard Eber whose contact was confined to his brother Oskar; Hans, on speaking terms with Karin but avoiding encounters with the captain; Karin, avoiding her father and, hoping against hope, clinging with almost doglike devotion to the father of her unborn child; the old housekeeper Anna, trying to please everybody and plying all day and all night between the warring parties. None of the simple solutions, usually the only possible ones in difficult situations, was thinkable and that was what oppressed Hans more than anything. One could not split up because there was no accommodation; one could not go to law because Allied legislation protected the sexual license of the Allied forces; a marriage was out of the question since the ban on such marriages provided the offender with a welcome excuse. The expectant mother could not even be moved from the house, because only her seducer could provide the milk, the foodstuffs and the other necessities required by her frail condition. The individual decisions which Hans considered time and again rebounded from the blank wall of the times he lived in. Against the monster called "circumstance"—circumstance springing from the collective fate of the occupied people—opposition was hopeless.

If it had not been for Adam Wild, times and circumstances would undoubtedly have driven Hans Eber on to the road which so many of his fellow-countrymen had now chosen. The Americans, more so than their allies, had missionary zeal and missionary talk in their blood: declaration and practice contrasted therefore more flagrantly in the American Zone than in the other parts of the occupied country. To distinguish between personal experience and a principle is not human nature; and though a principle need not be wrong because it is proclaimed by bad ambassadors, it would have been asking rather too much of the vanquished to believe in a salvation proclaimed by such patently sinful apostles. The fact that a girl had been got with child did not invalidate a crusade—but it made it difficult for the girl's brother to believe in that crusade. Only because Hans Eber had come to know the doctor whose ordering hand divided the wheat of the idea from the chaff of human frailty did he not get submerged in the mass of the confused and disappointed.

Towards the close of the year 1946, ex-Colonel in the General Staff Achim von Sibelius was still successfully resisting the threats and the invitations of the former regimental commander Werner Zobel, as well as his own increasing bitterness. This was the more difficult as Sibelius had lost his post in the "Mücke." Shortly after his visit to Colonel Zobel he had been informed by an extremely regretful Wedemeyer that the usefulness of the new headwaiter had come to an end. Too many customers, explained Wedemeyer, had got wind of the fact that the slight, gray-haired man was a former fellow-conspirator of Count Stauffenberg and Oberbürgermeister Gördeler: some of the clients had expressed objections to a man with such a questionable past, while others had simply felt embarrassed at being ministered to by a baron and an ex-colonel. He himself, Wedemeyer finally admitted, had been the butt of some quite unambiguous threats if Colonel von Sibelius were to continue in his employment any longer; he had never been a hero and did not now wish to risk an "accident" in his restaurant. No doubt, continued Wedemeyer, he might appeal for American protection, but then Sibelius had every reason to know from his own experience what unreliable patrons the Americans were. At the same time, having no intention of making an enemy of Sibelius, Wedemeyer recommended his former waiter to a friend, the director of a newly revived insurance firm, and that man gave him the chance of becoming an insurance salesman.

The chance, as Sibelius soon discovered, was not spectacular. Confidence in all public institutions—to which, in a manner of speaking, insurance companies belonged—was shaken and nobody felt like taking out a loan on the future. Eighteen months after the end of the war the words "life insurance" still had a highly ironical ring; only that of "endowment policy" was even more ironical. Since Sibelius drew no fixed salary, but received only a commission on the policies he sold, he had been eking out a miserable existence ever since his departure from the "Mücke." Eating a meager supper in his modest room, after a day spent wearing out his feet and knocking in vain at a multitude of doors, he often felt drawn to the Zobels' apartment where, to judge by various indications, they were still ready to clinch a profitable deal with him. True, most of his friends were no better off. One of the conspirators had received a license to publish a paper in a provincial town but, when local opposition began to show itself in a number of intrigues, it had again been withdrawn from him. Another, treated shabbily by the British, had gone over to the Russians who had promptly interned him as a militarist. But the fact that others had received no more recognition for their behavior held little consolation for Achim von Sibelius; on the contrary, it convinced him that his own fate was part of a certain gloomy pattern.

The reason why he would not join Zobel and Stappenhorst, or at least not just yet, was, oddly enough, that he had lost his position at the "Mücke," a position far from unprofitable in view of American tips in cigarette currency. Sibelius realized that it had been the intervention of Stappenhorst's crowd that had led to his dismissal, and that they had thus been trying to subject him to economic pressure. To this pressure Colonel von Sibelius's reaction was, as he put it, decidedly acid. In a conversation with Adam Wild he summed it up as follows, in one of his characteristic formulations: "You see, my dear Adam," he said, "the ethics of a regime are determined not so much by the degree of compulsion exercised by it—for every regime practices compulsion against its subjects—as by the magnitude of the risks faced by those who resist such compulsion. Freedom to die freely of starvation is, I concede, of limited value; but the risk has to be taken. And so long as nothing but a grumbling stomach induces me to sell my opinions I shall see if I can't deal with it for a while." That, then, was Baron Sibelius's philosophy and thus it came about that on New Year's Day 1947, the gentlemen assembled at Colonel Werner Zobel's apartment—which, by then, consisted once more of three nonrequisitioned rooms—waited in vain for the arrival of the conspirator.

Towards the close of the year 1946, the outlines of a strange circle began to take shape around Adam Wild. On Sunday afternoons a colorful company—so colorful as to be incomprehensible to any outsider—would collect in Frau Wild's antique-laden sitting-room. In the kitchen, Frau Wild would brew up whatever she had been able to save up throughout the week or conjure up all kinds of delicacies never dreamed of by any army cook, ably assisted by Inge Schmidt, daughter of an old-age pensioner and former streetwalker. Elisabeth von Zutraven, sometime one of the exalted ladies of the Third Reich and widow of a man who was not dead, would converse with Achim Freiherr von Sibelius, an officer of the 20th of July, interned as a militarist, subsequently headwaiter and now an insurance salesman. The student Hans Eber, son of the Führer's banker and former infantryman, would bring along old friends and new, Stefan Lester and others. Invited or uninvited friends would turn up, acquaintances and patients of Adam; and at least once a month, if he happened to be in Munich, Lieutenant Colonel Frank Green would arrive early in the afternoon, his American uniform providing a splash of color among the informal assembly. The talk was frequently, but by no means always, of political matters, of the latest events at home and abroad. But in the literal meaning of the word, these meetings had no purpose—firstly, because these people, who were not influential, did nothing beyond exchanging their thoughts; and secondly, because while they were all striving for clarity they did not really presume to arrive at generally valid conclusions. What it was that brought them so close to one another, so close in fact that they became indispensable to each other, none of them knew—with the possible exception of their host who spoke infrequently and said little, and who was yet profoundly happy at these meetings. For dimly he realized that there could be no darkness so long as, no matter where, a single candle was alight.

SIXTH CHAPTER

Black Market Supreme

𝔜ou're to see Colonel Hunter at once, Colonel," was the message brought to Lieutenant Colonel Frank Green by his sergeant one February morning in 1947. "Looks like the Colonel's having a fit."

But Frank found the Colonel quite collected; only his unusual pallor betrayed his emotion.

"Frank," Hunter began without preamble, "when did you last see your brother?"

"I don't know for certain," replied Frank, "about two weeks ago, in the officers' mess."

"That doesn't help at all," said the Colonel. "Let's make it short and painless: Captain Green has disappeared!"

"Disappeared?"

"You don't seem unduly surprised."

"Oh yes, I am," said Frank feebly.

"There's more to come," said Hunter. "Pfc. Harry S. Jones, O'Hara's former driver, has also vanished."

"Since when?"

"Exactly five days ago, at 1500 hours on January 30, they drove off to Regensburg."

"Had Jones been attached to my brother?"

"He'd asked for him for this particular trip. He'd done so a few times before; he hasn't got a driver of his own. The two never arrived at Regensburg. We've no report whatsoever of any accident. They've simply vanished into thin air. By tonight I must report them as AWOL. For the time being I've got to regard them as deserters." He looked at Frank searchingly. "Tell me, Frank, when are you going to start getting excited?"

"I don't know," said Frank. "Perhaps when I've heard more."

"You're welcome," said the Colonel. "The fact is, my boy, we're in the soup."

"You know something else, Colonel?"

"Nothing pleasant," said Hunter. "Lieutenant Colonel Wallace's branch pulled in some currency racketeer a few months ago, a man called . . ."—he glanced at the papers in front of him—"a man called Jakob Steiner. His case is to come up presently. Now this man, evidently hoping for some help at the last moment, has said that he'd been in touch with your brother. They're supposed to have done business together worth over a hundred thousand dollars."

"When did Steiner make this statement?" asked Frank.

"You've guessed right," said the Colonel. "The evening before Captain Green's disappearance. Naturally, Steiner's evidence had to be sifted first. Wallace only reported to me yesterday."

"Have Steiner's statements been corroborated?"

"There's not enough at the moment for a charge. Besides, I don't want to take the connection as absolutely granted. Maybe we are wronging your brother. As you know, he's been handling some extraordinarily confidential matters." He was speaking even more softly now. "He might have fallen into the hands of Soviet Intelligence."

"Did he carry confidential material?"

"Only in his head," said Hunter. "But that's enough."

Frank considered. "Maybe the thing's even more harmless, Colonel," he said. "Do you know the present whereabouts of the daughter of the banker Eber?"

"So you know about that business?"

"Yes."

"We've traced her already. She is with some friends of the Ebers' at Wasserburg-on-Inn. Her baby's due today or tomorrow. But Captain Green has not seen her for at least three weeks." He got up, circled his desk and remained standing in front of Frank, leaning against its edge. "Frank," he said, "I wasn't given this job because I don't know anything about people. I only have to look at you . . ."

"There's no need for a third degree, Colonel," said Frank. "I'll tell you what I know. On September 14 last year my brother came to me and told me about the Eber business. He asked me to intervene with you because he was afraid the business might put him in the General's bad books. At the same time he asked me to find out if that black-marketeer Steiner had mentioned his name. I declined to do either. Since then he has avoided me. That's all I know."

"How come you remember the exact date?"

"He had followed me to Augsburg. It was the day the Denazification Tribunal pronounced its verdict in the case of Elisabeth von Zutraven."

"Anyway," said Hunter. "That reassures me a little since it seems to suggest the black market. I'd rather have that than have the Russians collar him."

"What do you propose to do, Colonel?" asked Frank.

"You'll have to find him, Frank, and mighty quick!"

"Why me, of all people?"

"You don't seem to care at all whether he's found or not."

"You've got to understand, Colonel, that I don't expect the investigations to yield anything very pleasant."

"Pleasant or not," said Hunter. "He's got to be found."

Frank, who had been sitting in front of the desk, got up. "Colonel," he said, "I don't know why you insist on giving me the damnedest assignments. I'm the worst possible man for the job of finding my brother. Just picture my situation if I find him and have to convict him of some crime or even a simple offense. And if I don't find him everybody'll say I didn't want to find him. Why don't you put Captain Yates in charge. He is one of our most able officers."

"I know exactly how you feel, Frank," said Hunter. "If I were even half-convinced that Captain Green has taken a powder because of the Steiner business I wouldn't dream of bothering you with the case. But in spite of what you say it doesn't seem likely. Try it yourself some day: an American officer, accompanied by an army driver, riding in an official vehicle—there's been no trace of the jeep either—vanishing without the help of an organization."

"You're sticking to the Soviet version?"

"As the likeliest hypothesis."

"I still don't see . . ."

"You'll see it in a minute. The officer entrusted with this case must have the necessary tools for the job." He turned towards the desk and put his palm on a green folder. "This is top secret. It contains, among other things, the names of all the agents and contact men with whom Captain Green has been in touch. It also contains his reports. I can't give the assignment to Captain Yates, simply because he isn't authorized to see top-classified documents. On my whole staff only four men are entitled to do that—apart from the General whom I can't very well send chasing off after Captain Green. Lieutenant Colonel Steele is in London, Major Kovalsky has some other business right now, and Major Torreani is too stupid."

"Torreani is a splendid fellow," objected Frank.

"Will you please leave that to me," said Hunter. "Besides . . ."

Frank knew at once what this "besides" meant. Steele could be recalled from London; Kovalsky's present business was not all that pressing; and Torreani was not stupid. Now, Frank supposed, Hunter would tell him his real reason.

"Besides," continued Hunter, "I've no intention of alarming the entire HQ. I have my reasons for wishing to sort out the business quietly—even if it is only a black-market scandal."

"You aren't proposing to hush it up, Colonel?" said Frank.

Hunter picked up the army signal form that had been lying on the desk. Without a word he passed it to Frank.

Frank read: "From: Defense Department, Maj. Gen. John T. Payne, Adjutant General's Office. To: Lt. Gen. Theodore F. Mac-Callum, Military Governor of Bavaria. Promotion Colonel Graham T. Hunter, M.I., to permanent rank Brigadier General approved Secretary of Defense 4.15 P.M. today. Submission to Legislative earliest possible."

"Congratulations, Colonel," said Frank.

"Don't congratulate me too soon, my boy," said Hunter, unable to hide his emotion entirely. "Do you understand now?"

"I understand," said Frank. But it did not sound quite honest.

"I am convinced this would have come through last year," said Hunter. "But then the O'Hara business broke."

"I don't seem to have a lucky touch."

"Nothing to do with you, Frank. At least not the way you meant it. To whom am I to confide? We aren't going to hush up anything, Frank. But we're going to move tactfully. Take a week's leave. Go and look for your brother. You'll be searching for him not as a Military Intelligence officer, but as a man anxious to trace his vanished brother. You've no official assignment and you won't send in any written reports. At the same time you'll have my full support. You'll report to me in person. When the time's ripe we'll discuss the necessary steps together."

Frank hesitated. Then he said:

"Colonel, you know what recalcitrant GI's say when they don't want to do a thing? They ask the sergeant: 'Is that an order?' Is this an order, Colonel?"

Hunter frowned.

"Spare me the need to give you an order, Frank."

"All right, Colonel," said Frank.

The Colonel handed him the green folder. To cover up his embarrassment he said:

"You can always reach me at home—at any hour."

In spite of everything Hunter had said Frank remained convinced that George's disappearance was connected with the black market and not with his brother's intelligence work. There were much more important agents than George, he argued, and much more valuable prizes for any counterespionage from the East. And if the Colonel maintained that only a powerful organization could have kidnaped an American officer he evidently underrated the organization at the disposal of the black market.

For the moment, therefore, he left the green file marked "Top Secret" alone and decided to probe the mysteries of the black market in his own systematic way. Lieutenant Colonel Wallace, who was in charge of the branch dealing with the fight against the black market, was a successful exporter in Oregon in civil life. He was a capable man with that sound morality that springs not from saint-like indignation but from the knowledge that evil, as a rule, is highly practical and must therefore be fought with down-to-earth practical measures. When he opened up his channels and connections to Frank, the Intelligence officer found himself penetrating into realms which filled him with amazement.

A black web was spread over the occupied country. Manual workers, who received six thousand seven hundred grams of bread, four hundred and forty grams of fat and one hundred and fifty grams of cheese a month, and who therefore belonged to the privileged class, tried to save their children from starvation by sharing their rations with them. Shoelaces, wrapping paper, matches and combs were valuables—yet when a black marketeer was arrested in Nuremberg his store was found to contain two hundred kilograms of rancid butter. A miller in Ulm was caught with fifty tons of black-market flour. Black market gasoline flowed in a ceaseless stream from Army dumps into civilian hoards: an armored unit stationed at Kassel discovered one day that its entire supply had been bartered away by speculating GI's. For several months the Army had been looking for a deserter, a Negro, who had set up his headquarters in a ruined castle in the Bavarian mountains whence, like a black king, he commanded an army of deserters, DP's and all types of criminal elements. When the Constabulary captured the fortress after a pitched battle they found hundreds of pounds of flour, coffee, sugar and other foodstuffs. In Frankfurt they arrested a sergeant who had specialized in false teeth—one of the many shortages in Germany. He had had dentures sent to him from America by the thousand, packed in food parcels, and passed them on to German dentists and dental technicians. Tragedy and farce were never far apart: one night an American major appeared at the Berlin officers' club without shirt or trousers under his trench coat; he had sold both of them to a German driver. On the same day a military vehicle was stopped at the Austrian frontier: its skimpily-painted mudguard was found to consist of solid gold. The worthlessness of German currency led to a hectic dance around the currency of currencies—the dollar. Thousands of people wanted to emigrate and escape from the stricken country—but escape and emigration required green-backed currency. A collector sold a Rembrandt for a few dollars; another person sold stolen crown jewels; yet another bartered away his family silver. Anybody wanting to live had to get in touch with the black market, either as seller to buyer. A Munich doctor, struck off the medical register as a former Nazi Party member, became a big banker in black dollars. The studio of a Berlin sculptor served as a store for black marketeers in flour. The former proprietress of a fashion house in Duesseldorf ran a retail business in black-market penicillin.

What struck Frank most was the fact that, although Germany was cut off from the outside world, the black market seemed to know no frontiers: the first bridges linking postwar Germany with the world were built by criminals. There were transport organizations which would ship dollars, jewelry, gold and art treasures to Milan. Black marketeers in Frankfurt were able to order any article they needed from Copenhagen by the truckload. At the Café Royal, near the Möhlstrasse in Munich, stock exchange deals were concluded of which the effects were felt as far away as Wall Street.

The Möhlstrasse had not fortuitously acquired its truly legendary character. In 1947 the German peasants still only delivered some thirty-five per cent of the bread grain, thirty-three per cent of the barley, twelve per cent of the oats and twenty-six per cent of the hay they produced—and nobody could tell where the rest went. But in the Möhlstrasse one might purchase flour and carpets, French cognac and Spanish oranges, silver coffee jugs and cigarettes, English cloth and German cameras. Among the Eastern Jews, the Greeks, the Hungarians, Czechs, and Poles of the Möhlstrasse, whose miserable wooden huts contrasted with the wealth of their hidden goods, one might stroll up and down as if in a bazaar in Constantinople and order almost any article under the sun with a reasonable prospect of prompt delivery. But first and foremost the newly risen profiteers profited from the corruption of the victors and the lack of solidarity among the vanquished.

The black market reflected a distorted picture of the German scene. Former concentration camp inmates declared with solemn conviction that they were doing no more than recover, though with improper means, what had been stolen from them; they cared little that the dormant anti-Semitism derived welcome nourishment from their activities. Fists were clenched at the mention of the Möhlstrasse, but a good many victims of the black market praised it highly because the goods they had acquired there at usurious prices had saved their children from starvation. Thus, at times, the exploiters became saviors. A policeman who had photographed the local mafia sold the incriminating film to its members because his family was going hungry. Peasants who had hidden their grain would curse "those Galicians" from whom they had to buy fuel for their tractors. From a former slave laborer from the Baltic States, now the chief supplier of documents among the black-market dealers, a Nazi Party leader sought by Allied warrant obtained a forged passport for his escape to South America. Patrolling MP's got their Leicas in the street of shacks they were supposed to watch. The tragedy, it seemed to Frank was that the victors possessed what the vanquished were short of, and that the vanquished could offer things which the victors lacked. The victorious army had far too much food, tobacco, clothing, transport and fuel; the vanquished, on the other hand, still possessed a diminishing store of articles from a well-to-do past and an industry smashed only at the last moment. The German people were not the only ones who did not know why they had gone to war; the Allied nations did not know it either. The nations had fought as nations always will, but since they did not know the purpose of the war they had become un-worthy in victory and in defeat.

These matters were being increasingly borne in on Frank Green although, in his single-minded pursuit of a definite objective, he had no time to indulge in speculations about the history, character and sociology of the black market. He did not proceed at random. On the contrary: he regarded Hunter's casual remark that George had de-manded Pfc. Harry S. Jones, Major O'Hara's former driver, for his mysterious trip as his principal clue. The former auto stunt-man and reckless test-driver turned out to be a well-known figure among the shacks of the Möhlstrasse. From his own questioning of the arrested Jakob Steiner, Frank had gathered that Steiner had first approached George through Pfc. Jones; indeed the links had been so close that the black marketeer even remembered the unfortunate late major. When Frank finally discovered that the jeep driven by Pfc. Jones belonged to the regular black-market fleet serving the Möhlstrasse and had been through the Austrian and Italian frontier controls several times, he no longer doubted that he was on the right track.

Then suddenly, on the third day of his "leave," Frank's hypothesis was knocked in a heap. That morning Colonel Hunter informed him that another man, who had collaborated with Captain Green and who was a German espionage agent of some importance, was reported missing. The name was not unknown to Frank: he had made use of the man more than once himself. It was Josef Maurer, formerly a corporal in the Wehrmacht. But Jakob Steiner had never even heard Maurer's name. The trail now pointed unmistakably in the direction which Colonel Hunter had feared most of all.

"I've Always Been a Good Father"

"I'm afraid I must disturb you for a moment, Herr Doktor," said Elisabeth, entering Adam's surgery.

She was wearing a white coat. Adam too wore his white coat: he had just given his patient an injection. A little irritably he asked:

"What is it?"

Elisabeth drew him into a corner.

"Alois Schmidt is here—Inge's father," she said softly, struggling to keep the excitement out of her voice. "He is acting rather violently."

"Where's Inge?"

"Still at the PX."

"Any more patients waiting?"

"Only old man Weghaus. But he's quite prepared to come back tomorrow."

"Very well then. I shall be at Herr Schmidt's disposal in a minute."

He finished with his patient as quickly as he could. Then he asked for Alois Schmidt to be sent in.

The old-age pensioner, left alone with Adam, stopped short with surprise when he found himself faced by the impressive large man with the fair mustache. But he pulled himself together at once and said without further preamble:

"I have come to collect my daughter, Herr Doktor. You know who I am. You are hiding my daughter."

"Won't you sit down?" said Adam. "And, by the way, I'm not hiding anybody."

"But you're not denying that she is here?"

"I am not denying anything," replied Adam, still quite calmly.

"Well, then," said Schmidt without sitting down. "She's to pack her things and come along with me."

"She'll do nothing of the sort," said Adam.

Alois Schmidt changed color. "By what right," he asked, "are you detaining my daughter?"

"I am not detaining her, Herr Schmidt. She is my guest and will remain so as long as she pleases."

"She's under age," said Schmidt. "I'll get the police after you!"

Adam went over to the basin and washed his hands.

"I think not, Herr Schmidt," he said. "You sent Inge on to the streets once before and I shouldn't be surprised if you intended to do so again. If you go to the police, Herr Schmidt, it will be you that's locked up. And, so far as I can see, that wouldn't help anyone."

"It's only now that she walks the streets," retorted Schmidt. "I know very well where she works."

"Yes?"

"She works at the PX. Only Yankee whores work at the PX. No decent German girl would work for the Yanks."

Adam had dried his hands and turned back to the pensioner. He said:

"As the outraged German father you're cutting a rather ridiculous

»356«

figure, Herr Schmidt. Perhaps you'd better try that line on someone who knows less about you."

To his surprise Schmidt sat down slowly. In a changed voice he said:

"I've always been a good father, Herr Doktor." He began once more: "As a German father . . ."

Adam interrupted him. "Did you or did you not send Inge on to the streets?"

"She went of her own accord; believe me, Herr Doktor. She always was a bad girl—it's not my fault, Herr Doktor."

"How long has Inge lived away from you, Herr Schmidt?"

"Getting on for a year now," answered Schmidt. His voice was tearful.

"But till now you've done nothing to get her back?"

"I only found out yesterday that she works at the PX and lives at your place. If she weren't working for the Yanks . . ."

"You only had to go to the Registration Office," said Adam. "I'm wondering why you should have remembered your parental love all of a sudden. Did you think there might be some pickings for you at the PX?"

"You are trying to insult me, Herr Doktor. You are doing me a grave injustice. A few days ago I had my pension restored to me." He straightened up in his chair. "It is a starvation pension. But I can look after my child again. That is the reason, Herr Doktor."

Adam thoughtfully regarded the little man with his drink-flushed face. Even now he could not resist the temptation of finding out why human beings act in certain ways.

"How did Inge get on to the streets in the first place?" he asked.

"Ever since I lost my wife," said Schmidt, his stilted language attempting social equality with Adam, "Inge has been everything to me. The Yanks have robbed us of everything. Inge was spoilt. There were a few girls in the building, who set a bad example. But—" he added hastily—"I will let bygones be bygones. I am prepared to forget and forgive."

Adam sat down. "All right," he said; "no harm in asking her . . ."

"There's nothing to ask," replied Schmidt. He changed his tactics again. "She's not eighteen yet and she's got to obey. The idea of letting a girl of eighteen do as she pleases!"

"Herr Schmidt," said Adam, "the story you told me just doesn't stand up. Nevertheless I am not entirely averse to crediting you with a certain measure of good intentions. I have lately had a lot of dealings with people like you, Herr Schmidt. The collapse occurred two years ago and we are slowly beginning to recover. Some people, indeed, are having their pensions restored to them already. And with the pensions their conscience returns—conscience has a way of doing that, Herr Schmidt. But it is too late. Time—I don't know if I am making myself clear—excuses a lot of things, but it does not excuse everything. First you had to become a Nazi, Herr Schmidt, because Germany went National Socialist; then you became a knave because the occupation era favored that kind of character. And now, for a while, you may become a respectable citizen since respectability seems to be coming back into fashion. What you're going to be next I can't predict: I am no prophet. Come now, sit down again—there's a good fellow. Your indignation doesn't impress me a bit. A child—and Inge is a child, in spite of everything—is a delicate instrument. For yourself, you can do what you like, Herr Schmidt—that's your business. But you've kowtowed so low before the changing demands of our time that you've broken your backbone. You can't be trusted with a child any more. If you want to go to the police that's your business. But I promise you I'll give you a run for your money that you'll remember . . ."

Alois Schmidt leaped to his feet.

"I wanted to talk to you reasonably," he said. "You can bet your bottom dollar I'm going to the police. You talk about Nazis? You're hand in glove with that top Nazi Eber yourself! The small ones are hanged and the big ones get away with murder."

"This business has nothing to do with Nazis," said Adam, controlling himself with an effort. "Although I am getting rather tired of the protestation that one was only ever so small a Nazi. But that's by the way. What you don't seem to have noticed is that the idea of hereditary culpability is out. I am not acquainted with Herr Dr. Eber. His son is a decent young man, and but for him Inge wouldn't be alive now."

"A decent young man!" jeered Schmidt. His head was flushed crimson. "He's a pimp!"

Adam stood up.

"Herr Schmidt," he said, "I am getting near the end of my patience. If you hadn't previously interested me I should have kicked you down the stairs before now. Crooks are always the first to yell for the police when someone crosses their plans—but in this country they yell even louder than elsewhere. Sometimes I think that the only sound argument with a certain type of person is a good thrashing, and I'm not sure that the first man you denounced in your block wouldn't have done you a great favor by giving you a hearty kick in the pants. Maybe you don't think that's very democratic, Herr Schmidt—but frankly, I don't care. At all events you're now leaving my apartment before I lay hands on you!"

Alois Schmidt began his retreat towards the door. When he had reached the door he started shouting:

"You'll pay for this, you . . . I'll get the police on you . . . I know what you do with my daughter, you and your pimp! I know she hands over to you her earnings from the PX; I'll see you're struck off the register, you . . ."

With his back to the door he fumbled for the handle, but he had miscalculated Adam's earnestness. Elisabeth and Frau Wild, summoned by the shouting, looked on in horror as the giant in the white coat picked up the kicking little man by the collar and the seat of his pants, carried him through the apartment, opened the door with his elbow and then, almost gently, deposited his human bundle on the top stair.

"I've got to go over to the PX at once," said Adam, returning to the apartment. "I don't know if Hans is meeting her today." He stripped off his coat.

"I shall be getting ready to receive the police," said Frau Wild without rebuke. "Was this really necessary, Adam?"

"Necessary or not," muttered Adam as Elisabeth helped him on with his jacket, "but what can a man do when a pimp turns righteous . . . ?"

Forgive More and Forget Less

As the jeep wound its way out of Munich and reached the autobahn the heat, which had been lying heavily over the city for the past few days, abated. A light breeze ruffled Elisabeth's summer dress. She was sitting next to Frank, silent, absorbed in the rich landscape which lay dozing peacefully on both sides of the road.

It had required the gentle and persistent persuasion of Frau Wild and of Adam to induce Elisabeth to go on this drive to the Chiemsee. During the winter Frank had hardly ever come to Munich, and Elisabeth, while welcoming him cordially on his brief visits, had so far always declined his invitations.

The Non-Fraternization Law had been dropped at the beginning of 1947. It had been buried quietly—that law thought up by the prophets of collective guilt and mocked and infringed by life itself from the very start. The "normalization of relations," as the official justification termed it, was still no open reversal of the policy of the victors. The inhabitants of the disgraced country were still in disgrace and the law was merely the legalization of a state of affairs which had begun, illegally, at the moment when, with the guns silenced, the people had first talked to one another. Symbols of this state of affairs were the soldiers, especially the Negroes, who could be seen walking along with German women and pushing baby carriages: the babies in the carriages were living evidence of the fact that the unworldly law had been violated a year or more before its repeal. The procreation had been illegal, but its fruits were now legally paraded about in the summer sunshine. In the requistioned "Seehaus" restaurant by the artificial lake in the Englischer Garten in Munich, American officers were now dancing with German girls night after night, to the strains of a German jazz band—and the fact that these girls required a "Morality Pass" was not really designed to humiliate the Germans. On the contrary, it was a confession of weakness by the victorious army which, in its rocking boat, was terrified of every street-corner Lorelei. It was hardly surprising that it was precisely this type of girl who got the "Morality Pass"—the feeble joke was just then circulating that the abbreviation "VD" stood for "Veronika Dankeschön"—since girls and women with any self-respect at all did not apply for such a rubber-stamped certificate of their respectability. Besides, two years of Allied-decreed non-fraternization had produced among German women a resentment against the conquerors; and these, accustomed to conquer, were only looking for easy prey anyway.

Even if she had had no personal motives Elisabeth would have evaded Frank's invitation for fear of being reckoned among that doubtful company. But she had other, weightier motives—the chief one being that, yielding at last to Kurt von Zutraven's urgings, she had very quietly set about getting a divorce. Kurt von Zutraven was allowed to write to her every other month, and his wish and down-right demand that she should put an end to their false relationship leapt from every line. She had questioned herself very closely before taking the step, and she had only agreed to it when she was fully and wholly aware of her husband's motives. Kurt von Zutraven was obsessed with the desire to conclude at least his private life with a generous gesture; his letters were not self-torturing, but imbued with a pride to which he was now clinging like a drowning man. Even his political attitude, vacillating under the Third Reich just as his character, now hardened into self-congratulatory bitterness and vented itself in reproaches against his wife to whom he was generously giving her freedom and from whom he demanded his own, no matter how unreal, freedom. The divorce, which Elisabeth had not mentioned to Frank but of which he had accidentally learned through a stray remark of Adam's, did not smooth her path to Frank; on the contrary, she was afraid that he might suspect a connection between her decision and the relationship between them. Only when Frank suggested that they should drive out to the Chiemsee where fraternization had not yet penetrated in its more unrestrained forms, and only when Adam insisted that she could not wilt away all through the summer in the Schwabing caretaker's rooms or in his surgery, did she at last give in.

They had hardly exchanged a word since Munich. That first, long-missed, reunion with nature, the overwhelming contrast between the ruined city and the untouched countryside, completely took her breath away. Among the ruined houses lived ruined humans: walking about with downcast eyes and cautious step, dusty and crumbling and gray as the walls. The city was inhabited by the witnesses of the age—discharged prisoners of war in tattered uniforms with their white Afrika-Korps caps blackened with age; cripples on makeshift crutches; lonely women with the embittered eyes of widows; children prematurely aged and full of tragic cunning; mendicants desperately trying to preserve their dignity and the hundreds of characters that lived in the doorways. Elisabeth had always felt soothed and cheered by the countryside; but never before had the difference between it and the city been impressed on her with such urgency. Here, the land had not been destroyed, and neither had the people who walked over it. The grass stood tall and green; the trees bore an abundance of fruit; the ploughland stretched black and rich. Here, nothing was smashed, occupied or requisitioned. Neither the bustling, buzzing bees nor the lazily fluttering butterflies seemed aware that they were circling round doomed humans; calmly and confidently the peasants guided their ploughs, and when their womenfolk bent down to gather the cut crops their gesture held nothing of the servile bowing and scraping of the townspeople. In that great happiness that flooded Elisabeth there was also, as she readily admitted to herself, some happiness over the Germany which she loved. In the cities, those dark infested spots on the X-ray picture of life, Germany appeared to be dying; but one only had to look out over these valleys and forests and lakes to realize that the desert existed only in a few oases.

It was a weekday and the terrace of the officers' hotel by the lakeside was almost deserted when they sat down there late in the afternoon. Yet the tension which had hung between them throughout the journey did not abate even on that quiet terrace under the mild late-afternoon sunshine. The fact that they both wanted the same thing, that they desired each other, in the bright daylight of summer, with that overwhelming sobriety that is more powerful than any nighttime intoxication, did not bring them closer to one another. On the contrary, each of them seemed to be guarding their secret with redoubled bashfulness because they knew that it was the other's secret also. This was no case of conquest and refusal, but a shared fear lest a single word might betray everything; only the key was still needed to unlock the rooms they knew without ever having entered them.

At last Frank put an end to the silence—or rather to the flow of a conversation that had been about everyday things and hence, to both of them, a babbling brook of dissembling pretense.

"Elisabeth," he said abruptly. "We only have a few hours together. We've got to talk."

She suppressed the conventional objection that they had been talking all the time.

"I know about your divorce," he said. "Will you marry me?"

"This is so sudden," she said, trying to smile.

He said hastily: "I know all the obstacles. We can't get married over here. I've got to go back to America. But within a year I could get you an entry permit without much difficulty. Over there, they wouldn't make any difficulties." He had dropped his eyes, but now he looked up at her. He, too, tried to smile as he added: "The only question is: Do you want to?"

She was sitting opposite him. She took his hand which had been lying on the table.

"I'd sooner marry you today than tomorrow, Franz."

He squeezed her hand. "I can hear a 'But' in your voice," he said.

"A hundred 'Buts,'" she said, gently withdrawing her hand. "I have thought about it so many times, Franz. It isn't only the external circumstances. Just think of it: you and the divorced wife of Kurt von Zutraven in America! Oddly enough, things are much simpler here. Here I am who I am; and no matter who I am I have my own personality. Over there, they only know my name. I know, Franz, you would protect me, explain, and defend me. But do you know how wearying it is to convince people that everything is quite different? I have tried it often, and I know. The time would come when nothing would bind you to me except your determination to prove yourself right, before the rest of the world and before yourself."

"You think me weaker than I am," he said.

"No, I don't," she said. "I know how strong you are, Franz. But that isn't all. The people here . . . it may not be very important, but I don't deny that I am not indifferent to them. I love this country, Franz, and I don't love it any the less for the fact that it is in misfortune now and that it has probably deserved its misfortune." She gazed out across the lake which was so completely silent as if it were trying to eavesdrop. "Germany . . . it would always stand between us, Franz. I am full of admiration at the way you understand it, really understand it at times . . . and one day you'll understand it unreservedly. Perhaps I shall understand it less, but I shall always love it. There is bound to spring up a profound chill between us every time the word Germany is mentioned. . . . I have been afraid of that chill these past few months, whenever we have talked about Germany. Over there, I know, you would try to be generous, but your generosity would hurt me." Again she caught hold of his hand. "Franz . . . forgive me if I mention Kurt von Zutraven again. The comparison is bad, as all comparisons are. But I have come to know the misery caused by all lack of understanding, even if it is a failure to understand things which, properly speaking, have nothing to do with the relationship between a man and a woman. But in spite of all I've said, Franz, I would still risk it if . . ."

"Do finish," he said. "So long as you'll let me have my say afterwards . . ."

"These are only excuses," she said. "The truth is much worse."

"I can bear it," he said.

"The truth is the ghosts," she said. "The truth is the prisoner in Spandau. I am safe from him so long as I am certain that I did not leave him because it was expedient for me to leave him. But if I were to become your wife, an American wife, the wife of a conqueror —then I know that his ghost would come and haunt me till I could bear it no longer. I was his wife. I marched along with him. I fought with him, but I did not fight him in everything. When we lost Stalingrad he cried. And I sat at his side and cried with him. That day, as you told me yourself, you drank a toast at your officers' mess to the victory of Stalingrad. This is a thing that it's difficult to get over. Over there, you'd mention Stalingrad and you would clink your glasses, and one hundred and thirty thousand soldiers trudging into captivity with frost-bitten feet would be to you one hundred and thirty thousand rungs on the ladder of your victory. I fully understand it. But to me they would be one hundred and thirty thousand human beings. At such moments Kurt von Zutraven would stand before me and speak to me; and I should see him cry as he cried that time, and I should forget how much I hated him most of the time, and how much I despised him."

She stopped abruptly.

So suddenly had the evening descended over the Chiemsee that the dusk now hung between them, although they had not noticed it falling. Behind the gentle hills on the far side of the lake the sun was setting like a blazing ship, its fire sinking into the other, victorious, element.

Elisabeth leaned back instinctively, as though seeking support amidst the gathering shadows.

"And then," she said in a voice struggling for firmness, "and then there is your mother!" Now she had uttered the word which they had both avoided since their reunion at the villa in Nuremberg. Hurriedly she continued: "She will always stand between us, Franz. I don't know how, but I might have saved her. I knew that she was in the concentration camp: Dr. Wild had told my father. Your mother would despise you, Franz, if you made me your wife. You would betray the dead woman. Not today and not tomorrow . . . but some day she would remind you. I love you too much not to know that. One can't get over these things. . . ."

He did not reply to her immediately. He waited. She had spoken of the ghosts and the chill which the ghosts trailed behind them like white trains. Were the ghosts now closing in on them through the warm July evening? Had this mood been engineered by the ghosts, so that his proposal should look foolish, or even mean and treasonable? Should he not only renounce his love but even feel ashamed of it? But nothing happened: in him there were no ghostly voices and no chill. He said softly:

"One can't get over these things . . . you keep saying that, Elisabeth. But that's just it: one's got to get over them, and one can get over them. It's this great inertia which has to answer for so much, in big things as well as small, in personal affairs and in public affairs. Nations can't get over the fact that some other nation, a hundred years ago, robbed them of a piece of territory—so a hundred years later they've got to go to war. A man can't get over the fact that his wife once loved another man, and on this phantasm their marriage is shipwrecked. Nations can't get over their prejudices, and individuals can't get over the insults they have suffered. Nobody seems to be prepared to get over anything: tearfully and vainly they all regard their own wounds. Like a bad horse mankind refuses its jumps and anyone trying to leap over his shadow is considered a fool. I am not saying that love conquers all—I don't even know if it is true. But one can get over such things as having been too slow to realize this or that, having offended others or suffered offense, committing errors or seeing others commit them, or turning away from the path one ought to have followed. I don't believe in ghosts, Elisabeth; I do not believe that summoning the dead from their graves is a form of piety. My words have often hurt you because you are trying to forget; but I believe that too much is being forgotten and too little forgiven. Forgive more and forget less—that seems to me a better recipe. I can get over everything that you have mentioned—and in any case I'd known it all—and so can you if only you summon the courage."

The lights went up on the terrace.

"Let's walk a little," she said.

They took the narrow path which followed the bank. Frogs and crickets were competing in their nocturnal summer concert. There was a smell of water and wet earth.

She took his arm and said: "I can't answer you now, Franz. I just don't know if you are right. I only know that I love you."

She stopped, turned to him and offered him her lips. Their kiss was neither passionate nor chaste—it was as if the two wanted not to fan but to smother the flames that were burning within them. It was the first kiss after a thousand unkissed kisses.

Arm in arm they walked on, turning off the path when they reached the woods.

"We're adult people," she said, trying in vain to keep the tremor out of her voice, "we are in love with each other, Franz, and we don't have to make any plans."

Deeper in the forest they lay down. The night covered them, and the night was the only darkness in their love. Most overwhelming in their passion was their happy awareness of what they were doing; the conscious knowledge that did not leave them even now, and from which they did not flee; their pride in a mature decision that required no justification; the tranquil conscience in their throbbing bodies and that final victory without vanquished.

Late at night, as they drove back to Munich in the open car, with not a breath stirring in the hot night, they did not feel that they now had a secret before the world. They felt that there were no secrets left.

Sibelius Pays a Painful Visit

The year 1947 was not an eventful year in the history of Germany's occupation, yet in some respects it was the most eventful of all.

There was still great hardship in the occupied land. Only here and there did a house slowly rise from the debris. The one hundred and second food ration schedule was published; the Allied Combined Travel Board was still granting its foreign travel permits as if they were precious and exceptional awards; questionnaires were still being filled out, former Party members dismissed, black-market deals concluded and houses requisitioned. But Germany in 1947 was like a revolving stage: on the segment exposed to view Act One was still running, but at the back a new set was already being knocked together. "Poor as a Church Mouse" might have been the title of the play being staged; but just as in that successful German comedy of the Twenties the next act was going to show the poor mouse turned into an elegant lady.

That was the most significant thing about the year 1947—that anything of importance took place backstage. There, the cold war was being prepared, and now and again, as inevitably happens in the theater, the hammering behind the scenes could be heard by the audience. On the stage, Germany was still the defeated country, but in the dressing rooms she was already being made up for Act Two, when she would play the part of an ally in the cold war. The currency reform was in preparation, much earlier than originally planned; the Morgenthau plan was quietly buried outside the churchyard wall, so that nothing should testify to its recent existence; a blind eye was turned to the camouflaged ex-servicemen's associations; criticism of the Eastern Ally, until recently an offense punishable by imprisonment, was not only tolerated but surreptitiously encouraged; industrialists who had been expelled from their factories had their private villas quietly restored to them; and gray waistcoats, though perhaps not yet the black ones, came back from the Allied laundry white as the driven snow. On the stage Germany's misery, humiliation and persecution seemed to solidify into a permanent condition, and the masses were in despair—but behind the scenes everything was once more in a state of flux.

Worst off were those who belonged neither to the silent crowd in the darkened audience watching, open-mouthed and wide-eyed, their own fate being acted out on the stage, nor to the actors who knew the lines, the plot and the end of the play. Colonel Achim von Sibelius, who had tried his hand at a variety of jobs during the past nine months—after finding that his employment as insurance salesman did not bring in enough even to convert his ration cards into rations— was one of those who doubted the genuineness and permanence of what he saw before him, but his glimpses of what lay hidden behind the scenes were only sporadic and not necessarily convincing.

It was not conviction, either one way or another, that induced Sibelius on that raw and chilly September afternoon to pay the visit which he had put off time and again. That day, at long last, he called on Colonel Werner Zobel.

The baron was urged to his visit by a counsel both eloquent and bad—hunger. For the past four weeks he had not eaten a proper meal, with the exception of his Sunday visits to Adam Wild where, for the sake of good manners, he had forced himself to moderation so as not to wolf down the food on his plate. His lungs, weakened by a serious illness in his youth and subsequently, as he had believed, fully cured, had begun to trouble him again. Adam's opinion, when he had got him to examine him, had been: "My dear Achim, you've simply got to eat properly—which is about as frivolous a piece of advice as telling a man with a weak heart that he mustn't excite himself."

Even so, Sibelius had not gone stright to Colonel Zobel from Adam's consulting room; it required another occurrence to make up Sibelius's mind. It was indeed a very curious occurrence and it took place two or three days after his visit to the doctor. A former lieutenant of his acquaintance, whom Sibelius had since met at the "Mücke," made him a lucrative black-market proposition. Stripped of its camouflage trimmings, the offer meant that the politically non-incriminated colonel should obtain a travel permit for himself and should then ply between Munich and Milan as the courier of a syndicate of currency racketeers. The ex-lieutenant, now a flourishing black-market dealer, invited Sibelius to an opulent dinner, and when the Colonel, after several unaccustomed large glasses of French cognac, left the comfortable home of his former subordinate, there was an advance of twenty crisp dollar bills in his pocket.

That same night the Colonel conducted a strange dialogue with these dollar bills—or rather a monologue, since the greenbacks on his bedside table were merely staring at him in silence. Yes, my dears—Baron Sibelius addressed the dollar bills which to his drink-befuddled eyes took on the shape of goggling green frogs—my only choice now is between you and the visit which I have postponed so long. To earn one's livelihood in a respectable way seems to have gone out of fashion in this country; and to cough out my sick lungs or die of starvation does not appeal to me, any more than any other kind of unnecessary death. You may not know it—because at that time you were probably still circulating merrily in your bustling and boisterous native country—but I was not sorry to take off my uniform, and when a little later I put away my dreams as well, like a worn-out uniform, I did not suppose that a man must necessarily die of starvation merely because he believes in a civilian world. True enough, you have been offered to me in evidence of the fact that it is perfectly possible to make a living in our new democracy, but I happen to have my ingrained prejudices and would not really enjoy smuggling you or your kind across frontiers. I am ready to admit, my dear frogs, that this may be the fault of my conventional upbringing and not therefore necessarily justified: for who would maintain that it is more moral to conspire for the purpose of a new world conflagration than to make a temporary pact with some dealers and racketeers? But it appears once again that it is relatively less dangerous to play at soldiers than to take on civilian risks; besides, I very much doubt that I would cut a very successful figure as a currency broker. Your visit, dear frogs, seems to reduce my choice to the alternatives of black market or secret conspiracy, since I have tried everything else in vain. I trust that you will not take it amiss if, a slave to my tradition, I choose the latter. I am grateful to you for your kind visit, but I must ask you not to hop off my bedside table, as tomorrow morning I shall take you back to where you came from and thus redeem my rather limited freedom.

On the next morning the baron indeed returned the twenty dollars to the startled black marketeer, and on the same afternoon he presented himself at Colonel Zobel's apartment.

"A good job needs time," said the Colonel, amicably putting his arm round Sibelius's shoulder. "Your hesitation, my dear Baron, proves to me that you have carefully considered your step. I regard it is as particularly propitious that you have come today—a day which has brought me great happiness." He walked over to the piano and handed to his visitor a postcard which had lain there. "My son Jochen, a prisoner of war for more than five years, has arrived at Frankfurt-on-Oder. The Russians at last have let him go. He seems to be in good shape, and my daughter and I hope to have him here with us before long. I lost my two elder sons in the war, so you can imagine my joy at seeing Jochen again, and in reasonable health too."

"My congratulations, Herr Oberst," said Sibelius.

The Colonel glanced at the clock. "Yes indeed, your visit today is satisfactory in every respect, Baron. We are having a little meeting, in a private room at the 'Augustiner,' and I shall be pleased to introduce you to the old comrades."

Sibelius wanted to say something—such as that he was in no particular hurry, that he had come merely to convey his acceptance in principle and that he might make the acquaintance of the gentlemen of the ex-servicemen's association some other time.

But Zobel forestalled him. "We can have a little talk as we walk along," he said with a glance at the window, "provided you don't mind walking through the rain."

»369«

Sibelius put on his thin trench coat again. Martha, who had appeared in the hall simultaneously with the gentlemen, helped Zobel on with his winter coat.

From the Marienplatz the men walked down Kaufingerstrasse, towards the Stachus. Anyone seeing the two, the older man on the right and the younger one on the left, could not fail to identify them for what they were: two officers in civilian clothes. Both were walking more upright than was necessary, striding out boldly, and entirely untroubled by the rain which fell on them softly but steadily.

"I am glad that you gave up your post at the 'Mücke'—that, I think, was the name of the night club?" said Zobel. "But I suppose you have had rather a thin time since."

"As always, you are excellently informed, Herr Oberst," Sibelius said with a smile.

"Well," said the Colonel, in a casual voice that could not be taken as an affront, "you'll meet a few old comrades who may give you a tip or two. Myself, I've been working for the past few months for an American building firm—not a particularly lucrative but quite a decent job, at least until our pension claims are met."

"Is there any chance . . . ?" Sibelius asked without much genuine interest.

"Not at the moment, naturally. Wouldn't be worth it in the present currency. But it's just as well you've mentioned it, Herr Oberst. The Americans have advised us to put the emphasis in our activities on financial matters for the time being. You will find that this evening there will be disproportionately much talk of pension claims, widows' annuities and such like. We've always got to expect the presence of some American prompters. Besides, the Americans—business-like people all of them—are quite right. Our group, like all the others in the country, suffers from top-heaviness: too many officers, too few NCO's, and practically no privates. It's no tragedy in itself, especially as far as the privates are concerned—you can always recruit those in a hurry. But when we begin to show our faces, in public and political life I mean—next year at the latest—we mustn't create the impression that we are an officers' clique. You know what people are like. That is also why I have made an old Feldwebel from my regiment Vice-President. A good fellow, though a trifle dense and garrulous. But as I was saying . . . yes, the financial aspect, pensions and widows' benefits and such stuff, that has a pull all right and we're getting more enrolments from the lower classes—and that's what impresses the Americans. If therefore you have some privates among your crowd—I'm afraid your 20th of July was a bit of an aristocratic enterprise—then please don't hesitate, Baron. We are emphatically democratic."

"My crowd?" said Sibelius. "I hope I won't disappoint you, Herr Oberst. The men of the 20th of July are not an organized group; most of them will continue to waver . . ."

"Quite so, quite so," Zobel interrupted him. "We don't expect you to work miracles. But a beginning must be made, you understand."

They had arrived at the beer cellar soaked to the skin. Sibelius, who wore no hat, used his handkerchief to dry the white hair sticking to his forehead. As they stepped into the restaurant the steamy heat struck him so suddenly that he began to cough; he had to pause before following Zobel down a steep flight of stairs to a private room.

His coughing fit had brought tears to his eyes and he could not take in the scene at once. When his gaze cleared he saw eight men at a long table: in the middle a chair was vacant, evidently kept for the Colonel. The eight men facing the door stood up at Zobel's entry; the others turned and also rose. Informally or rigid as they stood, Sibelius was not only able to tell which of these civilians had been officers and which NCO's or privates, but he could have very nearly guessed their former ranks.

Sibelius sat down on the last free chair next to the chairman's table. He was glad that Zobel was paying no particular attention to him. As the Colonel declared the meeting open and while the items on the agenda were rattled off monotonously he was able to study the officials of the association and the rest of the assembly more closely.

On the Colonel's right sat a man who spoke more often than the rest, and who was addressed as "Herr General." Sibelius thought he recognized him from photographs: a former paratroop general of about fifty-five, with the face of a sullen bulldog. His pet hobbyhorse seemed to be the German soldier's honor, for whenever that subject was mentioned he would have something to say on it and in his own speeches the soldier's honor kept recurring like the chorus in a song. Whether indemnities for war widows were under discussion, or prisoners of war, or the release of some senior officers—invariably the General referred to the insulted honor of the soldier. On Zobel's left sat a former Feldwebel, a man of gaunt features, with restless eyes and prominent cheekbones, who nodded emphatically whenever the General or the Colonel were speaking and who gave a startled jump when once, presumably at the wrong moment, his fist came down rather too vigorously on the table right in front of Zobel. But most of all Sibelius was interested in a relatively young man at the end of the table, presumably the clerk, for he was taking copious notes. He was a thin man with the face of an ascetic carp, and Sibelius was sure that he knew him although he could not place him at the moment. For his part, the clerk, a "Herr Hauptmann," kept glancing over at the visitor with a searching, hostile look of gradual recognition.

The last item on the agenda had been reached: discussion of the impending war crimes trial of Field Marshall August Kadonitz. It was a disgrace without parallel, that trial to be held in the British Zone, declared the paratroop general: the Herr Feldmarschall had merely done his duty as a soldier and acted in accordance with his oath, as all German soldiers whose honor was now being trampled underfoot. Needless to say, the verdict was a foregone conclusion— after all, everyone knew what this so-called Allied justice was like— but it was nevertheless an obligation of soldierly loyalty to do everything humanly possible for the Herr Feldmarschall. In short, it was a case of finding witnesses who would testify to the unexceptional behavior of the Herr Feldmarschall. If any such potential witnesses were present would they report to the General immediately this meeting was over. Would those present also look out for any former soldiers who had served under the Herr Feldmarschall: any incidental expenses, and of course also the fare to Hanover, would be met by the association.

What was this strange game that was being played here, Sibelius asked himself, while the General, accompanied by unanimous applause, went on to describe the war crime trials as a mockery of democracy. A "No" rang out from a hundred throats in reply to his question whether there was in fact a so-called war crime that the Allies had not themselves committed. Was it his sickness that was nowadays apt to pounce on him suddenly, or was there really a veil of unreality over this assembly? Up above, in the Kaufingerstrasse, American troops moved about; notices of "Off Limits" were nailed to every other door; fast jeeps were tearing about among a few rickety old German vehicles—but down here, in the beer cellar, a paratroop general was inveighing against the Allies and handing out money to witnesses for the defense in the trial against Field Marshal Kadonitz. The money could only come from American sources—which meant that in Hanover a "war criminal" was to be tried by the Allies, while in Munich they were financing witnesses to disprove his guilt. Only a few months ago the Governor of the occupied country had spoken of the final destruction of German militarism; but here the gentlemen were once more addressing each other as "Herr Oberst" and "Herr Hauptmann" and "Herr Feldwebel," throwing smart salutes and standing at attention—and all under the eyes of "American prompters" who promoted this ghostly business and did not seem to care about being jeered at.

And what about himself, Colonel Achim von Sibelius? He who had once conspired to rid his country of these loyal servants of their masters-of-the-moment, of these fellow-culprits through obedience, these men obedient through conviction; he who had been prepared to jettison his entire tradition of military obedience because he had come to realize that obedience and slavery were all too apt to mean the same thing in Germany—by what strange tortuous paths had the supposed liberators forced him into a position where the unsuccessful gravedigger of obedience was to become the midwife of new enslavement?

Sibelius tried desperately to resolve these contradictions and riddles, and it was at that moment of ultimate mental effort that his eyes again met those of the minute-taking Herr Hauptmamn and that suddenly Sibelius recognized him. That time in Berlin, when everything had been topsy-turvy, when a certain Colonel Remer had occupied the Reich Chancellery but there had still been hope of last-minute salvation in the General Staff; that time when Colonel von Sibelius had picked up the telephone with a shaking hand to receive the latest news about success or failure of the plot—that time a young captain with the Knight's Cross round his neck, looking like an ascetic fish, had toured the offices accompanied by a few NCO's, walking from room to room, a self-appointed policeman on the lookout for unreliable elements, renegades and conspirators. By a mere chance Sibelius had not then fallen into the hands of the zealous young captain—the same who was now sitting at the end of the long table, taking down the minutes of a meeting of a very different crowd of conspirators.

Acting on an impulse, his first live impulse in weeks, Sibelius rose.

Yet immediately he slumped back into his chair. Colonel Zobel had stood up and was speaking.

"*Kameraden!*" he said. "I do not want to declare today's meeting closed without first making an announcement which, I hope, will fill you all with the same joy and satisfaction as it did me. It is my pleasure to welcome a new member, who is here today for the first time—Colonel in the General Staff Achim Freiherr von Sibelius." A low murmur ran through the smoke-filled room. "Herr Oberst von Sibelius, holder of the Knight's Cross with Oak Leaves, a most distinguished officer of the Wehrmacht, was—as some of you are perhaps aware—involved in that unfortunate 20th of July, though not in an essential capacity." The murmur in the room grew louder. "*Kameraden!*" the Colonel continued undismayed. "I know your objections, and indeed I share them. But I asked myself one decisive question: Who is a man, and who isn't?" The Colonel paused; from one or two places came sounds of approval. "Colonel von Sibelius is a man; we can all of us vouch for that. He has erred, but to err is human. To admit one's errors is the action of a brave man. We do not want to show ourselves less manly than the man Sibelius. He has proffered his hand and I, for one, will not reject it. There are many like Colonel von Sibelius—men who did not consider at the time the consequences of their action. We hope and believe that many who are still aloof today will follow the example of Colonel von Sibelius." He stopped and waited. As he could not perceive any demonstration either of approval or disapproval he concluded: "I call on all those in favor of the enrollment of Colonel Achim von Sibelius to raise their right hands."

Through the thick smoke Sibelius gazed across the room. All those at the chairman's table and about two dozen men at the beer tables raised their hands.

"Anbody against the enrollment of Colonel von Sibelius?" asked Zobel.

Five or six hands were raised.

Zobel turned to Sibelius.

"I am delighted, Herr Oberst," he said, "to be able to shake hands with you as one of us."

Sibelius stood up. He went over to the table, reeling almost like a drunk. As through a thick fog he heard the Feldwebel's voice:

"The meeting will be closed with the National Anthem."

Everyone stood up. Zobel released Sibelius's limp, clammy hand. Like a father leading his children in a merry roundel Zobel nodded encouragingly to his new protégé as he started up in a sonorous base:

"Deutschland, Deutschland über alles . . ."

You Need a Good Stomach

That day Inge was on duty at the PX only in the morning, and when she had not come home by two o'clock Adam and Frau Wild began to get worried. At half past two, at last, the front-door bell rang, but when Frau Wild went to answer it she found that it was Hans Eber, excitedly asking if they had heard from Inge.

"I was meeting her at twelve-thirty," Hans explained without sitting down, "but she didn't come out. In the end I buttonhole one of her colleagues and after much babbling she confessed that Inge had been 'chucked out.' She couldn't tell me what for—or I suspect she didn't want to. What are we to do, Dr. Wild?"

Adam at once reached for his coat.

"Come along," he said. "We've got to find out first of all what happened at the PX."

Through the misty October afternoon they hurried towards the Brienner Strasse.

"It won't be so easy to get in," said Hans.

"We've got to start somewhere," said Adam.

Hans had been right with his prediction. A great deal of time was spent negotiating with the Negro soldiers guarding the American paradise of consumer goods. Women, girls and children, and even a sprinkling of men, were hanging about on the opposite side of the street, and while Hans, who fortunately spoke English, tried all his persuasion on the sentries, Adam, who usually avoided this neighborhood, had an opportunity of studying the scene.

The words "Yankee Whore," which were appearing with increasing frequency on the walls of the city, filled Adam with disgust. But equally, he was unable to fight down a feeling of revulsion as he gazed at the women who were waiting for some heavily laden conqueror. For the most part they were women whom nobody but strange soldiers in a strange country could possibly find desirable: prematurely aged, sluttish, unkempt women with bad teeth and faulty gold fillings, with pale faces swollen with hunger and lips painted scarlet; with ineffectually dyed army blankets round their shoulders, from which the blue or green dye had begun to run so that the original brown color was beginning to spread again like a rash. But what struck Adam most was the uniform smile that played about the lips of these women: uncertain which way to go and ready to go off in any direction—apologetic when other women hurried past; accusing, challenging and defensive when a German man looked at them; and inviting whenever a richly laden soldier emerged from the land of plenty. The spineless changeability of that smile pained Adam, as did also the fact that these women stood rooted to the spot regardless of the lashing rain which had started to fall from a leaden sky. As they stood there, dripping, pushing children aside because they feared their competition, or sending children forward to slow down some hurrying GI, noisily bartering with the black marketeers who were waiting there for old or new customers—they seemed beggar women rather than prostitutes, or perhaps a blend of the two, ready either to humble or to sell themselves according to the whim of the possessing. One day, maybe very soon—thought Adam—this nightmare would vanish, but how were these beggar women to find their way back to themselves, to a hard daily round, to returning husbands or real lovers? Would they not come to hate the men from whom they were now begging alms; would they not hate themselves, and would they not hate us who were unable to protect them?

While Adam was watching the scene outside the PX, Hans had at last succeeded in persuading one of the Negro giants to call his immediate superior, an American in civilian clothes; that man in turn negotiated at some length with a lieutenant behind a glass door; the lieutenant had a protracted telephone conversation, and when Adam and Hans had filled in the proper forms they were at last allowed to penetrate to the German manager of the store.

As though through a fairy-tale land of plenty, the visitors, escorted by a vigilant soldier, walked through the American store. They passed counters with veritable mountains of white, yellow and red packs of cigarettes, in cartons of two hundred; their path was lined with pillars of cans; packages of toothpaste, Kleenex, fountain pens, face lotion and men's shirts were arranged in huge pyramids; boxes of chocolate had been piled up in massive square blocks. Between the counters bustled servicemen and American wives, some of them with children in blue jeans and short well-padded winter coats. The German girls behind the counters, in their black satin uniforms, had taken on a little of the American flavor—not only because they displayed their slight command of English with much zeal, but also because they looked better kept than the remainder of the German women and because in hair-style and in manner they had surprisingly quickly adjusted themselves to the tastes of their customers.

The German manager, Herr Fröhlich, received his callers in his overheated office. He was a sour-looking man of pedantic appearance: Adam felt that he would blindly trust him with the till, but with nothing else. Nevertheless Herr Fröhlich, the typical half-educated bureaucrat, seemed duly impressed by Adam's academic title and, having assured himself over the gleaming internal telephone that a certain Captain Mariani had no objections, condescended to explain Inge Schmidt's sudden dismissal.

"A major," he said, pronouncing the rank in the English way, "appeared in my office at about half-past ten this morning. He informed me that he recognized the Schmidt girl at the soap counter as a former prostitute. As an officer and family man he objected strongly to our employing girls of that sort. Naturally, gentlemen, this was a bolt from the blue for me, and I had the girl sent for at once."

"Was the major still present?" interposed Adam.

"No, he had left," the manager continued hastily. "But there was no need for a confrontation. Fräulein Schmidt was already in tears on entering my office and, in reply to my question, admitted at once to having been a prostitute—though, as she maintained, only prior to her employment here."

"How did she know in advance . . ." asked Adam.

The little man in the black suit began to polish his rimless spectacles with excessive energy.

"Please, Herr Doktor," he said sharply, "I am prepared to give you certain information but I must insist that you do not interrupt me. You may think what you like, but the fact is that Fräulein Schmidt knew herself to be discovered the moment I had her sent for. Moreover, she behaved in a most improper manner; as soon as she had recovered from her first shock she made certain indecent remarks about the major, which only convinced me that his complaint was justified. Only because I was anxious to avoid any further scandal—and I did not put it beyond her to cause some awkwardness—I gave instructions for her wages to be paid to her, including today's though she had only just started. I suppose she must have left some time before noon." He got up. "Your interest in the young lady," he continued sarcastically, "is no business of mine, but I feel sure that she will shortly turn up again like the proverbial bad penny. Goodbye, gentlemen."

"Goodbye," said Adam, and his English salutation was not without sarcasm.

The soldier who had been waiting for them outside the manager's office once more took charge of them and shepherded them through the store to the exit. Adam avoided looking at his young friend. Only when they were out in the street again did he say:

"We'll ride out to the Eastern Cemetery. In her despair she may well have gone back to her father."

They had a long wait at the trolley stop. Adam vented his anger:

"The Herr Major! Now that his wife's here he is afraid of Inge. A fine crusader!"

"Will she ever shake it off . . . ?" wondered Hans.

"That depends on you," said Adam, almost roughly.

The old-age pensioner Alois Schmidt was lying on the divan with the lion's heads when Adam and Hans entered the room. He was in shirt sleeves and bedroom slippers, and his suspenders dangled from his unbuttoned trousers. The room reeked like a huge bottle of spirits and it was obvious that Herr Schmidt had been in the middle of sleeping off his liquor. At the sight of Adam he sat up; he clearly intended to jump up and eject the bold intruders, but his head was too heavy and he slumped back on to the divan. Adam, who had thought up a number of stratagems on the way, so that he need not broach the awkward subject straight off, was able to save himself all tactical maneuvers—drunk though he was Schmidt instantly guessed the purpose of their visit.

"So she's run away from you too?" he said. "No good looking for the bitch here—she's not come to me." He laughed. "What did you expect? A girl who runs away from her own father . . ." He propped himself up on an elbow. "Run away from her father, she has!" With the persistency of the drunk he clung to that single idea which appeared to be new to him. "Left her father who's always looked after her. Yes, left her father in his old age when she ought to have been a support to him." Tears appeared in his bloodshot eyes. "An ungrateful girl . . . So she's also been ungrateful to you . . ." He lingered on that thought for a while. Then he looked at Adam and recollection appeared in his features. "You . . . Of course she ran away from you. . . . It's all your fault. First you stole my daughter and now she is lost. . . ."

At last he managed to get up. Swaying but determinedly, he made for the two men, and since he could not just then find any other weapon he began furiously to unbutton his dragging suspenders, But before he could carry out his intention he got hopelessly entangled in the loose ends. So there was nothing left for him but to shout "Get out! Get out!" and the two men retreated quietly since what they wanted was not another brush with Alois Schmidt but to find Inge.

It had got dark in the meantime, but the rain had ceased.

"Let's ring up my apartment," suggested Adam. "Maybe she's come back after all."

He put a call through from a restaurant. No, he said when he rejoined Hans; Frau Wild had no news of her.

"I am afraid . . ." began Hans as they made once more for the trolley stop.

"I know," Adam interrupted him. "But you are mistaken. I am convinced that she won't do anything foolish . . . at least not the way you think."

Hans laughed wryly. "But maybe in some other way," he said. "Perhaps she has gone to the tall blonde."

"The prostitute, you mean . . . ?"

"That's the one."

"Very well. Let's go there," said Adam. After a little hesitation he added: "All this is not very pleasant, Hans. You need a good stomach if you want to live in our times. That's the most important thing—a good stomach."

"It takes more than that," said Hans. "Will she ever shake off her past?"

"You asked that one before. Don't you get bitten by that German bug of turning every one-act play into a Shakespearean drama. We are all suffering from our past. Inge's was more dramatic, but it was also shorter. Come along! My stomach is still quite good, and yours is even younger."

It was getting on towards seven when they reached the house in the Sendlinger-Tor-Platz. There was a light in Ilse Joachim's window. They climbed up the chicken-ladder. When they rang a young girl with a strangely innocent face opened the door. She wore a dressing gown and looked as if she had just got out of bed.

"You can't see Ilse just now. She's got a visitor. But if you'd like to wait . . . in my room?"

"Thank you," said Hans. "We'll wait out here."

The girl shrugged her shoulders and disappeared into her room.

The two men stood uncertainly in the poorly-lit hall. From Ilse's room came the sound of laughter. Somewhere in the half-wrecked building a toilet was being flushed: it made the whole building shudder. Behind one of the three doors opening off the hall a bed creaked.

Suddenly the middle door opened—Ilse's door. An American soldier emerged. He stopped and tightened his belt under his short Eisenhower jacket. He looked at the two men and his good-natured face was screwed up in a grin. Pointing with his thumb over his shoulder, at Ilse's door, he said:

"*Prima Fräulein!*"

Hans knocked.

The tall blonde, to the surprise of her visitors, was fully dressed. She was in the middle of carefully folding a sheet that had been spread on the couch.

Hurriedly, before Ilse might misunderstand the purpose of their visit, Adam explained their business.

"So you're the fellow," said the tall blonde, measuring Hans from head to toe.

"And you've had no news of her?" asked Adam.

Ilse put the sheet away in the wardrobe on top of which, as always, there stood a row of rosy-cheeked apples.

"Twice," she said. "But not in person. Once she sent me a hundred cigarettes, and the other time three bars of chocolate. She sent word that she was working at the PX. She is a good girl."

"And you've no idea where she might have gone?" asked Hans.

Ilse sat down on the couch.

"She might have jumped into the river," she said. "Her generation suffers from air-raid nerves. Weakened by the air raids, I mean. You'd think they'd be hardened—but it's the other way round. The more they've been through, the weaker their nerves." She scrutinized Hans again. "But it's nice of you that you should be looking for her. Wouldn't have expected it of you."

Hans did not want to prolong the conversation, but her remark made him look at her questioningly.

"Well, you're one of the air-raid generation, too," she said contemptuously. She got up and walked over to the washbasin to run out the dirty water. "She didn't fit here," she said. "You ought to marry her, Herr Eber, if she hasn't jumped into the river. But probably you haven't got the courage . . . The younger a man is the more cowardly he is." Suddenly she stopped. "Something's just occurred to me . . . Have you looked in at the 'Mücke'?"

"No," said Adam. "Why the 'Mücke,' of all places?"

"If she has some money . . . she always liked going there—because of the elegant atmosphere."

"We'll be off," said Hans. "We'll try there. And in case you hear of her . . ." He gave Ilse Dr. Wild's address.

Quickly and in silence they walked to the night club behind the brewery. As they reached the brightly-lit entrance Adam said:

"Got any money on you? I haven't any."

"Just about enough, I think," said Hans.

"The "Mücke" was packed. They pushed their way past dancing girls and soldiers, cast a glance into the smaller room and finally, not having found Inge, pulled up at the bar.

"Maybe the barman has seen her," Hans suggested.

He walked round to the back of the bar in the hope of getting a few private words with the barman.

Adam's eyes followed him. If she hasn't jumped into the river, he thought. And suppose we do find her. And suppose his stomach is strong enough . . . why, then perhaps everything may come out right.

He felt a heavy arm settling round his shoulders. Turning his head he discovered a man perched on a high stool by his side, taking big gulps from a big glass. The glass said "Odol" in large blue letters, but the white liquid in it was not water but schnapps. The man's eyes, too, were floating in a sea of schnapps. He was about thirty-five and his sparse hair was hanging into a face that looked as though it had been exposed to the rain for days on end. His long legs hung limply from the tall stool, boneless, like those of a wooden marionette.

"A glass of schnapps for you?" asked the stranger.

"No, thank you," Adam replied amicably, "I've got to go in a minute."

"A double for the gentleman here," the man called across the bar. Adam's refusal did not seem to impress him. "You don't want a drink," he jabbered, "because you think I've got no money. But you're mistaken, mightily mistaken."

He began to rummage in his pockets. Only now did Adam notice that the man was wearing a Wehrmacht uniform, stripped of its insignia of rank and most of its buttons. A civilian, bankrupt, tattered uniform.

"*Kamerad*," said the man, leaning heavily on Adam's shoulder, "I've got oodles of money—" but at the same time he gave up his search in his pockets. "Fact is, I'm dead. And if a fellow's dead he doesn't need any money. Agreed?"

"Indubitably," said Adam, looking round for Hans.

But the stranger did not let him go. "You think, of course, that I'm drunk, but that's only an optical illusion. Fact is, I'm dead. And I bet you've never seen a drunken dead before—not with all your cleverness." Once again he started to dig into his pockets. "I can prove it to you in black and white, *Kamerad*; I'm dead all right. The Führer and Reich Chancellor regrets to inform you . . ." He began to laugh noisily; the laughter shook him so that for a while he was unable to speak. "Fancy now, the Führer and Reich Chancellor really regretted it. Unteroffizier Karl-Heinz Simmel is dead. . . . He was quite sad about it. But nothing like as sad as my wife!" He twisted his face into a grimace of caricatured grief. "Did she weep or did she weep? *Kamerad!* She wept for fully six weeks. And then she went and married another fellow, out of grief, of course—after all, what doesn't one do out of grief! The Führer regrets, and one's wife regrets: Unteroffizier Simmel is dead." He forced his glass on Adam. "Drink it up. I don't need it, and they won't give you anything anyway."

"And what happened then?" asked Adam. He had to know more about Unteroffizier Karl-Heinz Simmel.

"Now she's got two husbands," said the man. "Most women haven't one, but she's got two."

"That's nonsense," said Adam. "The second marriage is invalid."

The stranger laughed. "You're a scream. You talk just like the authorities. Invalid. Second marriage invalid." He described a circle with his hand as if to indicate that the authorities had thrown the second marriage out of the window with one fell swoop. "But my wife says: the first marriage is invalid. I'm invalid. Came home too late, she says. She ought to know. Dead is dead, she says." He shrugged his shoulders. "Strictly speaking, she's quite right. Dead is dead. If a fellow is dead he oughtn't to come back home." He gripped Adam's shoulder still more firmly. "What about you? You're not dead, are you? You think you're not dead." His index finger moved in a semicircle: "All these people think they're not dead. Guzzling themselves, and not knowing they're dead." At last he released Adam and turned to a man on his other side. "He thinks he's not dead," he said to him, scornfully pointing at Adam.

At that moment Adam spotted Hans engaged in earnest conversation with one of the barmen. Hans waved to him and Adam pushed his way through to the far end of the bar.

"He's seen her," said Hans breathlessly. "He knows her. She was here an hour ago. She can't have got far. Let's go!"

The rain had not started again, but a damp night mist lay on the streets. Systematically the two men began to search the neighborhood of the night club. Now that he knew that he might find her Hans was filled with new energy. Adam was watching his young friend and he felt almost merry at the sight of a love that could regenerate itself so quickly and that avoided with such sure instinct the traps which the age set for it. But why, he now wondered with redoubled intensity, why had Inge not hurried home to him and Frau Wild and Hans straight from the PX? What deep roots must distrust have driven in the few years of her life if, after all those months at his home, she still did not realize how they all felt about her. And yet it was not surprising, seeing that Hans himself had twice that evening asked if she would ever shake off the past—meaning, presumably, if he would ever be able to do so. Was there anybody living in this country without a ghost from the past? If it was not the ghost of the twelve years then it was one of the years that followed.

Hans had caught hold of Adam's arm and was pulling him along as though guided by an instinct not shared by his companion. An hour had passed in unavailing search; now Adam noticed that Hans, silent and filled with some inner tenseness, was steering him in the direction of the Isar.

"There is a little restaurant," Hans said at last, "where we sat at our first meeting. We went back there a few days ago . . ."

They walked quickly, the younger man a step or two ahead and Adam barely able to keep up with him.

As they crossed the vegetable market, passing between the shuttered stalls which rose from the mist like giant tombstones in a nocturnal graveyard, they suddenly stopped. Only a few steps in front of them walked the slim figure of a girl—swaying, stopping, and moving off again.

"I'd better leave you now," said Adam softly although nobody could hear him there. "Bring her home safely. We'll be waiting up."

Hans wanted to say "Thank you" before following the swaying figure. But Adam Wild had vanished among the market stalls.

The Colonel Has Three Interviews

A week before Christmas 1947 the street of villas in Harlaching had the appearance of the residential section of any American provincial city. "Every Englishman is an island," wrote the German Romantic Novalis. Evidently, he had had no experience of Americans. In the Harlaching district, now almost entirely requisitioned, as indeed wherever they settled down for any length of time, the sons of the great island had created their own little island.

What the Germans regarded as haughtiness, as contempt for the occupied country and its people and customs, was not haughtiness but simply a strange lack of capacity for assimilation. It was an erroneous conclusion—drawn not only by Germans but by all Europeans—that the Americans must be particularly gifted for assimilation since they themselves, or their parents or ancestors, had come to America from Europe. The very opposite was the case. The Americans regarded their own country not as a transatlantic extension of Europe, but as a more advanced stage of development of their old country, of a declining continent to which one could no more assimilate one's self than one would to a cemetery where one's ancestors were buried. Different people, of course, had different relationships to cemeteries: there were some who avoided the graveyard, others who discovered a certain macabre charm there, and still others who, every so often, paid their dutiful reverences. But very few of them felt any inclination to settle down and live in a cemetery. To all this was added a lack of assurance and of stability on the part of the new citizens, a circumstance recognized even by America's laws which prohibited new citizens from visiting their former homes for periods exceeding three years. The temptations which Germany held for a Frenchman, or Norway for an Italian, or England for a German, were slight; but the American legislators, and the Americans generally, were afraid, and perhaps not without justification, that the dying continent might attract, accept and eventually absorb its former children. The Americans did not want to assimilate themselves because they despised Europe and because they loved it—both to a marked degree even if they did not admit it to themselves.

With outward—one might almost say superficial—means, applied unwittingly and without the least evil intent, the Americans were defending themselves against the temptations of the "old country." The Commander in Chief of the American Occupation Forces, now established in the lacerated capital of Berlin, boasted, unaware of his admission, that he knew not a single word of German. No sooner did the Americans move into a new residential quarter than their womenfolk began to organize themselves into women's clubs. American children were demonstratively dressed in the most unsuitable "Wild West" clothes—and the defeated, of course, did not understand that such a demonstration was really an admission of weakness. Commissaries and the PX and the restaurants for "dependents" supplied the familiar pleasures of the table in treacherous plenitude, as though to offer a culinary resistance to the allurements of a European cuisine. American radio stations importunately filled the ear with the nourishments of American sentiment. To the defeated it must have seemed that the victors wanted to be "better" at any price, whereas in fact they were only desperately clinging to their "otherwiseness" laboriously acquired over only a few decades.

This difference emerged in its most striking form just before Christmas—for just as nothing differentiates people more than their mirth and the cause of their laughter, so nothing divides them more than the atmosphere of their feasts. Stubbornly, the Americans insisted even in the strange country on celebrating their Christmas on the morning of December 25; just as stubbornly they were putting up their Christmas trees in their front gardens, tying evergreen wreaths to their front doors, and lighting up their Christmas trees weeks before Christmas Eve. It was not only because of fire regulations that

MP's continually patrolled the American residential districts, making sure the Christmas trees bore no dangerous German candles but only modern electric fairy-lights.

A week before Christmas Eve the colored lights were also burning on the tree which Betty Hunter had fixed to the garden fence at their home in Harthauserstrasse and which, assisted by the children, she had lovingly decorated. The Colonel cast an approving glance at this tree as his car drove through the garden gate into his requisitioned property at about six P.M. on the 17th of December.

Betty, who for the past few days had been busy with her Christmas shopping, had not yet come home with the children, but, to the Colonel's surprise, Marianne was in. He had just made himself comfortable in the sitting-room, which was already decorated in preparation for the festival, and was about to have his regular evening glass of whisky when Marianne entered.

"I should like to speak to you, Colonel," she said, "if you can spare a few minutes."

"Of course," said Hunter. "Have a chair."

He offered her a glass of whisky, but she declined. He sat down by the fire, facing her, and waited.

Again he experienced that sense of uneasiness that invariably came to him in her proximity. Oddly enough, whenever they were left alone for a few minutes he was reminded of his Aunt Geraldine. During his childhood in Columbus, Ohio, his Aunt Geraldine, his mother's sister, had played a peculiar part. She had been as strange, exotic and exciting as her name. She had not visited often—only once or twice a year, en route from New York to California or back, with countless cases and hatboxes and clothes and presents. Hunter no longer remembered what she had looked like, or whether Marianne was anything like her in appearance: he only had a vague recollection of a dark and fiery elemental event that swept past old General Hunter's home like summer lightning. But he remembered quite clearly that her presence had always filled him with a sense of guilt, or perhaps a sense of inferiority: his perfectly decent suits had suddenly seemed to him awkward or childish, his speech uncouth and immature, and he himself several years younger than he actually was. He had avoided her, or else tried to show off, and on one occasion when, from boredom and after much persuasion by his father, she watched a baseball game, Graham, the star player of his club, had failed so utterly that it took him many months to recover from his defeat. More than once had Marianne's presence reminded him of that aunt—who, by the way, was not subsequently mentioned in the family as she had run away from her third husband and been drowned under mysterious circumstances from a row boat on Lake Michigan—with the only difference that now, on the threshold of old age, Colonel Hunter felt not younger but older than his years whenever her searching glance, like Aunt Geraldine's, rested upon him.

"Colonel," said the girl, "I want to make this brief and painless. I should like to give in my notice, and if possible I would like to leave even before Christmas."

"But Marianne," said Hunter, taken aback, "why this sudden decision? Has anything happened?"

"No," said Marianne. "Nothing has happened."

"Why then . . . ?"

"If you must have a reason, Colonel—my father has been denazified. We haven't anything left, of course, but at least we can start again. He is an old man and wants me with him."

"I understand," said Hunter. He did not understand. He knew that she was not telling the truth, or at least not the whole truth. "I am glad for your sake," he continued, "but this is going to be a bad blow to Mrs. Hunter. In fact, to all of us. . . ."

"It won't be a bad blow to Mrs. Hunter," said Marianne. Her dark eyes grew hard. "It will be a triumph for Mrs. Hunter."

"What do you mean . . . ?"

"You know very well what I mean, Colonel," she said. "And today I don't mind admitting my defeat."

"I am sorry, Marianne," he said, because he did not know what else to say.

"There's no need for you to be sorry, Graham," she said. Suddenly she was calling him Graham, as she had done during those hours or minutes when everything might have turned out differently from the way it had. "I played for high stakes, and I lost. Now I don't want you to think that I had hoped to get anything out of you. . . . I could have managed without American food tins. Nor did I want to become the wife of an American. . . . In a few years' time our passport will be as good as yours. I don't know if I was in love with you, Graham. But I wanted to take you away from that conqueror's woman. Please, don't interrupt me—I am leaving now, and on my departure I am entitled to having my say." She gave a short laugh. "I could have 'seduced' you, that time, in the summer, before your family arrived. You see, I am what you would call 'playing fair.' Otherwise I would not admit that the wish to take you away from her arose only after her arrival. It was only then that I realized what an American woman is capable of doing to a man. You are a man and you are young, even though you have forgotten both. That woman has made you an old man in your best years, Graham, so that you should become the way she is—old and ugly and undesirable. It means nothing to me that you are now jumping up and displaying chivalrous indignation. I'd sooner leave today than tomorrow, but I'm going to finish what I was going to say. I have wasted nearly two years of my life. I have tried to open your eyes. I have tried to demonstrate to you how ridiculous that woman is. You did not see it, or you did not want to see it." She stood up. "Just look around a bit yourself in this house. That collection of ghastly paintings on the wall. Your ugly, short, bespectacled wife in a dirndl. Your children, pampered and spoiled, turned into your wife's accomplices against you. What has she ever given you except gnawing ambition? These women marry their men when they are still boys, so that they are old men when they should be in their prime. You think, Graham, that I am bitter because you did not take me. It is true, I offered myself to you. But I have seen you tremble whenever I wore a tight-fitting sweater or a bathing suit. You did not resist because you didn't want me, nor out of puritanism, but because you'd been taught not to want anything any longer." She paused, but not long enough to allow him to retort anything. Much more quietly she continued: "I have been defeated, Graham, and I don't propose to lose any more time over you. I was not defeated by her. I was defeated by that dreadful American apple pie with cheese, which reminded you of your mother's cooking; by your wife's whisky-drinking at six in the evening; by her recognition of those barbarous cowboy songs on the radio; by the fact that those hideous beer jugs quite appeal to you too, and by that silly electrical tree outside the house. Stay as happy as you are, Graham, and when at last you get your general's star go out and buy her a pink-colored motor car and a pale-blue Easter bonnet!"

Perhaps she wanted to say more, but Hunter at last managed to interrupt her. His voice trembling with suppressed excitement, he said:

"I am sorry, Marianne, that your bitterness has led you to remarks which befit neither your character nor your upbringing. I should be grateful to you if you could leave this house before Mrs. Hunter returns. I shall find an excuse for you. Your salary will be ready for you at my office."

She went to the door. There she turned, as though to say something, but the long-repressed tears were now running down her cheeks. She was at pains to hide them when the old housekeeper entered to announce Lieutenant Colonel Green.

"Am I too early?" asked Frank, catching sight of the Colonel who was covered in confusion.

"No, no," said Hunter. "It's only . . . it doesn't matter. Scotch or bourbon, Frank?"

"Scotch, if I may."

The Colonel handed him a glass and refilled his own.

"I shall have to leave you presently for a minute," he said. "Our nurse has given notice. I must break the news to Betty."

"The Countess Artemstein?" said Frank. "I believe her father was recently denazified."

"Do you know her?"

"I examined her personal file at the time," said Frank. "I realized then that he was innocent."

"Yes," the Colonel said absently, "I suppose so. That's probably why she's leaving."

A moment later noise and children's laughter came from the hall. The Colonel excused himself.

Dinner à trois—with the Colonel taciturn, Frank conscious of a lurking uneasiness, and Betty vivacious and in good spirits—was over at last. But even when Mrs. Hunter had withdrawn and the two men were left alone in the sitting room the Colonel did not come straight to the purpose of his invitation.

They spoke at length about George Green. Not only had Frank's "leave"—so long ago now that it was almost forgotten—been unsuccessful, but many months had elapsed and George Green, his driver Jones and the ex-Corporal Josef Maurer were still missing. The American and German warrants were renewed every three months, but the investigation had long petered out for lack of clues. Now and again some occurrence would seem to confirm Frank's theory that George had become a victim of the black market, and then something else would prove the correctness of the Colonel's political anxieties. In the course of a large-scale black-market raid in Rome the police had arrested a man who answered to Maurer's description in every detail, but before the information from Italy could be sifted the black marketeer had escaped from prison. On the other hand—as Hunter had told Frank in strict confidence—four American agents had been arrested in the Eastern Zone: they were all men who had been in close contact with George.

"Forgive me for saying so," remarked the Colonel, "but I am afraid we haven't heard the last of your brother. But that's not what I have asked you here for."

"Not another O'Hara assignment, I hope," Frank tried to joke. Throughout the evening he had felt that the Colonel needed cheering up.

"No," said Hunter, lighting a cigar, "this time I have undertaken the delicate assignment myself. And it's an assignment that concerns you, Frank. Let me come straight to the point, no matter how awkward it is." He gazed at the smoke rings rising from his cigar and avoided looking at Frank's face. "For some time now anonymous denunications against you have been arriving at my office. Naturally, if only because of their anonymity, I have been throwing them straight into my wastebasket. But now, presumably because I ignored them, they have reached the General."

"Anonymous denunciations?" Frank asked in surprise.

"The point that they are anonymous doesn't enter into it any longer," said the Colonel. "The question now is how much of them is true and how much isn't. They concern your private life, Frank—and that's why this business is so embarrassing to me. It has always been my rule not to concern myself with the private affairs of my officers, so far as they did not affect the service. Unfortunately, it's not so easy to draw the line in this particular case."

"You are referring to Elisabeth von Zutraven, Colonel," said Frank.

The Colonel looked at him. There was an approving smile on his features.

"That's just like you, Frank," he said cordially. "You're even saving me the embarrassment of an accusation."

"You are overrating my cooperation, Colonel," said Frank. "I am confessing only because I do not feel guilty."

"In other words: occupation gossip."

"By no means. I don't know what the anonymous letters are saying, but I shouldn't be surprised if for once they spoke the truth. I am in love with Elisabeth von Zutraven and shall marry her as soon as the law permits it."

The Colonel leapt up. "You must be out of your mind, Frank!"

"And why?" asked Frank calmly. "Since when have we believed in family culpability? Besides, she is divorced from Zutraven. She was herself tried by a Denazification Tribunal and found not guilty."

"Please, Frank!" said the Colonel. "Don't address me as if I were a court-martial. I didn't examine your case with an eye to the precise text of the law and I've not the slightest intention of doing so. But surely you can't shut your eyes to the facts. This woman was one of the most prominent ladies in the Third Reich. You are not only an American officer, and an Intelligence officer in charge of investigating National Socialist activities, but you are also . . ."

"A Jew," completed Frank.

"Well yes," said Hunter, "since you mention it yourself. The thing's simply absurd."

"Is there a law prohibiting Jews from forgiving?"

"A law, a law . . . I'm telling you I'm not concerned with any law. But surely you can't simply forget those six million Jews . . ."

"Rest assured, Colonel," said Frank, "I am not forgetting them. But since you insist on talking about my Judaism . . . there are a few things that I have lately come to understand. For nearly two thousand years the Jews have been the victims of the biggest and crudest lie of collective guilt that history has ever known. That alone ought to teach them not to lend support to a new lie of collective guilt. So much my reason told me. But my feelings told me even more. I know that you, Colonel, would be the last person to do so deliberately—but the obligation of hatred that is being imposed on the Jews is basically an anti-Semitic invention. Christians are to forgive, but Jews must hate. . . . That is an unChristianlike Christian concept. The Old Testament God of vengeance is an anti-Semitic invention. If I have a specifically Jewish relationship to the defeated Germans, then it is only in the sense that I understand them better than most Americans. Suffering nations—it is a curious fact—are always similar to the Jews. Suffering seems to me more typical than the characteristics attaching to different nations. I cannot at every step examine the causes that have led to Germany's suffering—but as a Jew, even as an American Jew, I feel a kinship with suffering." He drained the glass of brandy which the Colonel had put in front of him. "Besides, this has little to do with Elisabeth von Zutraven. I am sorry I've drifted from the subject."

"Yes," said Hunter, "we have drifted from the subject. Your relationship with Frau von Zutraven is incompatible with your position. I can't understand how you can fail to see that."

"I don't see it at all," said Frank. "Surely there must be some logic in our policy. We can't release a man like Obersturmbannführer Gerd Mante—I gather that was done yesterday—and then forbid an American officer to marry a German woman."

"We are not talking about higher policy, Frank. Your own duties have been exclusively concerned with Nazi activities. They cannot possibly remain unaffected by your relationship. That precisely is what the anonymous letters are saying, and unfortunately there is some logic in it."

"And who is going to prove, or even to claim, that Elisabeth von Zutraven is influencing me in a National Socialist direction?"

"Surely you're not so blind as to deny the lady's past," said Hunter. "I don't want to make it difficult for you, Frank." He walked slowly over to the window and gazed out into the darkened garden. "You are young and unmarried," he continued, "and you can do as you please. I understand the fatal attraction of German women. One does not have to have been born over here to understand it. There is scarcely an occupation soldier who has not fallen for their charm. We come from a country that is ruled by women, and we are deeply impressed that these German women put our slippers in front of the fire. Our women have skipped the stage of emancipation: they have moved straight from slavery to dictatorship. Don't think, Frank," he said warmly, "that I am too old or ossified; I too have felt the temptation. There is no greater temptation than finding normalcy in an abnormal civilization such as ours." He turned back to Frank. "But it is your particular misfortune, Frank, that the woman whom you believe to have found bears one of the most prominent names of the defeated regime. I am not doubting her personal integrity: I know too little about her. But there is such a thing as convention, even in an occupation army." As Frank rose he added: "I don't want to rush you, Frank. But you must make your decision within the next few weeks. The General is extremely intolerant in such matters. I should be genuinely sorry to lose you."

"I can give you my answer now, Colonel."

"I am asking you not to do so, Frank," said Hunter.

"As you wish, Colonel."

He wanted to go, but Hunter kept him back. It was not only that the Colonel was anxious not to let their interview end on a jarring note; he did not want to be left alone. It had been impossible to avoid it: Marianne had still been in the house when Betty returned from her shopping. The girl had been quick to find an excuse: her father was seriously ill and urgently needed her help. But the hasty and unemotional parting, Betty's excellent spirits, and one or two remarks dropped at table convinced Hunter that Marianne had not been wrong in speaking of his wife's imminent triumph. The diabolical coincidence that, on this very evening, he had been compelled to have a discussion with Frank which continuously reminded of himself; the pain which the young woman's absence would undoubtedly give him and which was only temporarily suppressed by his horror over her sudden self-revelation; the unavoidable talk with Betty about Marianne's unexpected decision—all this caused Hunter to fear the next few days. For well over an hour he involved Frank in a general but particularly amicable conversation, and it was past midnight when his subordinate eventually took his leave and he mounted the stairs to his matrimonial bedroom.

He undressed in the dark; with relief he found that Betty was asleep. Carefully, so as not to wake her, he slipped into his bed. There he lay on his back, the way he had done ever since his youth, his hands folded behind his head, his eyes shut. He deliberately tried not to think because he was afraid his noisy thoughts might wake the sleeper.

Marianne's farewell amidst the Christmas decorations in the living-room once more passed before his eyes, and the more he, reluctantly, thought her words over the more he found himself entangled in a maze of falsehood and truth. He fastened on to her surprising vulgarity, hoping that the lively recollection of her ill-mannered behavior would bring final disenchantment. But her words, distorted by prejudice and disappointment, had held a good measure of truth, and the very lack of control that had led her into her vulgarity reflected a passion such as Hunter had missed in his married life and which he had now finally omitted to experience.

Sleep would not come to him, and he was about to grope cautiously for a cigarette when he heard his wife's voice beside him:

"Are you sorry, Graham?" Betty asked softly.

"What about?"

"That she has gone."

"Sure," he said, and his voice sounded strangled.

"Did you love her, Graham?"

"I don't know."

"But I did. She was beautiful and young and she was a German."

"Is that an advantage?" he asked, conscious of his hypocrisy.

"Yes," said Betty. "For a woman it is an advantage to be one of the defeated."

"It doesn't matter," said Hunter. "She is gone."

"There'll be another," said Betty.

"Nothing happened between us."

"I know. But you regret it."

"Do you want to torture me?"

"No, Graham. I admire you. It must have been difficult. I have learned a lot from her. Only I can't grow young and beautiful again."

"You don't have to change, Betty."

"I wasn't always fair, Graham. She was at home; I had to act as if I was at home, too."

He found her hand in the dark.

"Don't let's talk about it any more," he said.

"Can't we go home, Graham?" she asked.

"Escape?"

"If you like."

"They've postponed my promotion again," he said. "If I stay on for a little . . ."

"It'll only be the same again."

"Maybe not this time."

Her hand was as cold as ice. She said:

"Things are so confusing here, Graham. It was easier in the Philippines. At least the people looked different from us. Here they look like us and yet they are stranger to us than the Filipinos."

"Because they are defeated, Betty."

"Maybe," she said. "I hate living among these defeated people. I am afraid of them."

A near-by church clock struck one.

"We'd better sleep now," he said. "It's late."

"Why they must ring their church bells at night . . . ?" said Betty.

He held her hand and wondered if he ought to make love to her. His mind was as cold as her hand. Perhaps later, he thought. Perhaps somewhere far from here, from this terrible defeated country. Perhaps back home, where the church bells are silent at night. He squeezed her hand affectionately.

"Good night, Betty."

"Good night, Graham."

Bankhaus Eber Runs Up Its Flag

The solemn opening of the Banking House O. Eber took place at carnival time, 1948.

The carnival of 1948 differed considerably from the carnivals of 1946 and 1947, just as that of 1949 was to differ again from that of 1948.

The first two Munich carnivals after the war had been marked by surreptitious but intense gaiety. The war was over, and the misery had only just begun. In the first year there were only private parties, since it was inappropriate for the defeated Germans to make merry in public. In fact, the Allies saw to it that the sense of relief over the end of air raids, army communiqués and, in many instances, Gestapo terror should not manifest itself in explosive hilarity. The curfew was still in force, and anybody giving a party in the evening had to make arrangements to put up his guests until the early hours of the morning when they could again emerge into the streets. Needless to say, the coal ration was insufficient to heat more than one room, and even though one might expect the dancers to supply each other with some of their bodily warmth, a host would nevertheless expect his guests to bring along with them a few lumps of coal or a few logs of wood. The same applied to the indispensable drinks, which were likewise contributed by the guests, so that each new bottle produced by a new arrival from under his overcoat was hailed with howls of delight. The Munich carnival had always been a festival of fantasy, but now everybody's inventive genius was put to a special test; for at a time when every piece of rag became a garment and people seemed to be masquerading in their everyday clothes it was difficult to think up a fancy dress. In the second year of the occupation a few sporadic public celebrations made their appearance, but the mood of the guests had still to make up for the lack of those stimulants which had previously contributed so largely to the carnival atmosphere.

And yet the carnival days of 1946 and 1947 remained engraved in the memories of all those who took part in them. With amazement and disapproval the victors observed the manifestations of *joie de vivre* which the vanquished displayed by day and by night. Although it had been publicly announced that the Germans had been defeated, not liberated, there was nevertheless an improper air of liberation about everywhere. Never before had there been so much dancing, joking, flirting and even drinking as at the private and later at the public parties given during the carnival. A negative, and therefore more pronounced, sense of pleasure at not having suddenly to scramble from the dance floor into the air-raid shelter pervaded the celebrations. The fact that the gaiety was against regulations, and that by making merry the Germans were playing a trick on the Allies, heightened the general jollity. The need to overcome countless difficulties imparted a portion of triumphant satisfaction to every painted ornament, every hand-sewn fancy dress and every drop of liquor. The celebrations were not, as one might have expected, in the least macabre: although they took place in half-ruined homes, with reminders of human and material loss everywhere, yet the sense of having escaped jeopardy, danger and disaster proved stronger than all else. Perhaps the children, many of whom had never seen a carnival before, sensed this most clearly in a way but vaguely understood. For many days, well beyond the end of the carnival, they swarmed about the ruined buildings in their fancy dresses. Instead of a single fancy dress parade, the young pirates now had entire pirate castles at their disposal, and the vast bomb-flattened expanses served the little cowboys in their makeshift costumes as a prairie. The conquerors were perplexed and somewhat envious to see with what trifling means the stubborn spirit of merrymaking could be conjured up. They were shaking their heads over a people whose tough vitality found an expression even in cardboard Texan hats, threadbare Hungarian peasant costumes, ancient toppers and false noses.

The carnival of 1948 was entirely different. There was still a shortage of wine, fuel, food and materials, and fantasy was still the only luxury which the defeated could afford. But there was no curfew any longer; only few windows were left without panes; everybody knew a peasant or a black-market supplier; and *joie de vivre*, like life itself, had quieted down and got itself organized. People had got used to the surprising fact that they were not dead. Jollity was no longer entirely unconditional, and the equality which misery had produced was gradually yielding to carefully graded class distinctions. A few women, the wives of the newly rich, of the men swept to the crest by smuggling, black-marketing or foreign contacts, already owned evening gowns. Some people were still living in cellars while others were already laying up wine in them. The old Society, rising to the challenge of the new, tried to display a somewhat shabby elegance. One thing was abundantly clear: the carnivals of the past two years had been a tribute to a past that had been overcome; the carnival of 1948 was a salute to the future. Very few people doubted that a currency reform was imminent, probably even that year; behind the carnival revelries the switch-over to normalcy had begun. True, the new exponents of position and respect—licensed bankers, newspaper publishers, manufacturers or businessmen—still wore their "confirmation suits," as they mockingly called their shabby clothes; they arrived at parties and balls by streetcar or on bicycles; and their homes were modest and crowded. But many of them knew that the miracle would happen, that it would come as surely as Santa Claus's presents under the Christmas tree. Yesterday's poverty and tomorrow's wealth waltzed together through the Munich carnival.

The formal opening of the Eber bank took place on February 4, at the height of the carnival season. Thus it happened that many of the one-hundred-odd guests, although invited for five-thirty in the afternoon, arrived in evening clothes or deposited in the cloakroom huge parcels from which peeped out masks or items of fancy dress.

The new bank building was situated in Theatinerstrasse, once one of the busiest streets of the Bavarian capital, and provided a most striking contrast to its surroundings. A large part of Theatinerstrasse had been destroyed: only at its junction with Odeonsplatz did the noble yellow baroque structure of the Theatiner church tower into the gray February sky. Between the Theatiner church and the new bank, that is, on the right-hand side coming from Odeonsplatz, there were only several neatly arranged piles of debris and some of those low temporary buildings which were the hallmark of the German towns in 1948. By the side of these huts—for they were huts, even if they had nothing of the dirty shacks of the Balkans about them, but were German huts, neatly assembled of stone, with an air of temporary permanence—the two-story bank building, obviously designed with an eye to subsequent extension, looked like a palace of unbelievable sumptuousness. The Eber bank even had a marble entrance, simple and in good taste, as if to say "Have every hope in the currency reform, ye who enter." The letters over the entrance, not too small and only just managing to look discreet, were likewise of marble. They spelled "Bankhaus O. Eber"—for reasons of business economy and wise foresight the name Oskar had not been written in full, since only the totally ignorant could doubt that the "O" would shortly be replaced by an "E."

Moreover, anybody entering the premises of the bank on that dark February afternoon—the entire premises, including counting-rooms, boardrooms and offices, were open to the visiting public—would have found that the proprietors of the bank scarcely troubled to make a secret of the impending change of initials. True, the gray-haired O. Eber was present, doing the honors in a black coat and pin-striped trousers, but this gentleman with the pince-nez, who looked like a popular edition of his brother, moved among the visitors, of whom he barely knew a third, like a butler specially hired for the occasion. Whenever he was involved by one of the uniformed guests in a conversation, especially if it turned on business matters, he was quick to pass the visitor unobtrusively on to his brother who would then take charge of him, smiling, the man of the world, full of self-assurance. As to the number and position of those present, Dr. Eberhard Eber had nothing to complain of: two members of the Provincial Government, numerous representatives of the aristocracy, presidents and managing directors of old and new enterprises, three former Wehrmacht generals and half a dozen senior officers of the occupation army, together with their ladies, were doing full justice to the champagne which had been produced from unknown cellars.

Hans Eber had yielded to his father's insistence and had turned up for the occasion, but for other reasons than to celebrate the opening of the bank. Alone and unrecognized, a glass of champagne in his hand, he roamed through the building. Even before the war he had known few of his father's friends; the old friends were as much strangers to him now as the new ones. He had drunk a considerable quantity of the unaccustomed beverage and he was seeing the people around him with the knife-edge clarity that comes so often with the consumption of alcohol just before it blunts and blurs the senses.

Above all he saw Karin. Nearly a year had passed since she had returned to the parental home after giving birth to her child in the country. That Dr. Eber forgave her, or that he was able to forgive her, was no doubt due to Captain George Green's disappearance: the obstacle, as it were, had removed itself. And when Karin declared herself ready to hand her child over to strangers for good Dr. Eber magnanimously received her back. She had never seen her child, a healthy boy, since, and she seemed to bear the loss without pain. Indeed, on one occasion when Hans, acting on an impulse not quite clear to him, steered the conversation to her illegitimate baby he discovered that Karin's feelings were anything but maternal: she spoke of her son with horror and revulsion, the more so as she claimed him to be the spit and image of his father. Although they still lived under the same roof Hans and Karin had hardly spoken to each other since then. By mere chance he had heard that Friedrich Stettinus, the son of a Cologne bank president, had asked for Karin's hand in marriage, and this he now found confirmed by the fact that both the young man and his father had specially arrived for the occasion from Cologne. As he watched Karin sitting between Stettinus father and son, in a new white dress, her cheeks flushed, a picture of virtuous maidenliness—gay without being noisy, coquettish without being provocative—the phantasmagoria of the past years was brought home to him with crystal clarity. The world of the day before yesterday seemed closer to him than that of yesterday which was now being solemnly buried. He moved through the ostentatious rooms of the new bank as through a waxwork exhibition come to life. He did not know most of the guests, but the bald bull-necked gentleman who was raising his glass with an angular movement of his elbow and drinking to Dr. Eber's success reminded him of all those great financiers who had been in and out of the Ebers' house in his early childhood; the slim gentleman with the naked face and the close-fitting suit who, it was whispered, was none other than General Stappenhorst, the future head of German Intelligence, reminded him of many a uniformed visitor of the past; the polite gentlemen with the horn-rimmed glasses and black coats seemed to come from the same Government

Departments which used to send their messengers to Dr. Eber in the old days. Karin; his father who was trying so hard today to combine charm with dignity; his bowing and scraping uncle; the yellow faces from the waxwork exhibition—that whole carnival procession of his yesterdays pursued Hans from room to room. Like a fugitive who has at last managed to give his pursuers the slip he drew a deep breath when he finally found himself alone in the big boardroom.

He walked over to one of the four arched windows and looked out. The moon had risen early and cast her light on the ruins across the street. Snow lay on the burst brickwork and formed white steps from ruin to ruin. A group of revelers appeared in the moonlight—two men and two women. In their fancy dress they seemed, in this setting and in this light, like visitors from Mars.

Hans turned and sat down at the board table. He was tired and his head began to grow heavy. It was a long table, shining with newness, surrounded by fourteen or eighteen armchairs in cream hide. A monotonous murmur of voices came muted through the padded doors. Dr. Eberhard Eber's guests were leaving. Hans put down his glass, folded his arms and laid his head on the table. He did not know if he had dozed off for a few minutes when the creaking of the stiff new door roused him. His father had entered the room.

"Well, you don't seem to be having a very good time," Dr. Eber said with a smile.

"I didn't know I was supposed to have a good time," said Hans.

Dr. Eber sat down. They sat at the long table facing each other. Dr. Eber pretended not to have heard. He said:

"It was a fine celebration—one might almost say: a noble celebration. Tomorrow, of course, life starts in earnest. To open a bank in our days is a bold undertaking. On the other hand, we are bound for better times, and the platitude of 'first come, first served' will no doubt be proved true again. When you've got your degree in another eighteen months . . ."

Hans interrupted him: "I have no intention of joining the Bankhaus O. Eber. Nor, for that matter, the Bankhaus E. Eber."

Dr. Eber removed his pince-nez from his small stubby nose.

"Why this aggressive tone?" he asked.

"I'm sorry," said Hans. "I do not wish to disturb your festive mood."

»400«

"You are not disturbing it in the least. This is as good an opportunity as any . . ."

"All right," said Hans, still trying to avoid a conversation. "I don't want to be a banker."

"There's not much future in a law practice. On the other hand, a knowledge of the law in the banking business . . ."

"Are you deliberately trying to misunderstand me, Papa?"

Dr. Eber replaced his pince-nez and regarded him inquiringly.

"I have nothing for or against the banking business. But I've got something against the Bankhaus Eber," said Hans.

"Go on," said Dr. Eber. "I'm listening."

"You probably think that I'm drunk, Papa," said Hans. "But even if I had come here drunk this celebration would have sobered me up. Maybe I only came in order to summon the courage to tell you the truth. I am determined to leave your house, Papa, and to see how I can manage on my own. The celebration, of course, is only a convenient opportunity: it all began on the day I returned from captivity. . . ."

Dr. Eber was regarding him without irritation: he was clearly resolved to keep his temper at all costs.

"What began on that day?" he asked.

"My revulsion," said Hans. "I could not believe that Dr. Eberhard Eber's house should be exempted from requisitioning; that, amidst all the misery which you helped to bring about, we should escape suffering; that the Denazification Tribunal which sends a lot of slogan-parroting dunderheads to the labor camp for ten years should smooth the path of 'the Führer's banker' so that he can once again be first come and first served. I could not believe that I should see those gravediggers swilling champagne, ably assisted by our so-called re-educators. Maybe, Papa, you will once again be proved right—but if it has to be let it be without me."

He had expected a violent outburst from his father who had always been a stickler for discipline, had never allowed anybody to contradict him and had invariably nipped all rebellion in the bud. But Dr. Eber seemed to have chosen a different method. He said:

"In other words, you would rather see me in a labor camp."

"You misunderstand me deliberately," said Hans. "Retribution means nothing to me. Even if it did, the victors would have made me turn away from it. In fact, I don't even know whether there is any point in punishing anybody. . . . All I know is that one must try to prevent things. It starts with the opening of the Bankhaus Eber and it ends in the infantry trench."

"You are talking like a Communist."

"That's what you always say as soon as something doesn't suit your books. If I were a Communist I should be against the banks. I am not against the banks; I am against your bank."

"It would be cheap," observed Dr. Eber, "to remind you that when you were in need . . ."

"I know," interrupted Hans. "I am sorry I have eaten at your table. I needed time . . ."

"To work out your program of 'Without me'? Is that all that you and your friends have to offer? Is that going to be Germany's future program?"

"We aren't in such a hurry about a program. It'll do for the moment. You people are merely in such a hurry to go forward because you are afraid to look back. You've got to forget at all costs; for if you looked back you would only see yourselves and the things you have done. We can look back without wanting to die of shame. You are compelled to build on the wreckage; we would like to remove it first."

Dr. Eber looked about the quiet, elegant and comfortable board-room. There was a fragrance of new leather about. Still controlling himself he said:

"You talk like our enemies. For them, too, we are rebuilding too quickly. They are again afraid of us."

"The rebuilding can't be too quick for me," retorted Hans. He too looked around the room. "But it gives me the creeps to see ghosts do the rebuilding."

"Are you referring to me?"

"To you among others."

"And what gives you the right? The lost war? Would you speak in the same way if we had won it?"

"We couldn't win it. As for the right? The right of the victims, Papa. Your victims."

"One other question. Supposing you were right . . . in one way or another. Are you denying the possibility that I too may have learned something?"

"Yes," said Hans, "so long as you believe greatness to consist of being feared."

From outside came the muted sound of laughter, the clink of glasses, and a woman's voice.

"Your guests are still here," said Hans.

"Just the last ones. Talking to my son is more important to me." He sounded cordial as he continued: "I never had much time for you, Hans. If you've got yourself into the kind of company that betrays itself in your words then this is partly my fault. Your generation was born of chaos. You are not capable of putting things in order; we've got to do it for you. Once both your feet are again planted on firm ground . . ."

"Let it pass, Papa," said Hans. "The chaos that gave rise to us was created by you. From the order that you are setting up a new chaos will spring. You always call chaos order, and the fear of others you regard as greatness. . . . We don't want any share in it."

"I have listened to you patiently," said Dr. Eber, leaning back in his chair. "Now you listen to me! If I have made mistakes I have paid for them a hundredfold. I should have preferred to spend the rest of my days in a labor camp to having to watch the things that have been going on under my own eyes, in my own home. My daughter, your sister Karin, became a whore. The whore of an American and a Jew. If you think I don't know what you've been up to you're greatly mistaken. A certain Alois Schmidt came to see me a little while ago, needless to say with a view to blackmail. I don't think this needs amplification. You've got yourself involved with a prostitute and unless I am greatly deceived you have the crazy intention of marrying her. It's my turn now to say: 'Without me.' Even if I have done my duty by Karin, by receiving her back into my house; even though, fully aware of your own muddleheadedness, I offered to smooth out your road for you a few minutes ago, this does not alter the fact that I have lost my children. All you can see in this house is the leather armchairs and the marble doorway. I am an old man; I should have liked to retire long ago. For me there is nothing left but duty and work. And this work I propose to do, in spite of all personal bitterness and to the best of my knowledge and ability, so that stable conditions shall once more return to our country—the kind of stable conditions that would make it impossible for a Karin Eber to become the mistress of an American gangster or for a Hans Eber to become an an archist. I do not know how any of your friends, who boast of their tolerance, would have reacted to the accusations that you have today hurled at me—but I don't want to let you go without telling you that my house shall always be open to you when you have seen reason. That is all I have to say."

"Thank you, Papa," said Hans. It sounded final. And it did not sound ironical.

He stood up. Dr. Eber remained seated. For a moment neither of them knew how to say goodbye. Then Hans went to the door and said softly: "Good night."

The last guests had left. Only Karin was standing in the entrance hall, talking and laughing with the Cologne banker and young Stettinus. They were obviously waiting for Dr. Eber. Hans slipped on his overcoat and with a short greeting hurried out past them.

Snow was falling in large, ponderous flakes. Two drunks took Hans between them for a moment. One of them was dressed up as a clown, with a big red nose and a harlequin's hat. The other wore a Charlie Chaplin mask, but instead of waddling he reeled.

Hans shook them off and hurried on his way, past the temporary huts in the direction of the church on whose steeple the crescent moon sat like a weather vane. He was fleeing from the brightly lit bank building, from the lonely man in the boardroom, from the laughing girl in the marble vestibule. He was fleeing from the sentiments which had imperiled him for a moment, from the chaos that looked like order, from false greatness built on the ruins, from the ghosts which had seized control of the living. He did not know where he was going. But this was Germany in 1948, and it was something to know where one was not going.

Black Bird Among the Ruins

Lieutenant Colonel Frank Green's jeep was heading for Berlin at eighty miles an hour.

For reasons unknown to them, officers of the U. S. Army were forbidden to drive their vehicles themselves. In this case of a high-ranking Intelligence officer an exception had been made. His mission demanded the utmost discretion.

On June 20, 1948 Lieutenant Colonel Green had received a letter datelined from Berlin but posted in Frankfurt. It read:

"Dear Frank,

"No doubt you will be surprised to hear from me after such a long time. For reasons which I cannot explain in writing I should like to have a talk with you—in both our interests. A friend, who will reveal himself accordingly, is prepared to take you to me on June 17. On that day be at the Café Bremer in Berlin at six P.M. sharp. I can tell you this much: it concerns the possibility and the conditions of my return. For this reason it would be inadvisable for you to take any special 'precautions'—besides there is no need for them whatever. I ask you to trust me at least this once.

"Yours, George."

Frank at once reported to Colonel Hunter and showed him the letter.

"Why, this is tremendously interesting," Hunter said excitedly. "I was just going to have you sent for, Frank. Last night a report came in from Captain Symington, to the effect that he has had to call off the search for Agent G-101. That's a German agent whose name you may recall from the file which I lent you at the time, in connection with your search for your brother. Well, this man had been working with Captain Green. A few weeks ago he failed to return from the Soviet Sector. All inquiries have drawn a blank. Do you believe there is a connection between the disappearance of that agent and this letter?"

"I don't think it impossible."

"Do you believe your brother would act as a bait for you?"

"Possibly."

"There's no doubt of the genuineness of the letter?"

"None whatever. I know George's handwriting intimately. Of course, I can't tell under what conditions the letter was written."

"What do you want to do?"

"I'll go, of course."

"Right," said the Colonel. "Call back for your instructions in an hour. I'll make the necessary arrangements through Symington. Good luck!"

And now the jeep had passed Kassel and the ribbon of the motor road was disappearing under the hood of the stocky, massive military vehicle like an endless string of spaghetti swallowed up by a giant.

It was a clear, sunny June day. In anticipation of a hot noontime the fields were having a morning bath in dew. The Hessian pine forests were like green sunshades put up against the hot midday sun.

In this serene matutinal landscape Frank found it difficult to think of his Berlin assignment. He was thinking of Elisabeth with whom he had spent every free hour of his last few days in Munich and from whom he had taken a casual leave the previous afternoon, without even hinting at the purpose of his trip.

Similarly, he had not mentioned to her his conversation with Hunter, some time back, when his superior had faced him with his strict ultimatum. His time for "thinking it over" had expired, but Frank had not handed in his resignation although he could have done so under the points system in force since the end of the war. There were good reasons for that—though perhaps they did not seem so good to Frank. A few weeks after their conversation the Colonel had once more called him to his office. In the course of their business Hunter, who was a bad actor, observed with an unconvincing air of casualness that Frank might now forget his recent remarks about Elisabeth von Zutraven. But Frank had no intention of making things so easy for the Colonel. What, he asked, had changed since that ultimatum and why should a relationship which had quite recently been regarded as sufficient grounds for the dismissal of a distinguished officer suddenly appear proper to the military authorities? "Proper" was not quite the word, Hunter replied; perhaps "tolerable" would be nearer. There had been new instructions from Washington—as usual, they had not been very precise, but clear enough to indicate a "change of the wind." It was intended to permit marriages between Americans and Germans, under certain conditions; "social relations" between occupation troops and German women were no longer to be expressly discouraged; and the term "Nazi" was to be interpreted in a more generous spirit. The directives, said Hunter, were still vague and rather general, but one could not fail to see what they were aiming at, and the General would certainly not now regard the case of Elisabeth von Zutraven as a "cause célèbre." Frank, not without accusing himself of weakness, took note of the Colonel's changed attitude, but the disquieting feeling that the victors' morality was adapting itself with servile haste to the requirements of the hour remained with him ever since. If the Colonel had ordered an investigation into Elisabeth von Zutraven and had come to realize her innocence, Frank would have been content. But Hunter's opinion about Elisabeth had not changed—only the wind had. Frank disliked the idea of benefiting from the new trend, even though indirectly and through no effort on his part; he felt like a mariner who, on the point of shipwreck, drifts into a safe haven but finds that this is not the port he has been making for.

Beyond Kassel, however, the happenings on the road again fully absorbed Frank's attention, so much so that he could think neither of Elisabeth nor of his immediate plans for Berlin. Even back in Kassel, where he had spent the night, he had felt the unrest that reigned at the Zonal frontier. For some days rumors had been circulating that the Russians were preparing a coup in Berlin, and possibly even a blockade of the quadripartite city.

What had begun to appear in outline in 1947 was now taking clearer shape in this spring of 1948. Andrei Vyshinsky, the Soviet Deputy Foreign Minister, had referred to "the warlike intentions of the reactionaries, capitalists and imperialists"; the American Secretary of State George C. Marshall had called Europe "the U.S.A.'s first line of defense." At the 82nd meeting of the Allied Control Council in Berlin Soviet Marshal Sokolovsky had observed to his colleagues that this was perhaps the last meeting of the Allied Commanders in Chief. On January 5, the Bavarian Minister President Dr. Hans Ehard was still being sharply criticized by the Americans for having described the Yalta Agreement, with its mutual obligation for the extradition of war criminals, as "a deal in human beings"; but now all extraditions to the Soviets had been officially suspended. An American note to the Soviet Union referred to the violation of the Potsdam Agreement and "the suppression of human rights in Eastern Europe." The import of Soviet-licensed newspapers into Western Germany was prohibited. The Soviet garrison in Potsdam noisily proclaimed a "state of alert" and the three Western Powers set up a Co-Ordinating Authority in Berlin for the purpose of "common resistance." The censorship regulations which had forbidden the West German papers to criticize the Eastern Ally were tacitly withdrawn: the *Süddeutsche Zeitung* on March 23 carried the banner headline: "Cold War and Hot Heads in Berlin" and a few days later a leading article spoke openly about "the war of nerves and the danger of war." Almost overnight, the postwar period seemed to have changed into a prewar period.

Again and again Frank's jeep was caught up in military convoys making for the Zonal frontier. True enough, endless columns of tanks, heavy trucks and motorized patrols had been encountered on Germany's deserted autobahns before—but to the officer in the jeep the difference between those harmlessly promenading demonstration outings and the convoys which were now menacingly and ponderously rolling towards the Zonal boundary was instantly obvious. There were a few significant details: the American soldiers no longer wore the varnished featherweight inner hulls of their steel helmets, but the full heavy metal headgear: the muzzles of the guns no longer bore their peaceful little covers looking like dust-sheets in locked-up and moth-ball-reeking parlors. The GI's no longer wore their light-green "fatigues," those overalls like pajamas, but were in full battle dress. But what impressed Frank even more than these outward military signs was the seriousness which marked this silent move up to the frontier. An expert could easily tell the difference between the mock-serious maneuver expression on a soldier's face and the tension, alertness and, possibly, anxiety which was written on the features of the young men in the scout cars, the jeeps and the troop carriers.

If officers and men were infecting one another with their vague but all the more alarming information, then this was equally true of the German population along the Zonal boundary. The peasants, busy in their fields, would stop working and stand by the roadside, their astonished and anxious eyes following the steady eastward trek of military vehicles. In the villages, small groups of people stood leaning on their bicycles, discussing the news. There was an air of dull and perplexed passivity: the campaign might well be about Germany, but Germany was defeated and an inert plaything in the hands of the warring allies. The people who were principally concerned were not yet taking up positions: their humiliation had been so great that even the rupture of the grand alliance which had vanquished them was to them only a spectacle to be watched from the roadside, humbly and in meek submission to whatever fate had in store for them.

Meanwhile, through the cloudless blue sky overhead roared the dark squadrons of the Western air forces, bound for the former capital of the Reich and instructed to defend what they had but lately destroyed—deep-throbbing, swiftly flying proofs of human vacillation.

The nearer he got to the frontier at Helmstedt the more Frank feared to find it closed. With a sense of relief he discovered that this was not so. True, the German heavy trucks, the troop carriers and the sporadic private cars were lining up in their hundreds at the barrier, but Frank, who had pulled his jeep in behind an army convoy, was told that the frontier formalities, though performed with excessive tardiness, were nevertheless proceeding without incident. Sitting in his vehicle, so as to be able to move up yard by yard, he again ran his mind over George's letter. Whatever lay behind George's disappearance and strange reappearance, Frank now felt convinced that it was at least indirectly related to what was now happening on the road between the West and Berlin.

The American frontier guards examined Frank's papers politely but with exceptional care. A few minutes later the procedure was repeated on the Soviet side, again politely but with even greater mistrust and rigid bureaucratic pedantry. On his past journeys Frank had always been dealt with speedily and with indifference by the Russian soldiers; now the sentries in their grubby gray blouses almost disappeared among the dozens of bemedaled officers officiating in their faultlessly tailored dark-olive uniforms. A lieutenant of the Soviet police, with whom Frank, though unable to converse with him, had concluded almost a friendship based on his frequent frontier crossings, now handed him his papers without returning his greetings and without a sign of recognition.

On the autobahn, which led to Berlin through the Soviet Zone, Frank had an opportunity of studying the striking contrasts between American and Russian methods. The democracies found it difficult to keep a secret, even the most secret of military secrets. With the Soviets, on the other hand, keeping a secret had become second nature. The American officer was not permitted to deviate from the autobahn even by a hairbreadth or to stop, if only for a moment, on the stretch between Helmstedt and Berlin—but no traveling order, whether phrased in Russian, English, French or German, could prevent him from looking right and left. The woods on both sides of the autobahn were thick with trucks, tanks and scout cars—most of the vehicles, oddly enough, being of German or American manufacture. In the villages mobile radio transmitters had run up their aerial masts on the hilltops guns had been brought into position, their muzzles pointing westward. Yet all movements must have taken place at night, for the tanks were camouflaged with fresh green leaves, military vehicles and guns were covered with branches and twigs, and there was hardly a soldier in sight anywhere. It was almost as if vehicles and weapons had been moved up into position and then abandoned. Frank even had the impression, though he knew it to be incorrect, that the peasants, too, on this side of the boundary tilled their land at night: hardly anywhere was a peasant or a peasant woman to be seen in the fields. The villages, too, looked as though their inhabitants had fled, leaving their homes and livestock and implements behind. On the few occasions when the American officer's jeep passed a group of Germans they lowered their eyes and moved off hastily. Thus, right through the cold war, Frank drove towards the destroyed capital.

He did not go to headquarters but, in accordance with his instructions, put up at the Dahlem house of an artillery major. The nervous tension which reigned in Berlin infected him, even though he only went into the city for an hour in order to establish the location of the Café Bremer. Neither the traditional humor nor the raid-hardened sang-froid of the Berliners could disguise the electric atmosphere. The queues outside stores and foodshops were so long that, in some instances, they went right round a block. Everywhere stood small arguing groups of people who did not want to be left alone; American, French and British jeeps tore through the Western Sectors as if the city were one huge battle HQ. Again and again the lieutenant colonel was stopped by women eager for some encouraging remark; it was rumored that the Soviets had cut off the electric power supply to the Western Sectors; and nobody seemed willing to go to bed, because of a superstitious fear that while one slept things might befall which could not happen so long as one stayed awake exorcising them. The anemic newspapers were snatched from the vendors' hands; silent waiting crowds formed outside radio stores and around radio sound-trucks; the Tiergarten, where Germans, Russians and Western Allies were normally fraternizing in black-market deals, looked once more like a park, or like a garbage dump; at the Brandenburger Tor, Russian and British sentries were facing each other silently and expectantly. But the hearts of the West Berliners, so it seemed to Frank, went out to the Allies in uniform, to the conquerors who had become defenders. But no matter how oppressively a premonition of things to come lay over the hot city, Frank did not find in this beleaguered island the passiveness which had so struck him on his journey to Berlin, on both sides of the boundary. There was confidence here amidst anxiety, and determination amidst impotence. Among the ruins moved the "rubble women," as these true heroines of Berlin were called, steadily going about their laborious task. And this, to Frank, was the most promising sign—that there were still peo-ple who believed there was some point in removing debris.

On the following evening, at the appointed hour of six, he arrived at the Café Bremer. The place was situated, somewhat to Frank's misgivings, in the immediate neighborhood of the Sector boundary, in a small street off Potsdamer Platz. Although at that time the inhabitants of the Western Sectors did not yet differ so markedly from those from the East, it was nevertheless obvious to Frank that this was a café predominantly patronized by East Berliners. He did not see a single American soldier in the shabby room with its rough wooden tables.

The place was overcrowded: not a single table was free. However, a waitress wearing a grubby apron approached the hesitating American officer and said softly:

"You are expected."

Inconspicuously she pointed to a small corner table where a man was sitting in a polo-neck sweater that seemed quite inappropriate to the hot season. On his head was a dark-blue peaked cap of the kind usually worn by seamen. When Frank sat down by his side he looked, much to his surprise, into a pale, narrow, highly intellectual face.

"Good evening, Herr Green," said the man.

"Good evening."

"Shall we come straight to the point?"

Frank nodded.

"Your brother would like to speak to you," said the stranger without introducing himself. He spoke the German of Hamburg.

"I know."

"Will you come with me?"

"Where to?"

"He is waiting for you at the Alexanderplatz."

"I do not intend to go into the Eastern Sector."

A faint smile flitted over the features of the man with the chauffeur's cap. With a faultless English pronunciation he said:

" 'East is East and West is West, and never the twain shall meet,' as the poet has it. Your brother can't come over here: there is a warrant out for his arrest. But you needn't be afraid about coming along with me."

"Who says I needn't be afraid to enter the Eastern Sector? Too many have not returned."

"Only those who hadn't been invited over. You are cordially invited."

"I must think this over," said Frank.

In fact, he did not have to think it over. Or rather, he had thought it all over back in Munich. He had never doubted that the rendezvous would be arranged in the Eastern Sector. He had agreed with Hunter to take the risk.

"It's a case of now or never," said the stranger. And when Frank still seemed to hesitate he added: "We don't want any international incidents. We—" he emphasized the word—"we don't want war. Not even over the brothers Green. I shall deliver you back here unscathed."

"All right," said Frank and got up.

"My car is parked just round the corner," said the man. "A taxi. Follow me in a few minutes."

The ramshackle antediluvian vehicle, an East Sector taxi whose number Frank instantly committed to his memory, was standing at the corner. Frank got inside. He noted with relief that he was alone in the car. The fact that the driver calmly allowed him to sit behind him also seemed a favorable sign. Only the fact that the police sentries posted immediately behind the café let the vehicle pass without any formalit —they did not even demand Frank's properly made out Int onal Pass—seemed a little disturbing.

I   as getting dark as the vehicle pulled up in the Alexanderplatz. Th square was empty. Two or three street lamps shed a sick yellowish light.

The stranger, who had remained silent throughout the drive, pointed to the ruin of the former police headquarters. Frank got out.

From the ruin emerged George's figure. As far as Frank could judge he was wearing a well-fitting light-gray civilian suit. He approached his brother with a measured tread.

"Good evening, Frank," said George.

"Good evening, George."

"If it's all right with you," said George, "we can have our talk walking up and down. This will prove to you, better than anything else, that we aren't plotting anything against you. The car will wait for you here."

Frank nodded agreement. They started off round the square.

"First of all, thanks for coming," said George. He tried to speak as if he had last seen Frank the day before and as if the circumstances of their meeting were nothing out of the ordinary. But his voice was hoarse and unsteady. "The fact that you've come even increases the respect which I have always felt for you—though I did not always admit it to myself."

"What do you want from me?" asked Frank.

"To begin with, a few words about myself," said George, undismayed by Frank's unresponsive tone. "Whatever you may think—I crossed over out of conviction. Let us then accept this for granted . . ."

Frank interrupted him. "I don't know that it matters—but I don't believe it."

"Why not?"

"Because you had too many other reasons. You knew about Jakob Steiner's confession. Your affair with Karin. Your black-market deals worth hundreds of thousands. Deserters out of conviction are rare—on both sides. People's private lives always come first. Politics usually are only a convenient peg for their actions. But I didn't mean to interrupt you. I don't suppose the purpose of your letter was to convince me of your morality."

George stopped. "You are mistaken. In a certain sense it was the only purpose of my letter."

"In what sense?"

"I admit to having made crooked deals back there, Frank. But have you ever asked yourself why I transacted crooked deals? Because, instinctively at first and then consciously, I despised the world in which I lived. In a world of thieves only a fool remains honest."

He resumed his walk. Frank fell into step again.

"Ideological theft," said Frank, "is, at best, a justification invented afterwards. At any rate, you aren't thinking of returning?"

"No."

"Why then did you write to me?"

"I had to write to you." It was not clear what or who had com‐
pelled him to do so.

"I shouldn't think you're doing much work over here," said
Frank. He pointed towards the taxi which was still standing in the
deserted square. "You've made a deal with the local powers. Whom
did you sell to clinch your deal?"

"It's not my fault if they're mopping up those Western spies," said
George. "Although I didn't lift a finger to save them. But you were
wanting to know why I've asked you to come?"

"I'm listening."

"I'm putting my cards on the table, Frank. I should like to per‐
suade you to stay here."

Frank stopped in his tracks.

"You're out of your mind," he said.

A cyclist rode into the nocturnal square. Frank thought it rather
pointless that he should ride twice round the square before turning
into a side street.

George touched Frank's arm. They resumed their stroll.

"You've got to listen to me, Frank," he began. "You are blind.
Can't you see that over on your side they are preparing for a war?
Three years after the end of the war a new war is just round the
corner. The Americans want it; they want it at all costs." He dropped
his voice. "I might have stood for that, Frank. But think of your new
allies! Three years after our glorious crusade we are allying ourselves
with hangmen and murderers. You know as well as I that before
long the Americans are going to put the Germans back into uniform.
Do you remember our talk at the Ebers' house? Everything I told
you has come true. Over there, the Stappenhorsts will once more be at
the helm. When they go to war they'll again gas the Jews."

Their steps echoed on the asphalt. A policeman appeared under a
street lamp. He did not seem interested in the solitary motorcar.

"Assuming," continued George, "that war can still be avoided this
once—do you want to live in a world where the concentration camp
guards call the tune? In a few years German industry will again be‐
long to the war criminals. People like yourself will have to disappear.
Today they're making you a lieutenant colonel, and tomorrow
they'll chuck you on the scrap heap." He extended his arm and

ointed to the ruins which stood around the Alexanderplatz like so
many skeletons in an empty anatomy theater. "The currency reform
over there is now only a question of a few days. That's when German rehabilitation will start in full earnest. Can't you see that this
splendid Marshall Plan is only designed to rebuild the houses of the
criminals? I too was blind, Frank. So blind that I began to be proud
of German rehabilitation. Do you think the East, with its healthy
economic system, could not rebuild ten times as quickly? Maybe you
think these are clichés. I don't care. But you can believe me that here,
and only here, do they know how to keep the Germans enslaved for
ever. Have we really got to the point, you and I, that we should
begrudge a victor the fruits of his victory? Didn't we, you and I, go
to war with the determination to subject this nation for all times?
Or did we set forth to spoon-feed the murderers, nurse their children
and rebuild their homes? Who, I ask you, is the deserter now: you
or I?"

They had again arrived at the former police headquarters. A street
lamp stood to the right of the wrecked building. Frank caught sight
of two men who seemed to have emerged from the ruins. They made
or the car and stopped by it, talking to the driver.

"Who are these people?" asked Frank.

"I don't know," said George. "Passers-by. Maybe they're looking
or a taxi."

"Go on," said Frank.

"I have no instructions," said George, "to get you over here, and
what I've got to say to you will be the best proof of that. I'm not a
Communist—at least, not yet. What makes me sympathize with
them," he continued almost in a whisper, "is the fact that they lie.
They don't want to rebuild Germany. They are treating the Germans
as the Germans deserve to be treated—like pigs. There's a lot of fuss
being made now because the Russians have violated a few thousand
German women. I got that Nazi girl with child back there—only
over here they're doing it in a big way. So what? They are practicing
what we had intended to practice. I haven't become unfaithful to
America, but America has become unfaithful to me. The war—you've
got to admit it, Frank—has been the great event in our life. Can
we afford to have waged the war in vain? That would be like having lived in vain. This growing sense of futility . . . That's what

made me a criminal if you wish to call me one, Frank. Searc
yourself, I beseech you, and you will find that this feeling is as stro
in you as it is in me. Only you're better off than me. You've remain
clean. But even I have rediscovered my better self in this clean a
mosphere over here. I make you no other promise than that yo
won't have to make deals with Mama's murderers over here. Her
you don't have to become corrupt, nor do you have to march int
another war under the same flag as Mama's murderers. Here, yo
can remain the person you are. Take off this disgraced uniform
Let's forget our differences, Frank. You've never had any love fo
me, whereas I've always admired you. You don't have to have an
love for me tomorrow either. Myself, I was only accepted; but yo
will be received with open arms. It's your last opportunity, Frank

He had been speaking urgently, with a power of conviction tha
was a blend of his efficient sales talk of the past and the fire of
fanaticism soon to come. Only the last sentence sounded hard and
it seemed to Frank, even threatening.

"Is that all you've got to say to me?" asked Frank.

"Yes."

"Very well. I've listened to you attentively, George. I don't know i
you composed your speech—we'll leave that open. It certainly was a
effective speech since you touched upon a few things which hav
been disturbing me deeply. It was also a particularly effective speec
because, deliberately or spontaneously, you skilfully blended trutl
and falsehood."

He stopped abruptly. The two men who had been standing by th
taxi were getting into it.

"What's going on there?" he asked, drawing his brother's attentio
to the surprising spectacle.

George shrugged his shoulders.

"Friends of his, maybe," he said. It did not sound convincing

"If you're playing a dirty game it won't get you anywhere," saic
Frank.

"Why should I?" asked George. "But continue . . . you've onl
just begun."

"I will try," said Frank, "to leave out all personal aspects—such a
the fact that I don't believe your motives. Whatever one may thin
about revenge—revenge wasn't your motive, George. You didn't wan

"Tell them you want to walk with me to my apartment."

"Will they believe that?"

"I'm living just round the corner. I can't think of anything else."

They could hear their own footsteps. They had nearly reached the waiting taxi.

"All right," said Frank. "I'll try."

"You must knock me down afterwards," George said quickly.

They were now by the taxi. The driver was sitting behind the wheel, smoking a cigarette. Without turning to Frank he said:

"Two friends here want a lift."

Frank said: "I want to go to my brother's place."

"Right," said the driver. "Get in."

"I thought he lived just round the corner," said Frank.

"Get in!" repeated the driver. This time it sounded like an order.

The two men inside got out with a carefully rehearsed movement and planted themselves on both sides of Frank. George was standing a little way off, silent.

"Get in!" said the driver. He did not leave his seat.

"What's all this?" said Frank. "Is it forbidden to walk here?"

He was watching himself, as he had always done in dangerous situations. He wanted to gain time, though he did not know what for.

He took a step back, his hand going to his pistol. The two men grabbed him. The driver turned round and reached under the driving seat. He produced an enormous wrench.

But the blow never came. Round the corner by the former police headquarters a car appeared. It swerved wildly and came to a halt next to the taxi. A childhood memory rose up before Frank's eyes. At a circus he had once seen a funny act: a minute car had rolled into the ring, and to the delighted shrieks of the audience at least a dozen clowns had tumbled out of the vehicle. He was reminded of that scene now as the four hastily opened doors disgorged six or seven men into the street. They were in civilian clothes and each of them had a pistol in his hand.

The driver dropped his wrench. One of the two men holding Frank groped for his coat pocket, but the butt of a pistol cracked against his temple. He sagged to the ground. Frank could not see where George was or what he was doing.

"Let's go," said one of the men with the pistols. Two others dragged Frank to the car. They flung him, still bewildered, into the back and scrambled aboard themselves as best they could. A moment later the car was streaking across the Alexanderplatz towards the Sector boundary.

Frank recognized the voice as that of Captain Yates, the young officer who had replaced O'Hara.

"You didn't turn up a minute too soon," said Frank.

"We wanted to await developments," one of the men said. "You were never in danger for a moment, Frank."

A third voice remarked: "We could have picked up the lot of them."

"The Colonel's funny that way," said Yates. "He doesn't hold with kidnapping."

Yet another said: "Better hurry up before they give the alarm to the guys on the boundary."

"What, with those telephones?" Yates said contemptuously.

The car stopped at the boundary. A Russian soldier and a German policeman walked up slowly.

Yates produced his papers. The beam of a torch flashed round the inside of the car. "One too many," said the policeman.

Frank fished out his pass. For a never-ending minute the German and the Russian studied the piece of paper. Then the German nodded. A few minutes later the car rolled down the darkened Kurfürstendamm.

"Lucky this time," said one of the men.

"Pity we've got to leave the car behind," said Yates dryly.

"Leave the car behind?" asked Frank.

"Haven't you heard, Colonel?" said Yates. "We've got to fly out in the morning. The Russians have blockaded Berlin."

The Ghosts Are Stronger

The evening after Frank's dramatic escape from East Berlin three men and a woman were sitting around the laid table at the Munich apartment of ex-Colonel Werner Zobel—the Colonel himself, his daughter Martha, her fiancé Gerd Mante, and her brother Jochen.

In outward appearance it was a family idyl. The Colonel was smoking a fat American cigar; Martha had surreptitiously put her fleshy arm on her fiancé's thigh; Gerd Mante was doing justice to the excellent bottle of Moselle; and Jochen Zobel was sipping a long-missed cup of real coffee.

The outward picture, however, concealed much hidden tension. The Colonel had behind him some difficult weeks, and had not yet quite recovered from them. In May, his ex-servicemen's association had festively celebrated Field Marshal Joachim Sturzenbach's release from Allied detention. The Field Marshal, held by the Americans on charges of war crimes, had been released, and within a few days his old colleague, the paratroop general, had introduced him to the crowd at the Augustinerkeller. Colonel Zobel, who had made his former Feldwebel Vice-President of the Association, was bitterly disillusioned in his democratic beliefs when the General and the Field Marshal joined forces to overthrow Zobel. When, after some hesitation, he complained to General Stappenhorst, once his own proposer, that gentleman regretted the ungrateful treatment meted out to the deserving colonel, but pointed out that such a brilliant name as that of the ever-victorious Field Marshal would be of exceptional service to the cause. When Zobel objected that surely the relatively young Field Marshal did not belong to the old school, but was on the contrary a typical product of the Hitlerite Wehrmacht, he invited General Stappenhorst's barely disguised anger. Assuming that the officers and troops, most of whom had been personally enrolled by him, would undoubtedly remain loyal to him and would not wish to exchange his leadership for that of the highly-respected but nevertheless compromised Field Marshal, Zobel was rash enough to call for a vote which resulted in the overwhelming victory of the man used to victories. Zobel, for his part highly experienced in tactical withdrawals or, as they were more tactfully called, disengagements, after some initial hesitation accepted the post of Vice-President magnanimously offered to him, and his old Feldwebel was made collector of membership dues. Thus, to all appearances, the crisis resolved itself to everybody's satisfaction—but Zobel had not been getting the same pleasure out of his activities since.

Even his joy over his son's return was not undivided. Jochen, who did not arrive in Munich till early in 1948, showed various symptoms of what the Colonel could only regard as a psychosis born of six years of captivity.

Formerly a lively and adventurous young man, this thirty-year-old ex-lieutenant in an armored infantry regiment, though in good shape physically, was displaying a strange and indeed eccentric behavior. In spite of his father's offer of financial help Jochen wore an old, extremely shabby suit which he had unearthed in the attic; he refused persistently, and without giving any reason, to accompany his father to his weekly ex-servicemen's meetings; he treated his sister Martha, of whom he used to be extremely fond, with frosty politeness; and generally drove the Zobels' household into fits of frenzy by his habit of spending five, six or more hours a day playing chess—all by himself. When he finally got himself a job he did so without calling on his father's help, and it was only several weeks later that Colonel Zobel discovered that his son was working as a porter at the Munich central station.

There had also been an embarassing, though perhaps not surprising, change in the Colonel's relations with his lately discharged son-in-law-to-be—if indeed there was any hope left that Gerd Mante would ever marry the besotted Martha. The former Obersturmbann-führer, now one of General Stappenhorst's most intimate collaborators, was no longer staying at the Zobels' home: he now owned a bachelor's apartment in Tengstrasse, equipped with every comfort and convenience. His attitude to the Colonel was no longer hostile but insultingly condescending, which pained the old man even more. Zobel repeatedly implored his daughter to break off her relationship with Mante, but he was unsuccessful in this even when he proved to her beyond any doubt that her fiancé was carrying on an affair with at least one, but probably two, of General Stappenhorst's secretaries.

Earlier that day special editions of the newspapers had announced the Berlin blockade and the conversation in the Zobels' sitting-room turned to the situation in the beleaguered city.

"It seems the Americans intend to carry in supplies by means of an airlift," said the Colonel. "A difficult business. Colonel Howley, the City Commandant, believes that the stocks of food are enough for only thirty days."

"All this nonsense isn't going to last for thirty days," declared Mante.

"You think the Americans cannot organize an airlift?" asked Zobel.

"Oh, they can do that all right. They've got food and supplies enough to pour down the drain. But after a few weeks the Russians will lose their temper. They'll knock down a few Yankee planes and then we're off."

"That would be a misfortune," said the Colonel. "We haven't got anything; the Americans have been disarming—and there are the Russians in full battle order."

"Doesn't matter," replied Mante. "After Pearl Harbor the Yanks were also finished. . . ."

"You mean you have absolute confidence in the Americans?"

Mante shrugged his shoulders. "As human beings and as soldiers they're muck. But technologically they are and remain unsurpassed. They'll simply stage a little atomic bang or two for the Russians."

The conversation was only between the Colonel and the SS officer; Martha and Jochen were silent. Now and again Zobel cast a sidelong glance at Jochen, but he was unable to read his son's thoughts.

"So you think war is unavoidable?" the Colonel asked.

"Perfectly obvious," replied Mante. "And who foresaw the whole shemozzle? The Führer. If Washington hadn't been entirely Jew-ridden they could have concluded a separate peace with us as late as 1944 and could have marched right into Moscow. Now, of course, they've got to swallow their own mess. But it so happens we've no other choice than the Yanks or the Russkis, and so we've got to march along with the Yanks. The important thing is that we must not again pull other people's chestnuts out of the fire. . . ."

The Colonel nodded. "Certainly," he said, "if only we didn't have to be the battlefield . . ."

"Rather today than tomorrow," retorted Mante. "The Russians have no atom bombs—that's a fact. We've got no industry—thanks to Mr. Morgenthau. So at the most we'll have a few houses knocked down. But a year later the Russians will have built the whole thing up for us again."

The Colonel did not want to make a reply, though it seemed to him that quite a few observations called for one. Martha had put a caressing hand on Mante's knee and gazed at him with such adoration as though in the hero of yesterday she could already see the hero of tomorrow. Jochen Zobel was lounging back, his eyes closed. He seemed not to be listening.

But suddenly he opened his eyes and leaned forward. His voice shook with excitement as he turned to his father:

»423«

"Papa—how much longer are you going to listen to this rubbish?"

Mante straightened up on the sofa where he was sitting. The Colonel said placatingly:

"What do you mean, Jochen?"

"I'm asking how much longer you're going to listen to this rubbish."

"Jochen, please," the Colonel reproved him.

Mante had himself under control again. "Don't mind him," he said condescendingly. "And what do you consider such rubbish, Herr Leutnant?"

At last Jochen faced him.

"You can drop the 'Leutnant,' Herr Mante," he said. "I've taken off the 'Leutnant' and no power on earth is going to make me put him on again."

"That's your business," said Mante. "For all I care you can go back to slavery again if you wish."

"Herr Mante!" the Colonel tried to pacify him.

"You talk about slavery?" said Jochen, paying no attention to his father. "Who introduced slavery into this country? Who sacrificed hundreds of thousands in order to maintain slavery?"

Mante took a sip of wine and said to the Colonel:

"These celebrated ex-prisoners! Returning home with their packs full of Bolshevik ideas!"

"That's always been the favorite lie of you and your kind. Of course we're in your way. You are afraid of ghosts, Herr Mante, for the ghosts might tell stories of how they died for your lies."

A deep flush suffused Mante's head. He wanted to jump up, but Martha gently forced him back on to the sofa.

"Gerd . . . can't you see he's sick?" she said.

It was a mollifying remark and well-intentioned, but it was the most unfortunate thing she could have said. Jochen stood up. Taking no notice of his sister he addressed Mante:

"Yes, Herr Obersturmbannführer, I am sick. So incurably sick that, three years after the end of one mass murder, I feel no inclination to take part in another. I am so sick, so mentally deranged, that I am not hoping that someone will 'knock down' a few planes tomorrow or 'stage a little atomic bang or two.' I am so sick, Herr Mante, that I am not indifferent to a few hundred thousand civilian homes being 'knocked down.' But that isn't all. I am so sick that I refuse to take up arms against Germans, as I should have to do if your marvelous plans were to come to fruition. But I am even sicker than that, Herr Mante. Your 'Russkis' pushed me around for six years, from one lousy prison camp to another, while you were running around with your whores. Even so I have no desire to make war on those 'Russkis,' simply because war doesn't prove anything . . . not even if some slave nation rebuilds our 'knocked down' houses afterwards. I am so sick, Herr Obersturmbannführer, as to remember the words uttered by your late lamented Führer before he killed himself in his air-raid shelter—that the German people could go to the devil if they betrayed him. I am so sick as to think that you and the likes of you are still trying to get your revenge against the German people for their betrayal of Hitler. I wasn't quite so sick a few months ago when I returned from captivity in the vain hope of finding my sick nation recovering, my father awakening, and yourself dead or behind prison bars. Since then my condition has greatly deteriorated. I have since seen the Germany for which I had been homesick every minute throughout six long years; this country so full of vitality that it must once again die for you, Herr Mante; this country that is rebuilding without first removing the wreckage, and that is escaping from its memories into activity. The old man here is nodding his head in agreement, as he has done all his life whenever empty words have come from empty heads. Instead of giving his brain an airing he is airing his uniform again. Impertinent boneheads are again brandishing words and will presently brandish bombs, and my unhappy nation is once again marching down the road to perdition. I was once sentenced to twenty-eight days of solitary confinement in darkness, a punishment for something I didn't do, and when I came out from that blindness, Herr Mante, my eyes were opened. At that moment I was Germany—responsible for the crimes of a few and her eyes opened only when emerging from the dark. Sick? I'm not only sick but a public menace. For listen to this, Herr Mante, and get it into your head. This country is full of sick men like myself. You might also call us ghosts. We haven't rallied together yet—as always, you have stolen a march on us. But we're no less dangerous for all that— for every single man of us is determined to stay your hand, if need be by force. I shall now leave this house which has been spared by the bombs but which is nevertheless ruined because it has taken in a murderer who wants to go on murdering tomorrow. I shall not return so long as I am sick; and I shall be sick while I know that the plague is still in my father's house."

Gerd Mante had leapt up while Jochen spoke, and now the two men were facing each other—so closely that any attempt to separate them would have been futile. They were of much the same height, the one fair and the other dark; with little difference in their age but a great deal of difference in their features—the flushed, long since well-nourished skull of Gerd Mante, and the bony, emaciated, feverish head of Jochen Zobel.

"Traitor! Swine!" hissed Mante through his teeth. "I'll teach you . . ." He caught Jochen by the collar.

He did not get any further. Jochen struck him in the face with his clenched fist. Mante reeled back and stumbled. Behind him stood the Colonel's red armchair—empty now because Zobel too had sprung up. Mante fell, striking his head against the edge of one of the arms of the chair. The blood streamed down his face and over the red plush. He tried to pull himself up, but he fell back, unconscious. His blood ran on to the carpet.

"Water, quick!" called the Colonel, kneeling down by Mante.

Martha was unable to comply with the instruction.

"He's dead! He's dead!" she screamed. "You've killed him!"

Jochen turned away.

"He's not dead," he said dryly.

For a moment he stood over the bleeding man. As he stood there, with a faraway gaze, scarcely aware of the man he had knocked out, with empty eyes and sunken cheeks, he looked indeed sick and more helpless than his victim. Then he turned in silence and went to the next room. Quickly but calmly he threw his meager possessions into his rucksack.

When he returned to the sitting-room Gerd Mante, his face white and a makeshift bandage around his head, was sitting on the sofa. Martha was wringing out wet towels over a washbowl. The Colonel stood in the center of the room, undecided whether to encourage his lost son-in-law or hold back his retrieved son.

For a moment Jochen stood in the doorway. Then he nodded to his father and left. The three followed him with their eyes. It was indeed as though a ghost had passed through the room.

Towards a Splendid Future

"We are all set for a splendid future," said Adam, and the men and women who had gathered round at his house that Sunday did not know if he meant it seriously or sarcastically.

The miracle had come to pass almost overnight.

Just as the darkest hour of the night is just before the dawn, so the German night had also been at its darkest just before the break of the new day. Only a few days prior to the currency reform the papers had reported that it was quite impossible to obtain any articles, even on coupons—not vouchers but connections were needed if one wanted to buy a pair of stockings or a new pair of trousers. Within a matter of weeks the goods turnover had dropped to a third. The statistics were depressing and accusing—the ration for standard consumers was reduced to one thousand starvation calories; during the one hundred and tenth ration period the monthly cheese allocation of sixty-two grams was altogether deleted; the fat content of so-called unskimmed milk was now only two and a half per cent. In Munich fifty thousand people had applied for bicycles, but only one thousand eight hundred received their indispensable means of transport. Instead of twenty thousand pairs of shoes needed in the Ruhr, only eight hundred and eighty were issued. In Berlin, out of two thousand six hundred newborn babies, one thousand seven hundred died because of the milk shortage. In the Ruhr one hundred thousand desperate workers downed tools; in Bavaria two thousand breweries with thirty thousand employees were idle. In Erlangen the Chairman of the Economic Council made a speech accusing the Allies of supplying merely "chicken feed" and calling his fellow-countrymen "starvation wizards." The black market was celebrating its Black Mass: the cost of a suit of clothes soared to four thousand marks and that of a pair of children's shoes to four hundred. In Munich alone one hundred and eight cases of milk adulteration were brought to court in one week. In Berlin bricks were traded like gold ingots. Indignation began to outgrow fear: in the Möhlstrasse in Munich the police had to suppress anti-Semitic demonstrations; in Essen the few existing shopwindows were smashed; and in a public opinion poll organized by the *Süddeutsche Zeitung* a few weeks before the currency reform eight out of every ten answered "No" to the question: Do you believe that the situation will improve?

But those who could interpret the signs suspected that misery and exploitation were culminating so orgiastically only because the end of the big orgy was in sight. Things had to get better because they could not get any worse. Nobody knew how many new Deutsche Marks would be given for every one hundred Reichsmarks—but no doubt an inquiry among the profiteers would have shown them offering odds of eight to two on better times ahead. Peasants, manufacturers and tradesmen alike saved up all they produced or possessed for the new golden age, and even the black marketeers showed expectant restraint. Life was holding its breath: no more contracts were concluded; the fines imposed by the judiciary seemed a mockery of justice; nobody was thinking seriously of presenting or paying a bill; and the counting-rooms of the banks were like morgues. The mood was best expressed in a report published in one of the sporadic daily papers, which said under the coy headline "To Clay: Personal": "There they stand, the crates stenciled 'Clay AX 13689 C.' In them reposes tomorrow's capital: power still contained by metal straps, the currency reform still boxed in. At this moment we feel our hearts pounding as at every great crisis of our lives. The proximity of mammon, of the devil in a bundle of notes, heightens the expectant and anxious suspense of the past few months, weeks and days to a fever pitch of certainty. Now at last the moment has come! Here is the money that will herald in a new beginning and that will accompany us into a yet uncertain future. These crates hold the remainder of our days: they will play their part in determining our work, our efforts and our hopes, and they will enable us to make a fresh start and, we hope, achieve rehabilitation." It was not by accident that this report was a rhapsody of linguistic stupidity: no great love, no erotic passion, no noble idea and no startling discovery could have inspired that scribe to such ecstatic expressions as "power contained by metal straps," "the devil in a bundle of notes," or "hearts pounding." It was only "the proximity of mammon" that had turned the usually terse reporter into a babbling troubadour.

Then, suddenly, an important announcement of the Military Government was made over all German radio transmitters on June 19 —repeatedly and in the style of Hitler's "special communiqués," though this time with a markedly foreign accent. Nobody had realized that the currency reform had been secretly planned, like a military operation, several months beforehand. On April 20 the German currency experts had been collected from Bad Homburg by bus and taken to the former airfield of Rothwesten near Kassel. There, the gates of the barbed-wire ringed American camp closed behind them and there, housed in barracks, they were to deliberate about the forthcoming financial battle. It was impossible not to think in military symbols: there was the abduction by army bus, the silence en route, the barbed wire, the U. S. Army rations eagerly devoured by Germany's financial experts throughout those weeks, the first conference lasting till six in the morning and followed by dozens of further conferences, and finally the fact that the new German money had been printed in America and shipped across the ocean in food ration crates to the country to be blessed with it. And then, to keep to the reporter's flowery language, "at last the moment had come." Just as Hitler had loved springing his surprises on Saturdays so that no organized reaction could come on the day of rest either from his own people or from abroad, so this latest decision was likewise announced over the radio on a Saturday. On Sunday, a prayer of thanksgiving was offered up at a Cologne church, as if for salvation from the plague. Followed by jeeps with machine-guns in position the American heavy trucks, laden with the new currency, streaked over the autobahns. The police had been alerted to the highest degree of readiness, and the bank staffs, assisted by thousands of auxiliaries, began to gather at their premises at the crack of dawn. The entire German people was holding its breath, as if between two epochs.

On Monday the "German Monetary Reorganization," proclaimed in Currency Law No. 61 of the Western Military Governments, came officially into force; it abolished the Reichsmark, the Rentenmark and the Allied Military Mark, and established the Deutsche Mark— at a rate of one to ten—as the only legal tender. At that moment it seemed to conquerors and vanquished as if vice had turned to virtue over the Sunday. Nobody was in the mood for a more searching inquiry or for pondering the terrible moral degradation which only now revealed itself. It was a cheerful earthquake and nobody wanted to see the dirt which the reeling earth had thrown up. In misery there had been a certain reticence; a decent appearance had been observed even in under-the-counter deals. But now shamelessness was rampant. The merchant who had concealed his stock—often vital and lifesaving merchandise—did not wait a few weeks or even a few days before offering them for sale: twenty-four hours after the announcement the goods, hobgoblin-like, hopped up on to the shelves and into the shopwindows. A hundred times a day you could hear the remark: "They've got it in stock again. . . ." Sellers and buyers had joined in a silent conspiracy not to inquire why they had not "got it in stock" the day before. "Are vegetables growing more plentifully now?" a courageous daily paper ventured to ask as on the hitherto deserted greengrocers' stalls in the Munich market cabbages, cauliflowers, cucumbers, carrots, peas and cherries—"choice black hearts at seventy to eighty pfennigs"—appeared on the Monday. "Suddenly," wrote an astonished reporter, "you can buy brief cases (DM 15.—to 28.75), electric bulbs (40 Watts at DM 1.15), colored knitting wool (against textile waste coupons), brushes, snaps, thermos flasks, shoelaces, tools, milk cans, pocket knives, elastic, floor wax, leather gloves, ties, cutlery, alarm clocks of prewar quality, baby clothes of first-rate finish, and even novels and opera texts." Outside the front doors, in the sun, sat the children playing with the "blue scraps"—the now worthless hundred-mark notes. Outside the banks formed large, joking crowds: wrapped in brown paper, or even in tissue paper, they were carrying their wealth home. At street corners people were showing each other their purchases: cucumbers and watches, shirts and radio sets. The natural relationship between the exponents of supply and demand was restored with indecent haste: courtesy, obligingness and even servility had suddenly leaped from in front of the counter to behind the counter. Morality was writing a skit on itself. "Let others follow suit!" called the newspaper advertisements of shops, enterprises, publishing firms and various institutions, declaring that "the black market is the enemy of the working people" and adding that "any person found engaging in black-market activities on the premises" would be "dismissed on the spot." Nobody bothered to ask why such laudable measures had not been thought of at the time of the old rocking currency.

The Alois Schmidts were fast disappearing and fathers were again severely concerned about their daughters' virtuous behavior. The women who but yesterday had offered themselves outside the PX now walked past the store with an air of proud self-assurance. The police announced that they would "clean up" the Möhlstrasse. Morality was strutting through the German cities in a gold-bar reinforced corset.

"We are all set for a splendid future," said Adam exactly one week after that historic Sunday, as his friends were sitting around an exceptionally sumptuously laid coffee table.

They were present in strength: Frau Wild, Elisabeth, Hans, Inge, Stefan, Frank, and half a dozen others. Only Achim von Sibelius was absent; he had not attended their meetings for the past few months.

"Do you really mean it?" asked Hans.

Adam stood up and walked about the room restlessly while the others followed him with their eyes.

"Pessimism," he said, "is no longer popular nowadays, and I don't want to sound pessimistic. In some respects we are all set for a splendid future—no doubt of it. The rubble is going to disappear, and the ruins will disappear next. The Americans, who peer at them from the windows of their sight-seeing buses with such delectable horror, will have to hurry up. Soon there won't be a macabre sight left for them. We shall be creeping out of our cellars and the empty window frames will have panes again. Our clothes will begin to fill out again, and what's more they'll be new clothes. Who wouldn't be pleased? I'm sorry—I wish I were less clear-sighted and wouldn't see the fatal connection between a robust currency and robust health. The fact that we have made such a splendid recovery in only three years will blind us to our failure—or don't you think we have failed?"

"It's all forgotten now," said Stefan Lester.

"That's just it," said Adam. "We are a forgetful people. We're just like children who learn quickly and forget quickly."

"Is there a solution?" mused Stefan. "Sometimes the conflict seems to me insoluble. We want a happy Germany . . . and at the same time a Germany that won't forget. But a happy Germany is bound to forget. We are a foul-weather nation."

Adam sat down again. "Forget . . . ," he said. "Even this concept would have to be redefined. If at least we forgot everything . . . ! But our memory is selective. I don't know if I'm making myself clear. We won't forget the Möhlstrasse in a hurry—but the leather manufacturer who failed to deliver his shoe leather will be a respectable citizen again tomorrow. We won't forget that yesterday we gladly cycled some fifty miles in order to fill our stomachs properly—but we shall have forgotten that the day before yesterday we were cheering a Führer who led us straight into hunger. The fact that we weren't even allowed to touch our hat to a GI will stick in our memory for a long time—but who's going to remember why the GI's crossed the Rhine in the first place? I shall have to revise my ideas: it seems to me that it is not so much a case of trying not to forget as of careful distinction between the things we want to forget and those we want to remember."

"Maybe you're right," said Hans. "But I am afraid of something else. I am afraid of greatness. Do you think, Dr. Wild, we shall ever succeed in being happy without wanting to be great?"

A young doctor who had been coming to their Sunday meetings for several months intervened.

"Why are you afraid of greatness, Herr Eber?" he asked. "Surely there is a kind of—how shall I put it—greatness in goodness?"

"I don't know," Adam said thoughtfully. "No doubt it'll be a long time before we can again think of greatness—though perhaps not so long as we think. Greatness has always been a menace to us, and yet we seem to need it time and again."

"So long as we are occupied there can be no thought of greatness," interposed Stefan. "And here's another conflict. We are looking forward to the end of the occupation period—but I, for one, am afraid of it at the same time. Isn't this the real German tragedy: that some of us still have more confidence in the discredited conquerors than in ourselves?" He kept stopping as though to arrange his thoughts. "At the same time," he went on, "I believe that we are still too much wrapped up in the recent events. They do not mean the end of the occupation . . . There is talk of fifty, thirty, or at least twenty years."

Frank had listened in silence so far. Now he said:

"The occupation is over, Herr Lester. I don't know whether we're going to stay in Germany for five years or ten—I doubt if anybody does. I also doubt if my fellow-countrymen understand the significance of the currency reform. The occupation was a dictatorship"—he smiled—"even if in a democratic garb. It was one of the gravest mistakes not to have admitted this openly. To occupy a country democratically is a contradiction in terms. After all, even a military government is a form of government, and since it is not a government elected or desired by the people it is a form of despotism. Here, I think, was the root of our failure. We arrived here with the Bible in one hand and the knout in the other. We punished and preached, commanded and courted, hanged and healed. We believed ourselves to be missionaries, but we did not love those under our charge. Our efforts were marked by the motto: '. . . and unless you are willing I shall have to use force.' Not a suitable slogan for re-educators."

"Hitler managed all right with it," said Hans.

"Not in the long run," said Frank. "Besides, he didn't talk about democracy. And he was not a foreigner."

"Moreover," remarked Stefan, "it's been proved that no nation can be 're-educated.' Educated, perhaps—in the case of children."

"We were not deliberately hypocritical," said Frank, "but it was bound to look like hypocrisy. Our intentions were not always bad . . . but the packaging invariably was. The packaging and the carriers. When I am thinking of ideal exponents of democracy—exponents in the best sense of the word—I do not necessarily think of generals, not even American ones."

"You were saying, Frank," Adam interrupted him, "that the occupation is over. What makes you think so?"

"The occupation was a dictatorship—as I've said," Frank replied. "Dictatorships only thrive in misery. A moment ago, Adam, you were complaining that German pride was beginning to wake up only when the first Deutsche Mark was pressed into the German palm. It would have been the same with any other nation. You show me a single example from history of a nation being subjugated when it had an internationally recognized currency. Hitler conquered Germany only after the German currency collapsed outside the country. Don't you believe for a moment that the Soviets are really anxious to get their ruble internationally recognized. A ruined currency is the diabolically contrived plague cordon with which each dictatorship encircles its country. Freedom and escape are almost the same thing: their is no freedom if there is no escape from bondage. Worthless values, it seems to me, are the chains which bind the would-be escaper to his country. That, you see, is the strange thing, the incomprehensible thing, about my fellow-countrymen—they want to continue governing this country, but they are coining the money that will enable the governed to escape. You must not, of course, take the term 'escape' too literally. . . . I only mean the possibility of contacts, and free movement, and happiness, and—if you like—greatness." Tenderly and unnoticed by those present, he put his hand on Elisabeth's, who was sitting beside him. "I know that the occupation era is over, and although I am not actually regretting it I am nevertheless drawing the necessary conclusions for my own part." He smiled again.

"This is not meant to be a farewell party, Adam, because I'll not be going back to the States till the autumn. But I have applied for my discharge, and some time in September or October . . ."

A sudden hush descended on the room. It had not been Frank's intention to announce his departure so early. He had been carried away by his own arguments; he had wanted to illustrate his point by the most readily available example—his own. Now he regretted his words. Everybody's eyes were upon him, and from him, though haltingly and tactfully, they swiveled to the woman at his side. Frank found it difficult to control the emotion which overcame him, for the eyes that regarded him were full of friendship and regret at his decision. In embarrassment he stared at the open window through which the summer night was flooding in warm waves.

As always, Frau Wild was the first to collect herself.

"Are you leaving because everything has been in vain, Frank?" she asked.

But before Frank could make a reply Hans said:

"The proof that everything has not been in vain is right here with us. . . ."

THE YEARS THAT
FOLLOWED

SEVENTH CHAPTER

Colonel Hunter Declines Promotion

𝕴T WAS a sunny January day in 1949 and Lieutenant General Theodore E. MacCallum was wearing a pair of pale gray corduroy
trousers, top boots, and a dark-green uniform jacket. But the trousers
and boots were not visible to Colonel Hunter, for the General was
sitting behind his desk.

"Needless to say, you've got to use the utmost discretion," said the
General. "Stappenhorst is getting in touch with you tomorrow. Officially we have nothing to do with his service, but the exchange of
information must function promptly and in a spirit of mutual trust."

Hunter made no reply. His silence irritated the General. He continued hurriedly:

"What form German rearmament is to take hasn't been decided
yet. There's talk of a European Army. I shall probably be able to tell
you more about it when I come back from Washington. The thing
now is to provide for a healthy transition."

"What do you understand by a healthy transition?" Hunter came
out with at last.

The Governor was fond of issuing vague and general directives and
letting his subordinates worry about the details. He said:

"We must lay the psychological foundations. Close cooperation
with the Germans. Stiffening their will to resist. Gradual rehabilitation of the German soldier. No death sentences. Amnesties wherever
possible. Appeals to German patriotism." And impatiently he added:
"Come off it, Graham, you know quite well what I mean."

"I'm afraid I know only too well what you mean," said Hunter.

"Well then," said the General.

"There's no 'Well then' about it," said Hunter, and he did not
sound very respectful. "Perhaps you wouldn't mind explaining to me
how we are to bring about that 'healthy transition.' I have an in-

struction, with your signature to it, saying that German policemen must not carry firearms. The instruction also says that they are to be dressed in a uniform that doesn't look like a uniform."

"I wasn't talking about policemen," interrupted the General.

"I was only quoting an example," Hunter replied calmly. "Appeal to patriotism? We've only just thrashed their national pride out of them. A man's Nazi past? My instructions were that the severest possible Denazification Tribunals were to be set up. The instructions came from you."

"The instructions came from those blockheads in Washington. Once more they've completely failed to foresee developments."

"I remember distinctly, Ted, you telling me one evening—it was at your schloss—that you couldn't do anything with that German 'army of cripples.' Have their limbs grown since then?"

The General jumped up. He walked, or rather marched, over to the window.

"Please, Graham, take a look outside. Those people are hammering away till my head's humming. Look at what they've knocked together in less than a year. They are and remain the only nation in this rotten Europe. Give them a hand—and even their legs will grow again."

Hunter rose too and moved across to the window. There was a scaffolding across the way. The winter did not seem to interfere with the work: the men were as busy as bees in midsummer. The house was visibly growing under their hands.

"Is there going to be a war?" asked the Colonel.

"That depends on the Russians. One thing's certain: we can't manage without the krauts." He returned to his desk. "I'm flying over to Washington the day after tomorrow." For the first time he smiled. "You'll have to celebrate without me."

Hunter, still at the window, turned his head. "Celebrate?" he asked.

The General passed him a telegram. "It's come through at last," he said. "Your promotion is coming up before the Senate on Friday."

Hunter had come over to the desk. He picked up the form and walked back to the window. There was not a sound in the room: only from across the street, muted by the double windowpanes, came the hammering from the building site.

»438«

The silence made the General uneasy. "Aren't you pleased?" he asked.

Hunter was still silent. At last he said:

"I should like to decline my promotion, Ted."

"You must be out of your mind."

"The promotion puts me under the obligation of staying on over here," said Hunter. "I should like to retire, Ted."

"What's come over you?" the General expostulated.

"It doesn't have to be retirement," said Hunter. "If they can find some use for me—at home, or in the Philippines, or with some military mission . . . Perhaps you could fix it in Washington."

The General still failed to understand. "It's not my fault it's taken so long. These bastards of bureaucrats . . ."

"It has nothing to do with the delay," said Hunter. "I am extremely grateful to you, Ted. I just don't feel like it any longer. Let them send some new men to Germany. I should feel too much of a fool. First I stripped the police of their top boots, and now I'm to put all young men back into uniform. I've banned a paper because on one occasion they printed the word SS with the old angular Nazi characters—and now I'm to sit round a table with former SS officers. I'm an old soldier, Ted, and I don't doubt that they've got their reasons for it back at the Pentagon. But I have learned too much in this occupied country. I have punished hundreds of German officers because they did not think. That's what has made me think."

"I never knew you were so radically anti-German, Graham," said the General. "After all, they must be given a chance."

"I'm not anti-German," said the Colonel. "Perhaps they ought to have been given a change to rebuild from the very first. . . ."

"This isn't a moral problem," the General interrupted. "Not even a matter of taste. Personally, I can't stand them. Nor do I expect any gratitude from them: I know quite well what they think of us. But we are for them the lesser evil—and so are they for us. That's a healthy relationship."

"Most reasonable," said Hunter. Gazing at the window, as if at a mirror, he continued: "Only a man's got to look at himself in the mirror sometimes—if only while shaving each morning. And the Colonel Hunter who did the one thing yesterday can't do the other thing tomorrow. Not even if he disguises himself as a general. His image in the mirror would mock him. Let the demilitatization colonel go home and get yourself a remilitarization general. I won't mind. For five years it has been my task to make the Germans feel ashamed of themselves. I don't want them to make me feel ashamed."

"And all this hasn't occurred to you before? Stappenhorst, for one, isn't a new acquaintance . . ."

"Unfortunately not," said the Colonel. "To the officers of the 20th of July Hitler wasn't a new acquaintance either. The cup's got to be full to brim over."

"I hope you are not comparing us with the Nazis," snapped the General.

"I am comparing myself with those who one day had had enough of it."

"What is it you really disapprove of?" insisted the General. "Our policy of yesterday, our policy of tomorrow, or merely our inconsistency?"

"Probably all three," said Hunter. "Chiefly that we are so obviously doing only what is expedient instead of doing what is right."

"You're aware that you are seriously jeopardizing your promotion? I shall have to report in Washington . . ."

The General continued speaking but the Colonel was no longer listening. He was still holding the telegram. He was thinking of Betty. Walking out of the chapel under an archway of crossed swords. The band playing "Here comes the bride." His promise to Betty that he would be a general one day. The many miracles that happened at first. The miracles getting less frequent as he was getting older. Their homes without number. How many homes had they had? Post quarters in Fort Dix and in the Philippines, and in Camp Kilmer, and in Honolulu, and a villa in Puerto Rico, and a lot of other houses, and finally a house in Harthauserstrasse. Bob and Ruth were born in army hospitals; only Beverley was born in a nursing home. There had always been a general's star in the sky, but the sky had clouded over. The Colonel thought of Marianne. "When you get your general's star you can buy her a pink automobile and a pale-blue bonnet," she had said to him. Or words to that effect. Betty would not get a pink automobile now, nor a pale-blue bonnet. He would come home and say to her: "I was holding that star in my hand, but I let go of it again." She would ask why. "I don't know," he would reply. "Maybe because of the shaving mirror." She would not understand that. She had given him three children, and when he was in the hospital she had written to him twice a day—but she had never understood him. It did not matter much: at least he did not have to pretend with her. "Here comes the bride" rang through him again: it was as if the men across the way were beating it out with their hammers. Besides, it came from *Lohengrin*. No, thought the Colonel, he was no Lohengrin, or else he would have left long ago. There was nothing heroic and nothing logical in his going now. Pity about that fine house and garden in Harlaching. He wondered if Betty would take all those Bavarian beer mugs home with her. Five years—Ted was right. But the years before had been equally wasted; only he had not realized it so clearly then. It must be the *Föhn* atmosphere: everything seemed more clear over here.

He said: "I don't really mind, Ted. I shouldn't have made a good general. I'm afraid of responsibility." He crumpled the telegram up in his fist.

"Think it over!" said the General.

"There's nothing to think over," said Hunter, and his voice sounded firm.

He went up to the desk where he had put his brief case. The General made no attempt to detain him. Quickly Hunter returned to his own office. One could not hear the bridal march there.

Wedemeyer Conjures Again

Once more, seven or eight cars were standing by the edge of the wood between Tutzing and Garatshausen, not far from the Starnberger See. This time there were quite a few German private cars among them. It was February and the snow lay deep. Around Wedemeyer's country house the trees looked like huge snowmen built by merry angels. Inside, a little party was in full swing, celebrating the end of the Munich carnival.

Walter Wedemeyer was again calling himself a man of private means. He had sold the "Mücke." For the night club he had got nothing, but for the building site he had got a small fortune in Deutsche Marks. The night club would shortly disappear and an insurance company would run up its new office building there.

Wedemeyer had sold his restaurant for a variety of reasons. It was not enough to know when an era began: one must also know when it was over. There were still black marketeers and agents, but they no longer needed the "Mücke" to eat their fill, to quench their thirst, or to barter their food, drinks, cigarettes or information. In spite of that, though, Wedemeyer would not have dropped his restaurant in such a hurry. But he was a man of sudden and strong impulses. Twenty-four hours after the currency reform a guest had kicked up a row because his wiener schnitzel was a trifle burnt. Two days later somebody suggested that his champagne had been watered. People had such short memories. Life was easier for a man of private means.

In the house by the lake the guests were helping themselves freely to the champagne. But there was nothing to suggest the ecstasy of the carnival celebrations of before the recent great turning point. Then there had been less to drink and almost nothing to eat, and the room had been chilly. Yet eroticism had made the people feel replete, drunk and warm. The band now was no longer a band playing on a sinking ship.

"Our host must give us a conjuring display," said General Stappenhorst to Lieutenant General MacCallum. "Did you know, Herr General, that he is a first-rate conjurer?"

MacCallum nodded. It was none of Stappenhorst's business that MacCullum had himself attained considerable skill in that art.

Stappenhorst raised his champagne glass. He was holding it by its stem, German fashion. MacCallum had got used to it, even though he could not bring himself to do likewise. But at least he too raised his glass again after emptying it, as demanded by German custom.

"Your health, Herr General!" said Stappenhorst.

"Your health, Herr General!" said MacCullum.

The two gentlemen were sitting in Wedemeyer's little study, a room much too elegant for a bachelor's home. The white double doors stood open, and through them they could see the guests dancing in the drawing-room. Wedemeyer had deliberately left them alone. All over the house small discreet groups had formed. All one had to do was give people some place where they could meet, and they would get along with each other. That was part of Wedemeyer's philosophy.

From the drawing-room a young American officer entered the study. He was a youthful brigadier general, broad-shouldered, with the face of a college boy and a crew cut. Over his uniform he wore a black and white domino.

"Seem to be having a good time, Brisbane, eh?" MacCullum said benevolently.

"I'm settling down, General," said Brisbane. He joined the other two.

"I'm sure you'll get along fine with Brisbane," MacCullum said to Stappenhorst.

Stappenhorst bowed, a little stiffly but courteously.

"We passed your budget on to Washington yesterday," continued MacCallum. "Of course, fifteen million is quite a mouthful to start with. It's got to be authorized by the politicians." He uttered the word "politicians" as if it were an unpleasant disease.

"It's always the same," agreed Stappenhorst.

Brigadier General Brisbane was clearly disinclined to discuss politics at the moment.

"Daisy is a marvellous dancer," he said, nodding towards the drawing-room.

The wife of the lieutenant general was just spinning past.

"You weren't supposed to recognize her," laughed MacCallum.

Daisy was wearing a red mask. She was dressed as Madame Pompadour, in a full skirt of red silk. On her head sat a charming tricorn hat. She was dancing with the host, who was disguised as Mephistopheles, all in black. He had even glued a pointed black beard to his chin, but his dark horn-rimmed glasses somewhat mitigated his diabolical appearance. The next couple was Bank President Stettinus from Cologne with Karin Eber, his future daughter-in-law. Stettinus senior was wearing a brown monk's habit. Karin was in a plunging-neckline evening gown, the first dress she had again been able to order from Paris. She had taken off her black silk mask. The leading lady of the musical comedy theater had come dressed up as the currency reform, in a transparent dress made of old blue bank notes. She was dancing with an American colonel.

"Not bad," said Brisbane as she waltzed past.

"Not bad," agreed MacCallum.

"Of course," said Stappenhorst, "the whole business could easily be financed with German means. We might have a word with Dr. Eber presently. He called on me last week."

"That would be a mistake," MacCallum said hastily. He knew exactly what Stappenhorst was getting at. "I am convinced that you'll get your fifteen million. After all, that's not even four million dollars. We spend that much on toilet paper."

"On the black market," said Stappenhorst, "you can still get six or eight marks for a dollar."

"A transitional phenomenon," said MacCallum.

Outside the music stopped abruptly. The gentlemen in the small study could hear Wedemeyer's voice:

"I don't wish to disappoint my revered guests . . . in response to a general request . . . just a little performance . . ."

"I mustn't miss that," said Stappenhorst. "They say he's really superb."

Another tray of champagne-filled glasses was passed round. The guests arranged themselves around the grand piano on the little dais —evidently constructed specially for Wedemeyer's performances.

Dr. Eberhard Eber was now sitting with his daughter.

"I wonder if he's going to show us his old tricks," he whispered in her ear. "I used to see him frequently in the old days . . ."

"I know," said Karin.

An American lietuenant colonel whispered to the General's wife:

"The first time I was here he made a copy of *Mein Kampf* disappear. You know, that book Hitler wrote . . ."

But Dr. Eber and the lieutenant colonel underestimated their host. Wedemeyer never repeated himself.

"Our American friends," he said, "are well known for the fact that they can use their steel helmets either as military headgear, or as soup dishes, or as wash-basins. Let's see if we can't be more inventive than that!"

From a steel helmet he first produced a bunch of flowers, then a bottle of champagne, then a chimney-sweep's brush—"Good luck!"— and finally a parrot. MacCallum had sat down next to his wife and was busily explaining to her how Wedemeyer did it. The trick with the steel helmet was one he could do himself.

Wedemeyer noticed it. As he finished his number he said with the offhand negligence of the experienced performer:

"Of course, I'm a little nervous today. For one of my esteemed visitors all this is no mystery. We have among us one of America's greatest amateur conjurers."

A few intimates looked at General MacCallum. Others clapped. The General shook his head in embarrassment.

Wedemeyer next tried his hand at telepathy. His latest trick was as up to date as could be. From a pack of cards the leading lady of the musical comedy theater withdrew a card and, without Wedemeyer being able to see it, showed it to those present. He counted up to ten, and as he uttered "ten" the telephone rang. At his request Mrs. MacCallum rose to answer it. A voice on the line named the card: the ace of diamonds. A murmur of incredulous amazement ran through the room. The General said to Daisy:

"He hasn't let me in on that one, the old rascal!"

Next, Wedemeyer asked for one of the audience to write down a number on a slate. It may have been pure chance that he handed the slate and chalk to Stappenhorst. A moment later, his eyes bandaged, Wedemeyer said:

"The Herr General is immoderate. Fifteen million."

"I could have guessed that one," Brigadier General Brisbane whispered to his superior.

Finally, Wedemeyer once more picked up the steel helmet. In a voice unsteady with emotion he said:

"Ladies and gentlemen! Permit me to conclude with the number with which we servants of magic used to end our performances. To think that we may do so again . . ." He seemed too moved to continue. He reached for the glass of champagne on the piano.

From the steel helmet he produced the Stars and Stripes of the United States. As he unfolded the flag tremendous applause rang through the room. Only MacCallum and Brisbane exchanged anxious glances. But Wedemeyer was what he had always been—a man of infinite tact. Out of the empty helmet he now lifted the new black-red-and-gold flag of the future Federal Republic. Unfolding it, he draped the two flags, side by side, over the grand piano. MacCullum and Brisbane heaved sighs of relief.

A few minutes later the small band was again on the dais. They were playing a waltz. The General's wife had taken off her red mask and was dancing with her husband. Dr. Eberhard Eber, a scarlet domino over his old-fashioned dinner jacket, was courteously dancing with your Mrs. Brisbane. Karin had found her fiancé, who had arrived as Richard Wagner. General Stappenhorst was not dancing.

With a slight smile and a friendly "My congratulations" he returned the slate to his host.

Sibelius Writes to Adam Wild

On February 18, 1949 Dr. Adam Wild was visited by a stranger who introduced himself as Jochen Zobel and handed him a letter from his long-missed friend Achim von Sibelius. The letter ran as follows:

"My dear Adam,

"There were good reasons why I should have left Munich without saying goodbye to you, to your dear mother, or to our friends—if indeed I am still entitled to call them that. Although I have now been in Cologne for over two months, I have put off writing to you. 'Epistula non erubescit,' says Cicero in his Letters to his Friends. The paper upon which it is written does not, perhaps, blush—but there is still the danger that the writer may do so. Blushingly I admit therefore that I have so far evaded this feeling of shame before myself and before the recipient of my letter. And yet Cicero was not entirely wrong—in the sense, at least, that I have indeed avoided your house and any encounter with you since that day in the autumn of 1947 when I set out on the most difficult journey in my life. Even now I should still find it difficult to face you, unless I could make certain explanations in writing first.

"The bearer of these lines, the former Lieutenant Jochen Zobel, will be able to tell you more than I could hope to do. Indeed, the request that you will cordially receive my young friend is the immediate reason for this letter.

"I am greatly in debt to young Zobel. I know that my connection with his father and his ex-servicemen's association has not remained unknown to you. I disappeared from your sight on the day that I called on Colonel Zobel and joined his association; yet spiritually I resumed my contact with you on the very day that I made the acquaintance of Zobel's son, who has recently returned from Russian captivity.

"I cannot properly put forward any but opportunist reasons for having, at the time, joined Colonel Zobel's circle. You are aware, of course, that my health was seriously undermined and that I was suffering hunger and privations; in fact, I should not be surprised if you had quoted these very facts to exonerate me before yourself and others. But, for my own part, I have never been able to accept such arguments as altogether convincing.

It may be a fact that the voice of conscience does not make itself heard until that of a grumbling stomach is silenced, but it is nevertheless distasteful to me and I should not therefore like to put it forward as an excuse in my own case. Nor, for that matter, do I claim as an extenuating circumstance the fact that the victors were scattering disillusionment all around them like some bad seed, or that the futility of opposition drove me to the Zobels. Hope and opportunism, I fear, are closely related since both hinge upon one's personal well-being at a future date. Finally, I am not very happy over the fact that disillusionment is nowadays almost universally accepted as a justification of wrong actions—so I must waive that explanation too.

"As a matter of fact, I should not have dared to write to you even today if I had only found my way back to you—I might almost say: to us— when I saw more clearly because I ate better food, when I heard more clearly because I was in better health, and when I thought more clearly because the paper in my pocket had again turned into reliable money. Providence be praised: it was not quite as bad. Long before our glorious currency reform—at least several months prior to it—I said goodbye to Colonel Zobel and his friends. The occasion, I must confess, was of a personal nature—the fact that we require most things in our unimaginative lives to be demonstrated to us before our own eyes in order that we may understand them is one of the most depressing discoveries of my advancing years.

"The occasion for this salutary shock, which had an electrifying effect on me, was the release of Obersturmbannführer Gerd Mante from Allied captivity and the appearance of Field Marshal Sturzenbach in Zobel's circle. A remarkable, paradoxical process now took place. Surely the fact that the conquerors had let loose upon Germany a character like Mante, the fact that they were lending a helping hand to Sturzenbach, ought to have convinced me, more than anything that happened before, that it was futile to resist the trend of the times. But the very things which had induced me to give up my resistance shortly afterwards gave rise to that spirit of opposition which is probably nothing other than the human spirit itself. The false moralists, and frequently also the true ones, make the mistake of discovering the substance of evil only when they realize its quantity. Dirt, one would think, is dirt—but in actual fact we don't find dirt unbearable until it accumulates in considerable quantity. People like yourself—and this, perhaps, is the ultimate wisdom of ethics—discern the dirt in the grain; we who are weaker do not discern it until there is a heap of it.

The secret society headed by Colonel Zobel—himself a very insignificant and unsuspecting man—was no different after Mante's and Sturzenbach's appearance from what it had always been: yet only in the mass did I recognize its character. Unhappily, this is not a new experience to me, for the substance of National Socialism was likewise no different at birth from what it was at the moment when I decided to resist it. I am realizing more and more that our maturity is closely connected with our imagination. Children act the way they do because their imagination is inadequate to foresee fully the consequences of their actions: as we grow older and more mature we foresee these consequences more clearly. In this sense we Germans do not appear to belong to the mature nations: to see the visible does not require that imagination which I have come to regard as an integral constituent of maturity.

"At any rate, I have now, perhaps just in time, realized what the game is. The game, my dear Adam, is this: with the mirage of future greatness our nation is once more being driven into a course of action which it desires no more than any other nation on this earth, but for which it will one day be held responsible as no other nation ever has. Once more, my dear Adam, the drums of heroism will be beaten. Once more a few people will get their—to them profitable—way, and we shall realize too late that we have yielded to their vain will. Once more we shall be tempted in our most vulnerable spot—to wit, our pride in an impressive industriousness, a patent prosperity and an imaginary power. We shall be praised, my dear Adam, for the very qualities of which we ought to be ashamed; we shall be pushed forward into an action that we ought to refuse; we shall be commended and lauded until our vanity reaches the pitch of self-destruction; our vices will be turned into virtues and our virtues will be condemned as vices. It makes no difference whatever whether, as the disgruntled are claiming, we shall be sent in as a spearhead, or as I am inclined to believe myself, we shall merely march shoulder to shoulder with the others. In either case our national destiny will be fulfilled in the marching.

"If there are any grounds for optimism then they are with the Jochen Zobels. At the moment our young generation is still in the grips of an apathy that comes to people who are innocently punished for the sins of their fathers. But if we can give them another five or six years their chances will be better than the cynics are today disposed to believe. It seems to me that you, and others like you, ought to rally these young people around you, so as to shield them against a fatal tradition, a poisoned chronicle of the past, and a whitewashed yesterday.

"As for me, my dear Adam, I am working as a reader for a Cologne publisher whose address you will find at the head of this letter. Almost every day I am approached by people who try to persuade me to take an active part in the German Government that is shortly to be set up in our truncated country. I am still hanging back—not because I would not gladly cooperate in the creation of a new Germany but because—by an odd quirk of fate—I have to discover laboriously in each case whether they are after the former officer of the 20th of July, or the former member of the secret ex-servicemen's association in Munich, or simply after the ex-officer. I should like it best if they did not want any of the three.

"My thoughts are often with you and our friends in Munich. Not a Sunday passes but I am with you in my thoughts. If I may make a wish—and I feel that the wrong turnings that I have taken entitle me now to make a sincere wish—then it is this: Do not despair because you are few. I am not, as you are probably thinking with a smile, indulging in the illusion that every flame grows into a fire. All I want to know is that not even such disappointments as I have caused you can quench the flame. And lastly, I am deriving some consolation from the knowledge that young Jochen Zobel will be able to fill the place that has been vacant since my desertion.

"In old cordiality,

"Yours as ever,

"Achim von Sibelius."

In the Air-Raid Shelter All Men Were Equal

"How long now since I last saw you?" asked the tall blonde, drawing the curtain.

Inge was sitting by the fire. "It must be about a year," she said.

"It was nice of your Hans to let me know they'd found you. He seems a nice boy. I only hope he marries you."

"Why should he marry me?"

"Aren't you in love with each other?"

"Certainly."

"But he doesn't want to?"

"I don't want to!"

Ilse regarded her young friend in astonishment. Was there any woman who did not want to get married?

"I might have agreed before the currency reform," said Inge.

"What on earth are you talking about?"

"Things were just like wartime then," explained Inge. "Just as in the air-raid shelters, only without the bombs. You see, in the shelter all men were equal."

"So that's it," said Ilse. "And now he is acting the grand seigneur again?"

With an impatient gesture Inge flicked her cigarette into the fire.

"He hasn't changed in the least," she said. "It's my fault. It always has been my fault. Including that time they chucked me out of the PX. Dr. Wild has been reproaching me, in his paternal way. He says I ought to have trusted them more. Nobody is holding it against me that I used to walk the streets—only I keep acting as if it were written right across my face. That's what he said."

The tall blonde lit a cigarette.

"What does he mean: 'written right across your face'?" she said. "I can't stand people who ooze forgivingness. Most people sell things that don't belong to them. I at least . . ."

"I know," said Inge. "Besides, I've forgotten all about it now. That's the best thing about the currency reform. You can forget anything that happened before. I can't remember a thing."

"Well then," said Ilse without much conviction.

"You don't understand," said Inge. "Everything has such clear outlines now. The other night I dreamed that an empty picture frame was hanging on our wall. We were all sitting in the room, including yourself, when somebody called out: 'All into the frame!' The way they shout 'All aboard' on the railways. And then they all sat inside the frame, just as in a family group, only I couldn't get in and I stood there crying. You know I've always had these silly dreams. I can't explain it. But there was my father without a pension, and Hans's father coming up before the Denazification Tribunal, and I had only one dress, and he had only one old pair of shoes. At Dr. Wild's they talked of things which I understood. Not always of shoes or food or tribunals . . . but all the same, they were subjects I could follow. And now everything is changed, just as if everybody had jumped back into his own place."

"Well, you've a lot to learn," said Ilse. "When I was a mannequin

I ran around with a famous doctor. It lasted for six months, and I too had a lot to learn. Especially listening. That's all a woman's got to be good at: sleeping and listening. . . ."

"To you everythings comes easily," Inge said with a smile.

"But you've got a decent job," continued Ilse. "In a department store a girl can get on pretty well. The Yanks will soon be gone. I, for one, won't be sorry. Not that I have anything against them. I've got no prejudices: they're human too. Only they're so unpredictable. They're generous or stingy, according to whether you flatter them or hurt their feelings. When a German comes here he knows what he's buying. But the Yanks always want to buy sentiment as well. It's too exhausting."

"I felt happier in the past. You know, sometimes I think that only during the war was I really myself. And at the Sendlinger-Tor-Platz. Now everybody is so cheerful and the shops all have that pre-Christmas look . . . Somehow I can't share in the merrymaking—know what I mean?"

"Yes," said Ilse. "If you've grown up on a farm you think manure is perfume."

"Perhaps," said Inge.

She left after half an hour. She did not know why she had come in the first place. She felt an urge to talk to someone who spoke her language. But did the tall blonde speak her language? Did anyone speak it? Her father, or Hans, or Dr. Wild? She did not know. That was the worst of it: always asking questions and not knowing the answers. Why was Dr. Wild so indulgent and why had the major denounced her? Why did she not want to get married, and why did she feel hurt because Hans never mentioned marriage? Why did the manager at the department store shout at the assistants, and why did Stefan Lester have a hump? Why did she remember the funeral of a child which she had seen from her window at the Eastern Cemetery, and why had Hilde, the girl from next door, married a Yank? Why did Ilse think that all a woman need know was how to sleep and how to listen, and why did she not realize that one must also be able to answer questions? There was no urgent need for any of these questions to be answered, so why was she getting desperate over her inability to answer them?

She was walking across the Marienplatz and down the Theatinerstrasse, towards the Siegestor. It was past five o'clock and quite dark.

But the street lights were much brighter now than they had been a few weeks back. What did they want so much light for? She passed the Eber Bank. It was no longer a solitary building in a wilderness. On either side of it the scaffoldings of two new houses towered into the evening sky. A neon light was flickering above the letters "Bankhaus O. Eber." What made Hans walk over the bridge that time? The shopwindows of the temporary low stone buildings were brightly lit: the goods almost seemed to well out of them. What made beautiful things beautiful and ugly things ugly? And why were human intentions so difficult to read? She had money in her handbag, an unbelievable heap of money, because she had drawn her pay a couple of days ago. She might buy herself a new handbag. Why did she have to carry that childish red handbag for so long, and later that large black bag which Lincoln Washington Haymes had given her? Why did she have to celebrate Christmas with Lincoln, and why had she not heard from him lately?

She had got as far as the Odeonsplatz. She would cross over to the traffic safety zone in front of the Feldherrnhalle. The oblique beams of a street lamp lit up the two lions. They reminded her of the lions' heads on the divan at home. Why should she think: at home? Was the house by the cemetery still her home?

She would cross over at the corner of Brienner Strasse. The most expensive tarts used to stroll up and down the Brienner Strasse. She wondered if they had been chased away, now that there were once more elegant shops in the Brienner Strasse.

That was her last thought before it happened. A jeep swung out of the Brienner Strasse into the Theatinerstrasse at a furious pace. Too late did the driver sound his horn. Too late did he jam on his brakes. Too late did Inge jump back.

Or did she jump back at all? The driver disputed it a few minutes later when two MP jeeps, their sirens screaming, arrived on the scene to establish particulars of the accident. "She wanted to die," insisted the driver. The witnesses were unanimous in denying this. "Road hogs!" they muttered. Some of them were saying it quite audibly. The arrival of the ambulance turned the incident into a small-scale German-American clash. Those present—and they were quite a crowd now—forced their names and addresses on the doctor. Maybe something could be done about those American road hogs.

"It won't help her now," said the doctor.

He ought to know. The slim girl, occupying no more than half the width of the stretcher, was dead.

Adventure at the Cemetery Gate

In March the city had its own noises and its own smells. They were the noises and the smells of reconstruction. One would walk through the city as one might walk through a carpenter's workshop. One was scarcely aware of the hammering any longer, so much had it become part of the general background noise. The whole city smelled of cement, glue, paint and brick dust. It was curious that this dust could have two different smells—a dead one and a live one. Now the smell was live. At midday the workmen would sit on the scaffoldings, enjoying a short lunch break. For a while the smell of beer would mingle with the smell of building. Food was consumed in excessive quantities and at excessive speed. And a moment later the hammering would start again, because nobody wanted to be reminded of the silence that had held sway for so long.

Hans entered the Eber bank. Like a stranger he asked for the private office of the "Herr Doktor." The commissionaire conducted him to the elevator, with the obsequiousness of bank commissionaires who learn that a caller has a personal appointment with the President. The commissionaire wore a navy-blue uniform with a wealth of gold braid. It seemed as though he were carrying upon his person a substantial part of the gold cover of the Deutsche Mark.

Dr. Eber's new, paneled office was small—his private offices always had been—but it was furnished with that subtle elegance which substitutes solidity for old age. Behind the desk hung a painting representing Dr. Eber's father in a dignified posture. In the old days, thought Hans, the Führer's portrait used to hang by its side.

"I am grateful to you for coming," said Dr. Eber, somewhat formally but evidently trying to sound cordial. He offered his son a chair and sat down next to him at a small smoking table. "Cigar?"

"No, thank you." He took a cigarette.

"It's over a year now since we last saw one another," said Dr. Eber. "In a way I am hurt that you never came to see me, but at the same time I feel a certain pride in you. I believe you are about to take your final examination . . . ?"

Hans nodded assent.

Dr. Eber adjusted the pince-nez on his small nose. "I was sorry to hear . . ." he said.

Hans winced. "It was an accident," he said.

"In any case," said Dr. Eber, "I thought you might perhaps like to go abroad for a bit. We are now doing big business with the Arab countries. . . ."

"I heard you'd been to Egypt."

"Yes," said Dr. Eber with feigned modesty. "Saudi Arabia is next on the list. German reputation is again very high out there. We are about to open a branch in Spanish Morocco. Madrid has been most accommodating." After a short pause he added: "If the prophet doesn't come to the mountain . . . you know what I mean. I was going to suggest that you go to Morocco for a year. There would be no obligation on your part. If you didn't like it . . ."

"It's very good of you, Papa," said Hans. "But I don't want to repeat what I said last time. I am as determined as ever to go my own way."

"A pity," said Dr. Eber. "For a young man of your intelligence you're displaying a marked lack of foresight. Although, of course, you're not the only one that is still standing aloof. I just can't understand you people. The victors are no longer identifying themselves with themselves—only you still seem anxious to identify yourselves with them. Do you really want to perpetuate the state of defeat?"

"No," said Hans. "We just don't want another adventure."

"A strong Germany is the best guarantee of peace."

"Maybe. I don't like speaking for my generation because I don't know if I'm representative of it. But we young people are odd—or, at least, we must seem odd to you, Papa. You old ones, if you don't object to the term, are the adventurers—we young ones have no taste left for adventure."

"The impact of the war. Quite understandable," said Dr. Eber. "But nothing could be further from our 'adventurous' minds than the idea of another war."

"Neither do the people who play with fire intend to get burned. No, Papa; we won't take the risk. We are an unimaginative generation." Abruptly he added: "Have you ever read the American Declaration of Independence?"

"I don't quite see . . ."

"It guarantees to the citizen, in addition to life and liberty, the 'pursuit of happiness.' You'll probably be shocked, Papa—but we young people regard this pursuit of happiness as our noblest right. We are modest pursuers. You people are once again pursuing greatness and power and wealth."

"Just like the Americans with their fine Declaration of Independence," smiled Dr. Eber.

"I don't care what the Americans are doing. You people want to see a great Germany, whereas we merely want to see a happy one. That is the difference between your patriotism and ours."

"Why shouldn't a great Germany be happy as well? Does she have to be occupied in order to know happiness? To us the Americans have brought neither life nor liberty, nor yet permission to pursue happiness."

"I thought you were working closely with the Americans?" said Hans, trying to change the subject.

"I am working only for Germany," said Dr. Eber.

Why had he asked him to call, wondered Hans. A sunbeam fell obliquely between father and son; tiny motes were dancing in the pale spring sunlight. The beam was like an invisible wall between the two men. What was the use of talking, thought Hans. The wall would never disappear. He had probably summoned him because he had heard of Inge's death. A great bitterness welled up in him, drowning even the pain that had been with him for weeks and would not diminish. But now he was feeling less pain and more bitterness. How tactful of Papa to have waited a few weeks before inviting him. But then Papa had always been exceedingly tactful. Let a little grass grow over Inge's grave. And now the time had come for young Eber to pull himself together. The girl from the occupation era was dead. That had always been the strength of the Eberhard Ebers: to be able to march over graves. What was that line from Schiller? "And the right is with the living." A monstrous statement. The right was with the dead. He remembered those last dead by the Elbe, when the bullets had been flying only because everybody wanted to fire off their ammunition. The dead had been lying on the river bank, under the late April sunshine. Inge had been lying in the morgue when he and Adam had come to identify her. "Identify" was a horrible expression for someone who had been alive but an hour previously. They might so easily drift into a new adventure, the Eberhard Ebers, because they did not even know they were marching over graves. Adventure was waiting for them at the cemetery gate. How was one to make one's self understood to them? And to what end? That was it, thought Hans—to what end? There were those who were "still standing aloof," as Papa had put it. But it was not enough to stand aloof. One had to resist. Not feebly and apathetically and with the weariness of premature old age. After all, there was nothing feeble or apathetic or prematurely aged about the Eberhard Ebers.

He crushed his cigarette in the brilliantly polished glass ashtray and stood up.

"Surely," said Dr. Eber, "that doesn't mean that you can't come home. I won't stop you from going your own way, as you call it. We don't have to be enemies because of that. At times the house is uncannily empty. Oskar is having a house built at the Englischer Garten. Good old Anna is talking about you all the time. Since Karin left . . ."

"I forgot to offer my felicitations," said Hans.

Dr. Eber also got up. "She was a little sad," he said, "but she seems to be quite happy in Cologne now. Their carnival appears to have been even better than ours. Young Stettinus intends to go to London for a year."

"Give her my regards when you write to her," said Hans.

"Well, how about it . . . ?" said Dr. Eber.

"No, Papa," said Hans. "We shall never be enemies. But we had better not deceive ourselves over the fact that we shall remain adversaries."

"If you think so," said Dr. Eber.

He extended his hand to Hans. Hans shook it, bowed, and left.

For the first time since Inge's death there was a feeling of serenity in him. Was he feeling happy because he had hurt the old man, Hans wondered. No; he was happy merely because he had not let himself be bribed. They always talked of people who took bribes and did not realize how much more corrupt were those who offered them. They believed that the future belonged to them, and they were ready to offer advance payments drawn on that future. What would happen if one refused to accept the payment? Would they, perhaps, begin to lose confidence in their currency of tomorrow?

With a brief greeting he hurried past the gold-braided commission-aire. Outside the entrance was a small scaffolding. Hans looked up. Two men were removing the letter "O" from the legend "Bankhaus

O. Eber." By tomorrow morning it would again be the Bankhaus
E. Eber. But there was no bitterness left in Hans now.

Mante Breaks off the Engagement

Martha Zobel rang the bell on the new natural-wood door with its
inlays of dark brown.

For a long time nothing happened. Yet she knew that Gerd
Mante was at home. Muted voices could be heard through the door.

She had made herself beautiful. She was wearing a summer dress
although the weather was still cold. She had taken her coat off on the
stairs, for the coat was old and shabby and wintry. But the summer
dress was new. It had a deep neckline and left her shoulders bare.
She wore no brassiere and her big firm bosom was nearly bursting
out of her décolletage. She had no need of rouge, for her cheeks had
their usual fresh color. But there was lipstick on her mouth—a lot
of lipstick. She knew that Gerd liked lipstick: it was his concession
to modernity.

At last the door was opened.

Gerd stood in the door. He was wearing an old dressing gown—a
threadbare cross between a dressing gown and a bathrobe. His hairless white chest was bare. His legs with their covering of fair hair
were also naked. He was not wearing anything under his dressing
gown. His soft hair was hanging damp into his face and there were
feverish patches of red on his usually pale cheeks. She knew those
patches.

"What do you want here?" he asked.

He tried to bar her way, but the bachelor's apartment had no hall
and with one resolute step Martha was in the living-room.

The door to the bedroom was ajar. For a moment Martha considered if she should force her way into the bedroom. Then she
passed the door. All she could see was the lower end of the bed and
a woman's bare legs.

Before Mante could say anything Martha had sat down on the low
modern settee.

"Tell your whore to beat it," she said.

"Don't behave like a fishwife," said Mante. He was towering above
her. "I didn't invite you here."

"Tell her to beat it," repeated Martha. "I've got to talk to you."

"Some other time, my sweet," Mante mocked her. "I'm not in the mood now."

"I know," said Martha, loud enough to be heard in the bedroom. "You're never in the mood for talking afterwards. But you'll talk to me just the same."

"Get out before I lose my temper," said Mante.

"And what happens when you lose your temper?" said Martha.

"I'll throw you out," said Mante, but something in her voice made him sit down all the same.

"You wouldn't dare," said Martha, her voice trembling.

"Wouldn't I though? And who's going to scare me? Your father maybe? I know what you've come for. He's sent you. He can't take plain words. I've said a few plain words to him."

"I know nothing about that," said Martha. She sounded uncertain of herself.

"He was trying to make me marry you." He mimicked Zobel's speech: " 'We are living in normal conditions again.' So I was to marry you. But you ought to know that I cut up rough when someone tries to make me do something. Especially if it's someone like your father."

"I forbid you to talk like this about Papa," said Martha. But her eyes gave the lie to her words. She would not forbid him anything if he took her in his arms.

Mante was aware of this. He said: "Maybe I'd do it if it weren't for your father. But I am sick of him and all his clique. Your father is dead—only he doesn't know it. And that splendid brother of yours! One wants to give them a chance, and they mess it up. I never wanted any truck with him and the likes of him. Who got us stuck with that man Sibelius? He would have hung that brother of yours round our necks as well."

"We have apologized for Jochen."

"And I was fool enough to accept your apologies. Men like your brother ought to croak. Far too few have croaked."

Martha was pale. She had long sacrificed Jochen. She was prepared to sacrifice her father as well. But suddenly she knew that Gerd no longer wanted her. She made one more attempt:

"It was Jochen's fault. But Jochen is no longer with us. It's all over. Papa is quite sensible again."

"As sensible as a leaf in the wind," sneered Mante. "Here today and gone tomorrow. They can't get away from treason, the Zobels. But why are we talking about your father?"

"You started it. That's not what I came for."

"What did you come for?"

"Need you ask, Gerd? I haven't seen you for two weeks. Didn't you miss me at all?" There was a faint menace in her cajolery.

"I bore it with fortitude," said Mante. He said it loud enough to be audible in the bedroom.

"So you want to break it off?"

Mante got up, oblivious of the fact that his dressing gown had almost fallen open.

"I wanted to spare you," he said.

"It's all over then?" she repeated.

"If you insist: Yes!" He walked to the door. "If you wouldn't mind leaving now . . . ?"

About to open the door, he had turned his back on her.

When he faced her again she was standing upright in front of the settee. She was clutching her handbag, almost as if she was holding herself up by it.

"You're not throwing me out!" she said.

"And why not?"

"Because you can't live without me. You said so a hundred times."

"You shouldn't have taken it seriously."

"You used to love me," she said, trembling all over.

"I hate women who don't know when to disappear."

His hand was on the door handle. She opened her handbag. She did not open it quickly enough. By the time the shot rang out he had ducked. The revolver bullet buried itself in the door.

The woman in the next room started to scream. She did not scream for help: she just screamed helplessly.

With one leap Mante pounced on Martha. But there was no need for a struggle. Unresisting, she let him take the weapon from her hand. Her resolution and its sudden implementation had left her utterly exhausted: her face looked ashen, her shoulders dropped, and her teeth were chattering.

"And now scram," he said through his teeth. "Scram before I call the police!"

»459«

She reeled like a drunk. Then she threw herself down before him, her arms gripping his knees. Tears poured down her face. The color on her lips had begun to smudge.

Roughly he freed himself from her embrace, tossed the revolver on to the settee, lifted up the kneeling woman and dragged her to the door.

On the stairs she encountered the concierge who had been brought up by what had sounded like shooting in Mante's flat.

"Is anything wrong?" he asked the woman leaning against the banisters.

"No, nothing . . ." said Martha Zobel.

". . . And All We Want is One Little Thing"

For a whole week they had given themselves over to the illusion that the week would never end. Now it was ending.

Frank and Elisabeth were sitting in the dusky bar of the hotel in Reichenhall where for all that week they had been practically the only visitors. In the morning they would have to return to the city. Frank's train left tomorrow evening.

The Lieutenant Colonel had not got his discharge several months ago, in the autumn, as he had wanted. Time and again his departure had been delayed: first, Hunter had asked him to stay on, and then, after Hunter's return to the States, the General himself had insisted on Frank's staying.

They were talking about Hunter.

"I had a letter from him," said Frank. "He is teaching at West Point and seems quite contented. Although, of course, even if he were unhappy he wouldn't say so. I am glad he is so near New York."

"I don't suppose he'll ever be a general now," said Elisabeth.

"No. I rather admire him. . . ."

"You'd have done just the same."

"I don't know. Adam said something the other day which struck me as very true. Isn't passive resistance perhaps more heroic than active opposition? In other words, isn't resignation perhaps greater than action? Or is resignation not perhaps the best kind of action? In any event, of all actions resignation brings the least satisfaction."

She looked at him, aware that his thoughts were no longer with Hunter. He looked at her, and he too knew what she was thinking.

"We aren't resigning, Elisabeth," he said.

She attempted a smile. "Didn't we promise each other . . . ?"

"This is our last evening," he said. "We've got to talk about it. You must know that I never accept resignation. Why do you insist on it . . . ?"

"Haven't we discussed it often enough, Frank?"

"That hasn't made it any truer."

His hand was lying on the table, and she covered it with hers. "You know the poem by Richard Dehmel," she said. " '. . . and all we need is one little thing to be as free as the birds on the wing —Time.' Nothing can replace time, Frank. We need time."

"Isn't that escapism?" he asked. "Escape into the miracle of time. It is like holding up our wounds to Time and saying: 'Come, Time, and heal them!' Are our wounds really so deep still? Haven't we made them heal ourselves?"

"That's not it at all," she said. "You only heard the last line of the poem, Frank. But the line I love is this: 'to be as free as the birds on the wing . . .' We don't want to content ourselves with a condition of feverish half-health. We want to be free."

He kissed her hand.

"You are right," he said. "Sometimes I feel as if we were surrounded by a lot of sick people who believe they are well. Their rude health often seems uncanny to me, as though it were full of the germs of relapse. The whole country consists of people who have risen from their sickbed too soon. There is something profoundly unhealthy about this vigorous German health." After a little hesitation he added: "But what I have just said proves to me that you and I are on the right road. . . . You know what I mean? A year ago, or even a few months ago, you would have misunderstood me. You would have thought that I didn't want Germany to be healthy . . . when in fact I am hoping for a complete recovery."

"That's just it . . . Time," said Elisabeth. "But I know it won't be long now."

"Will you be angry if I ask again: How long?"

"Until we are certain of being free."

"Do you think one can know that moment?"

"Yes," she said firmly.

Yet that last night was full of temptations, more so than any previous night. Night meant a desperate fight against parting, and the knowledge that the parting was not final counted for nothing. The meaningless nature of the parting made all promise of reunion meaningless. In their soaring flight they asked themselves why a pair of eagles had to learn to fly; at the summits, why the conquerors of peaks still had to yearn for mountain air; in their plunging, why the sea which engulfed all rivers still had to wait for one little stream.

But when morning came they spoke no longer about parting or reunion. They stepped out into a world which remains enchained because it is so self-assured of its soaring flight, which remains earth-bound because it boasts of its heights, and which dries up because in its presumption it believes itself to be the ocean.

There was the world, but it no longer frightened them. In Frank and Elisabeth there was not resignation but the calm of assured union. In their waiting was the pride of the humble, exalting itself over nothing but vainglory. In their love was the certainty of ultimate recovery.

The Unquenched Flame

The last patient had left. Dr. Wild hung his white coat on a hook on the door. As he washed his hands in the basin by the window he glanced out into the street. Directly opposite a house had sprung up. The low May sun drew bright flashes from its windowpanes.

He crossed the old-fashioned waiting-room and entered the living-room. Frau Wild was sitting in a tall armchair, reading. She was reading without glasses.

She looked up and put down the letter she had been reading. "A beautiful letter. And so wise," she said.

Adam nodded in agreement. "He writes to Elisabeth every day."

She rose and opened the window. "I was reminded today of his first visit here," she said.

"Nearly five years ago," said Adam.

"They were not meaningless years," said the old woman.

"Are there meaningless years?"

"There are war years." And without a transition, as was her habit, she added: "I must go to the kitchen now. The cakes for tomorrow."

He followed her out. They liked talking together in the kitchen.

"Aren't these Sunday parties getting too much for you?" he wondered.

"I'm not as old as that! Do you think I've aged much in these five years?"

He laughed. "I wish I were as young . . ."

"So I should think," she said.

"Sometimes you must think me crazy," he said. "I've always been dragging people along . . . Professor Huber's students, and the Interpreter Company, and the people around Sibelius. And now this lot of conspirators who don't know yet what they are conspiring against."

"Nonsense!" she said. "The trouble with you is things aren't romantic enough for you. You don't really like the idea that there is no danger in it for the moment."

Adam frowned. "You're pulling my leg," he said lovingly. "This has nothing to do with romanticism. Sometimes I ask myself quite seriously if I am not perhaps becoming a sort of professional conspirator. After all, everything is fine just now. We are growing rich and powerful. And we've got our democracy which allows even our dear old ex-Nazis to become members of Parliament. Soon we shall have an army—and, when all is said and done, what's wrong with that? After all, the Swiss have an army too. A lot of people now think it quite in order to write off the East Germans—didn't somebody say something to that effect on the radio yesterday? Haven't they consumed too much and produced too little, those East Germans? Why, we don't even object to the occupation and longer. Didn't Americans distribute presents to the German children last Christmas? Chewing gum for the children and guns for the Government. The Russians are wooing us, and the Americans are wooing us, and even the British and French think we are quite nice now. And there we sit on your antiques every Sunday and quarrel with God and the world."

"There must be a *Föhn*," said Frau Wild, seemingly engrossed in her baking. "You always talk like that when there's a *Föhn*."

"The *Föhn* is all superstition," said Adam.

"You tell that to your patients."

"No, seriously, Mother . . . Do you think I'm possessed by the devil? Perhaps I am just a bad German. Why don't I share in the general rejoicing? Why am I not jubilant at what we've come through? We've made a magnificent recovery—there's no denying that. We've even succeeded in forgetting, and the world is forgetting, too. Only in our sitting-room is there still talk of war and gas chambers and concentration camps, and the Dresden might still be standing and Rotterdam need not have been razed to the ground. What reason have we, we alone, for refusing to forget?"

"But that's not true," said Frau Wild. "We do not only talk of the distant past. We also speak about the requistioned houses and the American prison camps, about starvation and about Denazification Tribunals."

"Well?" said Adam. "Does our resentment against the occupation make us better Germans? Besides, these too are subjects of yesterday. They ought to be buried with the rest."

Frau Wild reached up for some aluminum pastry cutters on the wall. She was too short. Adam picked her up. Wriggling, like a small child, she extended her arm towards the neatly arranged row.

"Besides," he continued. "What's the use of our talking? Sometimes there are ten of us; sometimes there are twenty. All we do is preach to the converted. We don't want any barrack-room nonsense any more. We don't want the old Feldwebels and we don't want the old generals. We have no inclination to take part in a conspiracy that will end in our marching upon Leipzig, or in those from Leipzig marching against Munich. I say: We. Who are we? Some twenty people in a Schwabing house, perching on old dowry chests and sipping Frau Wild's coffee. An American lieutenant colonel is one of us, and he writes letters to us from across the water, assuring us that we are right. And an old colonel has returned home because he shared our opinions. A handful of cranks gathering around an eccentric. And what's even worse: an eccentric who is stubbornly convinced that he and his faithful twenty are right, and that the rest of the world is wrong—and who is therefore doing the very thing he professes to fight against. And meanwhile the wheel of history keeps turning. On the one hand an American lieutenant colonel, now demobilized and a teacher of history at some small university—and on the other a few hundred American generals. The divorced wife of a war criminal living in a porter's apartment—and all those other women who are gradually having their jewelry and their castles restored to them. A student pigheaded enough to dissociate himself from his father's past—and the rearmament deals of the Bankhaus Eber. In Cologne an ex-colonel who does not want to be a colonel again—but on the Rhine, only a few miles further south, hundreds of colonels who hope to be field marshals some day. Seriously, Mother, don't you think I am crazy?"

Frau Wild slammed her oven door shut. She turned and sat down on a kitchen stool.

"Now then," she said, "I've listened to this nonsense long enough. Now you keep quiet for a change and listen to me. The other day I read a Chinese legend in an old book." And she began to tell her story as Adam had not heard her tell a story for many years, or possibly decades. "It was about a man," she continued, "who possessed nothing except a piece of burning pinewood. It was a strange piece of wood, for it burned all the time, yet it was never burned up. He did not speak of his treasure to anyone for fear they would laugh at him. A burning piece of pinewood is no great treasure. Then one day the rivers burst their banks and flooded the fields. Everybody tried to save their belongings. But the man thought of nothing but his burning piece of pinewood. He waded through the water, which came up to his chin, and in his hand, aloft, he carried the burning pinewood. But then the waters rose so high he could wade no longer. He tried to save himself by swimming, but the waves closed over him and over his burning pinewood. Coming up again he espied a piece of dry land. And as he stepped upon it, behold the pinewood was still burning: the great waters had not put out the tiny flame. Years passed and still the man possessed nothing but his piece of pinewood which burned without being consumed by the flames. Then one day a terrible fire broke out. Now the man might have cast away his piece of pinewood, for there were enough pieces of burning wood everywhere. Even if he were to survive the conflagration, of which he had little hope, he might collect a hundred pieces of burning wood. But he was a persistent man, probably an eccentric, and he held on to his piece of pinewood. The huts were burned down, the cattle perished in the flames, and the fields themselves were scorched. Only the piece of pinewood was not burned." Abruptly she paused. "Can you guess the end of the story, Adam?" she asked.

"No, Mother."

"When the man was on his deathbed he had his son called to him, and to him he bequeathed the burning piece of pinewood. And his son left it to his son, and he in turn to his son. And thus there is in the world today, in some place, a piece of pinewood that goes on burning. The great floods come and the great fires—but there is always one man to hold on to the piece of pinewood whose flame is not put out by water or fire." She got up and again busied herself at the oven. "Perhaps you think that it is a pointless story, Adam," she said. "We are so used to thinking that a story must have an end. But the eternal stories have no ending. Or else their ending is in eternity. One day the great-grandson of a great-grandson may discover why the man held on to the piece of pinewood in the first place. I do not know, and the man who wrote the story did not know either."

Adam went over to his mother. From her hand he took the spoon with which she had begun to stir some mixture while she was talking. He lifted her up and carried her back into the living room. Dusk had fallen and spread a veil of violet over the old furniture. He still held her in his arms when he said:

"Mother, you haven't told me a story since I was a child. But then they must have been stories like the one about the burning piece of pinewood."

She laughed. "So you think it's all my fault?"

He too was laughing. "Very likely. That's why you mustn't complain if I now carry forward the piece of pinewood."

Gently he put her down. She looked up at him.

"Through fire and water?" she asked.

"Through fire and water," said Adam.

About the Author

HANS HABE was born in 1911 in Budapest, Hungary, but was raised in Vienna, Austria, and considers himself a German writer. Descending from a long line of newspapermen, Hans Habe became at the age of twenty-one the youngest chief editor in Europe, heading up the staff of *Der Morgen* of Vienna. A year later, he earned world-wide fame by discovering the fact that Hitler's real name was Schicklgruber. He was subsequently black-listed by the Nazis. In the middle Thirties, he wrote his first novel in Geneva where he was a League of Nations correspondent for the famous *Prager Tagblatt* of Prague. He traveled extensively throughout the world, interviewing rulers and statesmen until 1939, when he enlisted in the French army, was captured by the Nazis but escaped. The story of his first war adventures, and of that escape, was described in his book published in the United States under the title *A Thousand Shall Fall*, and which became a best-seller throughout the world. Other books of his have been translated into eighteen languages.

In 1940, Hans Habe came to America and enlisted in the American Army as a private and rose to the rank of major. He numbers among his seven decorations the Bronze Star and the Oak Leaf Cluster. He landed with the first wave at Salerno and was instrumental in the liberation of Luxembourg. After the war he was entrusted with the rebuilding of the German press. He was editor-in-chief of the first eighteen German-language American newspapers in Germany after the war and was founder of the Military Government's *Neue Zeitung*.

After returning to this country, Hans Habe devoted himself to writing his books as well as an unusually popular column in the Los Angeles *Daily News*. He repeatedly returned to Europe, and was for two years editor-in-chief of the *Münchner Illustrierte* and the *Echo der Woche*. Several of Hans Habe's books have been filmed. Metro-Goldwyn-Meyer produced "A Thousand Shall Fall" under the title "Cross of Lorraine."

Hans Habe now lives in a chateau at the Lake of St. Wolfgang, Austria. He has been married five times and has a son and a daughter, aged thirteen and five. *Off Limits*, published originally in Germany, became at once the leading best-seller in that country. Hans Habe's own life and post-war experiences contributed greatly, of course, to the intimate knowledge displayed in these pages of the U. S. Army of Occupation.